this book
belongs to:

DISCARD

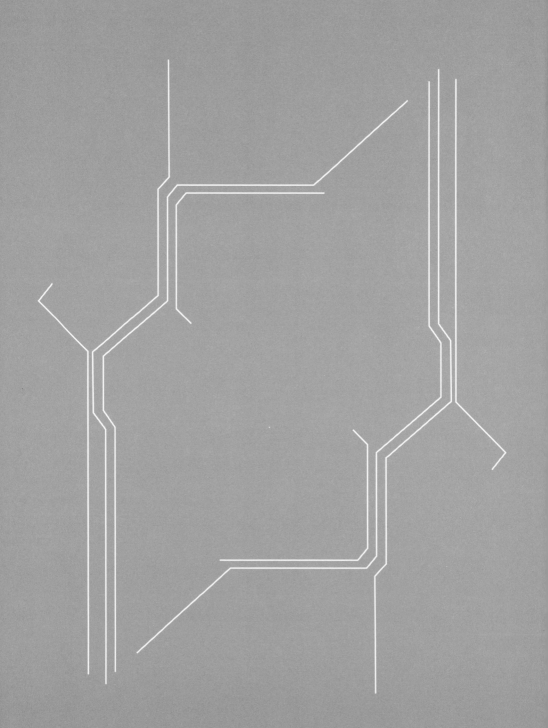

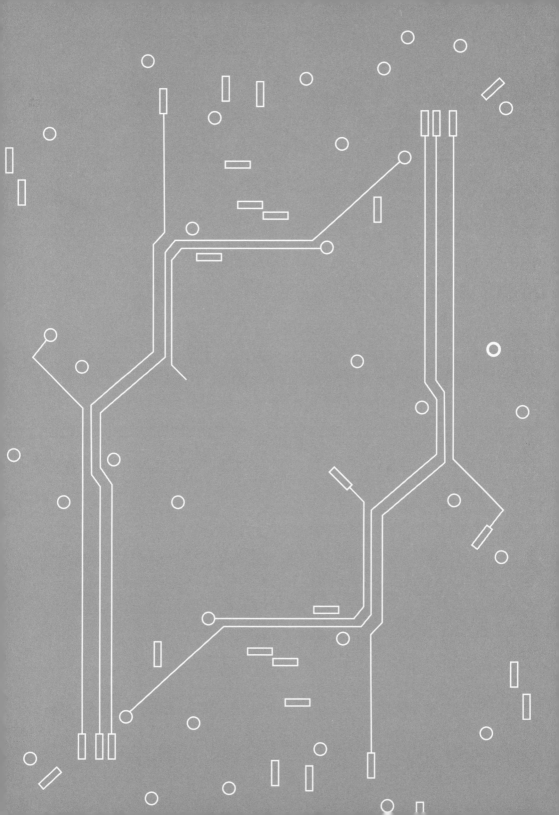

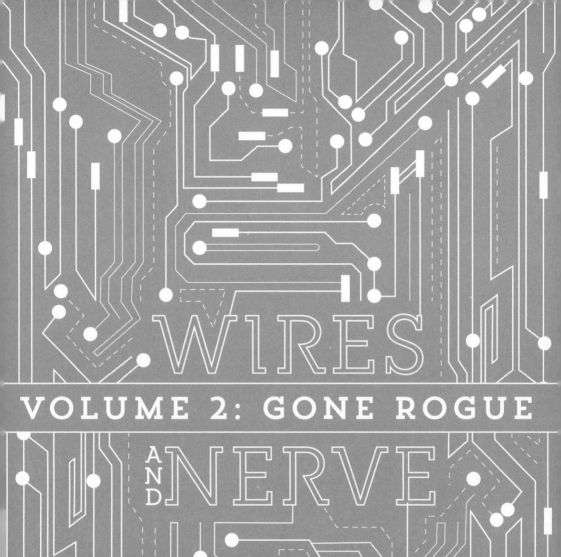

WIRES

VOLUME 2: GONE ROGUE

AND NERVE

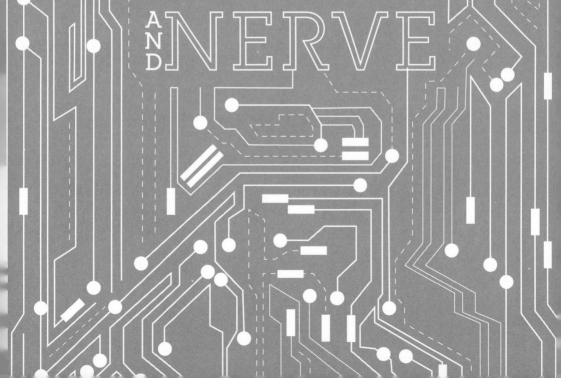

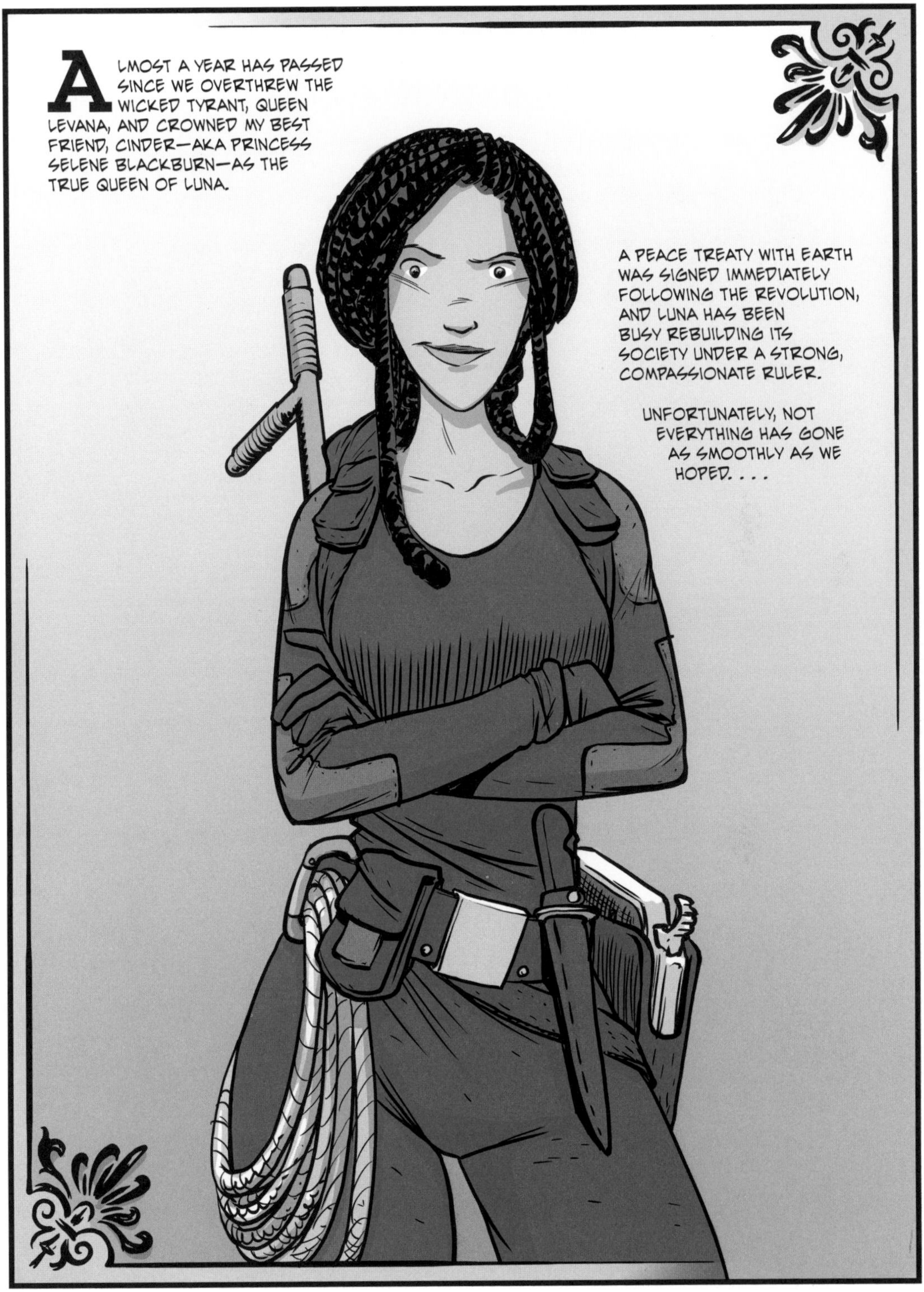
ALMOST A YEAR HAS PASSED SINCE WE OVERTHREW THE WICKED TYRANT, QUEEN LEVANA, AND CROWNED MY BEST FRIEND, CINDER—AKA PRINCESS SELENE BLACKBURN—AS THE TRUE QUEEN OF LUNA.
A PEACE TREATY WITH EARTH WAS SIGNED IMMEDIATELY FOLLOWING THE REVOLUTION, AND LUNA HAS BEEN BUSY REBUILDING ITS SOCIETY UNDER A STRONG, COMPASSIONATE RULER.
UNFORTUNATELY, NOT EVERYTHING HAS GONE AS SMOOTHLY AS WE HOPED. . . .

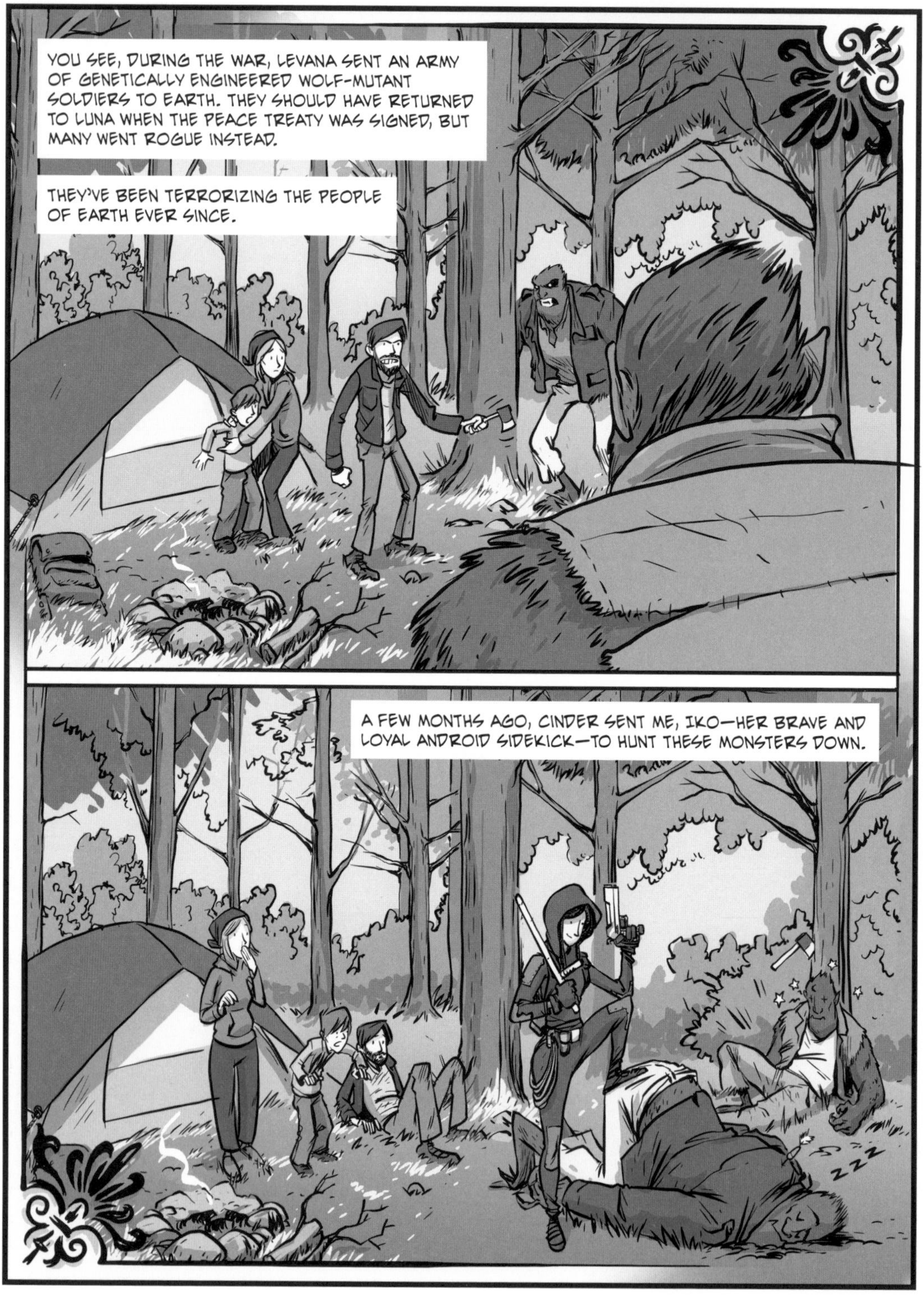
YOU SEE, DURING THE WAR, LEVANA SENT AN ARMY OF GENETICALLY ENGINEERED WOLF-MUTANT SOLDIERS TO EARTH. THEY SHOULD HAVE RETURNED TO LUNA WHEN THE PEACE TREATY WAS SIGNED, BUT MANY WENT ROGUE INSTEAD.
THEY'VE BEEN TERRORIZING THE PEOPLE OF EARTH EVER SINCE.
A FEW MONTHS AGO, CINDER SENT ME, IKO—HER BRAVE AND LOYAL ANDROID SIDEKICK—TO HUNT THESE MONSTERS DOWN.
Z Z Z

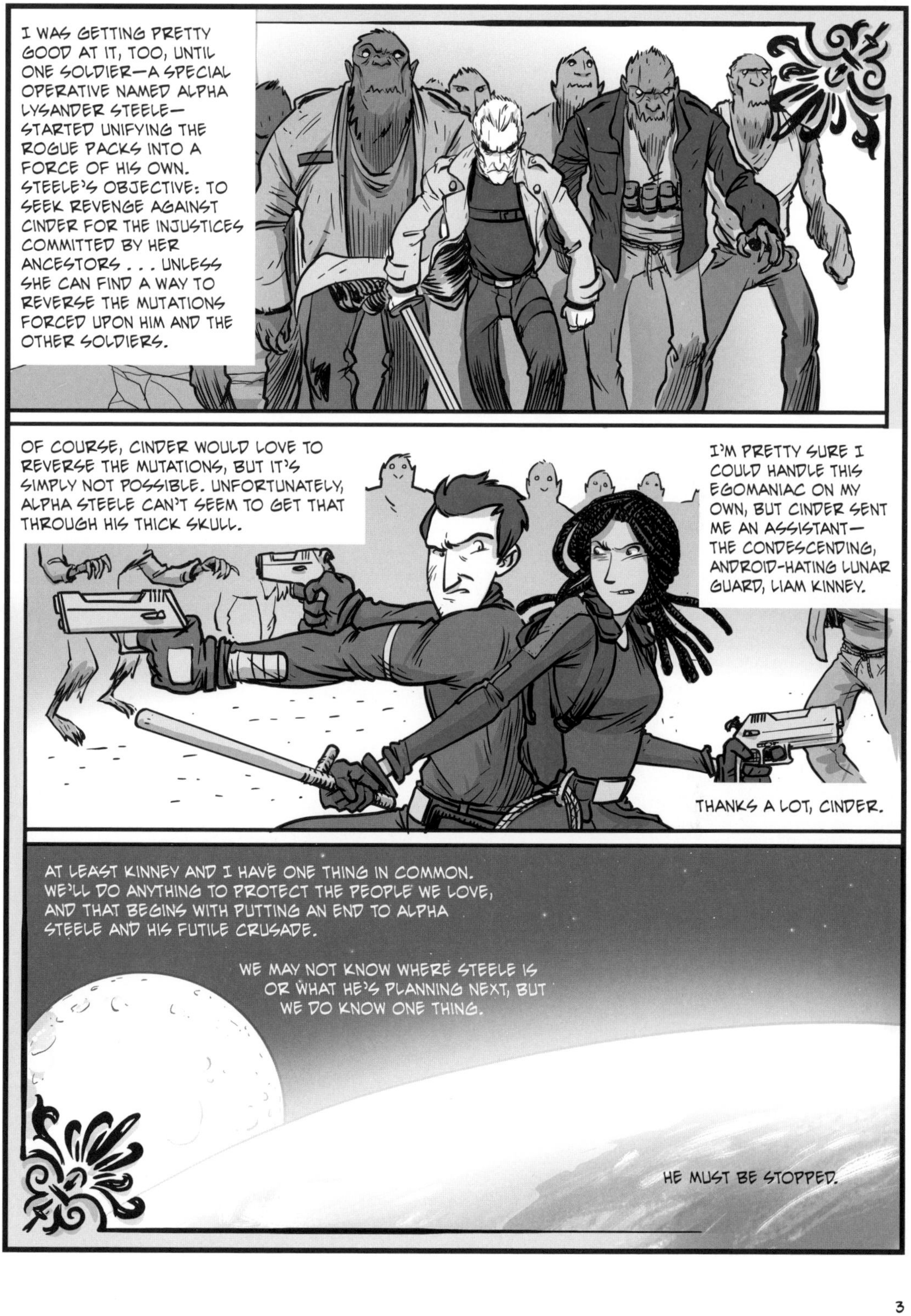

I WAS GETTING PRETTY GOOD AT IT, TOO, UNTIL ONE SOLDIER—A SPECIAL OPERATIVE NAMED ALPHA LYSANDER STEELE—STARTED UNIFYING THE ROGUE PACKS INTO A FORCE OF HIS OWN. STEELE'S OBJECTIVE: TO SEEK REVENGE AGAINST CINDER FOR THE INJUSTICES COMMITTED BY HER ANCESTORS . . . UNLESS SHE CAN FIND A WAY TO REVERSE THE MUTATIONS FORCED UPON HIM AND THE OTHER SOLDIERS.
OF COURSE, CINDER WOULD LOVE TO REVERSE THE MUTATIONS, BUT IT'S SIMPLY NOT POSSIBLE. UNFORTUNATELY, ALPHA STEELE CAN'T SEEM TO GET THAT THROUGH HIS THICK SKULL.
I'M PRETTY SURE I COULD HANDLE THIS EGOMANIAC ON MY OWN, BUT CINDER SENT ME AN ASSISTANT—THE CONDESCENDING, ANDROID-HATING LUNAR GUARD, LIAM KINNEY.
THANKS A LOT, CINDER.
AT LEAST KINNEY AND I HAVE ONE THING IN COMMON. WE'LL DO ANYTHING TO PROTECT THE PEOPLE WE LOVE, AND THAT BEGINS WITH PUTTING AN END TO ALPHA STEELE AND HIS FUTILE CRUSADE.
WE MAY NOT KNOW WHERE STEELE IS OR WHAT HE'S PLANNING NEXT, BUT WE DO KNOW ONE THING.
HE MUST BE STOPPED.

A FEIWEL AND FRIENDS BOOK

An imprint of Macmillan Publishing Group, LLC · 175 Fifth Ave, New York, NY 10010

WIRES AND NERVE, VOLUME 2. Copyright © 2018 by Rampion Books. All rights reserved.

Printed in China by RR Donnelley Asia Printing Solutions Ltd., Dongguan City, Guangdong Province.

Our books may be purchased in bulk for promotional, educational, or business use. Please contact your
local bookseller or the Macmillan Corporate and Premium Sales Department at (800) 221-7945 ext. 5442
or by e-mail at MacmillanSpecialMarkets@macmillan.com.

Library of Congress Control Number: 2017944825

ISBN 978-1-250-07828-5

Book design by Rich Deas

First edition, 2018

10 9 8 7 6 5 4 3 2 1

fiercereads.com

WIRES

AND

NERVE

VOLUME 2: GONE ROGUE

MARISSA MEYER

art by

STEPHEN GILPIN
Based on art by Doug Holgate

Feiwel and Friends
New York

CHAPTER 1

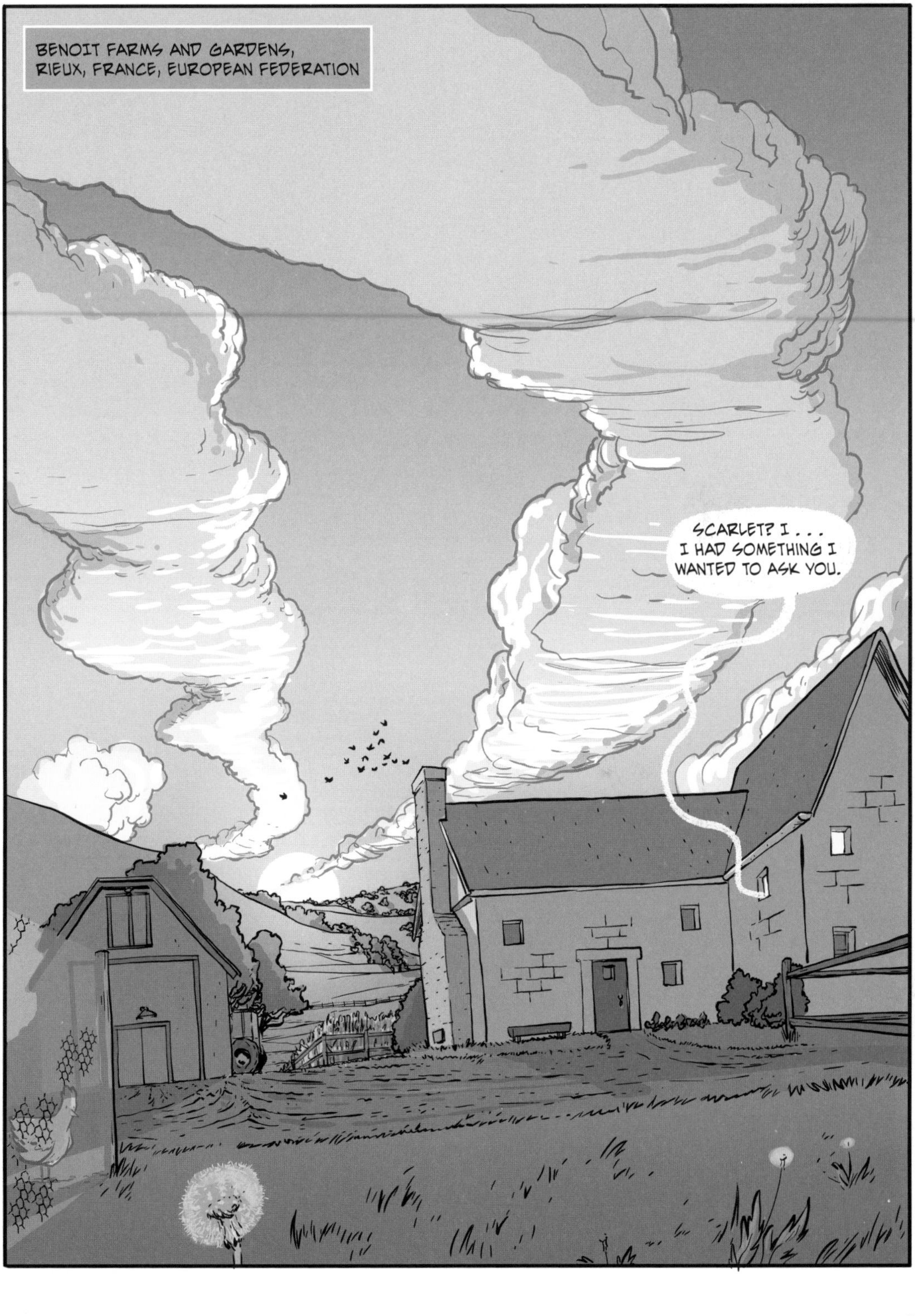
BENOIT FARMS AND GARDENS,
RIEUX, FRANCE, EUROPEAN FEDERATION
SCARLET? I . . . I HAD SOMETHING I WANTED TO ASK YOU.

YOU AND I HAVE BEEN THROUGH SO MUCH TOGETHER.

REVOLUTIONS . . . KIDNAPPINGS . . .

THAT ONE TIME I BETRAYED YOU . . .

AND THAT OTHER TIME I TRIED TO KILL YOU . . .

UGH.

MY POINT IS . . . I . . . I LOVE YOU, SCARLET. YOU'RE MY ALPHA, MY LIFE, MY EVERYTHING.

SO, WILL YOU . . .

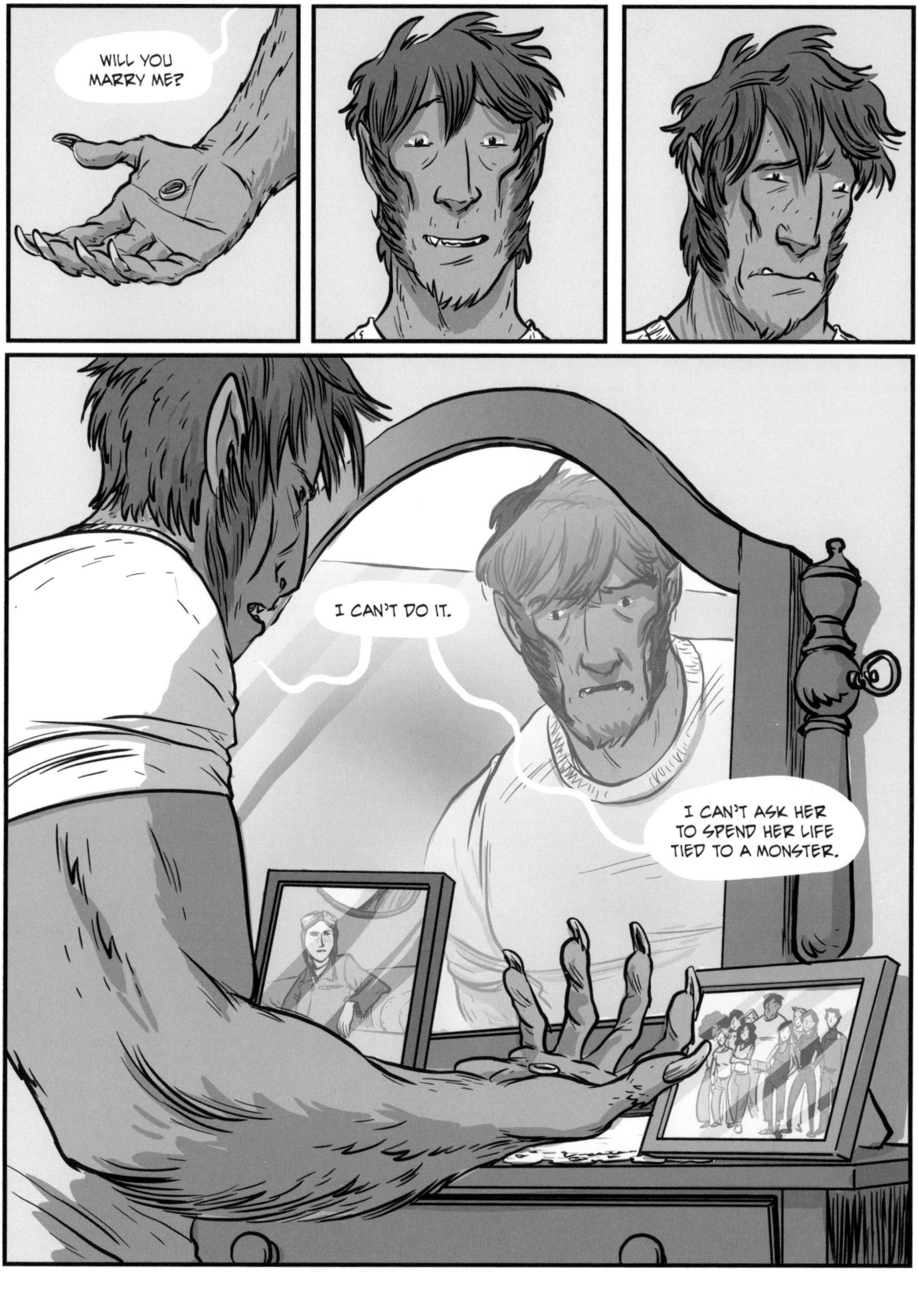
WILL YOU MARRY ME?
I CAN'T DO IT.
I CAN'T ASK HER TO SPEND HER LIFE TIED TO A MONSTER.

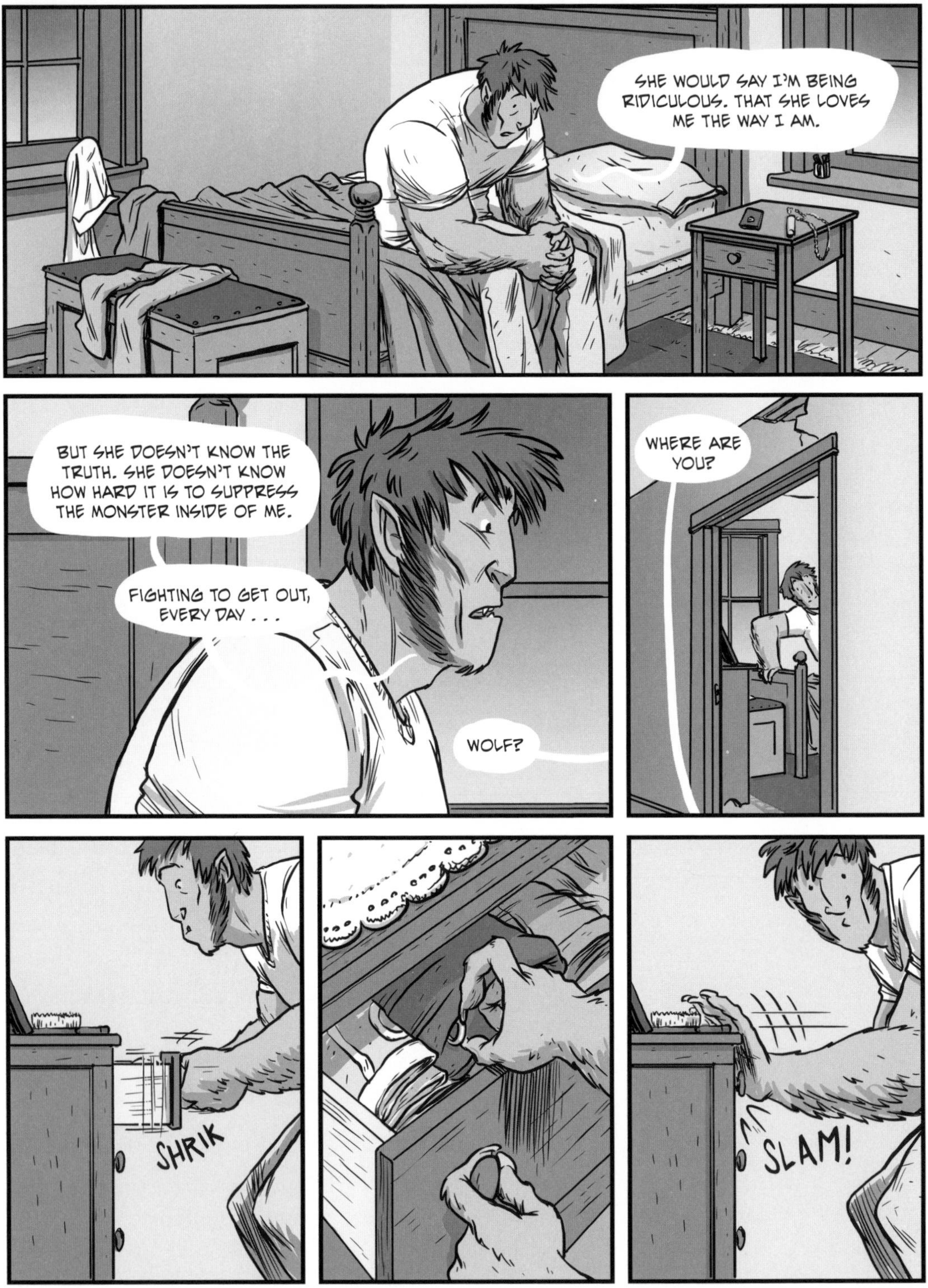
SHE WOULD SAY I'M BEING RIDICULOUS. THAT SHE LOVES ME THE WAY I AM.
BUT SHE DOESN'T KNOW THE TRUTH. SHE DOESN'T KNOW HOW HARD IT IS TO SUPPRESS THE MONSTER INSIDE OF ME.
FIGHTING TO GET OUT, EVERY DAY . . .
WOLF?
WHERE ARE YOU?
SHRIK
SLAM!

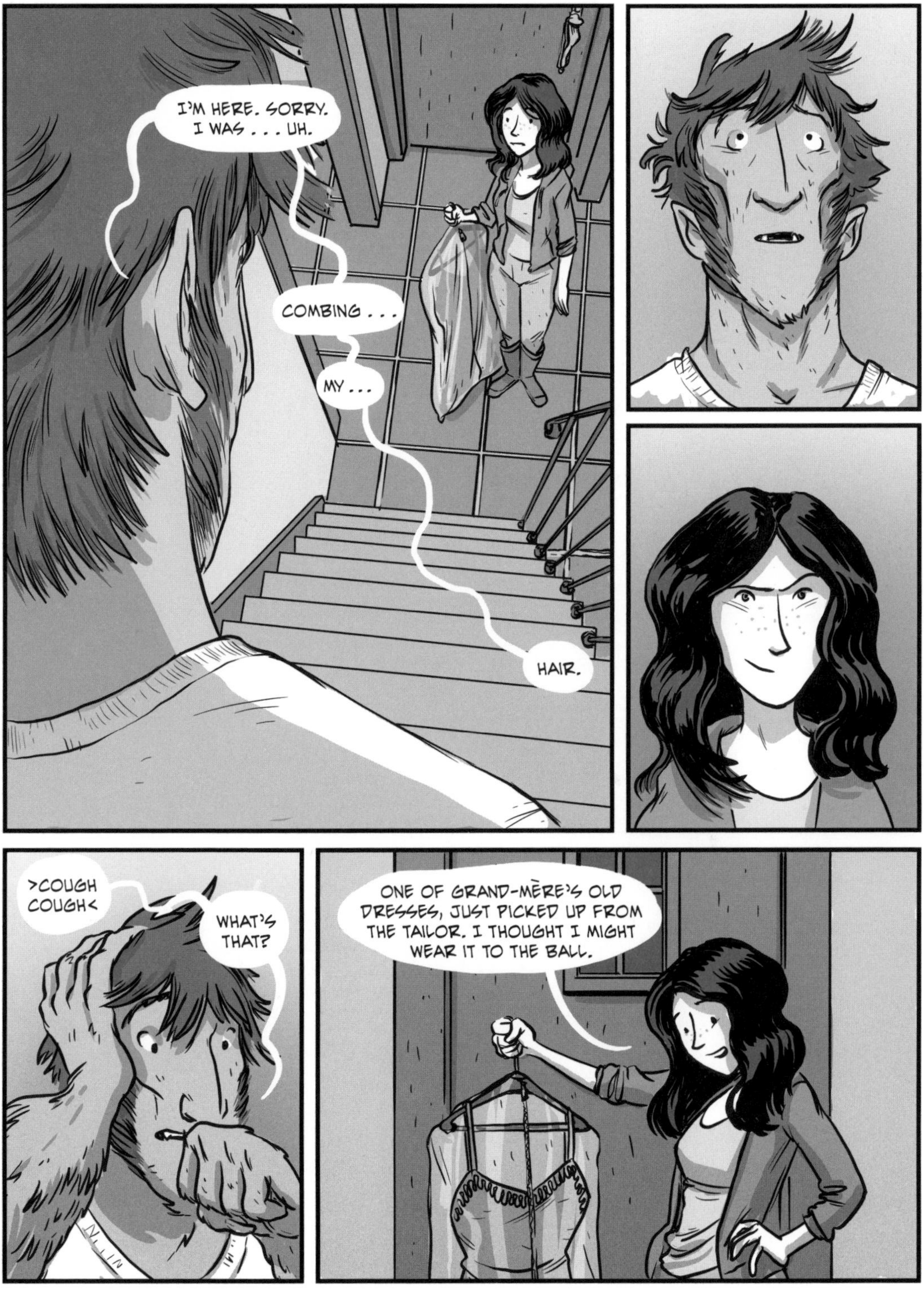
I'M HERE. SORRY. I WAS . . . UH.
COMBING . . .
MY . . .
HAIR.
>COUGH COUGH<
WHAT'S THAT?
ONE OF GRAND-MÈRE'S OLD DRESSES, JUST PICKED UP FROM THE TAILOR. I THOUGHT I MIGHT WEAR IT TO THE BALL.

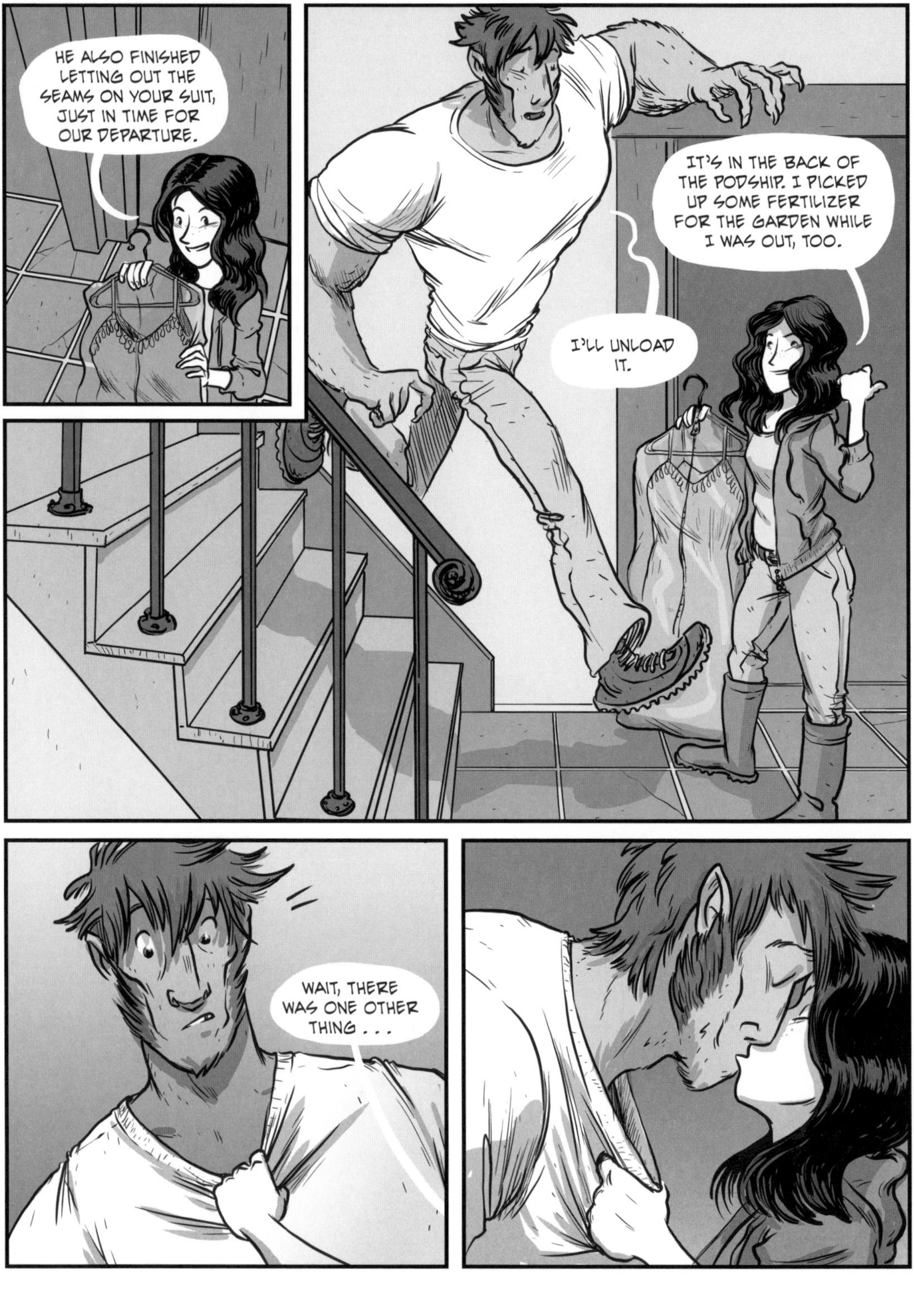
HE ALSO FINISHED LETTING OUT THE SEAMS ON YOUR SUIT, JUST IN TIME FOR OUR DEPARTURE.
IT'S IN THE BACK OF THE PODSHIP. I PICKED UP SOME FERTILIZER FOR THE GARDEN WHILE I WAS OUT, TOO.
I'LL UNLOAD IT.
WAIT, THERE WAS ONE OTHER THING . . .

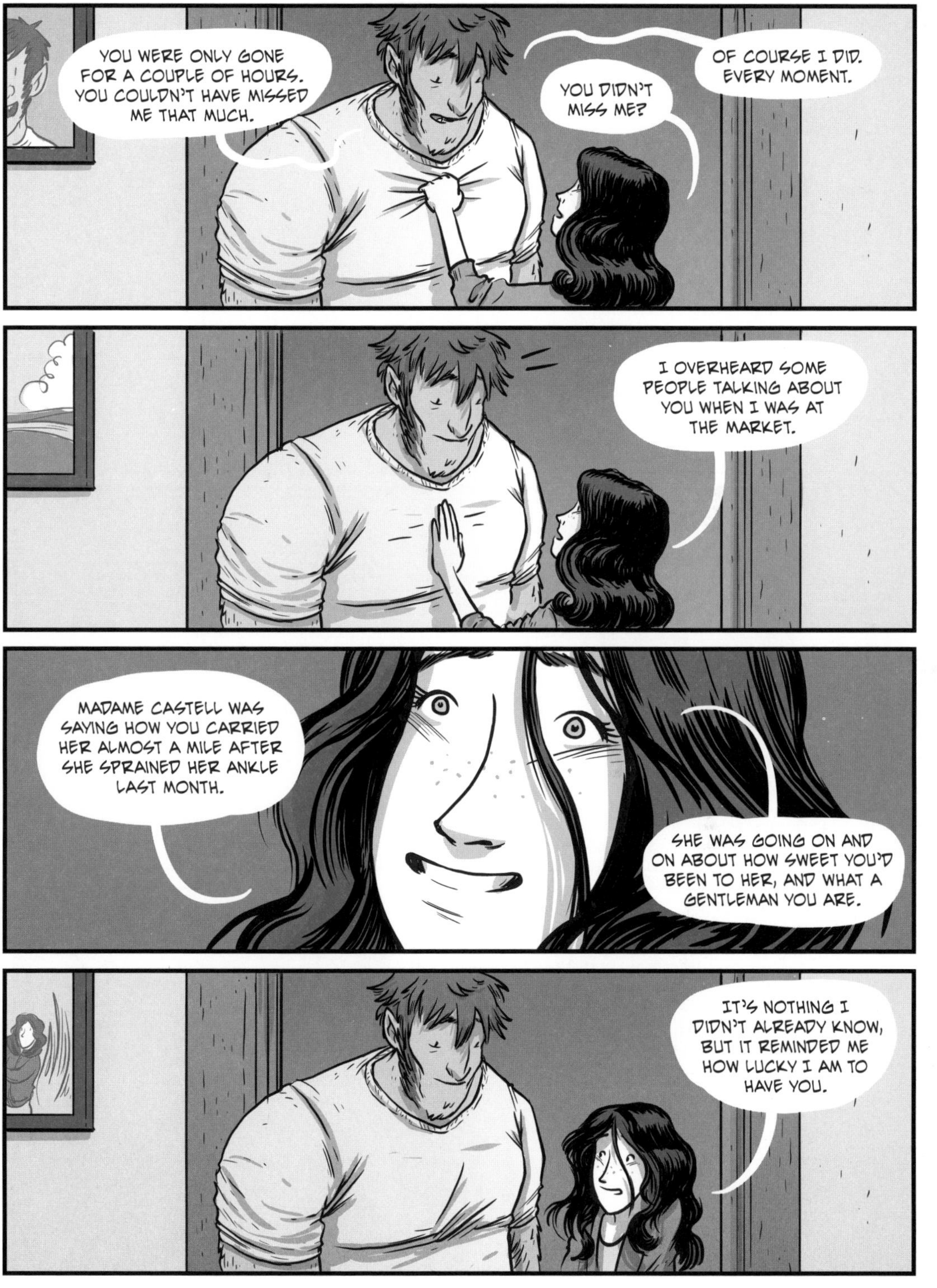
YOU WERE ONLY GONE FOR A COUPLE OF HOURS. YOU COULDN'T HAVE MISSED ME THAT MUCH.
YOU DIDN'T MISS ME?
OF COURSE I DID. EVERY MOMENT.
I OVERHEARD SOME PEOPLE TALKING ABOUT YOU WHEN I WAS AT THE MARKET.
MADAME CASTELL WAS SAYING HOW YOU CARRIED HER ALMOST A MILE AFTER SHE SPRAINED HER ANKLE LAST MONTH.
SHE WAS GOING ON AND ON ABOUT HOW SWEET YOU'D BEEN TO HER, AND WHAT A GENTLEMAN YOU ARE.
IT'S NOTHING I DIDN'T ALREADY KNOW, BUT IT REMINDED ME HOW LUCKY I AM TO HAVE YOU.

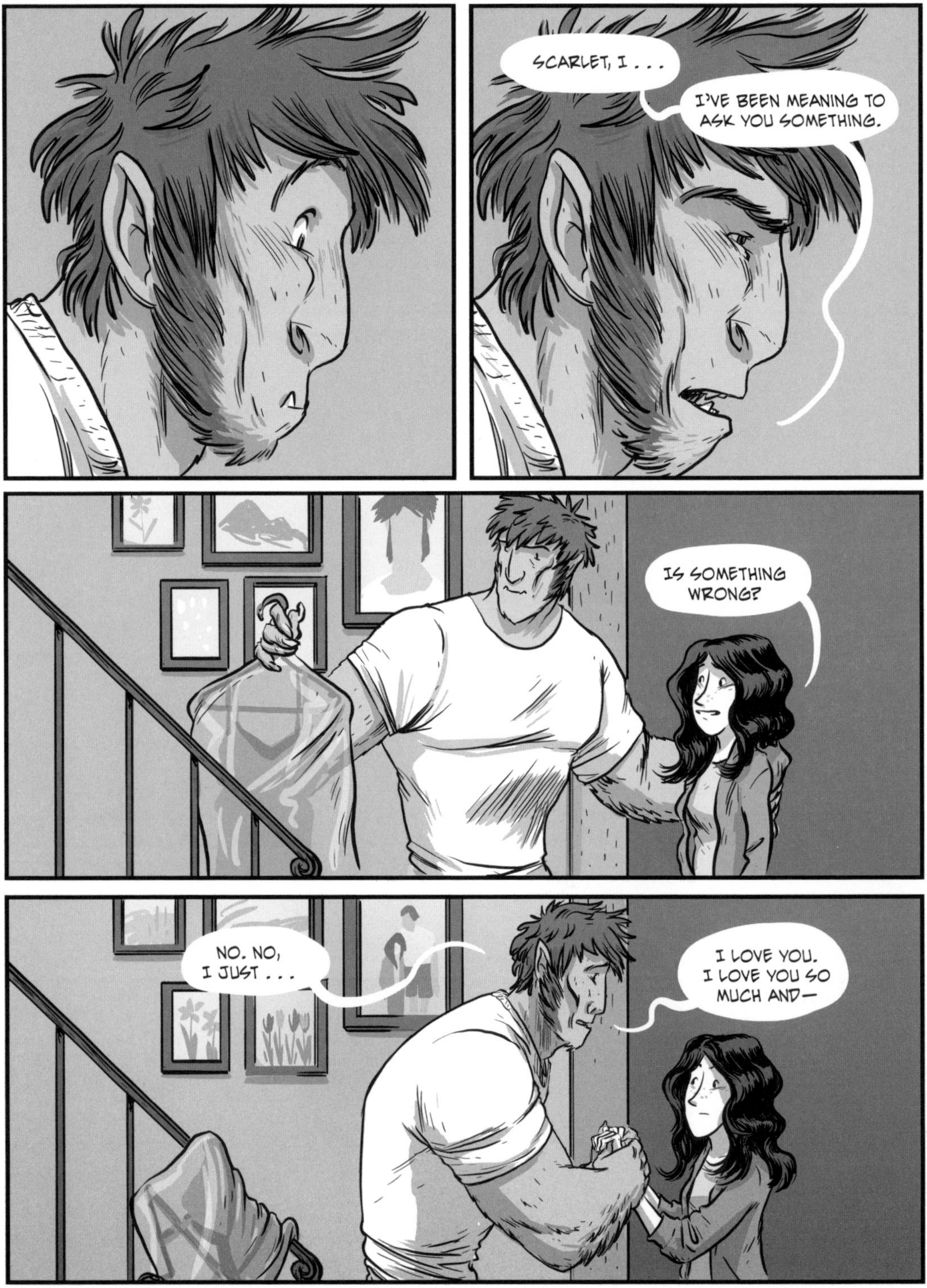
SCARLET, I . . .
I'VE BEEN MEANING TO ASK YOU SOMETHING.
IS SOMETHING WRONG?
NO. NO, I JUST . . .
I LOVE YOU. I LOVE YOU SO MUCH AND—

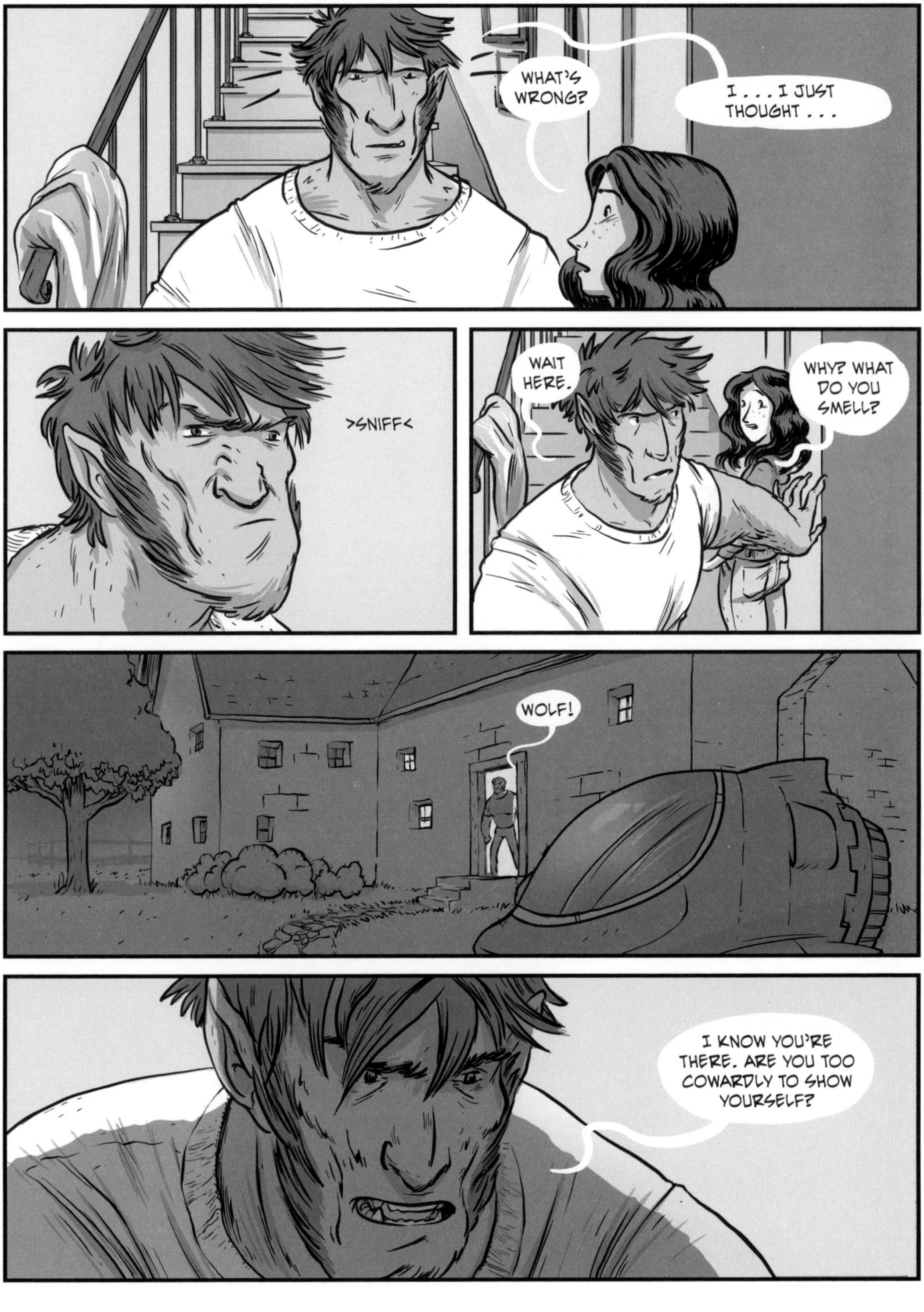
WHAT'S WRONG?
I . . . I JUST THOUGHT . . .
>SNIFF<
WAIT HERE.
WHY? WHAT DO YOU SMELL?
WOLF!
I KNOW YOU'RE THERE. ARE YOU TOO COWARDLY TO SHOW YOURSELF?

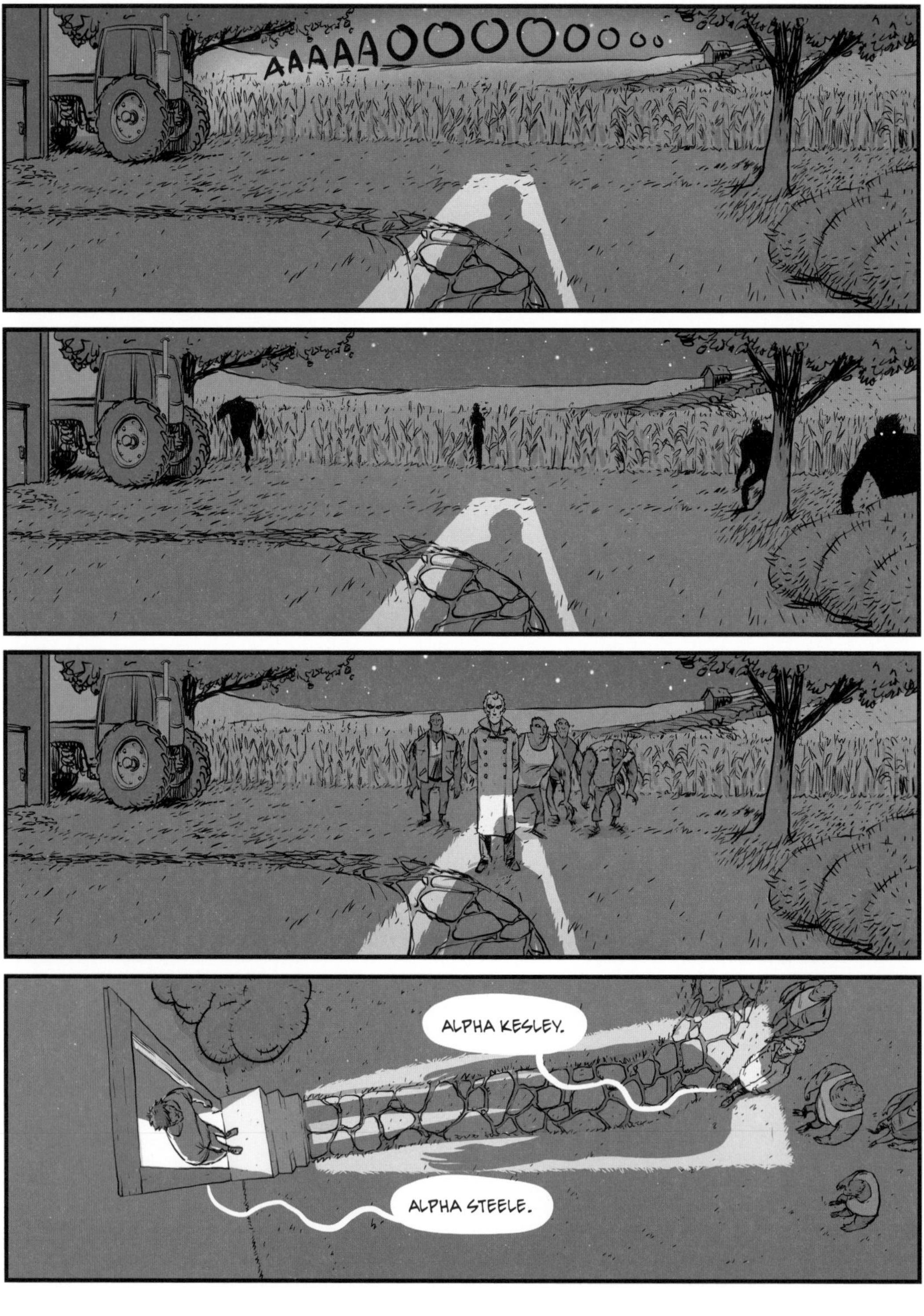
AAAAAOOOOOOooo
ALPHA KESLEY.
ALPHA STEELE.

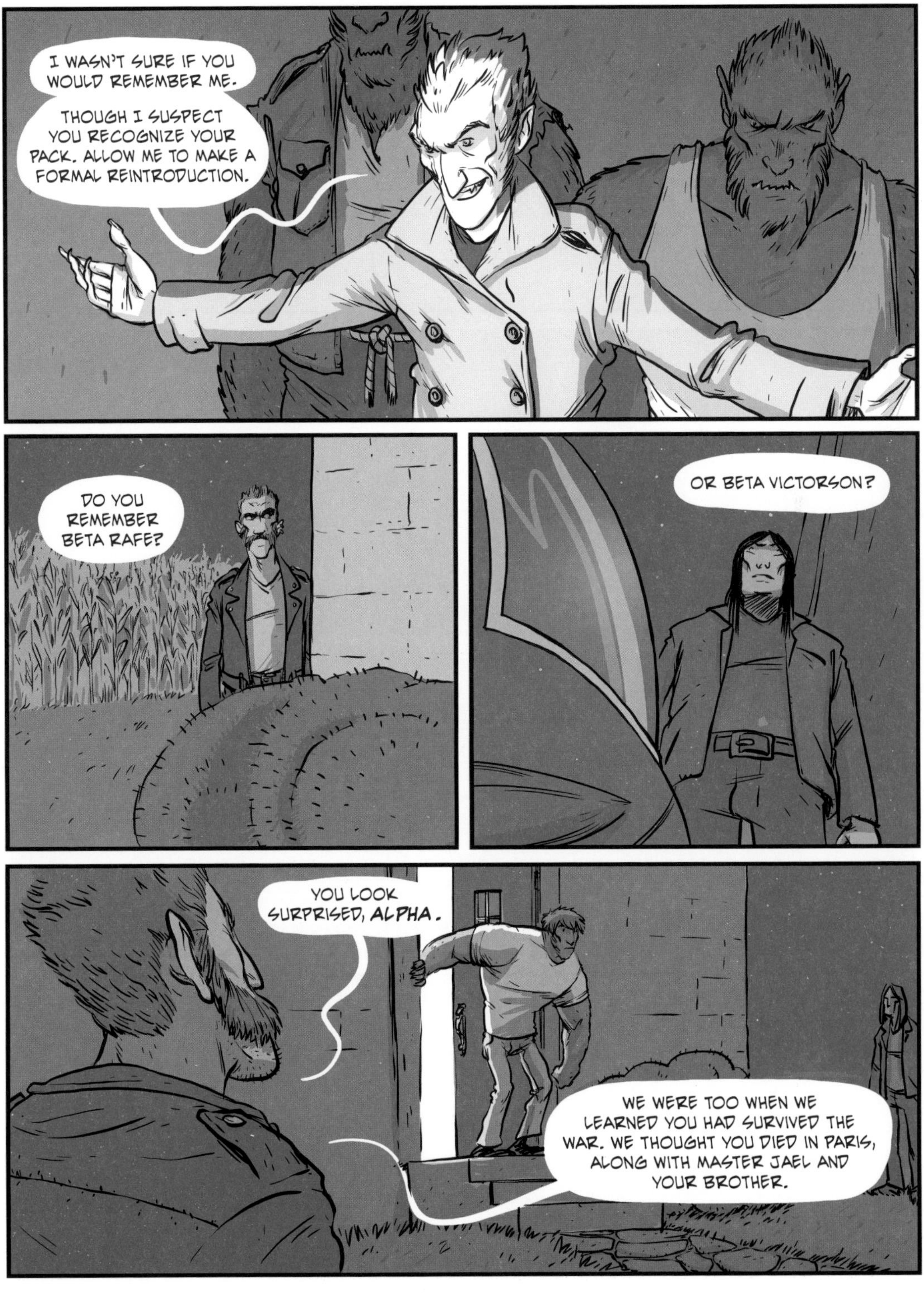
I WASN'T SURE IF YOU WOULD REMEMBER ME.
THOUGH I SUSPECT YOU RECOGNIZE YOUR PACK. ALLOW ME TO MAKE A FORMAL REINTRODUCTION.
DO YOU REMEMBER BETA RAFE?
OR BETA VICTORSON?
YOU LOOK SURPRISED, **ALPHA**.
WE WERE TOO WHEN WE LEARNED YOU HAD SURVIVED THE WAR. WE THOUGHT YOU DIED IN PARIS, ALONG WITH MASTER JAEL AND YOUR BROTHER.

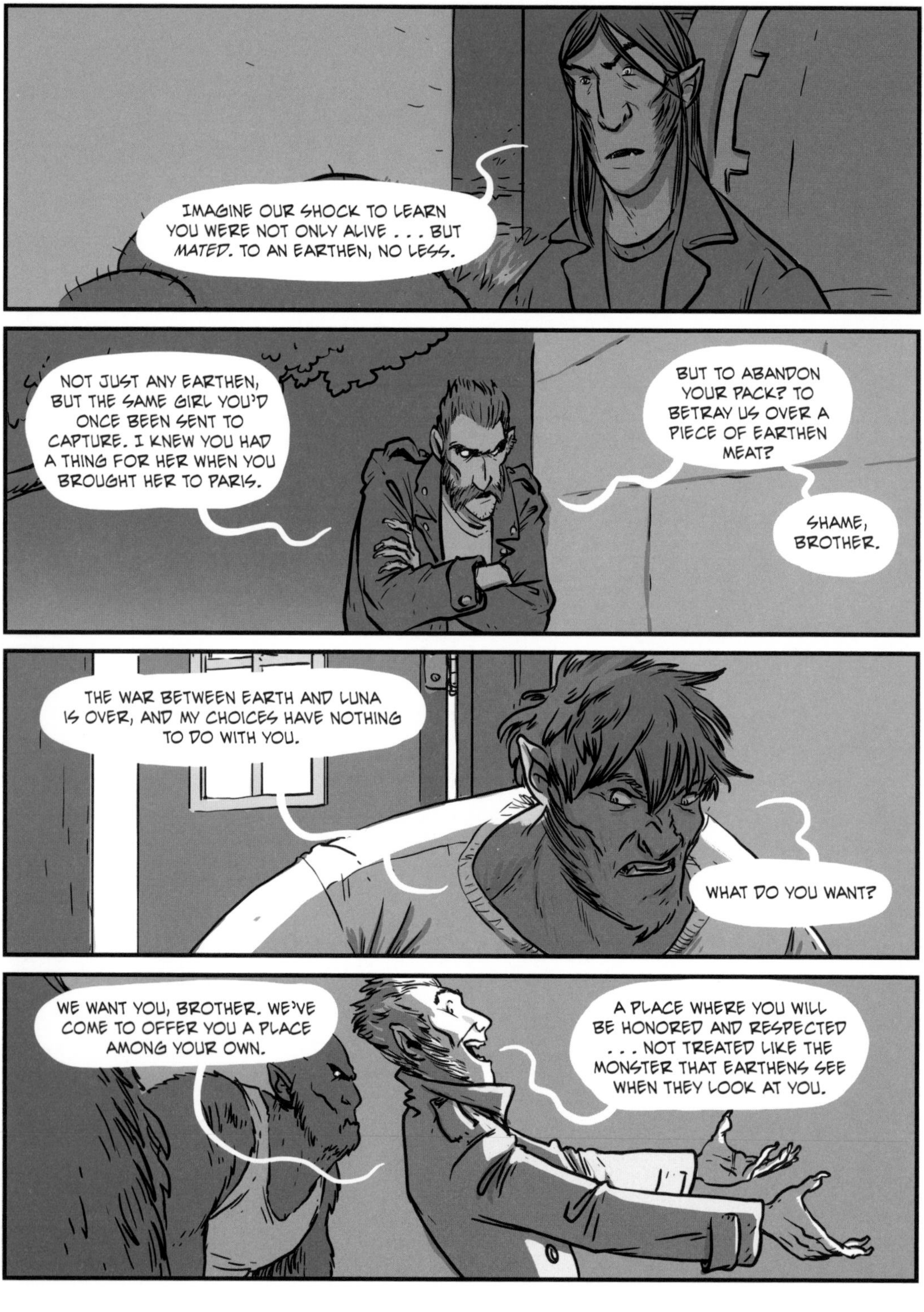
IMAGINE OUR SHOCK TO LEARN YOU WERE NOT ONLY ALIVE . . . BUT *MATED*. TO AN EARTHEN, NO LESS.
NOT JUST ANY EARTHEN, BUT THE SAME GIRL YOU'D ONCE BEEN SENT TO CAPTURE. I KNEW YOU HAD A THING FOR HER WHEN YOU BROUGHT HER TO PARIS.
BUT TO ABANDON YOUR PACK? TO BETRAY US OVER A PIECE OF EARTHEN MEAT?
SHAME, BROTHER.
THE WAR BETWEEN EARTH AND LUNA IS OVER, AND MY CHOICES HAVE NOTHING TO DO WITH YOU.
WHAT DO YOU WANT?
WE WANT YOU, BROTHER. WE'VE COME TO OFFER YOU A PLACE AMONG YOUR OWN.
A PLACE WHERE YOU WILL BE HONORED AND RESPECTED . . . NOT TREATED LIKE THE MONSTER THAT EARTHENS SEE WHEN THEY LOOK AT YOU.

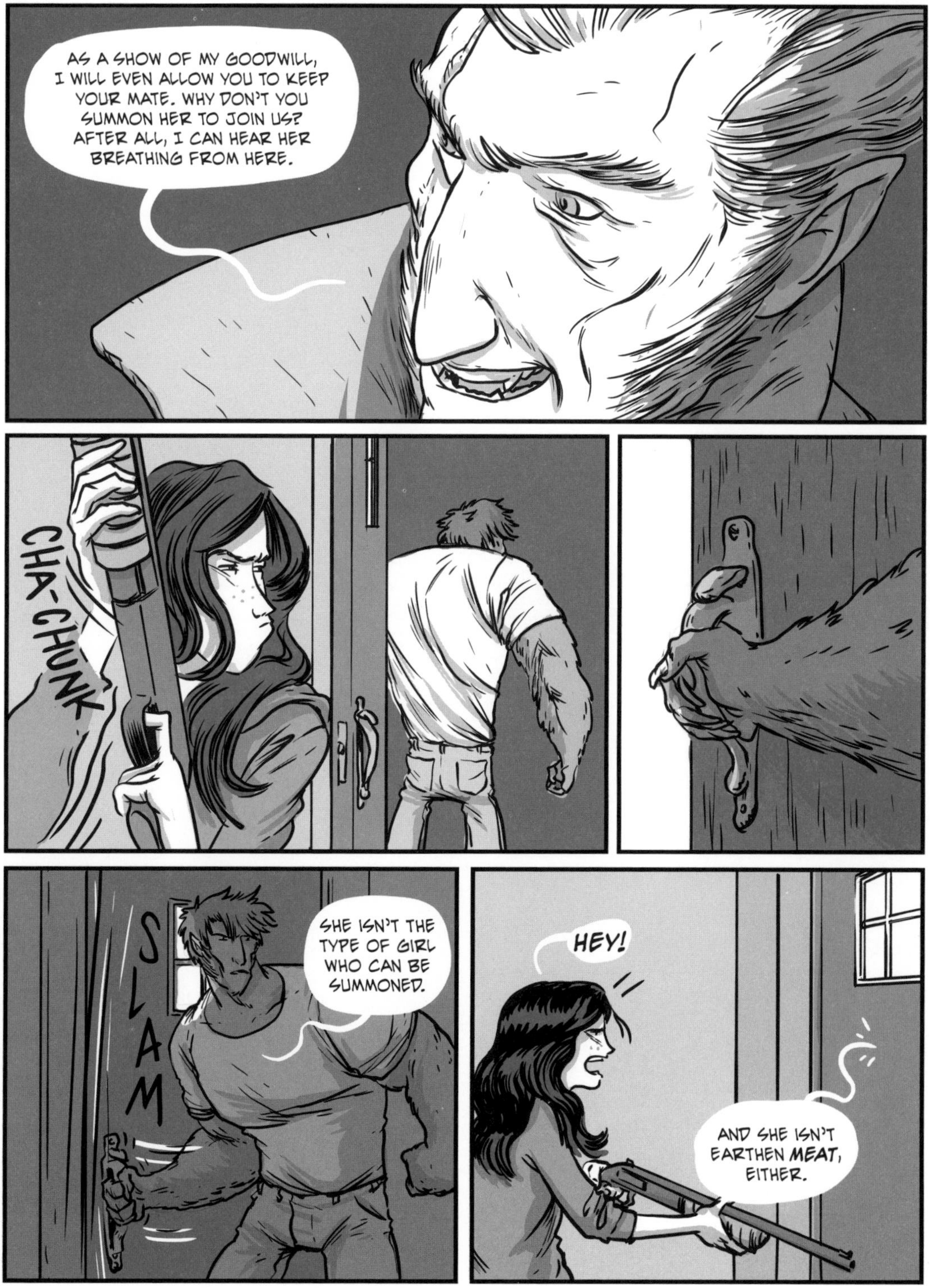
AS A SHOW OF MY GOODWILL, I WILL EVEN ALLOW YOU TO KEEP YOUR MATE. WHY DON'T YOU SUMMON HER TO JOIN US? AFTER ALL, I CAN HEAR HER BREATHING FROM HERE.
CHA-CHUNK
SLAM
SHE ISN'T THE TYPE OF GIRL WHO CAN BE SUMMONED.
HEY!
AND SHE ISN'T EARTHEN *MEAT*, EITHER.

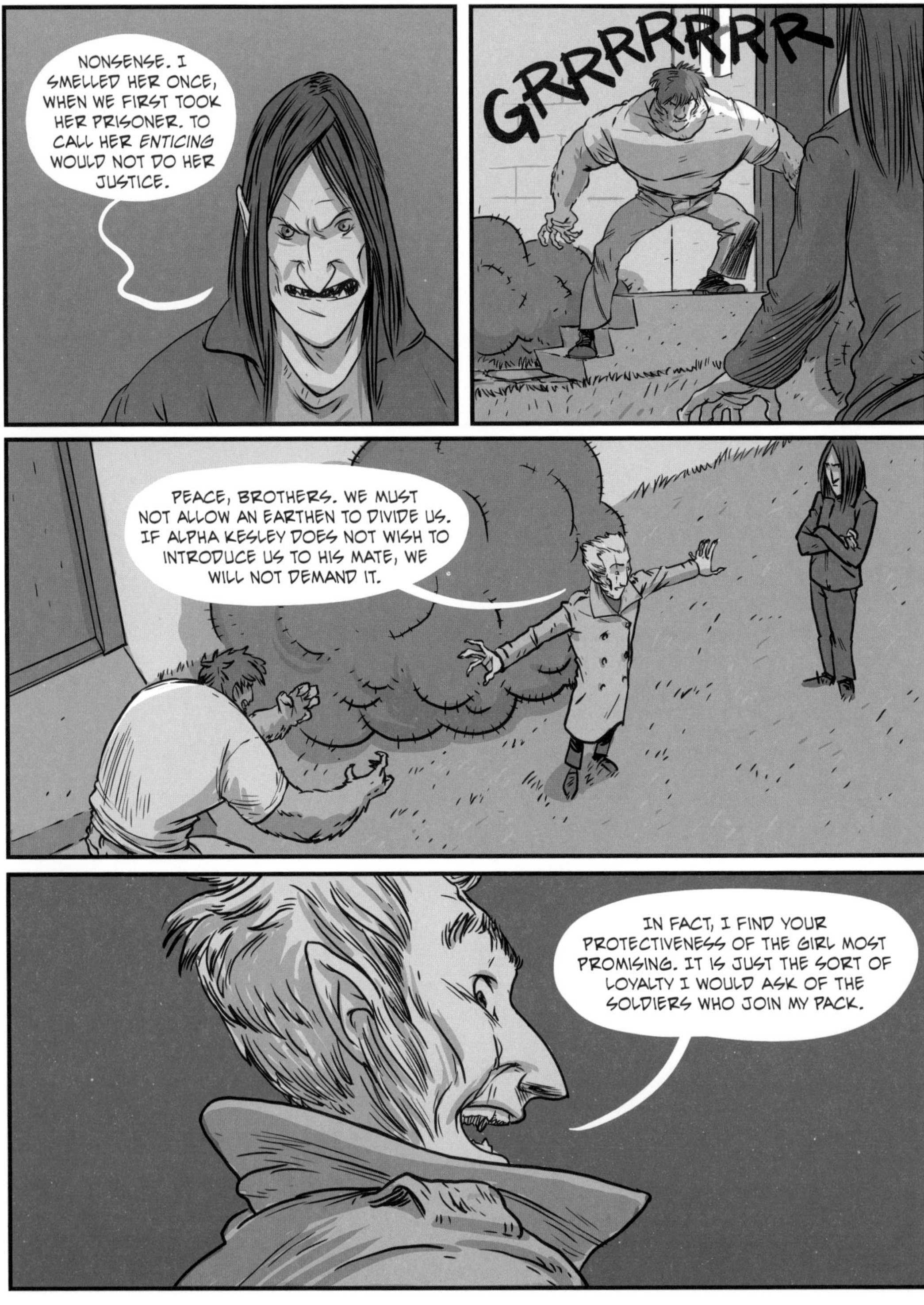
NONSENSE. I SMELLED HER ONCE, WHEN WE FIRST TOOK HER PRISONER. TO CALL HER *ENTICING* WOULD NOT DO HER JUSTICE.
GRRRRRRR
PEACE, BROTHERS. WE MUST NOT ALLOW AN EARTHEN TO DIVIDE US. IF ALPHA KESLEY DOES NOT WISH TO INTRODUCE US TO HIS MATE, WE WILL NOT DEMAND IT.
IN FACT, I FIND YOUR PROTECTIVENESS OF THE GIRL MOST PROMISING. IT IS JUST THE SORT OF LOYALTY I WOULD ASK OF THE SOLDIERS WHO JOIN MY PACK.

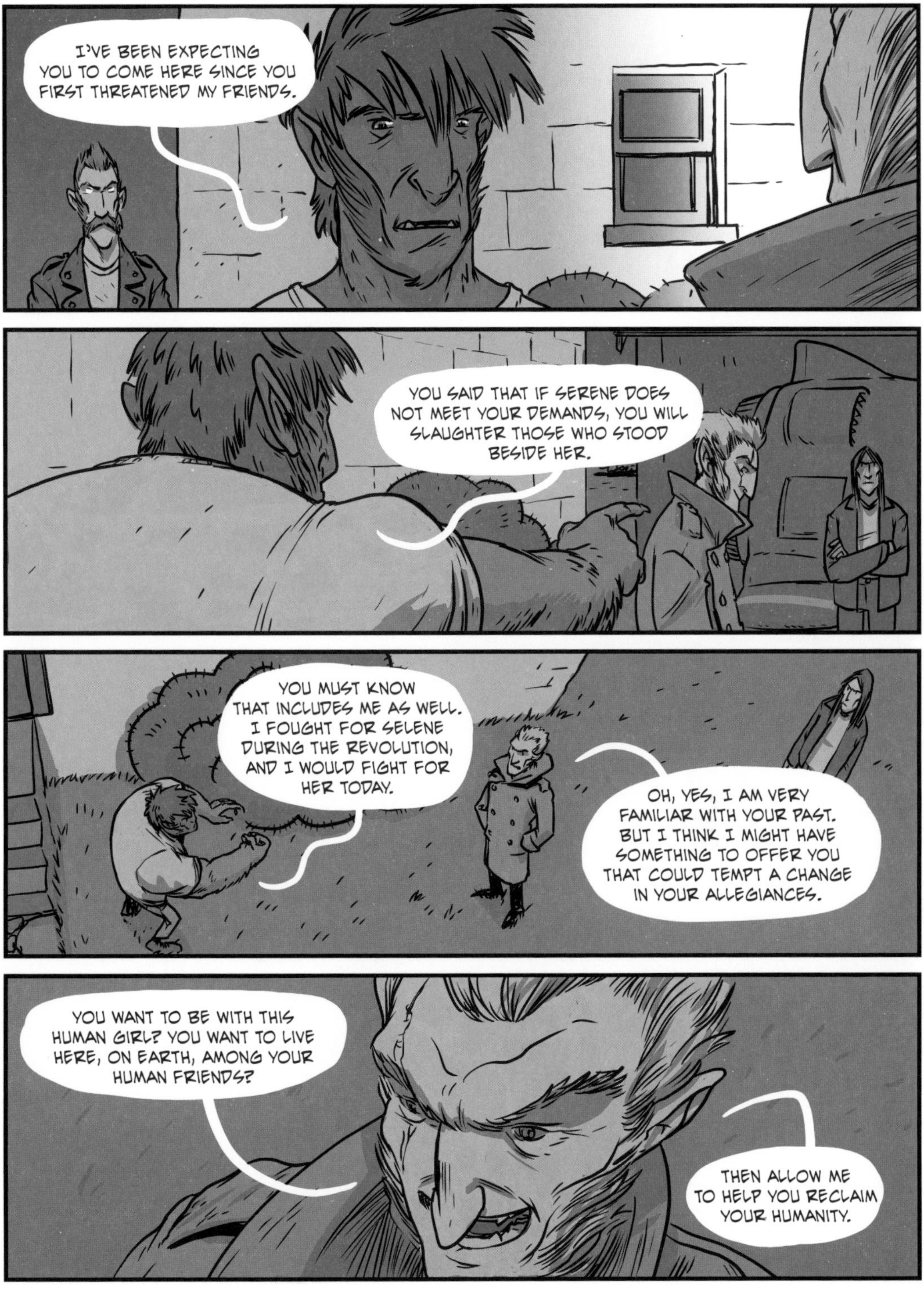
I'VE BEEN EXPECTING YOU TO COME HERE SINCE YOU FIRST THREATENED MY FRIENDS.
YOU SAID THAT IF SERENE DOES NOT MEET YOUR DEMANDS, YOU WILL SLAUGHTER THOSE WHO STOOD BESIDE HER.
YOU MUST KNOW THAT INCLUDES ME AS WELL. I FOUGHT FOR SELENE DURING THE REVOLUTION, AND I WOULD FIGHT FOR HER TODAY.
OH, YES, I AM VERY FAMILIAR WITH YOUR PAST. BUT I THINK I MIGHT HAVE SOMETHING TO OFFER YOU THAT COULD TEMPT A CHANGE IN YOUR ALLEGIANCES.
YOU WANT TO BE WITH THIS HUMAN GIRL? YOU WANT TO LIVE HERE, ON EARTH, AMONG YOUR HUMAN FRIENDS?
THEN ALLOW ME TO HELP YOU RECLAIM YOUR HUMANITY.

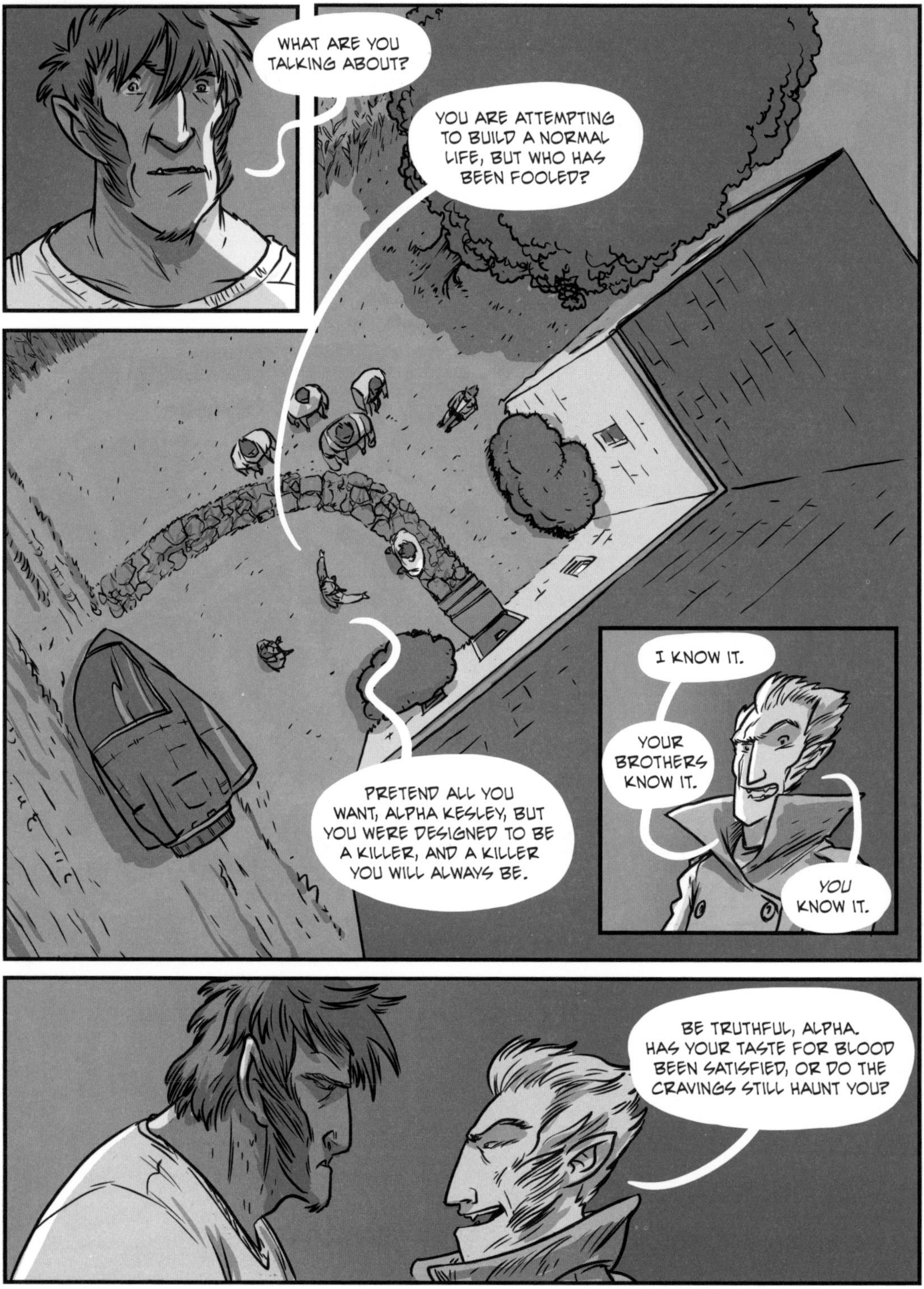
WHAT ARE YOU TALKING ABOUT?
YOU ARE ATTEMPTING TO BUILD A NORMAL LIFE, BUT WHO HAS BEEN FOOLED?
PRETEND ALL YOU WANT, ALPHA KESLEY, BUT YOU WERE DESIGNED TO BE A KILLER, AND A KILLER YOU WILL ALWAYS BE.
I KNOW IT.
YOUR BROTHERS KNOW IT.
YOU KNOW IT.
BE TRUTHFUL, ALPHA. HAS YOUR TASTE FOR BLOOD BEEN SATISFIED, OR DO THE CRAVINGS STILL HAUNT YOU?

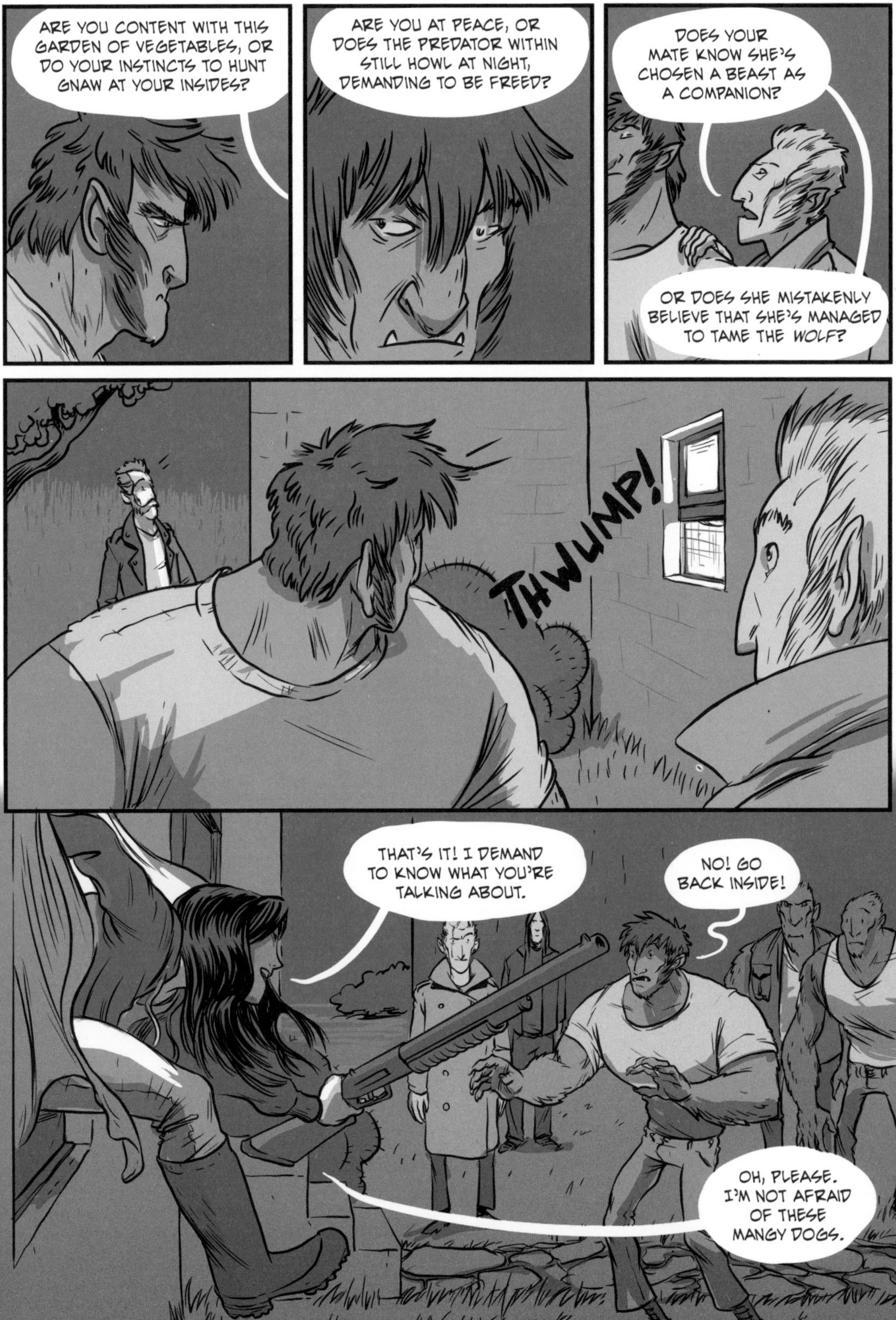
ARE YOU CONTENT WITH THIS GARDEN OF VEGETABLES, OR DO YOUR INSTINCTS TO HUNT GNAW AT YOUR INSIDES?
ARE YOU AT PEACE, OR DOES THE PREDATOR WITHIN STILL HOWL AT NIGHT, DEMANDING TO BE FREED?
DOES YOUR MATE KNOW SHE'S CHOSEN A BEAST AS A COMPANION?
OR DOES SHE MISTAKENLY BELIEVE THAT SHE'S MANAGED TO TAME THE *WOLF*?
THWUMP!
THAT'S IT! I DEMAND TO KNOW WHAT YOU'RE TALKING ABOUT.
NO! GO BACK INSIDE!
OH, PLEASE. I'M NOT AFRAID OF THESE MANGY DOGS.

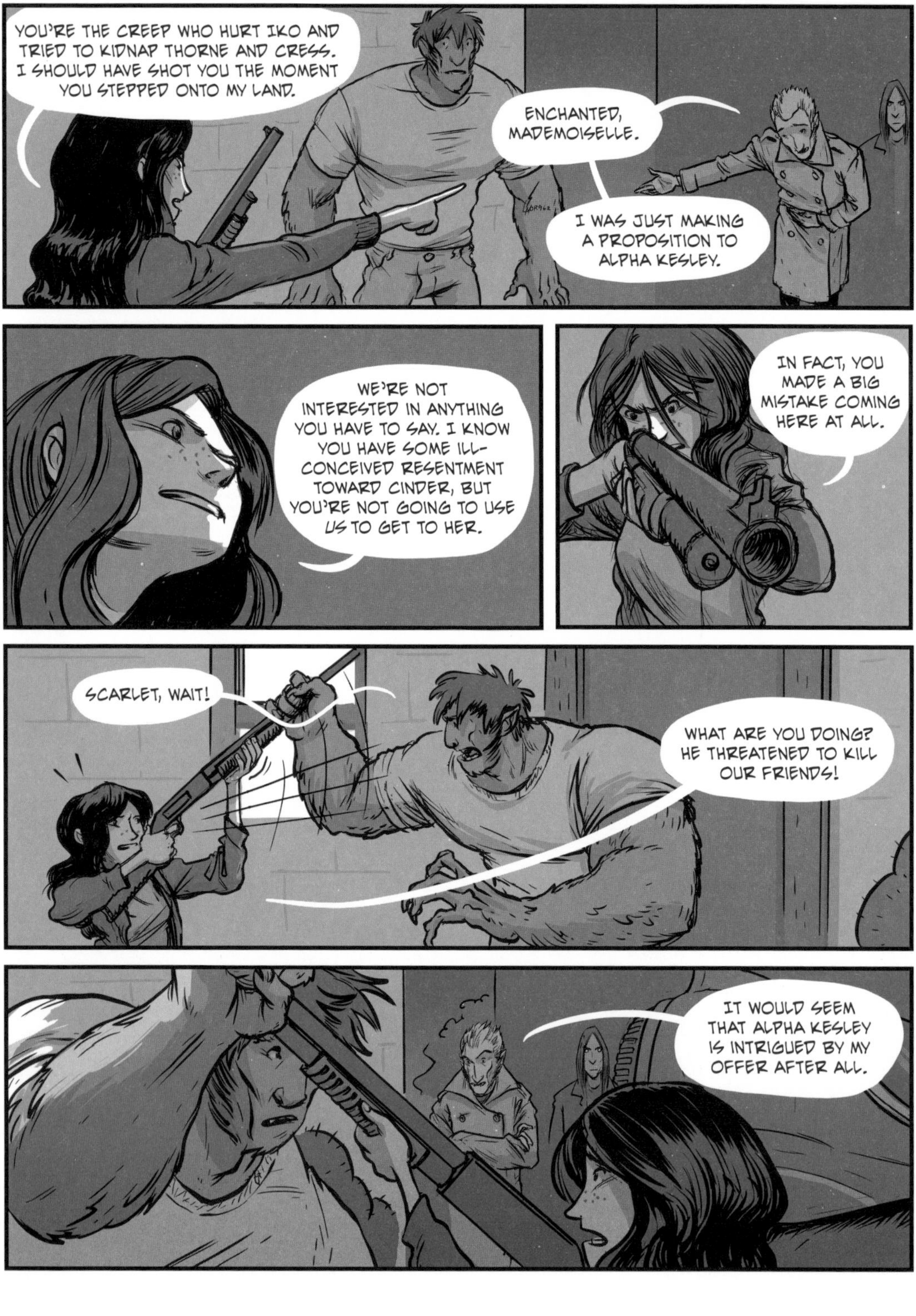
YOU'RE THE CREEP WHO HURT IKO AND TRIED TO KIDNAP THORNE AND CRESS. I SHOULD HAVE SHOT YOU THE MOMENT YOU STEPPED ONTO MY LAND.
ENCHANTED, MADEMOISELLE.
I WAS JUST MAKING A PROPOSITION TO ALPHA KESLEY.
WE'RE NOT INTERESTED IN ANYTHING YOU HAVE TO SAY. I KNOW YOU HAVE SOME ILL-CONCEIVED RESENTMENT TOWARD CINDER, BUT YOU'RE NOT GOING TO USE US TO GET TO HER.
IN FACT, YOU MADE A BIG MISTAKE COMING HERE AT ALL.
SCARLET, WAIT!
WHAT ARE YOU DOING? HE THREATENED TO KILL OUR FRIENDS!
IT WOULD SEEM THAT ALPHA KESLEY IS INTRIGUED BY MY OFFER AFTER ALL.

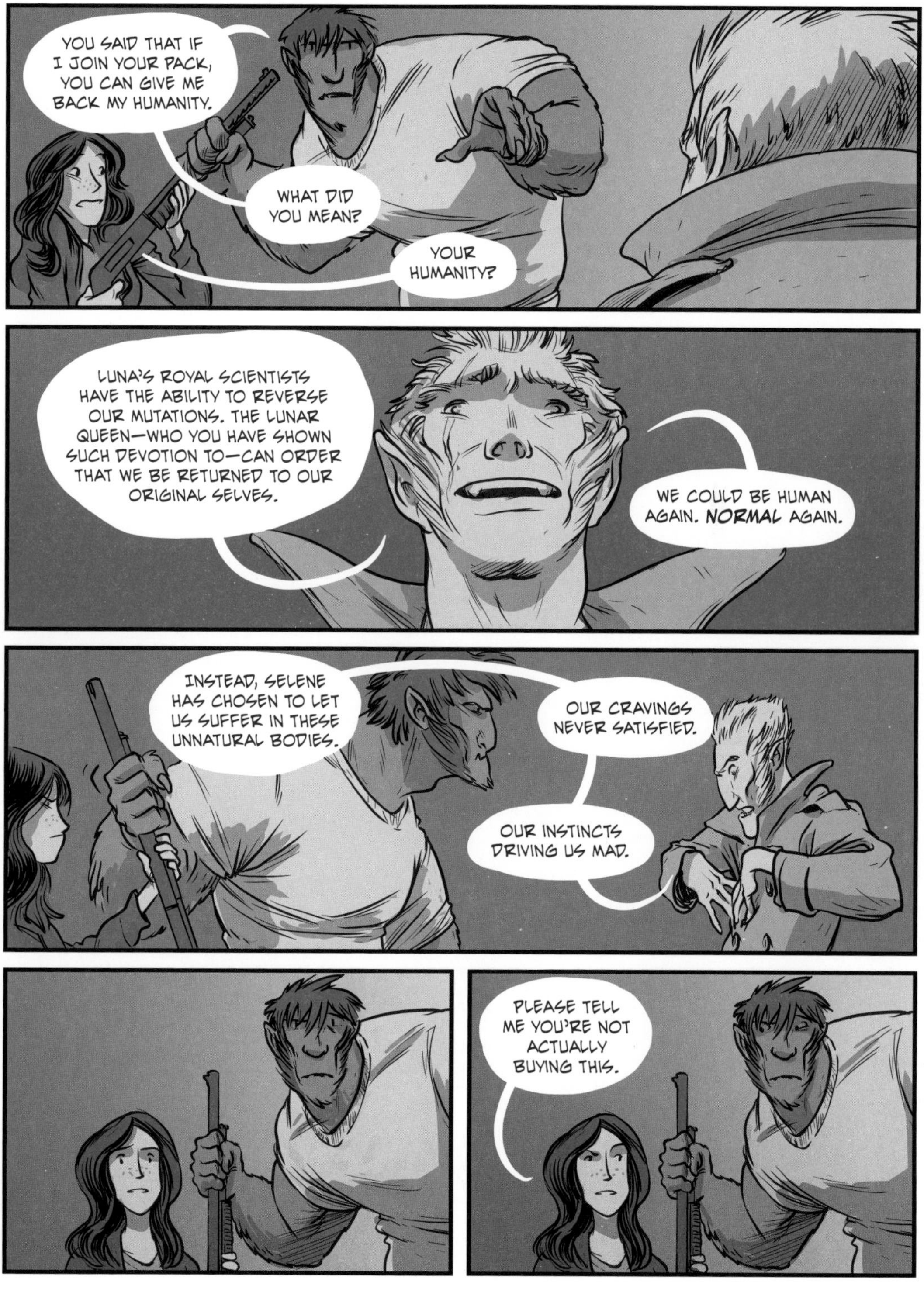

YOU SAID THAT IF I JOIN YOUR PACK, YOU CAN GIVE ME BACK MY HUMANITY.
WHAT DID YOU MEAN?
YOUR HUMANITY?
LUNA'S ROYAL SCIENTISTS HAVE THE ABILITY TO REVERSE OUR MUTATIONS. THE LUNAR QUEEN—WHO YOU HAVE SHOWN SUCH DEVOTION TO—CAN ORDER THAT WE BE RETURNED TO OUR ORIGINAL SELVES.
WE COULD BE HUMAN AGAIN. ***NORMAL*** AGAIN.
INSTEAD, SELENE HAS CHOSEN TO LET US SUFFER IN THESE UNNATURAL BODIES.
OUR CRAVINGS NEVER SATISFIED.
OUR INSTINCTS DRIVING US MAD.
PLEASE TELL ME YOU'RE NOT ACTUALLY BUYING THIS.

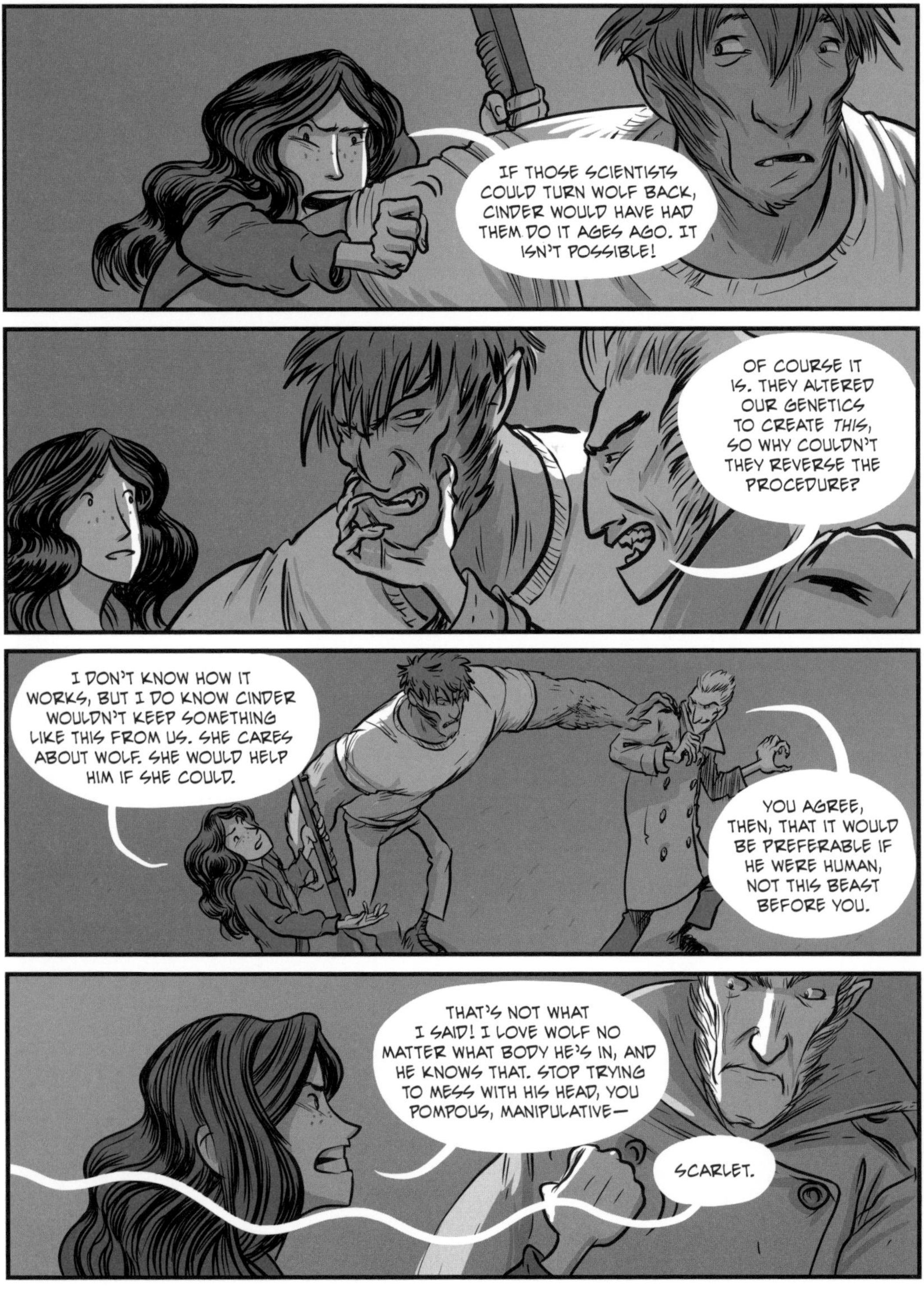
IF THOSE SCIENTISTS COULD TURN WOLF BACK, CINDER WOULD HAVE HAD THEM DO IT AGES AGO. IT ISN'T POSSIBLE!
OF COURSE IT IS. THEY ALTERED OUR GENETICS TO CREATE *THIS*, SO WHY COULDN'T THEY REVERSE THE PROCEDURE?
I DON'T KNOW HOW IT WORKS, BUT I DO KNOW CINDER WOULDN'T KEEP SOMETHING LIKE THIS FROM US. SHE CARES ABOUT WOLF. SHE WOULD HELP HIM IF SHE COULD.
YOU AGREE, THEN, THAT IT WOULD BE PREFERABLE IF HE WERE HUMAN, NOT THIS BEAST BEFORE YOU.
THAT'S NOT WHAT I SAID! I LOVE WOLF NO MATTER WHAT BODY HE'S IN, AND HE KNOWS THAT. STOP TRYING TO MESS WITH HIS HEAD, YOU POMPOUS, MANIPULATIVE—
SCARLET.

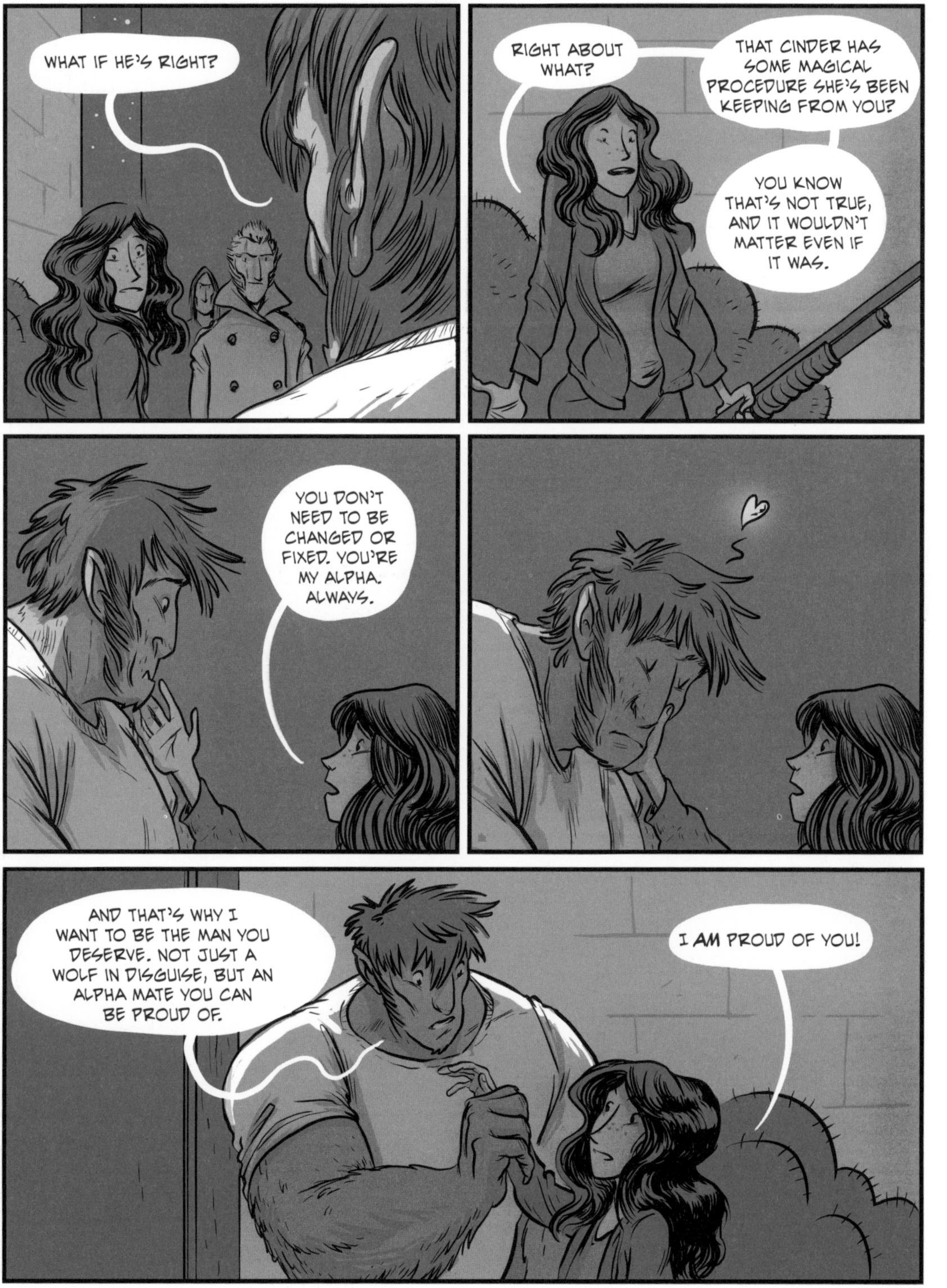
WHAT IF HE'S RIGHT?
RIGHT ABOUT WHAT?
THAT CINDER HAS SOME MAGICAL PROCEDURE SHE'S BEEN KEEPING FROM YOU?
YOU KNOW THAT'S NOT TRUE, AND IT WOULDN'T MATTER EVEN IF IT WAS.
YOU DON'T NEED TO BE CHANGED OR FIXED. YOU'RE MY ALPHA. ALWAYS.
AND THAT'S WHY I WANT TO BE THE MAN YOU DESERVE. NOT JUST A WOLF IN DISGUISE, BUT AN ALPHA MATE YOU CAN BE PROUD OF.
I **AM** PROUD OF YOU!

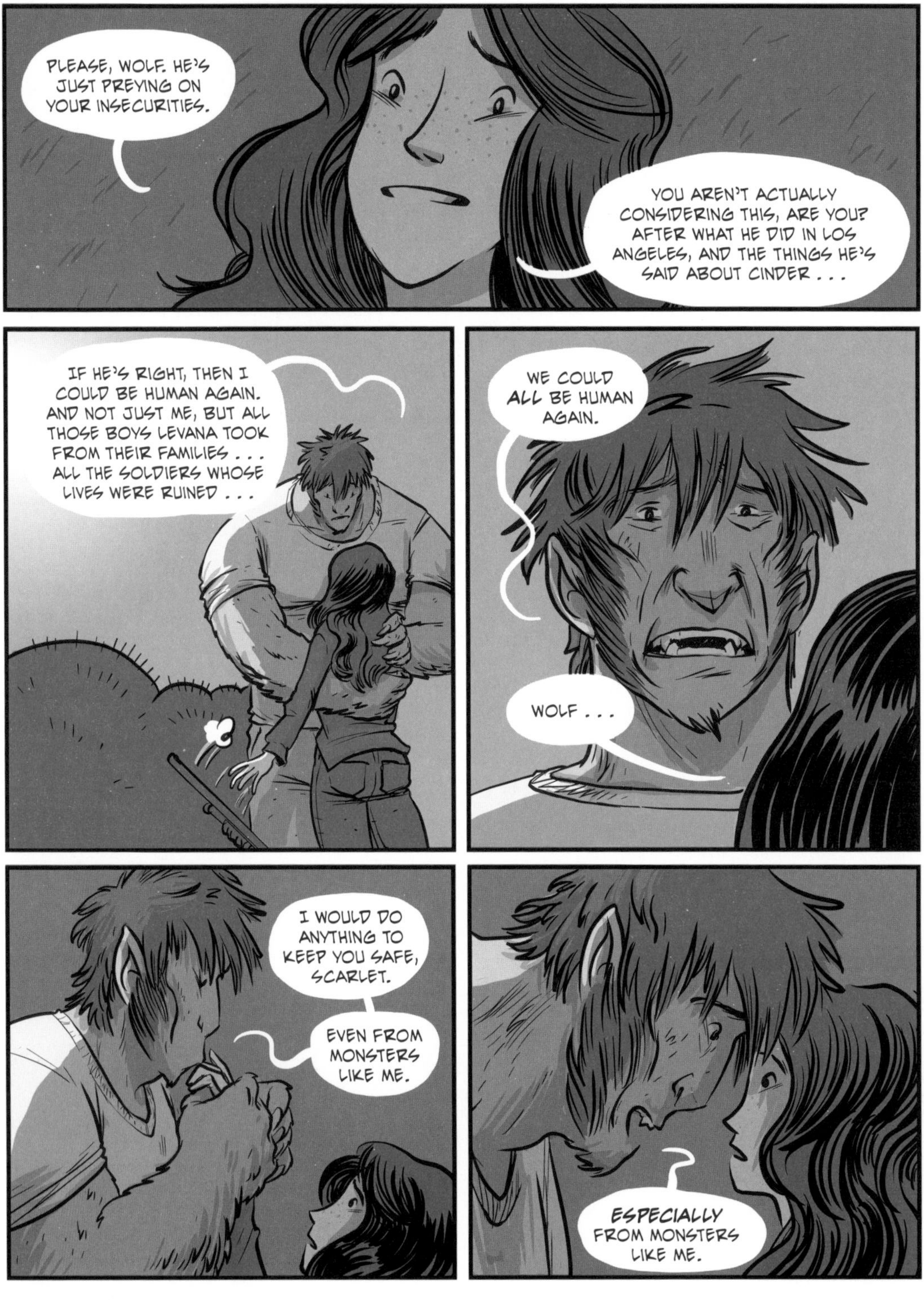
PLEASE, WOLF. HE'S JUST PREYING ON YOUR INSECURITIES.
YOU AREN'T ACTUALLY CONSIDERING THIS, ARE YOU? AFTER WHAT HE DID IN LOS ANGELES, AND THE THINGS HE'S SAID ABOUT CINDER . . .
IF HE'S RIGHT, THEN I COULD BE HUMAN AGAIN. AND NOT JUST ME, BUT ALL THOSE BOYS LEVANA TOOK FROM THEIR FAMILIES . . . ALL THE SOLDIERS WHOSE LIVES WERE RUINED . . .
WE COULD ALL BE HUMAN AGAIN.
WOLF . . .
I WOULD DO ANYTHING TO KEEP YOU SAFE, SCARLET.
EVEN FROM MONSTERS LIKE ME.
ESPECIALLY FROM MONSTERS LIKE ME.

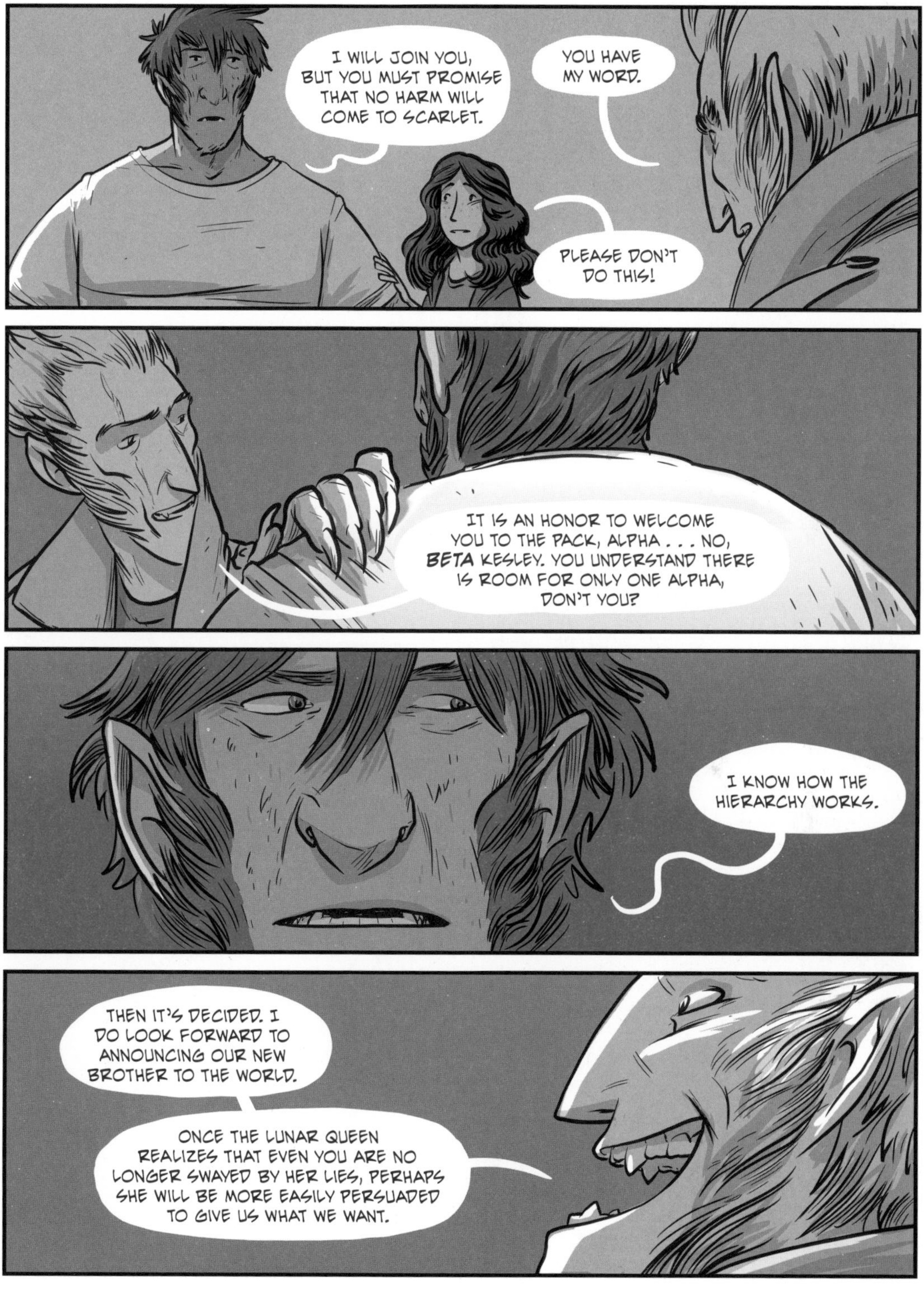
I WILL JOIN YOU, BUT YOU MUST PROMISE THAT NO HARM WILL COME TO SCARLET.
YOU HAVE MY WORD.
PLEASE DON'T DO THIS!
IT IS AN HONOR TO WELCOME YOU TO THE PACK, ALPHA . . . NO, BETA KESLEY. YOU UNDERSTAND THERE IS ROOM FOR ONLY ONE ALPHA, DON'T YOU?
I KNOW HOW THE HIERARCHY WORKS.
THEN IT'S DECIDED. I DO LOOK FORWARD TO ANNOUNCING OUR NEW BROTHER TO THE WORLD.
ONCE THE LUNAR QUEEN REALIZES THAT EVEN YOU ARE NO LONGER SWAYED BY HER LIES, PERHAPS SHE WILL BE MORE EASILY PERSUADED TO GIVE US WHAT WE WANT.

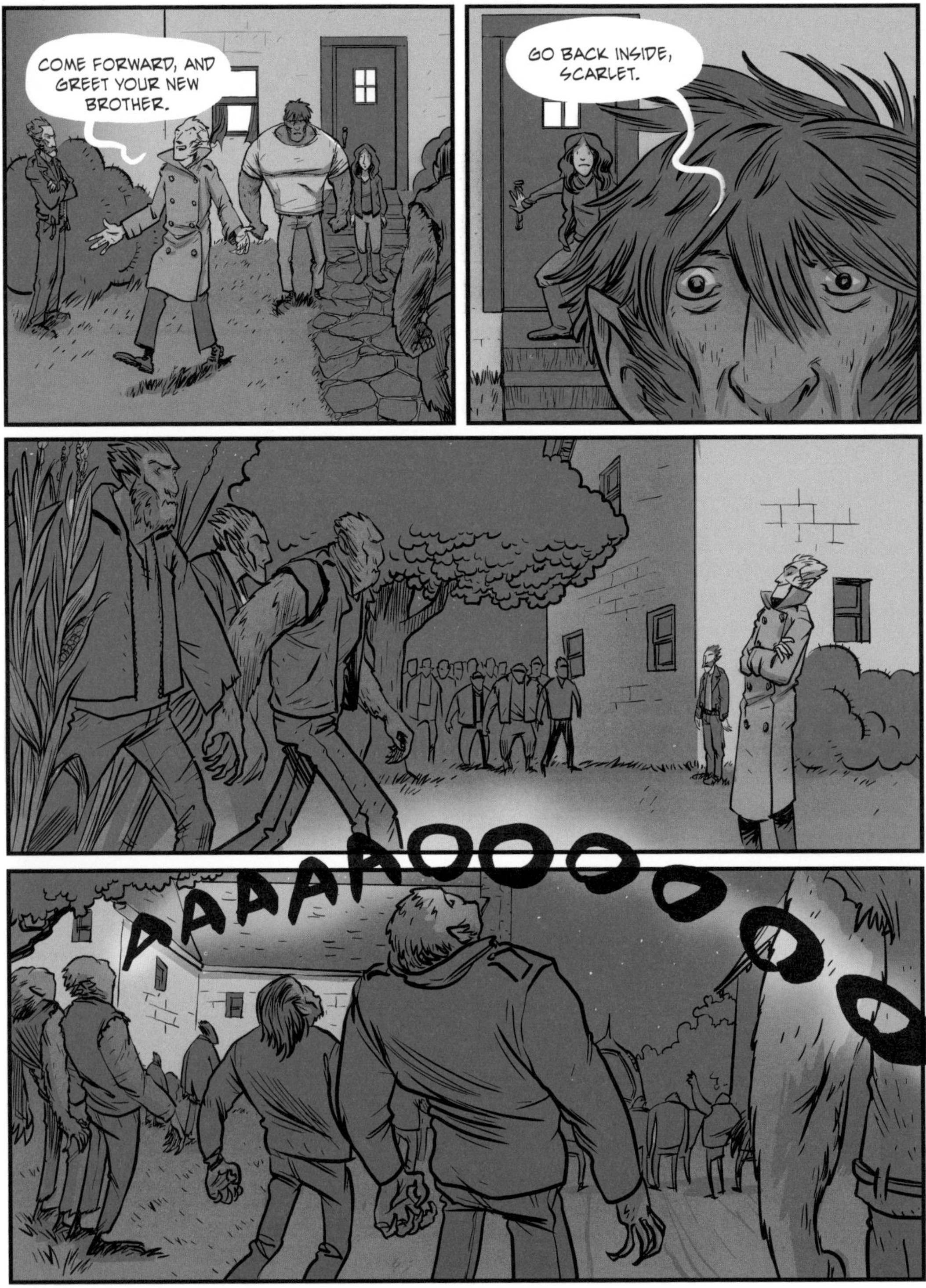
COME FORWARD, AND GREET YOUR NEW BROTHER.
GO BACK INSIDE, SCARLET.
AAAAAOOOOOO

CHAPTER 11

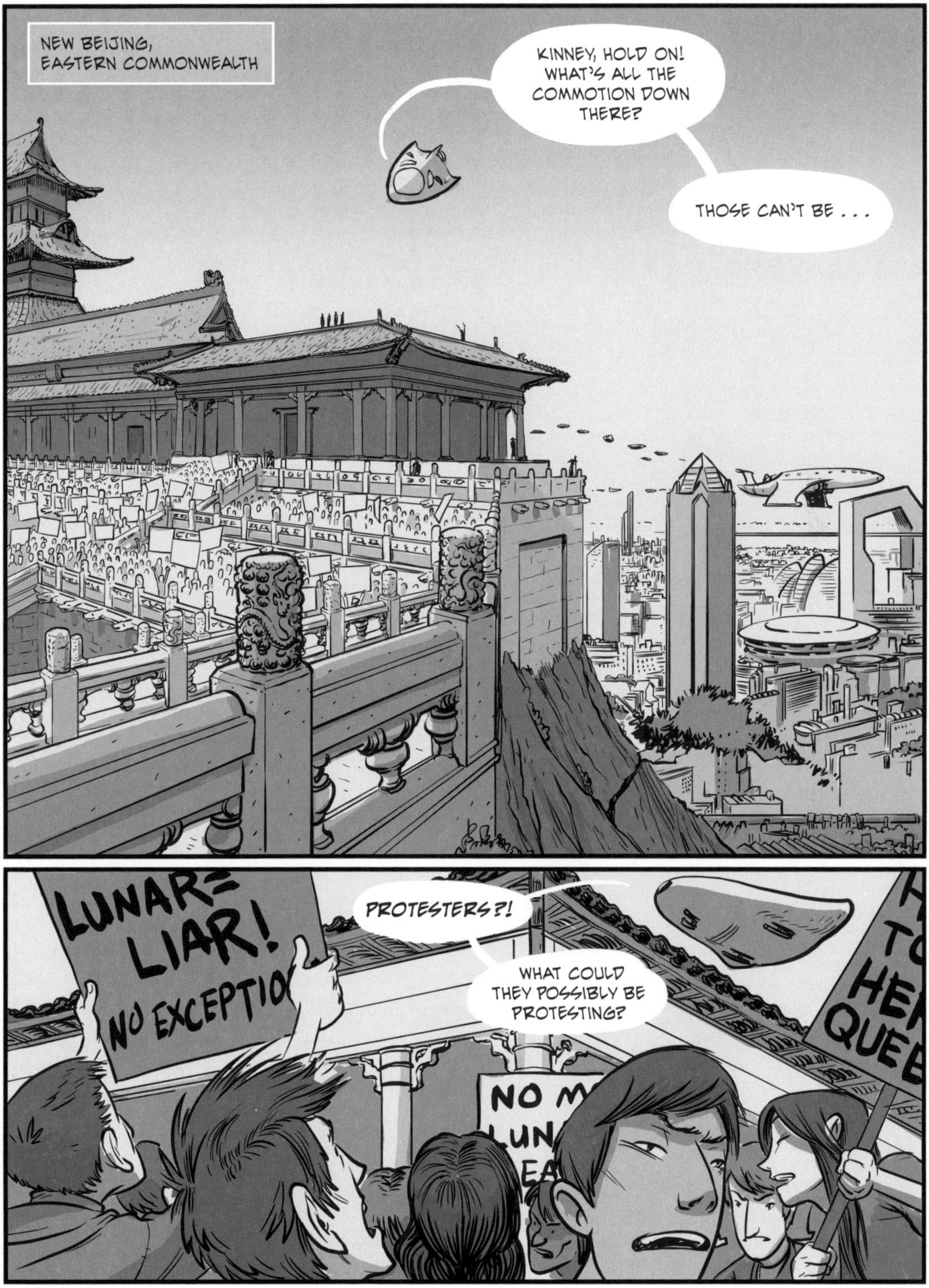
NEW BEIJING, EASTERN COMMONWEALTH
KINNEY, HOLD ON! WHAT'S ALL THE COMMOTION DOWN THERE?
THOSE CAN'T BE . . .
LUNAR= LIAR!
PROTESTERS?!
WHAT COULD THEY POSSIBLY BE PROTESTING?

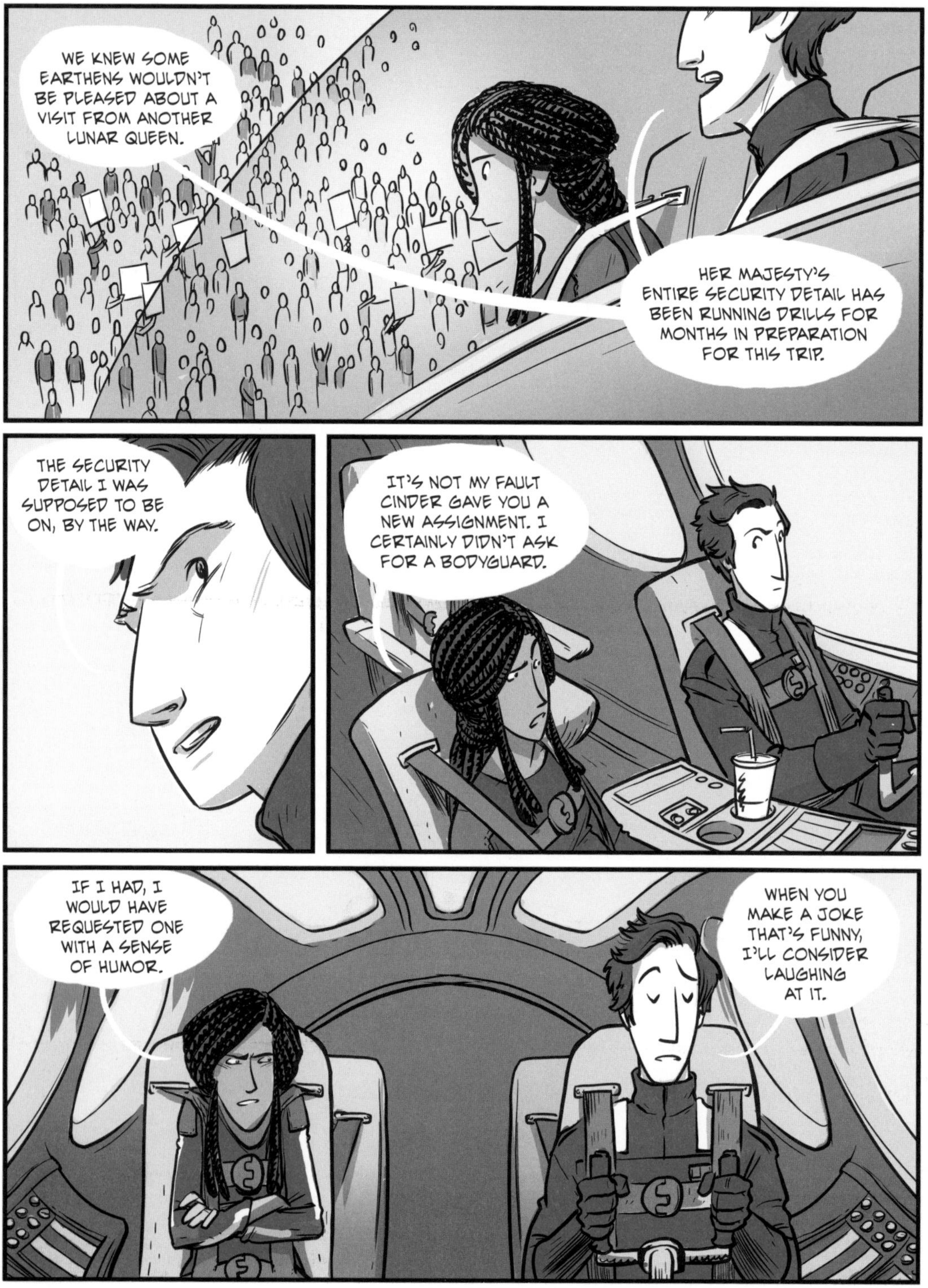
WE KNEW SOME EARTHENS WOULDN'T BE PLEASED ABOUT A VISIT FROM ANOTHER LUNAR QUEEN.
HER MAJESTY'S ENTIRE SECURITY DETAIL HAS BEEN RUNNING DRILLS FOR MONTHS IN PREPARATION FOR THIS TRIP.
THE SECURITY DETAIL I WAS SUPPOSED TO BE ON, BY THE WAY.
IT'S NOT MY FAULT CINDER GAVE YOU A NEW ASSIGNMENT. I CERTAINLY DIDN'T ASK FOR A BODYGUARD.
IF I HAD, I WOULD HAVE REQUESTED ONE WITH A SENSE OF HUMOR.
WHEN YOU MAKE A JOKE THAT'S FUNNY, I'LL CONSIDER LAUGHING AT IT.

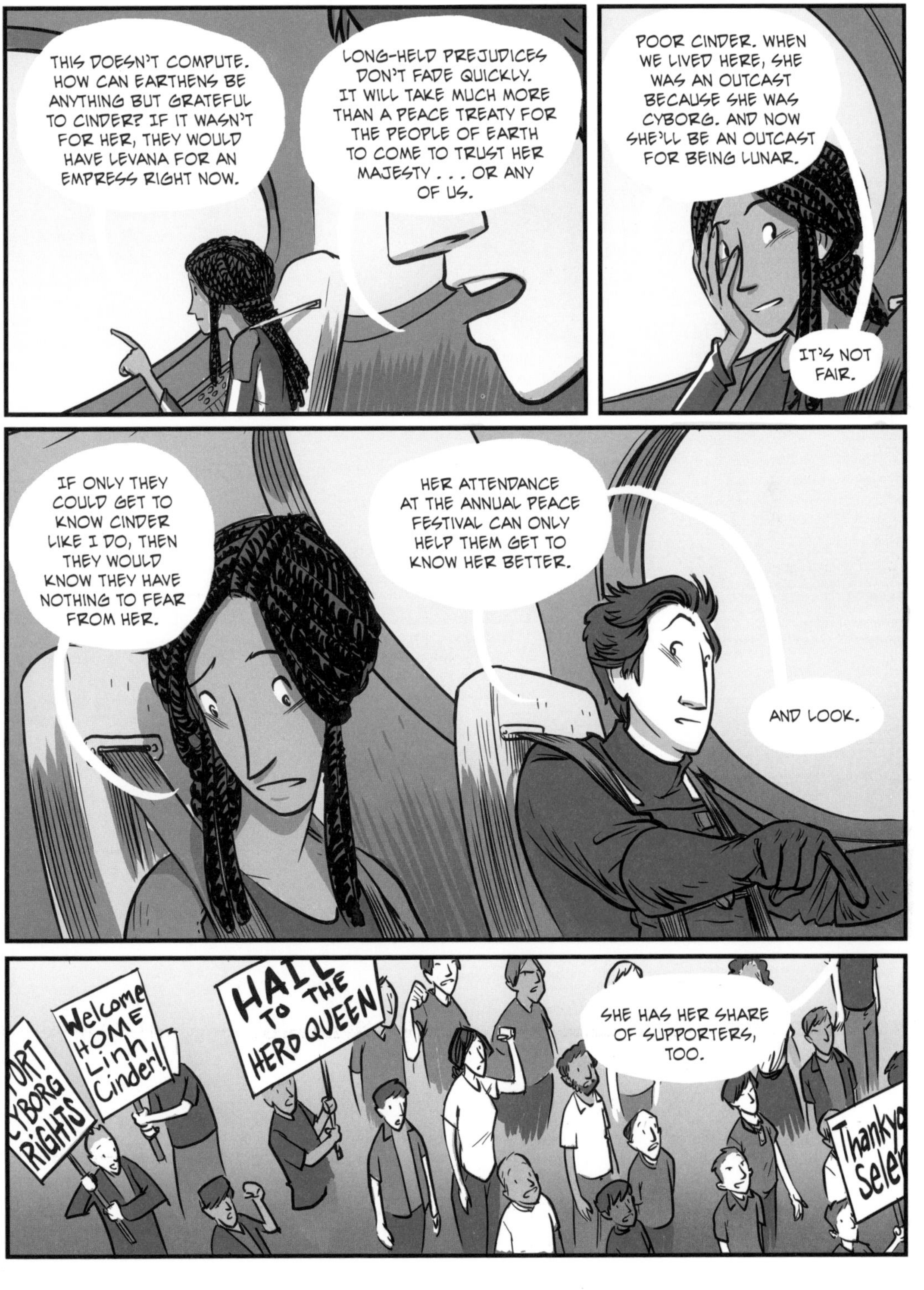
THIS DOESN'T COMPUTE. HOW CAN EARTHENS BE ANYTHING BUT GRATEFUL TO CINDER? IF IT WASN'T FOR HER, THEY WOULD HAVE LEVANA FOR AN EMPRESS RIGHT NOW.
LONG-HELD PREJUDICES DON'T FADE QUICKLY. IT WILL TAKE MUCH MORE THAN A PEACE TREATY FOR THE PEOPLE OF EARTH TO COME TO TRUST HER MAJESTY . . . OR ANY OF US.
POOR CINDER. WHEN WE LIVED HERE, SHE WAS AN OUTCAST BECAUSE SHE WAS CYBORG. AND NOW SHE'LL BE AN OUTCAST FOR BEING LUNAR.
IT'S NOT FAIR.
IF ONLY THEY COULD GET TO KNOW CINDER LIKE I DO, THEN THEY WOULD KNOW THEY HAVE NOTHING TO FEAR FROM HER.
HER ATTENDANCE AT THE ANNUAL PEACE FESTIVAL CAN ONLY HELP THEM GET TO KNOW HER BETTER.
AND LOOK.
CYBORG RIGHTS
Welcome HOME Linh Cinder!
HAIL TO THE HERO QUEEN
SHE HAS HER SHARE OF SUPPORTERS, TOO.

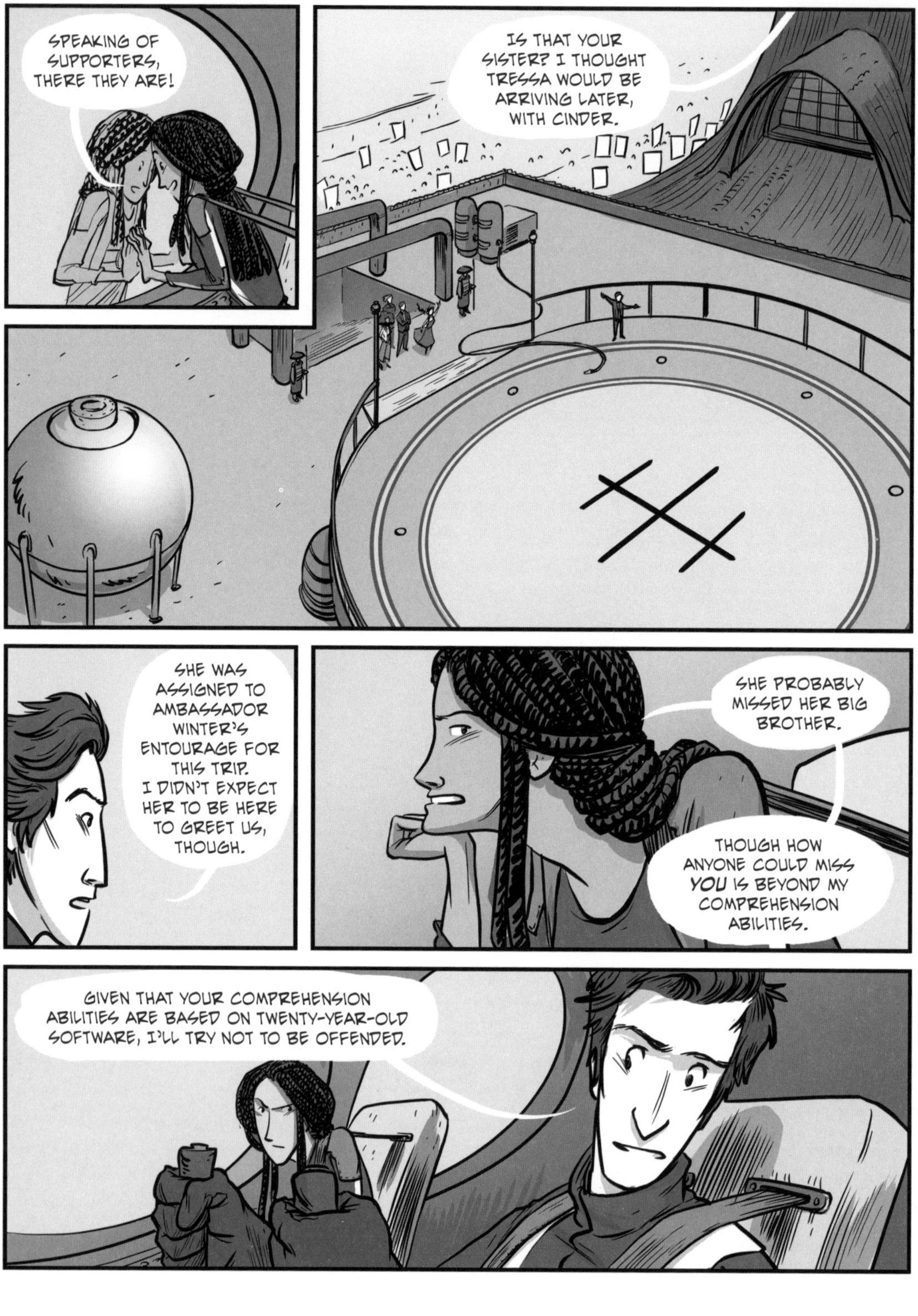
SPEAKING OF SUPPORTERS, THERE THEY ARE!
IS THAT YOUR SISTER? I THOUGHT TRESSA WOULD BE ARRIVING LATER, WITH CINDER.
SHE WAS ASSIGNED TO AMBASSADOR WINTER'S ENTOURAGE FOR THIS TRIP. I DIDN'T EXPECT HER TO BE HERE TO GREET US, THOUGH.
SHE PROBABLY MISSED HER BIG BROTHER.
THOUGH HOW ANYONE COULD MISS *YOU* IS BEYOND MY COMPREHENSION ABILITIES.
GIVEN THAT YOUR COMPREHENSION ABILITIES ARE BASED ON TWENTY-YEAR-OLD SOFTWARE, I'LL TRY NOT TO BE OFFENDED.

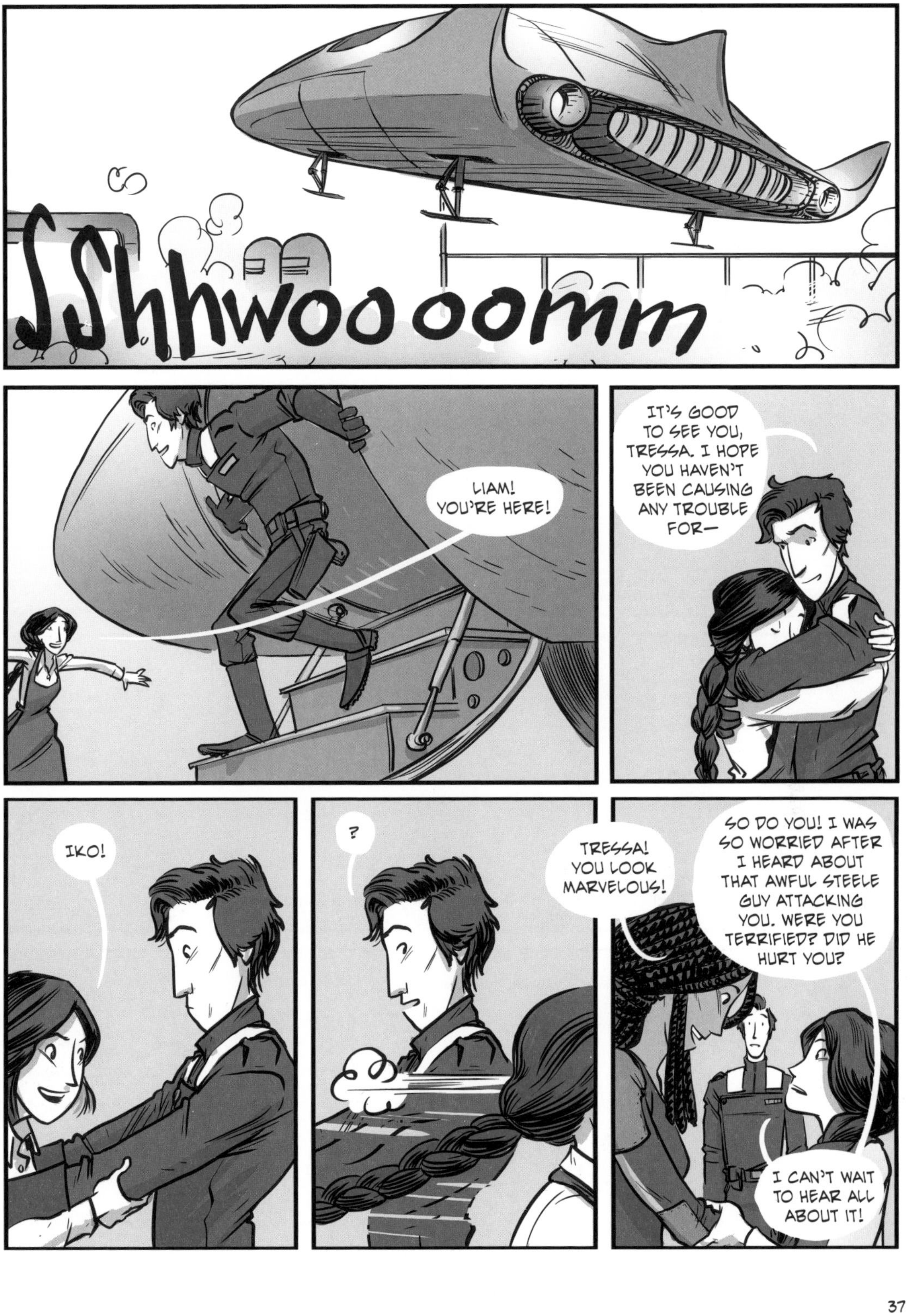
SShwooOomm
LIAM! YOU'RE HERE!
IT'S GOOD TO SEE YOU, TRESSA. I HOPE YOU HAVEN'T BEEN CAUSING ANY TROUBLE FOR—
IKO!
?
TRESSA! YOU LOOK MARVELOUS!
SO DO YOU! I WAS SO WORRIED AFTER I HEARD ABOUT THAT AWFUL STEELE GUY ATTACKING YOU. WERE YOU TERRIFIED? DID HE HURT YOU?
I CAN'T WAIT TO HEAR ALL ABOUT IT!

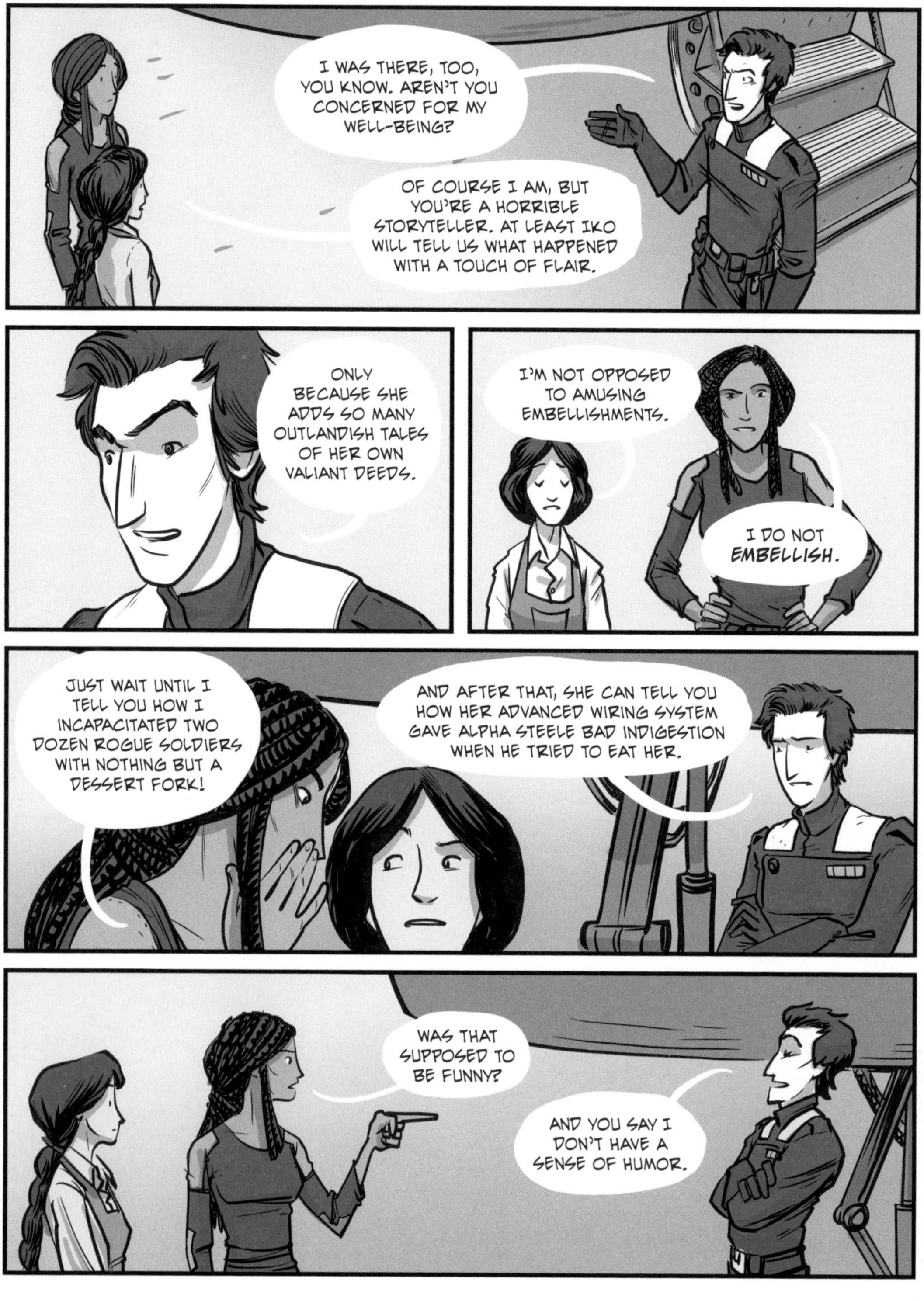
I WAS THERE, TOO, YOU KNOW. AREN'T YOU CONCERNED FOR MY WELL-BEING?
OF COURSE I AM, BUT YOU'RE A HORRIBLE STORYTELLER. AT LEAST IKO WILL TELL US WHAT HAPPENED WITH A TOUCH OF FLAIR.
ONLY BECAUSE SHE ADDS SO MANY OUTLANDISH TALES OF HER OWN VALIANT DEEDS.
I'M NOT OPPOSED TO AMUSING EMBELLISHMENTS.
I DO NOT EMBELLISH.
JUST WAIT UNTIL I TELL YOU HOW I INCAPACITATED TWO DOZEN ROGUE SOLDIERS WITH NOTHING BUT A DESSERT FORK!
AND AFTER THAT, SHE CAN TELL YOU HOW HER ADVANCED WIRING SYSTEM GAVE ALPHA STEELE BAD INDIGESTION WHEN HE TRIED TO EAT HER.
WAS THAT SUPPOSED TO BE FUNNY?
AND YOU SAY I DON'T HAVE A SENSE OF HUMOR.

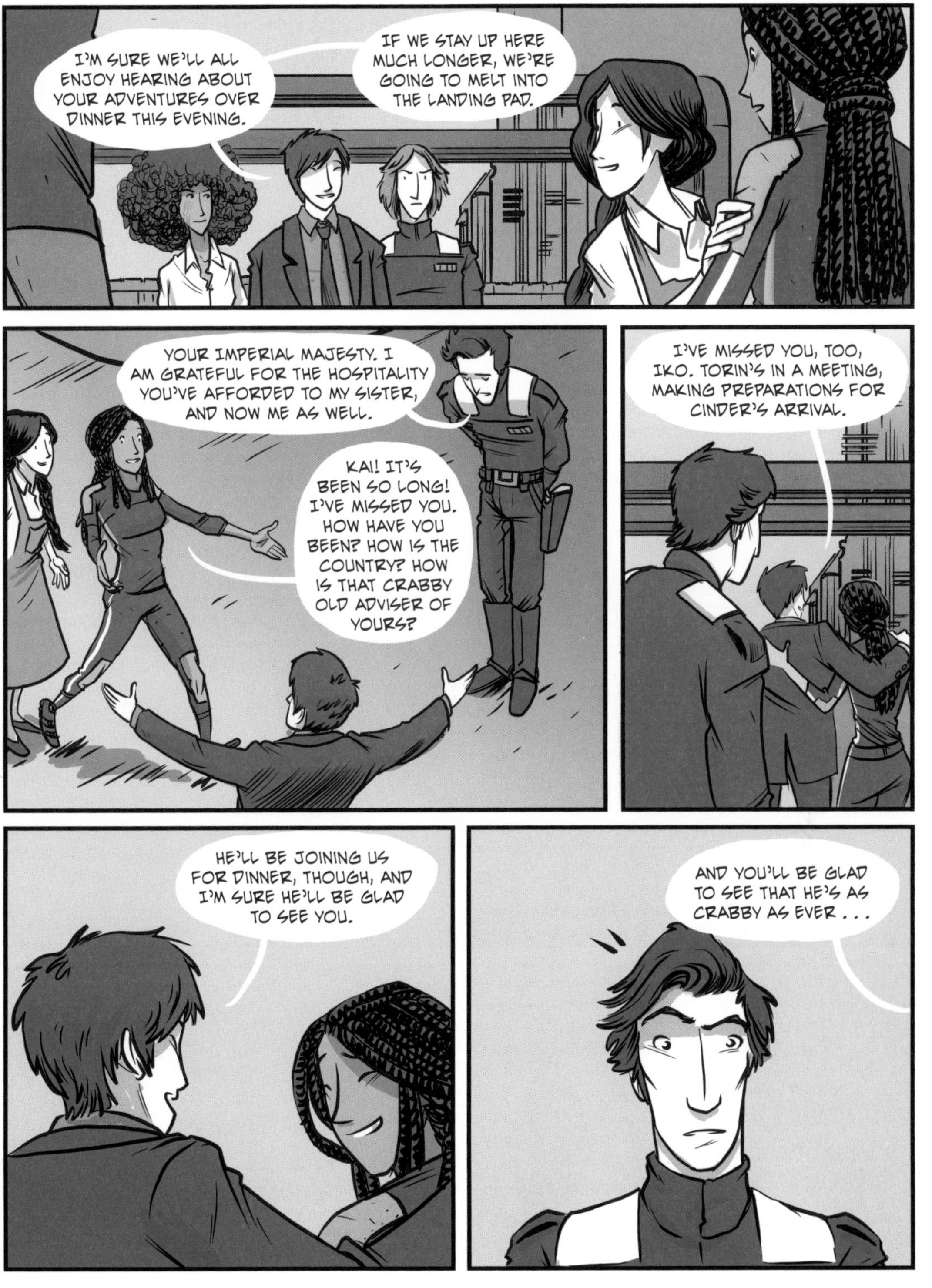
I'M SURE WE'LL ALL ENJOY HEARING ABOUT YOUR ADVENTURES OVER DINNER THIS EVENING.
IF WE STAY UP HERE MUCH LONGER, WE'RE GOING TO MELT INTO THE LANDING PAD.
YOUR IMPERIAL MAJESTY. I AM GRATEFUL FOR THE HOSPITALITY YOU'VE AFFORDED TO MY SISTER, AND NOW ME AS WELL.
KAI! IT'S BEEN SO LONG! I'VE MISSED YOU. HOW HAVE YOU BEEN? HOW IS THE COUNTRY? HOW IS THAT CRABBY OLD ADVISER OF YOURS?
I'VE MISSED YOU, TOO, IKO. TORIN'S IN A MEETING, MAKING PREPARATIONS FOR CINDER'S ARRIVAL.
HE'LL BE JOINING US FOR DINNER, THOUGH, AND I'M SURE HE'LL BE GLAD TO SEE YOU.
AND YOU'LL BE GLAD TO SEE THAT HE'S AS CRABBY AS EVER . . .

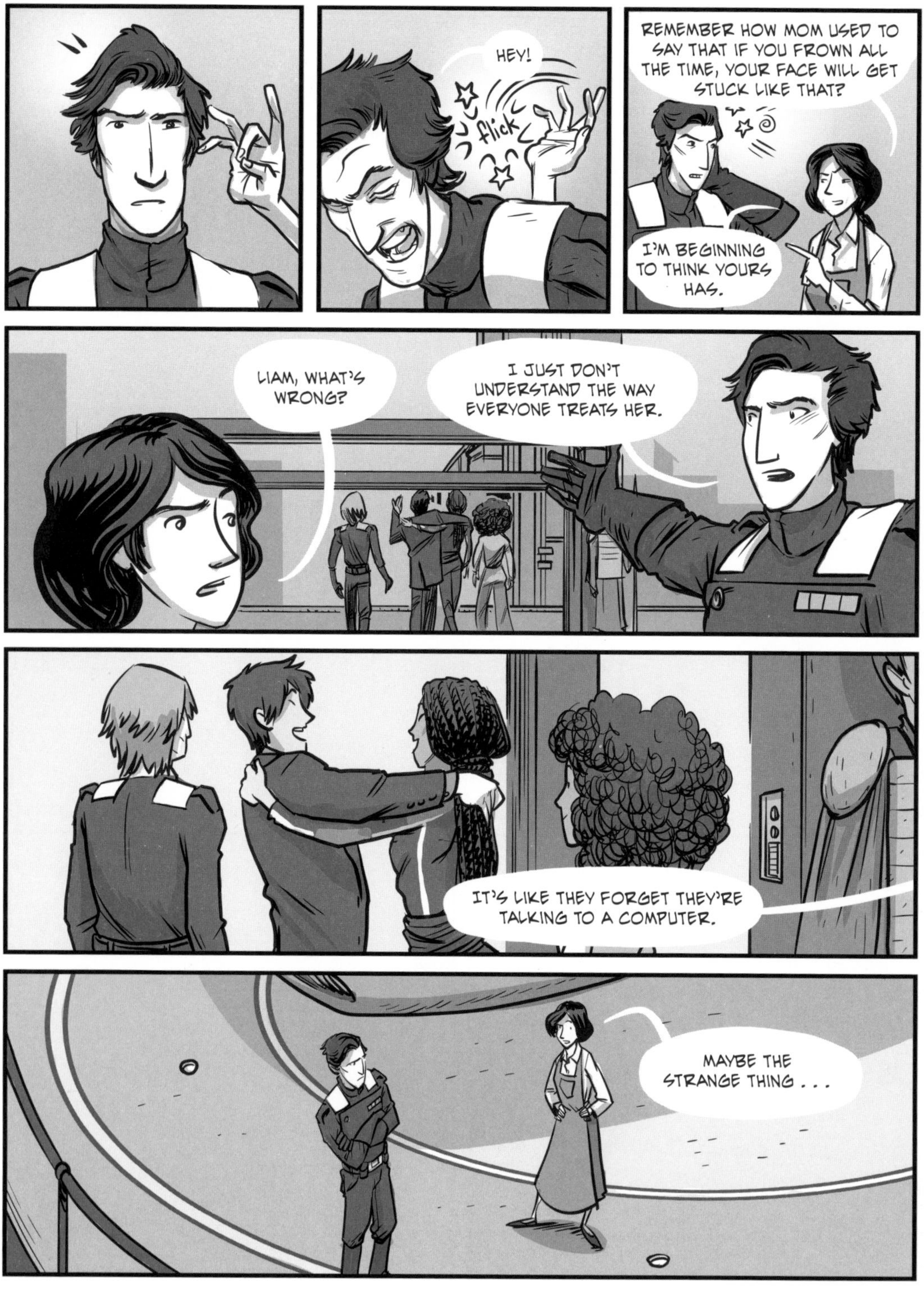
HEY!
flick
REMEMBER HOW MOM USED TO SAY THAT IF YOU FROWN ALL THE TIME, YOUR FACE WILL GET STUCK LIKE THAT?
I'M BEGINNING TO THINK YOURS HAS.
LIAM, WHAT'S WRONG?
I JUST DON'T UNDERSTAND THE WAY EVERYONE TREATS HER.
IT'S LIKE THEY FORGET THEY'RE TALKING TO A COMPUTER.
MAYBE THE STRANGE THING . . .

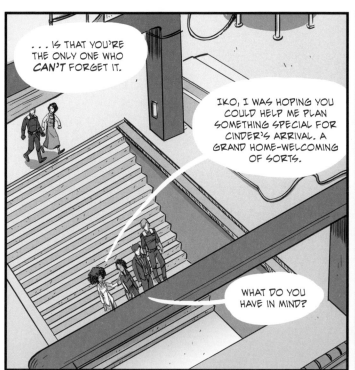

. . . IS THAT YOU'RE THE ONLY ONE WHO *CAN'T* FORGET IT.

IKO, I WAS HOPING YOU COULD HELP ME PLAN SOMETHING SPECIAL FOR CINDER'S ARRIVAL. A GRAND HOME-WELCOMING OF SORTS.

WHAT DO YOU HAVE IN MIND?

I THOUGHT WE COULD ENGAGE THE ENTIRE PALACE STAFF IN ONE ELABORATE CHOREOGRAPHED DANCE.

JUST IMAGINE . . . WE ALL SIT DOWN FOR A PEACEFUL, SOPHISTICATED FEAST IN THE ROYAL BANQUET HALL WHEN SUDDENLY THE LIGHTS DIM, MUSIC FLOODS THE ROOM . . .

. . . AND THE WHOLE STAFF EMERGES IN A GRAND SPECTACLE REMINISCENT OF SECOND-ERA MUSICAL THEATER!

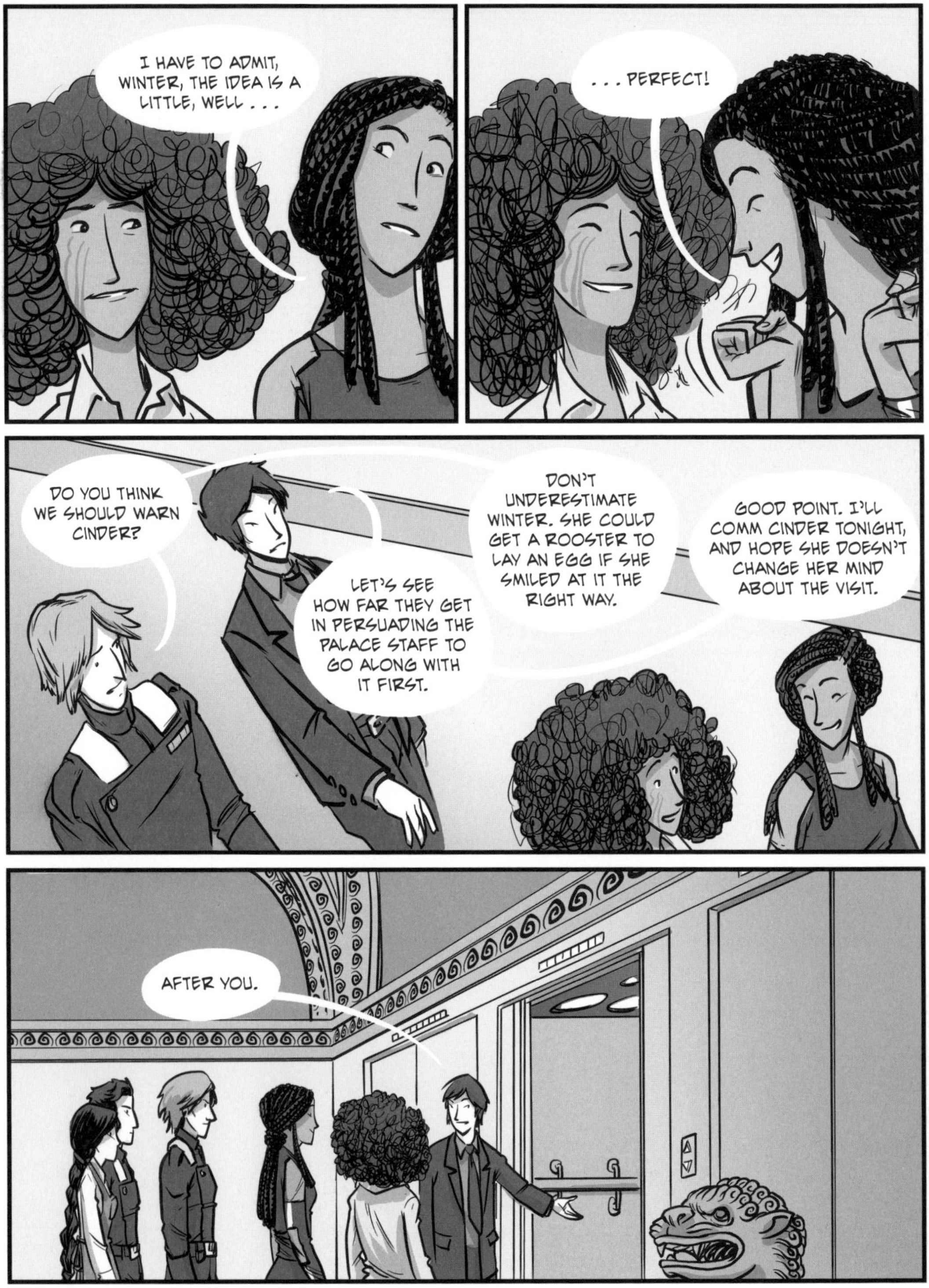
I HAVE TO ADMIT, WINTER, THE IDEA IS A LITTLE, WELL . . .
. . . PERFECT!
DO YOU THINK WE SHOULD WARN CINDER?
LET'S SEE HOW FAR THEY GET IN PERSUADING THE PALACE STAFF TO GO ALONG WITH IT FIRST.
DON'T UNDERESTIMATE WINTER. SHE COULD GET A ROOSTER TO LAY AN EGG IF SHE SMILED AT IT THE RIGHT WAY.
GOOD POINT. I'LL COMM CINDER TONIGHT, AND HOPE SHE DOESN'T CHANGE HER MIND ABOUT THE VISIT.
AFTER YOU.

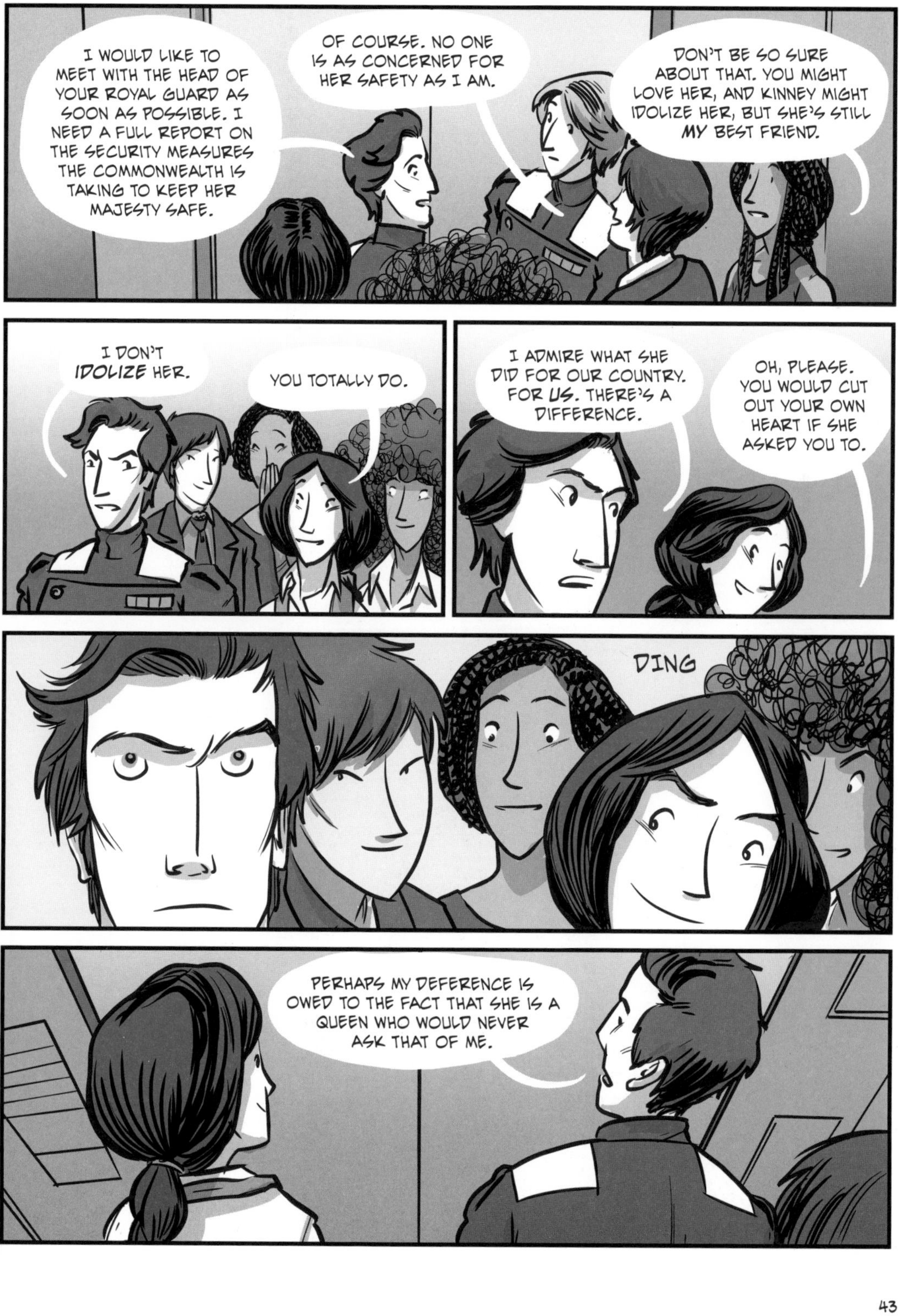
I WOULD LIKE TO MEET WITH THE HEAD OF YOUR ROYAL GUARD AS SOON AS POSSIBLE. I NEED A FULL REPORT ON THE SECURITY MEASURES THE COMMONWEALTH IS TAKING TO KEEP HER MAJESTY SAFE.
OF COURSE. NO ONE IS AS CONCERNED FOR HER SAFETY AS I AM.
DON'T BE SO SURE ABOUT THAT. YOU MIGHT LOVE HER, AND KINNEY MIGHT IDOLIZE HER, BUT SHE'S STILL *MY* BEST FRIEND.
I DON'T *IDOLIZE* HER.
YOU TOTALLY DO.
I ADMIRE WHAT SHE DID FOR OUR COUNTRY. FOR *US*. THERE'S A DIFFERENCE.
OH, PLEASE. YOU WOULD CUT OUT YOUR OWN HEART IF SHE ASKED YOU TO.
DING
PERHAPS MY DEFERENCE IS OWED TO THE FACT THAT SHE IS A QUEEN WHO WOULD NEVER ASK THAT OF ME.

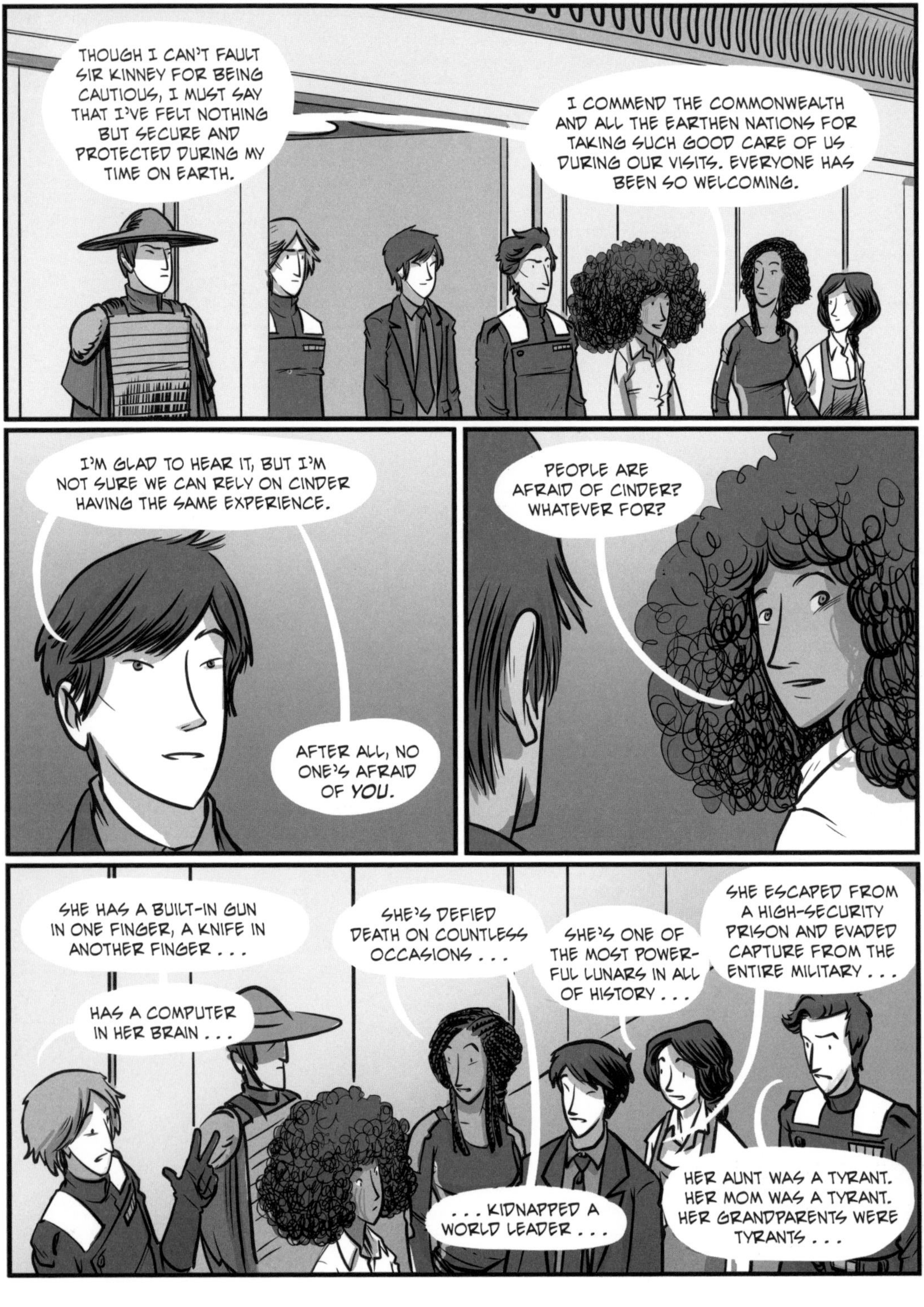
THOUGH I CAN'T FAULT SIR KINNEY FOR BEING CAUTIOUS, I MUST SAY THAT I'VE FELT NOTHING BUT SECURE AND PROTECTED DURING MY TIME ON EARTH.
I COMMEND THE COMMONWEALTH AND ALL THE EARTHEN NATIONS FOR TAKING SUCH GOOD CARE OF US DURING OUR VISITS. EVERYONE HAS BEEN SO WELCOMING.
I'M GLAD TO HEAR IT, BUT I'M NOT SURE WE CAN RELY ON CINDER HAVING THE SAME EXPERIENCE.
AFTER ALL, NO ONE'S AFRAID OF *YOU*.
PEOPLE ARE AFRAID OF CINDER? WHATEVER FOR?
SHE HAS A BUILT-IN GUN IN ONE FINGER, A KNIFE IN ANOTHER FINGER . . .
HAS A COMPUTER IN HER BRAIN . . .
SHE'S DEFIED DEATH ON COUNTLESS OCCASIONS . . .
. . . KIDNAPPED A WORLD LEADER . . .
SHE'S ONE OF THE MOST POWERFUL LUNARS IN ALL OF HISTORY . . .
SHE ESCAPED FROM A HIGH-SECURITY PRISON AND EVADED CAPTURE FROM THE ENTIRE MILITARY . . .
HER AUNT WAS A TYRANT. HER MOM WAS A TYRANT. HER GRANDPARENTS WERE TYRANTS . . .

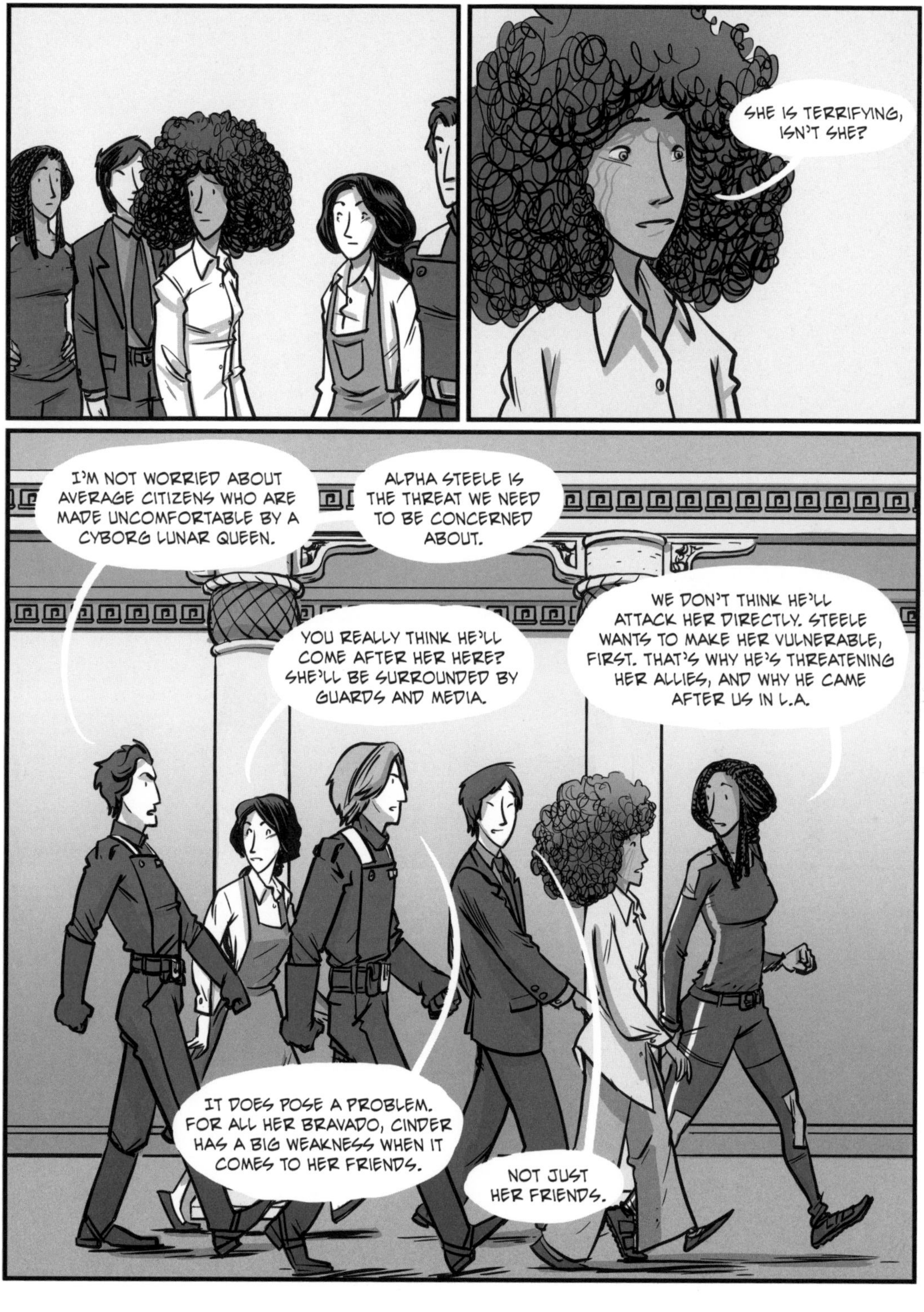
SHE IS TERRIFYING, ISN'T SHE?
I'M NOT WORRIED ABOUT AVERAGE CITIZENS WHO ARE MADE UNCOMFORTABLE BY A CYBORG LUNAR QUEEN.
ALPHA STEELE IS THE THREAT WE NEED TO BE CONCERNED ABOUT.
YOU REALLY THINK HE'LL COME AFTER HER HERE? SHE'LL BE SURROUNDED BY GUARDS AND MEDIA.
WE DON'T THINK HE'LL ATTACK HER DIRECTLY. STEELE WANTS TO MAKE HER VULNERABLE, FIRST. THAT'S WHY HE'S THREATENING HER ALLIES, AND WHY HE CAME AFTER US IN L.A.
IT DOES POSE A PROBLEM. FOR ALL HER BRAVADO, CINDER HAS A BIG WEAKNESS WHEN IT COMES TO HER FRIENDS.
NOT JUST HER FRIENDS.

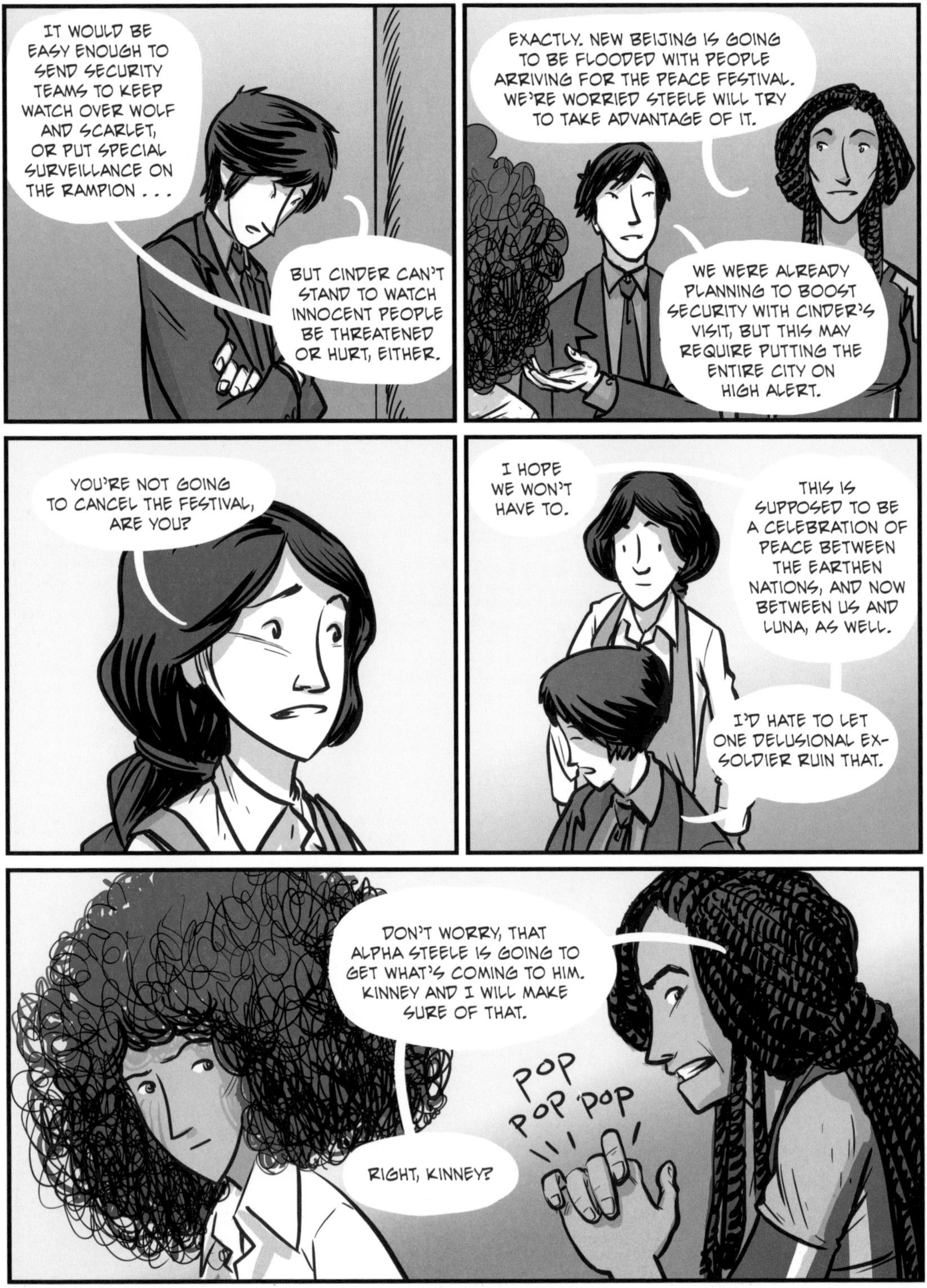
IT WOULD BE EASY ENOUGH TO SEND SECURITY TEAMS TO KEEP WATCH OVER WOLF AND SCARLET, OR PUT SPECIAL SURVEILLANCE ON THE RAMPION . . .
BUT CINDER CAN'T STAND TO WATCH INNOCENT PEOPLE BE THREATENED OR HURT, EITHER.
EXACTLY. NEW BEIJING IS GOING TO BE FLOODED WITH PEOPLE ARRIVING FOR THE PEACE FESTIVAL. WE'RE WORRIED STEELE WILL TRY TO TAKE ADVANTAGE OF IT.
WE WERE ALREADY PLANNING TO BOOST SECURITY WITH CINDER'S VISIT, BUT THIS MAY REQUIRE PUTTING THE ENTIRE CITY ON HIGH ALERT.
YOU'RE NOT GOING TO CANCEL THE FESTIVAL, ARE YOU?
I HOPE WE WON'T HAVE TO.
THIS IS SUPPOSED TO BE A CELEBRATION OF PEACE BETWEEN THE EARTHEN NATIONS, AND NOW BETWEEN US AND LUNA, AS WELL.
I'D HATE TO LET ONE DELUSIONAL EX-SOLDIER RUIN THAT.
DON'T WORRY, THAT ALPHA STEELE IS GOING TO GET WHAT'S COMING TO HIM. KINNEY AND I WILL MAKE SURE OF THAT.
RIGHT, KINNEY?
POP POP POP

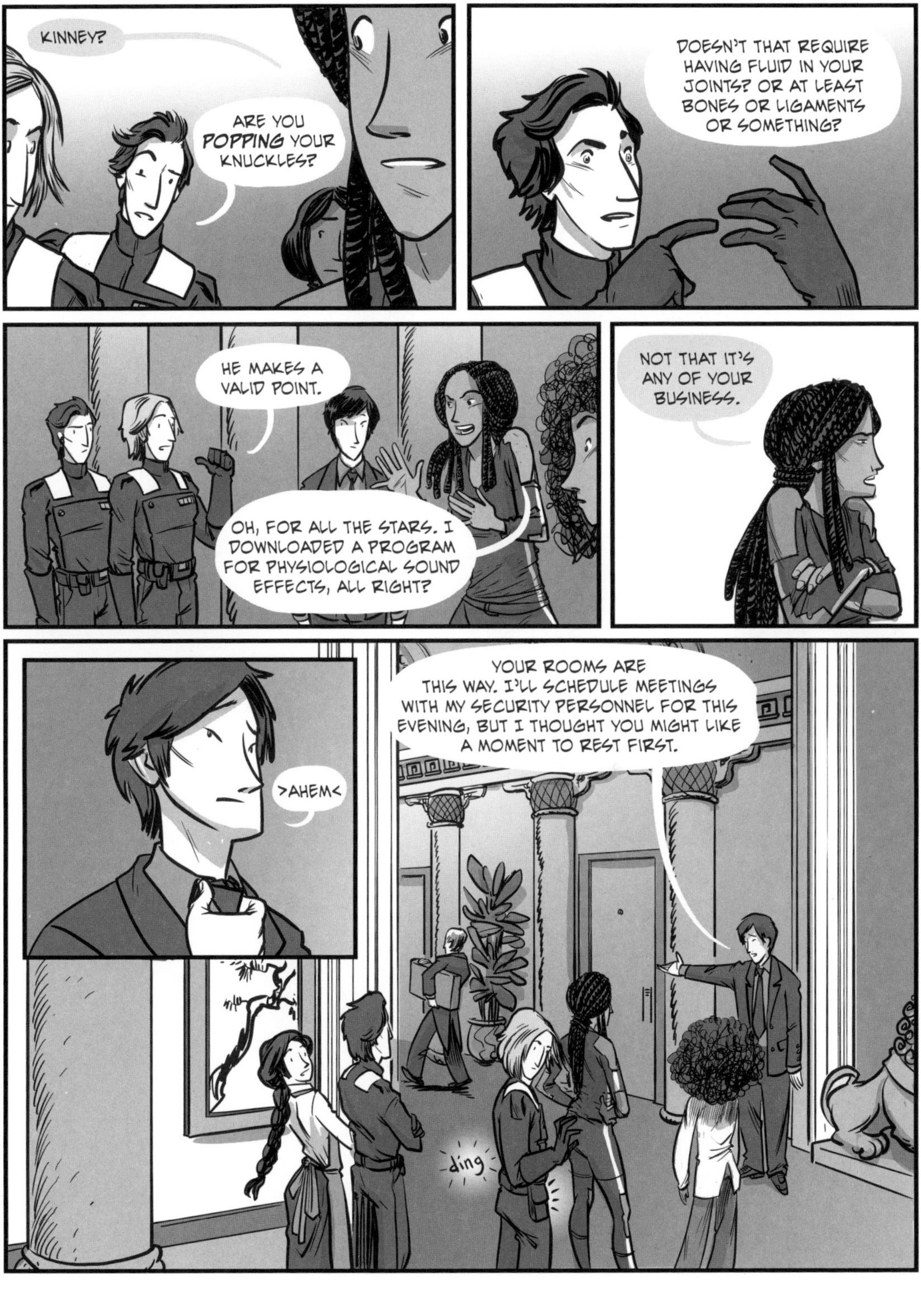
KINNEY?
ARE YOU POPPING YOUR KNUCKLES?
DOESN'T THAT REQUIRE HAVING FLUID IN YOUR JOINTS? OR AT LEAST BONES OR LIGAMENTS OR SOMETHING?
HE MAKES A VALID POINT.
OH, FOR ALL THE STARS. I DOWNLOADED A PROGRAM FOR PHYSIOLOGICAL SOUND EFFECTS, ALL RIGHT?
NOT THAT IT'S ANY OF YOUR BUSINESS.
>AHEM<
YOUR ROOMS ARE THIS WAY. I'LL SCHEDULE MEETINGS WITH MY SECURITY PERSONNEL FOR THIS EVENING, BUT I THOUGHT YOU MIGHT LIKE A MOMENT TO REST FIRST.
ding

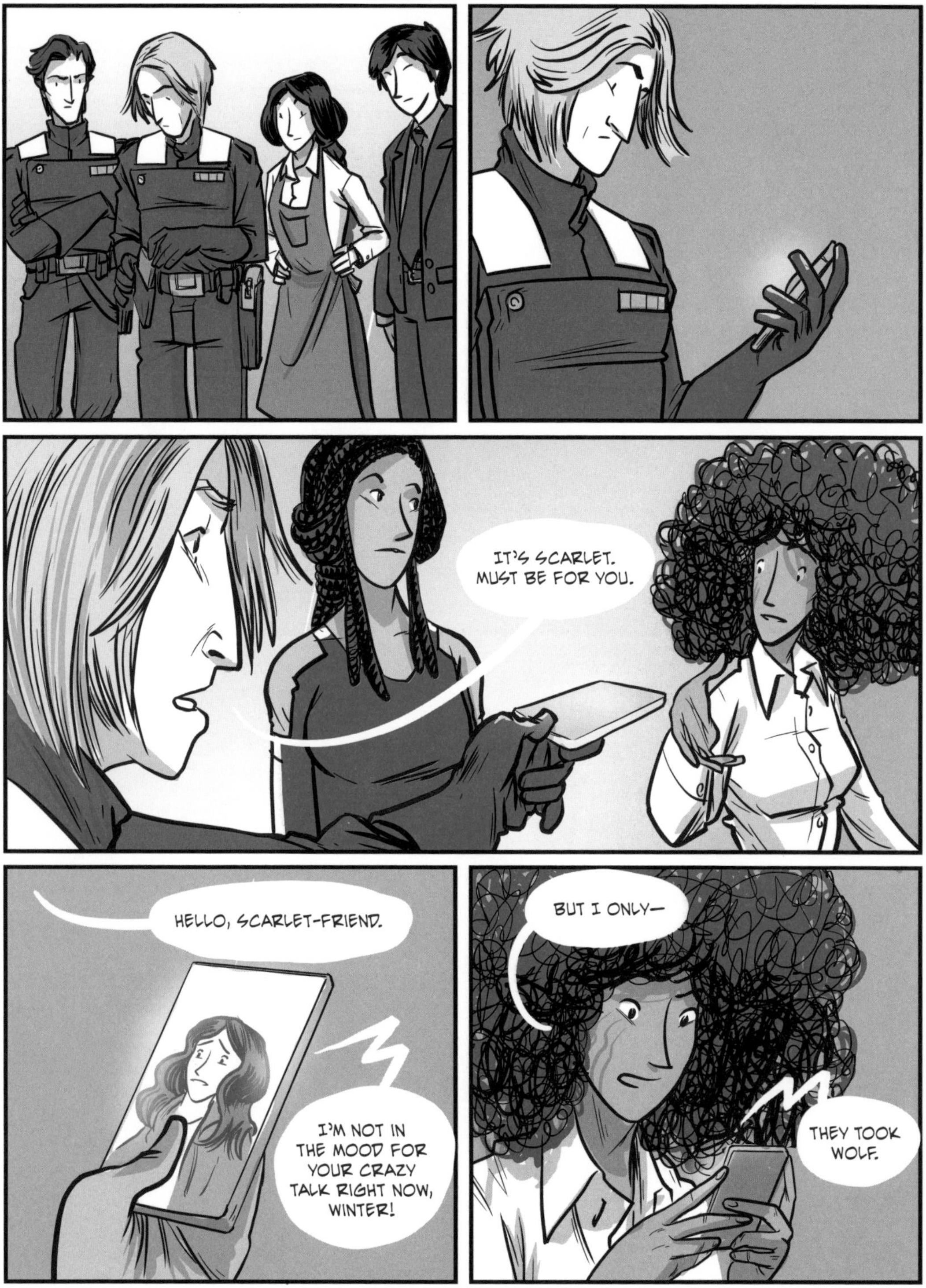

IT'S SCARLET. MUST BE FOR YOU.
HELLO, SCARLET-FRIEND.
I'M NOT IN THE MOOD FOR YOUR CRAZY TALK RIGHT NOW, WINTER!
BUT I ONLY—
THEY TOOK WOLF.

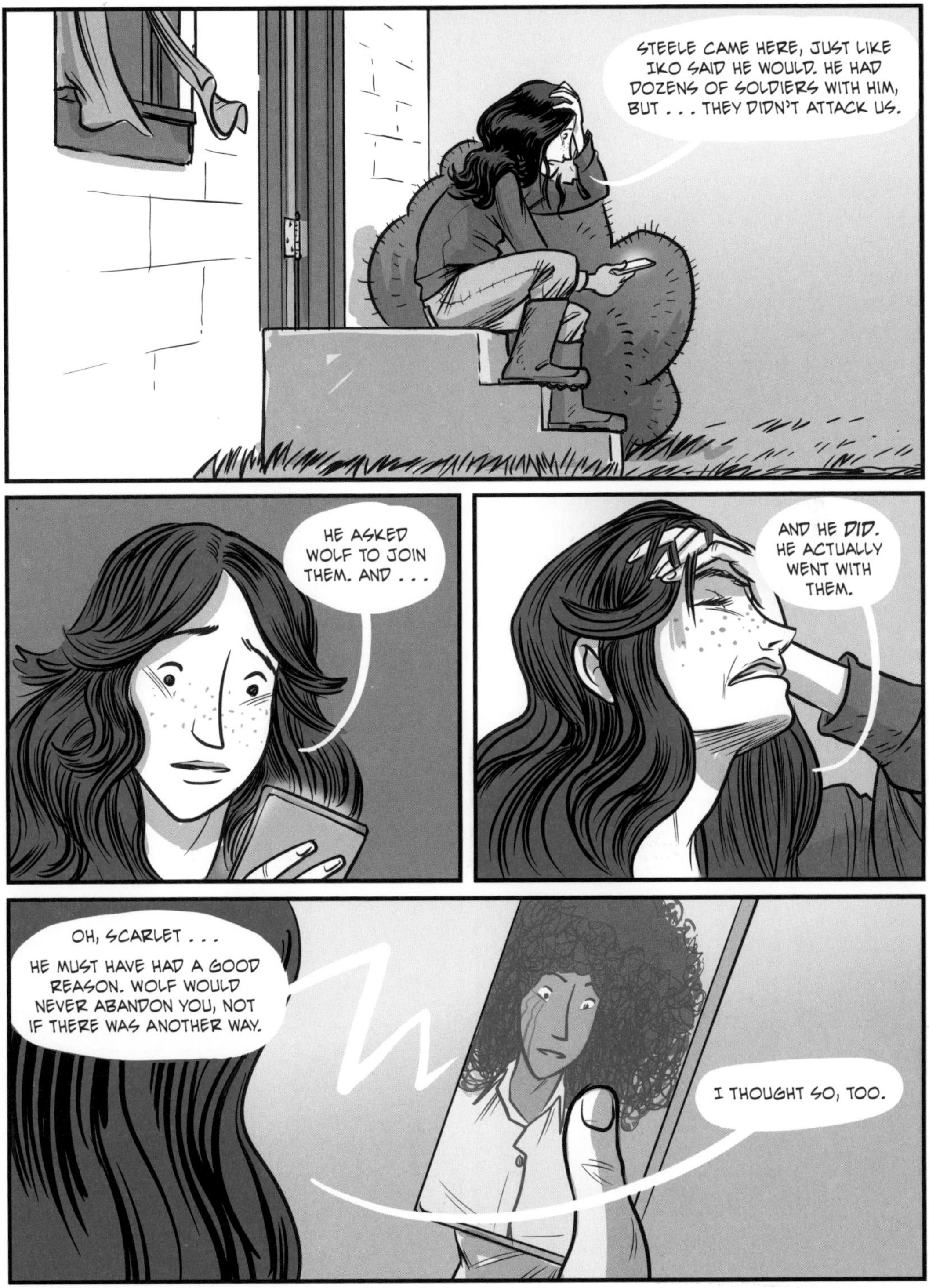
STEELE CAME HERE, JUST LIKE IKO SAID HE WOULD. HE HAD DOZENS OF SOLDIERS WITH HIM, BUT . . . THEY DIDN'T ATTACK US.
HE ASKED WOLF TO JOIN THEM. AND . . .
AND HE *DID*. HE ACTUALLY WENT WITH THEM.
OH, SCARLET . . .
HE MUST HAVE HAD A GOOD REASON. WOLF WOULD NEVER ABANDON YOU, NOT IF THERE WAS ANOTHER WAY.
I THOUGHT SO, TOO.

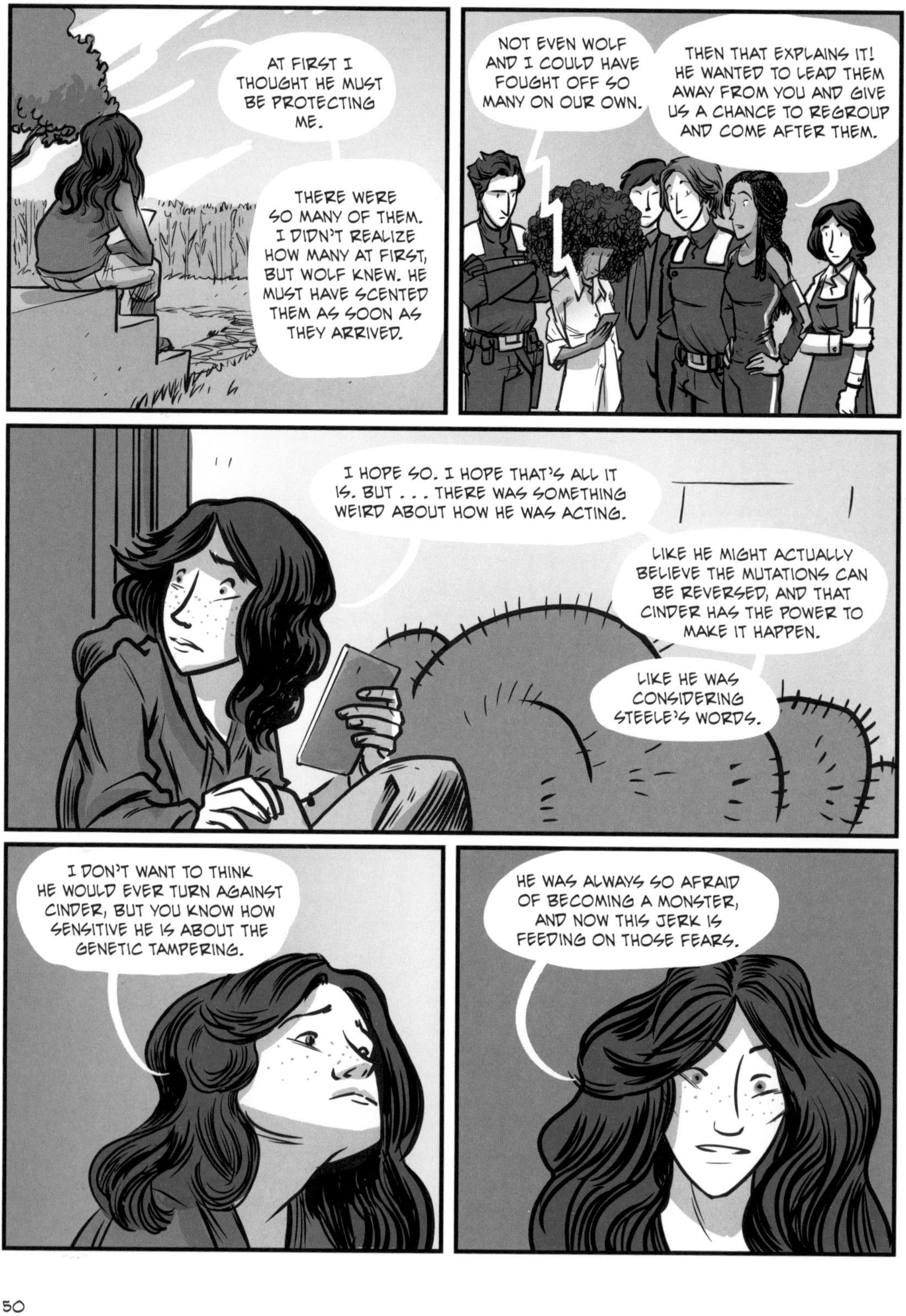
AT FIRST I THOUGHT HE MUST BE PROTECTING ME.
THERE WERE SO MANY OF THEM. I DIDN'T REALIZE HOW MANY AT FIRST, BUT WOLF KNEW. HE MUST HAVE SCENTED THEM AS SOON AS THEY ARRIVED.
NOT EVEN WOLF AND I COULD HAVE FOUGHT OFF SO MANY ON OUR OWN.
THEN THAT EXPLAINS IT! HE WANTED TO LEAD THEM AWAY FROM YOU AND GIVE US A CHANCE TO REGROUP AND COME AFTER THEM.
I HOPE SO. I HOPE THAT'S ALL IT IS. BUT . . . THERE WAS SOMETHING WEIRD ABOUT HOW HE WAS ACTING.
LIKE HE MIGHT ACTUALLY BELIEVE THE MUTATIONS CAN BE REVERSED, AND THAT CINDER HAS THE POWER TO MAKE IT HAPPEN.
LIKE HE WAS CONSIDERING STEELE'S WORDS.
I DON'T WANT TO THINK HE WOULD EVER TURN AGAINST CINDER, BUT YOU KNOW HOW SENSITIVE HE IS ABOUT THE GENETIC TAMPERING.
HE WAS ALWAYS SO AFRAID OF BECOMING A MONSTER, AND NOW THIS JERK IS FEEDING ON THOSE FEARS.

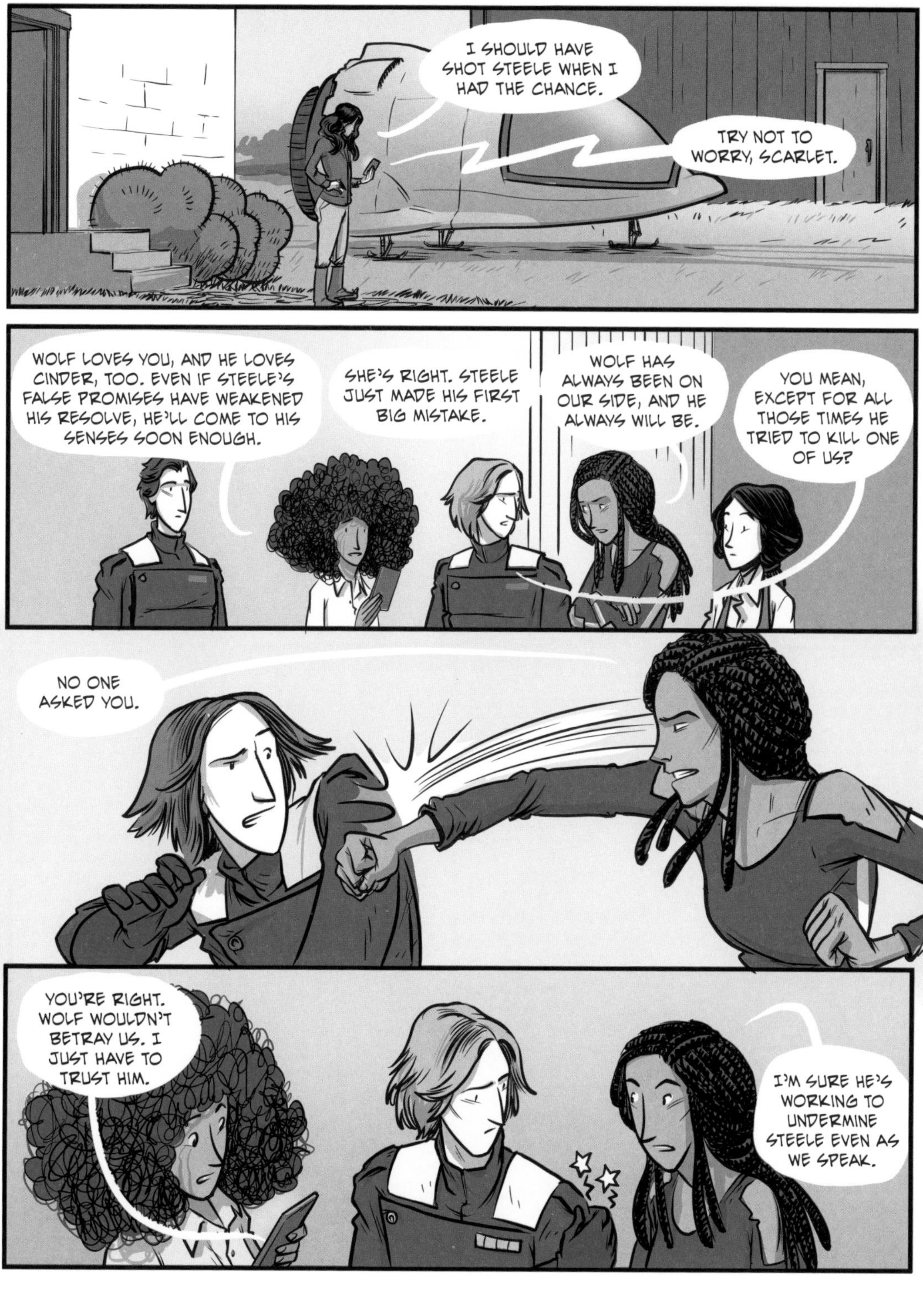
I SHOULD HAVE SHOT STEELE WHEN I HAD THE CHANCE.
TRY NOT TO WORRY, SCARLET.
WOLF LOVES YOU, AND HE LOVES CINDER, TOO. EVEN IF STEELE'S FALSE PROMISES HAVE WEAKENED HIS RESOLVE, HE'LL COME TO HIS SENSES SOON ENOUGH.
SHE'S RIGHT. STEELE JUST MADE HIS FIRST BIG MISTAKE.
WOLF HAS ALWAYS BEEN ON OUR SIDE, AND HE ALWAYS WILL BE.
YOU MEAN, EXCEPT FOR ALL THOSE TIMES HE TRIED TO KILL ONE OF US?
NO ONE ASKED YOU.
YOU'RE RIGHT. WOLF WOULDN'T BETRAY US. I JUST HAVE TO TRUST HIM.
I'M SURE HE'S WORKING TO UNDERMINE STEELE EVEN AS WE SPEAK.

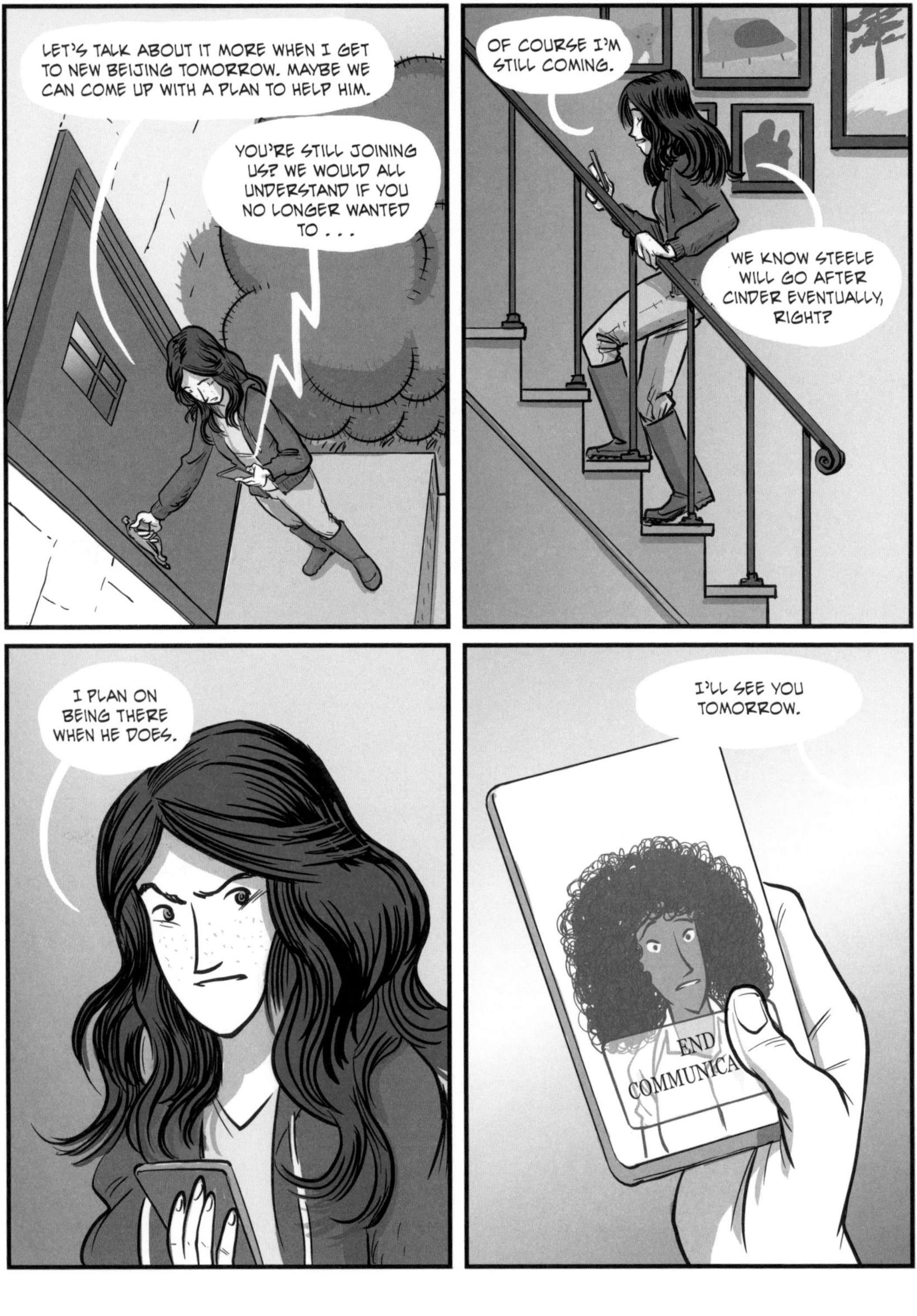
LET'S TALK ABOUT IT MORE WHEN I GET TO NEW BEIJING TOMORROW. MAYBE WE CAN COME UP WITH A PLAN TO HELP HIM.
YOU'RE STILL JOINING US? WE WOULD ALL UNDERSTAND IF YOU NO LONGER WANTED TO . . .
OF COURSE I'M STILL COMING.
WE KNOW STEELE WILL GO AFTER CINDER EVENTUALLY, RIGHT?
I PLAN ON BEING THERE WHEN HE DOES.
I'LL SEE YOU TOMORROW.
END
COMMUNICA

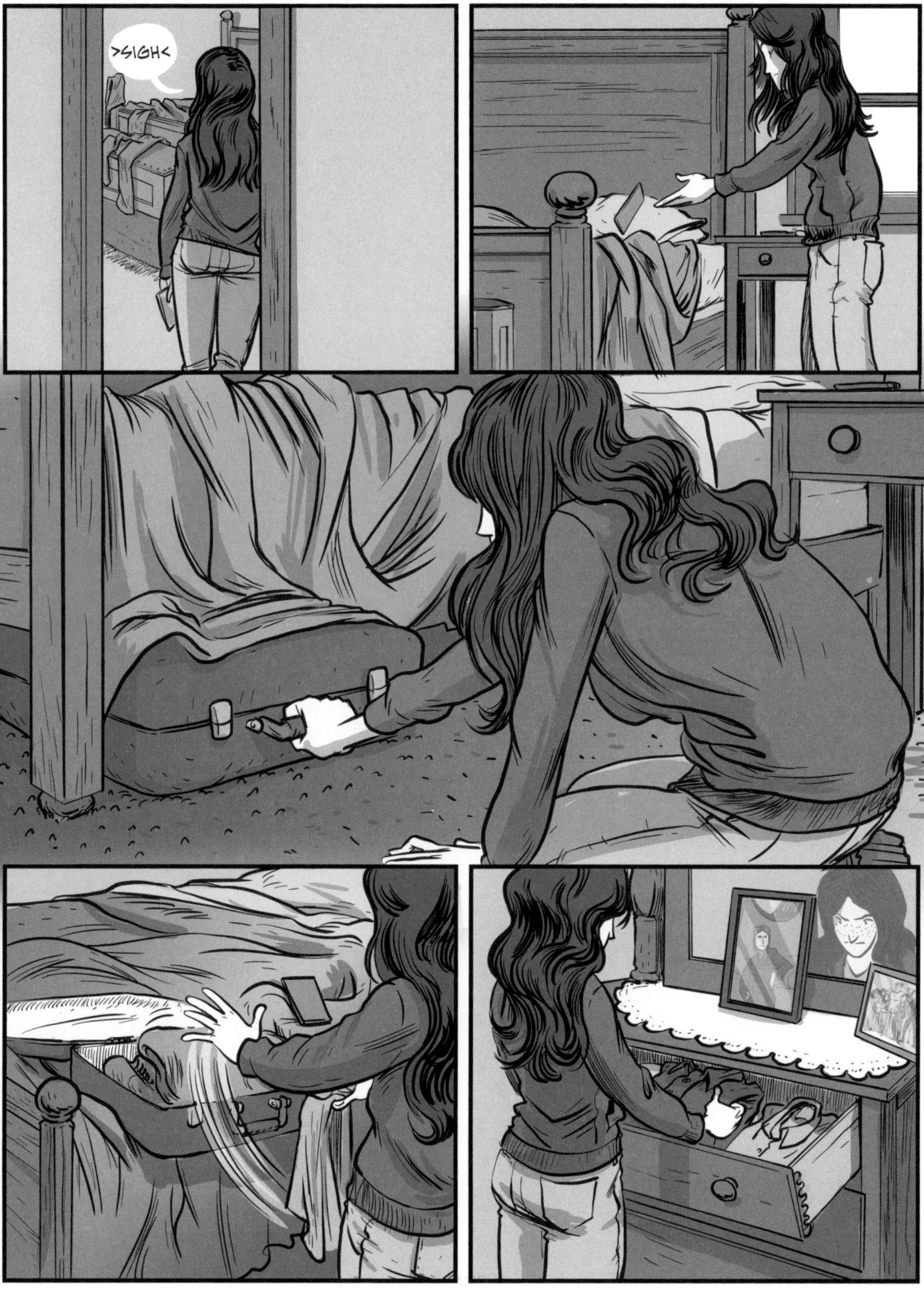
>SIGH<

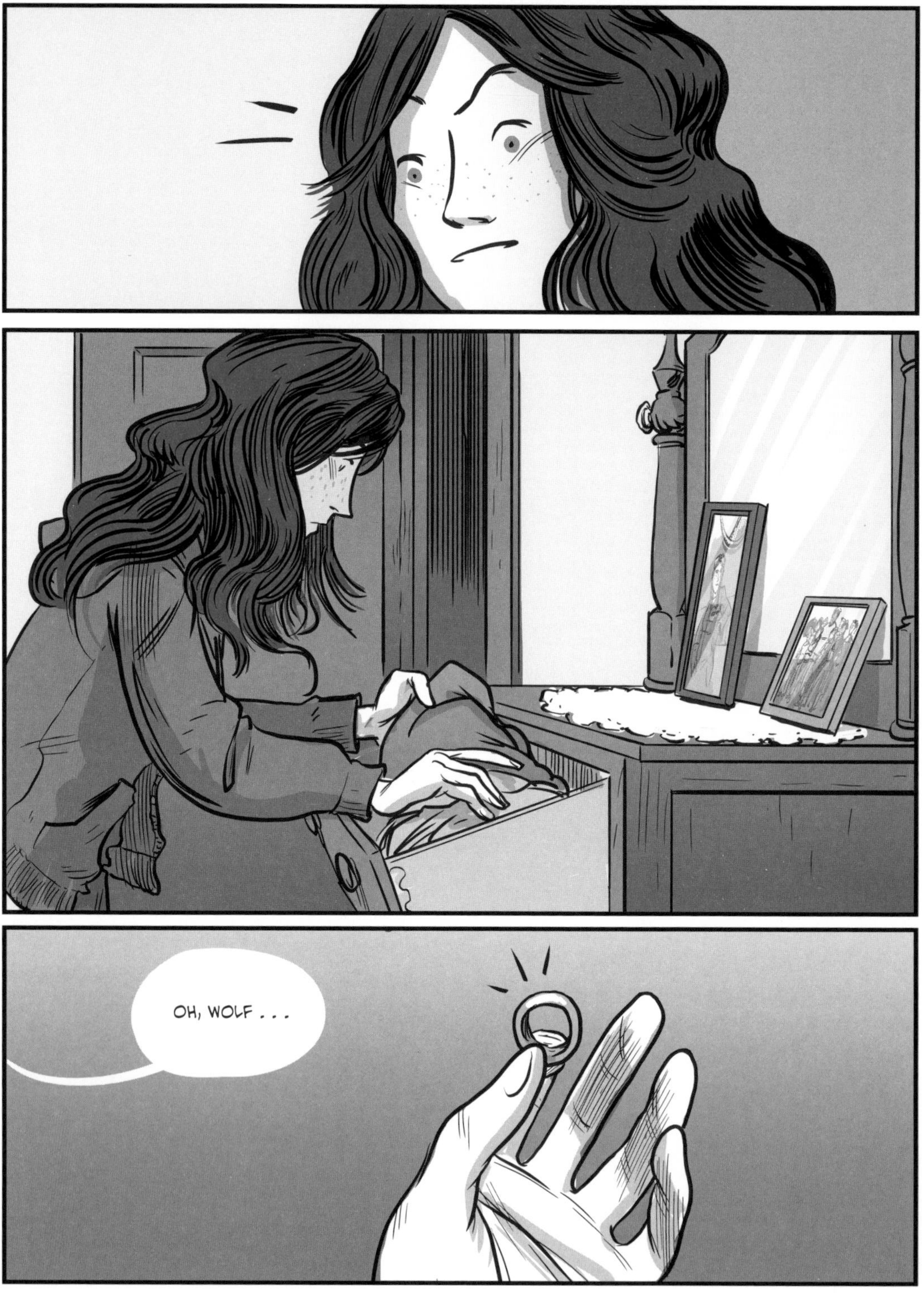
OH, WOLF . . .

CHAPTER III

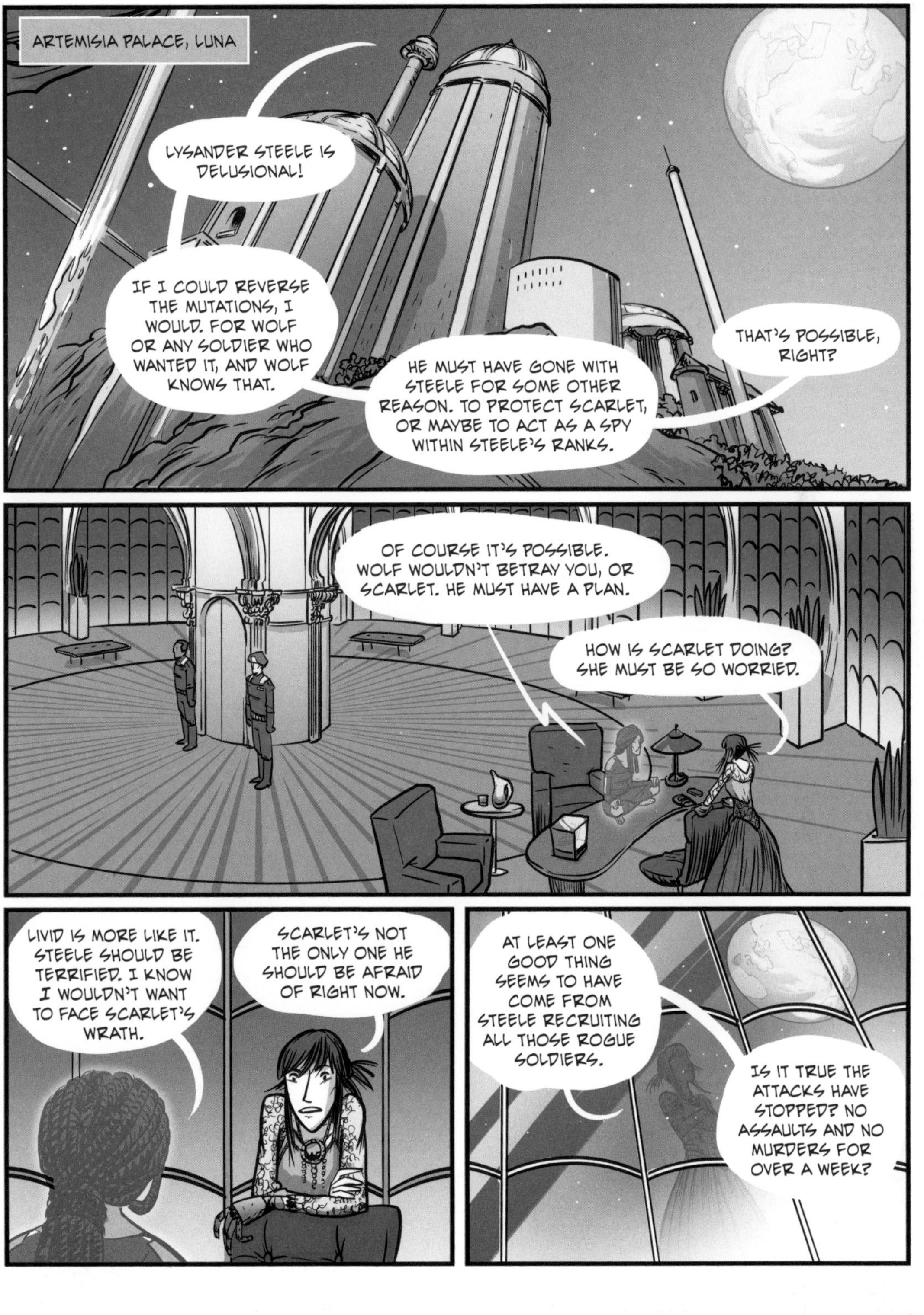
ARTEMISIA PALACE, LUNA
LYSANDER STEELE IS DELUSIONAL!
IF I COULD REVERSE THE MUTATIONS, I WOULD. FOR WOLF OR ANY SOLDIER WHO WANTED IT, AND WOLF KNOWS THAT.
HE MUST HAVE GONE WITH STEELE FOR SOME OTHER REASON. TO PROTECT SCARLET, OR MAYBE TO ACT AS A SPY WITHIN STEELE'S RANKS.
THAT'S POSSIBLE, RIGHT?
OF COURSE IT'S POSSIBLE. WOLF WOULDN'T BETRAY YOU, OR SCARLET. HE MUST HAVE A PLAN.
HOW IS SCARLET DOING? SHE MUST BE SO WORRIED.
LIVID IS MORE LIKE IT. STEELE SHOULD BE TERRIFIED. I KNOW I WOULDN'T WANT TO FACE SCARLET'S WRATH.
SCARLET'S NOT THE ONLY ONE HE SHOULD BE AFRAID OF RIGHT NOW.
AT LEAST ONE GOOD THING SEEMS TO HAVE COME FROM STEELE RECRUITING ALL THOSE ROGUE SOLDIERS.
IS IT TRUE THE ATTACKS HAVE STOPPED? NO ASSAULTS AND NO MURDERS FOR OVER A WEEK?

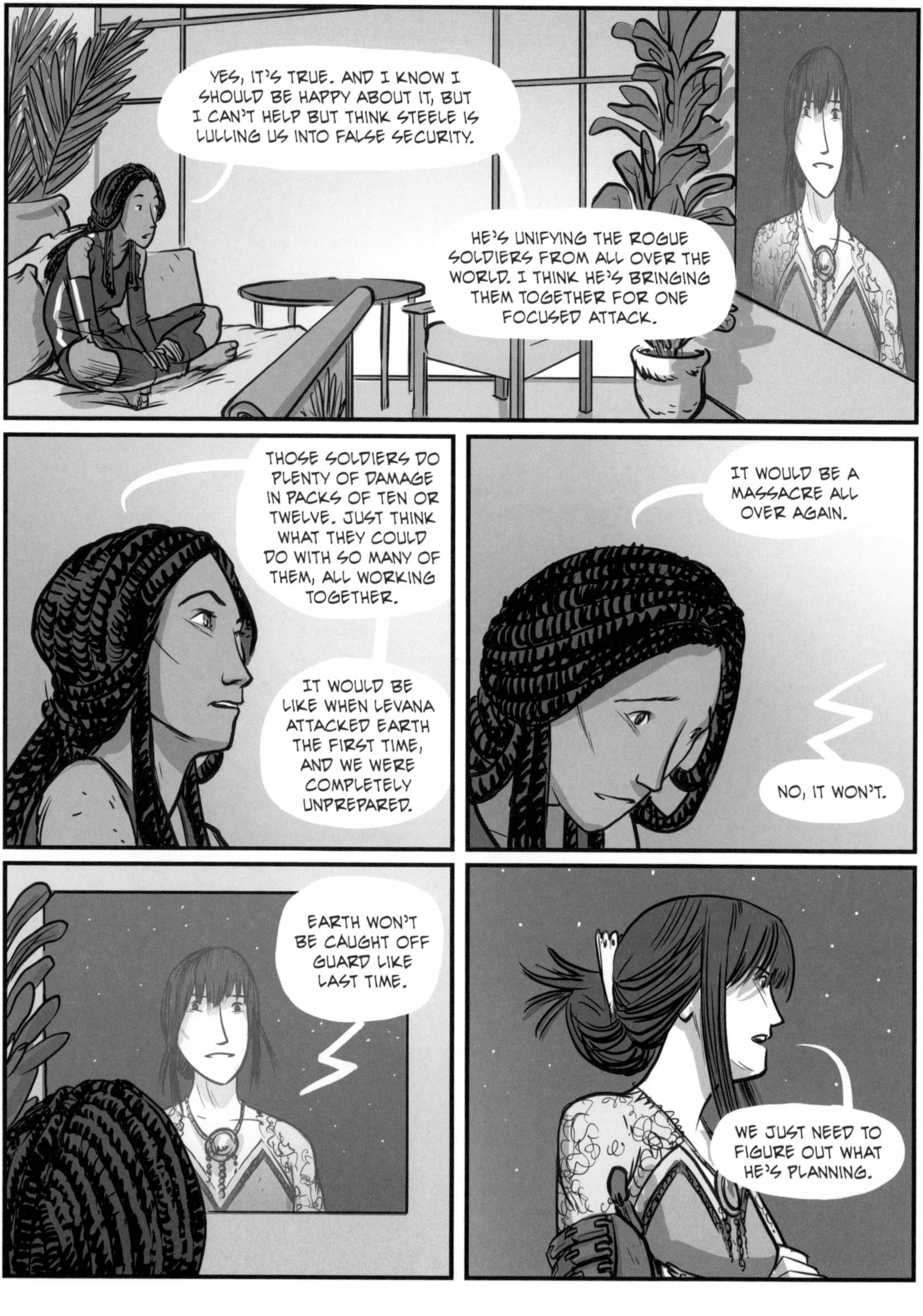
YES, IT'S TRUE. AND I KNOW I SHOULD BE HAPPY ABOUT IT, BUT I CAN'T HELP BUT THINK STEELE IS LULLING US INTO FALSE SECURITY.
HE'S UNIFYING THE ROGUE SOLDIERS FROM ALL OVER THE WORLD. I THINK HE'S BRINGING THEM TOGETHER FOR ONE FOCUSED ATTACK.
THOSE SOLDIERS DO PLENTY OF DAMAGE IN PACKS OF TEN OR TWELVE. JUST THINK WHAT THEY COULD DO WITH SO MANY OF THEM, ALL WORKING TOGETHER.
IT WOULD BE LIKE WHEN LEVANA ATTACKED EARTH THE FIRST TIME, AND WE WERE COMPLETELY UNPREPARED.
IT WOULD BE A MASSACRE ALL OVER AGAIN.
NO, IT WON'T.
EARTH WON'T BE CAUGHT OFF GUARD LIKE LAST TIME.
WE JUST NEED TO FIGURE OUT WHAT HE'S PLANNING.

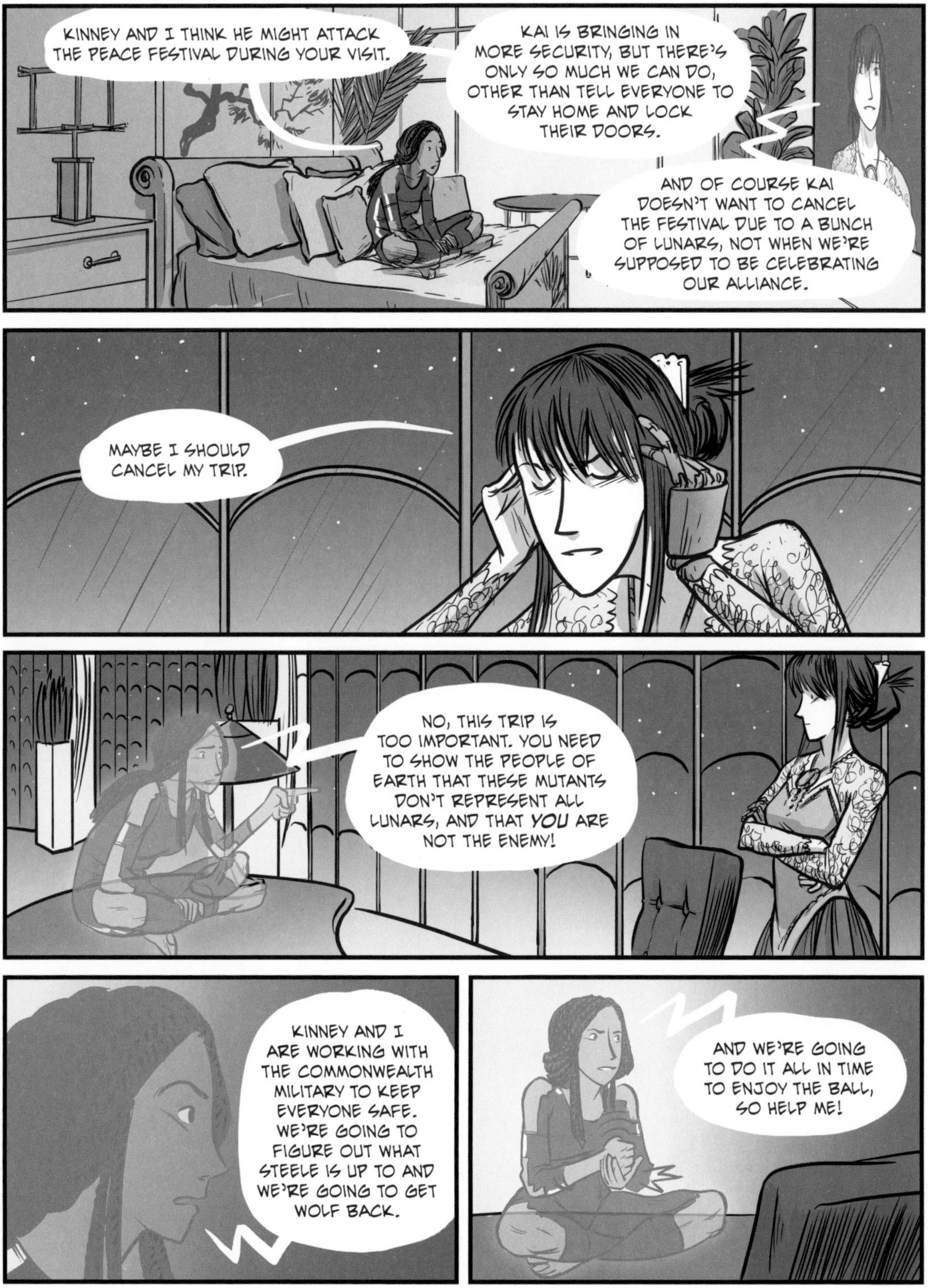

KINNEY AND I THINK HE MIGHT ATTACK THE PEACE FESTIVAL DURING YOUR VISIT.
KAI IS BRINGING IN MORE SECURITY, BUT THERE'S ONLY SO MUCH WE CAN DO, OTHER THAN TELL EVERYONE TO STAY HOME AND LOCK THEIR DOORS.
AND OF COURSE KAI DOESN'T WANT TO CANCEL THE FESTIVAL DUE TO A BUNCH OF LUNARS, NOT WHEN WE'RE SUPPOSED TO BE CELEBRATING OUR ALLIANCE.
MAYBE I SHOULD CANCEL MY TRIP.
NO, THIS TRIP IS TOO IMPORTANT. YOU NEED TO SHOW THE PEOPLE OF EARTH THAT THESE MUTANTS DON'T REPRESENT ALL LUNARS, AND THAT *YOU* ARE NOT THE ENEMY!
KINNEY AND I ARE WORKING WITH THE COMMONWEALTH MILITARY TO KEEP EVERYONE SAFE. WE'RE GOING TO FIGURE OUT WHAT STEELE IS UP TO AND WE'RE GOING TO GET WOLF BACK.
AND WE'RE GOING TO DO IT ALL IN TIME TO ENJOY THE BALL, SO HELP ME!

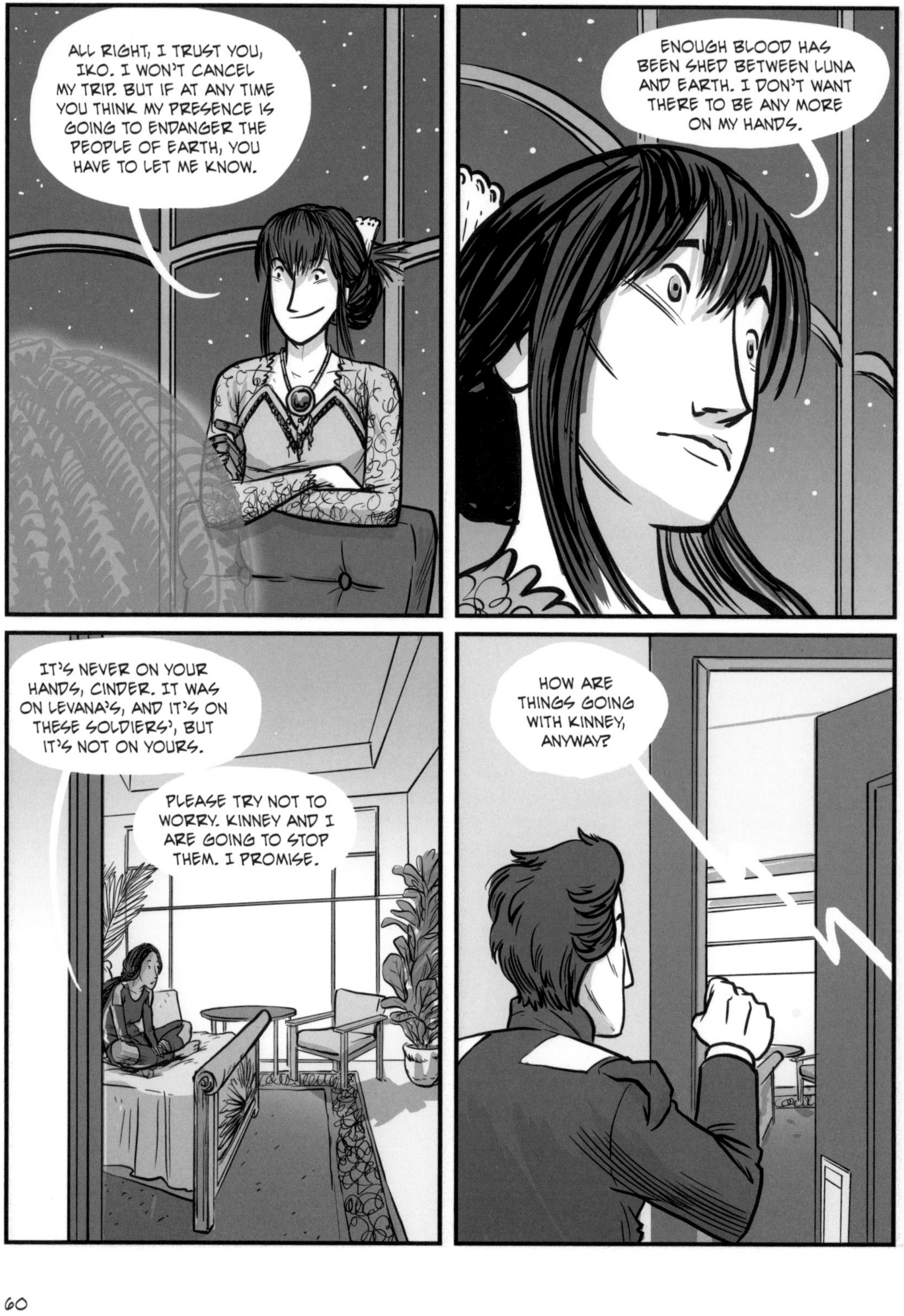
ALL RIGHT, I TRUST YOU, IKO. I WON'T CANCEL MY TRIP. BUT IF AT ANY TIME YOU THINK MY PRESENCE IS GOING TO ENDANGER THE PEOPLE OF EARTH, YOU HAVE TO LET ME KNOW.
ENOUGH BLOOD HAS BEEN SHED BETWEEN LUNA AND EARTH. I DON'T WANT THERE TO BE ANY MORE ON MY HANDS.
IT'S NEVER ON YOUR HANDS, CINDER. IT WAS ON LEVANA'S, AND IT'S ON THESE SOLDIERS', BUT IT'S NOT ON YOURS.
PLEASE TRY NOT TO WORRY. KINNEY AND I ARE GOING TO STOP THEM. I PROMISE.
HOW ARE THINGS GOING WITH KINNEY, ANYWAY?

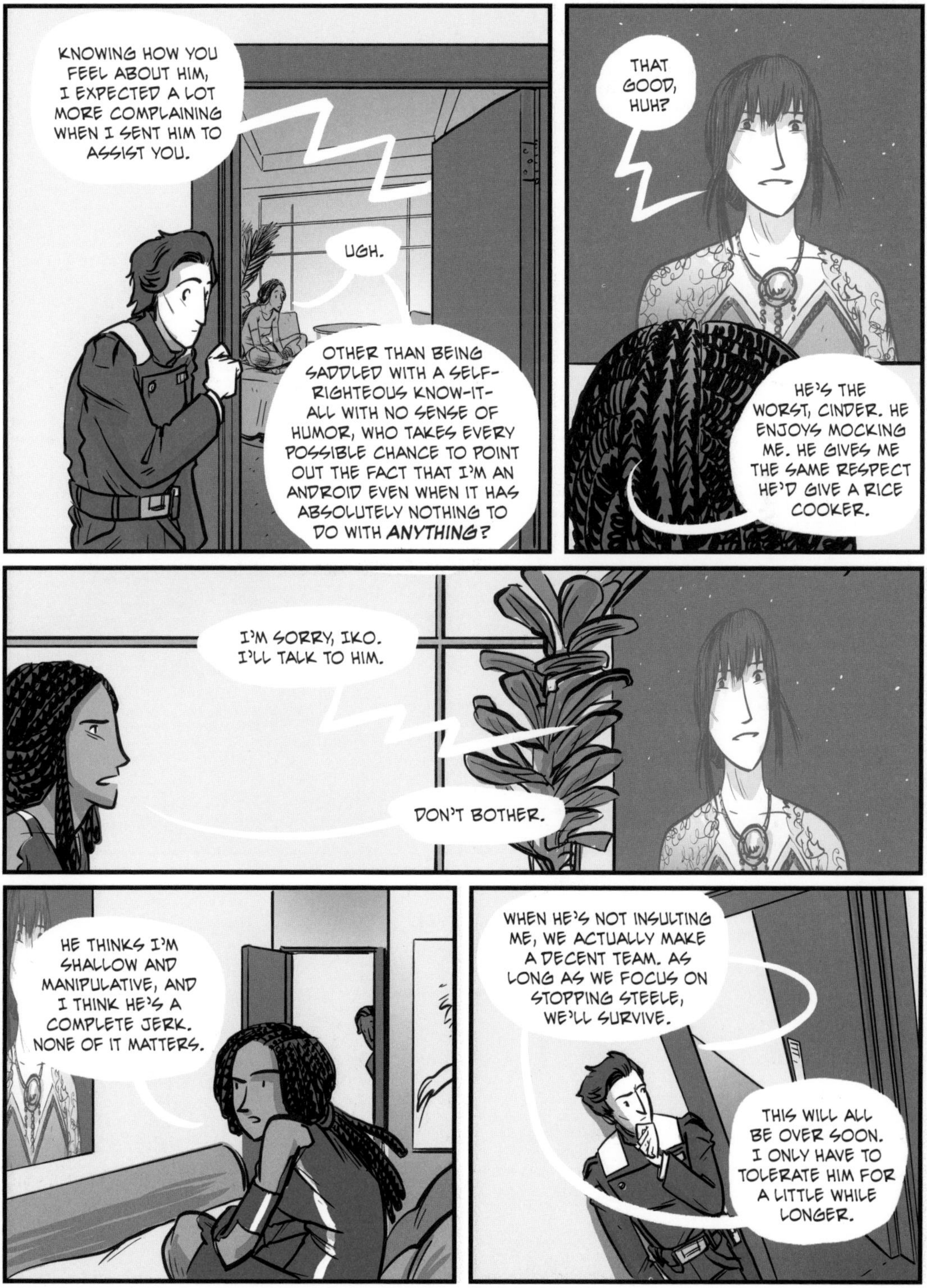
KNOWING HOW YOU FEEL ABOUT HIM, I EXPECTED A LOT MORE COMPLAINING WHEN I SENT HIM TO ASSIST YOU.
UGH.
OTHER THAN BEING SADDLED WITH A SELF-RIGHTEOUS KNOW-IT-ALL WITH NO SENSE OF HUMOR, WHO TAKES EVERY POSSIBLE CHANCE TO POINT OUT THE FACT THAT I'M AN ANDROID EVEN WHEN IT HAS ABSOLUTELY NOTHING TO DO WITH **ANYTHING**?
THAT GOOD, HUH?
HE'S THE WORST, CINDER. HE ENJOYS MOCKING ME. HE GIVES ME THE SAME RESPECT HE'D GIVE A RICE COOKER.
I'M SORRY, IKO. I'LL TALK TO HIM.
DON'T BOTHER.
HE THINKS I'M SHALLOW AND MANIPULATIVE, AND I THINK HE'S A COMPLETE JERK. NONE OF IT MATTERS.
WHEN HE'S NOT INSULTING ME, WE ACTUALLY MAKE A DECENT TEAM. AS LONG AS WE FOCUS ON STOPPING STEELE, WE'LL SURVIVE.
THIS WILL ALL BE OVER SOON. I ONLY HAVE TO TOLERATE HIM FOR A LITTLE WHILE LONGER.

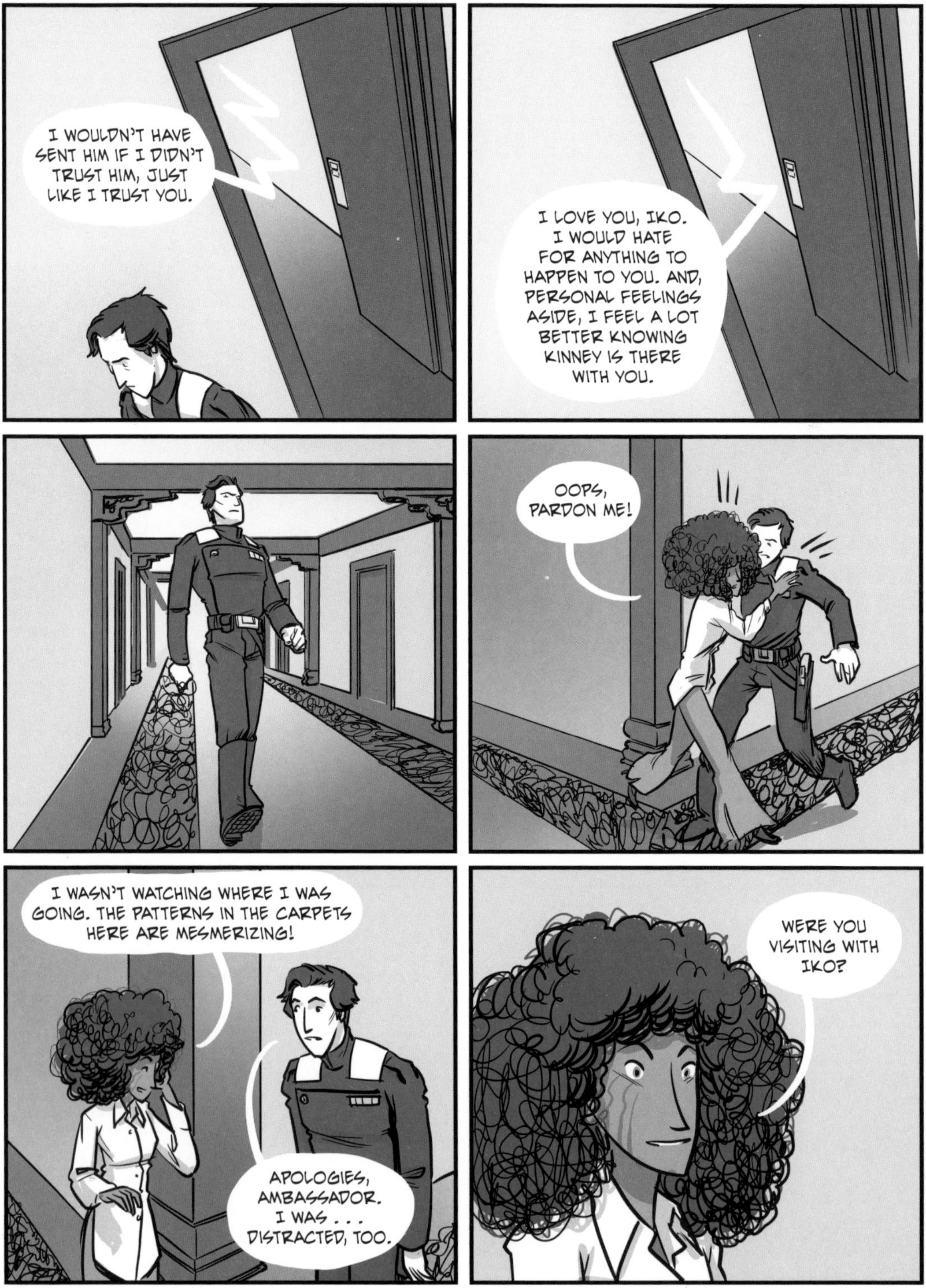
I WOULDN'T HAVE SENT HIM IF I DIDN'T TRUST HIM, JUST LIKE I TRUST YOU.
I LOVE YOU, IKO. I WOULD HATE FOR ANYTHING TO HAPPEN TO YOU. AND, PERSONAL FEELINGS ASIDE, I FEEL A LOT BETTER KNOWING KINNEY IS THERE WITH YOU.
OOPS, PARDON ME!
I WASN'T WATCHING WHERE I WAS GOING. THE PATTERNS IN THE CARPETS HERE ARE MESMERIZING!
APOLOGIES, AMBASSADOR. I WAS . . . DISTRACTED, TOO.
WERE YOU VISITING WITH IKO?

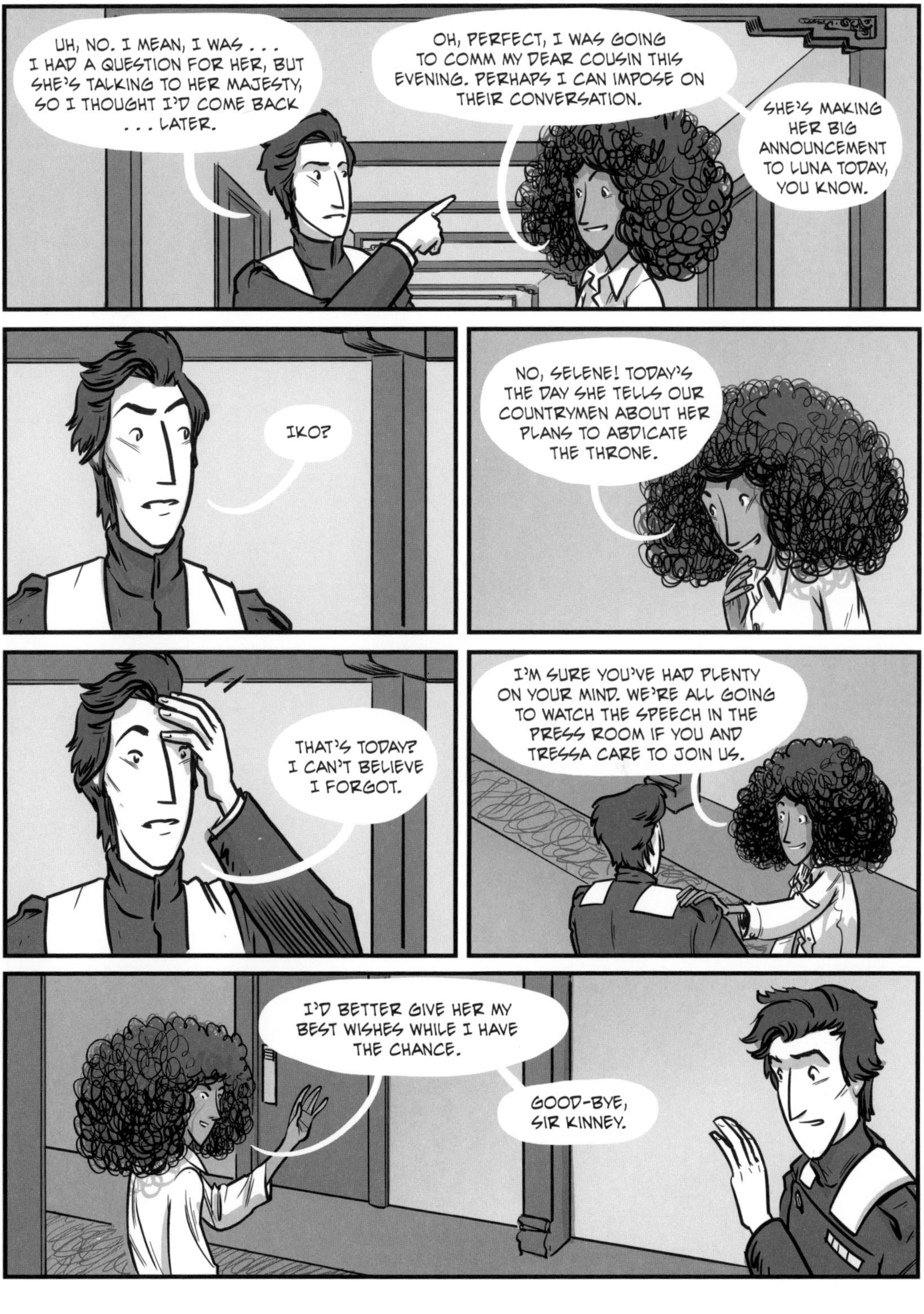
UH, NO. I MEAN, I WAS . . . I HAD A QUESTION FOR HER, BUT SHE'S TALKING TO HER MAJESTY, SO I THOUGHT I'D COME BACK . . . LATER.
OH, PERFECT, I WAS GOING TO COMM MY DEAR COUSIN THIS EVENING. PERHAPS I CAN IMPOSE ON THEIR CONVERSATION.
SHE'S MAKING HER BIG ANNOUNCEMENT TO LUNA TODAY, YOU KNOW.
IKO?
NO, SELENE! TODAY'S THE DAY SHE TELLS OUR COUNTRYMEN ABOUT HER PLANS TO ABDICATE THE THRONE.
THAT'S TODAY? I CAN'T BELIEVE I FORGOT.
I'M SURE YOU'VE HAD PLENTY ON YOUR MIND. WE'RE ALL GOING TO WATCH THE SPEECH IN THE PRESS ROOM IF YOU AND TRESSA CARE TO JOIN US.
I'D BETTER GIVE HER MY BEST WISHES WHILE I HAVE THE CHANCE.
GOOD-BYE, SIR KINNEY.

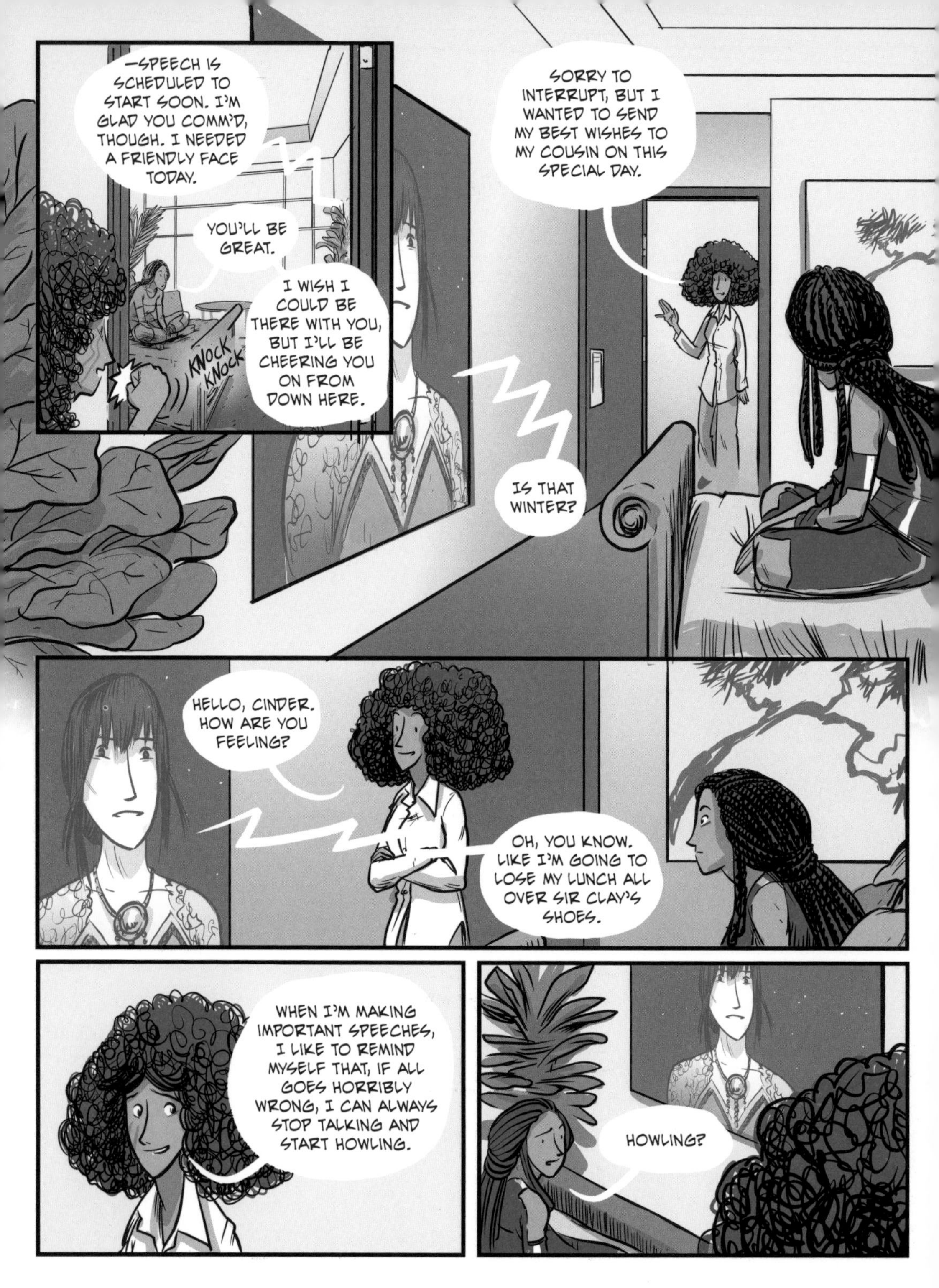
—SPEECH IS SCHEDULED TO START SOON. I'M GLAD YOU COMM'D, THOUGH. I NEEDED A FRIENDLY FACE TODAY.
YOU'LL BE GREAT.
I WISH I COULD BE THERE WITH YOU, BUT I'LL BE CHEERING YOU ON FROM DOWN HERE.
KNOCK KNOCK
SORRY TO INTERRUPT, BUT I WANTED TO SEND MY BEST WISHES TO MY COUSIN ON THIS SPECIAL DAY.
IS THAT WINTER?
HELLO, CINDER. HOW ARE YOU FEELING?
OH, YOU KNOW. LIKE I'M GOING TO LOSE MY LUNCH ALL OVER SIR CLAY'S SHOES.
WHEN I'M MAKING IMPORTANT SPEECHES, I LIKE TO REMIND MYSELF THAT, IF ALL GOES HORRIBLY WRONG, I CAN ALWAYS STOP TALKING AND START HOWLING.
HOWLING?

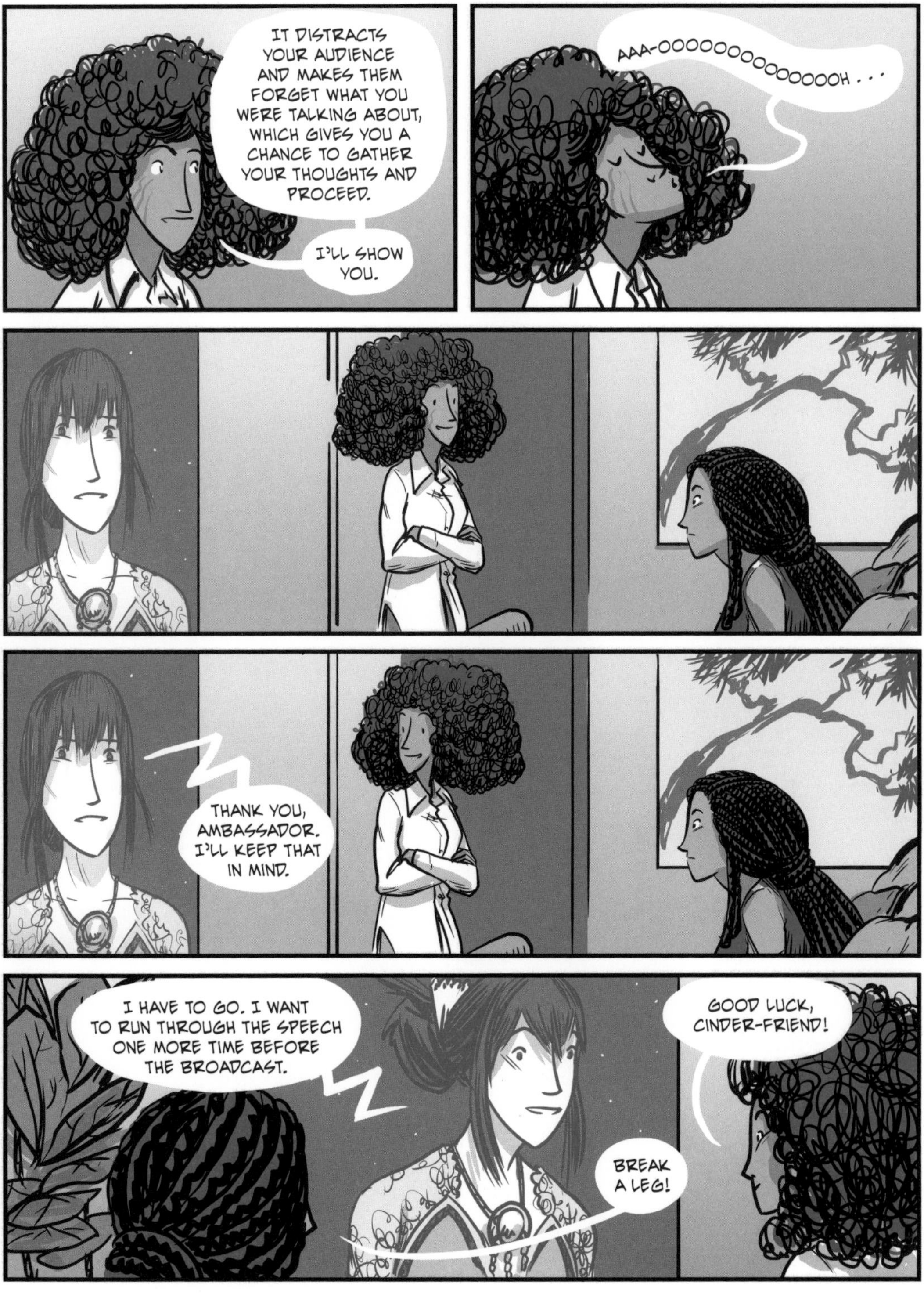
IT DISTRACTS YOUR AUDIENCE AND MAKES THEM FORGET WHAT YOU WERE TALKING ABOUT, WHICH GIVES YOU A CHANCE TO GATHER YOUR THOUGHTS AND PROCEED.
I'LL SHOW YOU.
AAA-OOOOOOOOOOOOOOOH . . .
THANK YOU, AMBASSADOR. I'LL KEEP THAT IN MIND.
I HAVE TO GO. I WANT TO RUN THROUGH THE SPEECH ONE MORE TIME BEFORE THE BROADCAST.
GOOD LUCK, CINDER-FRIEND!
BREAK A LEG!

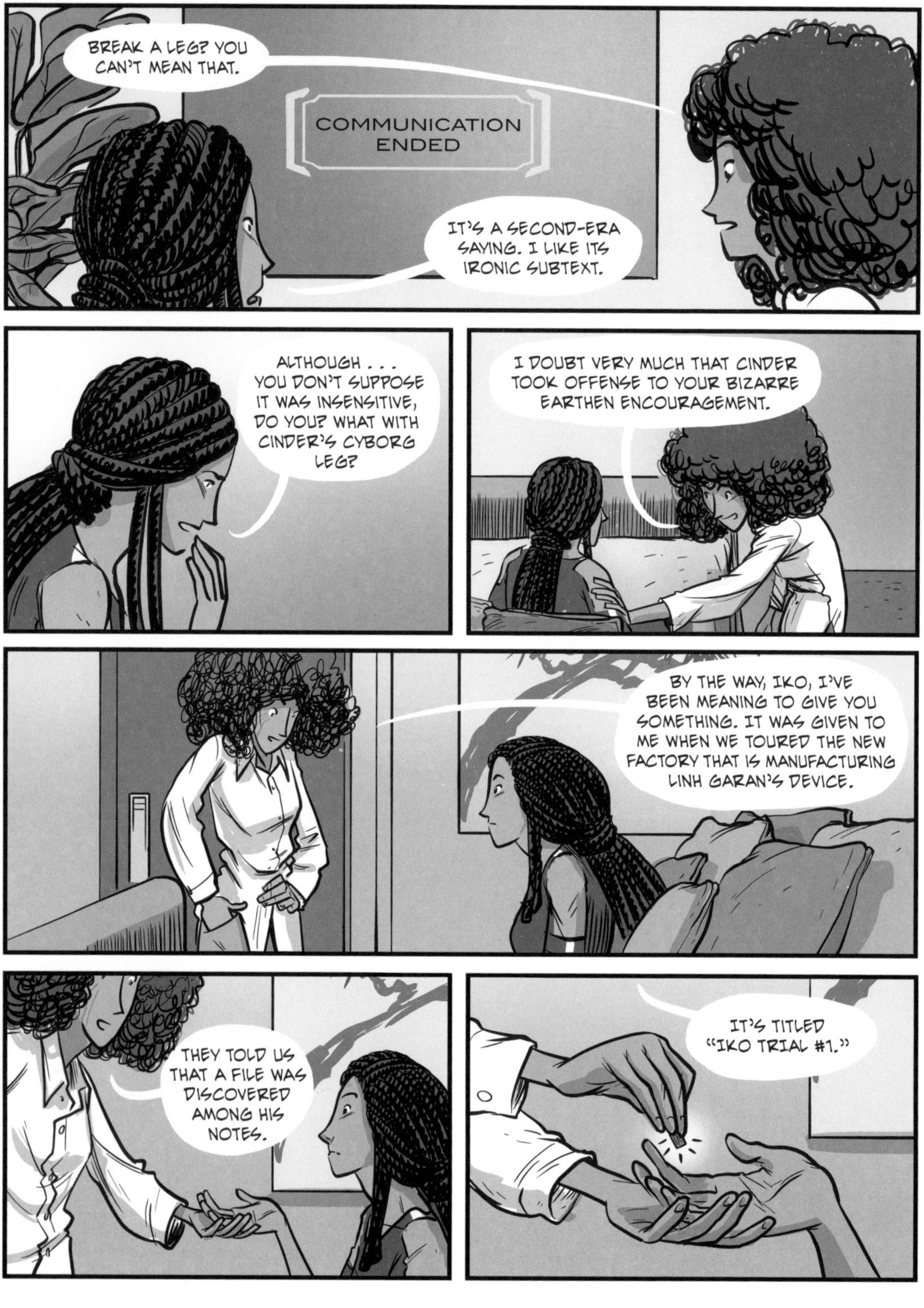
BREAK A LEG? YOU CAN'T MEAN THAT.
COMMUNICATION ENDED
IT'S A SECOND-ERA SAYING. I LIKE ITS IRONIC SUBTEXT.
ALTHOUGH . . . YOU DON'T SUPPOSE IT WAS INSENSITIVE, DO YOU? WHAT WITH CINDER'S CYBORG LEG?
I DOUBT VERY MUCH THAT CINDER TOOK OFFENSE TO YOUR BIZARRE EARTHEN ENCOURAGEMENT.
BY THE WAY, IKO, I'VE BEEN MEANING TO GIVE YOU SOMETHING. IT WAS GIVEN TO ME WHEN WE TOURED THE NEW FACTORY THAT IS MANUFACTURING LINH GARAN'S DEVICE.
THEY TOLD US THAT A FILE WAS DISCOVERED AMONG HIS NOTES.
IT'S TITLED "IKO TRIAL #1."

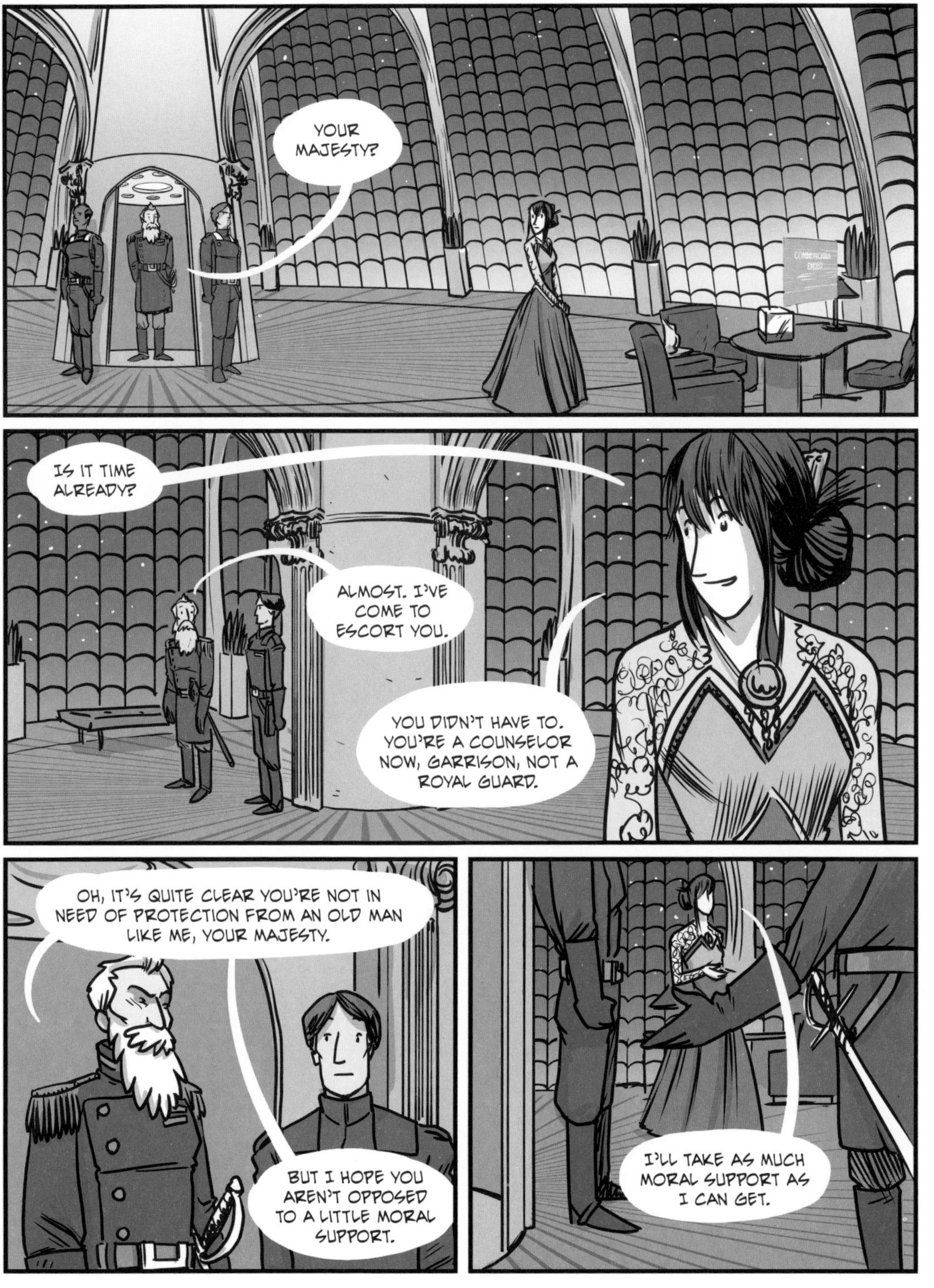
YOUR MAJESTY?
IS IT TIME ALREADY?
ALMOST. I'VE COME TO ESCORT YOU.
YOU DIDN'T HAVE TO. YOU'RE A COUNSELOR NOW, GARRISON, NOT A ROYAL GUARD.
OH, IT'S QUITE CLEAR YOU'RE NOT IN NEED OF PROTECTION FROM AN OLD MAN LIKE ME, YOUR MAJESTY.
BUT I HOPE YOU AREN'T OPPOSED TO A LITTLE MORAL SUPPORT.
I'LL TAKE AS MUCH MORAL SUPPORT AS I CAN GET.

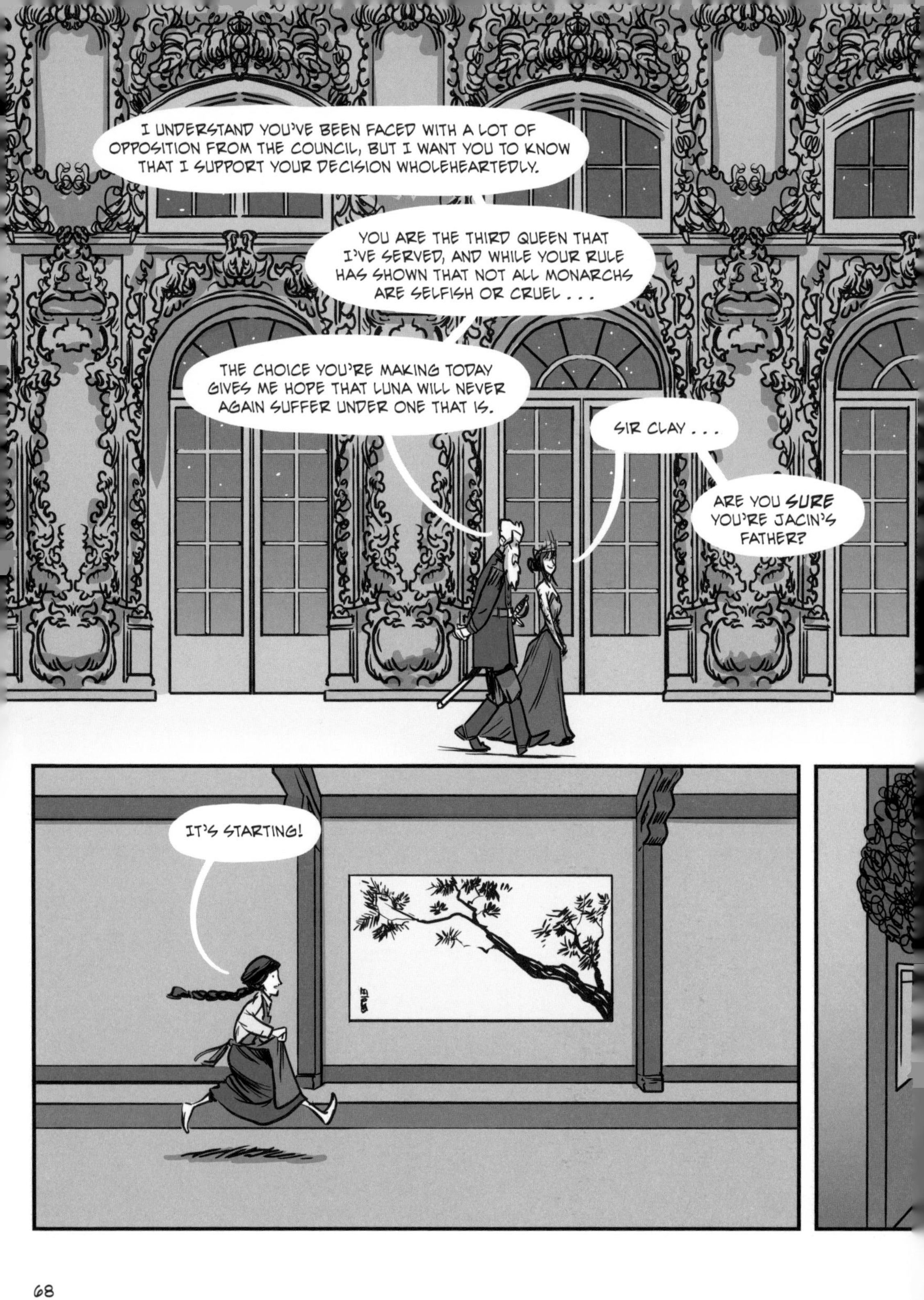
I UNDERSTAND YOU'VE BEEN FACED WITH A LOT OF OPPOSITION FROM THE COUNCIL, BUT I WANT YOU TO KNOW THAT I SUPPORT YOUR DECISION WHOLEHEARTEDLY.
YOU ARE THE THIRD QUEEN THAT I'VE SERVED, AND WHILE YOUR RULE HAS SHOWN THAT NOT ALL MONARCHS ARE SELFISH OR CRUEL . . .
THE CHOICE YOU'RE MAKING TODAY GIVES ME HOPE THAT LUNA WILL NEVER AGAIN SUFFER UNDER ONE THAT IS.
SIR CLAY . . .
ARE YOU **SURE** YOU'RE JACIN'S FATHER?
IT'S STARTING!

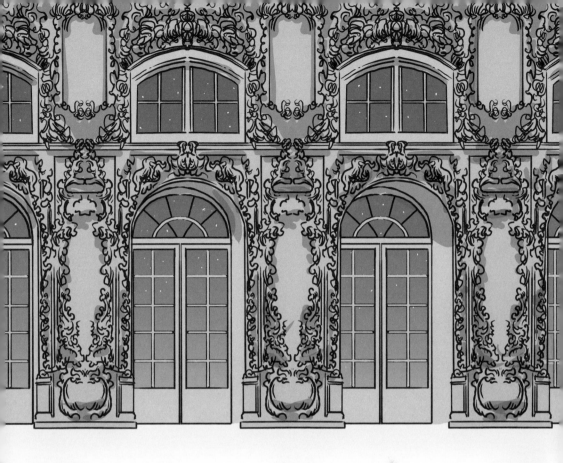

CINDER'S ABOUT TO GIVE HER SPEECH.

COME ON!

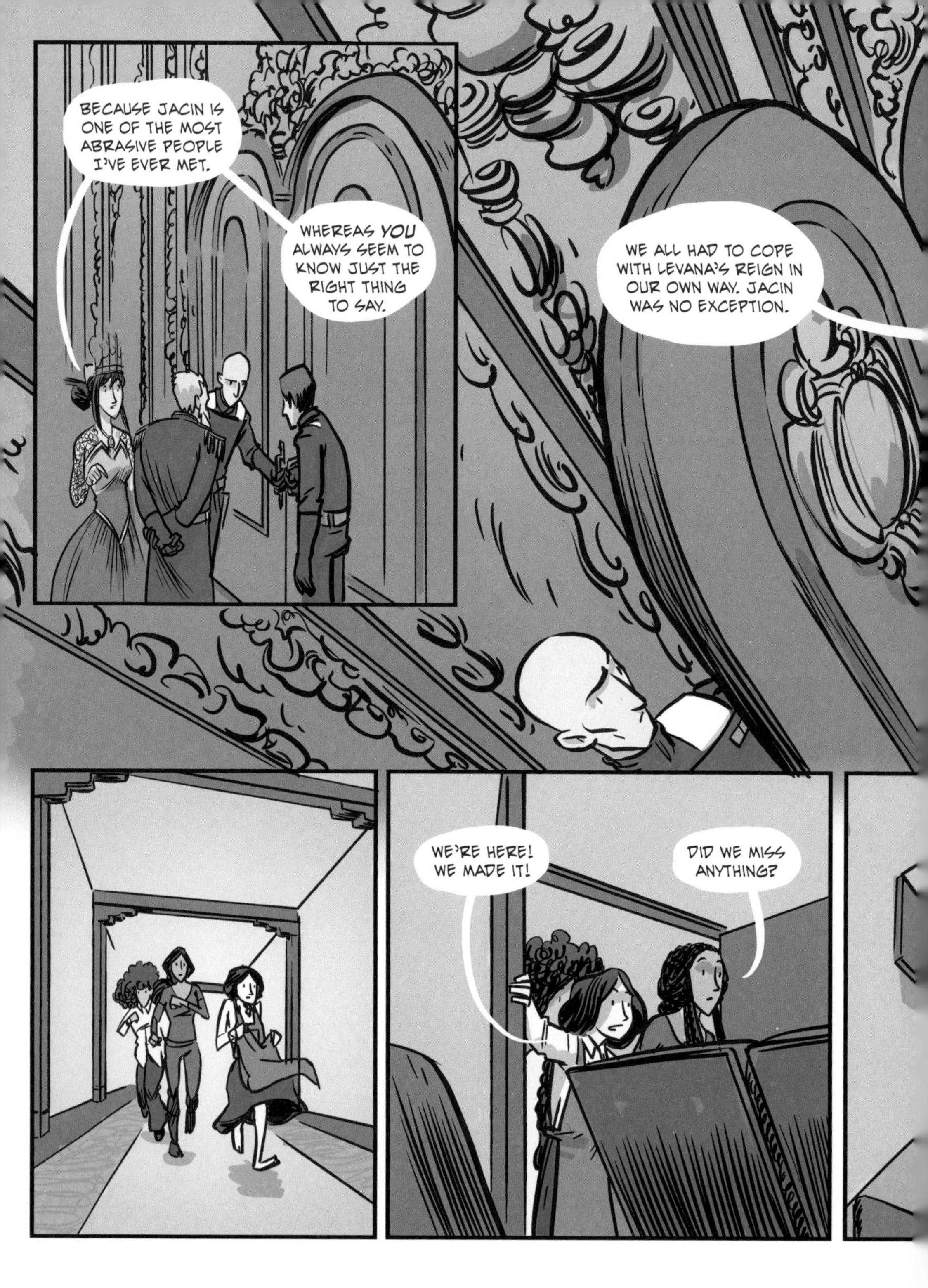
BECAUSE JACIN IS ONE OF THE MOST ABRASIVE PEOPLE I'VE EVER MET.
WHEREAS YOU ALWAYS SEEM TO KNOW JUST THE RIGHT THING TO SAY.
WE ALL HAD TO COPE WITH LEVANA'S REIGN IN OUR OWN WAY. JACIN WAS NO EXCEPTION.
WE'RE HERE! WE MADE IT!
DID WE MISS ANYTHING?

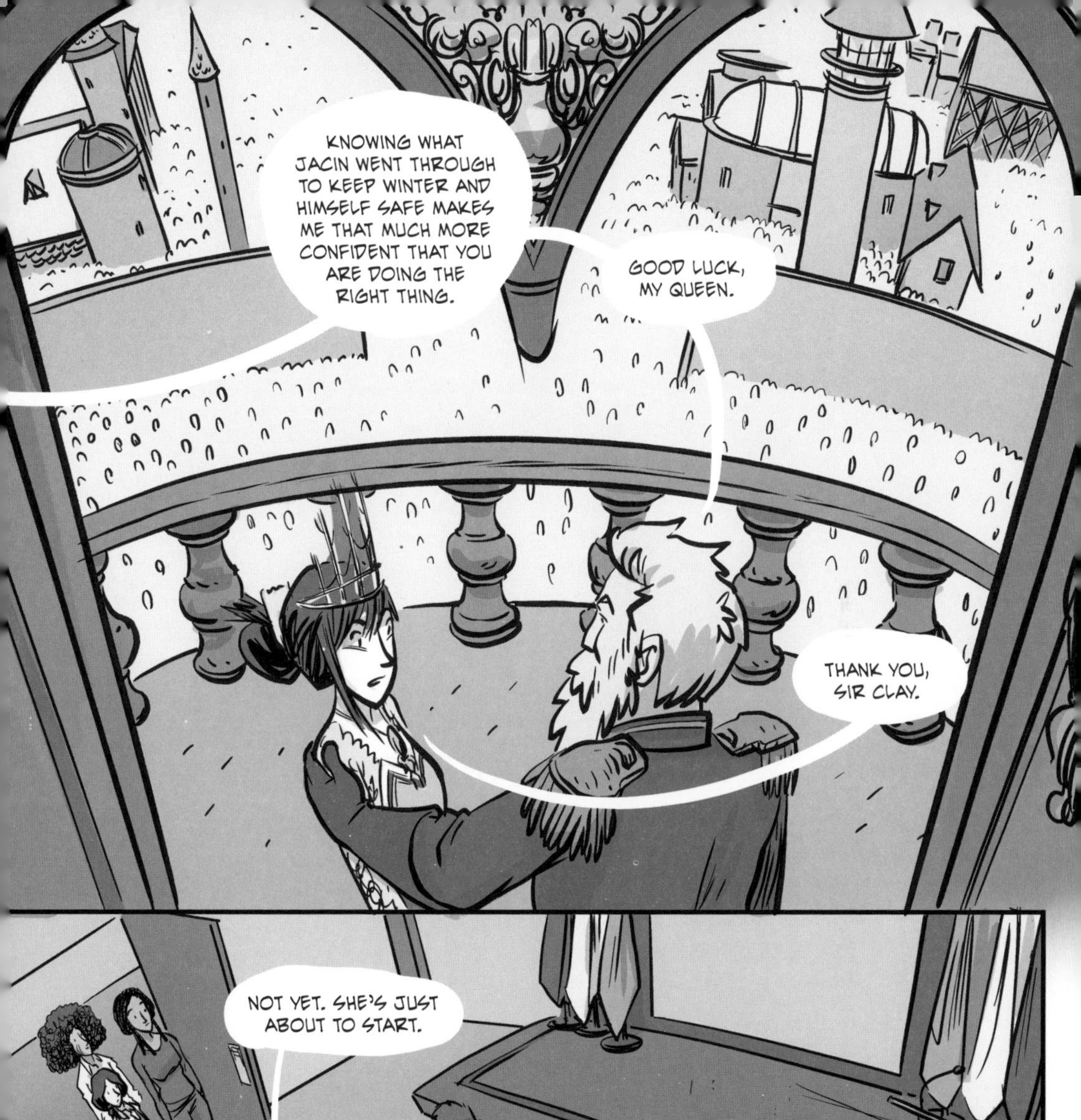
KNOWING WHAT JACIN WENT THROUGH TO KEEP WINTER AND HIMSELF SAFE MAKES ME THAT MUCH MORE CONFIDENT THAT YOU ARE DOING THE RIGHT THING.
GOOD LUCK, MY QUEEN.
THANK YOU, SIR CLAY.

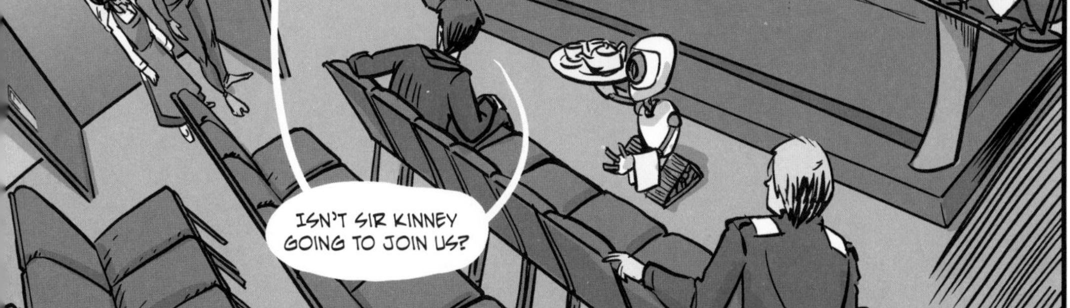
ISN'T SIR KINNEY GOING TO JOIN US?
NOT YET. SHE'S JUST ABOUT TO START.

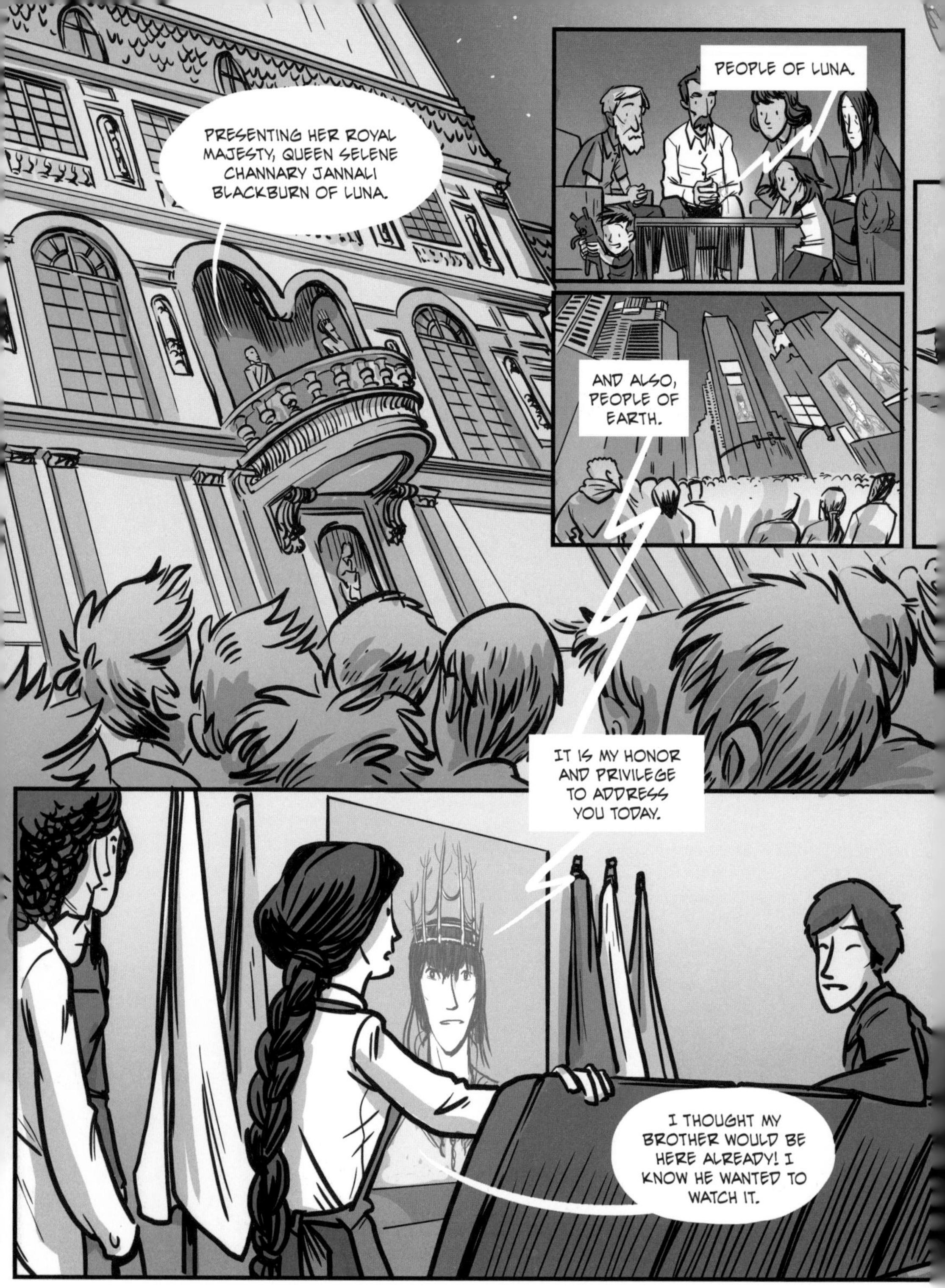
PRESENTING HER ROYAL MAJESTY, QUEEN SELENE CHANNARY JANNALI BLACKBURN OF LUNA.
PEOPLE OF LUNA.
AND ALSO, PEOPLE OF EARTH.
IT IS MY HONOR AND PRIVILEGE TO ADDRESS YOU TODAY.
I THOUGHT MY BROTHER WOULD BE HERE ALREADY! I KNOW HE WANTED TO WATCH IT.

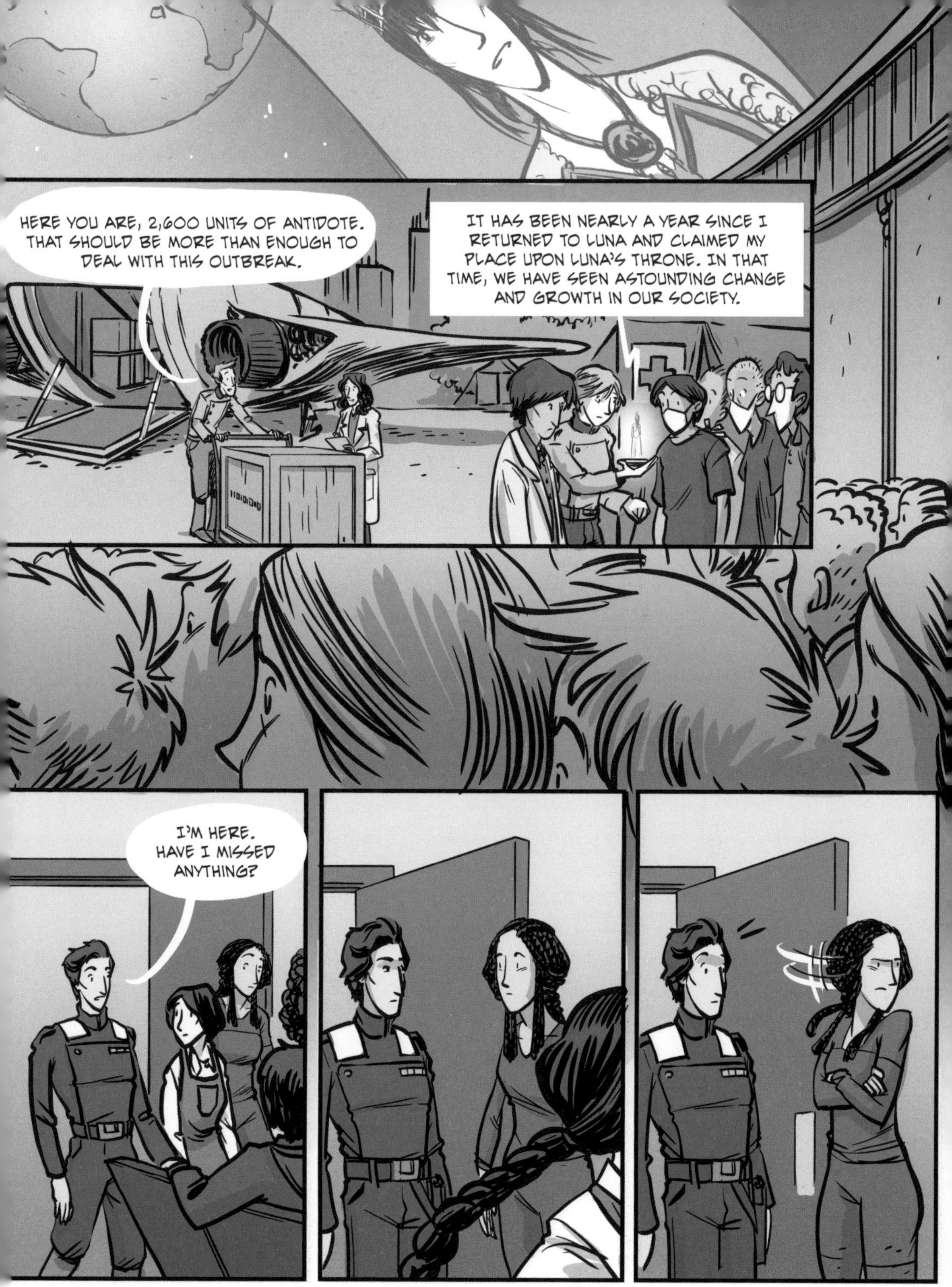
HERE YOU ARE, 2,600 UNITS OF ANTIDOTE. THAT SHOULD BE MORE THAN ENOUGH TO DEAL WITH THIS OUTBREAK.
IT HAS BEEN NEARLY A YEAR SINCE I RETURNED TO LUNA AND CLAIMED MY PLACE UPON LUNA'S THRONE. IN THAT TIME, WE HAVE SEEN ASTOUNDING CHANGE AND GROWTH IN OUR SOCIETY.
I'M HERE. HAVE I MISSED ANYTHING?

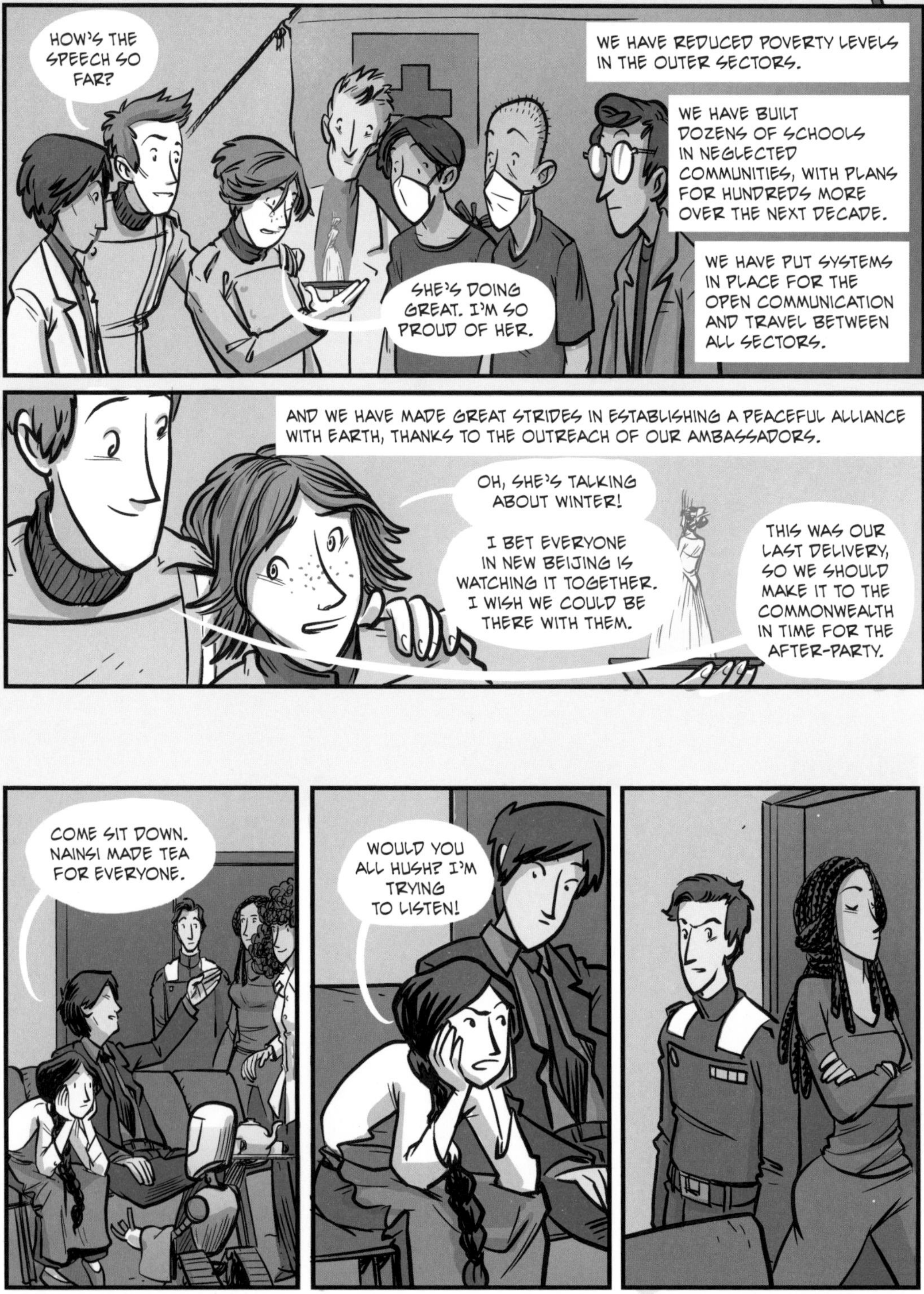
HOW'S THE SPEECH SO FAR?
WE HAVE REDUCED POVERTY LEVELS IN THE OUTER SECTORS.
WE HAVE BUILT DOZENS OF SCHOOLS IN NEGLECTED COMMUNITIES, WITH PLANS FOR HUNDREDS MORE OVER THE NEXT DECADE.
WE HAVE PUT SYSTEMS IN PLACE FOR THE OPEN COMMUNICATION AND TRAVEL BETWEEN ALL SECTORS.
SHE'S DOING GREAT. I'M SO PROUD OF HER.
AND WE HAVE MADE GREAT STRIDES IN ESTABLISHING A PEACEFUL ALLIANCE WITH EARTH, THANKS TO THE OUTREACH OF OUR AMBASSADORS.
OH, SHE'S TALKING ABOUT WINTER!
I BET EVERYONE IN NEW BEIJING IS WATCHING IT TOGETHER. I WISH WE COULD BE THERE WITH THEM.
THIS WAS OUR LAST DELIVERY, SO WE SHOULD MAKE IT TO THE COMMONWEALTH IN TIME FOR THE AFTER-PARTY.
COME SIT DOWN. NAINSI MADE TEA FOR EVERYONE.
WOULD YOU ALL HUSH? I'M TRYING TO LISTEN!

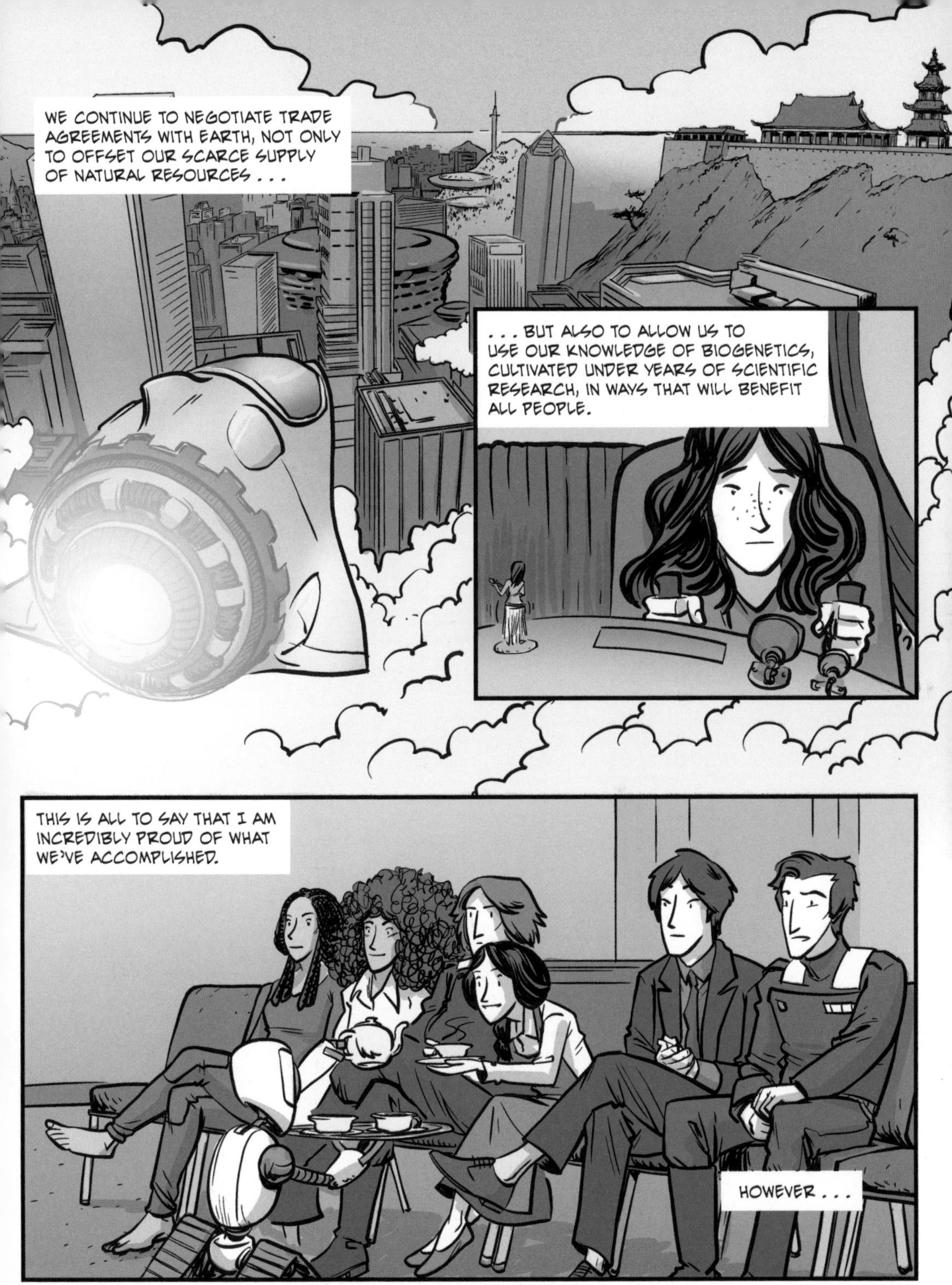
WE CONTINUE TO NEGOTIATE TRADE AGREEMENTS WITH EARTH, NOT ONLY TO OFFSET OUR SCARCE SUPPLY OF NATURAL RESOURCES . . .
. . . BUT ALSO TO ALLOW US TO USE OUR KNOWLEDGE OF BIOGENETICS, CULTIVATED UNDER YEARS OF SCIENTIFIC RESEARCH, IN WAYS THAT WILL BENEFIT ALL PEOPLE.
THIS IS ALL TO SAY THAT I AM INCREDIBLY PROUD OF WHAT WE'VE ACCOMPLISHED.
HOWEVER . . .

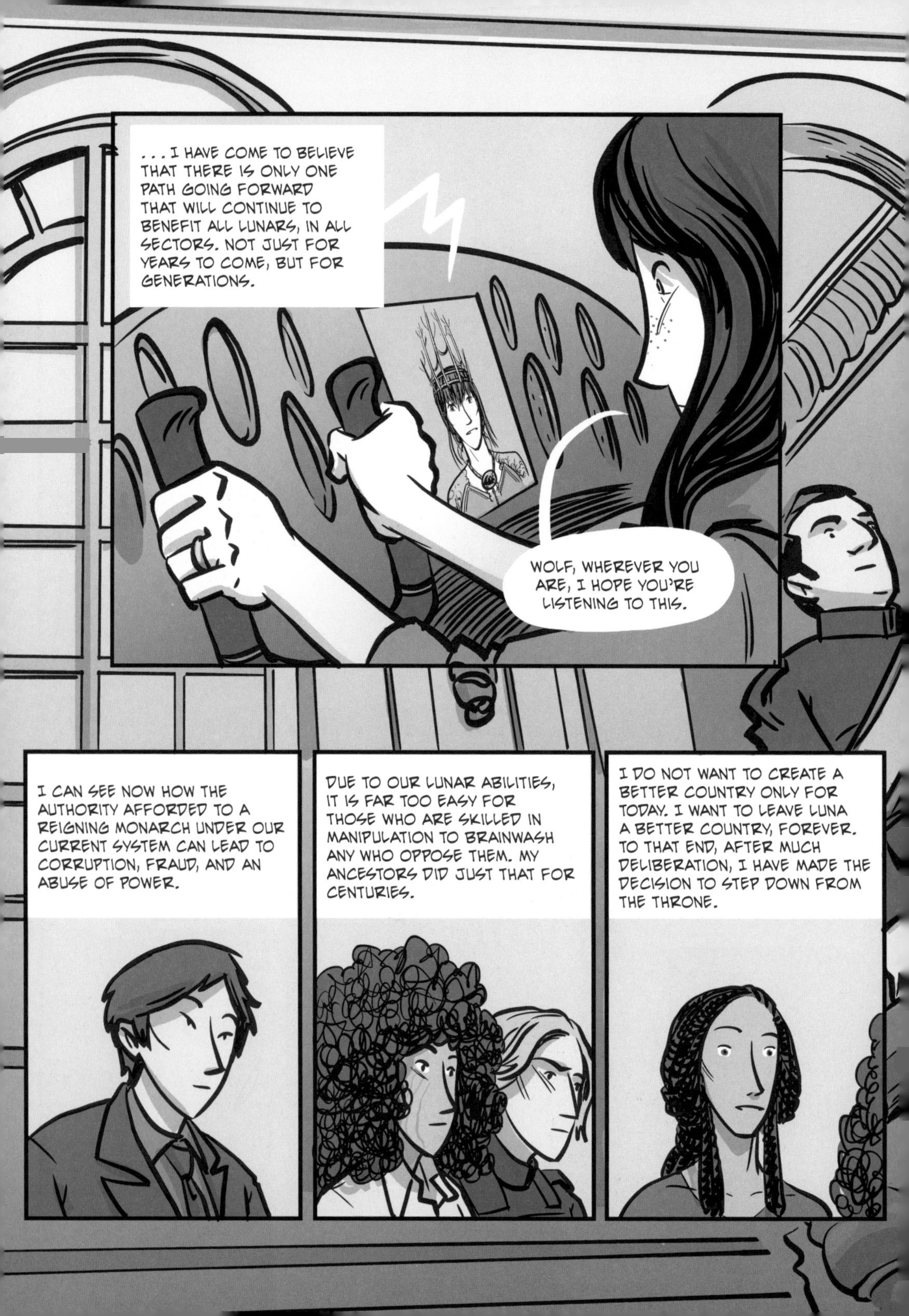
. . . I HAVE COME TO BELIEVE THAT THERE IS ONLY ONE PATH GOING FORWARD THAT WILL CONTINUE TO BENEFIT ALL LUNARS, IN ALL SECTORS. NOT JUST FOR YEARS TO COME, BUT FOR GENERATIONS.
WOLF, WHEREVER YOU ARE, I HOPE YOU'RE LISTENING TO THIS.
I CAN SEE NOW HOW THE AUTHORITY AFFORDED TO A REIGNING MONARCH UNDER OUR CURRENT SYSTEM CAN LEAD TO CORRUPTION, FRAUD, AND AN ABUSE OF POWER.
DUE TO OUR LUNAR ABILITIES, IT IS FAR TOO EASY FOR THOSE WHO ARE SKILLED IN MANIPULATION TO BRAINWASH ANY WHO OPPOSE THEM. MY ANCESTORS DID JUST THAT FOR CENTURIES.
I DO NOT WANT TO CREATE A BETTER COUNTRY ONLY FOR TODAY. I WANT TO LEAVE LUNA A BETTER COUNTRY, FOREVER. TO THAT END, AFTER MUCH DELIBERATION, I HAVE MADE THE DECISION TO STEP DOWN FROM THE THRONE.

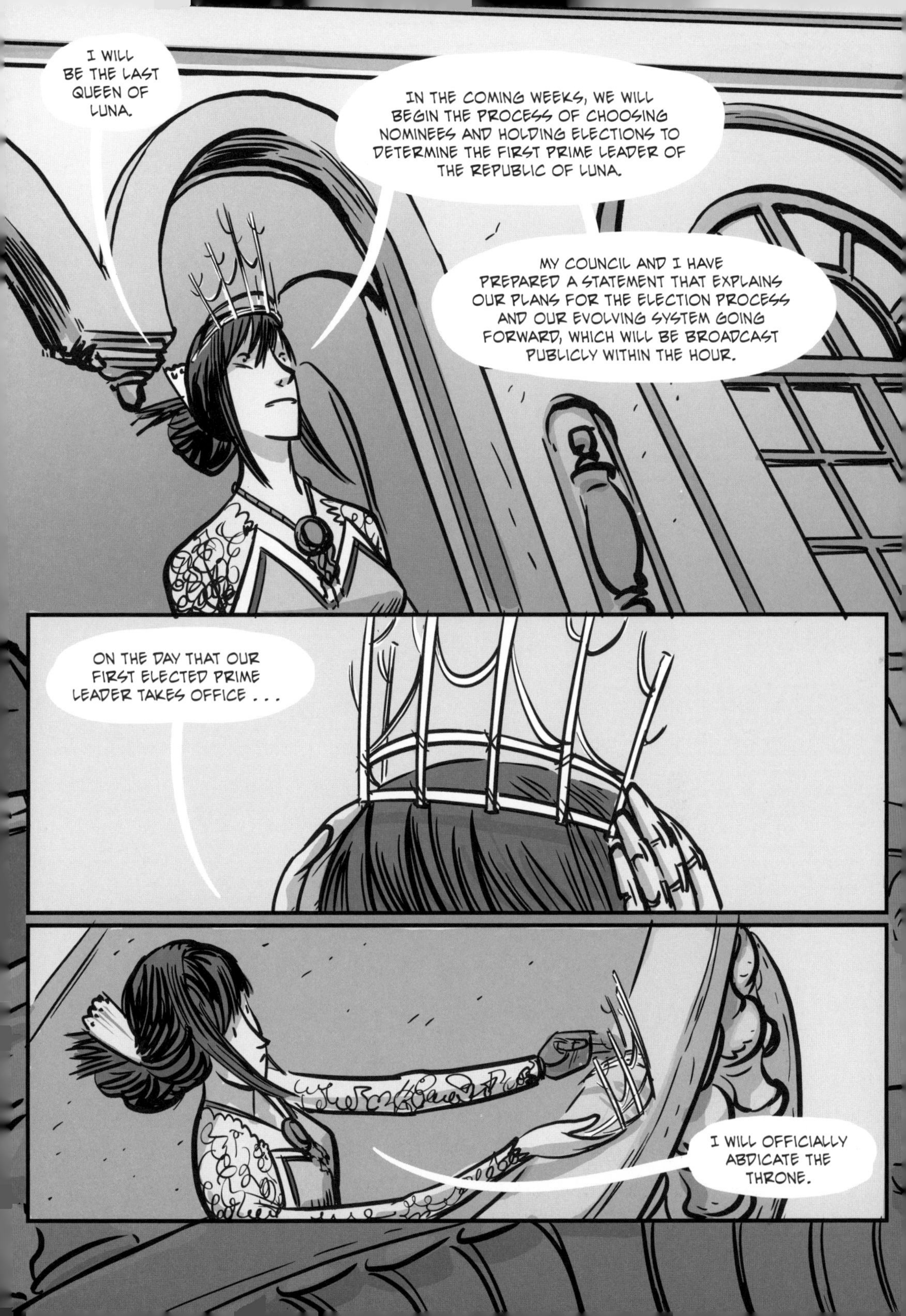
I WILL BE THE LAST QUEEN OF LUNA.
IN THE COMING WEEKS, WE WILL BEGIN THE PROCESS OF CHOOSING NOMINEES AND HOLDING ELECTIONS TO DETERMINE THE FIRST PRIME LEADER OF THE REPUBLIC OF LUNA.
MY COUNCIL AND I HAVE PREPARED A STATEMENT THAT EXPLAINS OUR PLANS FOR THE ELECTION PROCESS AND OUR EVOLVING SYSTEM GOING FORWARD, WHICH WILL BE BROADCAST PUBLICLY WITHIN THE HOUR.
ON THE DAY THAT OUR FIRST ELECTED PRIME LEADER TAKES OFFICE . . .
I WILL OFFICIALLY ABDICATE THE THRONE.

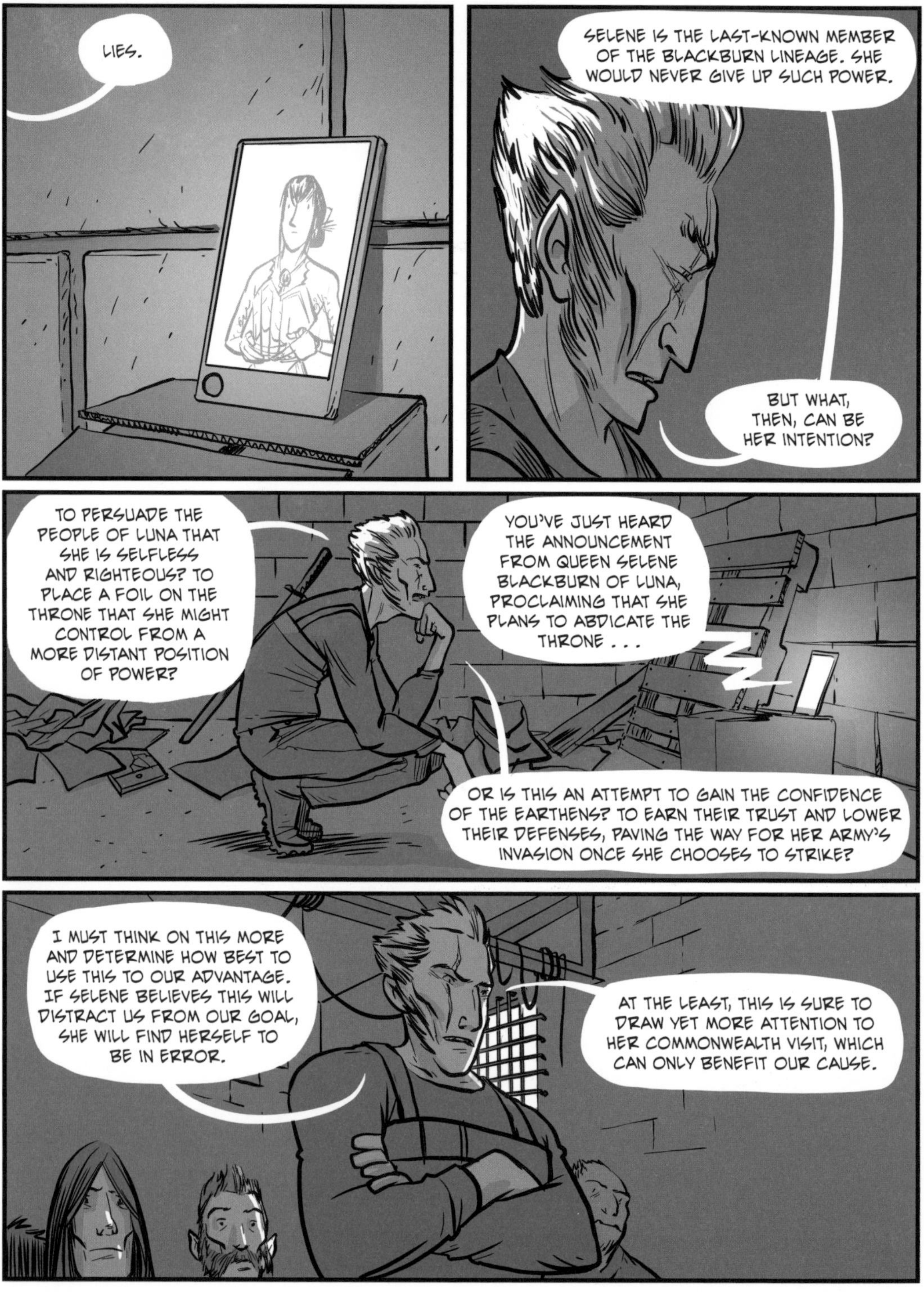
LIES.
SELENE IS THE LAST-KNOWN MEMBER OF THE BLACKBURN LINEAGE. SHE WOULD NEVER GIVE UP SUCH POWER.
BUT WHAT, THEN, CAN BE HER INTENTION?
TO PERSUADE THE PEOPLE OF LUNA THAT SHE IS SELFLESS AND RIGHTEOUS? TO PLACE A FOIL ON THE THRONE THAT SHE MIGHT CONTROL FROM A MORE DISTANT POSITION OF POWER?
YOU'VE JUST HEARD THE ANNOUNCEMENT FROM QUEEN SELENE BLACKBURN OF LUNA, PROCLAIMING THAT SHE PLANS TO ABDICATE THE THRONE . . .
OR IS THIS AN ATTEMPT TO GAIN THE CONFIDENCE OF THE EARTHENS? TO EARN THEIR TRUST AND LOWER THEIR DEFENSES, PAVING THE WAY FOR HER ARMY'S INVASION ONCE SHE CHOOSES TO STRIKE?
I MUST THINK ON THIS MORE AND DETERMINE HOW BEST TO USE THIS TO OUR ADVANTAGE. IF SELENE BELIEVES THIS WILL DISTRACT US FROM OUR GOAL, SHE WILL FIND HERSELF TO BE IN ERROR.
AT THE LEAST, THIS IS SURE TO DRAW YET MORE ATTENTION TO HER COMMONWEALTH VISIT, WHICH CAN ONLY BENEFIT OUR CAUSE.

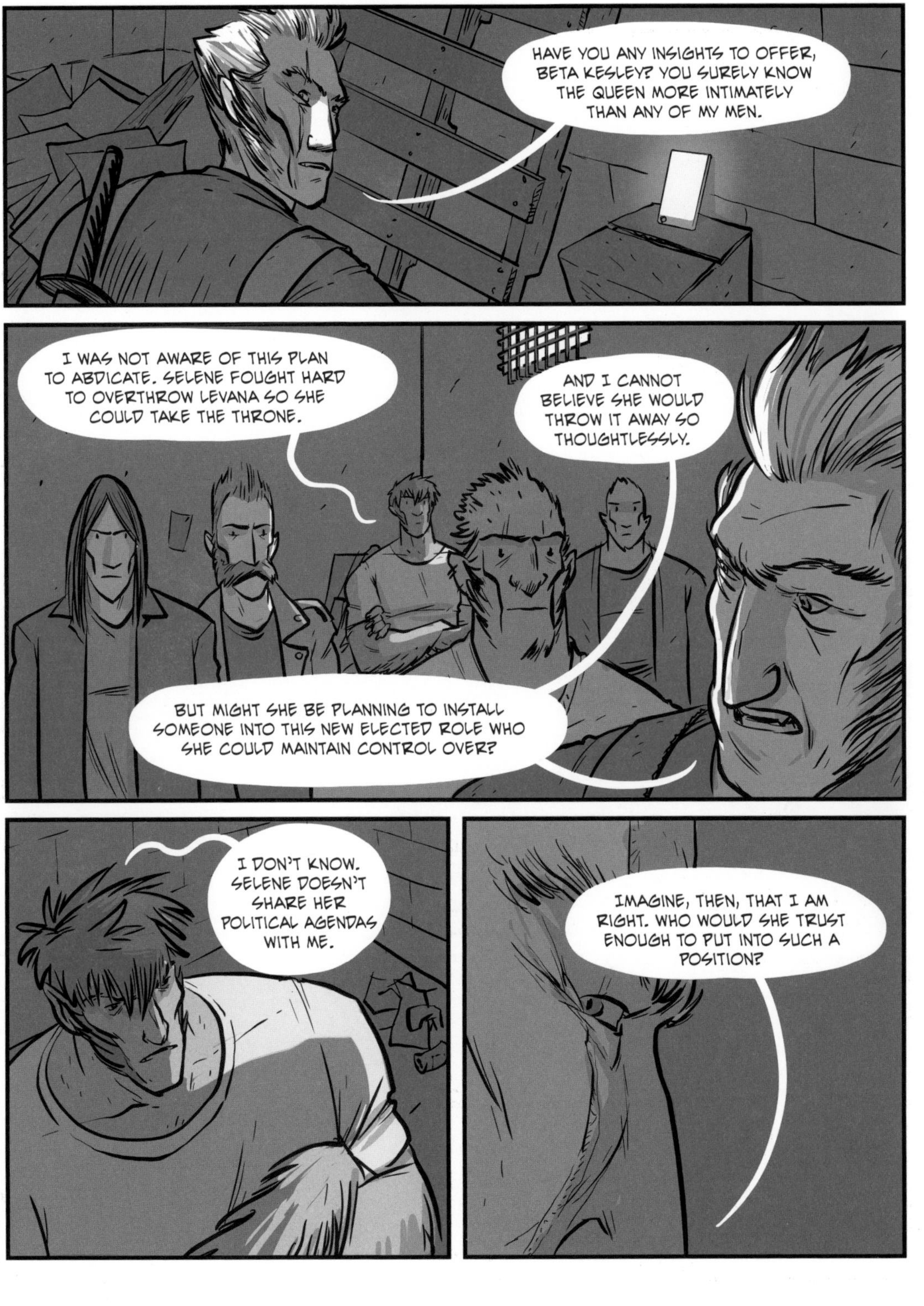
HAVE YOU ANY INSIGHTS TO OFFER, BETA KESLEY? YOU SURELY KNOW THE QUEEN MORE INTIMATELY THAN ANY OF MY MEN.
I WAS NOT AWARE OF THIS PLAN TO ABDICATE. SELENE FOUGHT HARD TO OVERTHROW LEVANA SO SHE COULD TAKE THE THRONE.
AND I CANNOT BELIEVE SHE WOULD THROW IT AWAY SO THOUGHTLESSLY.
BUT MIGHT SHE BE PLANNING TO INSTALL SOMEONE INTO THIS NEW ELECTED ROLE WHO SHE COULD MAINTAIN CONTROL OVER?
I DON'T KNOW. SELENE DOESN'T SHARE HER POLITICAL AGENDAS WITH ME.
IMAGINE, THEN, THAT I AM RIGHT. WHO WOULD SHE TRUST ENOUGH TO PUT INTO SUCH A POSITION?

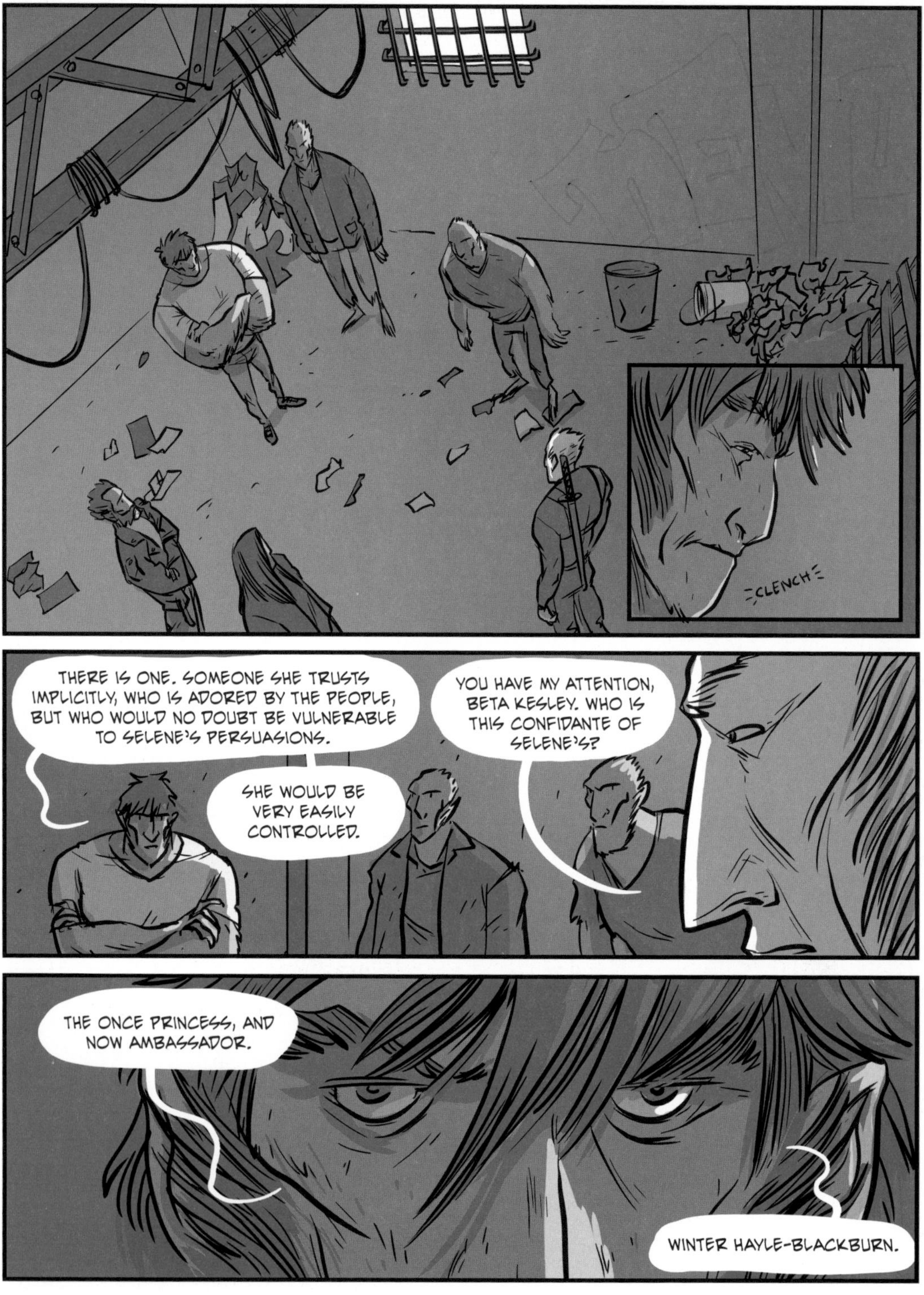
CLENCH
THERE IS ONE. SOMEONE SHE TRUSTS IMPLICITLY, WHO IS ADORED BY THE PEOPLE, BUT WHO WOULD NO DOUBT BE VULNERABLE TO SELENE'S PERSUASIONS.
SHE WOULD BE VERY EASILY CONTROLLED.
YOU HAVE MY ATTENTION, BETA KESLEY. WHO IS THIS CONFIDANTE OF SELENE'S?
THE ONCE PRINCESS, AND NOW AMBASSADOR.
WINTER HAYLE-BLACKBURN.

CHAPTER IV

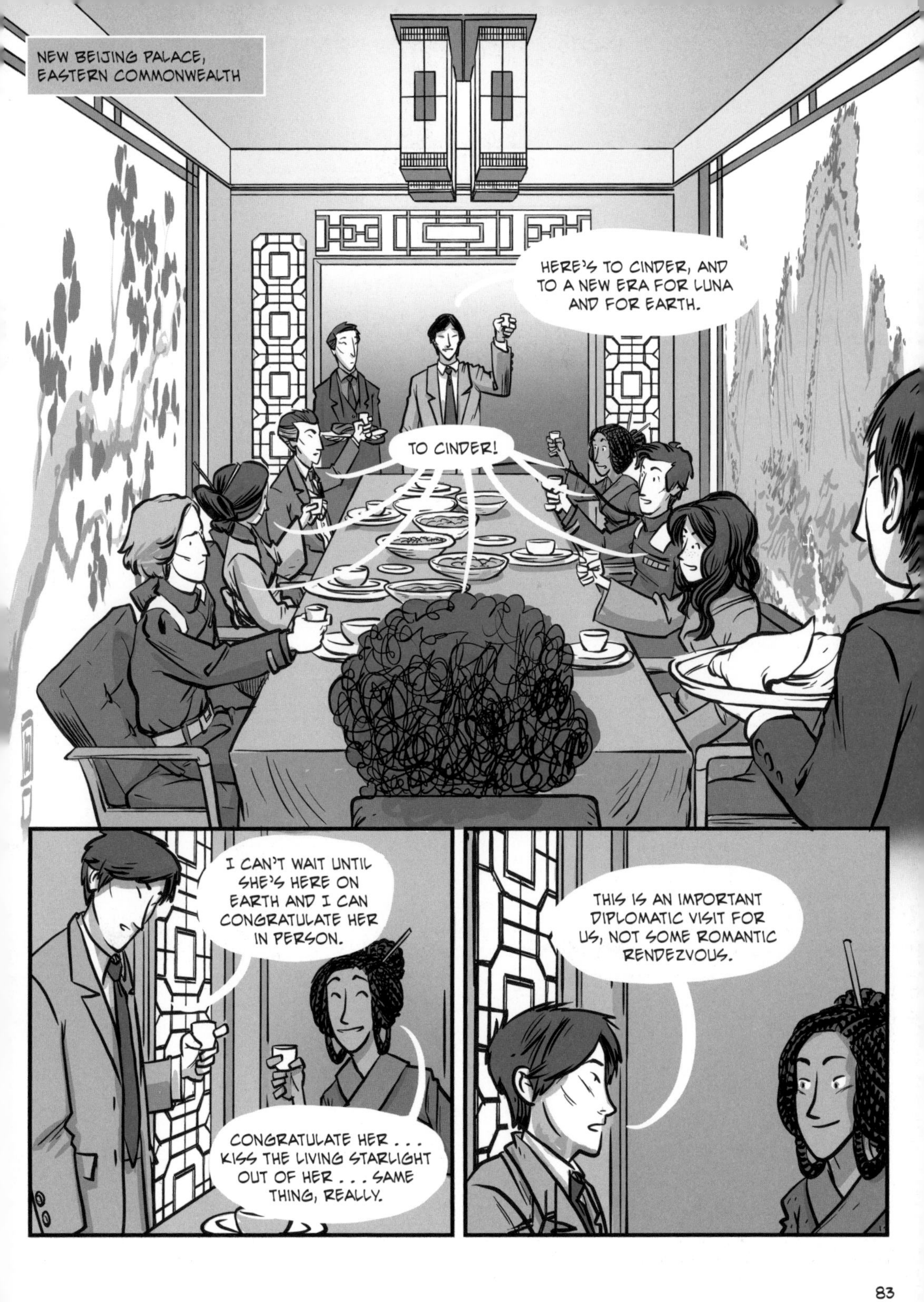
NEW BEIJING PALACE, EASTERN COMMONWEALTH
HERE'S TO CINDER, AND TO A NEW ERA FOR LUNA AND FOR EARTH.
TO CINDER!
I CAN'T WAIT UNTIL SHE'S HERE ON EARTH AND I CAN CONGRATULATE HER IN PERSON.
CONGRATULATE HER . . . KISS THE LIVING STARLIGHT OUT OF HER . . . SAME THING, REALLY.
THIS IS AN IMPORTANT DIPLOMATIC VISIT FOR US, NOT SOME ROMANTIC RENDEZVOUS.

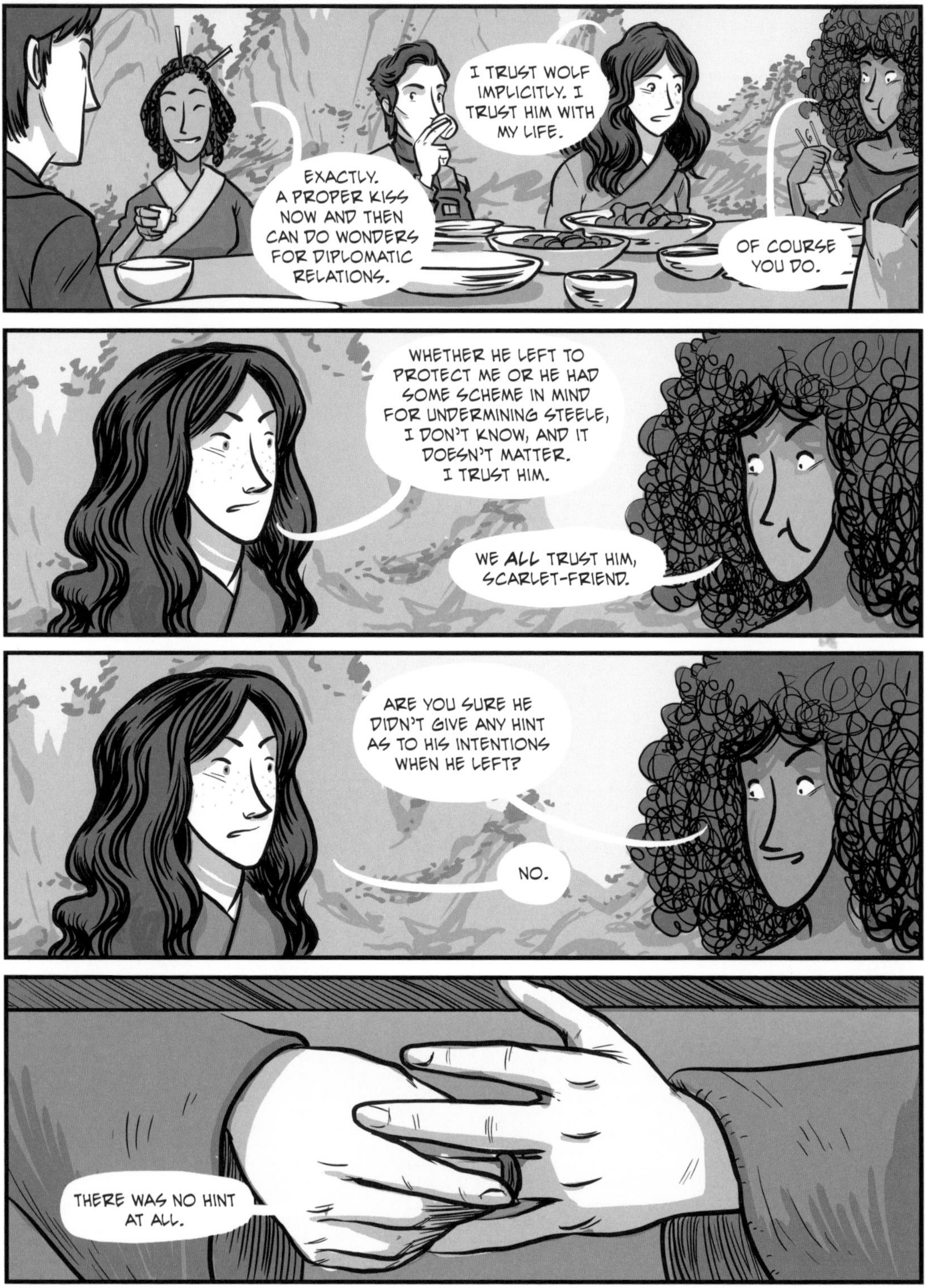
I TRUST WOLF IMPLICITLY. I TRUST HIM WITH MY LIFE.
EXACTLY. A PROPER KISS NOW AND THEN CAN DO WONDERS FOR DIPLOMATIC RELATIONS.
OF COURSE YOU DO.
WHETHER HE LEFT TO PROTECT ME OR HE HAD SOME SCHEME IN MIND FOR UNDERMINING STEELE, I DON'T KNOW, AND IT DOESN'T MATTER. I TRUST HIM.
WE **ALL** TRUST HIM, SCARLET-FRIEND.
ARE YOU SURE HE DIDN'T GIVE ANY HINT AS TO HIS INTENTIONS WHEN HE LEFT?
NO.
THERE WAS NO HINT AT ALL.

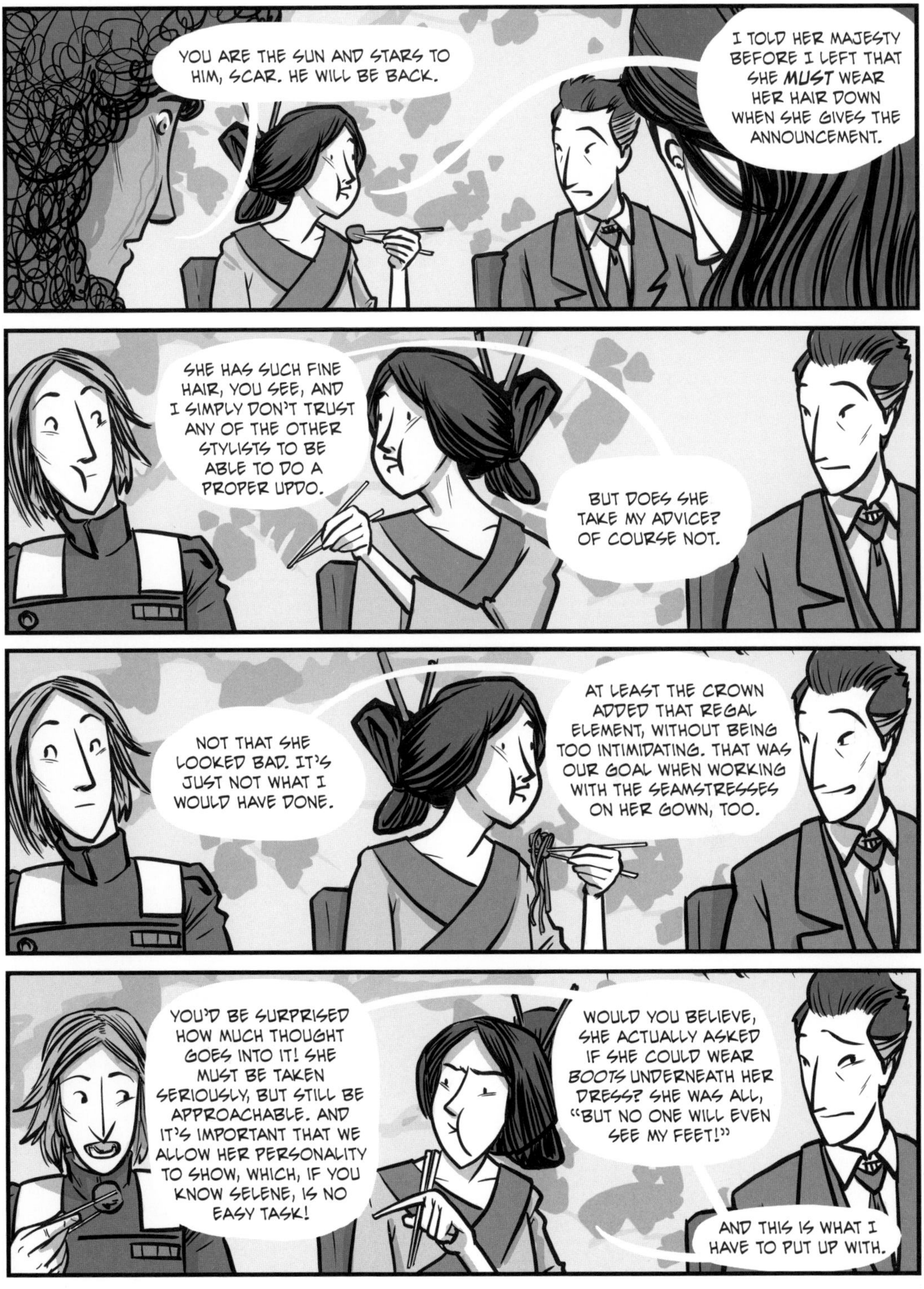
YOU ARE THE SUN AND STARS TO HIM, SCAR. HE WILL BE BACK.
I TOLD HER MAJESTY BEFORE I LEFT THAT SHE **MUST** WEAR HER HAIR DOWN WHEN SHE GIVES THE ANNOUNCEMENT.
SHE HAS SUCH FINE HAIR, YOU SEE, AND I SIMPLY DON'T TRUST ANY OF THE OTHER STYLISTS TO BE ABLE TO DO A PROPER UPDO.
BUT DOES SHE TAKE MY ADVICE? OF COURSE NOT.
NOT THAT SHE LOOKED BAD. IT'S JUST NOT WHAT I WOULD HAVE DONE.
AT LEAST THE CROWN ADDED THAT REGAL ELEMENT, WITHOUT BEING TOO INTIMIDATING. THAT WAS OUR GOAL WHEN WORKING WITH THE SEAMSTRESSES ON HER GOWN, TOO.
YOU'D BE SURPRISED HOW MUCH THOUGHT GOES INTO IT! SHE MUST BE TAKEN SERIOUSLY, BUT STILL BE APPROACHABLE. AND IT'S IMPORTANT THAT WE ALLOW HER PERSONALITY TO SHOW, WHICH, IF YOU KNOW SELENE, IS NO EASY TASK!
WOULD YOU BELIEVE, SHE ACTUALLY ASKED IF SHE COULD WEAR *BOOTS* UNDERNEATH HER DRESS? SHE WAS ALL, "BUT NO ONE WILL EVEN SEE MY FEET!"
AND THIS IS WHAT I HAVE TO PUT UP WITH.

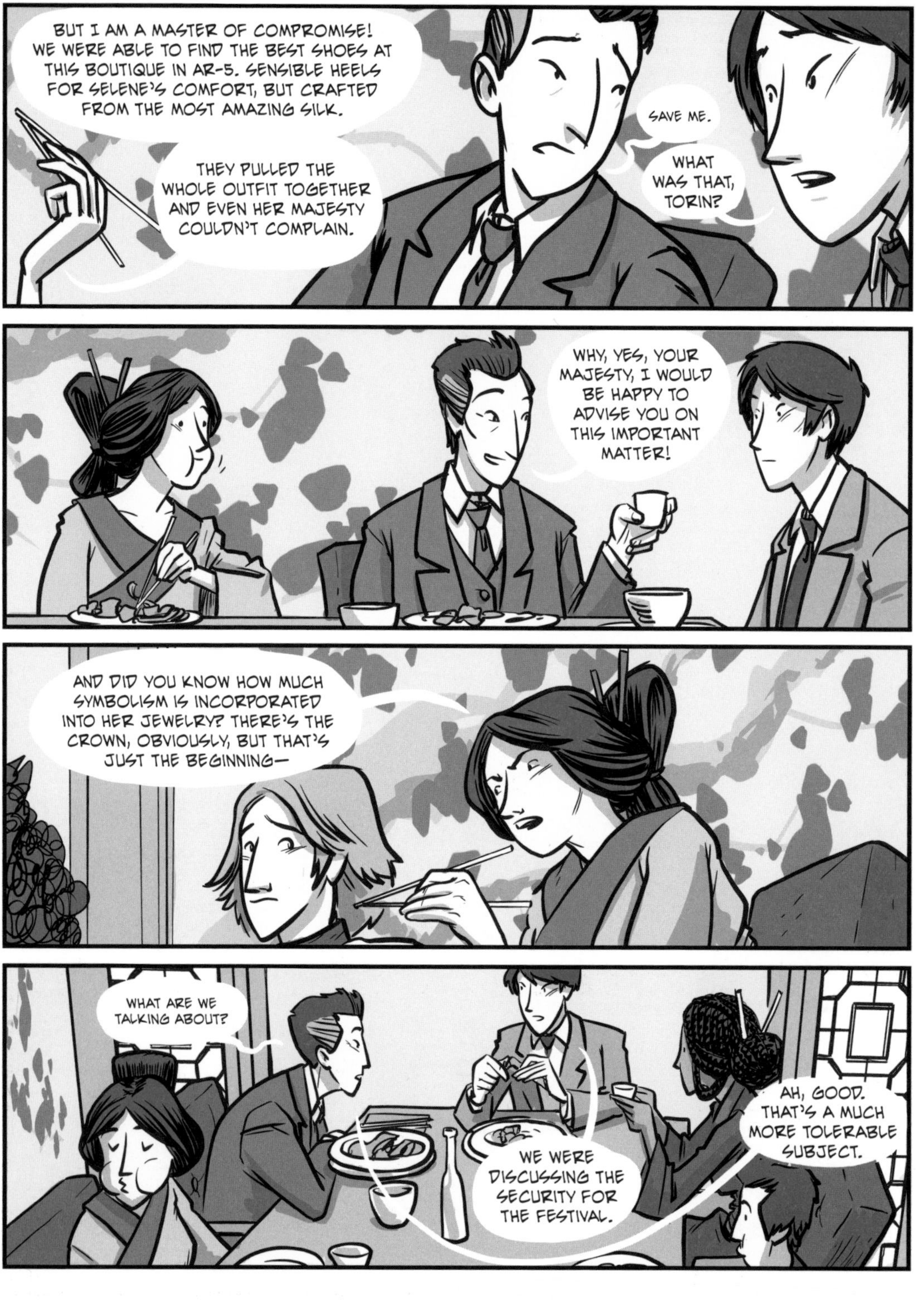
BUT I AM A MASTER OF COMPROMISE! WE WERE ABLE TO FIND THE BEST SHOES AT THIS BOUTIQUE IN AR-5. SENSIBLE HEELS FOR SELENE'S COMFORT, BUT CRAFTED FROM THE MOST AMAZING SILK.
THEY PULLED THE WHOLE OUTFIT TOGETHER AND EVEN HER MAJESTY COULDN'T COMPLAIN.
SAVE ME.
WHAT WAS THAT, TORIN?
WHY, YES, YOUR MAJESTY, I WOULD BE HAPPY TO ADVISE YOU ON THIS IMPORTANT MATTER!
AND DID YOU KNOW HOW MUCH SYMBOLISM IS INCORPORATED INTO HER JEWELRY? THERE'S THE CROWN, OBVIOUSLY, BUT THAT'S JUST THE BEGINNING—
WHAT ARE WE TALKING ABOUT?
WE WERE DISCUSSING THE SECURITY FOR THE FESTIVAL.
AH, GOOD. THAT'S A MUCH MORE TOLERABLE SUBJECT.

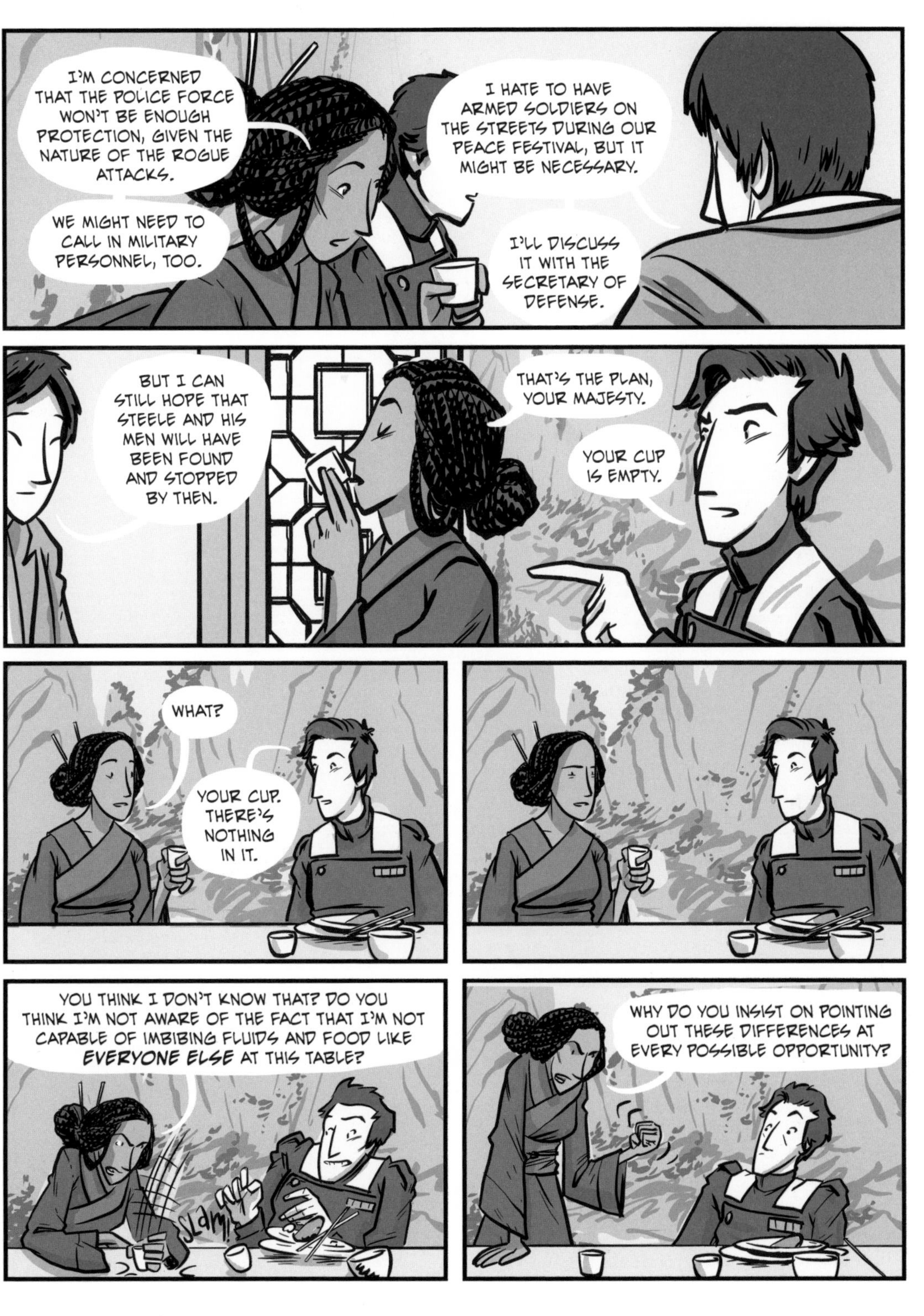
I'M CONCERNED THAT THE POLICE FORCE WON'T BE ENOUGH PROTECTION, GIVEN THE NATURE OF THE ROGUE ATTACKS.
WE MIGHT NEED TO CALL IN MILITARY PERSONNEL, TOO.
I HATE TO HAVE ARMED SOLDIERS ON THE STREETS DURING OUR PEACE FESTIVAL, BUT IT MIGHT BE NECESSARY.
I'LL DISCUSS IT WITH THE SECRETARY OF DEFENSE.
BUT I CAN STILL HOPE THAT STEELE AND HIS MEN WILL HAVE BEEN FOUND AND STOPPED BY THEN.
THAT'S THE PLAN, YOUR MAJESTY.
YOUR CUP IS EMPTY.
WHAT?
YOUR CUP. THERE'S NOTHING IN IT.
YOU THINK I DON'T KNOW THAT? DO YOU THINK I'M NOT AWARE OF THE FACT THAT I'M NOT CAPABLE OF IMBIBING FLUIDS AND FOOD LIKE EVERYONE ELSE AT THIS TABLE?
SLAM!
WHY DO YOU INSIST ON POINTING OUT THESE DIFFERENCES AT EVERY POSSIBLE OPPORTUNITY?

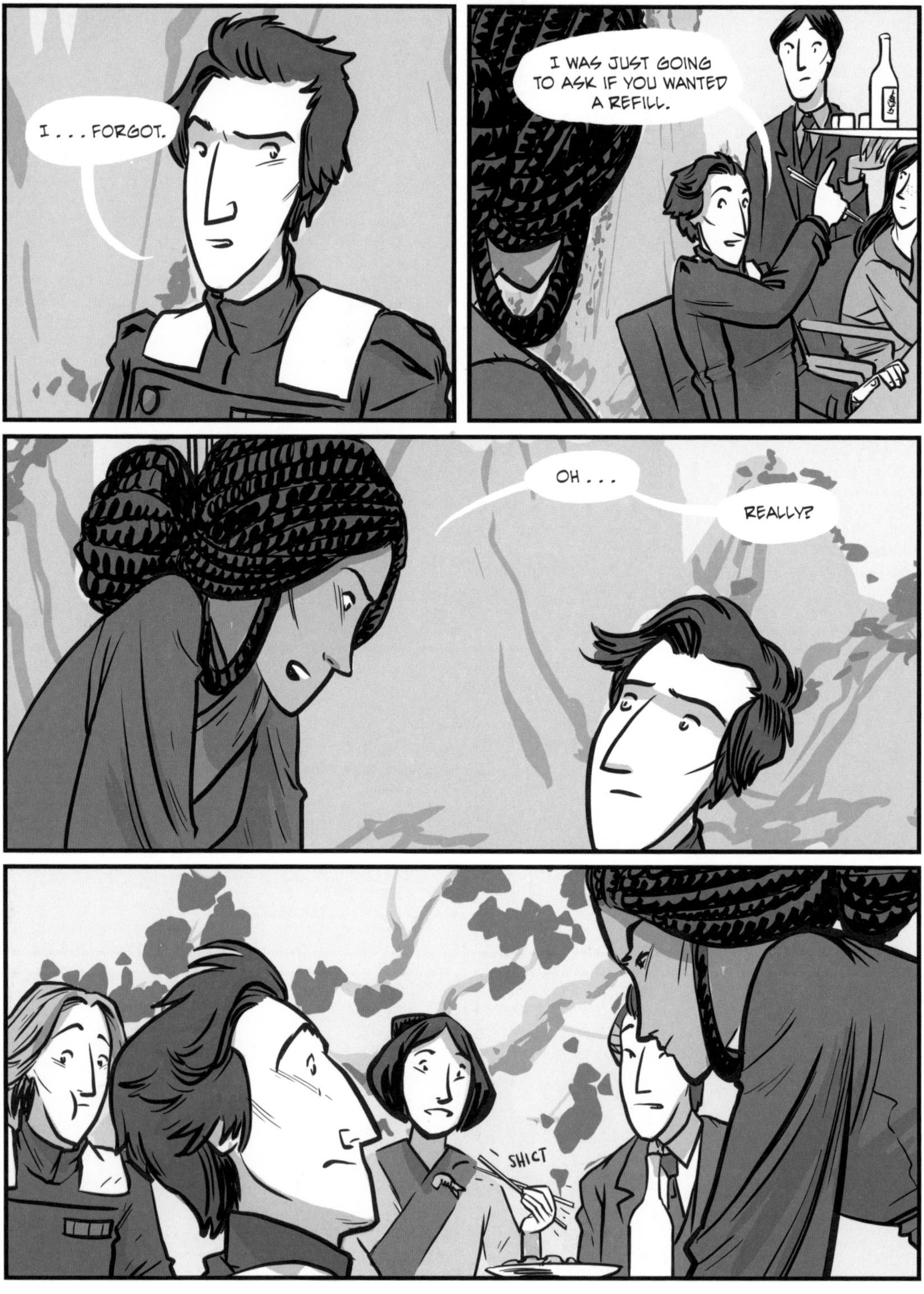

I . . . FORGOT.
I WAS JUST GOING TO ASK IF YOU WANTED A REFILL.
OH . . .
REALLY?
SHICT

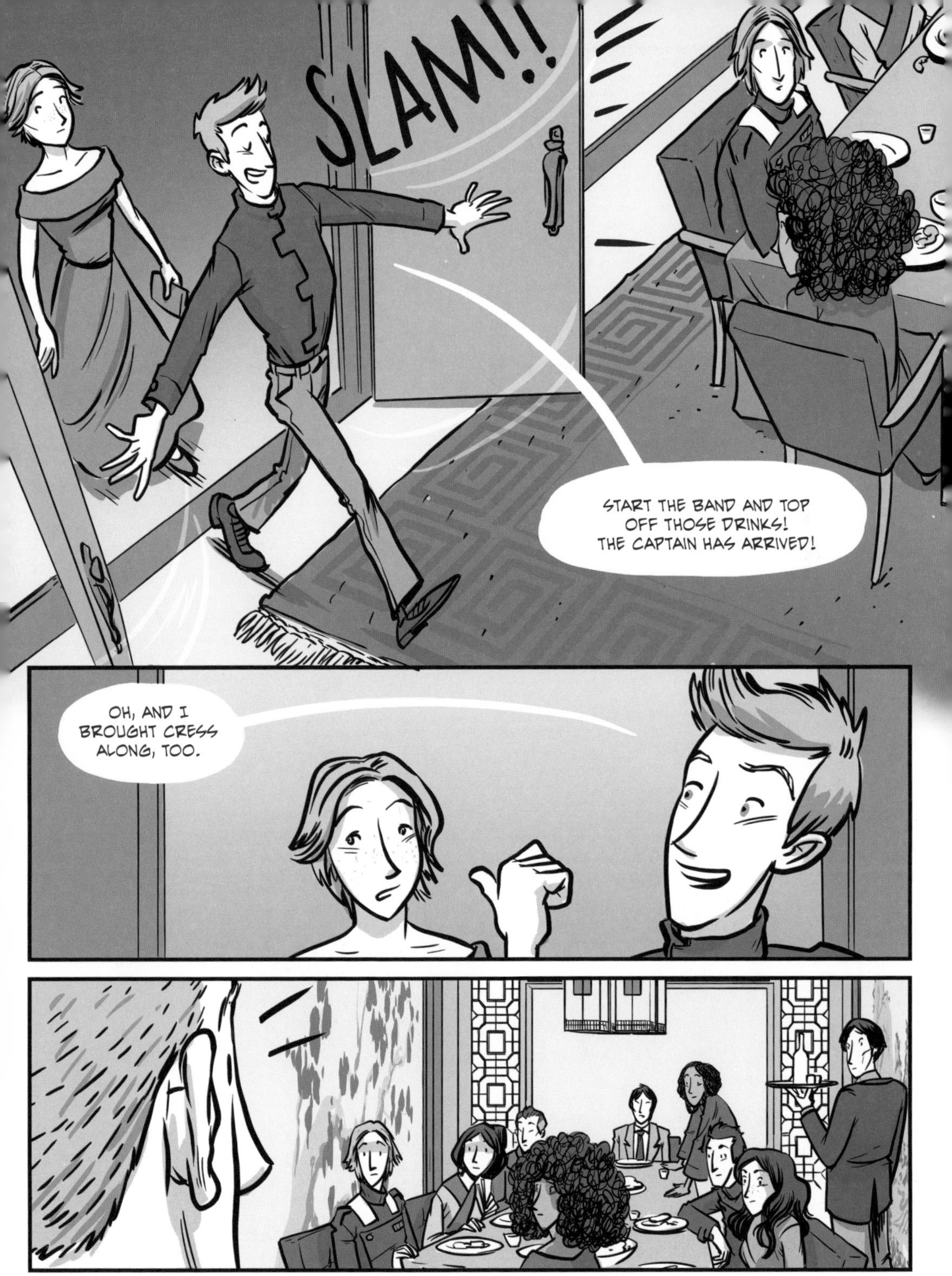
SLAM!!
START THE BAND AND TOP OFF THOSE DRINKS! THE CAPTAIN HAS ARRIVED!
OH, AND I BROUGHT CRESS ALONG, TOO.

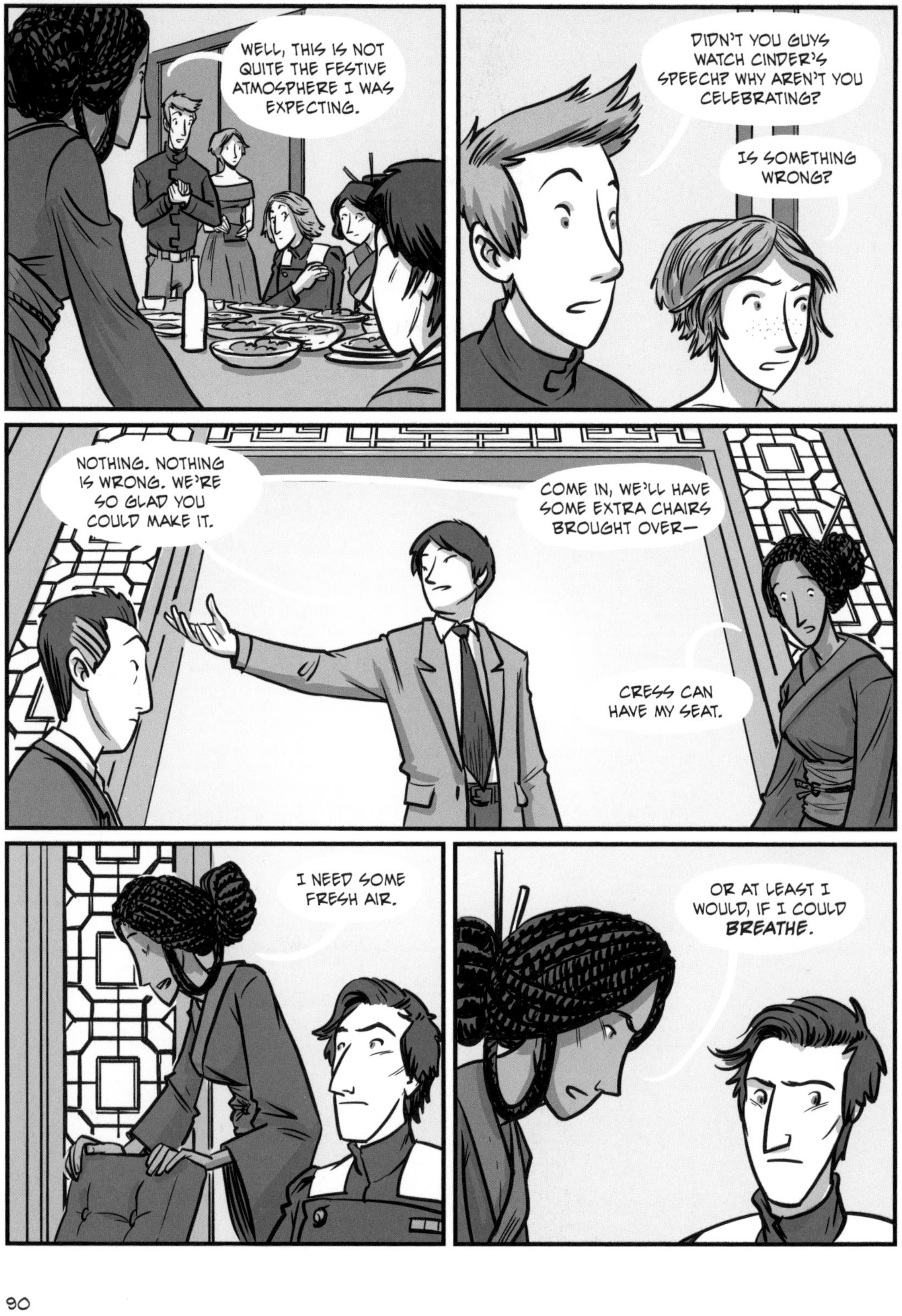
WELL, THIS IS NOT QUITE THE FESTIVE ATMOSPHERE I WAS EXPECTING.
DIDN'T YOU GUYS WATCH CINDER'S SPEECH? WHY AREN'T YOU CELEBRATING?
IS SOMETHING WRONG?
NOTHING. NOTHING IS WRONG. WE'RE SO GLAD YOU COULD MAKE IT.
COME IN, WE'LL HAVE SOME EXTRA CHAIRS BROUGHT OVER—
CRESS CAN HAVE MY SEAT.
I NEED SOME FRESH AIR.
OR AT LEAST I WOULD, IF I COULD **BREATHE**.

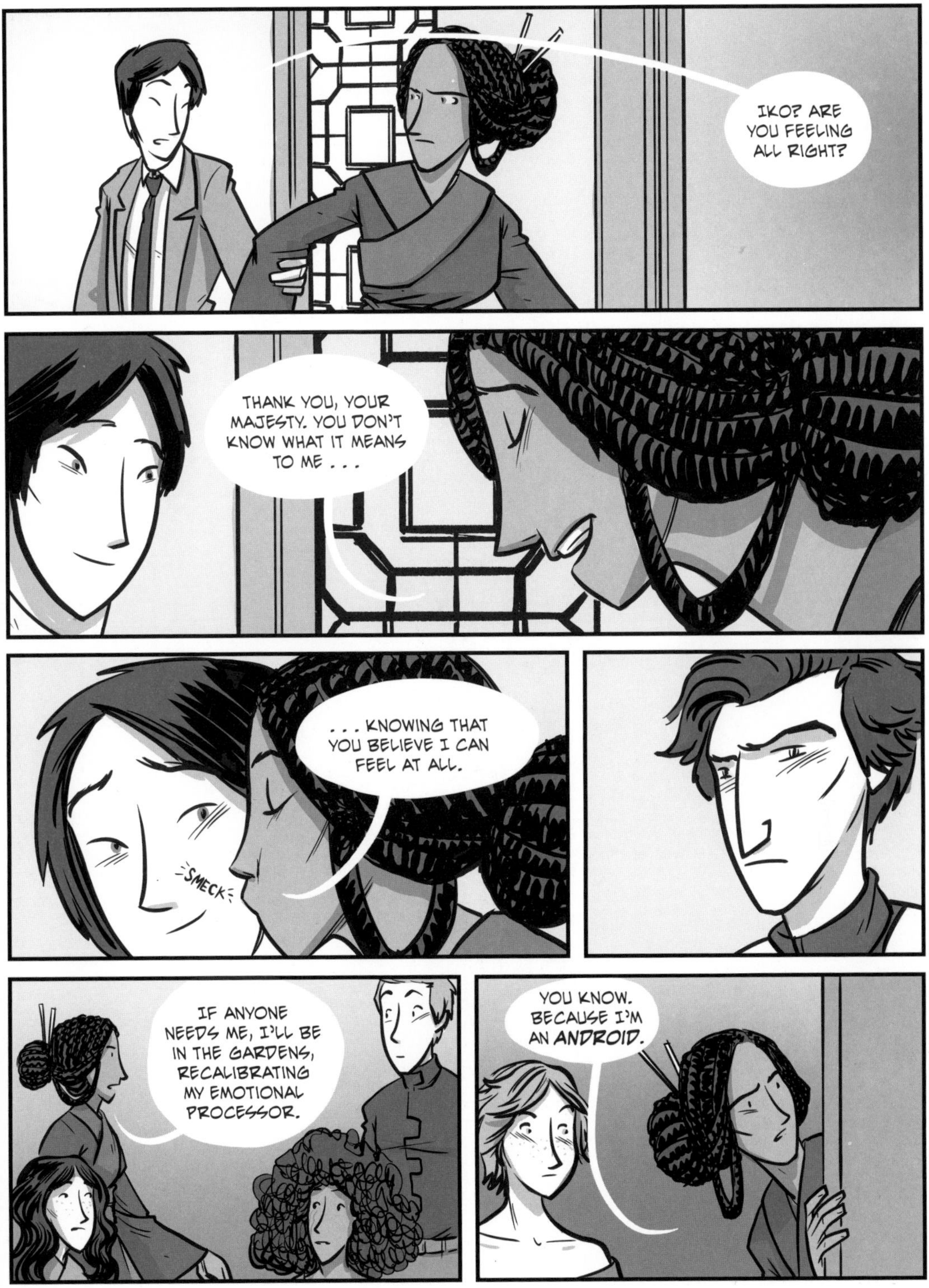
IKO? ARE YOU FEELING ALL RIGHT?
THANK YOU, YOUR MAJESTY. YOU DON'T KNOW WHAT IT MEANS TO ME . . .
. . . KNOWING THAT YOU BELIEVE I CAN FEEL AT ALL.
SMECK
IF ANYONE NEEDS ME, I'LL BE IN THE GARDENS, RECALIBRATING MY EMOTIONAL PROCESSOR.
YOU KNOW. BECAUSE I'M AN ANDROID.

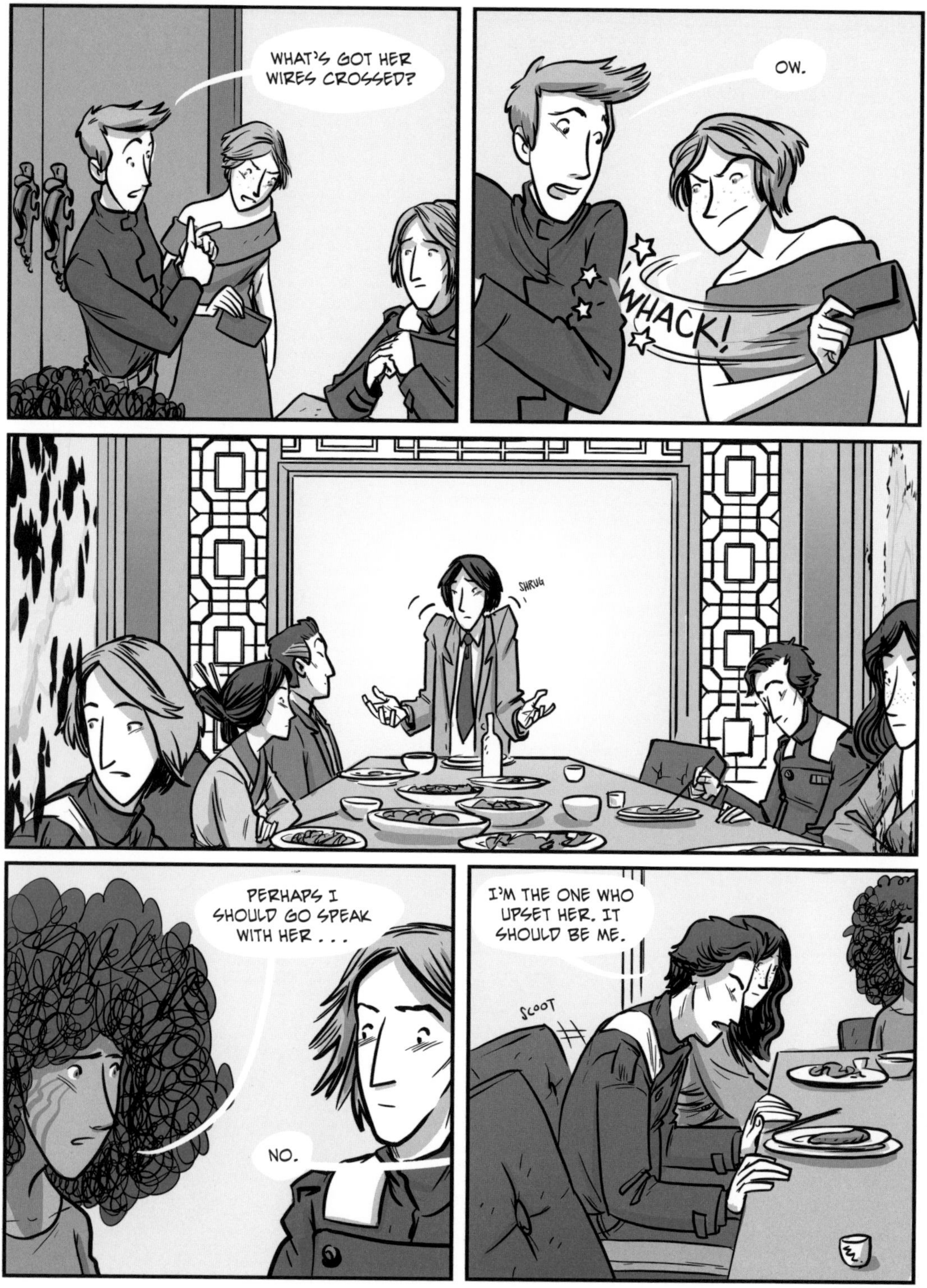
WHAT'S GOT HER WIRES CROSSED?
OW.
WHACK!
SHRUG
PERHAPS I SHOULD GO SPEAK WITH HER . . .
NO.
I'M THE ONE WHO UPSET HER. IT SHOULD BE ME.
SCOOT

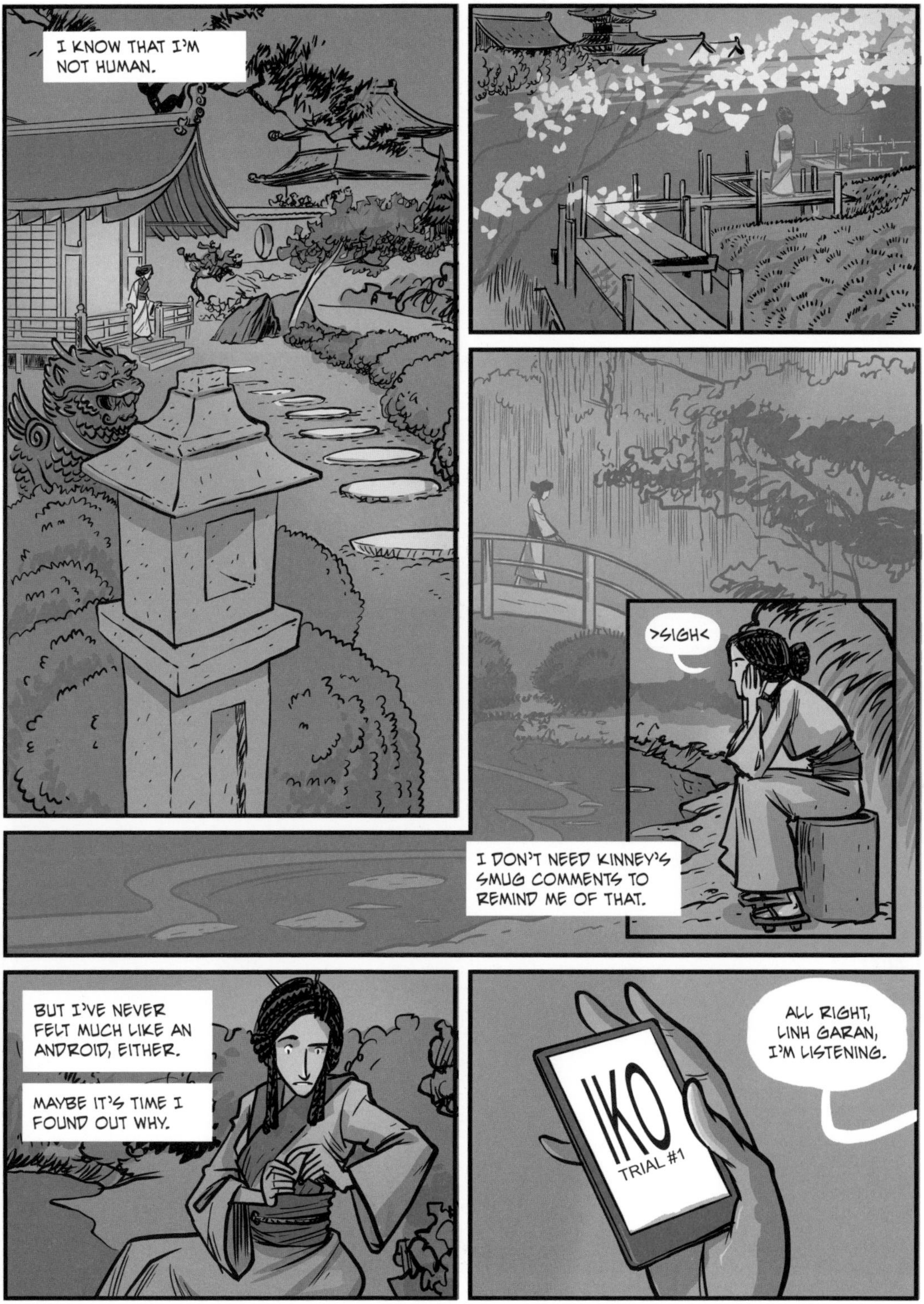
I KNOW THAT I'M NOT HUMAN.
>SIGH<
I DON'T NEED KINNEY'S SMUG COMMENTS TO REMIND ME OF THAT.
BUT I'VE NEVER FELT MUCH LIKE AN ANDROID, EITHER.
MAYBE IT'S TIME I FOUND OUT WHY.
IKO
TRIAL #1
ALL RIGHT, LINH GARAN, I'M LISTENING.

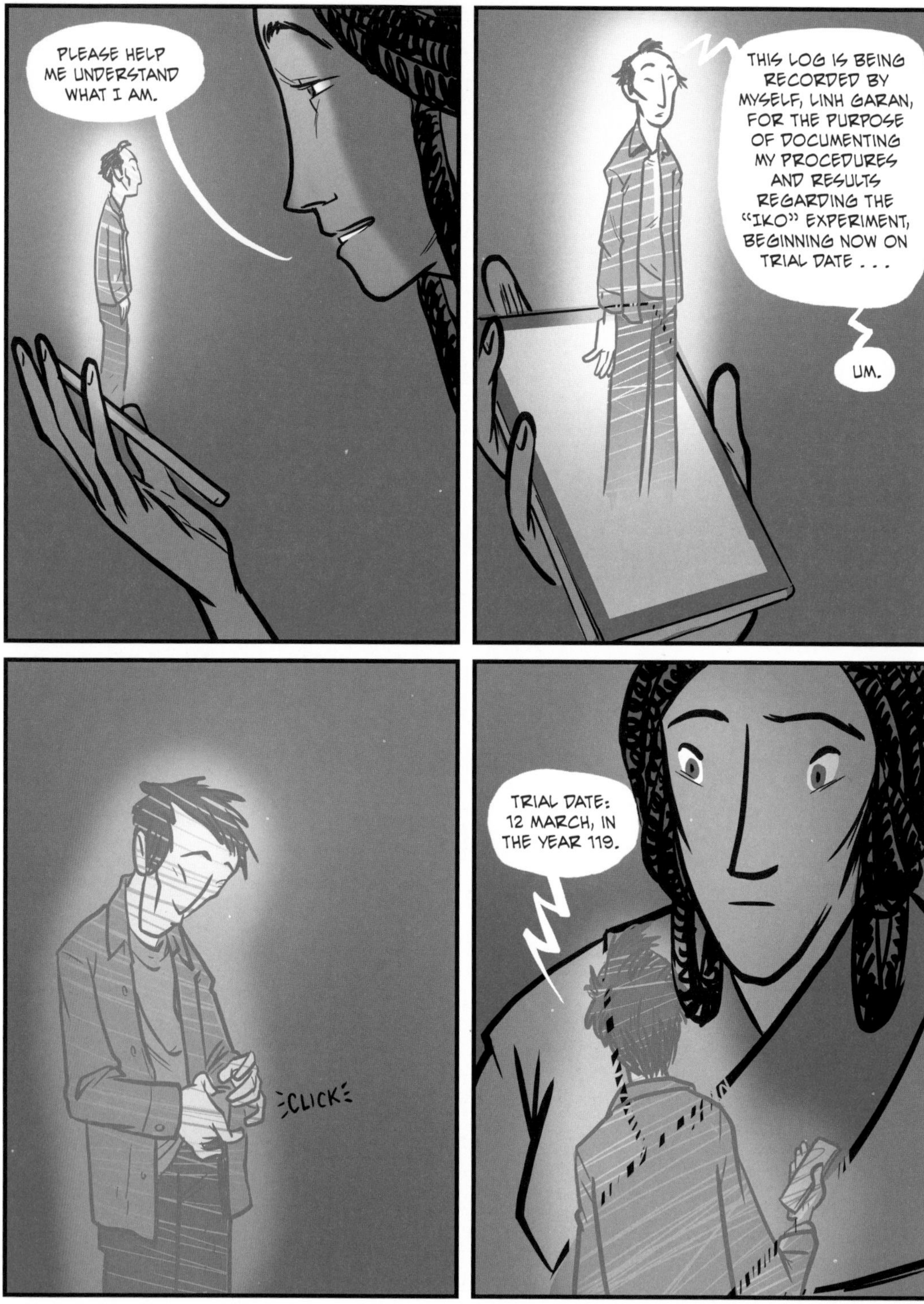
PLEASE HELP ME UNDERSTAND WHAT I AM.
THIS LOG IS BEING RECORDED BY MYSELF, LINH GARAN, FOR THE PURPOSE OF DOCUMENTING MY PROCEDURES AND RESULTS REGARDING THE "IKO" EXPERIMENT, BEGINNING NOW ON TRIAL DATE . . .
UM.
CLICK
TRIAL DATE: 12 MARCH, IN THE YEAR 119.

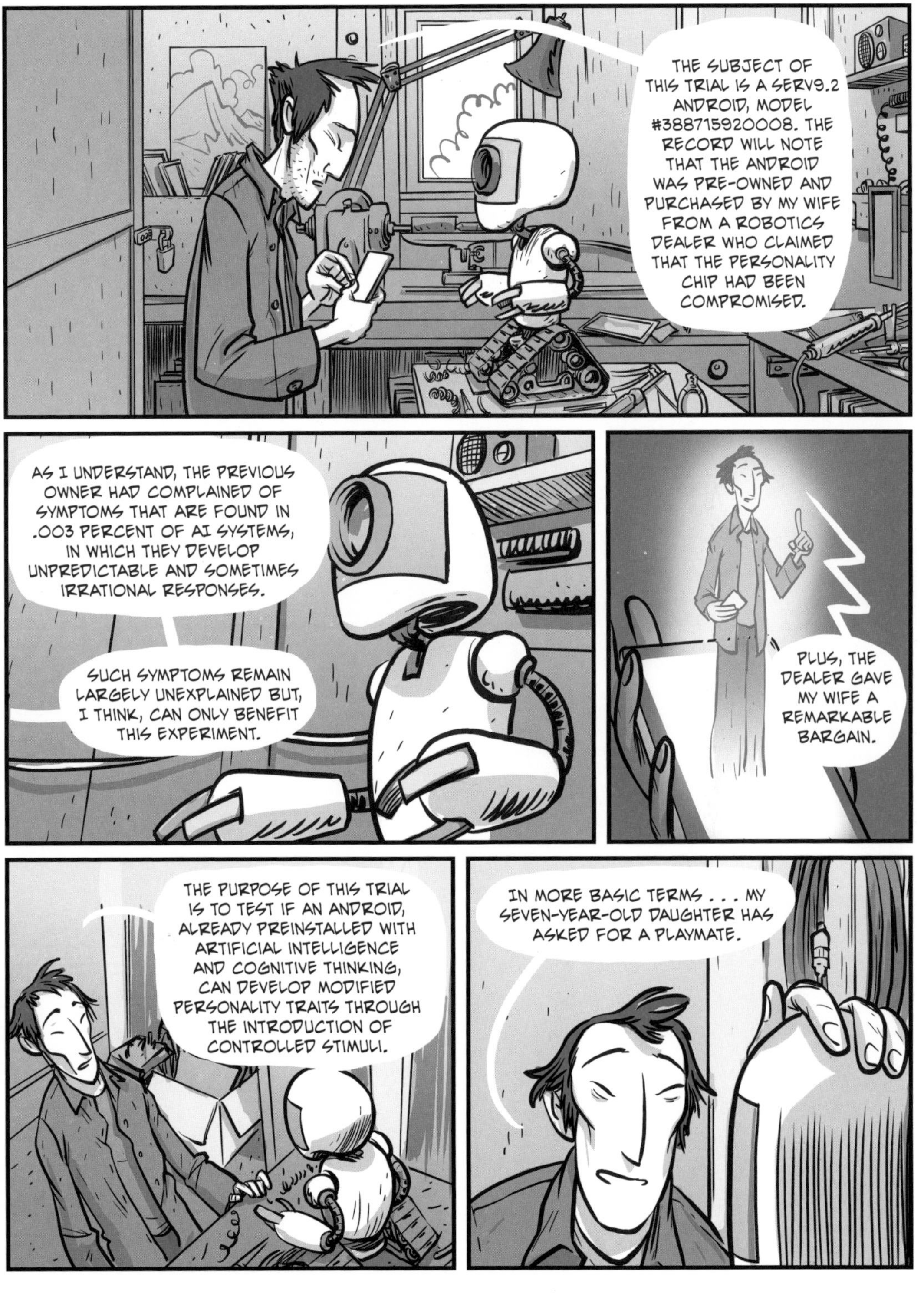
THE SUBJECT OF THIS TRIAL IS A SERV9.2 ANDROID, MODEL #388715920008. THE RECORD WILL NOTE THAT THE ANDROID WAS PRE-OWNED AND PURCHASED BY MY WIFE FROM A ROBOTICS DEALER WHO CLAIMED THAT THE PERSONALITY CHIP HAD BEEN COMPROMISED.
AS I UNDERSTAND, THE PREVIOUS OWNER HAD COMPLAINED OF SYMPTOMS THAT ARE FOUND IN .003 PERCENT OF AI SYSTEMS, IN WHICH THEY DEVELOP UNPREDICTABLE AND SOMETIMES IRRATIONAL RESPONSES.
SUCH SYMPTOMS REMAIN LARGELY UNEXPLAINED BUT, I THINK, CAN ONLY BENEFIT THIS EXPERIMENT.
PLUS, THE DEALER GAVE MY WIFE A REMARKABLE BARGAIN.
THE PURPOSE OF THIS TRIAL IS TO TEST IF AN ANDROID, ALREADY PREINSTALLED WITH ARTIFICIAL INTELLIGENCE AND COGNITIVE THINKING, CAN DEVELOP MODIFIED PERSONALITY TRAITS THROUGH THE INTRODUCTION OF CONTROLLED STIMULI.
IN MORE BASIC TERMS . . . MY SEVEN-YEAR-OLD DAUGHTER HAS ASKED FOR A PLAYMATE.

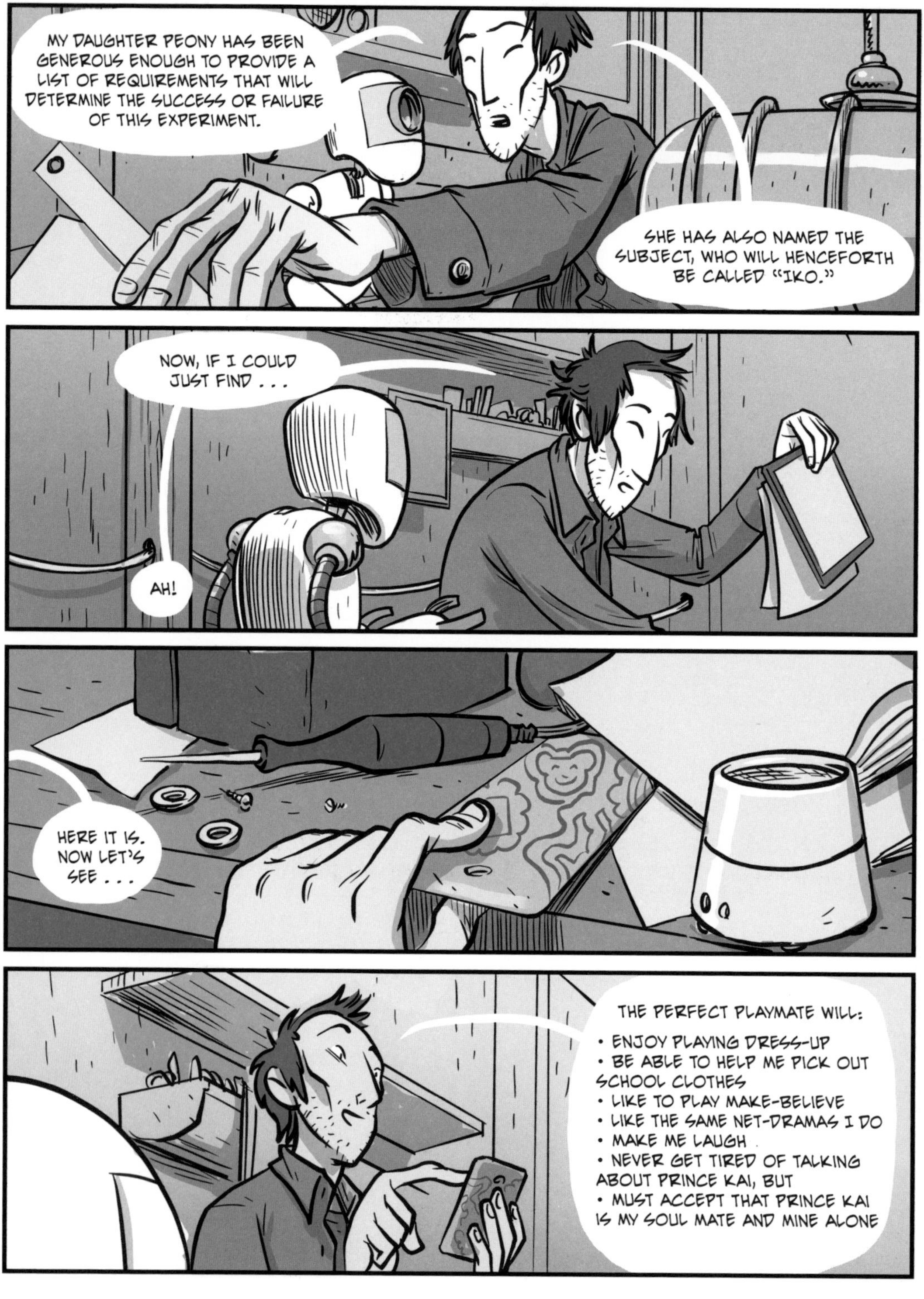
MY DAUGHTER PEONY HAS BEEN GENEROUS ENOUGH TO PROVIDE A LIST OF REQUIREMENTS THAT WILL DETERMINE THE SUCCESS OR FAILURE OF THIS EXPERIMENT.
SHE HAS ALSO NAMED THE SUBJECT, WHO WILL HENCEFORTH BE CALLED "IKO."
NOW, IF I COULD JUST FIND . . .
AH!
HERE IT IS. NOW LET'S SEE . . .
THE PERFECT PLAYMATE WILL:
• ENJOY PLAYING DRESS-UP
• BE ABLE TO HELP ME PICK OUT SCHOOL CLOTHES
• LIKE TO PLAY MAKE-BELIEVE
• LIKE THE SAME NET-DRAMAS I DO
• MAKE ME LAUGH
• NEVER GET TIRED OF TALKING ABOUT PRINCE KAI, BUT
• MUST ACCEPT THAT PRINCE KAI IS MY SOUL MATE AND MINE ALONE

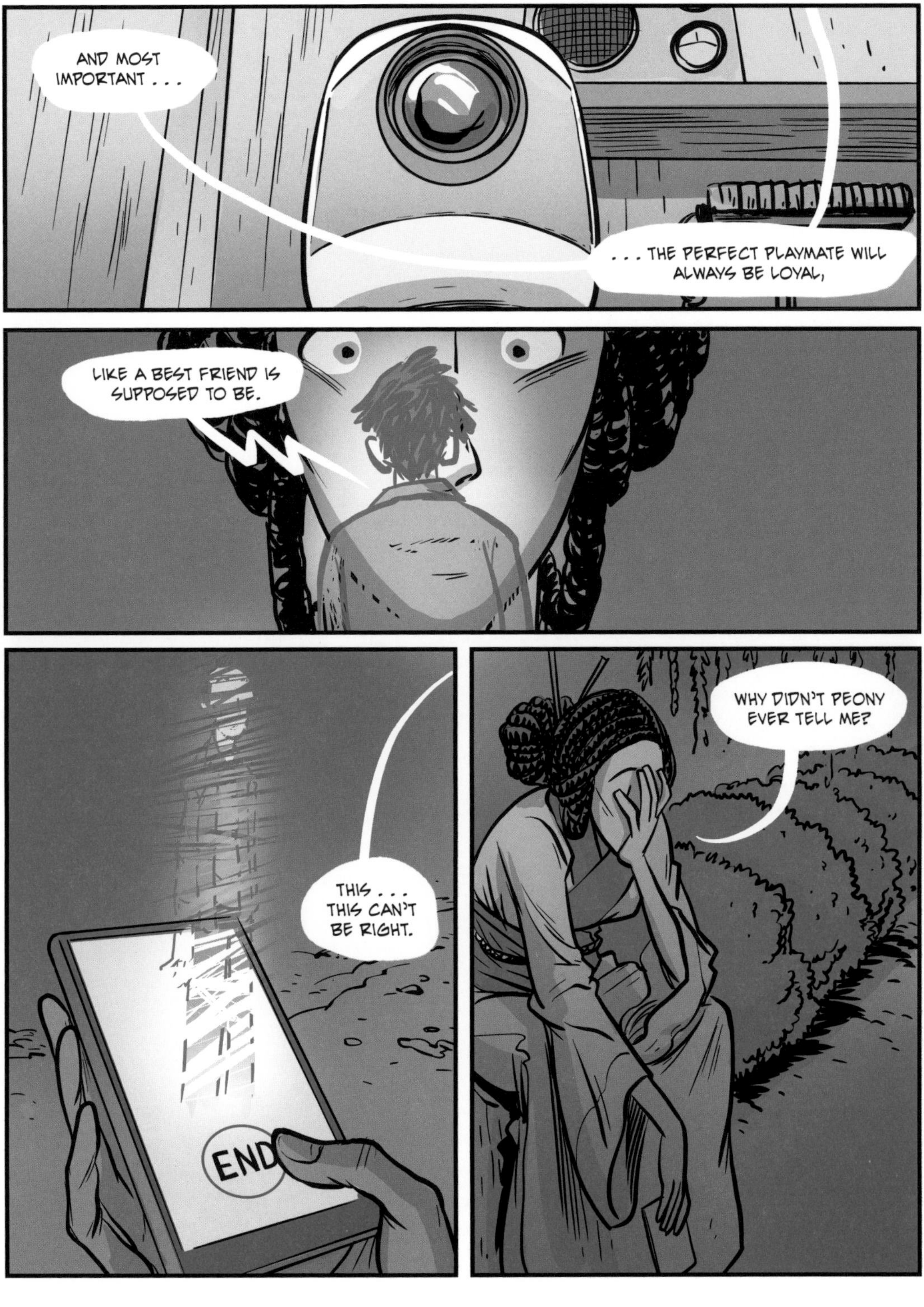
AND MOST IMPORTANT . . .
. . . THE PERFECT PLAYMATE WILL ALWAYS BE LOYAL,
LIKE A BEST FRIEND IS SUPPOSED TO BE.
THIS . . . THIS CAN'T BE RIGHT.
END
WHY DIDN'T PEONY EVER TELL ME?

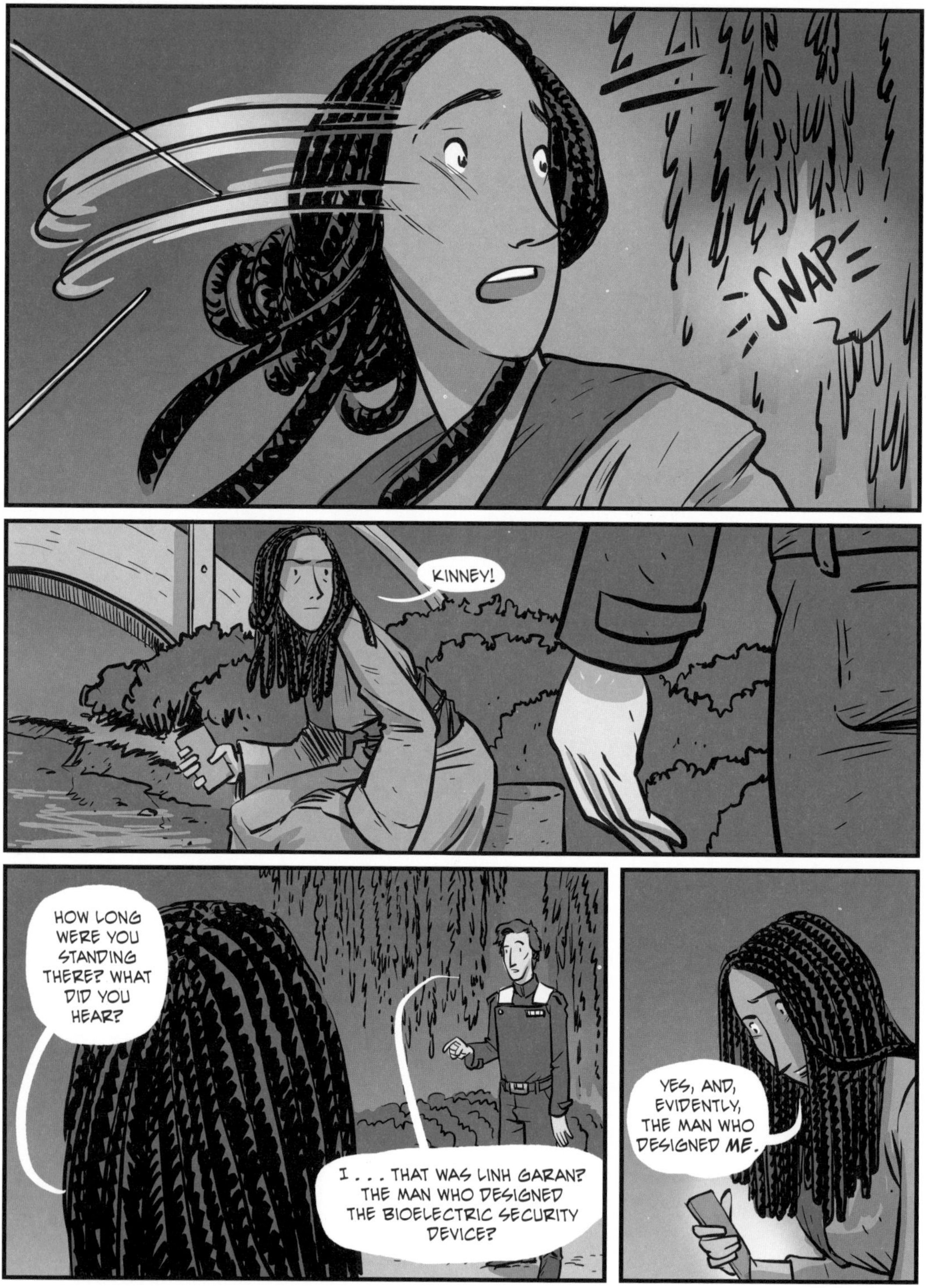
SNAP
KINNEY!
HOW LONG WERE YOU STANDING THERE? WHAT DID YOU HEAR?
I . . . THAT WAS LINH GARAN? THE MAN WHO DESIGNED THE BIOELECTRIC SECURITY DEVICE?
YES, AND, EVIDENTLY, THE MAN WHO DESIGNED ***ME***.

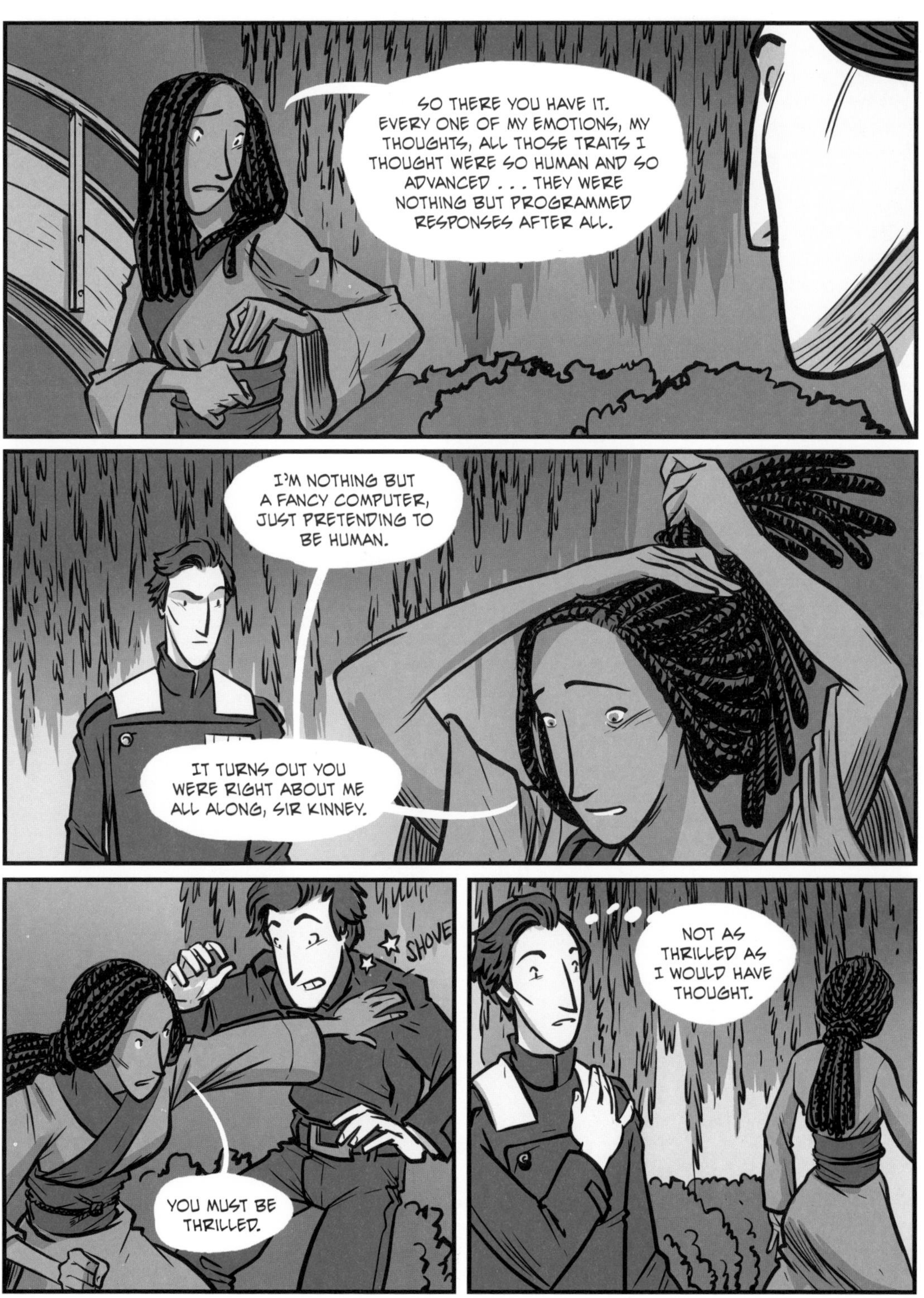
SO THERE YOU HAVE IT. EVERY ONE OF MY EMOTIONS, MY THOUGHTS, ALL THOSE TRAITS I THOUGHT WERE SO HUMAN AND SO ADVANCED . . . THEY WERE NOTHING BUT PROGRAMMED RESPONSES AFTER ALL.
I'M NOTHING BUT A FANCY COMPUTER, JUST PRETENDING TO BE HUMAN.
IT TURNS OUT YOU WERE RIGHT ABOUT ME ALL ALONG, SIR KINNEY.
SHOVE
YOU MUST BE THRILLED.
NOT AS THRILLED AS I WOULD HAVE THOUGHT.

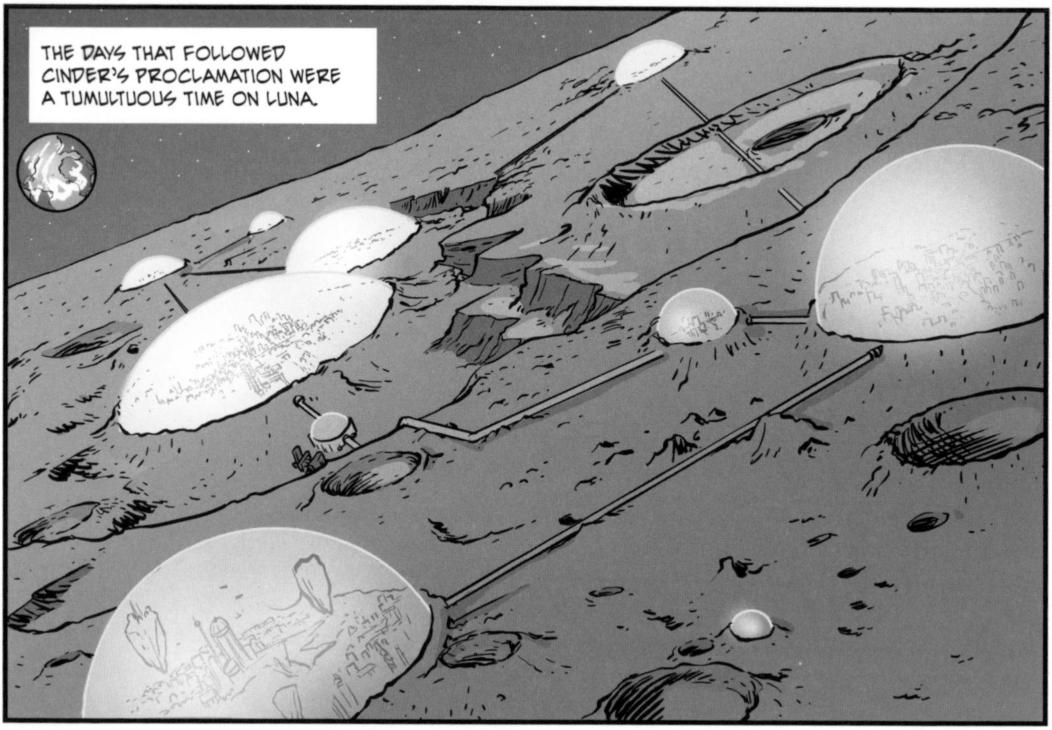
THE DAYS THAT FOLLOWED CINDER'S PROCLAMATION WERE A TUMULTUOUS TIME ON LUNA.

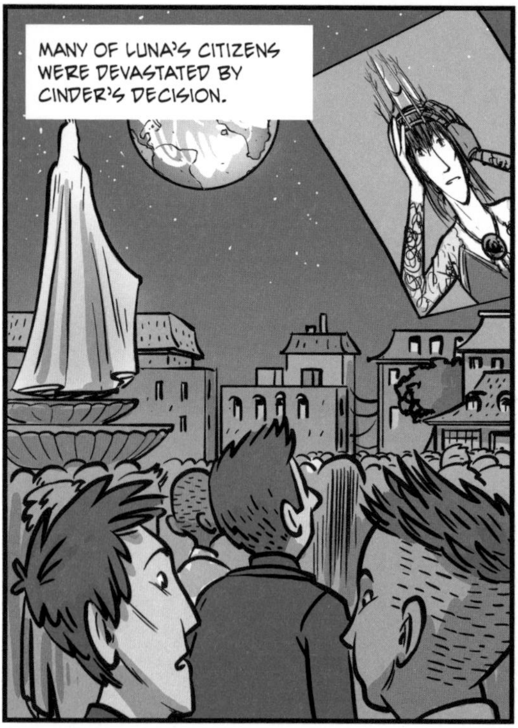
MANY OF LUNA'S CITIZENS WERE DEVASTATED BY CINDER'S DECISION.

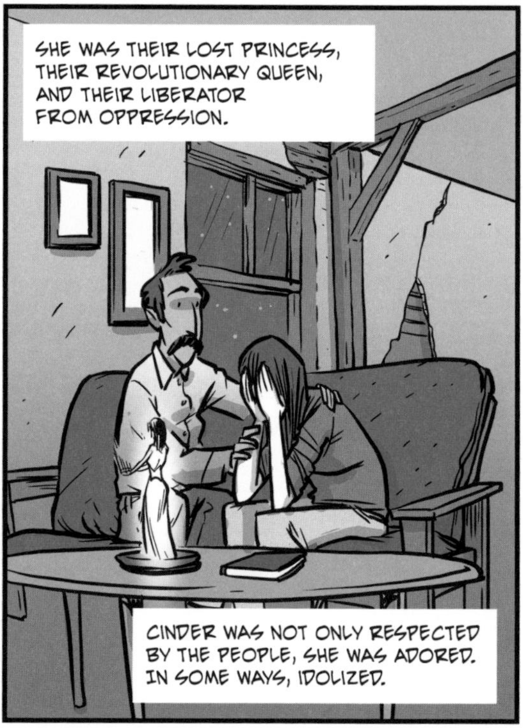
SHE WAS THEIR LOST PRINCESS, THEIR REVOLUTIONARY QUEEN, AND THEIR LIBERATOR FROM OPPRESSION.
CINDER WAS NOT ONLY RESPECTED BY THE PEOPLE, SHE WAS ADORED. IN SOME WAYS, IDOLIZED.

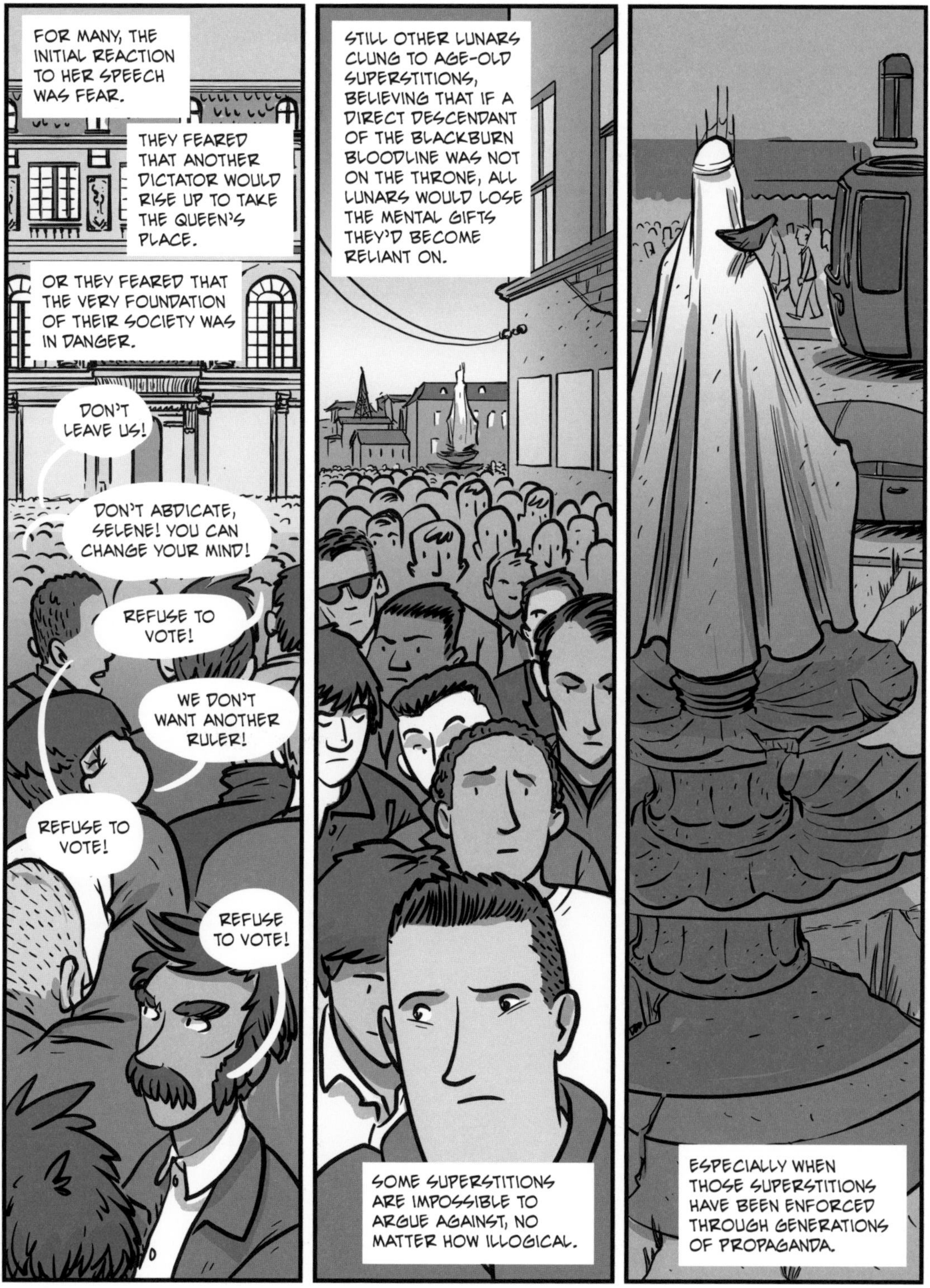

FOR MANY, THE INITIAL REACTION TO HER SPEECH WAS FEAR.
THEY FEARED THAT ANOTHER DICTATOR WOULD RISE UP TO TAKE THE QUEEN'S PLACE.
OR THEY FEARED THAT THE VERY FOUNDATION OF THEIR SOCIETY WAS IN DANGER.
DON'T LEAVE US!
DON'T ABDICATE, SELENE! YOU CAN CHANGE YOUR MIND!
REFUSE TO VOTE!
WE DON'T WANT ANOTHER RULER!
REFUSE TO VOTE!
REFUSE TO VOTE!
STILL OTHER LUNARS CLUNG TO AGE-OLD SUPERSTITIONS, BELIEVING THAT IF A DIRECT DESCENDANT OF THE BLACKBURN BLOODLINE WAS NOT ON THE THRONE, ALL LUNARS WOULD LOSE THE MENTAL GIFTS THEY'D BECOME RELIANT ON.
SOME SUPERSTITIONS ARE IMPOSSIBLE TO ARGUE AGAINST, NO MATTER HOW ILLOGICAL.
ESPECIALLY WHEN THOSE SUPERSTITIONS HAVE BEEN ENFORCED THROUGH GENERATIONS OF PROPAGANDA.

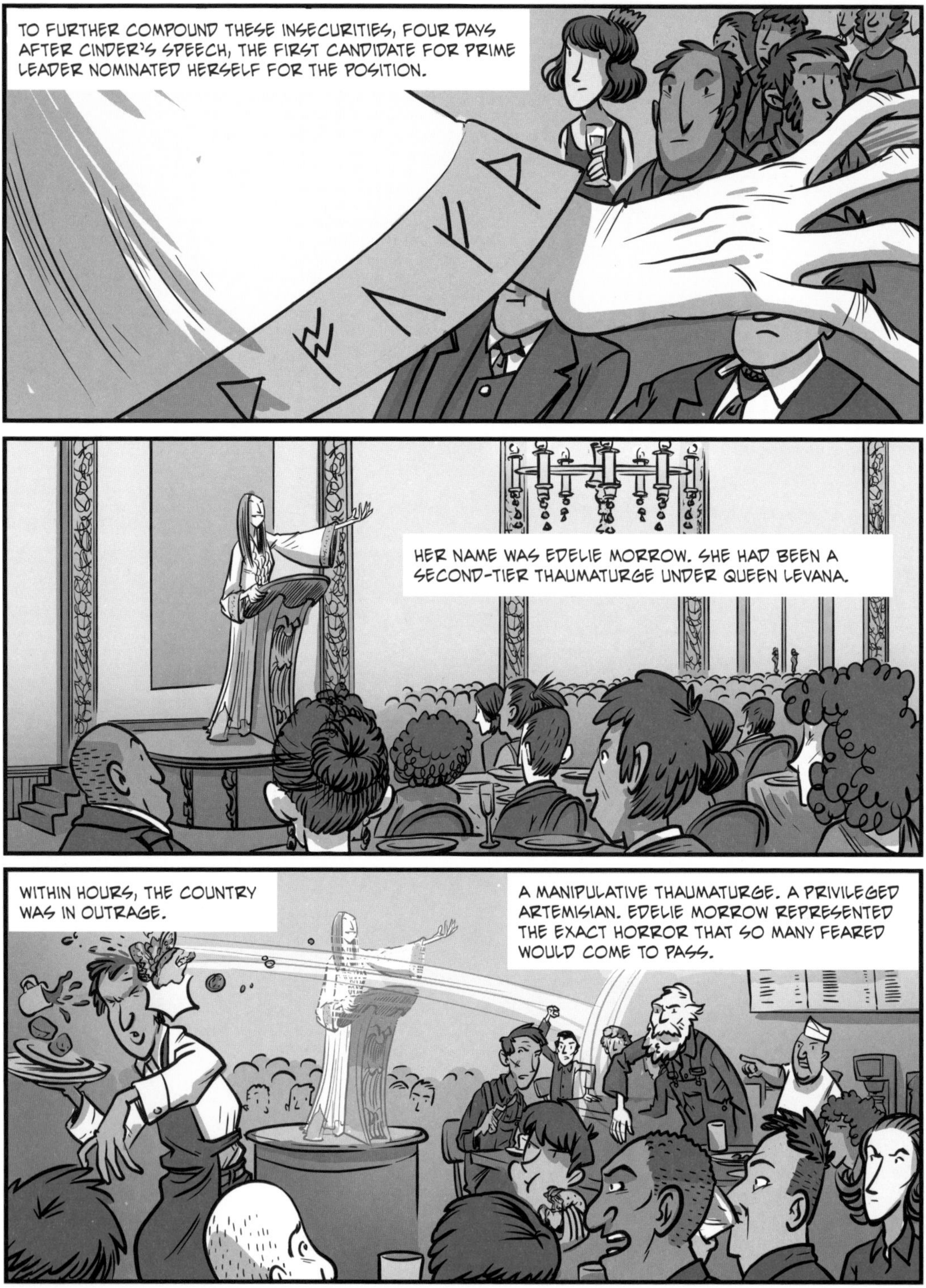
TO FURTHER COMPOUND THESE INSECURITIES, FOUR DAYS AFTER CINDER'S SPEECH, THE FIRST CANDIDATE FOR PRIME LEADER NOMINATED HERSELF FOR THE POSITION.
HER NAME WAS EDELIE MORROW. SHE HAD BEEN A SECOND-TIER THAUMATURGE UNDER QUEEN LEVANA.
WITHIN HOURS, THE COUNTRY WAS IN OUTRAGE.
A MANIPULATIVE THAUMATURGE. A PRIVILEGED ARTEMISIAN. EDELIE MORROW REPRESENTED THE EXACT HORROR THAT SO MANY FEARED WOULD COME TO PASS.

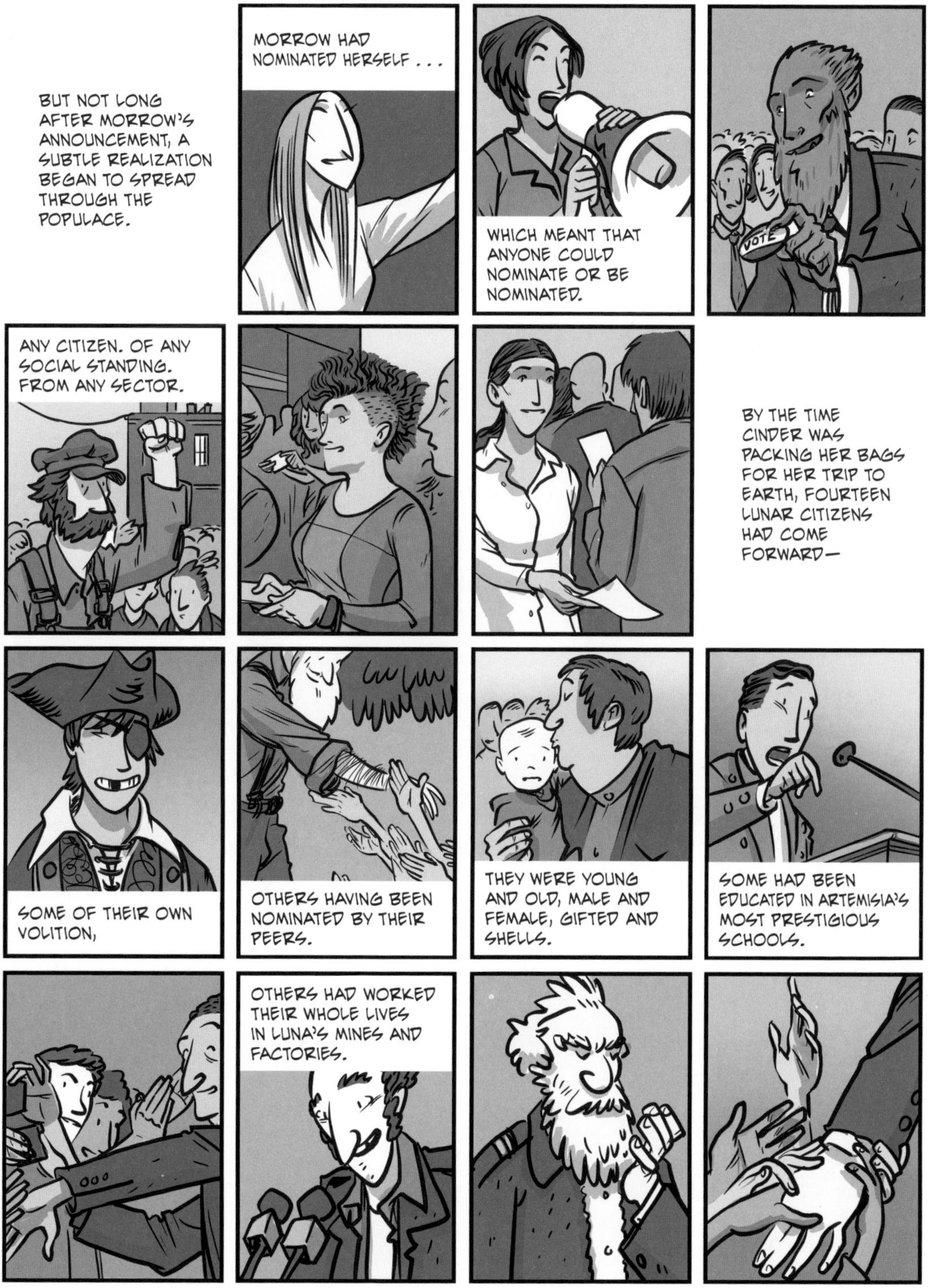
BUT NOT LONG AFTER MORROW'S ANNOUNCEMENT, A SUBTLE REALIZATION BEGAN TO SPREAD THROUGH THE POPULACE.
MORROW HAD NOMINATED HERSELF . . .
WHICH MEANT THAT ANYONE COULD NOMINATE OR BE NOMINATED.
VOTE
ANY CITIZEN. OF ANY SOCIAL STANDING. FROM ANY SECTOR.
BY THE TIME CINDER WAS PACKING HER BAGS FOR HER TRIP TO EARTH, FOURTEEN LUNAR CITIZENS HAD COME FORWARD—
SOME OF THEIR OWN VOLITION,
OTHERS HAVING BEEN NOMINATED BY THEIR PEERS.
THEY WERE YOUNG AND OLD, MALE AND FEMALE, GIFTED AND SHELLS.
SOME HAD BEEN EDUCATED IN ARTEMISIA'S MOST PRESTIGIOUS SCHOOLS.
OTHERS HAD WORKED THEIR WHOLE LIVES IN LUNA'S MINES AND FACTORIES.

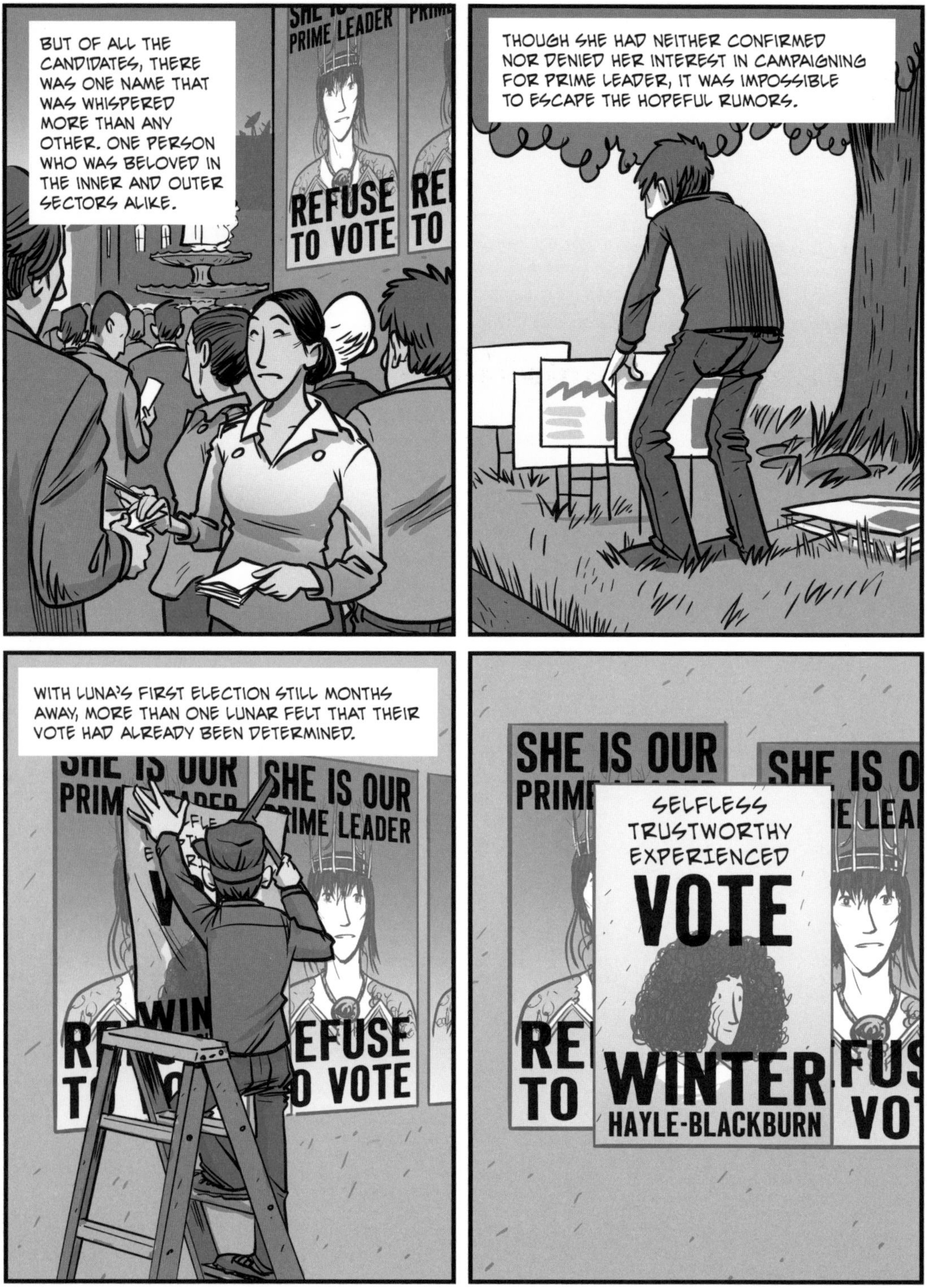

BUT OF ALL THE CANDIDATES, THERE WAS ONE NAME THAT WAS WHISPERED MORE THAN ANY OTHER. ONE PERSON WHO WAS BELOVED IN THE INNER AND OUTER SECTORS ALIKE.
SHE IS OUR PRIME LEADER
REFUSE TO VOTE
THOUGH SHE HAD NEITHER CONFIRMED NOR DENIED HER INTEREST IN CAMPAIGNING FOR PRIME LEADER, IT WAS IMPOSSIBLE TO ESCAPE THE HOPEFUL RUMORS.
WITH LUNA'S FIRST ELECTION STILL MONTHS AWAY, MORE THAN ONE LUNAR FELT THAT THEIR VOTE HAD ALREADY BEEN DETERMINED.
SHE IS OUR PRIME LEADER
REFUSE TO VOTE
SELFLESS
TRUSTWORTHY
EXPERIENCED
VOTE
WINTER
HAYLE-BLACKBURN

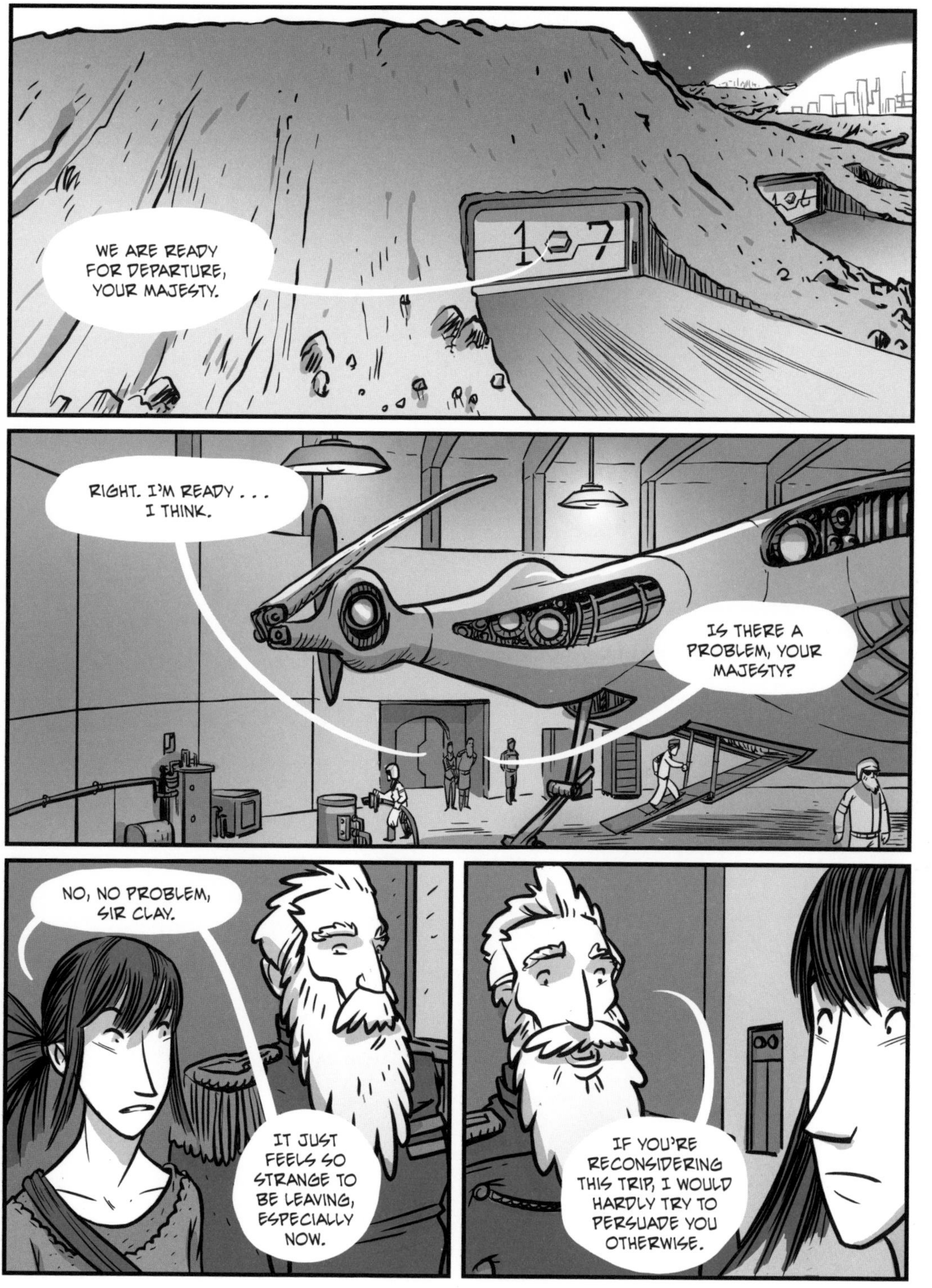
1o7
1o6
WE ARE READY FOR DEPARTURE, YOUR MAJESTY.
RIGHT. I'M READY . . . I THINK.
IS THERE A PROBLEM, YOUR MAJESTY?
NO, NO PROBLEM, SIR CLAY.
IT JUST FEELS SO STRANGE TO BE LEAVING, ESPECIALLY NOW.
IF YOU'RE RECONSIDERING THIS TRIP, I WOULD HARDLY TRY TO PERSUADE YOU OTHERWISE.

YOU THINK I SHOULD STAY, DON'T YOU?

WE ALL UNDERSTAND THE IMPORTANCE OF OUR EARTHEN RELATIONS AND THE SYMBOLISM OF THIS VISIT.

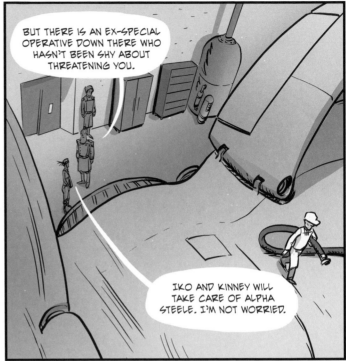

BUT THERE IS AN EX-SPECIAL OPERATIVE DOWN THERE WHO HASN'T BEEN SHY ABOUT THREATENING YOU.

IKO AND KINNEY WILL TAKE CARE OF ALPHA STEELE. I'M NOT WORRIED.

I'M MORE CONCERNED THAT THE PEOPLE OF LUNA WILL THINK I'M ABANDONING THEM.

IF THEY DO, THEY'LL GET OVER IT WHEN YOU RETURN.

BESIDES, THEY WILL HAVE PLENTY TO KEEP THEIR THOUGHTS OCCUPIED IN YOUR ABSENCE.

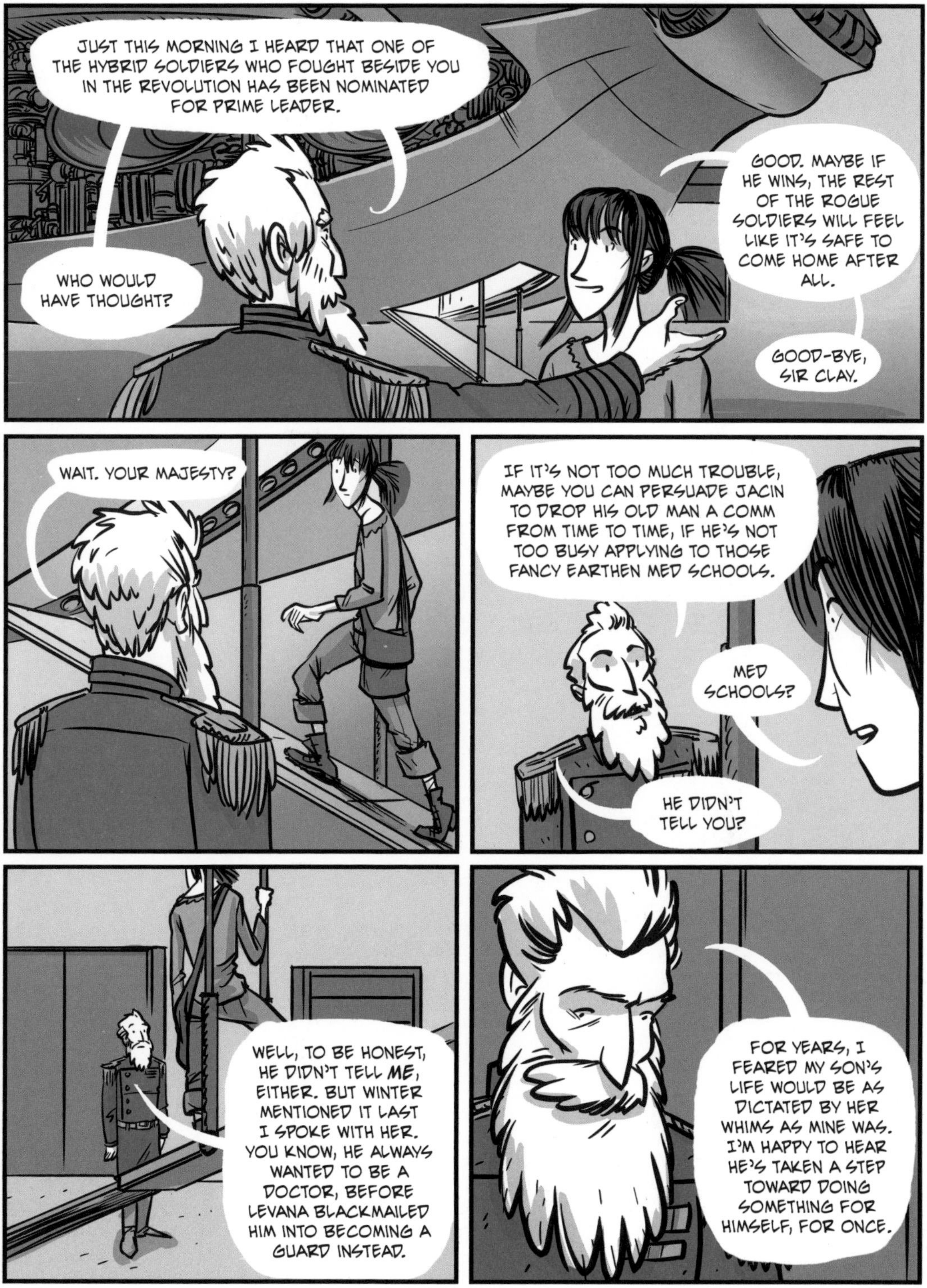
JUST THIS MORNING I HEARD THAT ONE OF THE HYBRID SOLDIERS WHO FOUGHT BESIDE YOU IN THE REVOLUTION HAS BEEN NOMINATED FOR PRIME LEADER.
WHO WOULD HAVE THOUGHT?
GOOD. MAYBE IF HE WINS, THE REST OF THE ROGUE SOLDIERS WILL FEEL LIKE IT'S SAFE TO COME HOME AFTER ALL.
GOOD-BYE, SIR CLAY.
WAIT. YOUR MAJESTY?
IF IT'S NOT TOO MUCH TROUBLE, MAYBE YOU CAN PERSUADE JACIN TO DROP HIS OLD MAN A COMM FROM TIME TO TIME, IF HE'S NOT TOO BUSY APPLYING TO THOSE FANCY EARTHEN MED SCHOOLS.
MED SCHOOLS?
HE DIDN'T TELL YOU?
WELL, TO BE HONEST, HE DIDN'T TELL *ME*, EITHER. BUT WINTER MENTIONED IT LAST I SPOKE WITH HER. YOU KNOW, HE ALWAYS WANTED TO BE A DOCTOR, BEFORE LEVANA BLACKMAILED HIM INTO BECOMING A GUARD INSTEAD.
FOR YEARS, I FEARED MY SON'S LIFE WOULD BE AS DICTATED BY HER WHIMS AS MINE WAS. I'M HAPPY TO HEAR HE'S TAKEN A STEP TOWARD DOING SOMETHING FOR HIMSELF, FOR ONCE.

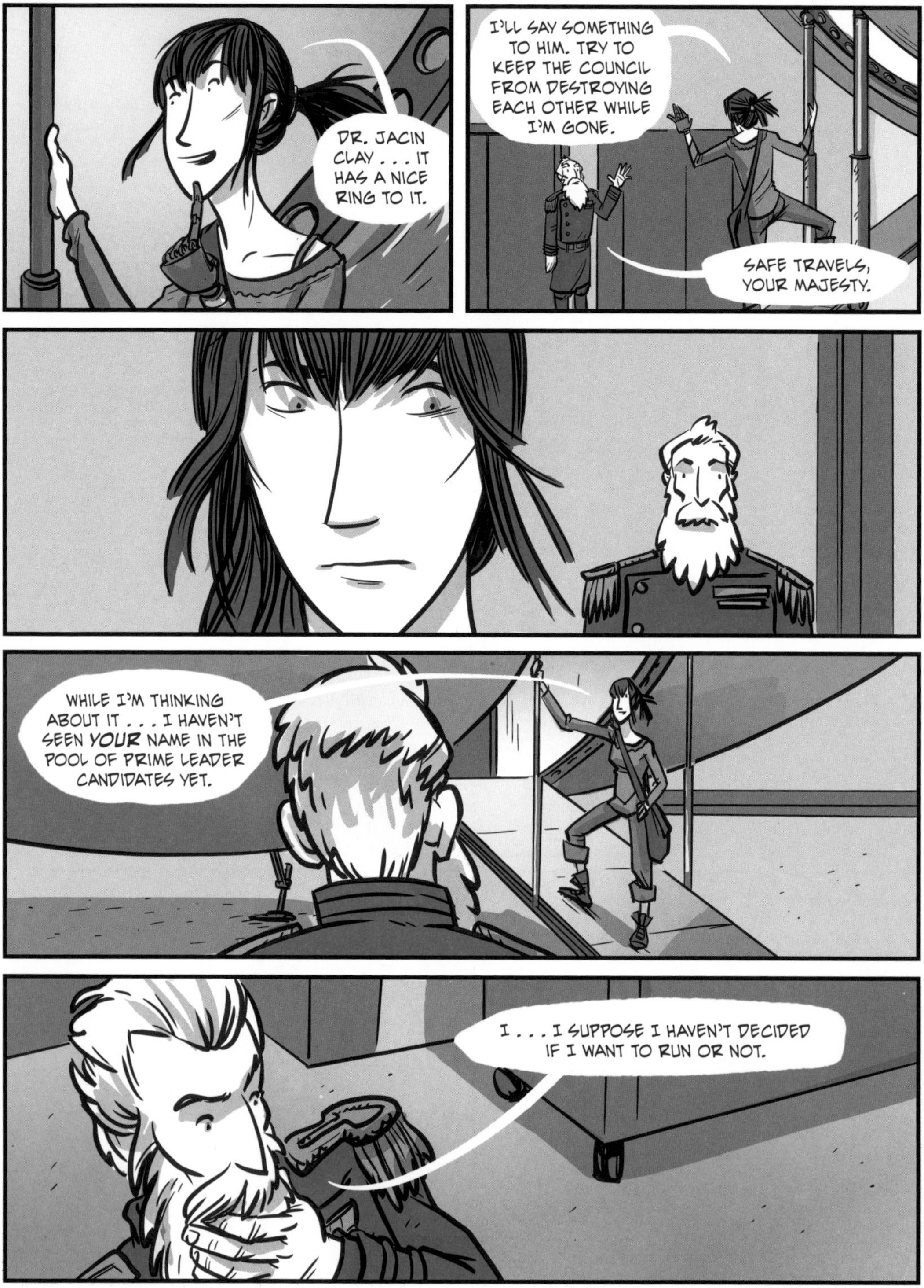
DR. JACIN CLAY . . . IT HAS A NICE RING TO IT.
I'LL SAY SOMETHING TO HIM. TRY TO KEEP THE COUNCIL FROM DESTROYING EACH OTHER WHILE I'M GONE.
SAFE TRAVELS, YOUR MAJESTY.
WHILE I'M THINKING ABOUT IT . . . I HAVEN'T SEEN *YOUR* NAME IN THE POOL OF PRIME LEADER CANDIDATES YET.
I . . . I SUPPOSE I HAVEN'T DECIDED IF I WANT TO RUN OR NOT.

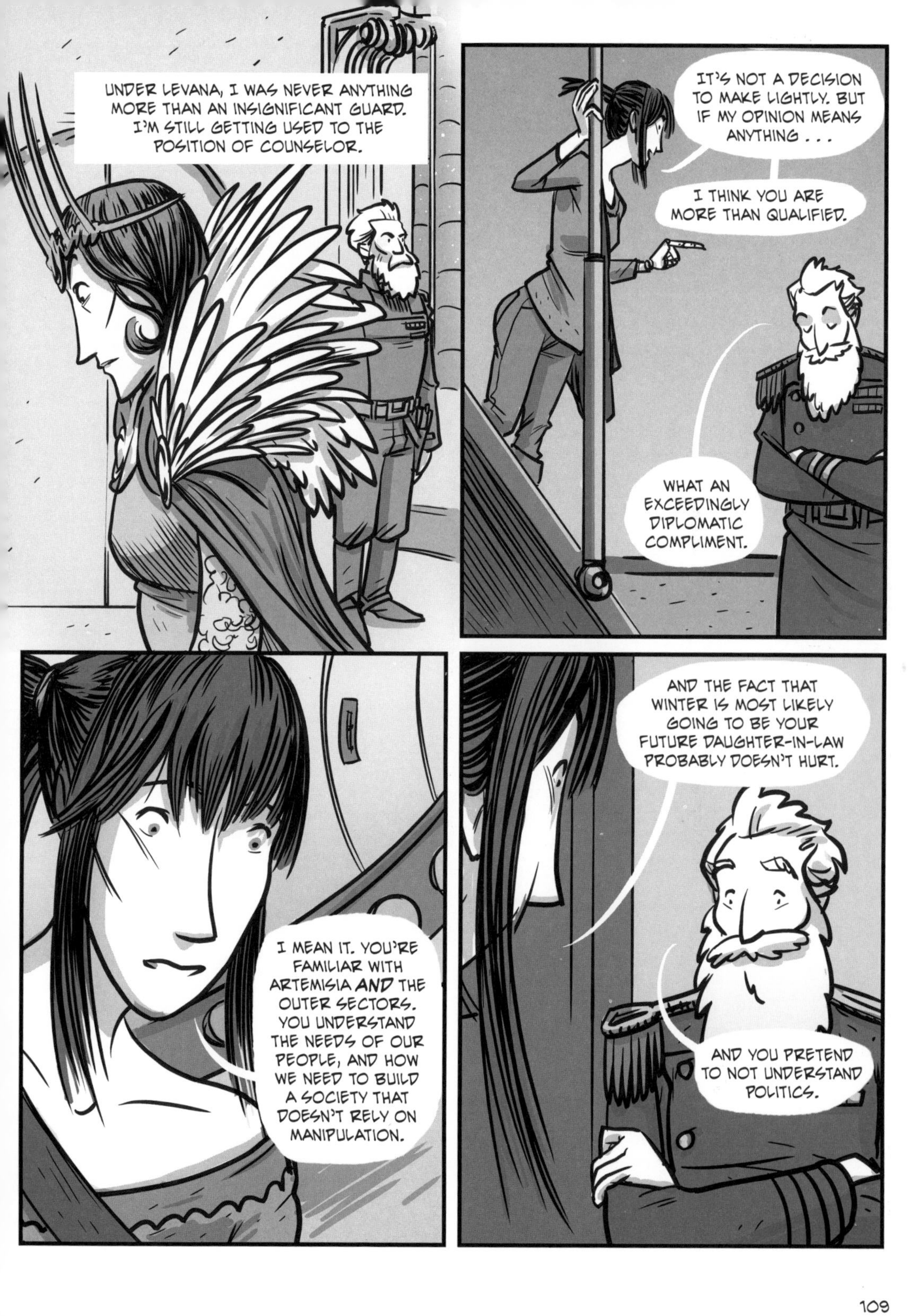
UNDER LEVANA, I WAS NEVER ANYTHING MORE THAN AN INSIGNIFICANT GUARD. I'M STILL GETTING USED TO THE POSITION OF COUNSELOR.
IT'S NOT A DECISION TO MAKE LIGHTLY. BUT IF MY OPINION MEANS ANYTHING . . .
I THINK YOU ARE MORE THAN QUALIFIED.
WHAT AN EXCEEDINGLY DIPLOMATIC COMPLIMENT.
I MEAN IT. YOU'RE FAMILIAR WITH ARTEMISIA AND THE OUTER SECTORS. YOU UNDERSTAND THE NEEDS OF OUR PEOPLE, AND HOW WE NEED TO BUILD A SOCIETY THAT DOESN'T RELY ON MANIPULATION.
AND THE FACT THAT WINTER IS MOST LIKELY GOING TO BE YOUR FUTURE DAUGHTER-IN-LAW PROBABLY DOESN'T HURT.
AND YOU PRETEND TO NOT UNDERSTAND POLITICS.

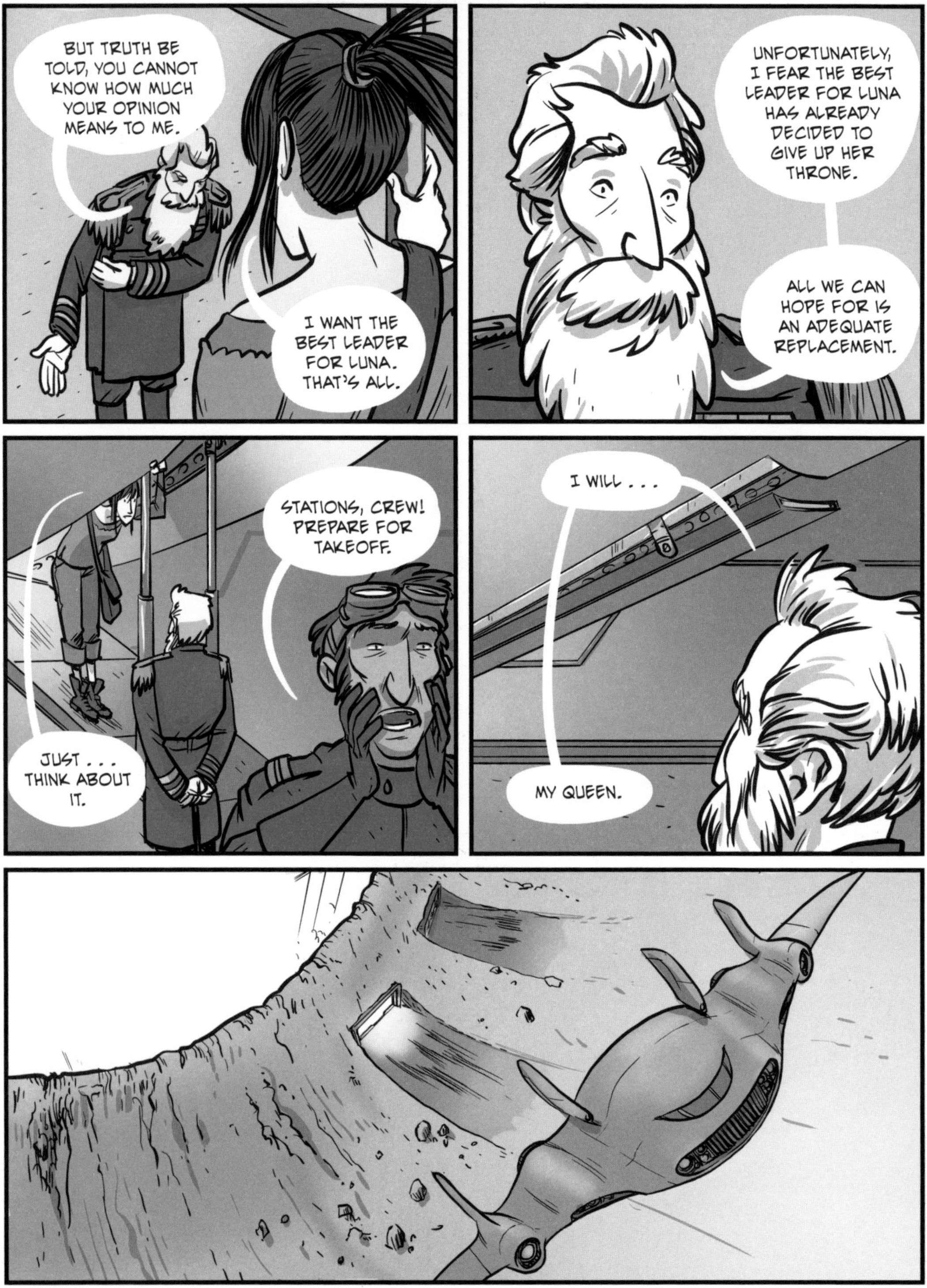
BUT TRUTH BE TOLD, YOU CANNOT KNOW HOW MUCH YOUR OPINION MEANS TO ME.
I WANT THE BEST LEADER FOR LUNA. THAT'S ALL.
UNFORTUNATELY, I FEAR THE BEST LEADER FOR LUNA HAS ALREADY DECIDED TO GIVE UP HER THRONE.
ALL WE CAN HOPE FOR IS AN ADEQUATE REPLACEMENT.
JUST . . . THINK ABOUT IT.
STATIONS, CREW! PREPARE FOR TAKEOFF.
I WILL . . .
MY QUEEN.

CHAPTER V

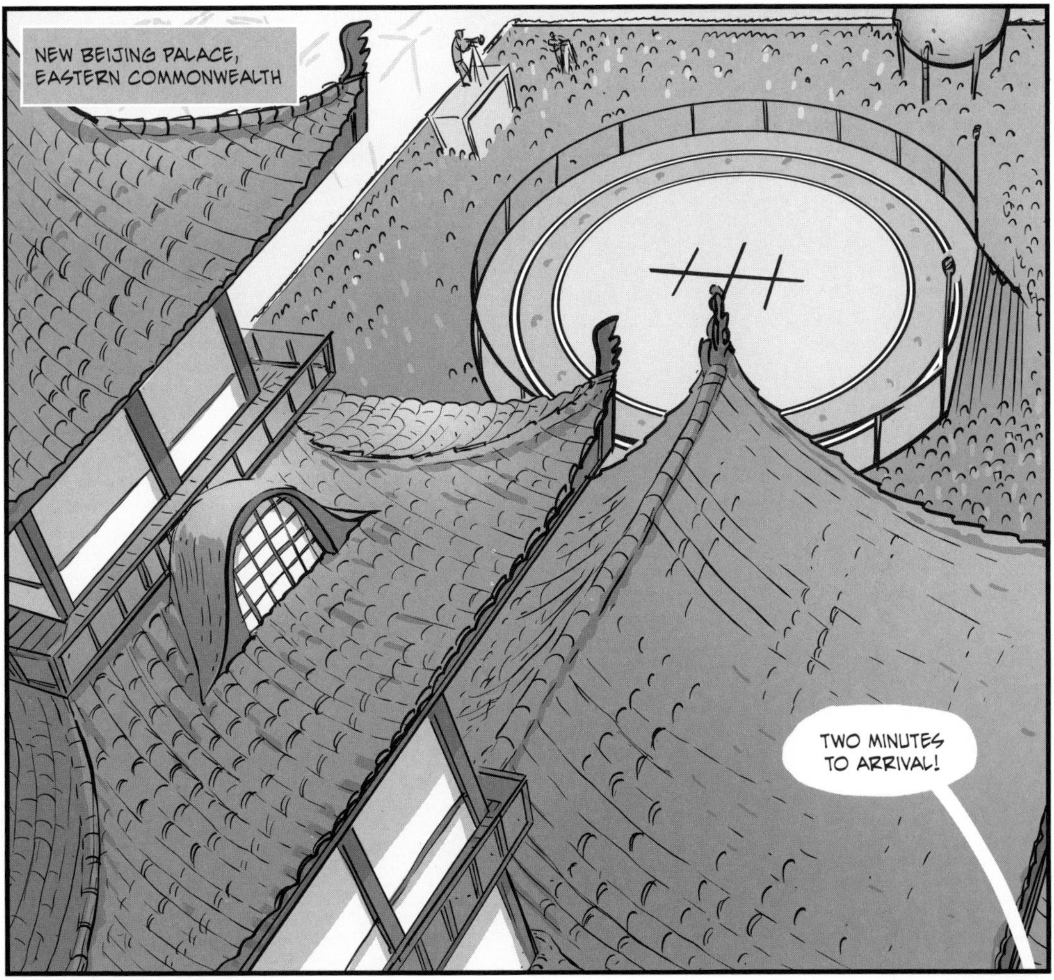
NEW BEIJING PALACE, EASTERN COMMONWEALTH
TWO MINUTES TO ARRIVAL!

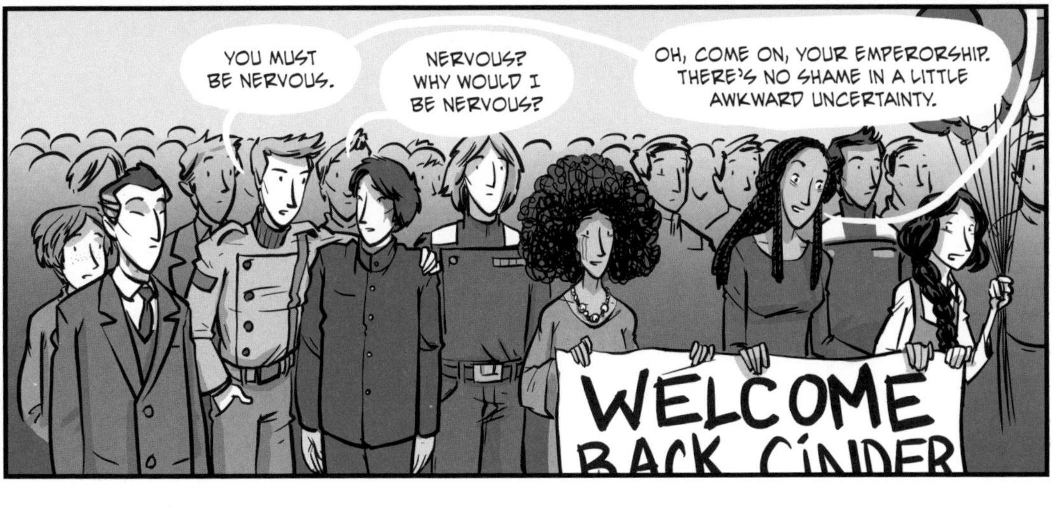
YOU MUST BE NERVOUS.
NERVOUS? WHY WOULD I BE NERVOUS?
OH, COME ON, YOUR EMPERORSHIP. THERE'S NO SHAME IN A LITTLE AWKWARD UNCERTAINTY.
WELCOME BACK CINDER

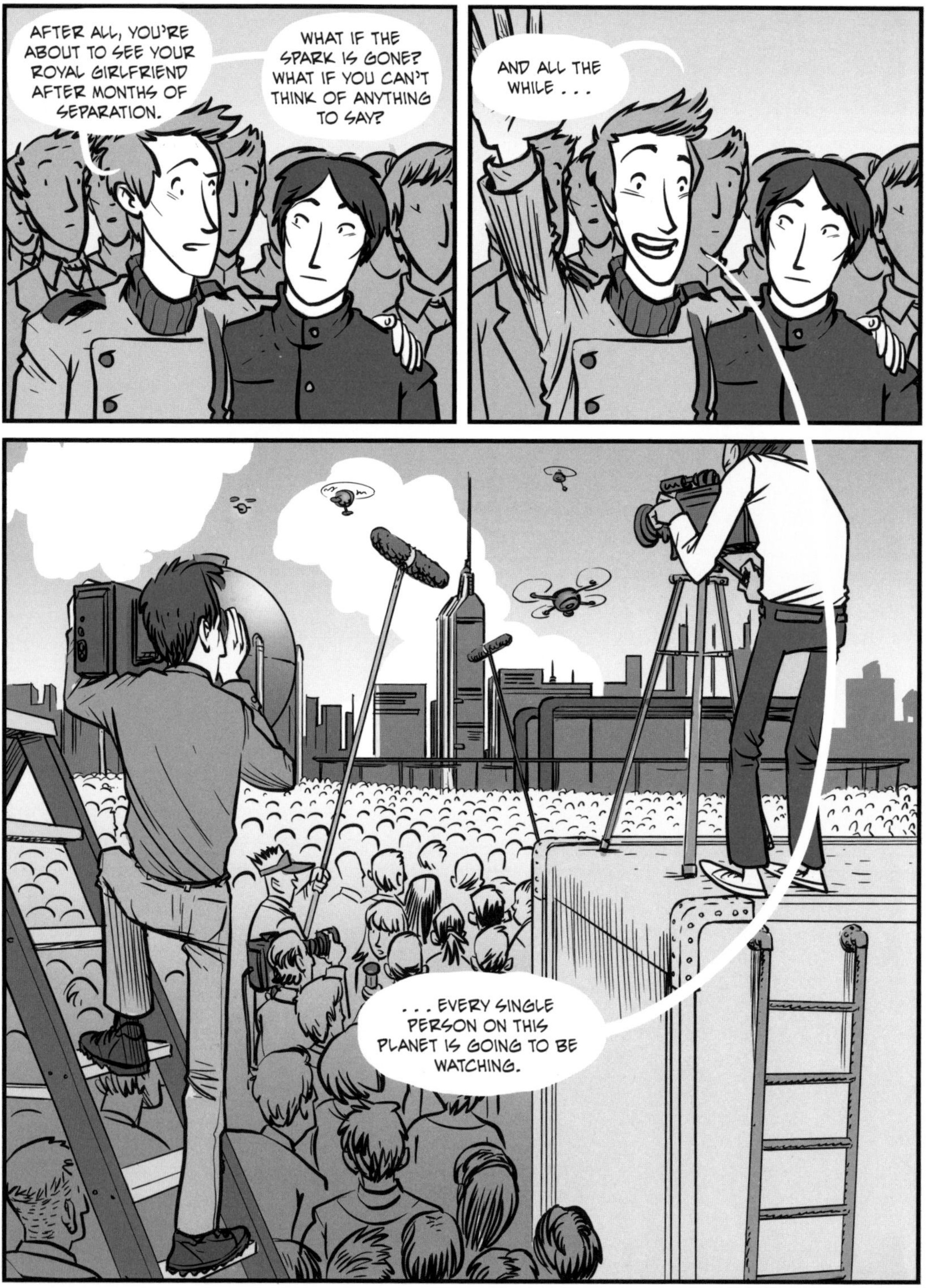
AFTER ALL, YOU'RE ABOUT TO SEE YOUR ROYAL GIRLFRIEND AFTER MONTHS OF SEPARATION.
WHAT IF THE SPARK IS GONE? WHAT IF YOU CAN'T THINK OF ANYTHING TO SAY?
AND ALL THE WHILE . . .
. . . EVERY SINGLE PERSON ON THIS PLANET IS GOING TO BE WATCHING.

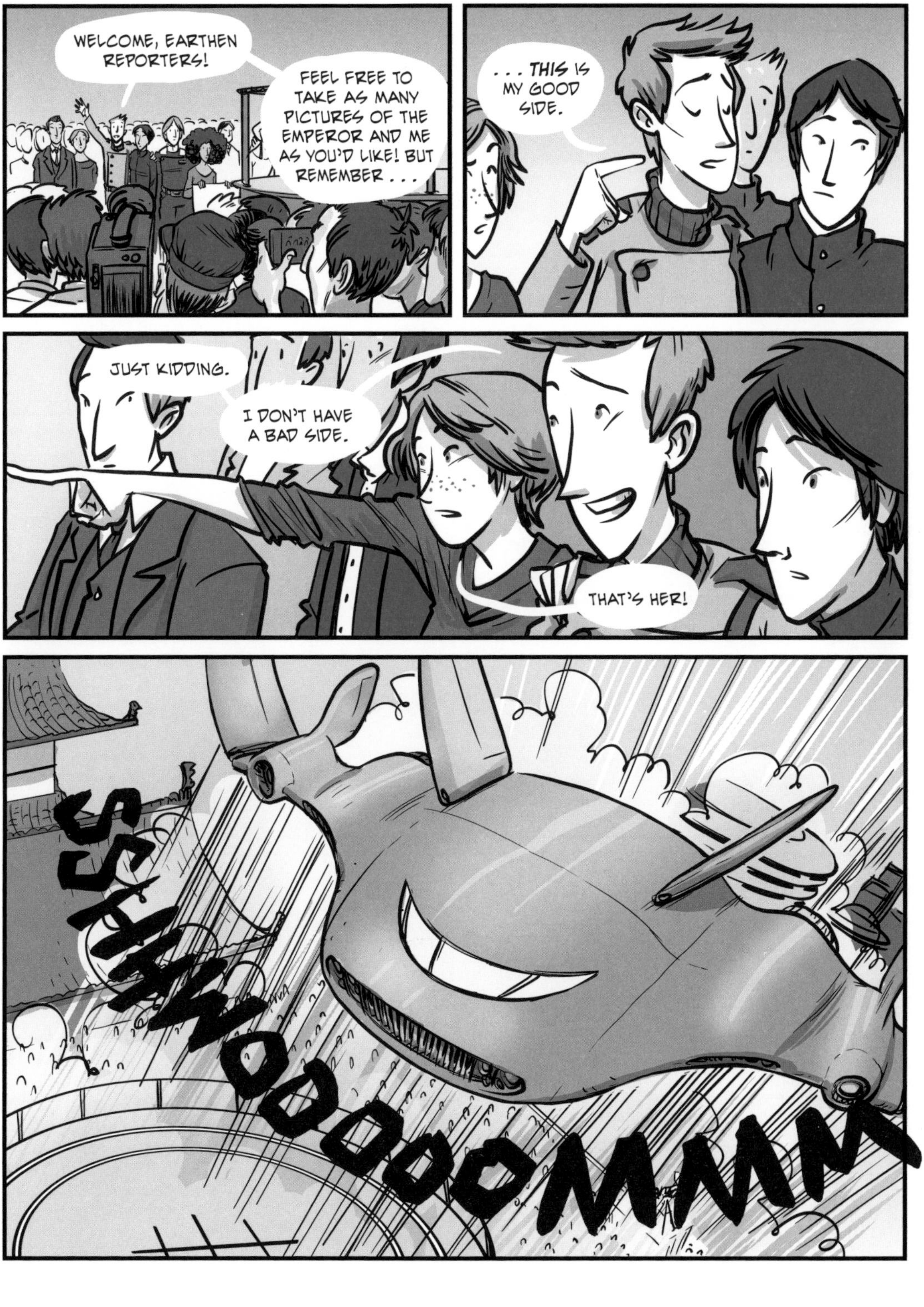
WELCOME, EARTHEN REPORTERS!
FEEL FREE TO TAKE AS MANY PICTURES OF THE EMPEROR AND ME AS YOU'D LIKE! BUT REMEMBER . . .
. . . THIS IS MY GOOD SIDE.
JUST KIDDING.
I DON'T HAVE A BAD SIDE.
THAT'S HER!
SSHWOOOOOMMMM

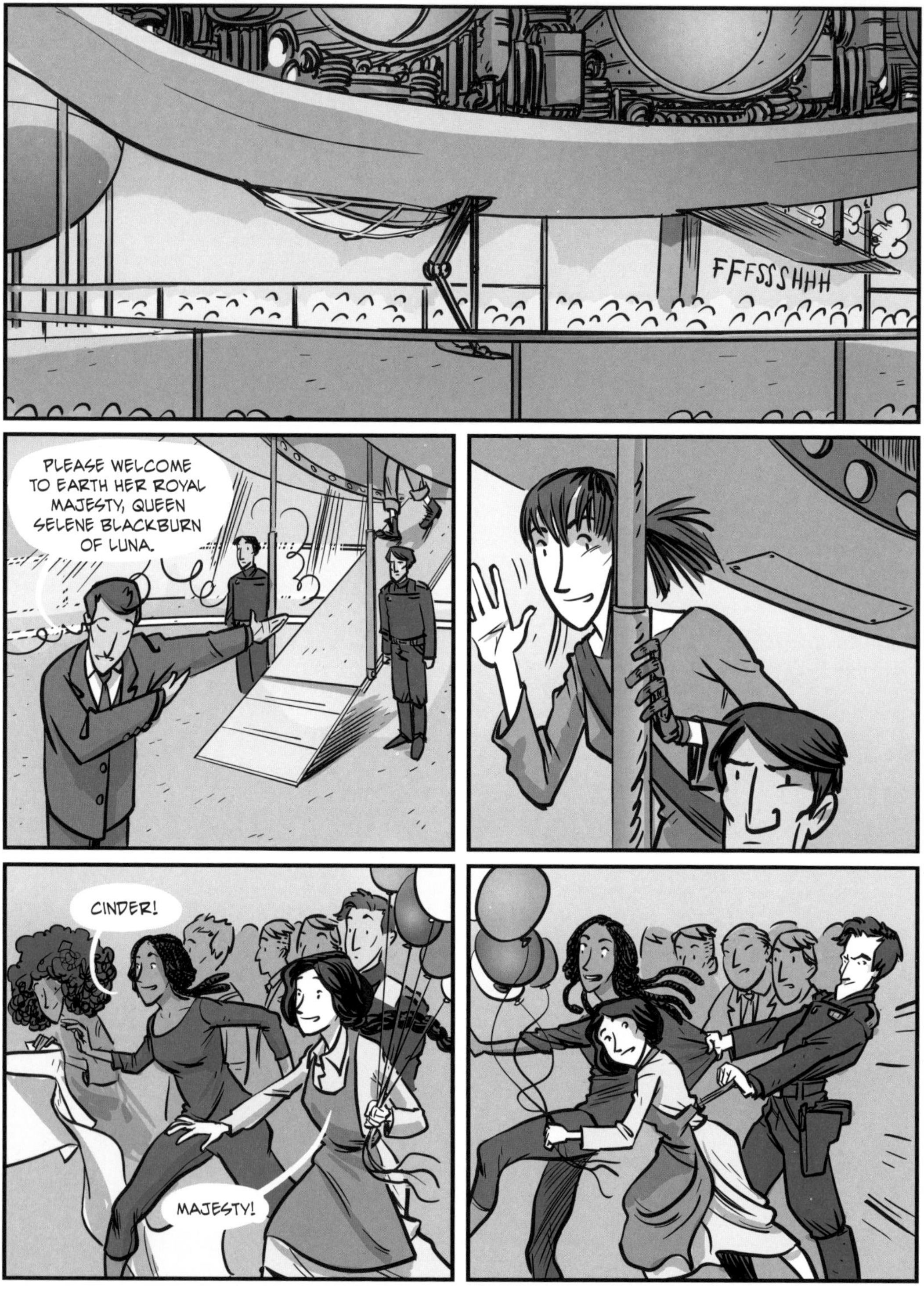
FFFSSSHHH
PLEASE WELCOME TO EARTH HER ROYAL MAJESTY, QUEEN SELENE BLACKBURN OF LUNA.
CINDER!
MAJESTY!

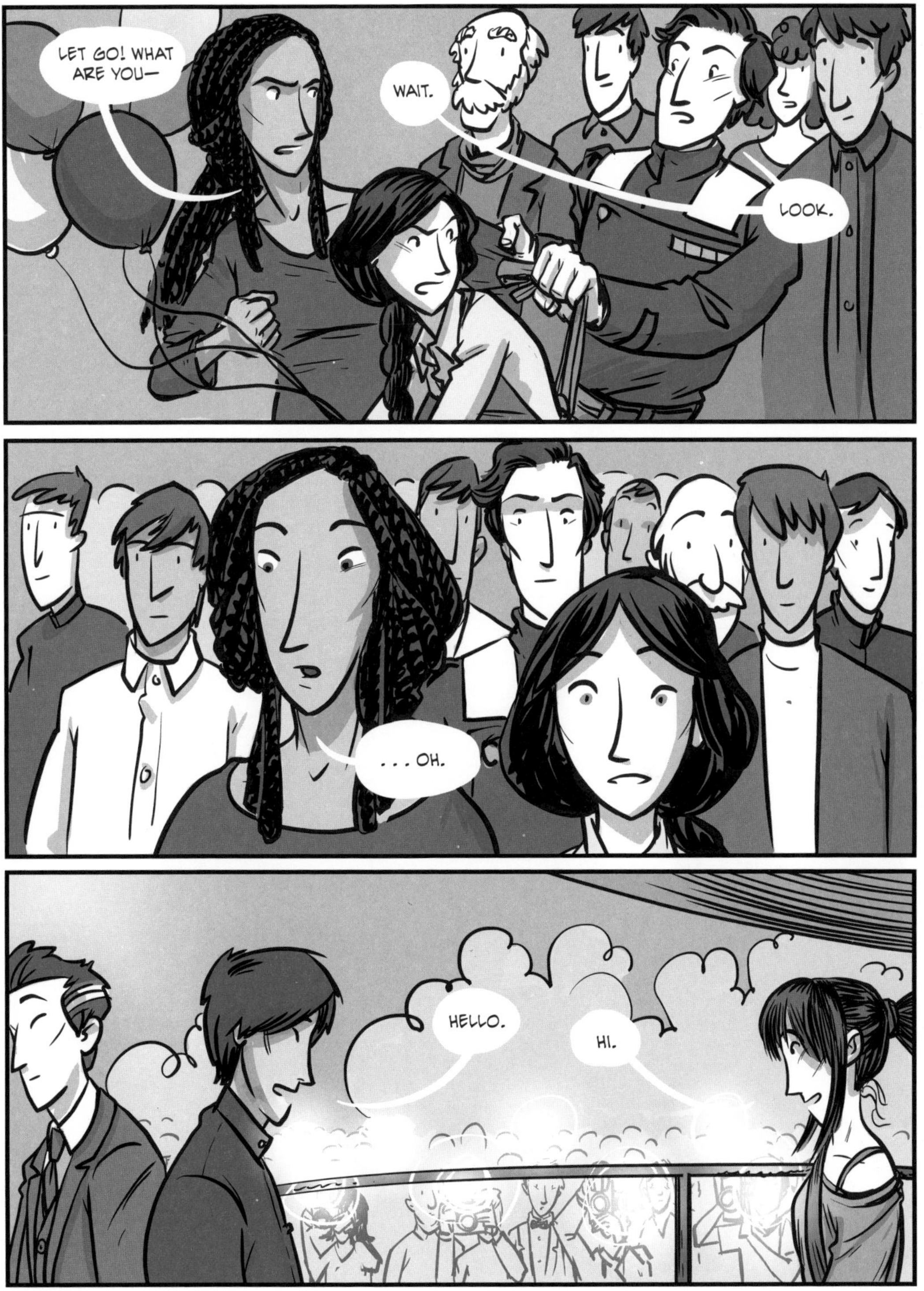
LET GO! WHAT ARE YOU—
WAIT.
LOOK.
. . . OH.
HELLO.
HI.

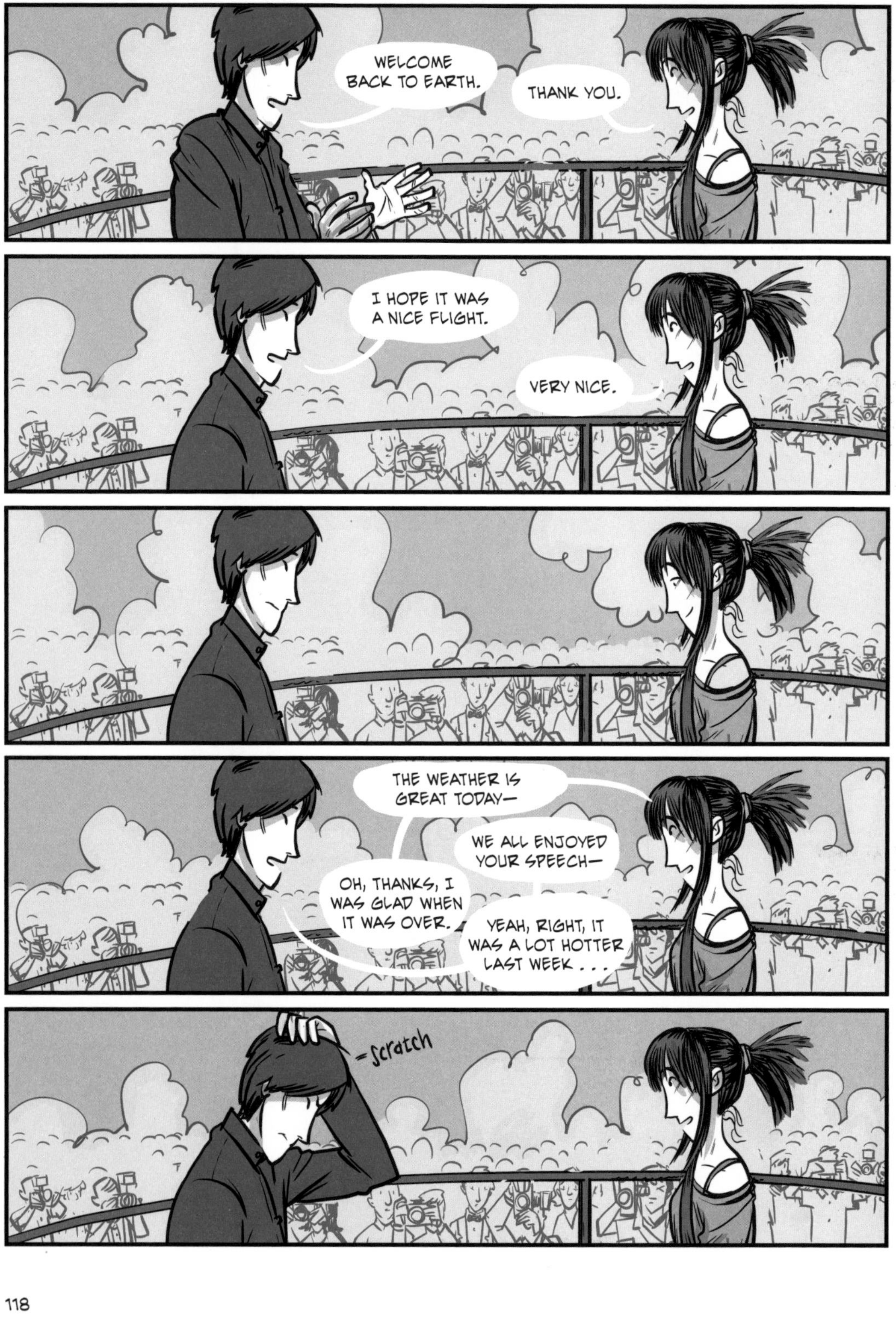
WELCOME BACK TO EARTH.
THANK YOU.
I HOPE IT WAS A NICE FLIGHT.
VERY NICE.
THE WEATHER IS GREAT TODAY—
WE ALL ENJOYED YOUR SPEECH—
OH, THANKS, I WAS GLAD WHEN IT WAS OVER.
YEAH, RIGHT, IT WAS A LOT HOTTER LAST WEEK . . .
scratch

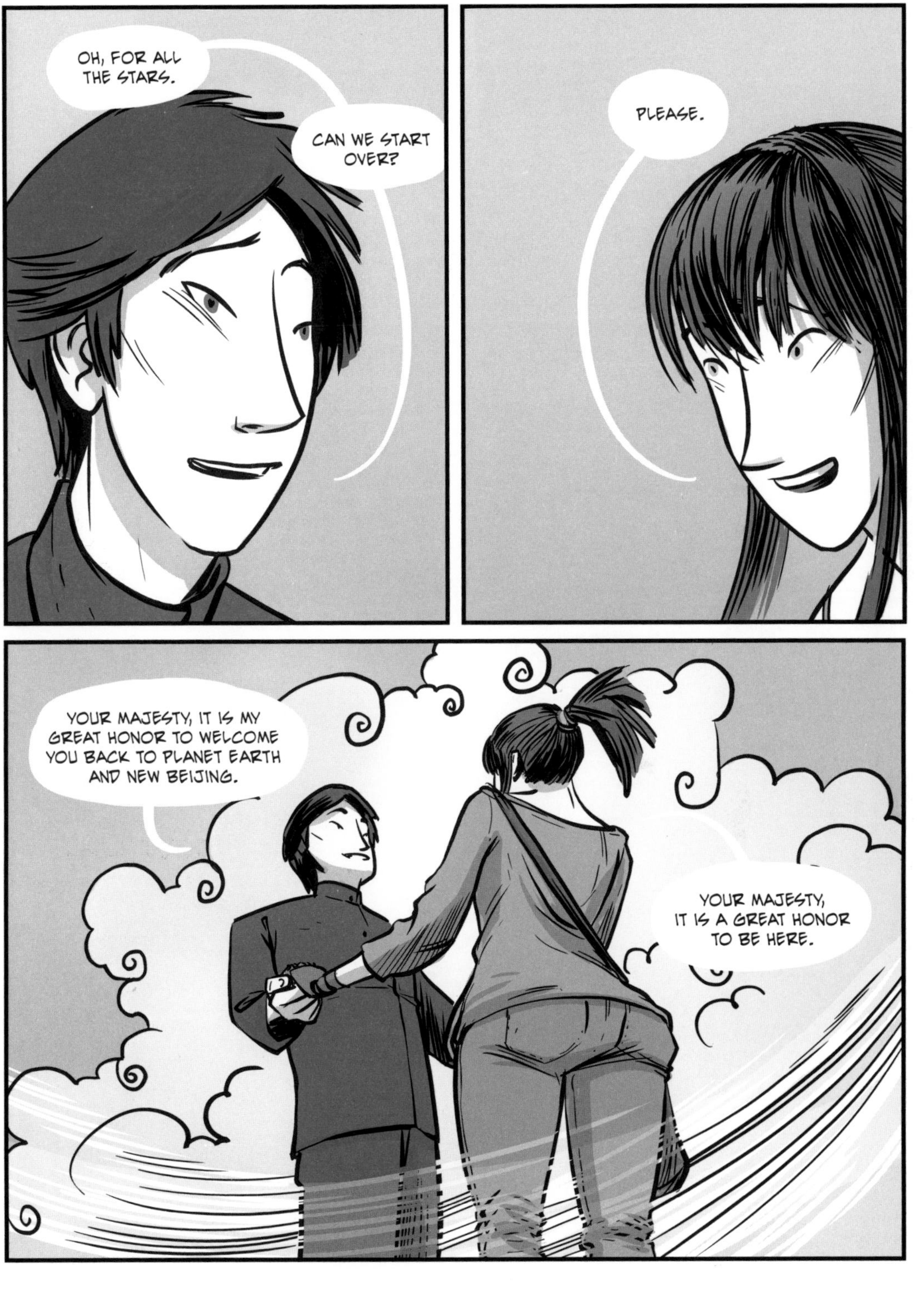
OH, FOR ALL THE STARS.
CAN WE START OVER?
PLEASE.
YOUR MAJESTY, IT IS MY GREAT HONOR TO WELCOME YOU BACK TO PLANET EARTH AND NEW BEIJING.
YOUR MAJESTY, IT IS A GREAT HONOR TO BE HERE.

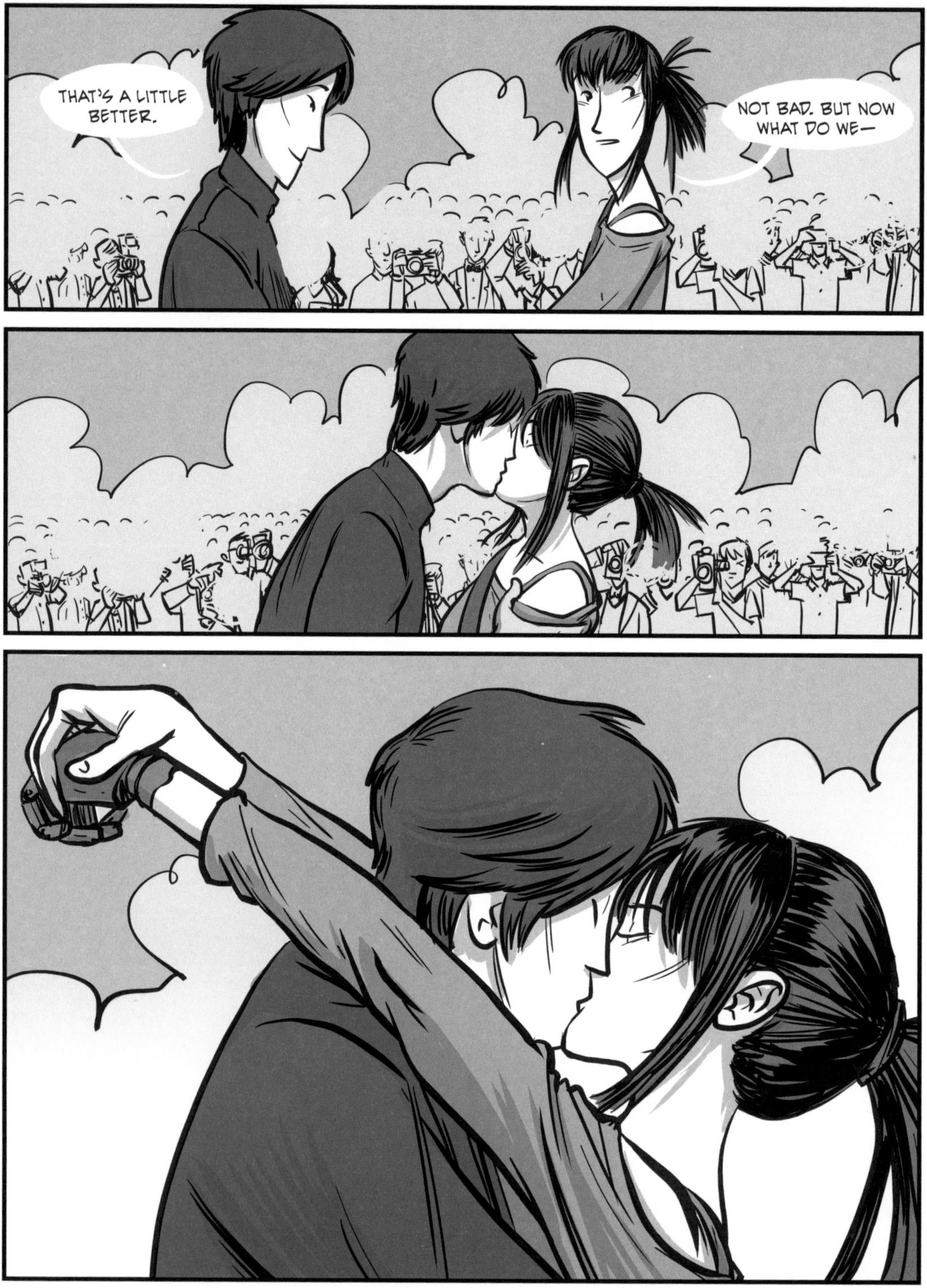
THAT'S A LITTLE BETTER.
NOT BAD. BUT NOW WHAT DO WE—

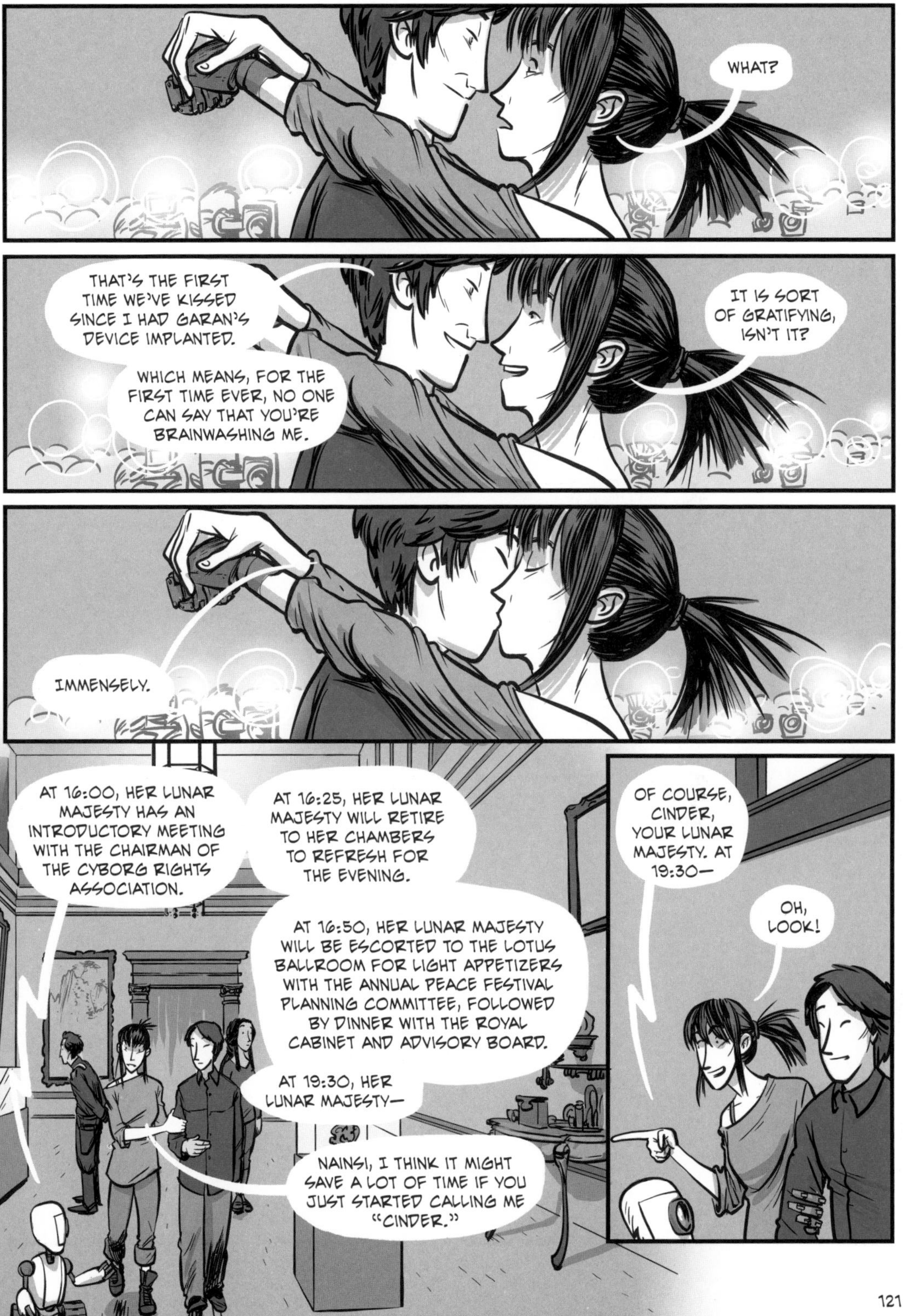
WHAT?
THAT'S THE FIRST TIME WE'VE KISSED SINCE I HAD GARAN'S DEVICE IMPLANTED.
WHICH MEANS, FOR THE FIRST TIME EVER, NO ONE CAN SAY THAT YOU'RE BRAINWASHING ME.
IT IS SORT OF GRATIFYING, ISN'T IT?
IMMENSELY.
AT 16:00, HER LUNAR MAJESTY HAS AN INTRODUCTORY MEETING WITH THE CHAIRMAN OF THE CYBORG RIGHTS ASSOCIATION.
AT 16:25, HER LUNAR MAJESTY WILL RETIRE TO HER CHAMBERS TO REFRESH FOR THE EVENING.
AT 16:50, HER LUNAR MAJESTY WILL BE ESCORTED TO THE LOTUS BALLROOM FOR LIGHT APPETIZERS WITH THE ANNUAL PEACE FESTIVAL PLANNING COMMITTEE, FOLLOWED BY DINNER WITH THE ROYAL CABINET AND ADVISORY BOARD.
AT 19:30, HER LUNAR MAJESTY—
NAINSI, I THINK IT MIGHT SAVE A LOT OF TIME IF YOU JUST STARTED CALLING ME "CINDER."
OF COURSE, CINDER, YOUR LUNAR MAJESTY. AT 19:30—
OH, LOOK!

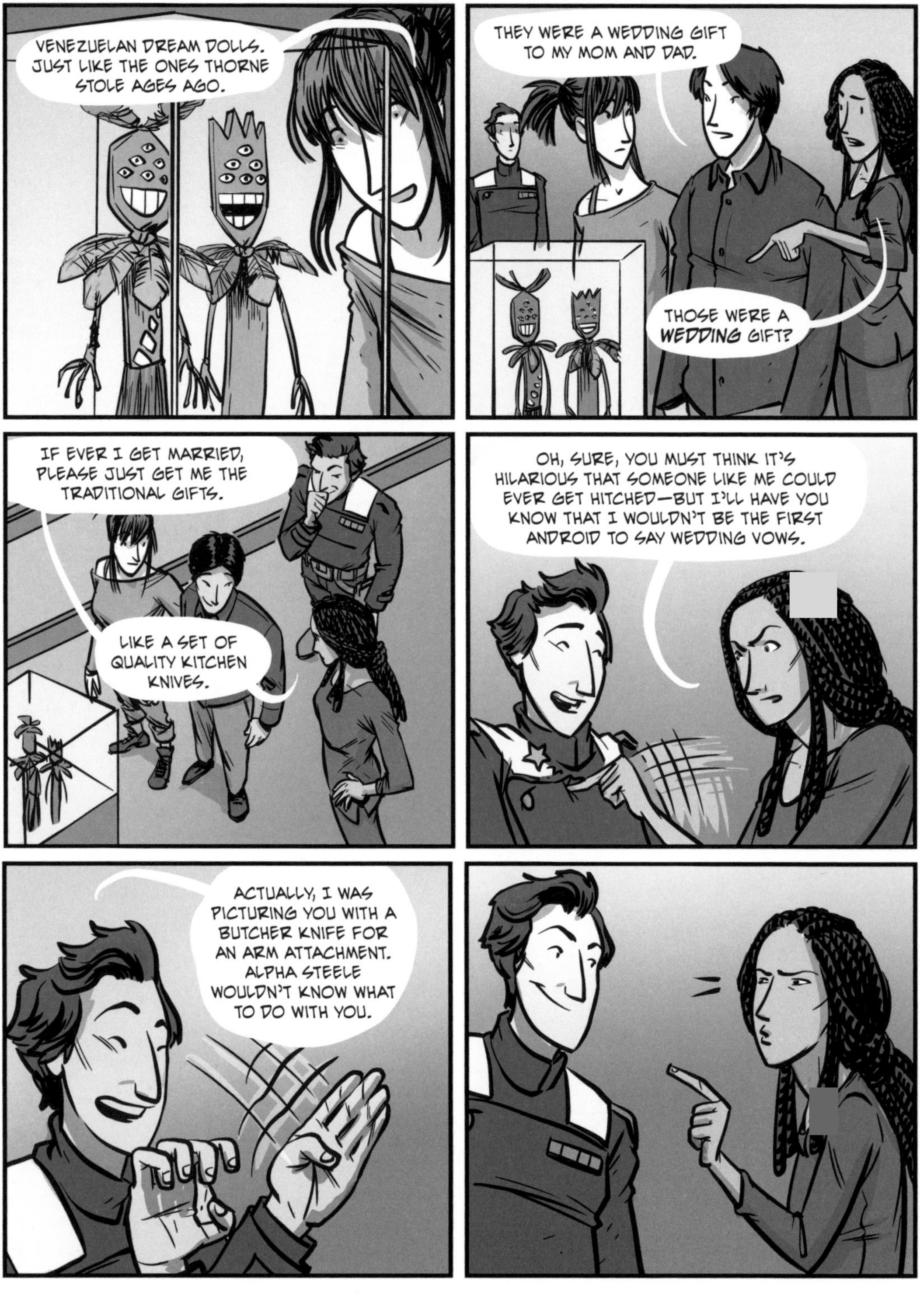
VENEZUELAN DREAM DOLLS. JUST LIKE THE ONES THORNE STOLE AGES AGO.
THEY WERE A WEDDING GIFT TO MY MOM AND DAD.
THOSE WERE A WEDDING GIFT?
IF EVER I GET MARRIED, PLEASE JUST GET ME THE TRADITIONAL GIFTS.
LIKE A SET OF QUALITY KITCHEN KNIVES.
OH, SURE, YOU MUST THINK IT'S HILARIOUS THAT SOMEONE LIKE ME COULD EVER GET HITCHED—BUT I'LL HAVE YOU KNOW THAT I WOULDN'T BE THE FIRST ANDROID TO SAY WEDDING VOWS.
ACTUALLY, I WAS PICTURING YOU WITH A BUTCHER KNIFE FOR AN ARM ATTACHMENT. ALPHA STEELE WOULDN'T KNOW WHAT TO DO WITH YOU.

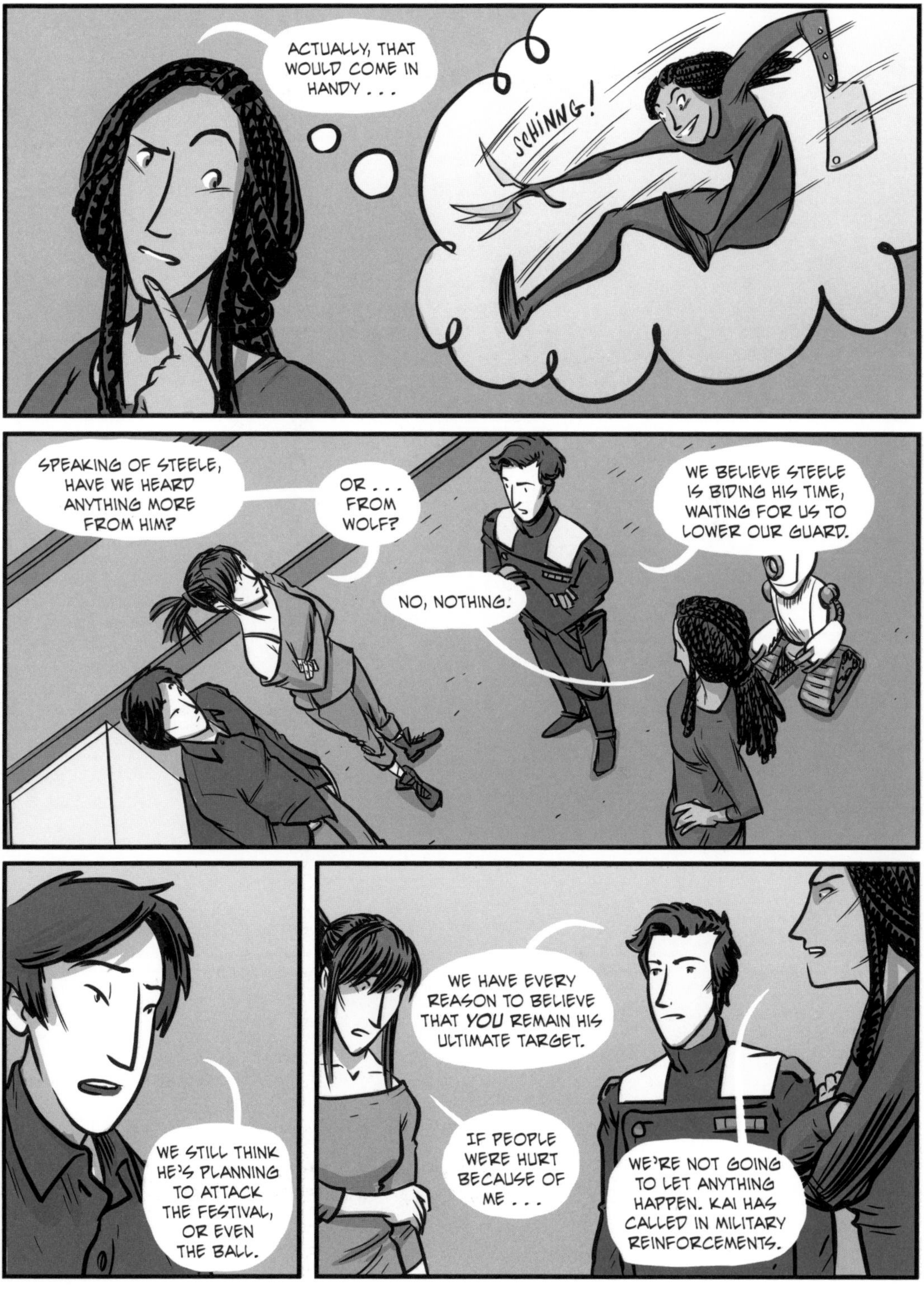
ACTUALLY, THAT WOULD COME IN HANDY . . .
SCHINNG!
SPEAKING OF STEELE, HAVE WE HEARD ANYTHING MORE FROM HIM?
OR . . . FROM WOLF?
NO, NOTHING.
WE BELIEVE STEELE IS BIDING HIS TIME, WAITING FOR US TO LOWER OUR GUARD.
WE STILL THINK HE'S PLANNING TO ATTACK THE FESTIVAL, OR EVEN THE BALL.
WE HAVE EVERY REASON TO BELIEVE THAT *YOU* REMAIN HIS ULTIMATE TARGET.
IF PEOPLE WERE HURT BECAUSE OF ME . . .
WE'RE NOT GOING TO LET ANYTHING HAPPEN. KAI HAS CALLED IN MILITARY REINFORCEMENTS.

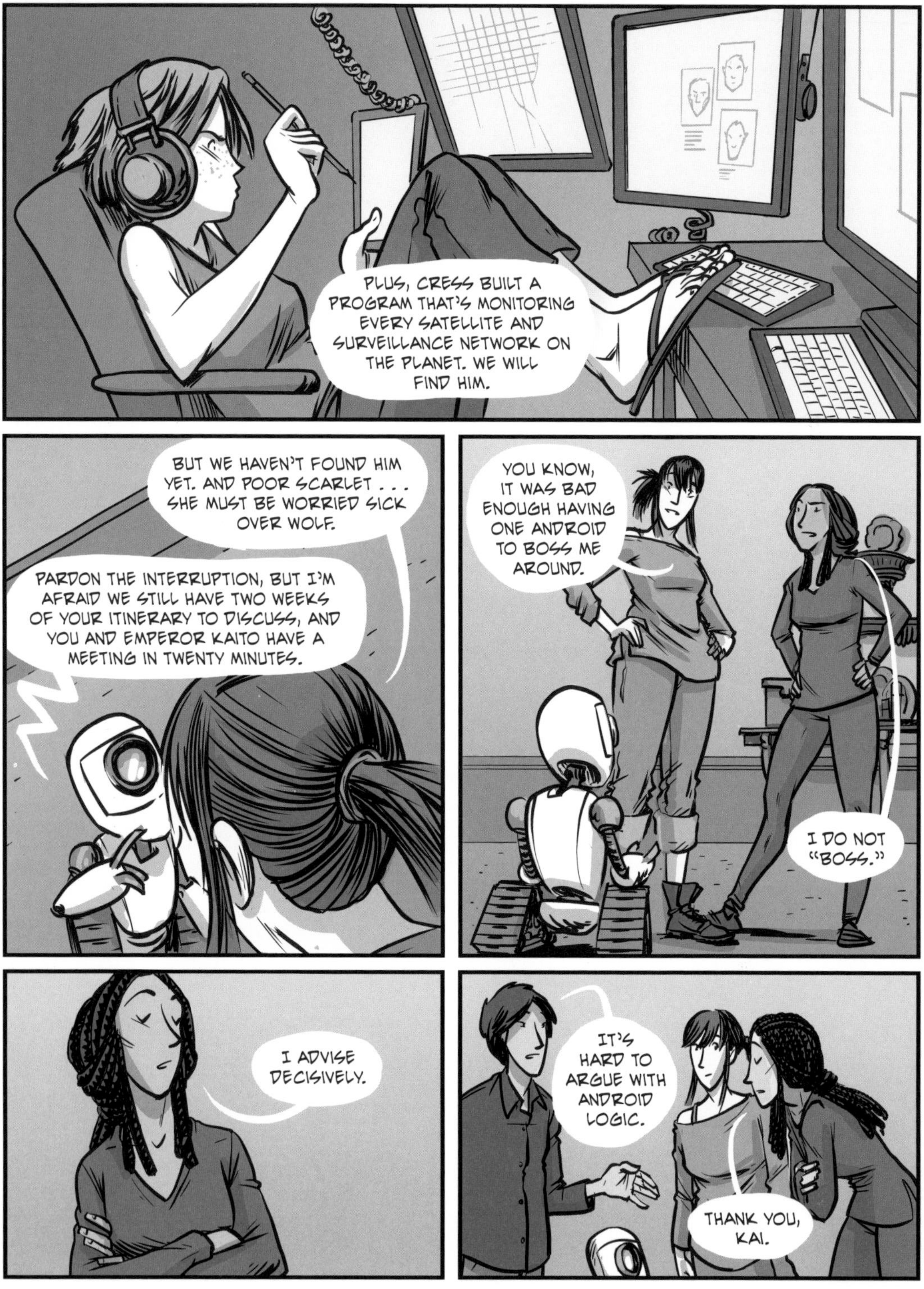
PLUS, CRESS BUILT A PROGRAM THAT'S MONITORING EVERY SATELLITE AND SURVEILLANCE NETWORK ON THE PLANET. WE WILL FIND HIM.
BUT WE HAVEN'T FOUND HIM YET. AND POOR SCARLET . . . SHE MUST BE WORRIED SICK OVER WOLF.
PARDON THE INTERRUPTION, BUT I'M AFRAID WE STILL HAVE TWO WEEKS OF YOUR ITINERARY TO DISCUSS, AND YOU AND EMPEROR KAITO HAVE A MEETING IN TWENTY MINUTES.
YOU KNOW, IT WAS BAD ENOUGH HAVING ONE ANDROID TO BOSS ME AROUND.
I DO NOT "BOSS."
I ADVISE DECISIVELY.
IT'S HARD TO ARGUE WITH ANDROID LOGIC.
THANK YOU, KAI.

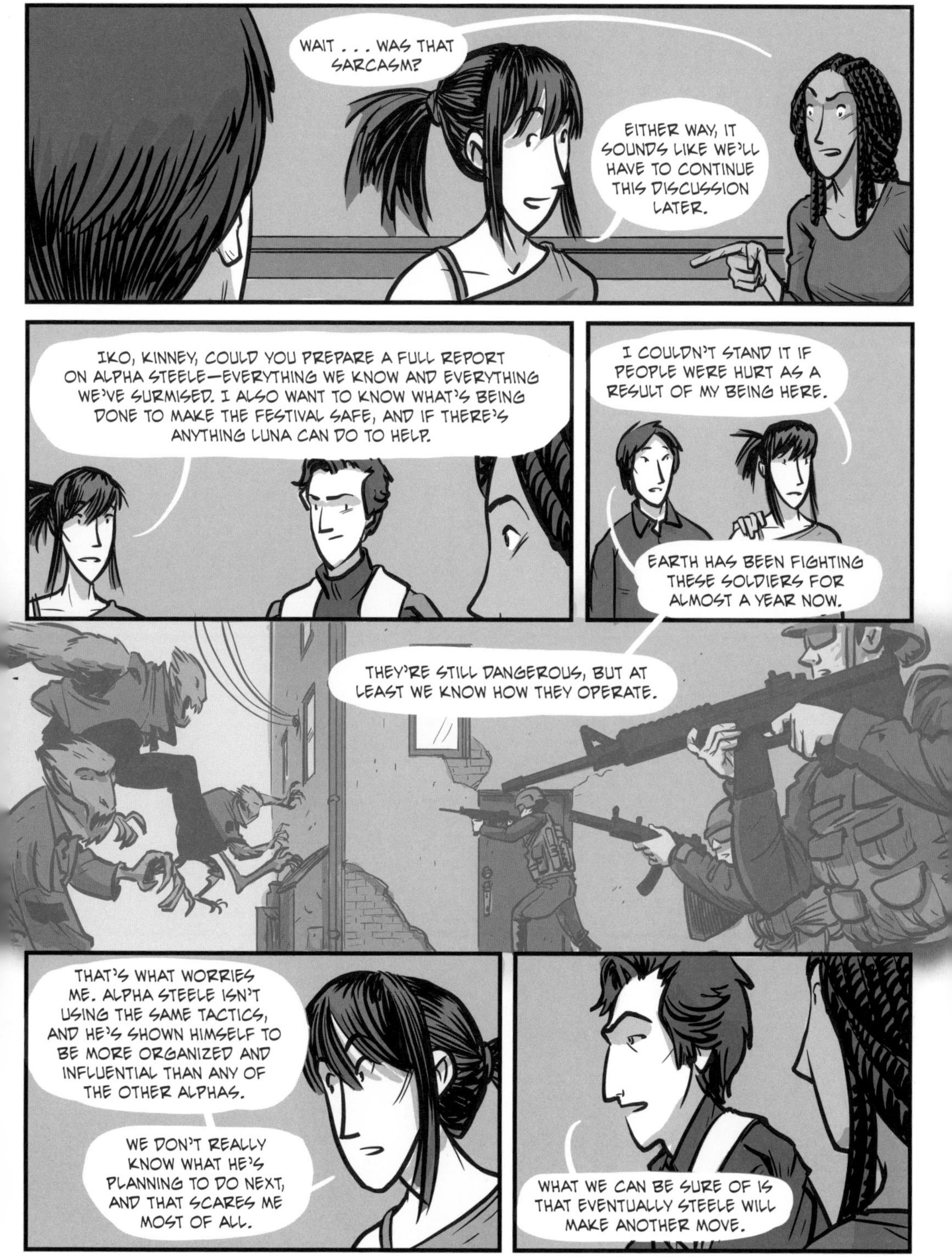
WAIT . . . WAS THAT SARCASM?
EITHER WAY, IT SOUNDS LIKE WE'LL HAVE TO CONTINUE THIS DISCUSSION LATER.
IKO, KINNEY, COULD YOU PREPARE A FULL REPORT ON ALPHA STEELE—EVERYTHING WE KNOW AND EVERYTHING WE'VE SURMISED. I ALSO WANT TO KNOW WHAT'S BEING DONE TO MAKE THE FESTIVAL SAFE, AND IF THERE'S ANYTHING LUNA CAN DO TO HELP.
I COULDN'T STAND IT IF PEOPLE WERE HURT AS A RESULT OF MY BEING HERE.
EARTH HAS BEEN FIGHTING THESE SOLDIERS FOR ALMOST A YEAR NOW.
THEY'RE STILL DANGEROUS, BUT AT LEAST WE KNOW HOW THEY OPERATE.
THAT'S WHAT WORRIES ME. ALPHA STEELE ISN'T USING THE SAME TACTICS, AND HE'S SHOWN HIMSELF TO BE MORE ORGANIZED AND INFLUENTIAL THAN ANY OF THE OTHER ALPHAS.
WE DON'T REALLY KNOW WHAT HE'S PLANNING TO DO NEXT, AND THAT SCARES ME MOST OF ALL.
WHAT WE CAN BE SURE OF IS THAT EVENTUALLY STEELE WILL MAKE ANOTHER MOVE.

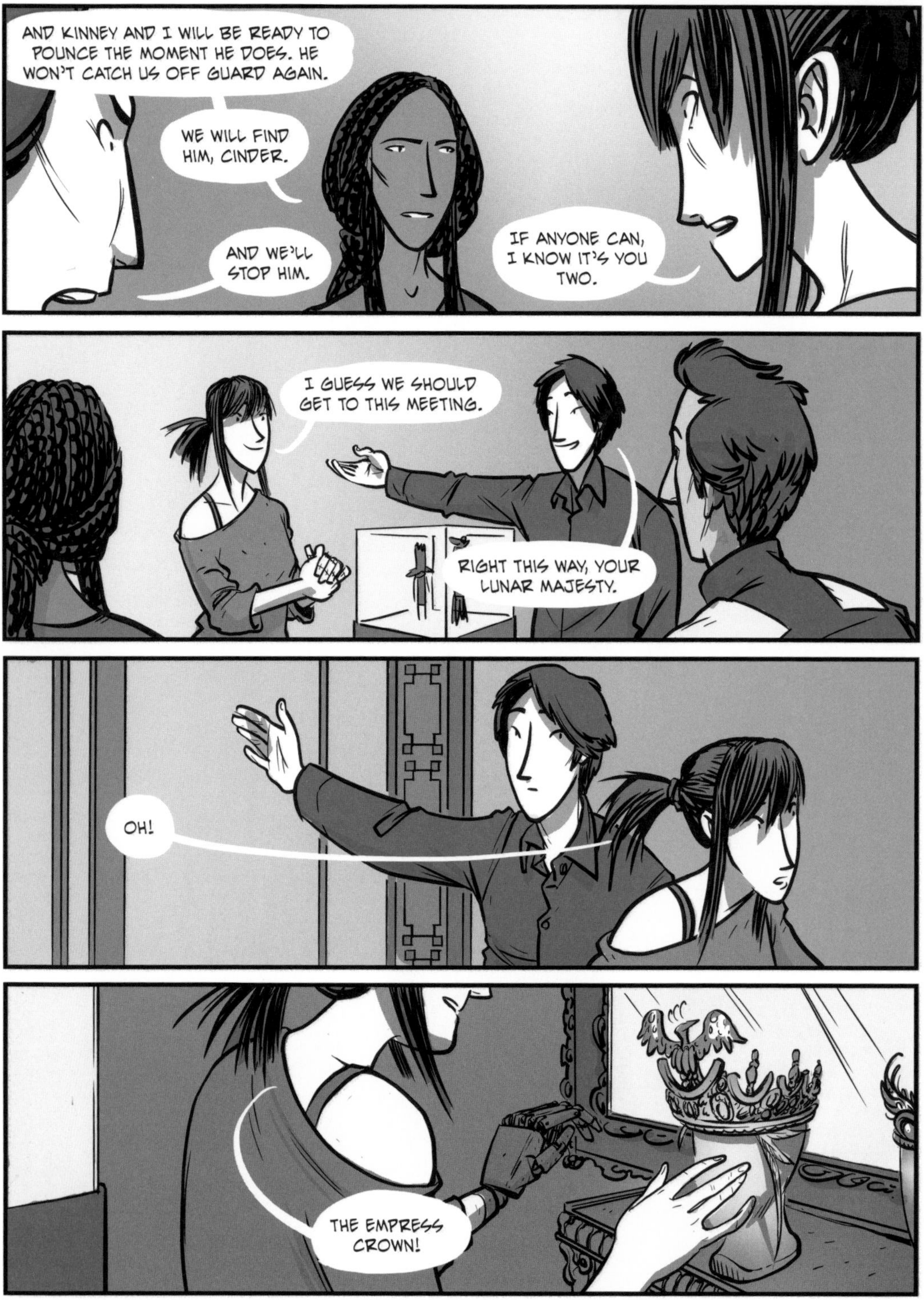
AND KINNEY AND I WILL BE READY TO POUNCE THE MOMENT HE DOES. HE WON'T CATCH US OFF GUARD AGAIN.
WE WILL FIND HIM, CINDER.
AND WE'LL STOP HIM.
IF ANYONE CAN, I KNOW IT'S YOU TWO.
I GUESS WE SHOULD GET TO THIS MEETING.
RIGHT THIS WAY, YOUR LUNAR MAJESTY.
OH!
THE EMPRESS CROWN!

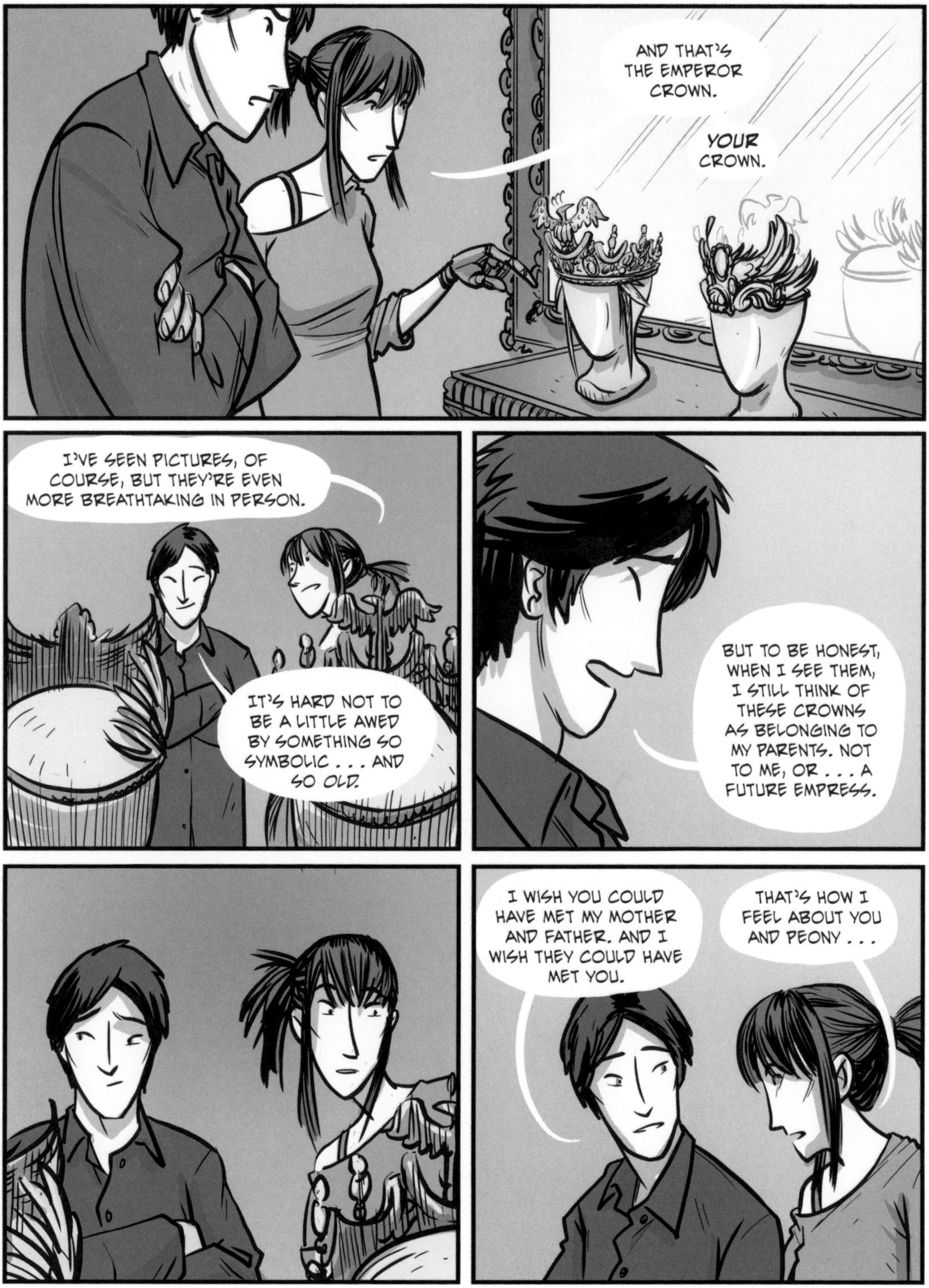
AND THAT'S THE EMPEROR CROWN.
YOUR CROWN.
I'VE SEEN PICTURES, OF COURSE, BUT THEY'RE EVEN MORE BREATHTAKING IN PERSON.
IT'S HARD NOT TO BE A LITTLE AWED BY SOMETHING SO SYMBOLIC . . . AND SO OLD.
BUT TO BE HONEST, WHEN I SEE THEM, I STILL THINK OF THESE CROWNS AS BELONGING TO MY PARENTS. NOT TO ME, OR . . . A FUTURE EMPRESS.
I WISH YOU COULD HAVE MET MY MOTHER AND FATHER. AND I WISH THEY COULD HAVE MET YOU.
THAT'S HOW I FEEL ABOUT YOU AND PEONY . . .

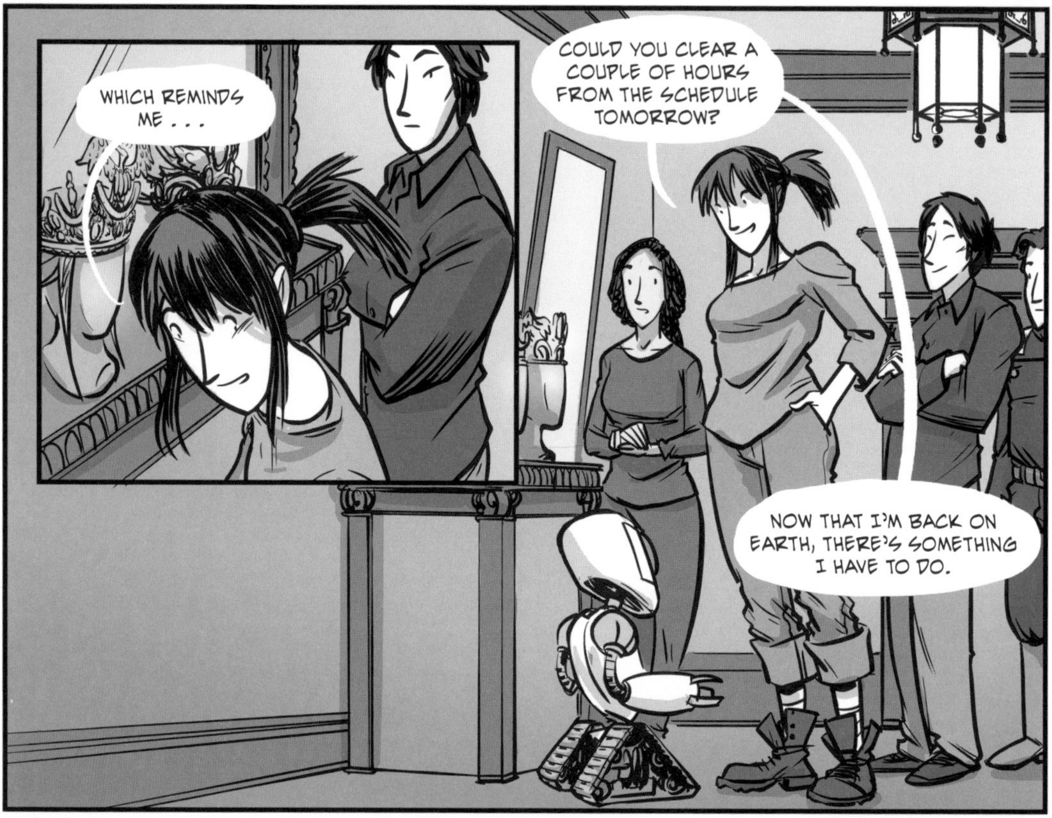
WHICH REMINDS ME . . .
COULD YOU CLEAR A COUPLE OF HOURS FROM THE SCHEDULE TOMORROW?
NOW THAT I'M BACK ON EARTH, THERE'S SOMETHING I HAVE TO DO.

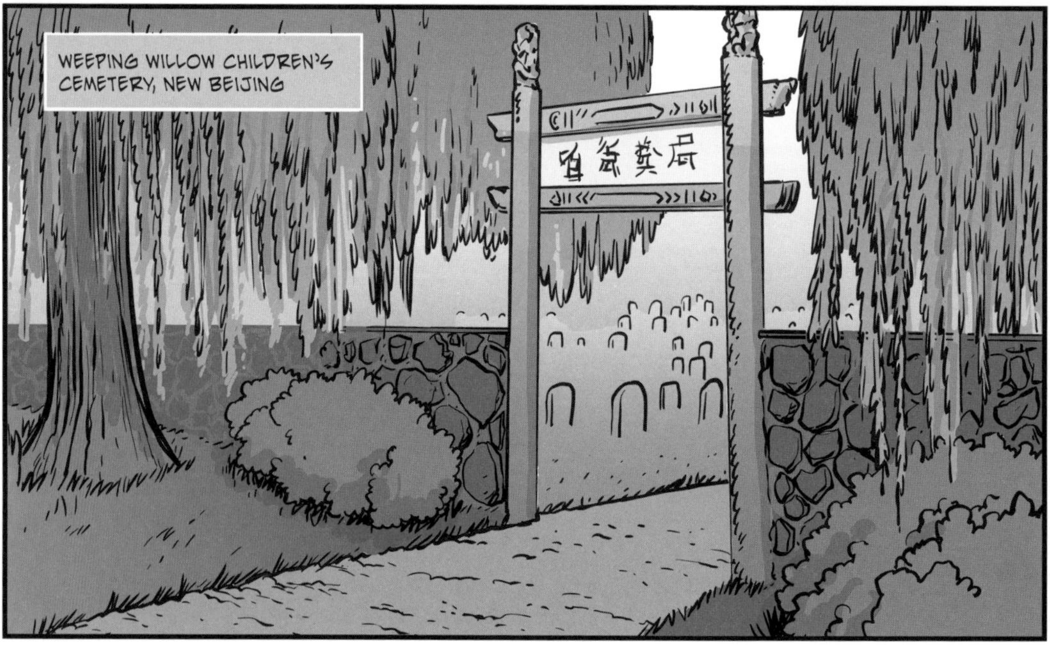
WEEPING WILLOW CHILDREN'S CEMETERY, NEW BEIJING

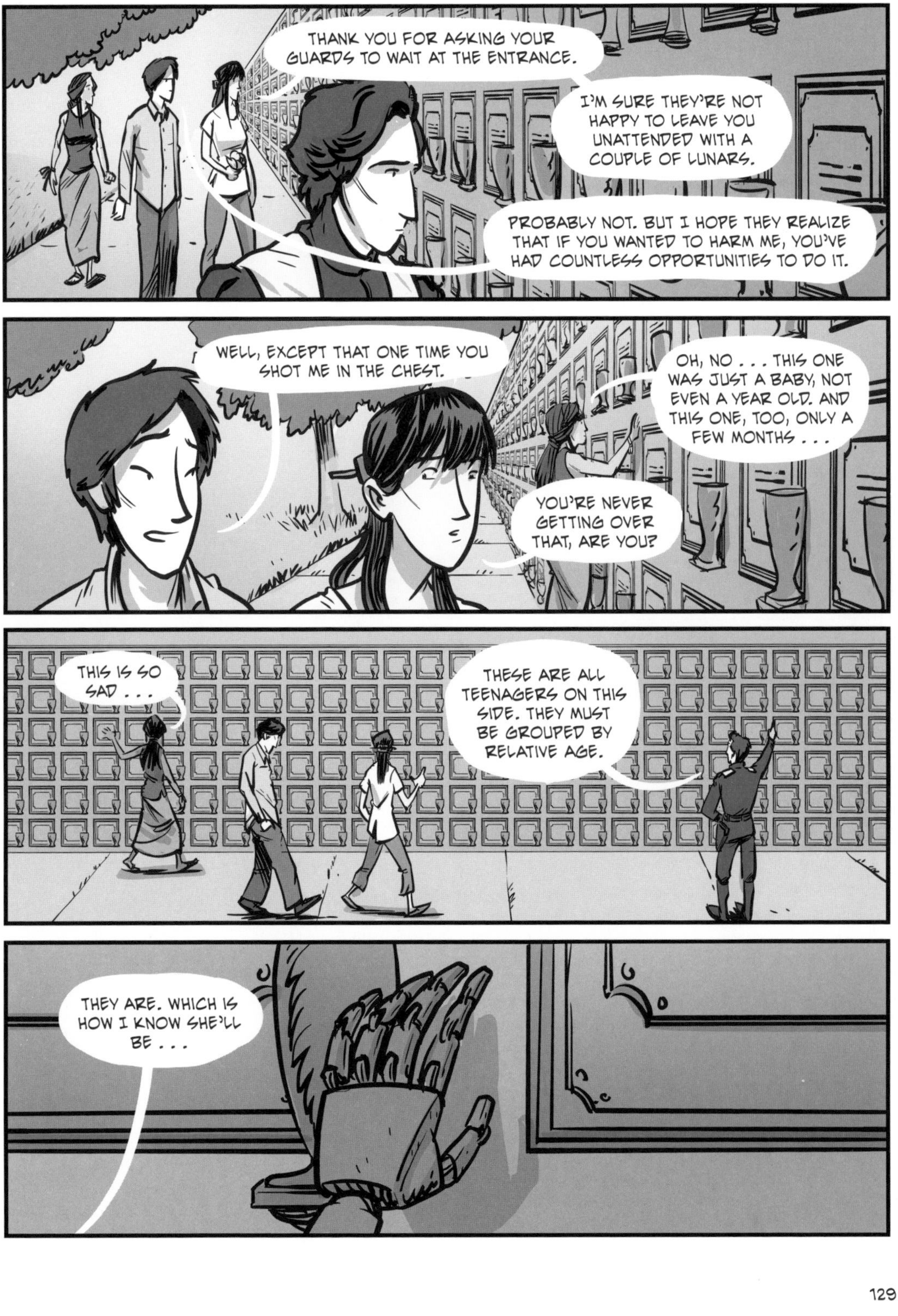
THANK YOU FOR ASKING YOUR GUARDS TO WAIT AT THE ENTRANCE.
I'M SURE THEY'RE NOT HAPPY TO LEAVE YOU UNATTENDED WITH A COUPLE OF LUNARS.
PROBABLY NOT. BUT I HOPE THEY REALIZE THAT IF YOU WANTED TO HARM ME, YOU'VE HAD COUNTLESS OPPORTUNITIES TO DO IT.
WELL, EXCEPT THAT ONE TIME YOU SHOT ME IN THE CHEST.
OH, NO . . . THIS ONE WAS JUST A BABY, NOT EVEN A YEAR OLD. AND THIS ONE, TOO, ONLY A FEW MONTHS . . .
YOU'RE NEVER GETTING OVER THAT, ARE YOU?
THIS IS SO SAD . . .
THESE ARE ALL TEENAGERS ON THIS SIDE. THEY MUST BE GROUPED BY RELATIVE AGE.
THEY ARE. WHICH IS HOW I KNOW SHE'LL BE . . .

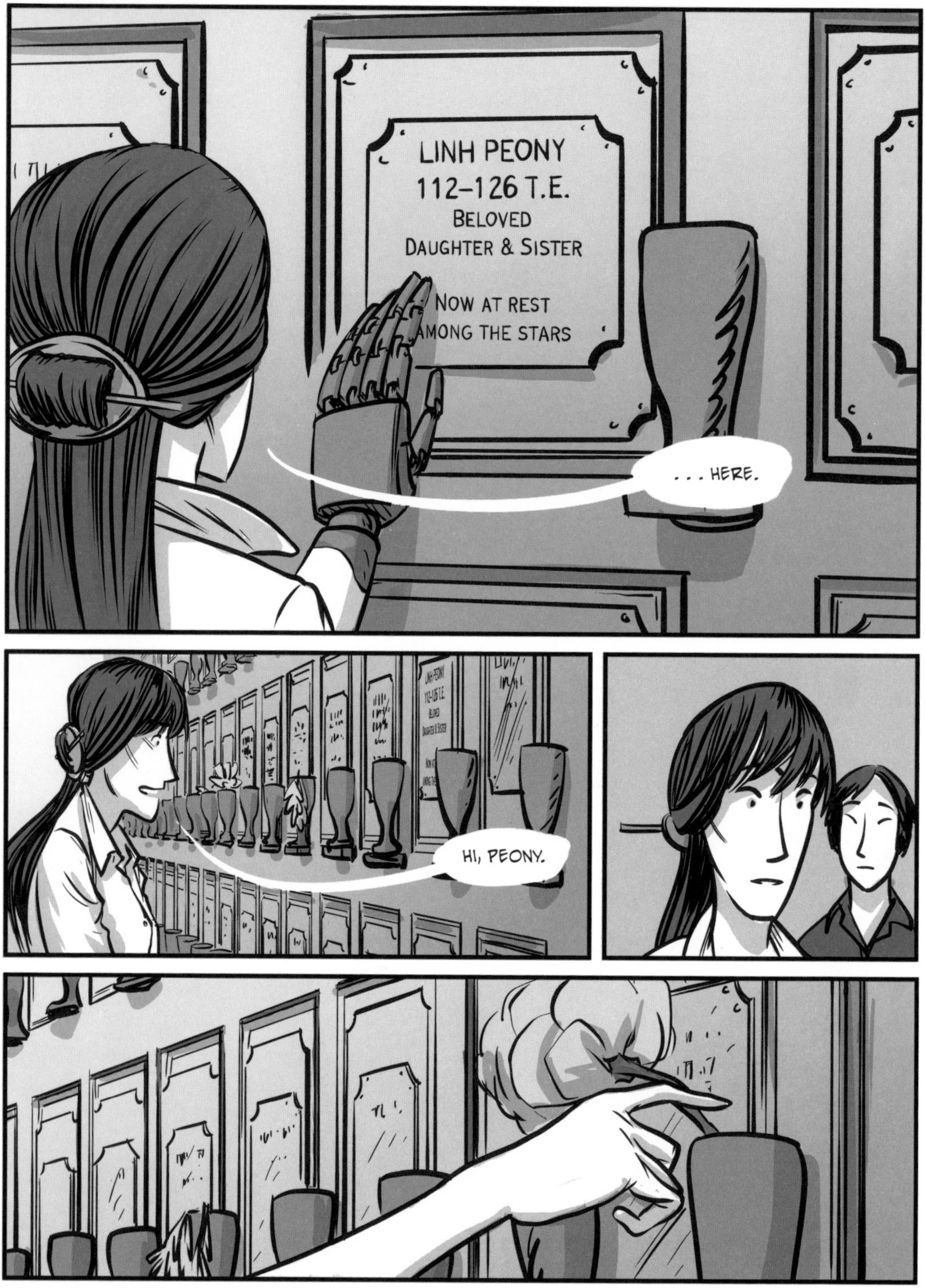
LINH PEONY
112–126 T.E.
BELOVED
DAUGHTER & SISTER
NOW AT REST
AMONG THE STARS
. . . HERE.
HI, PEONY.

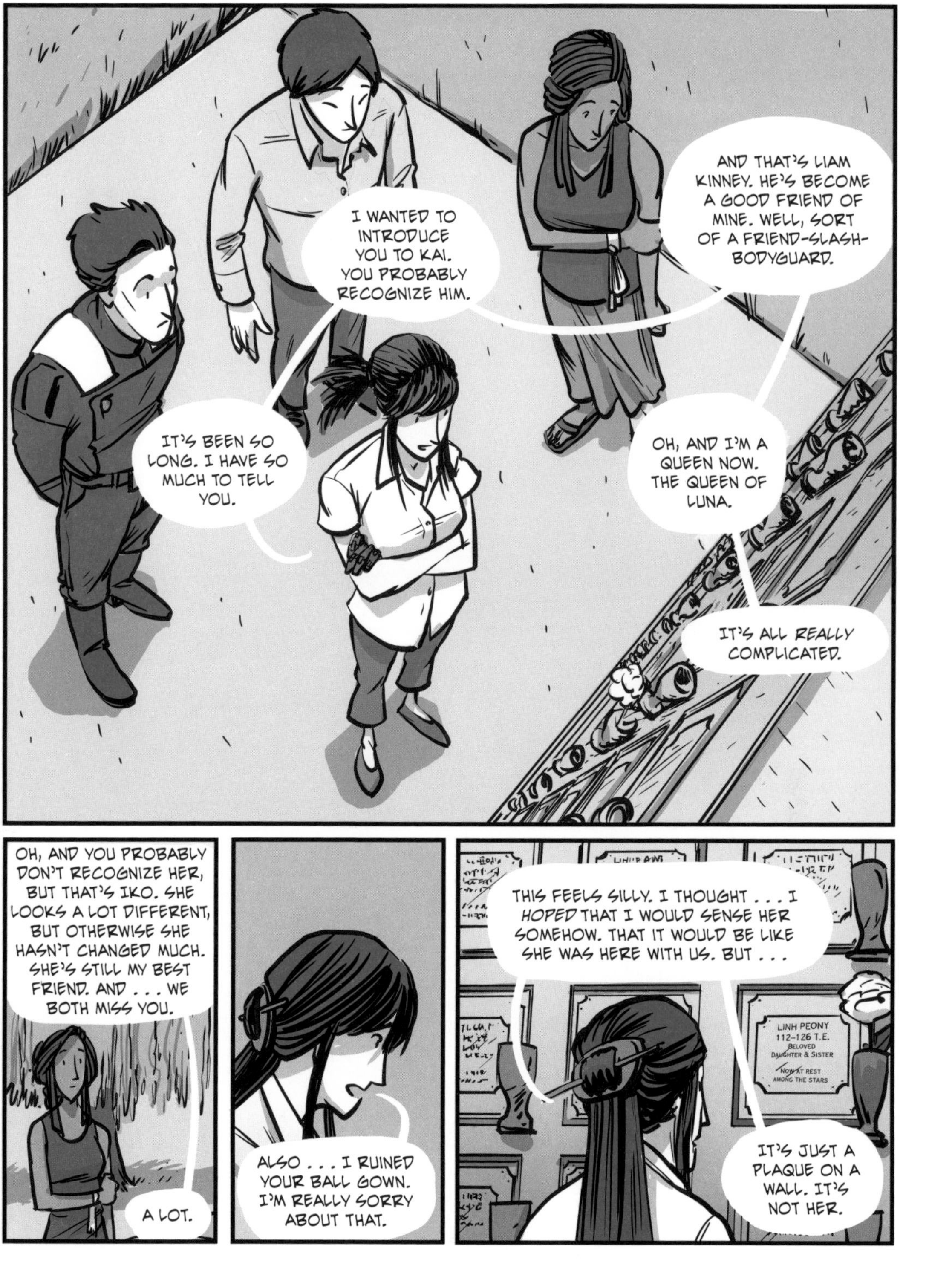
I WANTED TO INTRODUCE YOU TO KAI. YOU PROBABLY RECOGNIZE HIM.
AND THAT'S LIAM KINNEY. HE'S BECOME A GOOD FRIEND OF MINE. WELL, SORT OF A FRIEND-SLASH-BODYGUARD.
IT'S BEEN SO LONG. I HAVE SO MUCH TO TELL YOU.
OH, AND I'M A QUEEN NOW. THE QUEEN OF LUNA.
IT'S ALL *REALLY* COMPLICATED.
OH, AND YOU PROBABLY DON'T RECOGNIZE HER, BUT THAT'S IKO. SHE LOOKS A LOT DIFFERENT, BUT OTHERWISE SHE HASN'T CHANGED MUCH. SHE'S STILL MY BEST FRIEND. AND . . . WE BOTH MISS YOU.
A LOT.
ALSO . . . I RUINED YOUR BALL GOWN. I'M REALLY SORRY ABOUT THAT.
THIS FEELS SILLY. I THOUGHT . . . I *HOPED* THAT I WOULD SENSE HER SOMEHOW. THAT IT WOULD BE LIKE SHE WAS HERE WITH US. BUT . . .
LINH PEONY
112–126 T.E.
BELOVED DAUGHTER & SISTER
NOW AT REST AMONG THE STARS
IT'S JUST A PLAQUE ON A WALL. IT'S NOT HER.

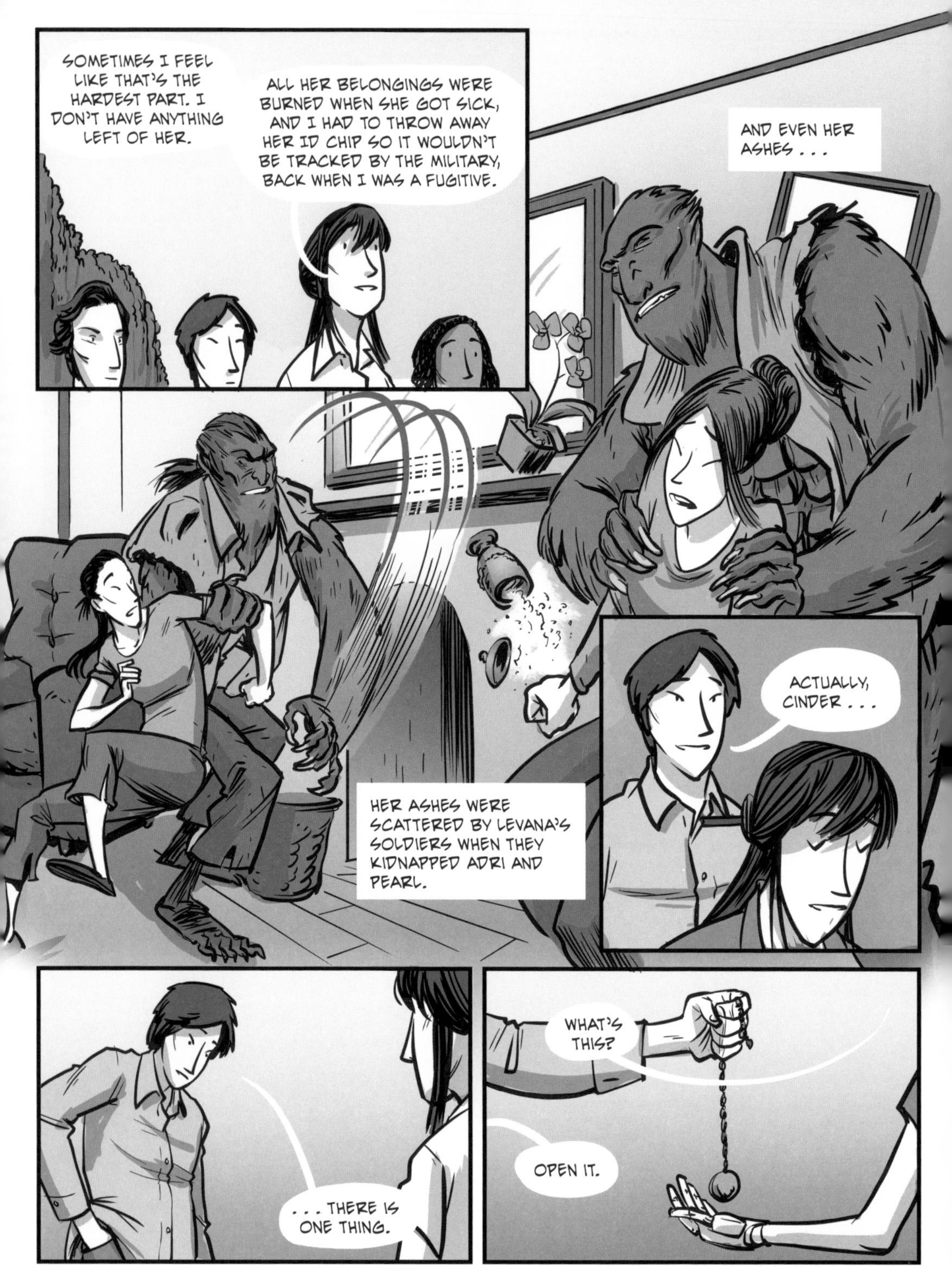
SOMETIMES I FEEL LIKE THAT'S THE HARDEST PART. I DON'T HAVE ANYTHING LEFT OF HER.
ALL HER BELONGINGS WERE BURNED WHEN SHE GOT SICK, AND I HAD TO THROW AWAY HER ID CHIP SO IT WOULDN'T BE TRACKED BY THE MILITARY, BACK WHEN I WAS A FUGITIVE.
AND EVEN HER ASHES . . .
HER ASHES WERE SCATTERED BY LEVANA'S SOLDIERS WHEN THEY KIDNAPPED ADRI AND PEARL.
ACTUALLY, CINDER . . .
. . . THERE IS ONE THING.
WHAT'S THIS?
OPEN IT.

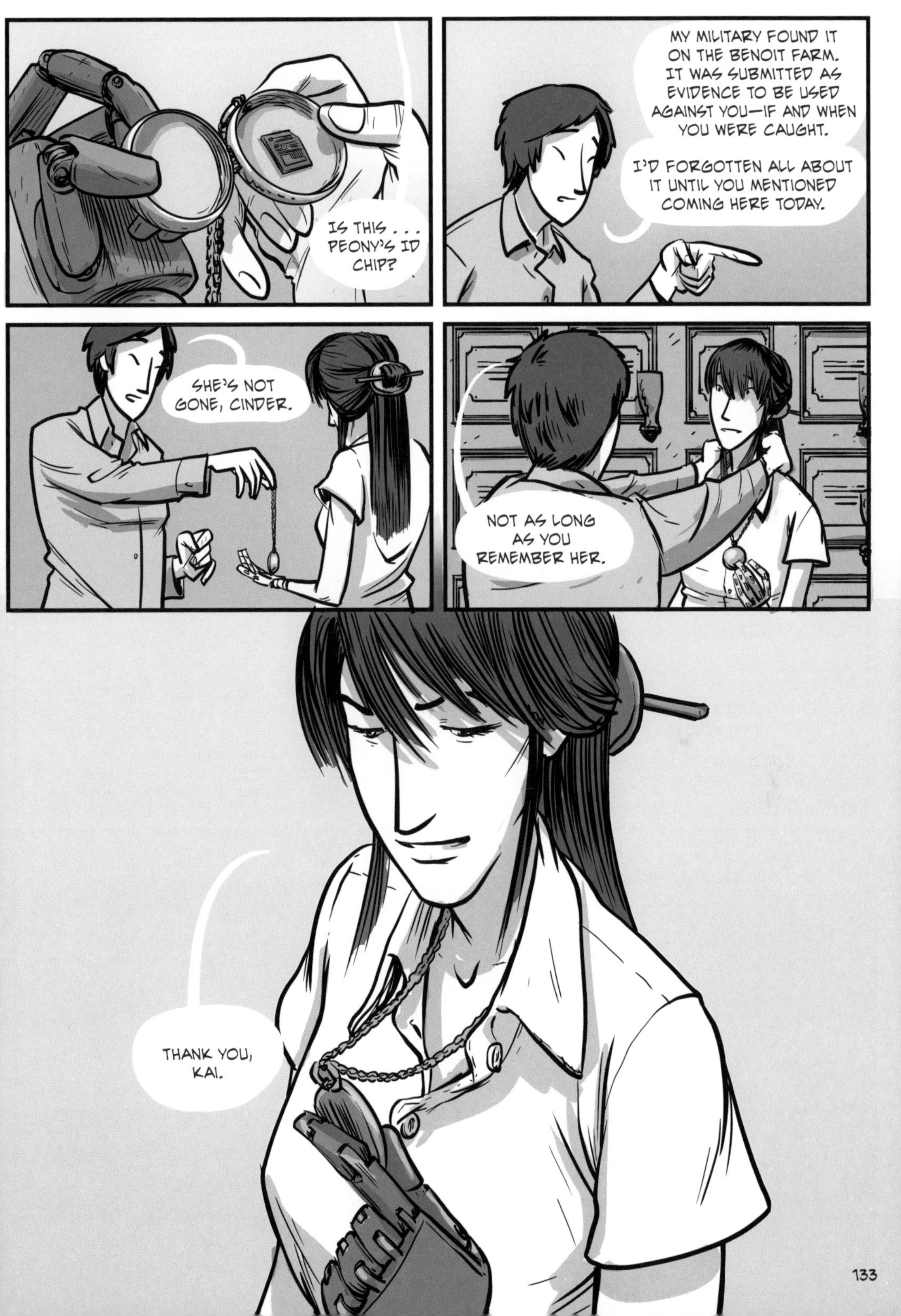
IS THIS . . . PEONY'S ID CHIP?
MY MILITARY FOUND IT ON THE BENOIT FARM. IT WAS SUBMITTED AS EVIDENCE TO BE USED AGAINST YOU—IF AND WHEN YOU WERE CAUGHT.
I'D FORGOTTEN ALL ABOUT IT UNTIL YOU MENTIONED COMING HERE TODAY.
SHE'S NOT GONE, CINDER.
NOT AS LONG AS YOU REMEMBER HER.
THANK YOU, KAI.

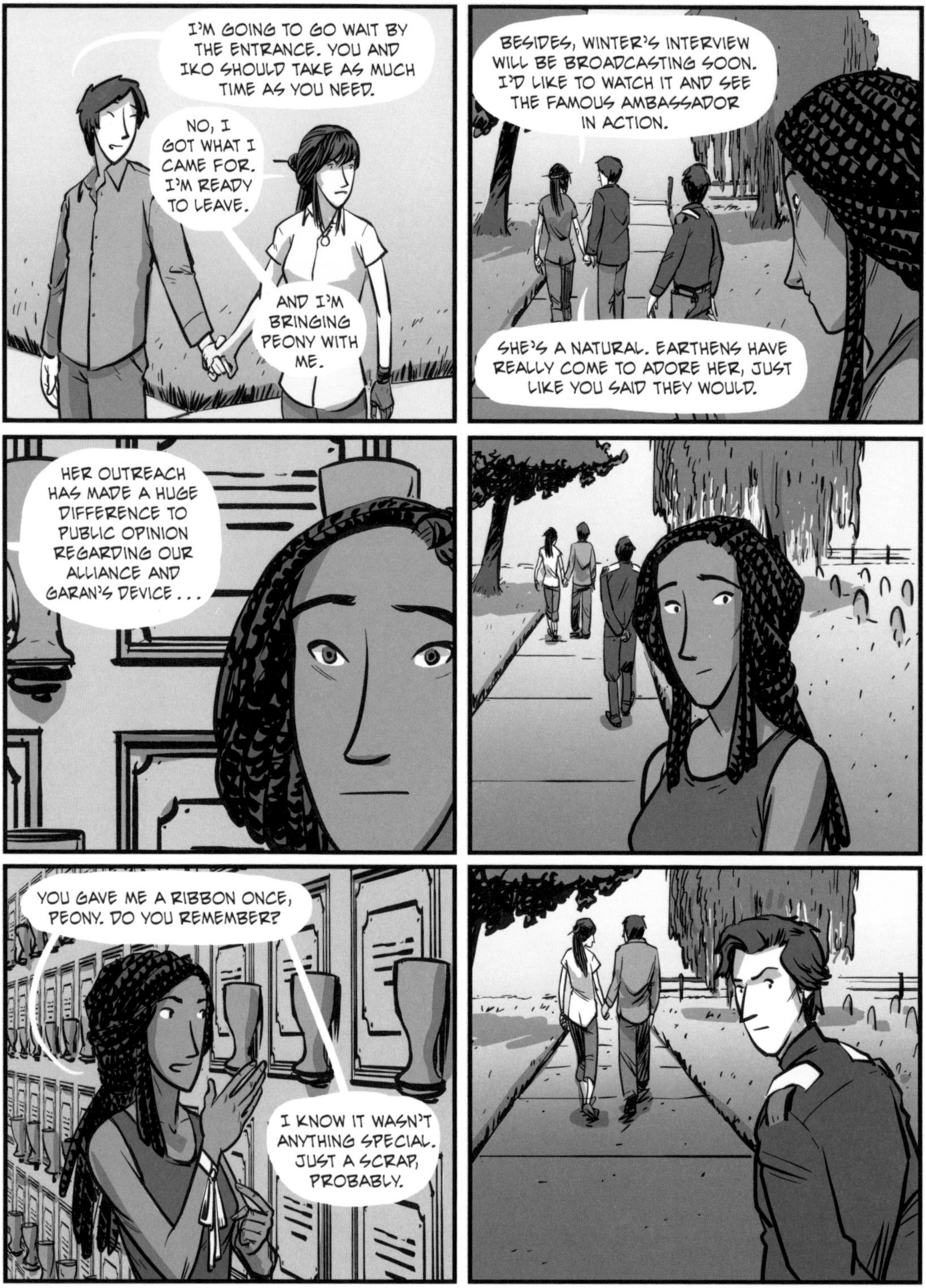

I'M GOING TO GO WAIT BY THE ENTRANCE. YOU AND IKO SHOULD TAKE AS MUCH TIME AS YOU NEED.
NO, I GOT WHAT I CAME FOR. I'M READY TO LEAVE.
AND I'M BRINGING PEONY WITH ME.
BESIDES, WINTER'S INTERVIEW WILL BE BROADCASTING SOON. I'D LIKE TO WATCH IT AND SEE THE FAMOUS AMBASSADOR IN ACTION.
SHE'S A NATURAL. EARTHENS HAVE REALLY COME TO ADORE HER, JUST LIKE YOU SAID THEY WOULD.
HER OUTREACH HAS MADE A HUGE DIFFERENCE TO PUBLIC OPINION REGARDING OUR ALLIANCE AND GARAN'S DEVICE . . .
YOU GAVE ME A RIBBON ONCE, PEONY. DO YOU REMEMBER?
I KNOW IT WASN'T ANYTHING SPECIAL. JUST A SCRAP, PROBABLY.

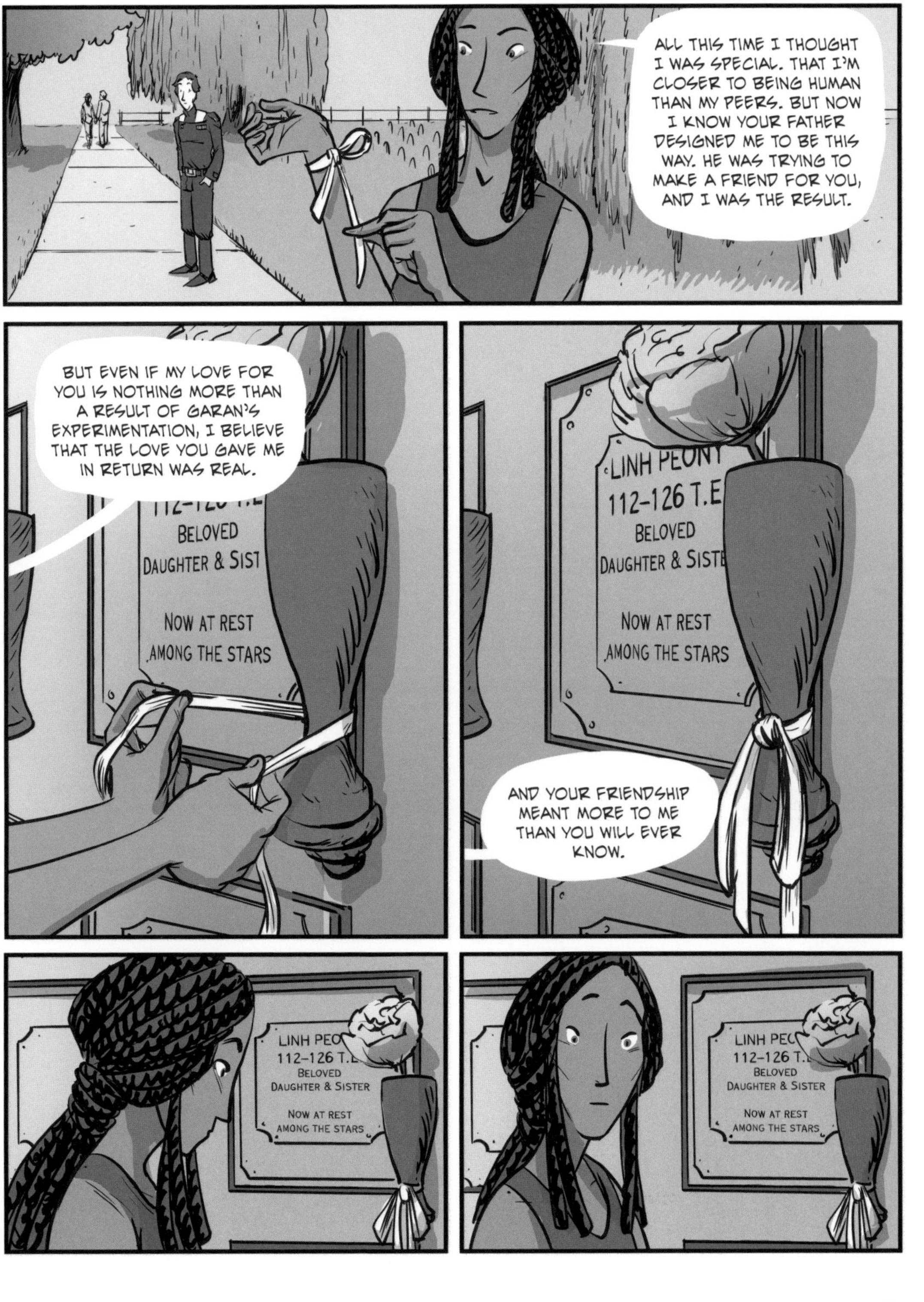
ALL THIS TIME I THOUGHT I WAS SPECIAL. THAT I'M CLOSER TO BEING HUMAN THAN MY PEERS. BUT NOW I KNOW YOUR FATHER DESIGNED ME TO BE THIS WAY. HE WAS TRYING TO MAKE A FRIEND FOR YOU, AND I WAS THE RESULT.
BUT EVEN IF MY LOVE FOR YOU IS NOTHING MORE THAN A RESULT OF GARAN'S EXPERIMENTATION, I BELIEVE THAT THE LOVE YOU GAVE ME IN RETURN WAS REAL.
112-126 T.E
BELOVED
DAUGHTER & SIST
NOW AT REST
AMONG THE STARS
LINH PEONY
112-126 T.E
BELOVED
DAUGHTER & SISTE
NOW AT REST
AMONG THE STARS
AND YOUR FRIENDSHIP MEANT MORE TO ME THAN YOU WILL EVER KNOW.
LINH PEO
112-126 T.E
BELOVED
DAUGHTER & SISTER
NOW AT REST
AMONG THE STARS
LINH PEO
112-126 T.
BELOVED
DAUGHTER & SISTER
NOW AT REST
AMONG THE STARS

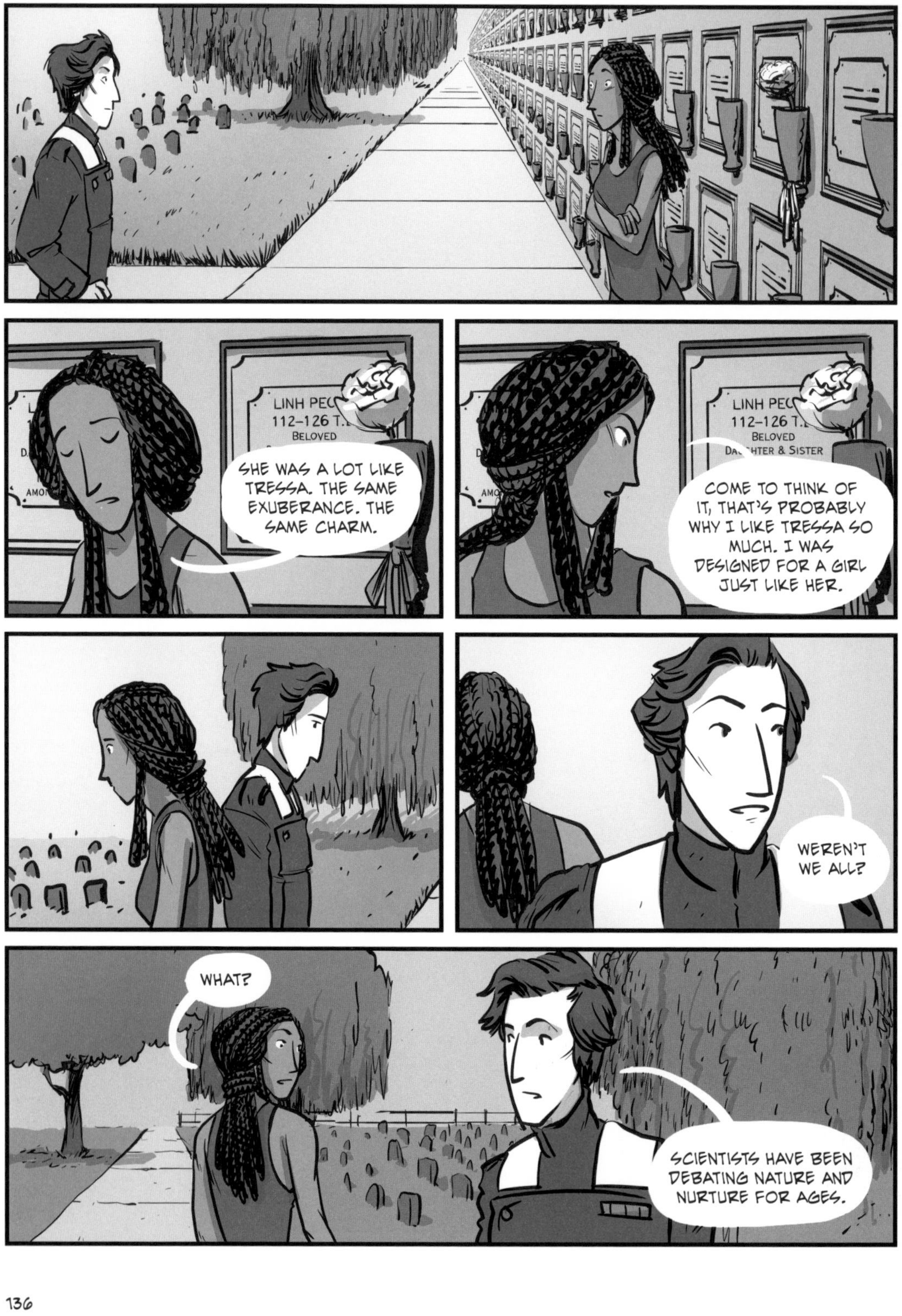
BELOVED
SHE WAS A LOT LIKE TRESSA. THE SAME EXUBERANCE. THE SAME CHARM.
COME TO THINK OF IT, THAT'S PROBABLY WHY I LIKE TRESSA SO MUCH. I WAS DESIGNED FOR A GIRL JUST LIKE HER.
WEREN'T WE ALL?
WHAT?
SCIENTISTS HAVE BEEN DEBATING NATURE AND NURTURE FOR AGES.

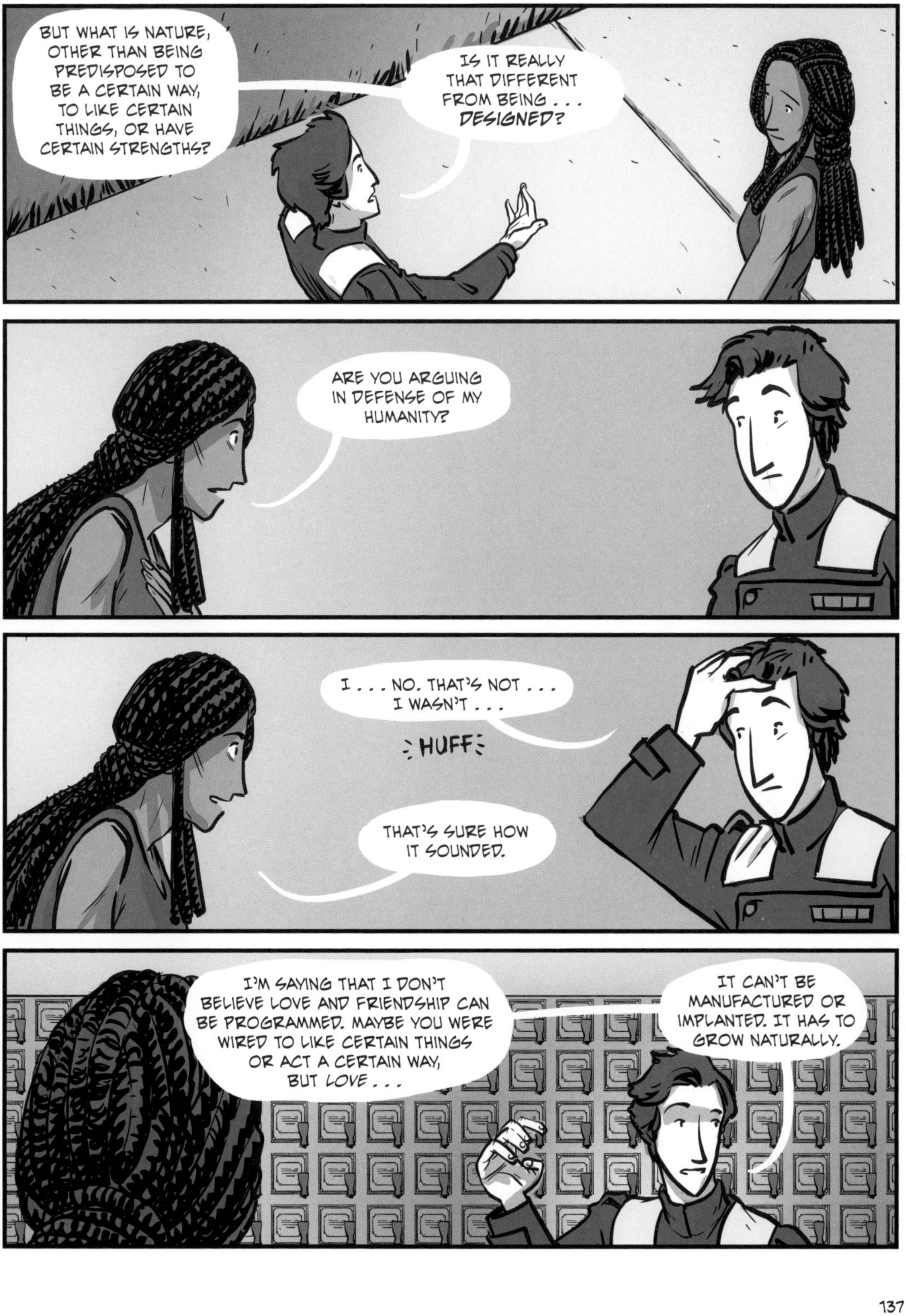
BUT WHAT IS NATURE, OTHER THAN BEING PREDISPOSED TO BE A CERTAIN WAY, TO LIKE CERTAIN THINGS, OR HAVE CERTAIN STRENGTHS?
IS IT REALLY THAT DIFFERENT FROM BEING . . . *DESIGNED*?
ARE YOU ARGUING IN DEFENSE OF MY HUMANITY?
I . . . NO. THAT'S NOT . . . I WASN'T . . .
HUFF
THAT'S SURE HOW IT SOUNDED.
I'M SAYING THAT I DON'T BELIEVE LOVE AND FRIENDSHIP CAN BE PROGRAMMED. MAYBE YOU WERE WIRED TO LIKE CERTAIN THINGS OR ACT A CERTAIN WAY, BUT *LOVE* . . .
IT CAN'T BE MANUFACTURED OR IMPLANTED. IT HAS TO GROW NATURALLY.

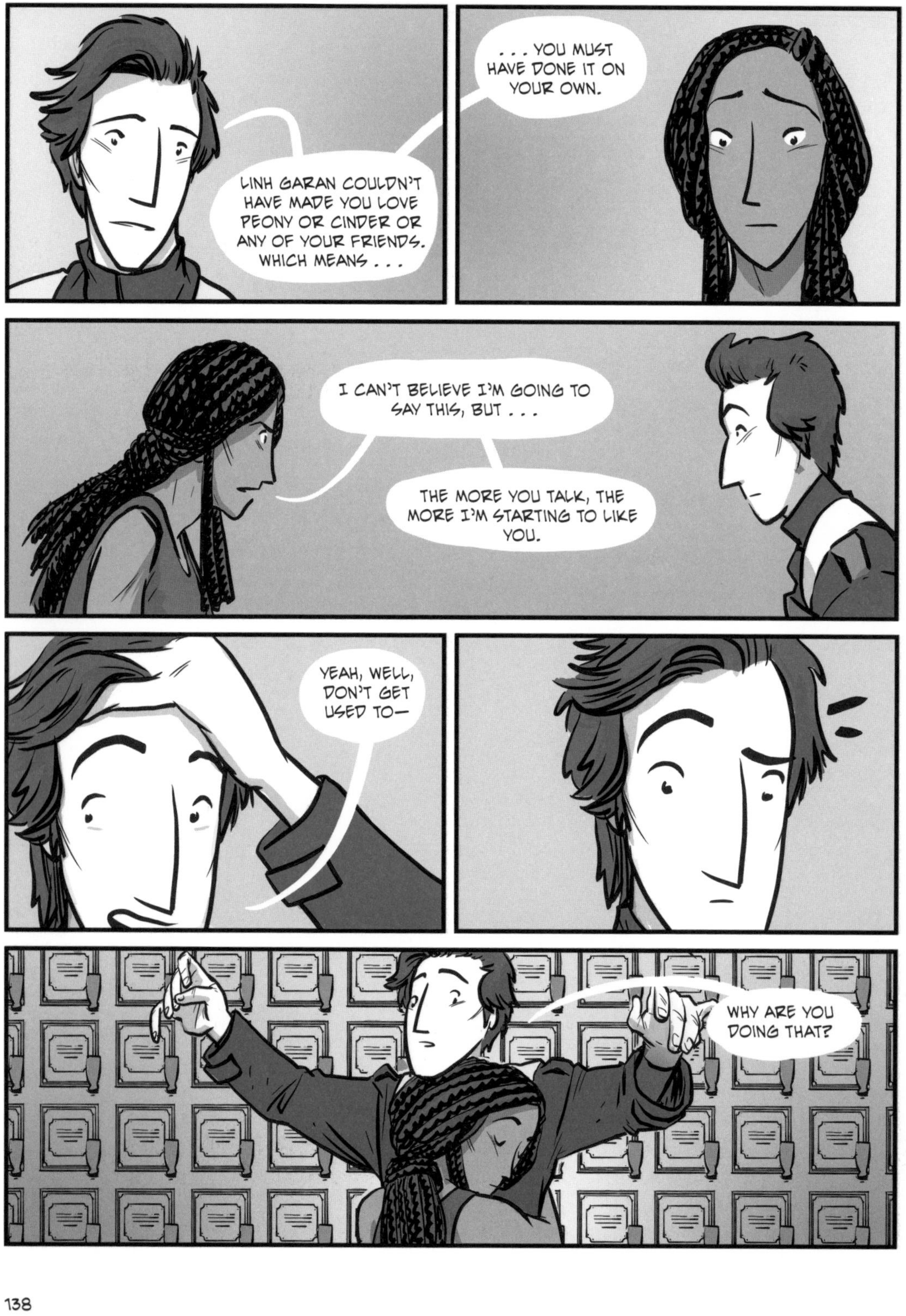
LINH GARAN COULDN'T HAVE MADE YOU LOVE PEONY OR CINDER OR ANY OF YOUR FRIENDS. WHICH MEANS . . .
. . . YOU MUST HAVE DONE IT ON YOUR OWN.
I CAN'T BELIEVE I'M GOING TO SAY THIS, BUT . . .
THE MORE YOU TALK, THE MORE I'M STARTING TO LIKE YOU.
YEAH, WELL, DON'T GET USED TO—
WHY ARE YOU DOING THAT?

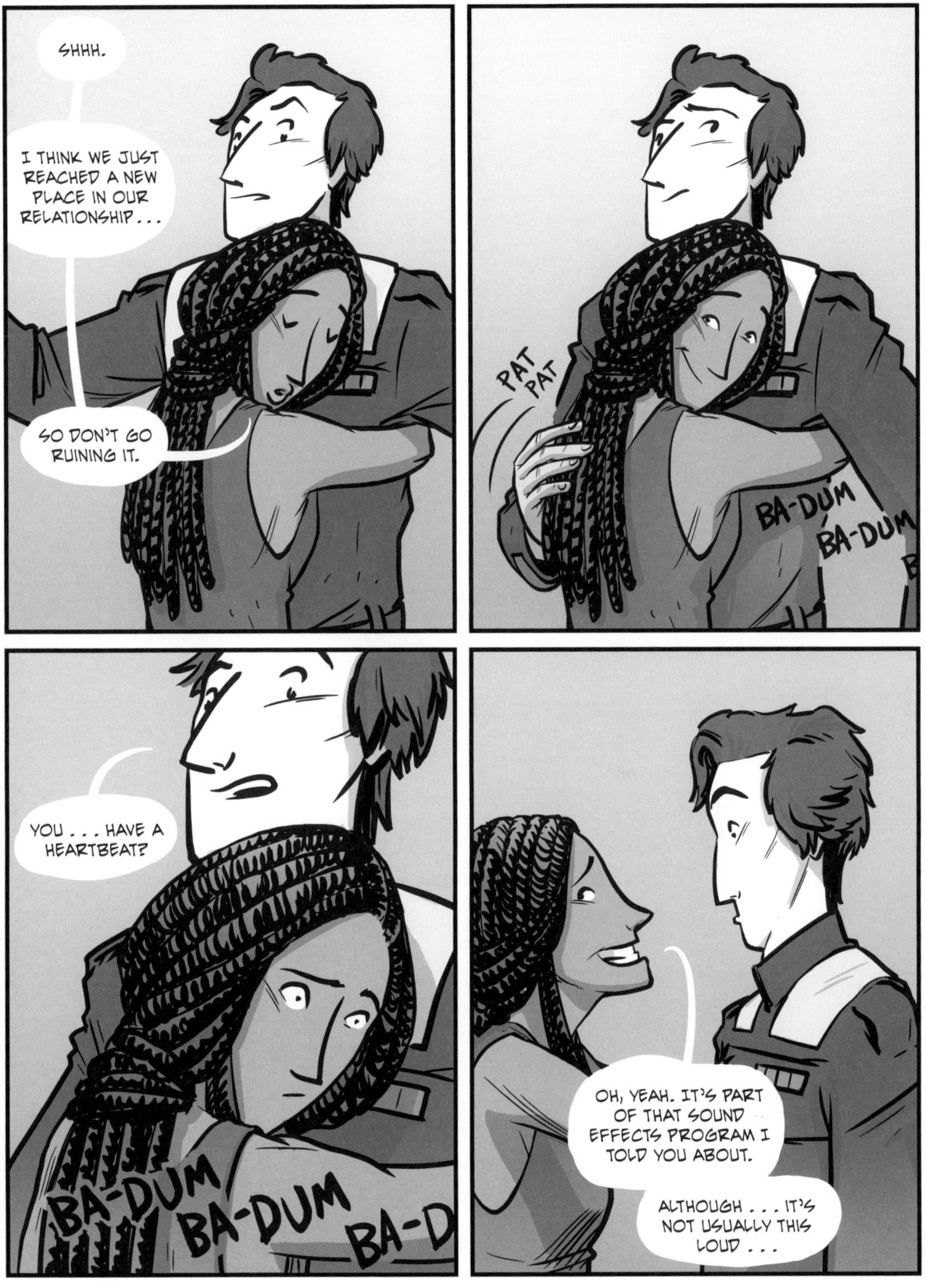
SHHH.
I THINK WE JUST REACHED A NEW PLACE IN OUR RELATIONSHIP . . .
SO DON'T GO RUINING IT.
PAT PAT
BA-DUM
BA-DUM
YOU . . . HAVE A HEARTBEAT?
BA-DUM
BA-DUM
OH, YEAH. IT'S PART OF THAT SOUND EFFECTS PROGRAM I TOLD YOU ABOUT.
ALTHOUGH . . . IT'S NOT USUALLY THIS LOUD . . .

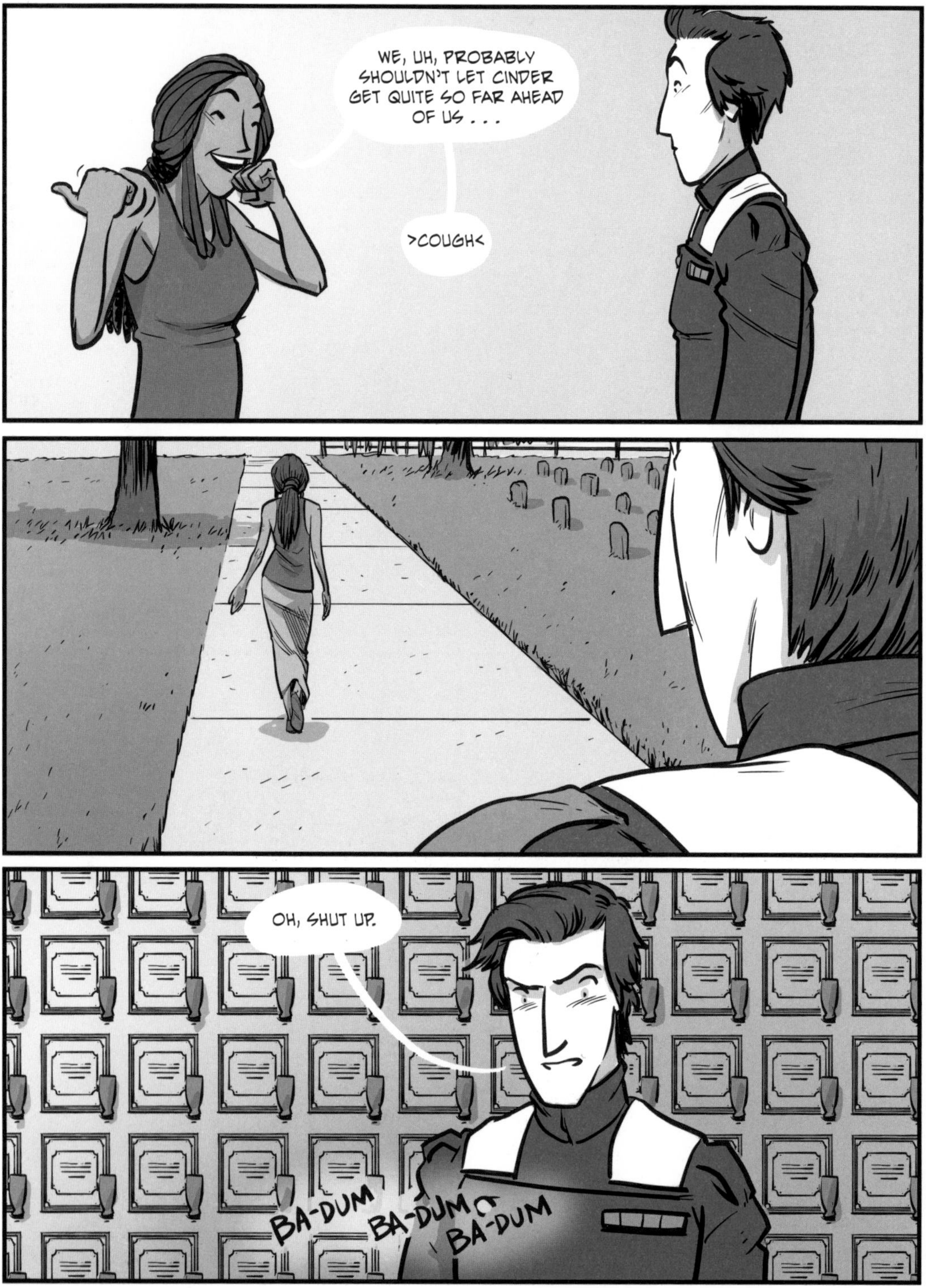
WE, UH, PROBABLY SHOULDN'T LET CINDER GET QUITE SO FAR AHEAD OF US . . .
>COUGH<
OH, SHUT UP.
BA-DUM
BA-DUM
BA-DUM

CHAPTER VI

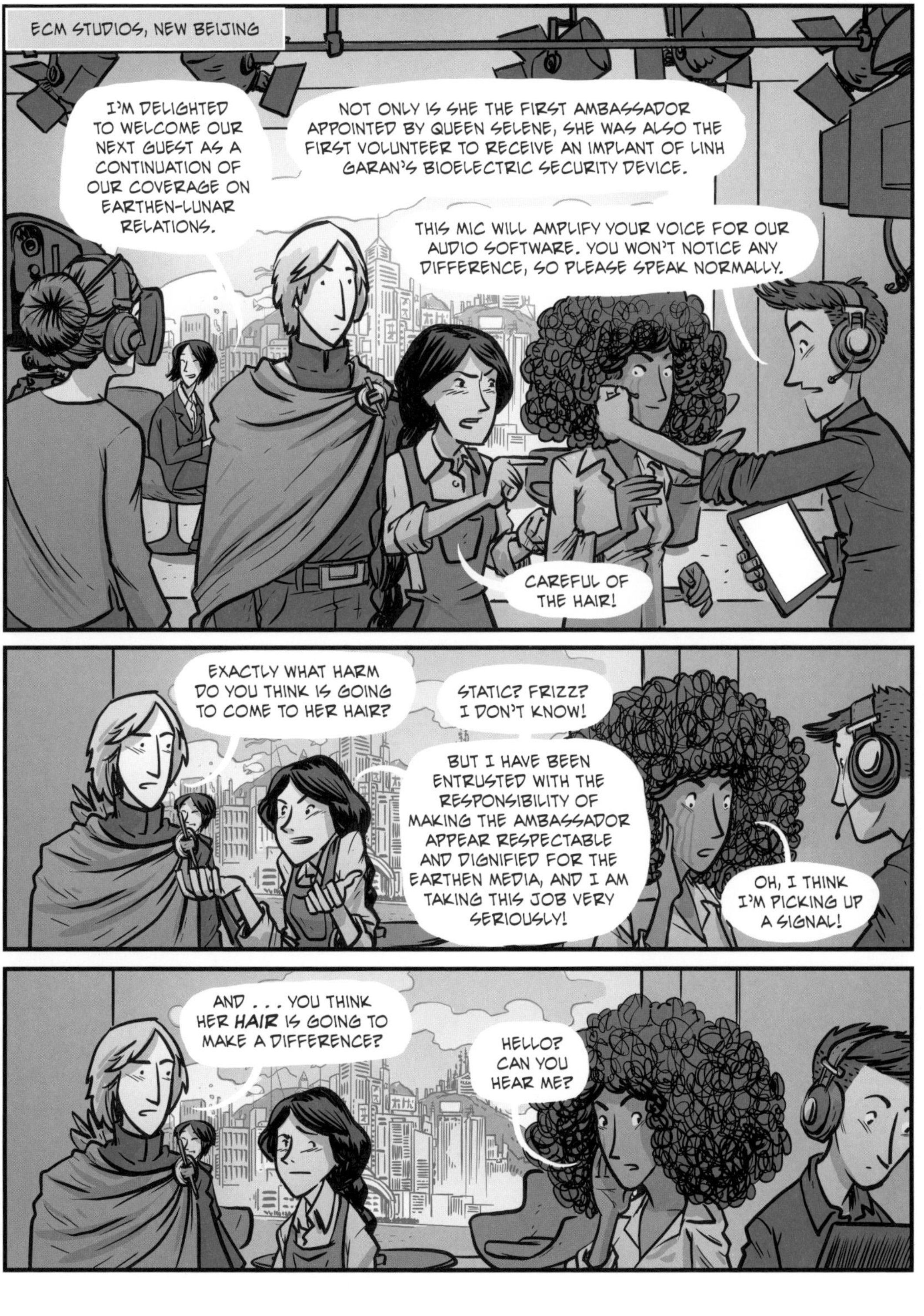
ECM STUDIOS, NEW BEIJING
I'M DELIGHTED TO WELCOME OUR NEXT GUEST AS A CONTINUATION OF OUR COVERAGE ON EARTHEN-LUNAR RELATIONS.
NOT ONLY IS SHE THE FIRST AMBASSADOR APPOINTED BY QUEEN SELENE, SHE WAS ALSO THE FIRST VOLUNTEER TO RECEIVE AN IMPLANT OF LINH GARAN'S BIOELECTRIC SECURITY DEVICE.
THIS MIC WILL AMPLIFY YOUR VOICE FOR OUR AUDIO SOFTWARE. YOU WON'T NOTICE ANY DIFFERENCE, SO PLEASE SPEAK NORMALLY.
CAREFUL OF THE HAIR!
EXACTLY WHAT HARM DO YOU THINK IS GOING TO COME TO HER HAIR?
STATIC? FRIZZ? I DON'T KNOW!
BUT I HAVE BEEN ENTRUSTED WITH THE RESPONSIBILITY OF MAKING THE AMBASSADOR APPEAR RESPECTABLE AND DIGNIFIED FOR THE EARTHEN MEDIA, AND I AM TAKING THIS JOB VERY SERIOUSLY!
OH, I THINK I'M PICKING UP A SIGNAL!
AND . . . YOU THINK HER **HAIR** IS GOING TO MAKE A DIFFERENCE?
HELLO? CAN YOU HEAR ME?

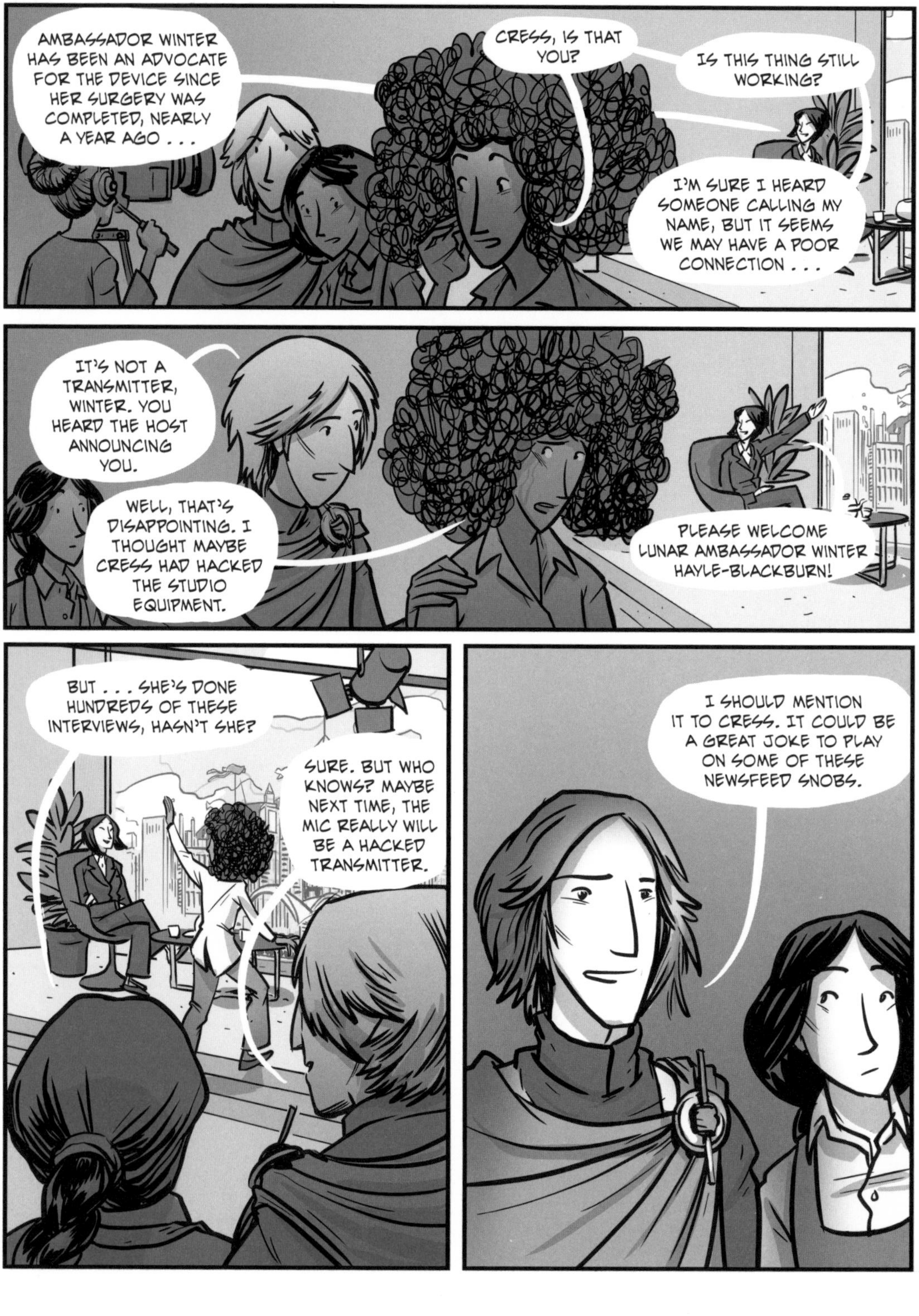
AMBASSADOR WINTER HAS BEEN AN ADVOCATE FOR THE DEVICE SINCE HER SURGERY WAS COMPLETED, NEARLY A YEAR AGO . . .
CRESS, IS THAT YOU?
IS THIS THING STILL WORKING?
I'M SURE I HEARD SOMEONE CALLING MY NAME, BUT IT SEEMS WE MAY HAVE A POOR CONNECTION . . .
IT'S NOT A TRANSMITTER, WINTER. YOU HEARD THE HOST ANNOUNCING YOU.
WELL, THAT'S DISAPPOINTING. I THOUGHT MAYBE CRESS HAD HACKED THE STUDIO EQUIPMENT.
PLEASE WELCOME LUNAR AMBASSADOR WINTER HAYLE-BLACKBURN!
BUT . . . SHE'S DONE HUNDREDS OF THESE INTERVIEWS, HASN'T SHE?
SURE. BUT WHO KNOWS? MAYBE NEXT TIME, THE MIC REALLY WILL BE A HACKED TRANSMITTER.
I SHOULD MENTION IT TO CRESS. IT COULD BE A GREAT JOKE TO PLAY ON SOME OF THESE NEWSFEED SNOBS.

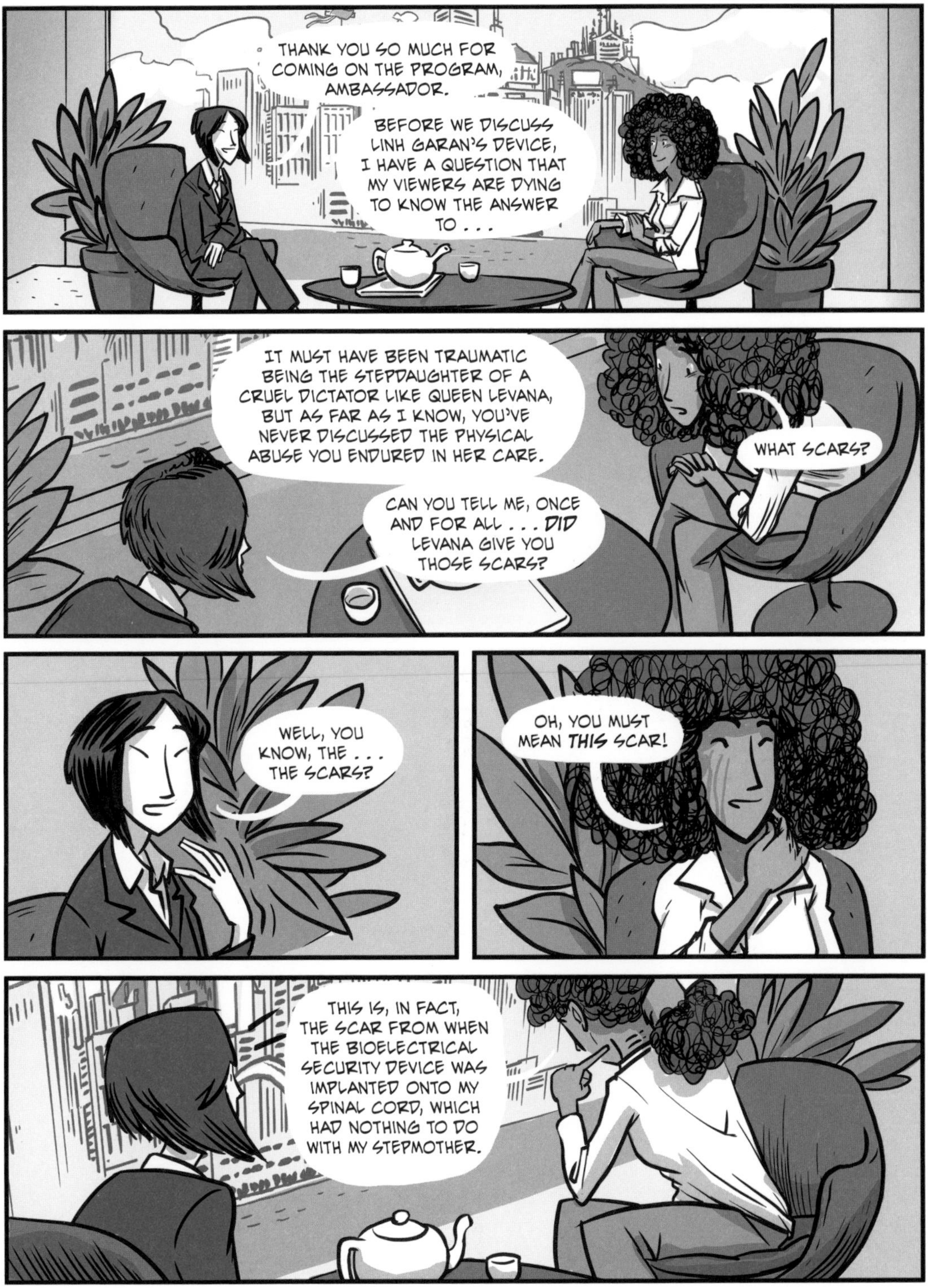
THANK YOU SO MUCH FOR COMING ON THE PROGRAM, AMBASSADOR.
BEFORE WE DISCUSS LINH GARAN'S DEVICE, I HAVE A QUESTION THAT MY VIEWERS ARE DYING TO KNOW THE ANSWER TO . . .
IT MUST HAVE BEEN TRAUMATIC BEING THE STEPDAUGHTER OF A CRUEL DICTATOR LIKE QUEEN LEVANA, BUT AS FAR AS I KNOW, YOU'VE NEVER DISCUSSED THE PHYSICAL ABUSE YOU ENDURED IN HER CARE.
CAN YOU TELL ME, ONCE AND FOR ALL . . . DID LEVANA GIVE YOU THOSE SCARS?
WHAT SCARS?
WELL, YOU KNOW, THE . . . THE SCARS?
OH, YOU MUST MEAN THIS SCAR!
THIS IS, IN FACT, THE SCAR FROM WHEN THE BIOELECTRICAL SECURITY DEVICE WAS IMPLANTED ONTO MY SPINAL CORD, WHICH HAD NOTHING TO DO WITH MY STEPMOTHER.

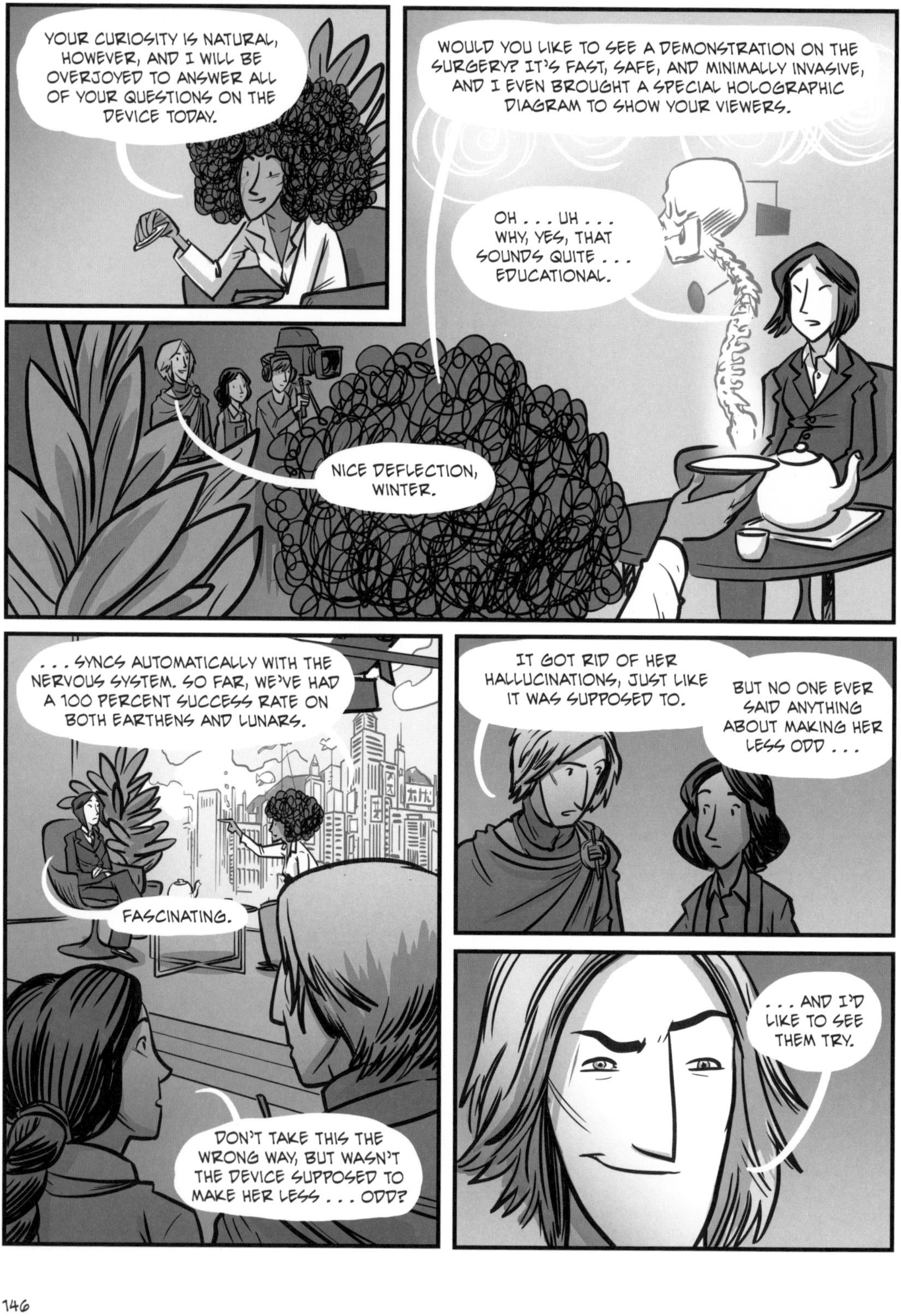
YOUR CURIOSITY IS NATURAL, HOWEVER, AND I WILL BE OVERJOYED TO ANSWER ALL OF YOUR QUESTIONS ON THE DEVICE TODAY.
WOULD YOU LIKE TO SEE A DEMONSTRATION ON THE SURGERY? IT'S FAST, SAFE, AND MINIMALLY INVASIVE, AND I EVEN BROUGHT A SPECIAL HOLOGRAPHIC DIAGRAM TO SHOW YOUR VIEWERS.
OH . . . UH . . . WHY, YES, THAT SOUNDS QUITE . . . EDUCATIONAL.
NICE DEFLECTION, WINTER.
. . . SYNCS AUTOMATICALLY WITH THE NERVOUS SYSTEM. SO FAR, WE'VE HAD A 100 PERCENT SUCCESS RATE ON BOTH EARTHENS AND LUNARS.
FASCINATING.
DON'T TAKE THIS THE WRONG WAY, BUT WASN'T THE DEVICE SUPPOSED TO MAKE HER LESS . . . ODD?
IT GOT RID OF HER HALLUCINATIONS, JUST LIKE IT WAS SUPPOSED TO.
BUT NO ONE EVER SAID ANYTHING ABOUT MAKING HER LESS ODD . . .
. . . AND I'D LIKE TO SEE THEM TRY.

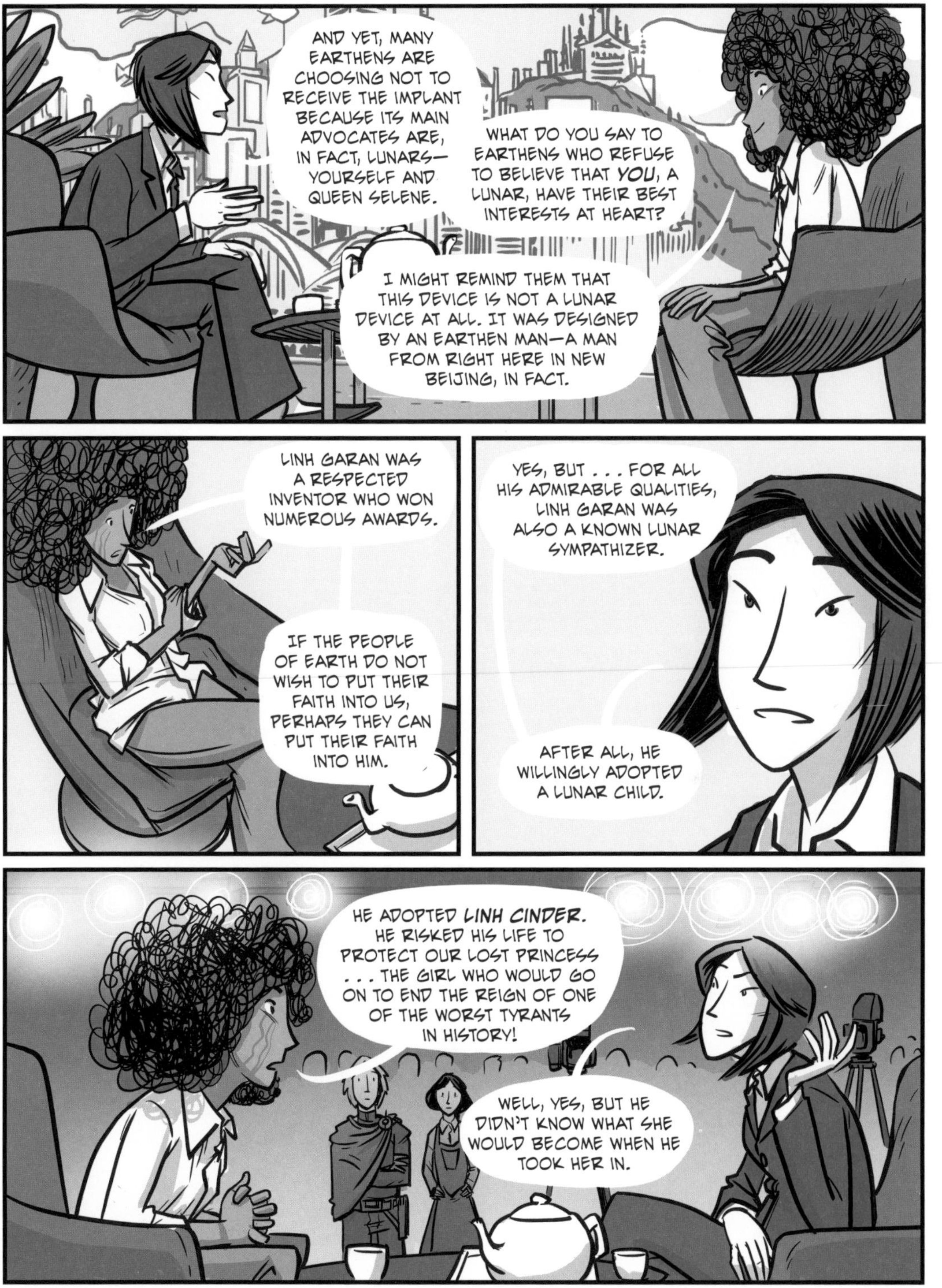
AND YET, MANY EARTHENS ARE CHOOSING NOT TO RECEIVE THE IMPLANT BECAUSE ITS MAIN ADVOCATES ARE, IN FACT, LUNARS—YOURSELF AND QUEEN SELENE.
WHAT DO YOU SAY TO EARTHENS WHO REFUSE TO BELIEVE THAT *YOU*, A LUNAR, HAVE THEIR BEST INTERESTS AT HEART?
I MIGHT REMIND THEM THAT THIS DEVICE IS NOT A LUNAR DEVICE AT ALL. IT WAS DESIGNED BY AN EARTHEN MAN—A MAN FROM RIGHT HERE IN NEW BEIJING, IN FACT.
LINH GARAN WAS A RESPECTED INVENTOR WHO WON NUMEROUS AWARDS.
IF THE PEOPLE OF EARTH DO NOT WISH TO PUT THEIR FAITH INTO US, PERHAPS THEY CAN PUT THEIR FAITH INTO HIM.
YES, BUT . . . FOR ALL HIS ADMIRABLE QUALITIES, LINH GARAN WAS ALSO A KNOWN LUNAR SYMPATHIZER.
AFTER ALL, HE WILLINGLY ADOPTED A LUNAR CHILD.
HE ADOPTED ***LINH CINDER.*** HE RISKED HIS LIFE TO PROTECT OUR LOST PRINCESS . . . THE GIRL WHO WOULD GO ON TO END THE REIGN OF ONE OF THE WORST TYRANTS IN HISTORY!
WELL, YES, BUT HE DIDN'T KNOW WHAT SHE WOULD BECOME WHEN HE TOOK HER IN.

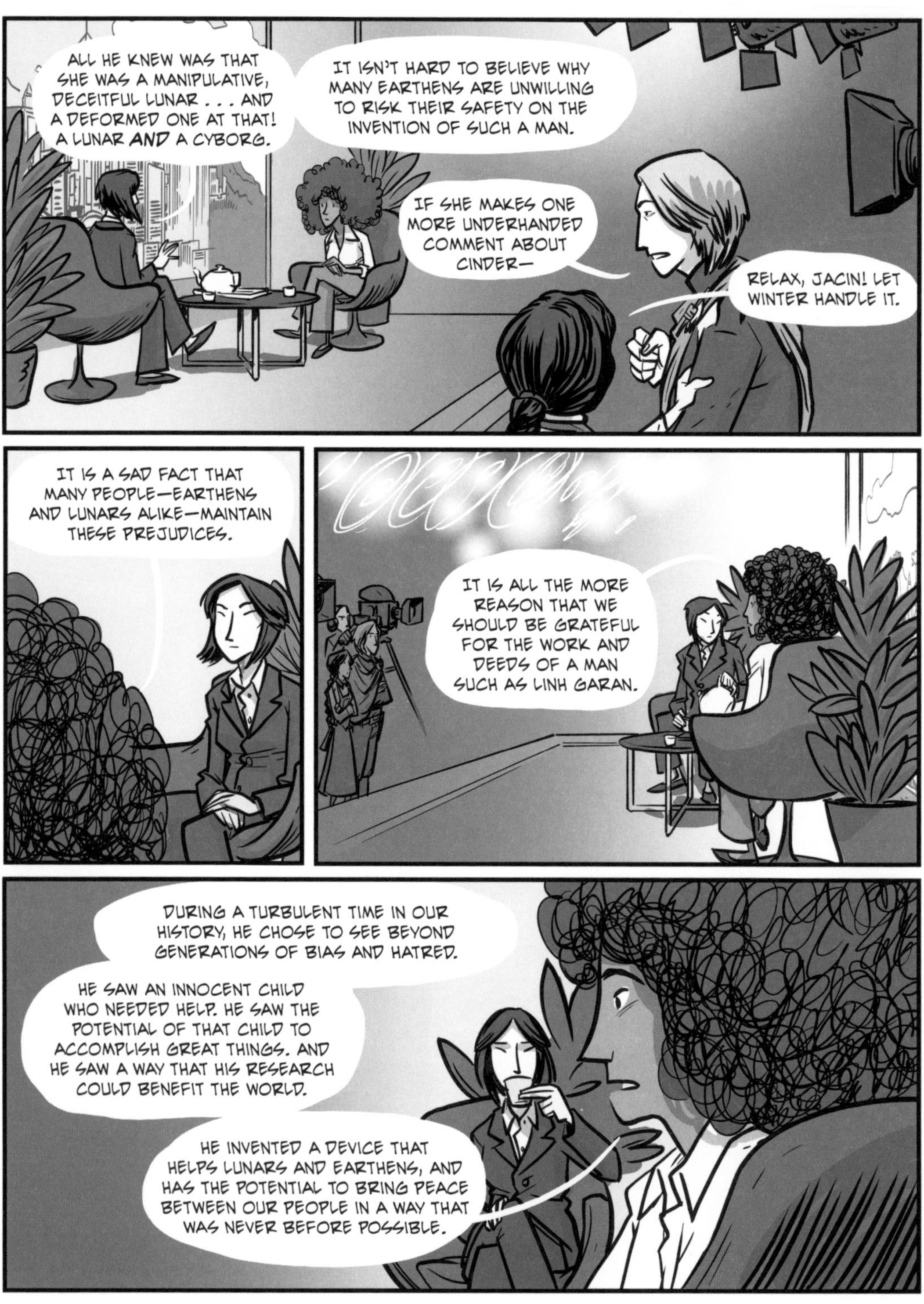
ALL HE KNEW WAS THAT SHE WAS A MANIPULATIVE, DECEITFUL LUNAR . . . AND A DEFORMED ONE AT THAT! A LUNAR AND A CYBORG.
IT ISN'T HARD TO BELIEVE WHY MANY EARTHENS ARE UNWILLING TO RISK THEIR SAFETY ON THE INVENTION OF SUCH A MAN.
IF SHE MAKES ONE MORE UNDERHANDED COMMENT ABOUT CINDER—
RELAX, JACIN! LET WINTER HANDLE IT.
IT IS A SAD FACT THAT MANY PEOPLE—EARTHENS AND LUNARS ALIKE—MAINTAIN THESE PREJUDICES.
IT IS ALL THE MORE REASON THAT WE SHOULD BE GRATEFUL FOR THE WORK AND DEEDS OF A MAN SUCH AS LINH GARAN.
DURING A TURBULENT TIME IN OUR HISTORY, HE CHOSE TO SEE BEYOND GENERATIONS OF BIAS AND HATRED.
HE SAW AN INNOCENT CHILD WHO NEEDED HELP. HE SAW THE POTENTIAL OF THAT CHILD TO ACCOMPLISH GREAT THINGS. AND HE SAW A WAY THAT HIS RESEARCH COULD BENEFIT THE WORLD.
HE INVENTED A DEVICE THAT HELPS LUNARS AND EARTHENS, AND HAS THE POTENTIAL TO BRING PEACE BETWEEN OUR PEOPLE IN A WAY THAT WAS NEVER BEFORE POSSIBLE.

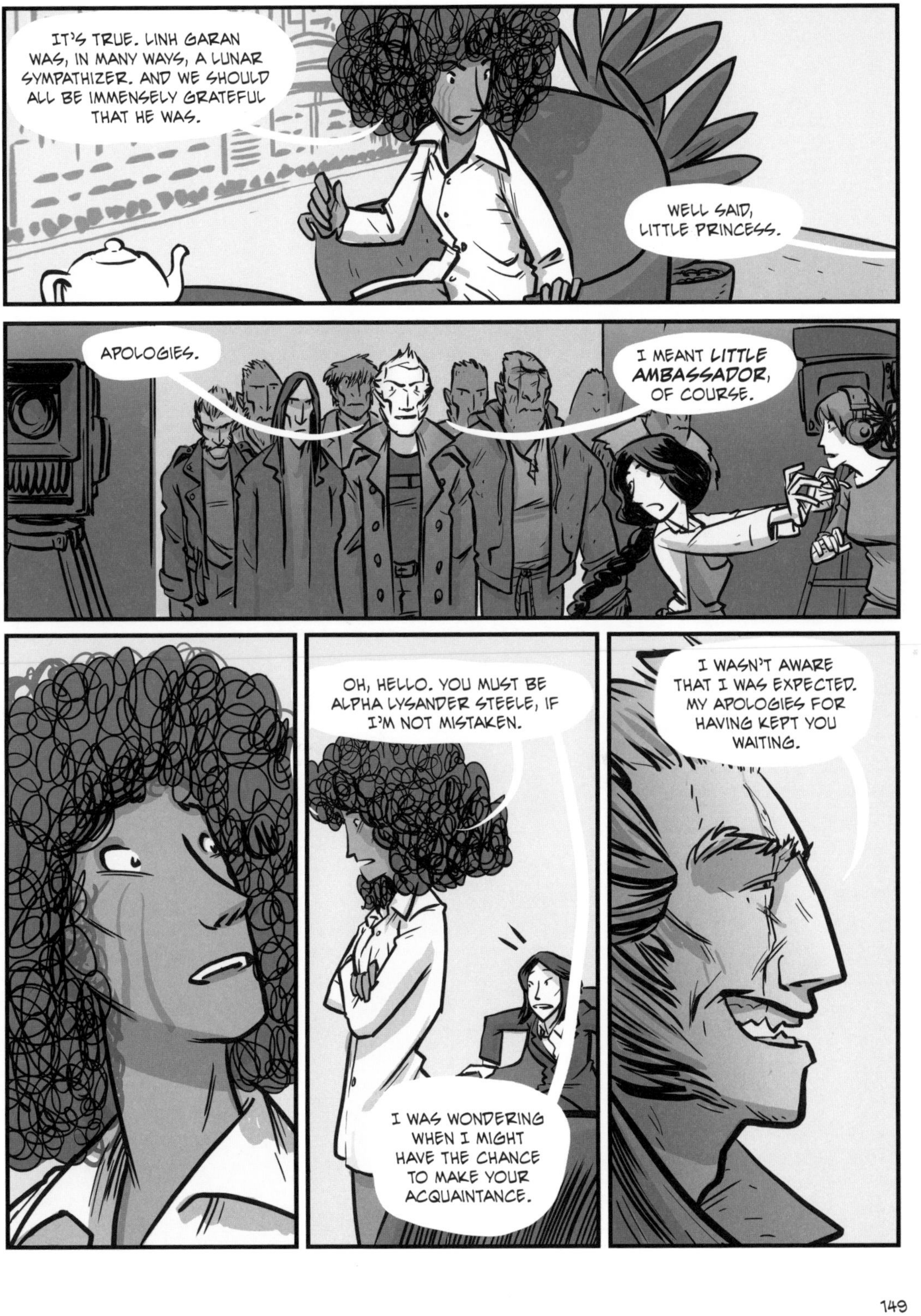
IT'S TRUE. LINH GARAN WAS, IN MANY WAYS, A LUNAR SYMPATHIZER. AND WE SHOULD ALL BE IMMENSELY GRATEFUL THAT HE WAS.
WELL SAID, LITTLE PRINCESS.
APOLOGIES.
I MEANT LITTLE AMBASSADOR, OF COURSE.
OH, HELLO. YOU MUST BE ALPHA LYSANDER STEELE, IF I'M NOT MISTAKEN.
I WAS WONDERING WHEN I MIGHT HAVE THE CHANCE TO MAKE YOUR ACQUAINTANCE.
I WASN'T AWARE THAT I WAS EXPECTED. MY APOLOGIES FOR HAVING KEPT YOU WAITING.

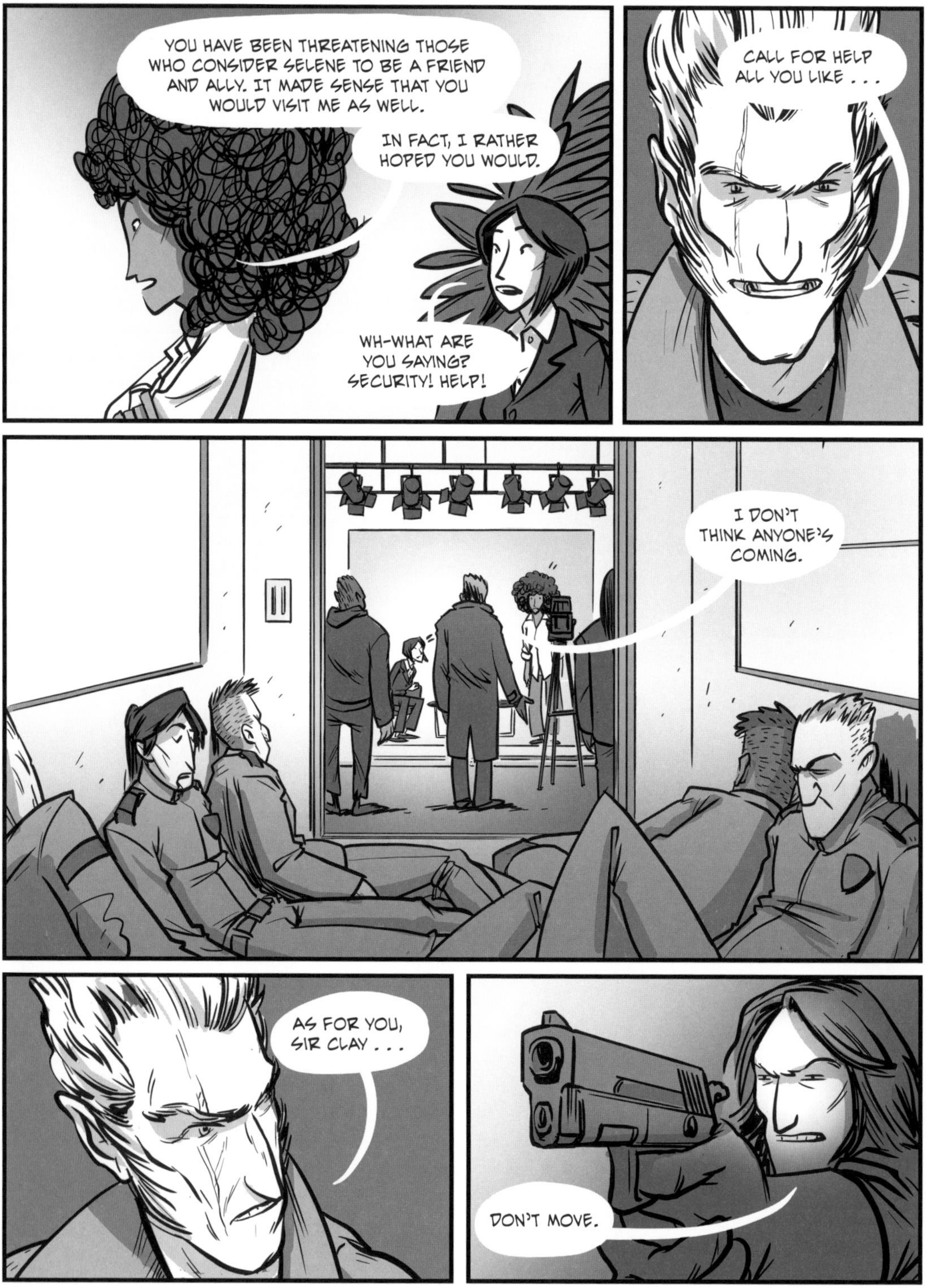
YOU HAVE BEEN THREATENING THOSE WHO CONSIDER SELENE TO BE A FRIEND AND ALLY. IT MADE SENSE THAT YOU WOULD VISIT ME AS WELL.
IN FACT, I RATHER HOPED YOU WOULD.
WH-WHAT ARE YOU SAYING? SECURITY! HELP!
CALL FOR HELP ALL YOU LIKE . . .
I DON'T THINK ANYONE'S COMING.
AS FOR YOU, SIR CLAY . . .
DON'T MOVE.

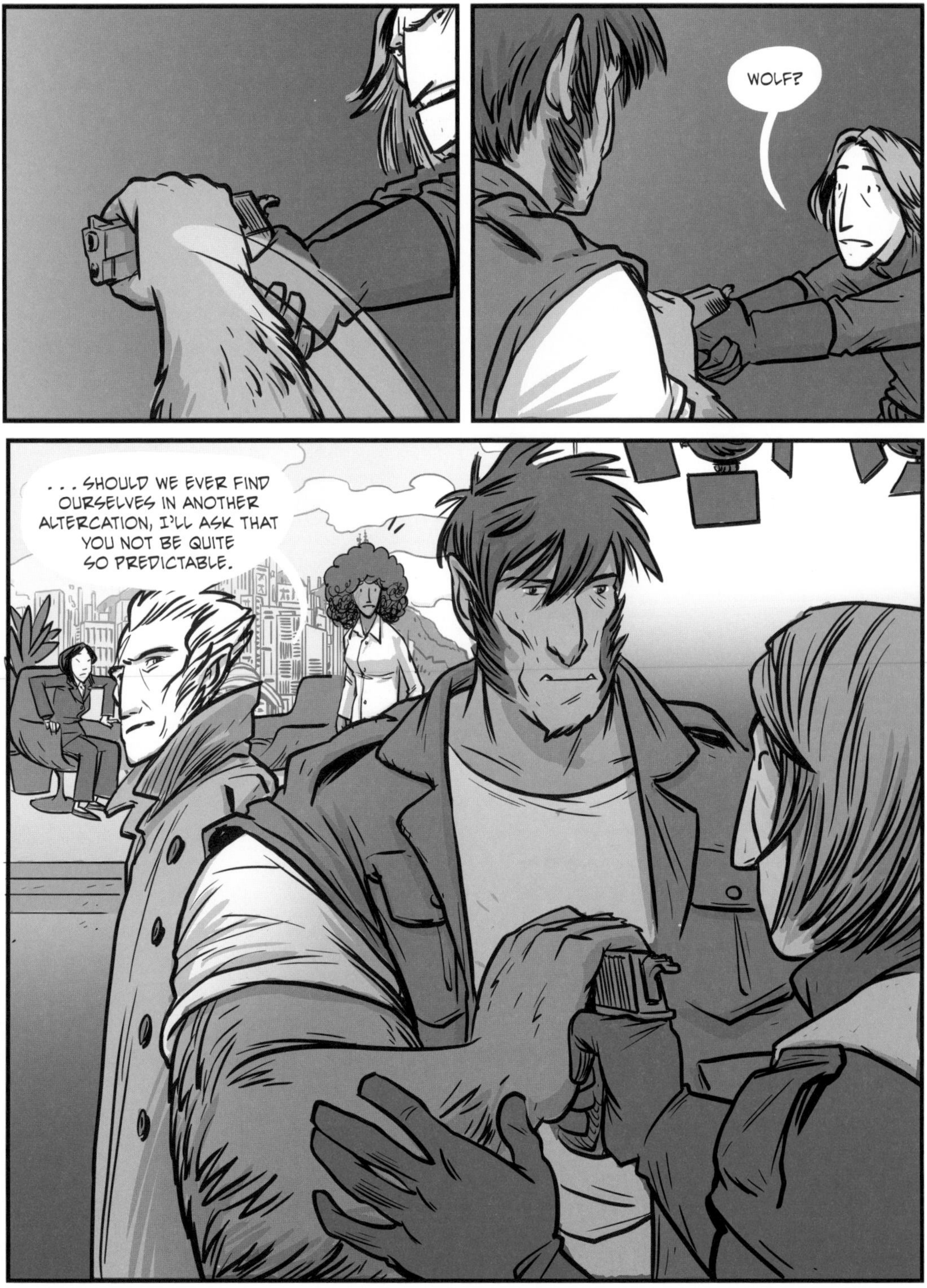
WOLF?
. . . SHOULD WE EVER FIND OURSELVES IN ANOTHER ALTERCATION, I'LL ASK THAT YOU NOT BE QUITE SO PREDICTABLE.

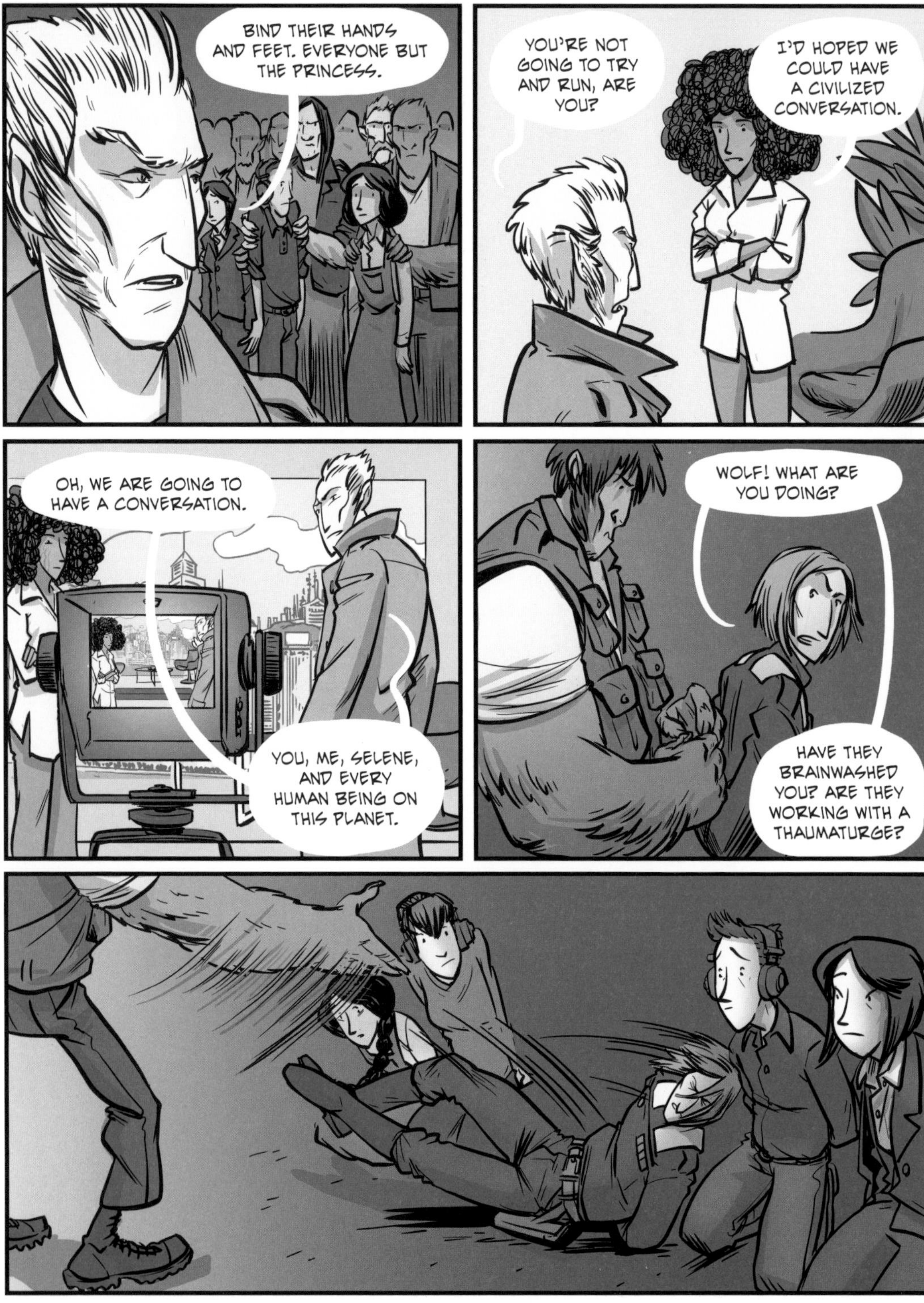
BIND THEIR HANDS AND FEET. EVERYONE BUT THE PRINCESS.
YOU'RE NOT GOING TO TRY AND RUN, ARE YOU?
I'D HOPED WE COULD HAVE A CIVILIZED CONVERSATION.
OH, WE ARE GOING TO HAVE A CONVERSATION.
YOU, ME, SELENE, AND EVERY HUMAN BEING ON THIS PLANET.
WOLF! WHAT ARE YOU DOING?
HAVE THEY BRAINWASHED YOU? ARE THEY WORKING WITH A THAUMATURGE?

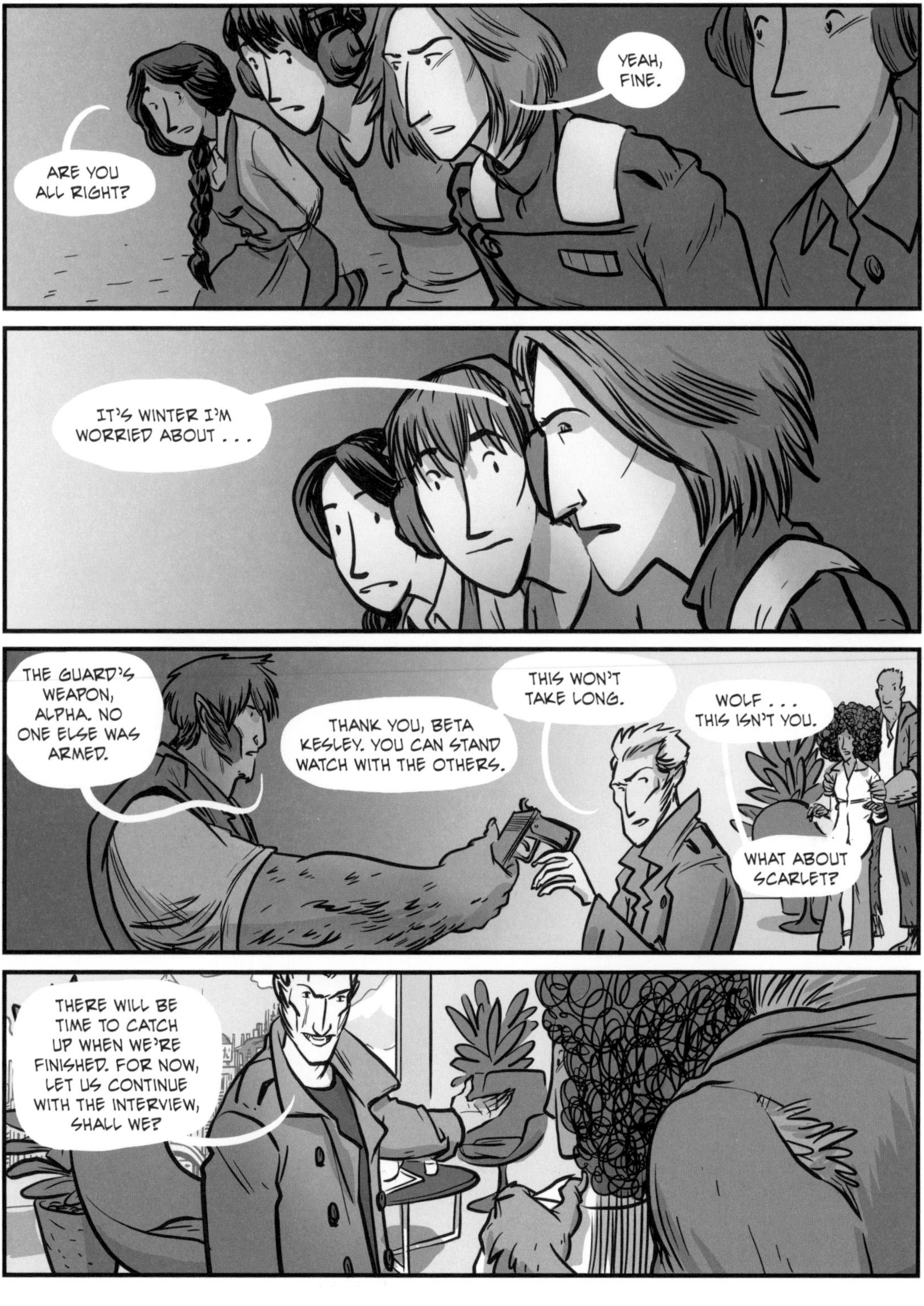
ARE YOU ALL RIGHT?
YEAH, FINE.
IT'S WINTER I'M WORRIED ABOUT . . .
THE GUARD'S WEAPON, ALPHA. NO ONE ELSE WAS ARMED.
THANK YOU, BETA KESLEY. YOU CAN STAND WATCH WITH THE OTHERS.
THIS WON'T TAKE LONG.
WOLF . . . THIS ISN'T YOU.
WHAT ABOUT SCARLET?
THERE WILL BE TIME TO CATCH UP WHEN WE'RE FINISHED. FOR NOW, LET US CONTINUE WITH THE INTERVIEW, SHALL WE?

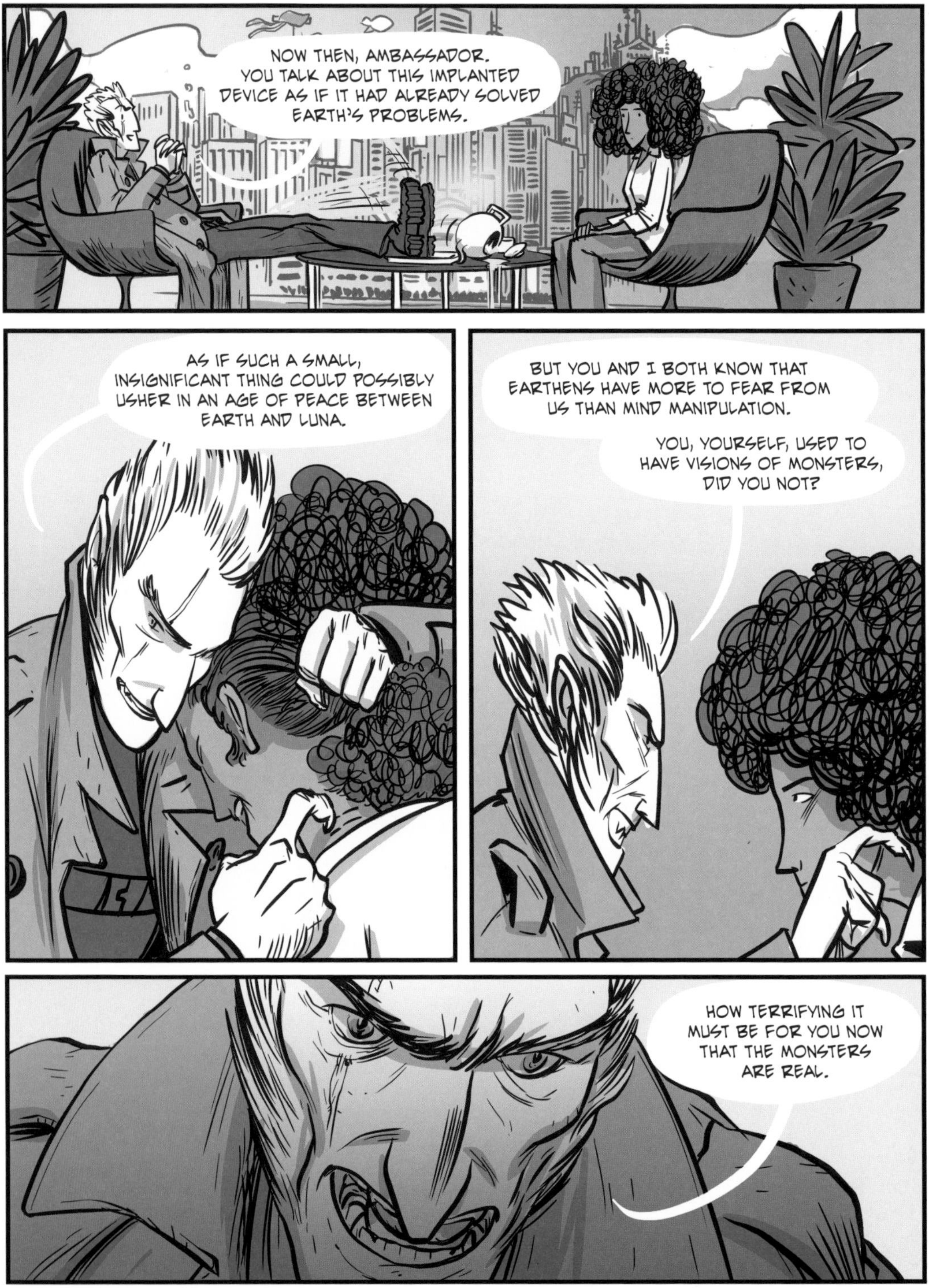
NOW THEN, AMBASSADOR. YOU TALK ABOUT THIS IMPLANTED DEVICE AS IF IT HAD ALREADY SOLVED EARTH'S PROBLEMS.
AS IF SUCH A SMALL, INSIGNIFICANT THING COULD POSSIBLY USHER IN AN AGE OF PEACE BETWEEN EARTH AND LUNA.
BUT YOU AND I BOTH KNOW THAT EARTHENS HAVE MORE TO FEAR FROM US THAN MIND MANIPULATION.
YOU, YOURSELF, USED TO HAVE VISIONS OF MONSTERS, DID YOU NOT?
HOW TERRIFYING IT MUST BE FOR YOU NOW THAT THE MONSTERS ARE REAL.

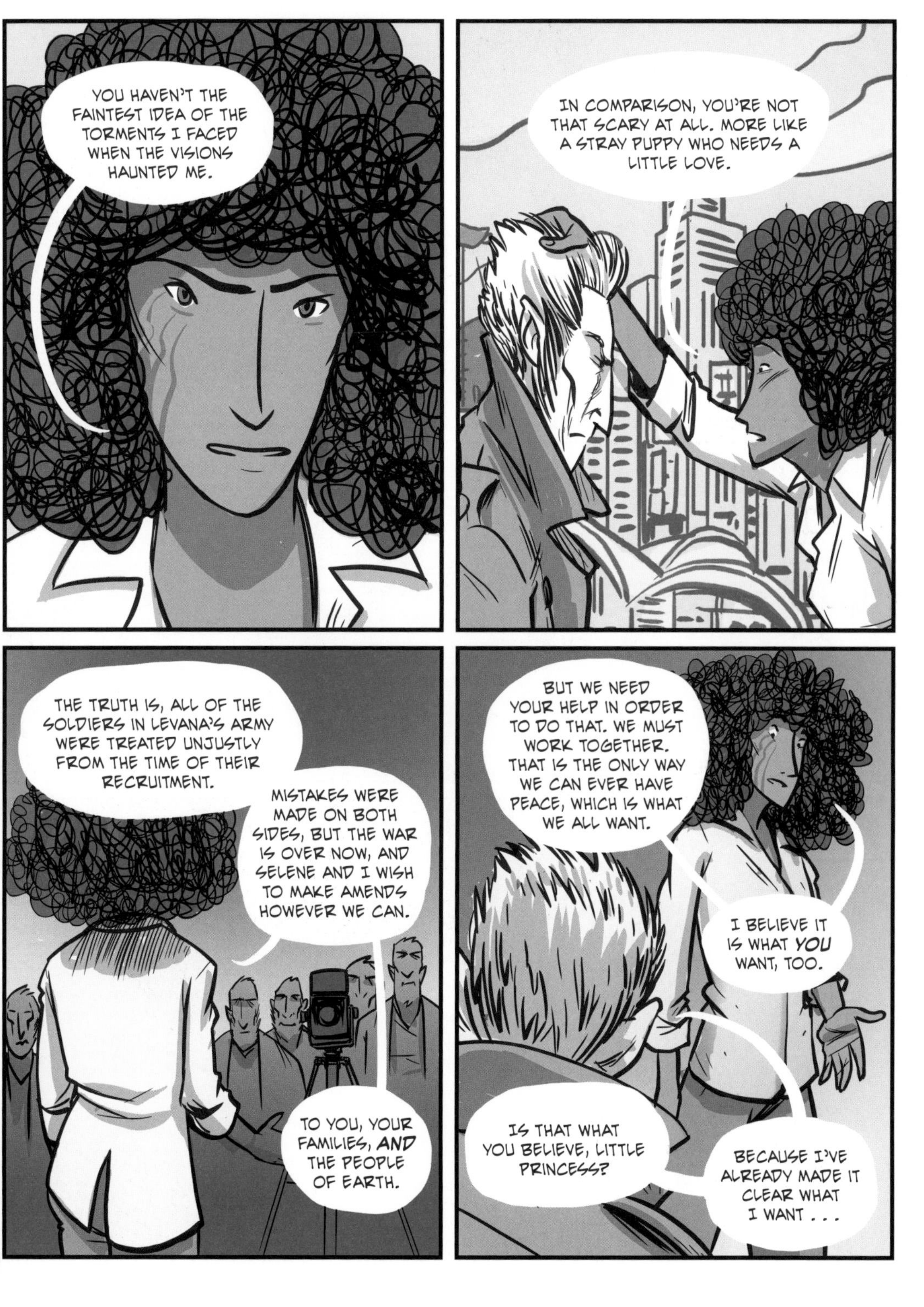

YOU HAVEN'T THE FAINTEST IDEA OF THE TORMENTS I FACED WHEN THE VISIONS HAUNTED ME.
IN COMPARISON, YOU'RE NOT THAT SCARY AT ALL. MORE LIKE A STRAY PUPPY WHO NEEDS A LITTLE LOVE.
THE TRUTH IS, ALL OF THE SOLDIERS IN LEVANA'S ARMY WERE TREATED UNJUSTLY FROM THE TIME OF THEIR RECRUITMENT.
MISTAKES WERE MADE ON BOTH SIDES, BUT THE WAR IS OVER NOW, AND SELENE AND I WISH TO MAKE AMENDS HOWEVER WE CAN.
TO YOU, YOUR FAMILIES, **AND** THE PEOPLE OF EARTH.
BUT WE NEED YOUR HELP IN ORDER TO DO THAT. WE MUST WORK TOGETHER. THAT IS THE ONLY WAY WE CAN EVER HAVE PEACE, WHICH IS WHAT WE ALL WANT.
I BELIEVE IT IS WHAT ***YOU*** WANT, TOO.
IS THAT WHAT YOU BELIEVE, LITTLE PRINCESS?
BECAUSE I'VE ALREADY MADE IT CLEAR WHAT I WANT . . .

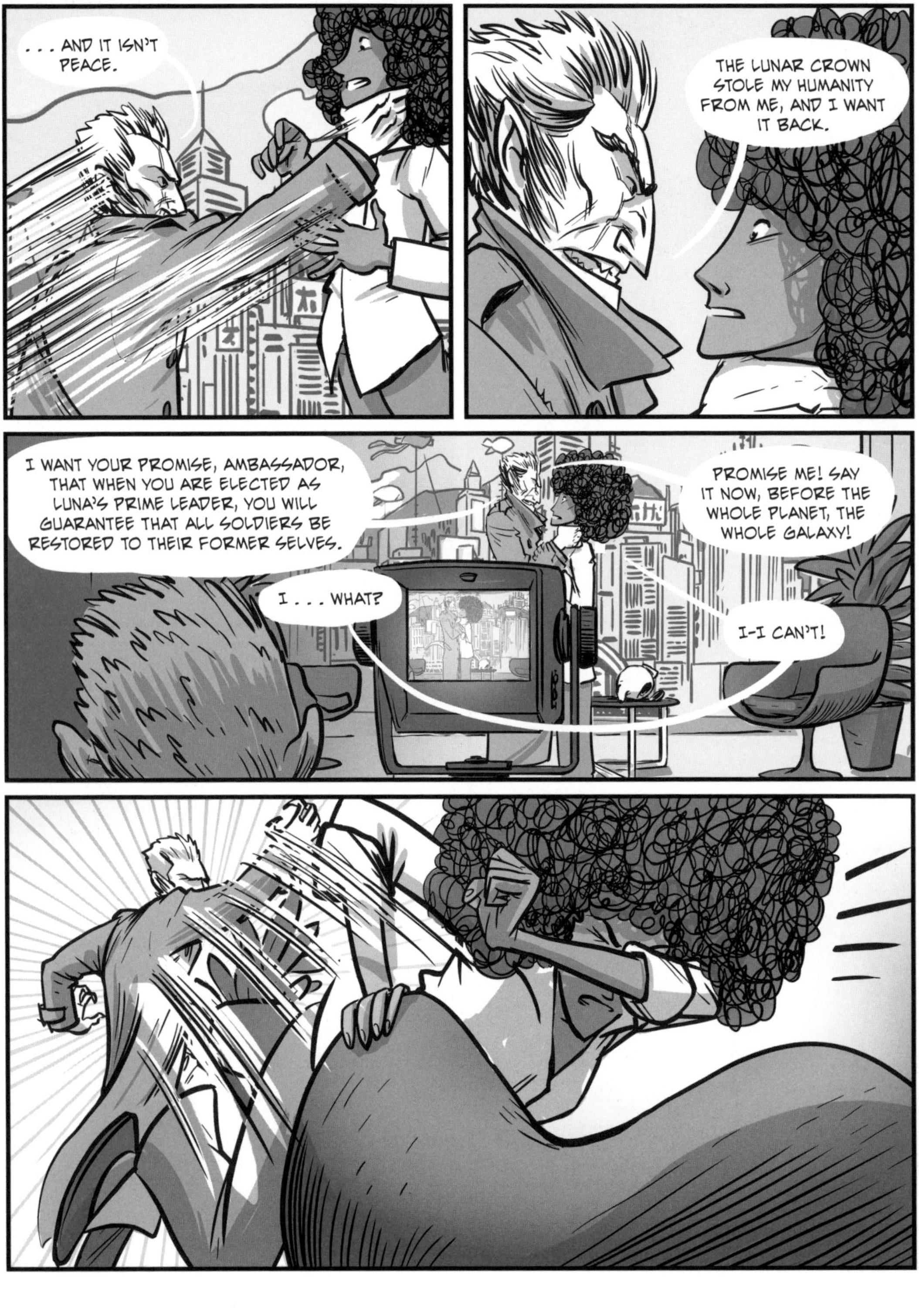
. . . AND IT ISN'T PEACE.
THE LUNAR CROWN STOLE MY HUMANITY FROM ME, AND I WANT IT BACK.
I WANT YOUR PROMISE, AMBASSADOR, THAT WHEN YOU ARE ELECTED AS LUNA'S PRIME LEADER, YOU WILL GUARANTEE THAT ALL SOLDIERS BE RESTORED TO THEIR FORMER SELVES.
PROMISE ME! SAY IT NOW, BEFORE THE WHOLE PLANET, THE WHOLE GALAXY!
I . . . WHAT?
I-I CAN'T!

I WANT YOUR WORD, AMBASSADOR.

I HAVE NO INTENTION OF BECOMING THE PRIME LEADER, AND EVEN IF I DID—

DO NOT LIE TO ME!

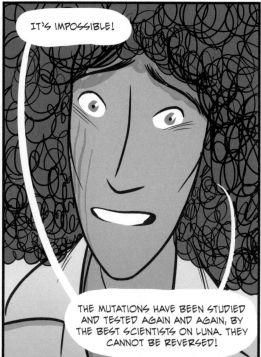

IT'S IMPOSSIBLE!

THE MUTATIONS HAVE BEEN STUDIED AND TESTED AGAIN AND AGAIN, BY THE BEST SCIENTISTS ON LUNA. THEY CANNOT BE REVERSED!

I SWEAR TO YOU. WE WOULD GLADLY RETURN YOUR HUMANITY IF WE COULD, BUT IT CANNOT BE DONE.

IF THIS IS TRUE, THEN WHAT AMENDS CAN YOU POSSIBLY THINK TO MAKE US?

WE CAN BRING YOU HOME AGAIN. WE CAN HELP YOU BECOME PART OF OUR SOCIETY ONCE MORE. AFTER ALL, WE ARE ALL LEARNING OUR PLACE IN THIS NEW WORLD.

LET US HELP YOU!

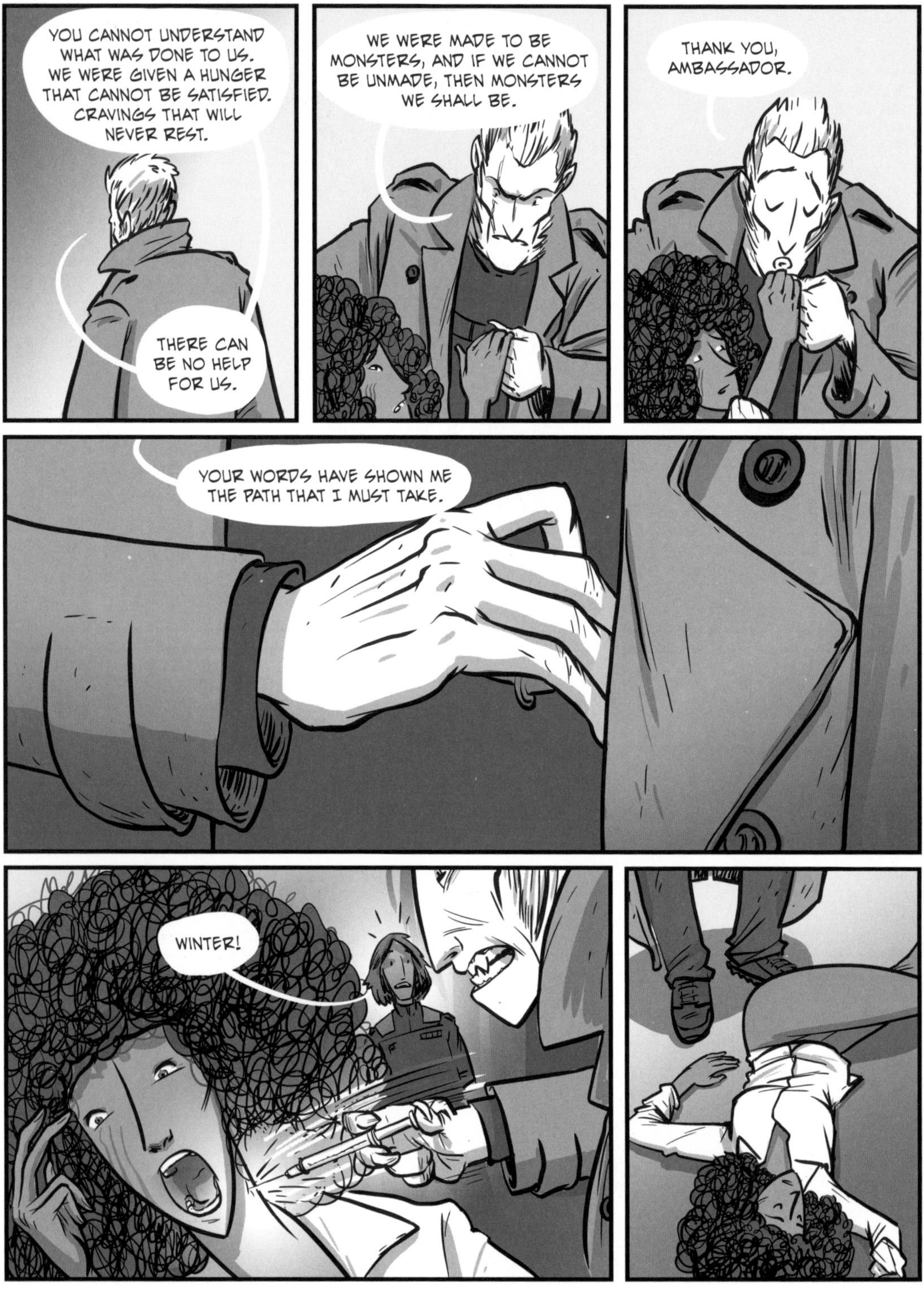
YOU CANNOT UNDERSTAND WHAT WAS DONE TO US. WE WERE GIVEN A HUNGER THAT CANNOT BE SATISFIED. CRAVINGS THAT WILL NEVER REST.
THERE CAN BE NO HELP FOR US.
WE WERE MADE TO BE MONSTERS, AND IF WE CANNOT BE UNMADE, THEN MONSTERS WE SHALL BE.
THANK YOU, AMBASSADOR.
YOUR WORDS HAVE SHOWN ME THE PATH THAT I MUST TAKE.
WINTER!

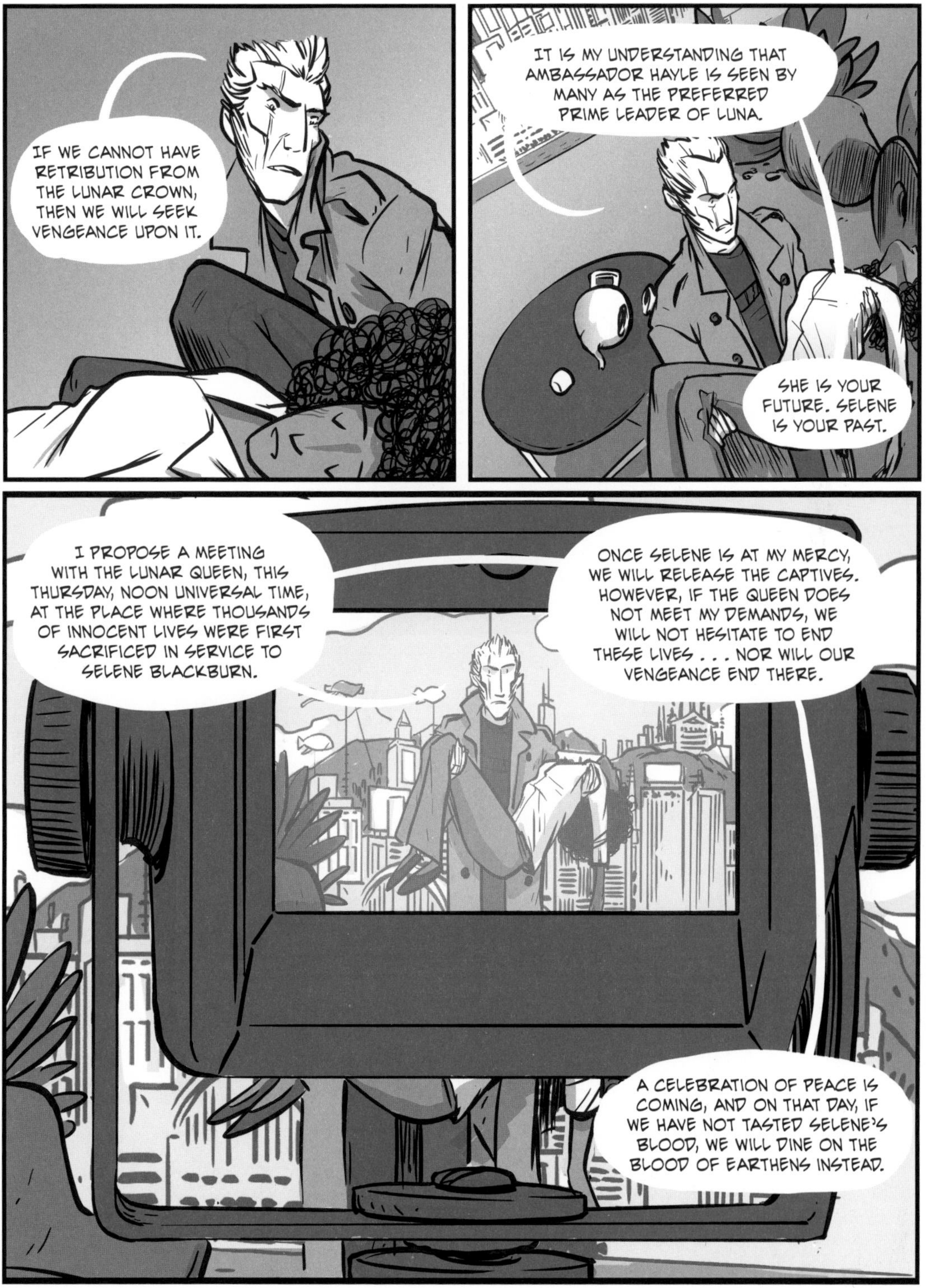
IF WE CANNOT HAVE RETRIBUTION FROM THE LUNAR CROWN, THEN WE WILL SEEK VENGEANCE UPON IT.
IT IS MY UNDERSTANDING THAT AMBASSADOR HAYLE IS SEEN BY MANY AS THE PREFERRED PRIME LEADER OF LUNA.
SHE IS YOUR FUTURE. SELENE IS YOUR PAST.
I PROPOSE A MEETING WITH THE LUNAR QUEEN, THIS THURSDAY, NOON UNIVERSAL TIME, AT THE PLACE WHERE THOUSANDS OF INNOCENT LIVES WERE FIRST SACRIFICED IN SERVICE TO SELENE BLACKBURN.
ONCE SELENE IS AT MY MERCY, WE WILL RELEASE THE CAPTIVES. HOWEVER, IF THE QUEEN DOES NOT MEET MY DEMANDS, WE WILL NOT HESITATE TO END THESE LIVES . . . NOR WILL OUR VENGEANCE END THERE.
A CELEBRATION OF PEACE IS COMING, AND ON THAT DAY, IF WE HAVE NOT TASTED SELENE'S BLOOD, WE WILL DINE ON THE BLOOD OF EARTHENS INSTEAD.

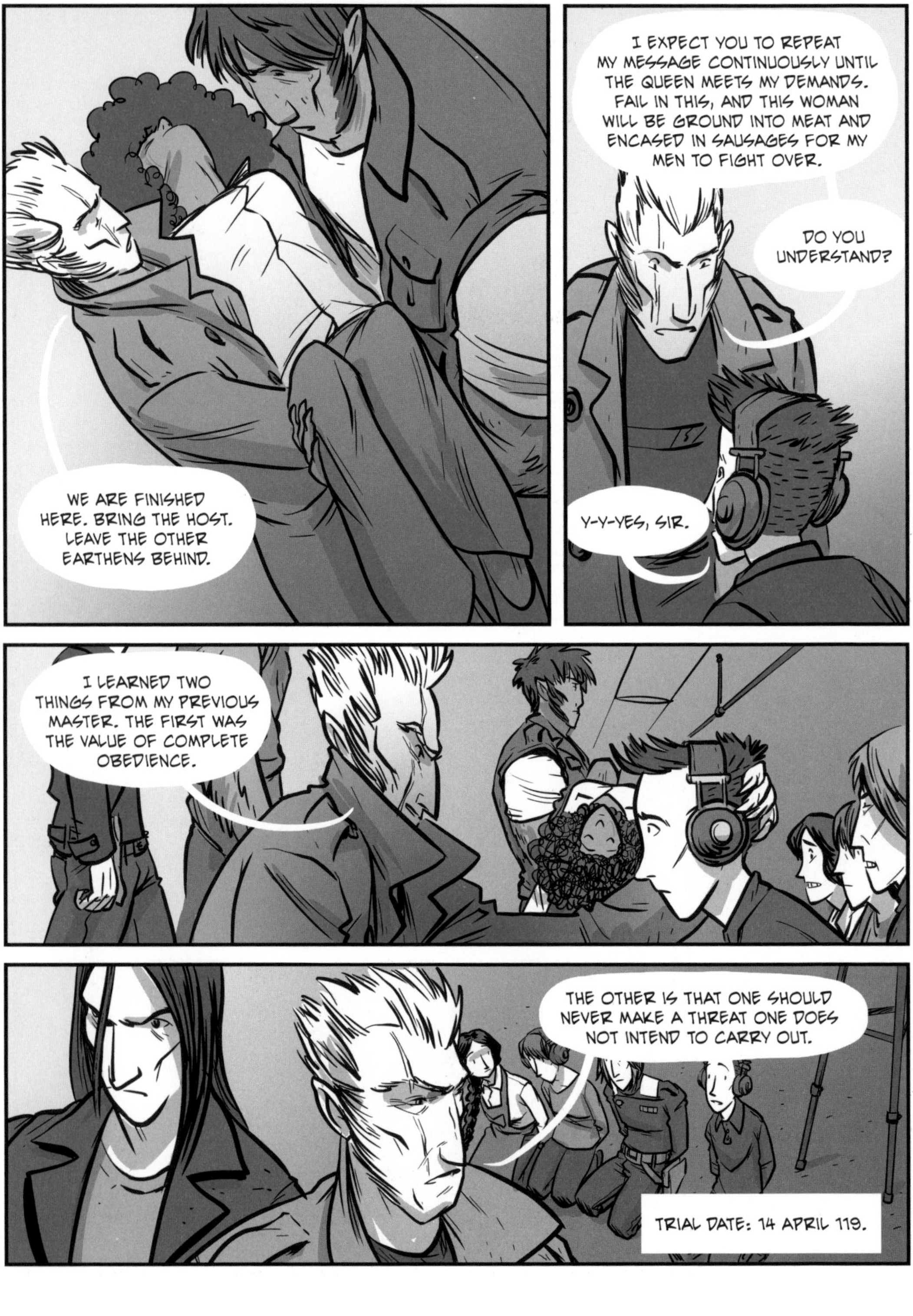
WE ARE FINISHED HERE. BRING THE HOST. LEAVE THE OTHER EARTHENS BEHIND.
I EXPECT YOU TO REPEAT MY MESSAGE CONTINUOUSLY UNTIL THE QUEEN MEETS MY DEMANDS. FAIL IN THIS, AND THIS WOMAN WILL BE GROUND INTO MEAT AND ENCASED IN SAUSAGES FOR MY MEN TO FIGHT OVER.
DO YOU UNDERSTAND?
Y-Y-YES, SIR.
I LEARNED TWO THINGS FROM MY PREVIOUS MASTER. THE FIRST WAS THE VALUE OF COMPLETE OBEDIENCE.
THE OTHER IS THAT ONE SHOULD NEVER MAKE A THREAT ONE DOES NOT INTEND TO CARRY OUT.
TRIAL DATE: 14 APRIL 119.

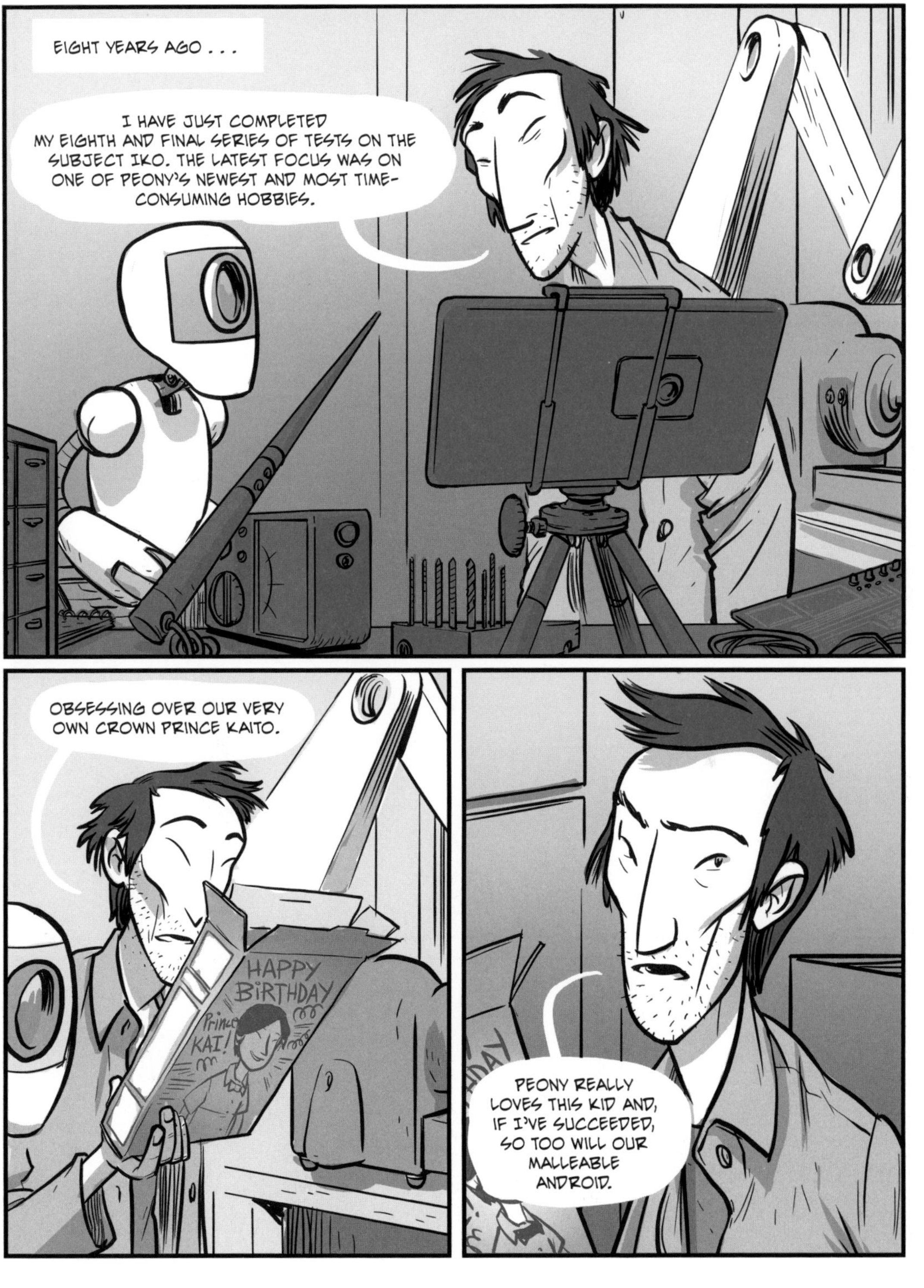
EIGHT YEARS AGO . . .
I HAVE JUST COMPLETED MY EIGHTH AND FINAL SERIES OF TESTS ON THE SUBJECT IKO. THE LATEST FOCUS WAS ON ONE OF PEONY'S NEWEST AND MOST TIME-CONSUMING HOBBIES.
OBSESSING OVER OUR VERY OWN CROWN PRINCE KAITO.
HAPPY BIRTHDAY
Prince KAI!
PEONY REALLY LOVES THIS KID AND, IF I'VE SUCCEEDED, SO TOO WILL OUR MALLEABLE ANDROID.

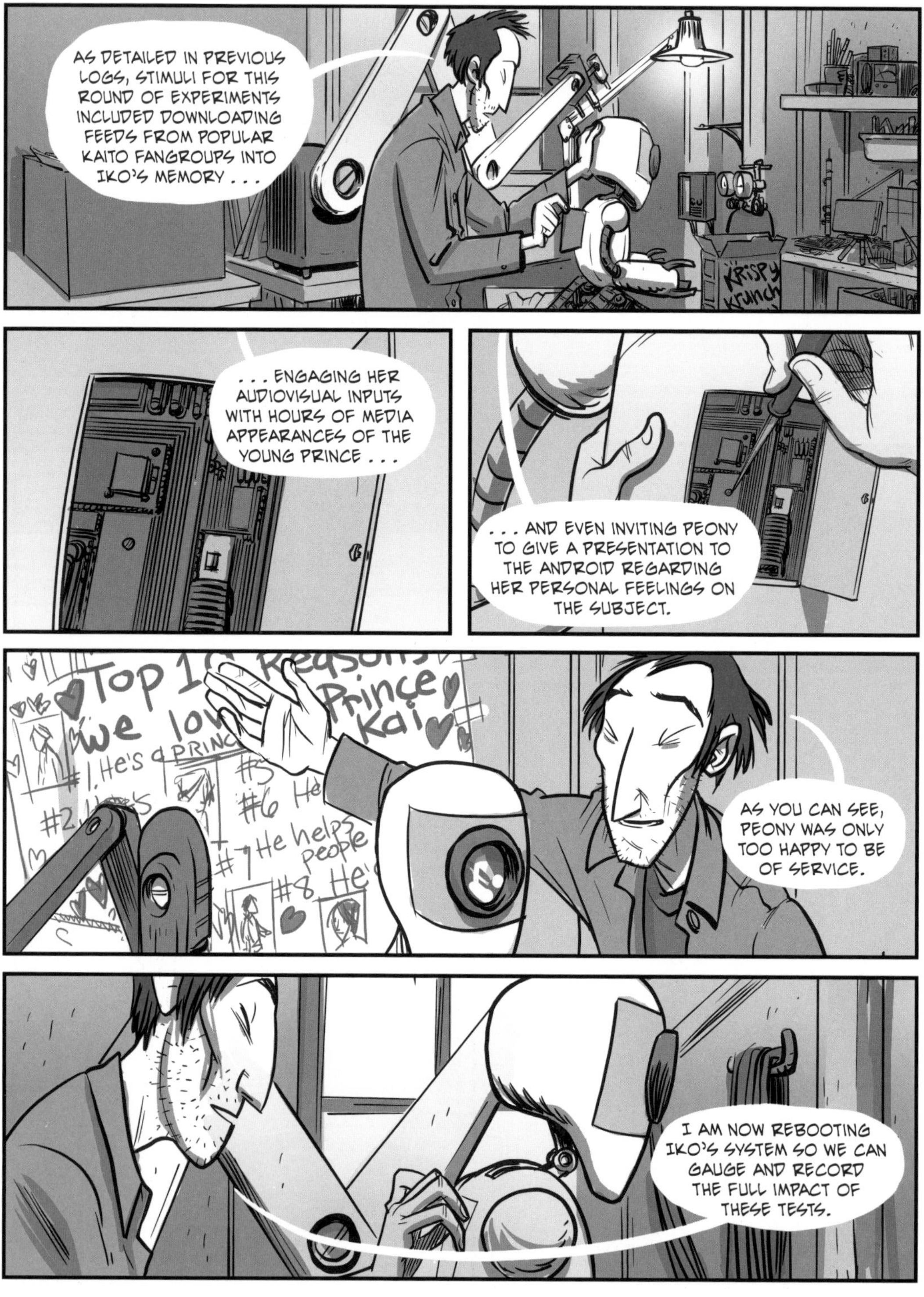
AS DETAILED IN PREVIOUS LOGS, STIMULI FOR THIS ROUND OF EXPERIMENTS INCLUDED DOWNLOADING FEEDS FROM POPULAR KAITO FANGROUPS INTO IKO'S MEMORY . . .
Krispy Krunch
. . . ENGAGING HER AUDIOVISUAL INPUTS WITH HOURS OF MEDIA APPEARANCES OF THE YOUNG PRINCE . . .
. . . AND EVEN INVITING PEONY TO GIVE A PRESENTATION TO THE ANDROID REGARDING HER PERSONAL FEELINGS ON THE SUBJECT.
Prince Kai
#7 He helps people
AS YOU CAN SEE, PEONY WAS ONLY TOO HAPPY TO BE OF SERVICE.
I AM NOW REBOOTING IKO'S SYSTEM SO WE CAN GAUGE AND RECORD THE FULL IMPACT OF THESE TESTS.

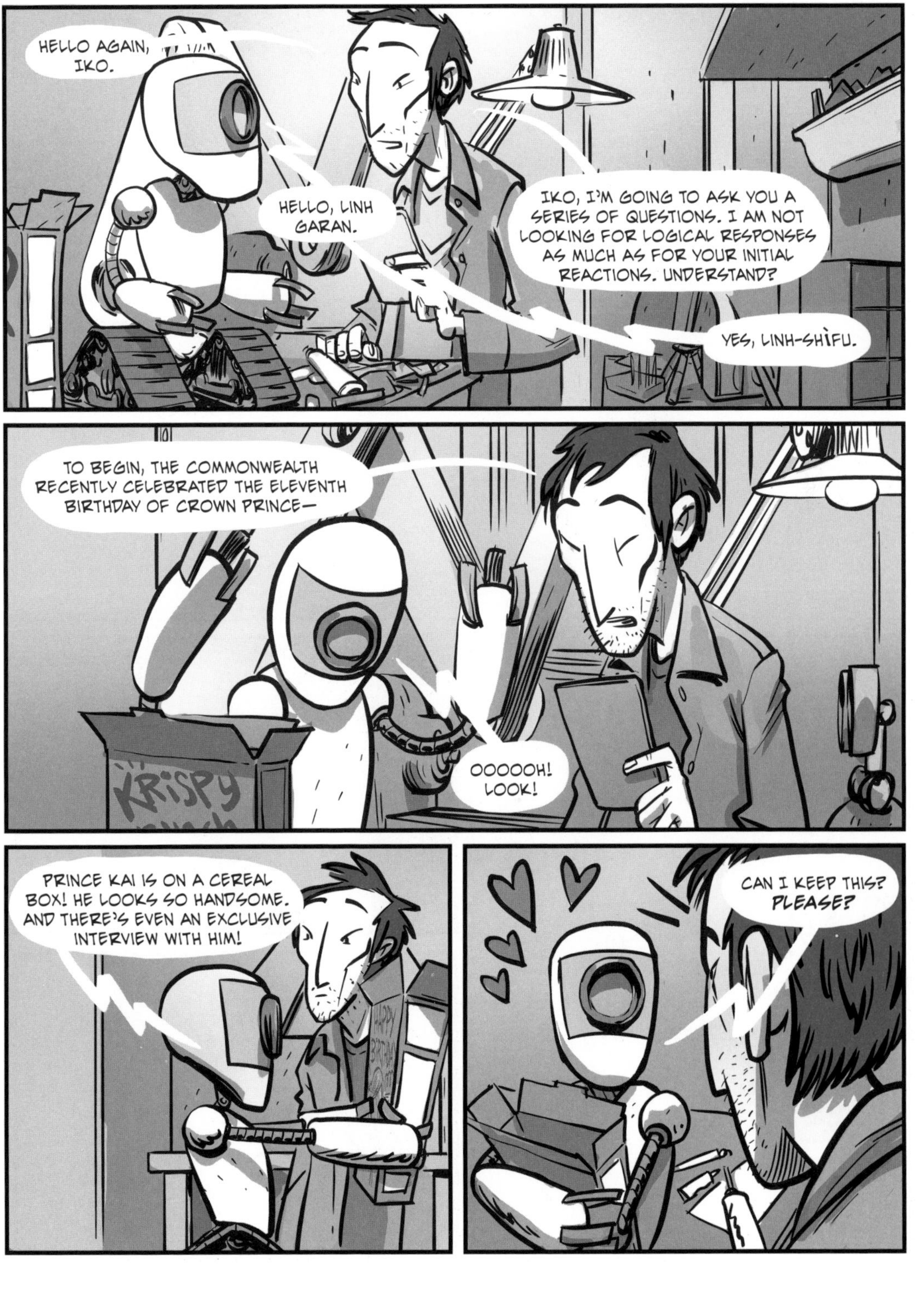
HELLO AGAIN, IKO.
HELLO, LINH GARAN.
IKO, I'M GOING TO ASK YOU A SERIES OF QUESTIONS. I AM NOT LOOKING FOR LOGICAL RESPONSES AS MUCH AS FOR YOUR INITIAL REACTIONS. UNDERSTAND?
YES, LINH-SHIFU.
TO BEGIN, THE COMMONWEALTH RECENTLY CELEBRATED THE ELEVENTH BIRTHDAY OF CROWN PRINCE—
OOOOOH! LOOK!
KRISPY
PRINCE KAI IS ON A CEREAL BOX! HE LOOKS SO HANDSOME. AND THERE'S EVEN AN EXCLUSIVE INTERVIEW WITH HIM!
CAN I KEEP THIS? **PLEASE?**

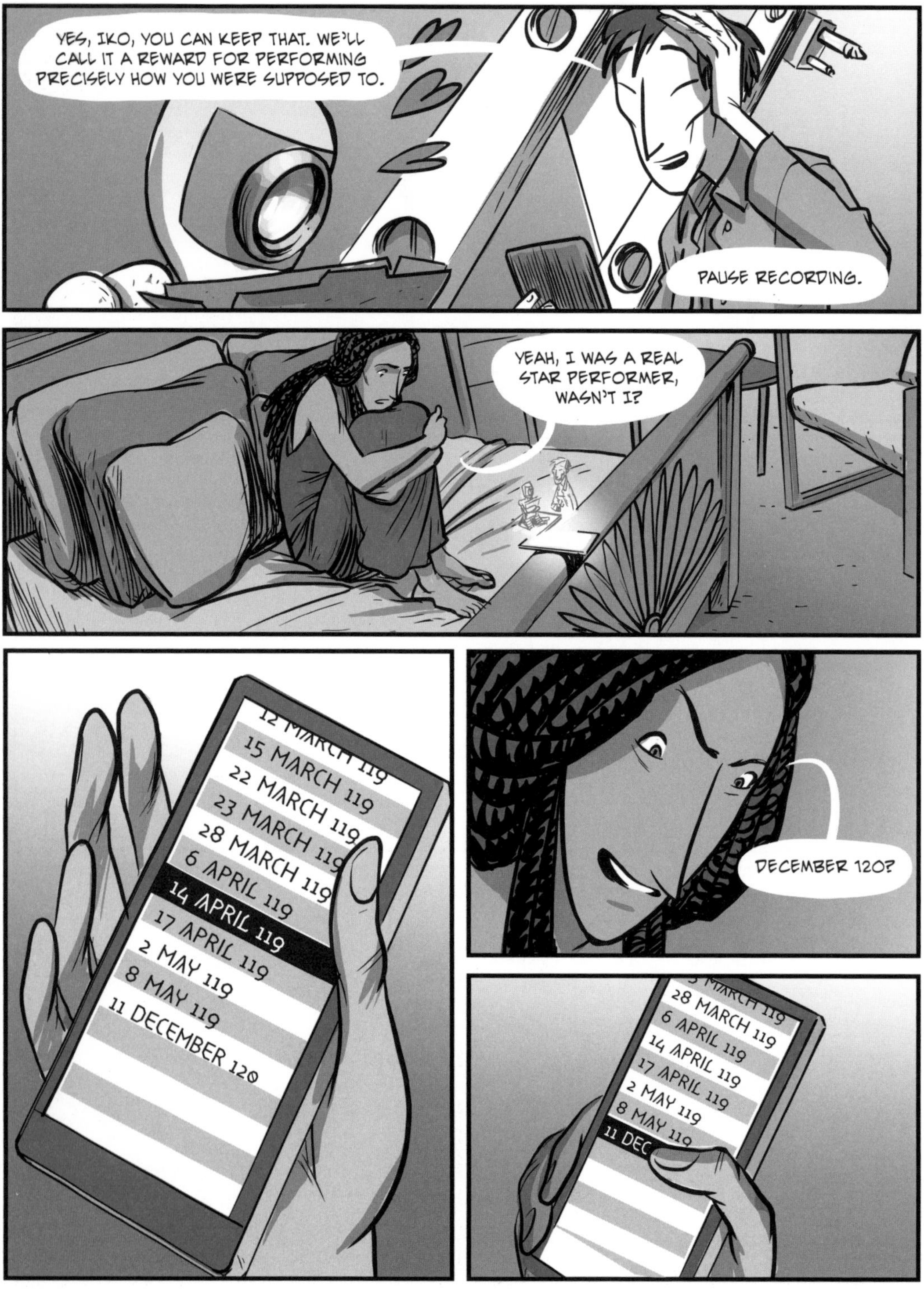
YES, IKO, YOU CAN KEEP THAT. WE'LL CALL IT A REWARD FOR PERFORMING PRECISELY HOW YOU WERE SUPPOSED TO.
PAUSE RECORDING.
YEAH, I WAS A REAL STAR PERFORMER, WASN'T I?
15 MARCH 119
22 MARCH 119
23 MARCH 119
28 MARCH 119
6 APRIL 119
14 APRIL 119
17 APRIL 119
2 MAY 119
8 MAY 119
11 DECEMBER 120
DECEMBER 120?
28 MARCH 119
6 APRIL 119
14 APRIL 119
17 APRIL 119
2 MAY 119
8 MAY 119
11 DEC

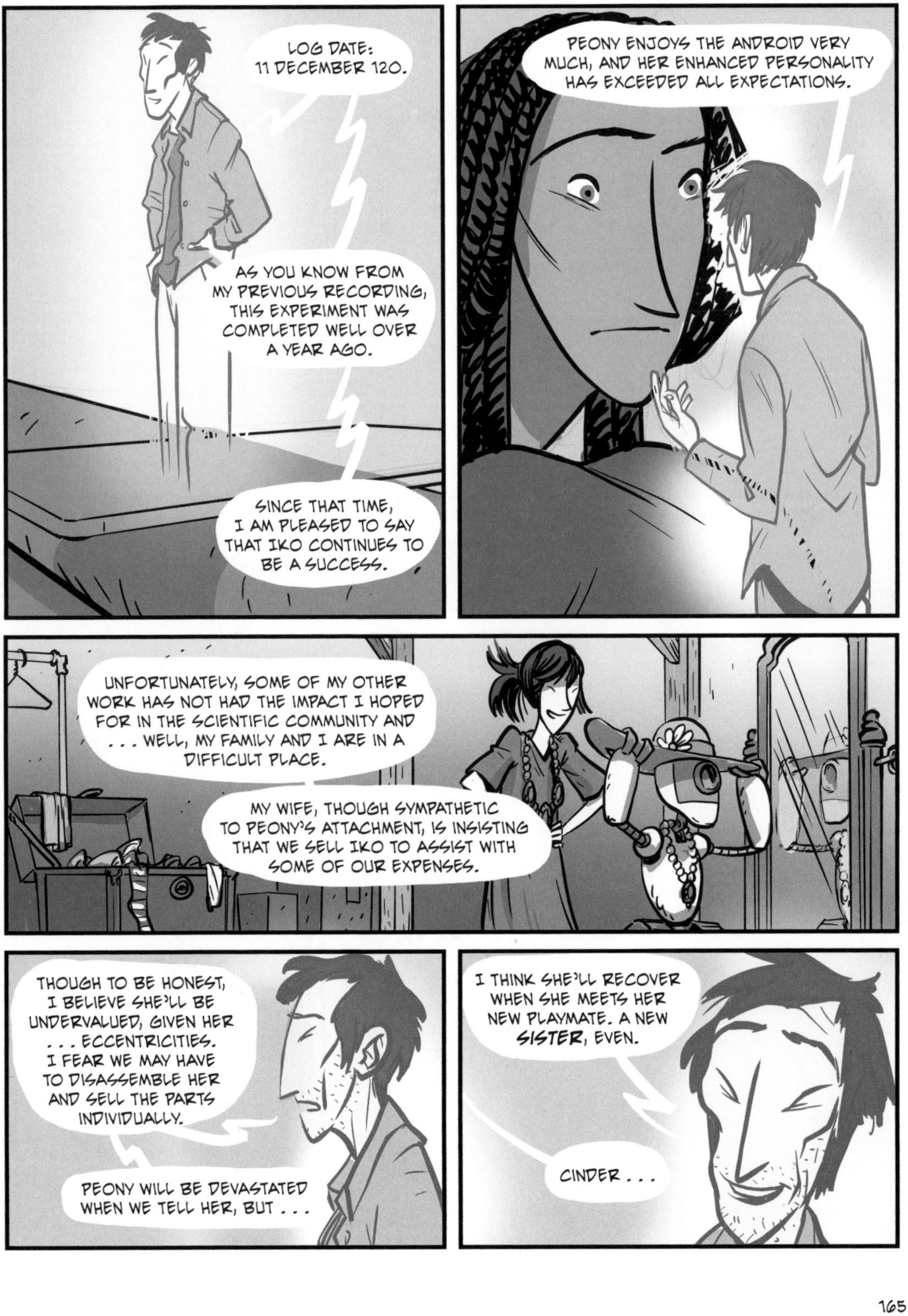
LOG DATE: 11 DECEMBER 120.
AS YOU KNOW FROM MY PREVIOUS RECORDING, THIS EXPERIMENT WAS COMPLETED WELL OVER A YEAR AGO.
SINCE THAT TIME, I AM PLEASED TO SAY THAT IKO CONTINUES TO BE A SUCCESS.
PEONY ENJOYS THE ANDROID VERY MUCH, AND HER ENHANCED PERSONALITY HAS EXCEEDED ALL EXPECTATIONS.
UNFORTUNATELY, SOME OF MY OTHER WORK HAS NOT HAD THE IMPACT I HOPED FOR IN THE SCIENTIFIC COMMUNITY AND . . . WELL, MY FAMILY AND I ARE IN A DIFFICULT PLACE.
MY WIFE, THOUGH SYMPATHETIC TO PEONY'S ATTACHMENT, IS INSISTING THAT WE SELL IKO TO ASSIST WITH SOME OF OUR EXPENSES.
THOUGH TO BE HONEST, I BELIEVE SHE'LL BE UNDERVALUED, GIVEN HER . . . ECCENTRICITIES. I FEAR WE MAY HAVE TO DISASSEMBLE HER AND SELL THE PARTS INDIVIDUALLY.
PEONY WILL BE DEVASTATED WHEN WE TELL HER, BUT . . .
I THINK SHE'LL RECOVER WHEN SHE MEETS HER NEW PLAYMATE. A NEW **SISTER**, EVEN.
CINDER . . .

THIS IS RIGHT BEFORE HE ADOPTED CINDER.

FWMP!

PEONY AND I WERE BEST FRIENDS FOR A YEAR AND A HALF, AND YOU THOUGHT YOU COULD JUST REPLACE ME?

AT THE LEAST, I DO INTEND TO PRESERVE IKO'S PERSONALITY CHIP. NO ONE ELSE WILL WANT IT, ANYHOW, AND SHE'S BECOME A CONVENIENT BACKUP SYSTEM FOR MY WORK.

WHO KNOWS?

MAYBE SOMEDAY IKO WILL BE BROUGHT TO LIFE AGAIN.

YEAH, NO THANKS TO YOU OR YOUR GREEDY WIFE!

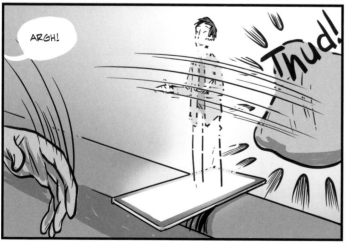

ARGH!

Thud!

WHY AM I LETTING THIS GET TO ME?

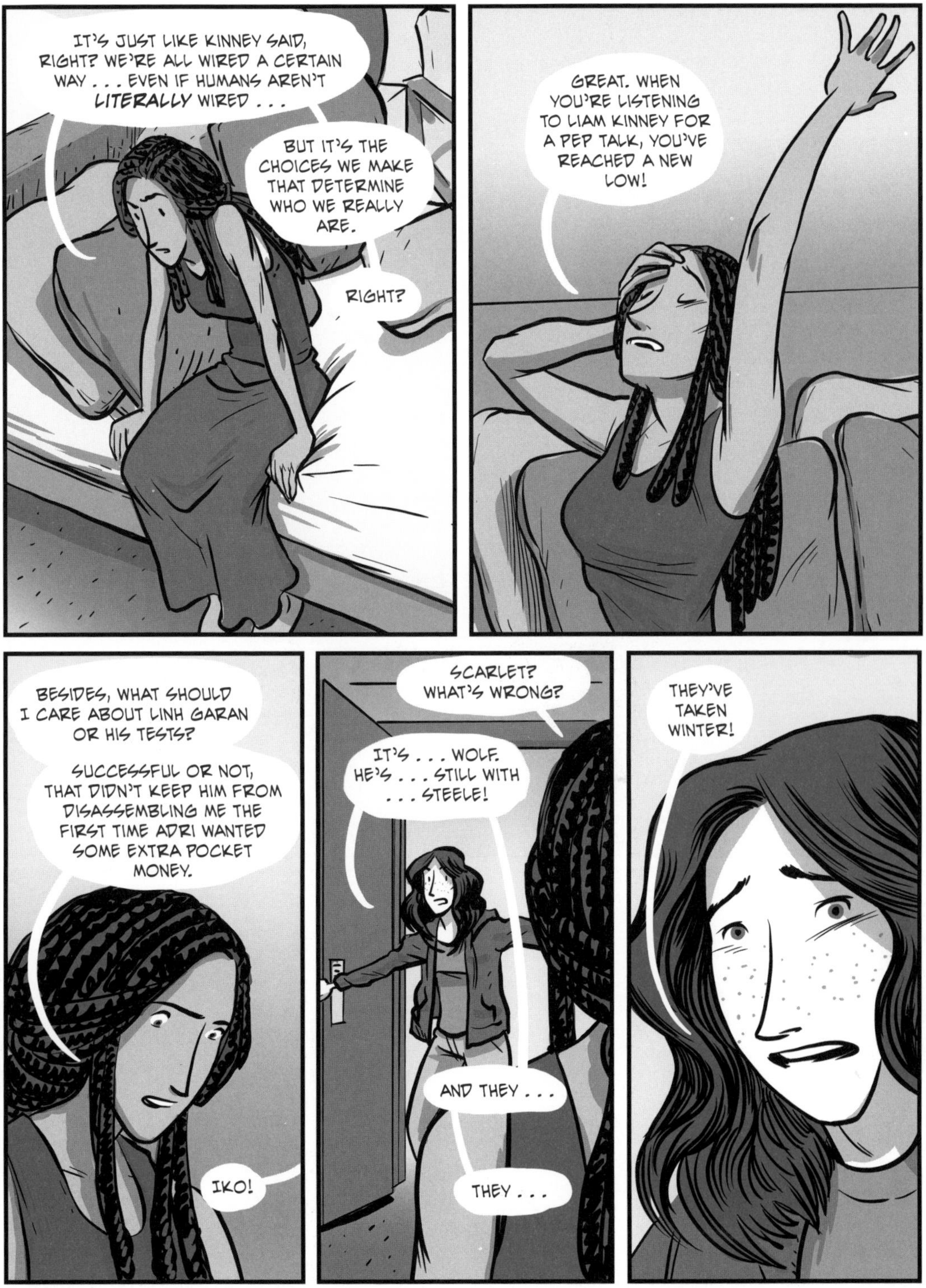
IT'S JUST LIKE KINNEY SAID, RIGHT? WE'RE ALL WIRED A CERTAIN WAY . . . EVEN IF HUMANS AREN'T *LITERALLY* WIRED . . .
BUT IT'S THE CHOICES WE MAKE THAT DETERMINE WHO WE REALLY ARE.
RIGHT?
GREAT. WHEN YOU'RE LISTENING TO LIAM KINNEY FOR A PEP TALK, YOU'VE REACHED A NEW LOW!
BESIDES, WHAT SHOULD I CARE ABOUT LINH GARAN OR HIS TESTS?
SUCCESSFUL OR NOT, THAT DIDN'T KEEP HIM FROM DISASSEMBLING ME THE FIRST TIME ADRI WANTED SOME EXTRA POCKET MONEY.
IKO!
SCARLET? WHAT'S WRONG?
IT'S . . . WOLF. HE'S . . . STILL WITH . . . STEELE!
AND THEY . . .
THEY . . .
THEY'VE TAKEN WINTER!

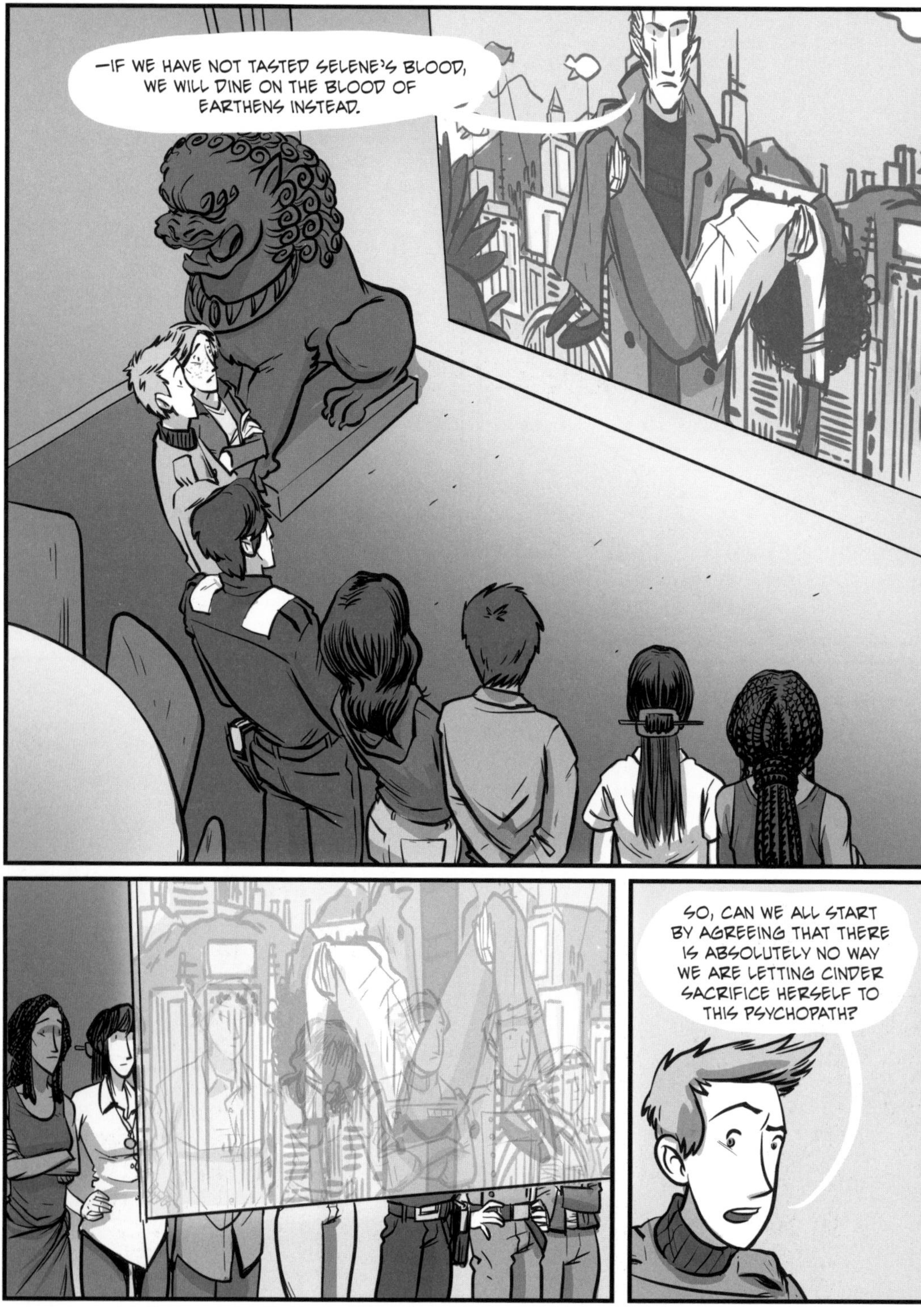
—IF WE HAVE NOT TASTED SELENE'S BLOOD, WE WILL DINE ON THE BLOOD OF EARTHENS INSTEAD.
SO, CAN WE ALL START BY AGREEING THAT THERE IS ABSOLUTELY NO WAY WE ARE LETTING CINDER SACRIFICE HERSELF TO THIS PSYCHOPATH?

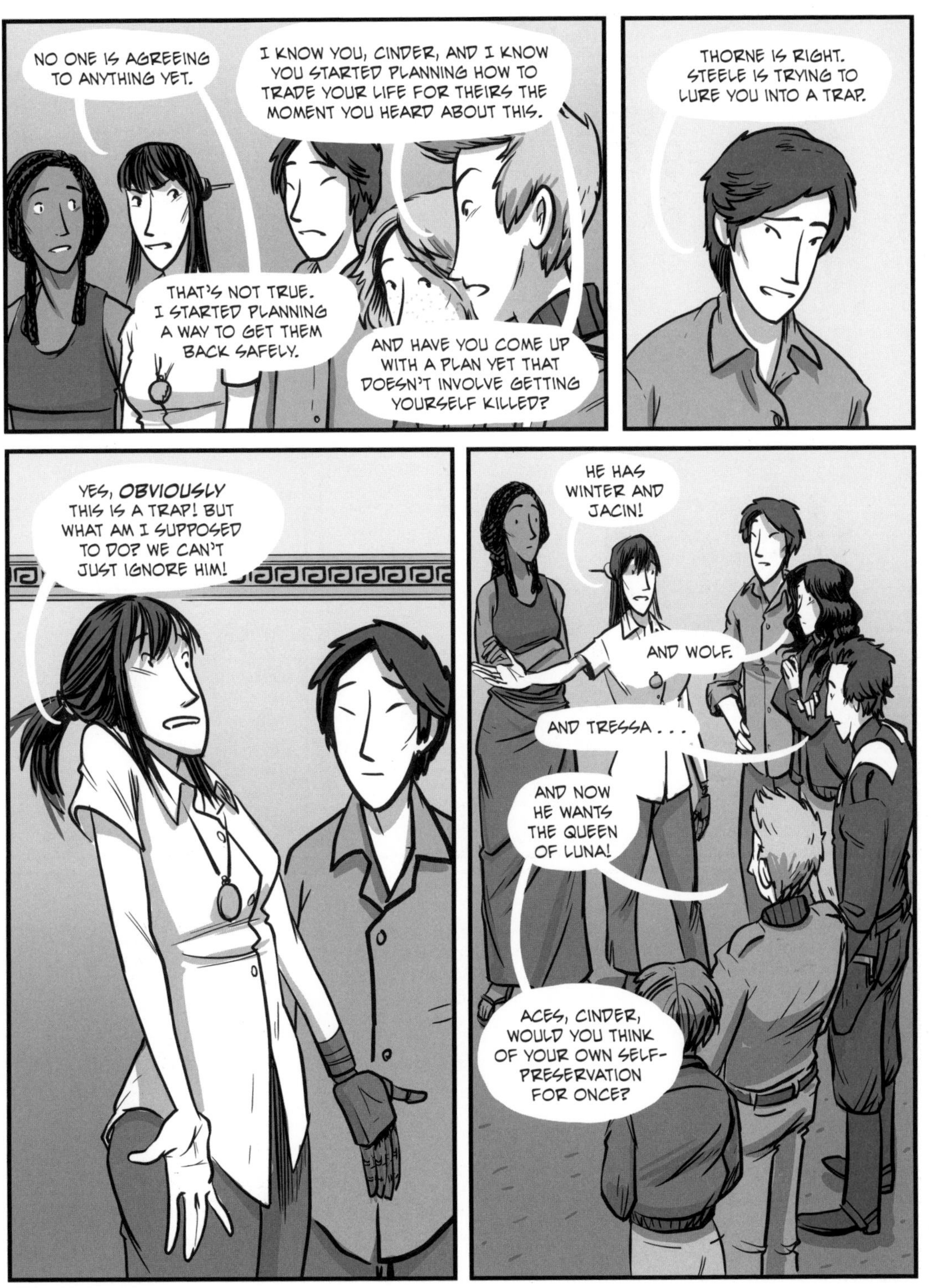
NO ONE IS AGREEING TO ANYTHING YET.
I KNOW YOU, CINDER, AND I KNOW YOU STARTED PLANNING HOW TO TRADE YOUR LIFE FOR THEIRS THE MOMENT YOU HEARD ABOUT THIS.
THAT'S NOT TRUE. I STARTED PLANNING A WAY TO GET THEM BACK SAFELY.
AND HAVE YOU COME UP WITH A PLAN YET THAT DOESN'T INVOLVE GETTING YOURSELF KILLED?
THORNE IS RIGHT. STEELE IS TRYING TO LURE YOU INTO A TRAP.
YES, **OBVIOUSLY** THIS IS A TRAP! BUT WHAT AM I SUPPOSED TO DO? WE CAN'T JUST IGNORE HIM!
HE HAS WINTER AND JACIN!
AND WOLF.
AND TRESSA . . .
AND NOW HE WANTS THE QUEEN OF LUNA!
ACES, CINDER, WOULD YOU THINK OF YOUR OWN SELF-PRESERVATION FOR ONCE?

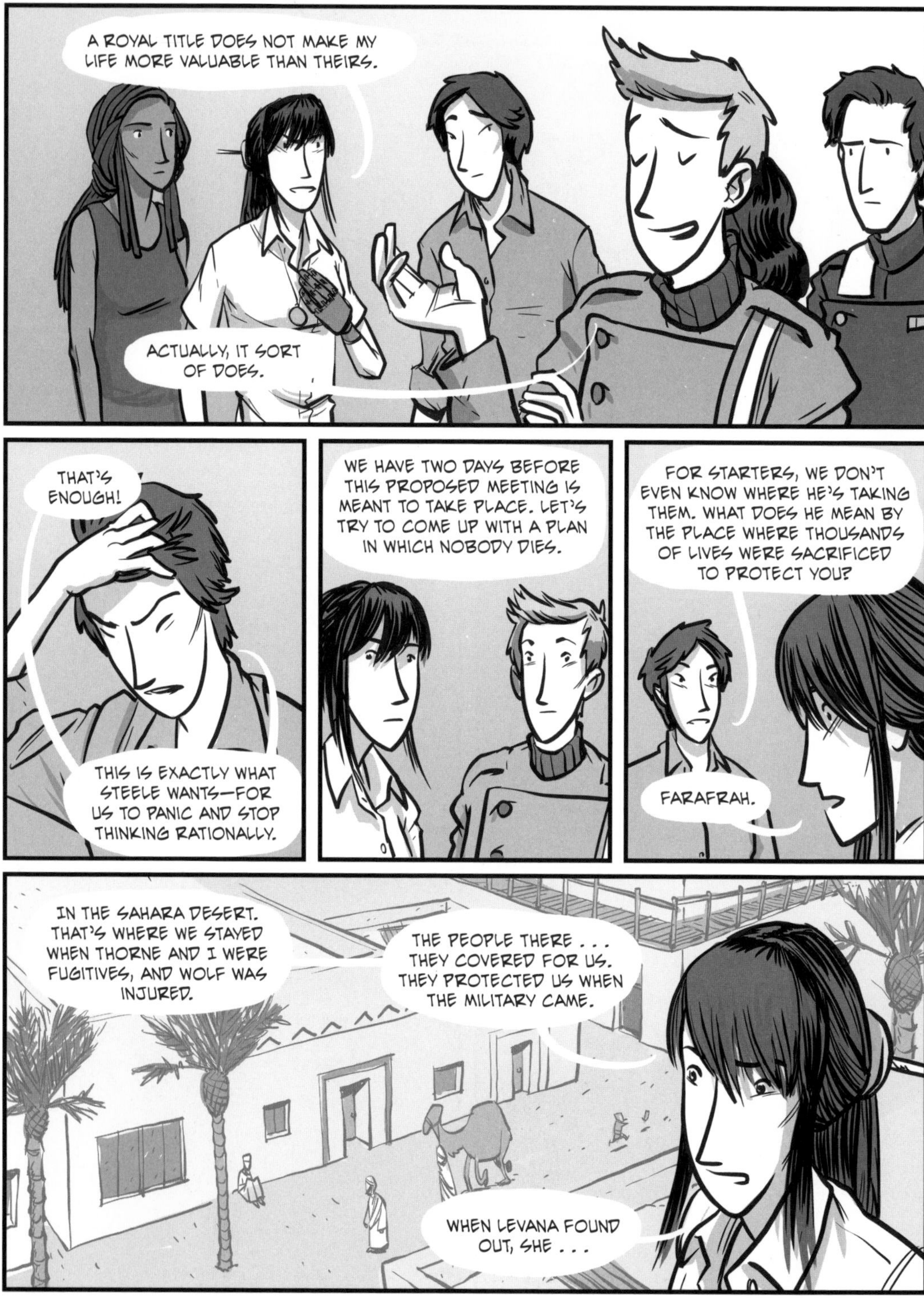
A ROYAL TITLE DOES NOT MAKE MY LIFE MORE VALUABLE THAN THEIRS.
ACTUALLY, IT SORT OF DOES.
THAT'S ENOUGH!
THIS IS EXACTLY WHAT STEELE WANTS—FOR US TO PANIC AND STOP THINKING RATIONALLY.
WE HAVE TWO DAYS BEFORE THIS PROPOSED MEETING IS MEANT TO TAKE PLACE. LET'S TRY TO COME UP WITH A PLAN IN WHICH NOBODY DIES.
FOR STARTERS, WE DON'T EVEN KNOW WHERE HE'S TAKING THEM. WHAT DOES HE MEAN BY THE PLACE WHERE THOUSANDS OF LIVES WERE SACRIFICED TO PROTECT YOU?
FARAFRAH.
IN THE SAHARA DESERT. THAT'S WHERE WE STAYED WHEN THORNE AND I WERE FUGITIVES, AND WOLF WAS INJURED.
THE PEOPLE THERE . . . THEY COVERED FOR US. THEY PROTECTED US WHEN THE MILITARY CAME.
WHEN LEVANA FOUND OUT, SHE . . .

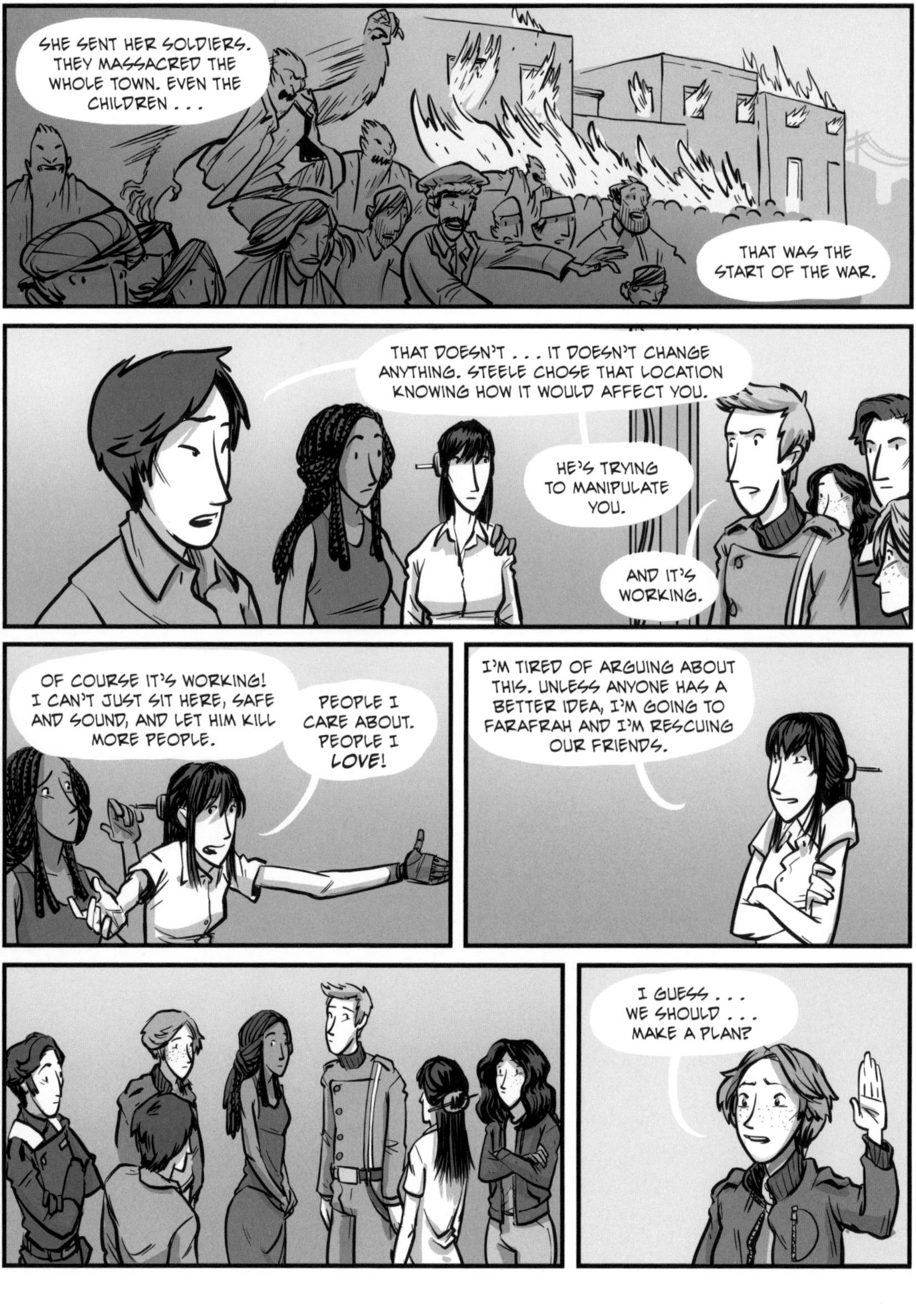
SHE SENT HER SOLDIERS. THEY MASSACRED THE WHOLE TOWN. EVEN THE CHILDREN . . .
THAT WAS THE START OF THE WAR.
THAT DOESN'T . . . IT DOESN'T CHANGE ANYTHING. STEELE CHOSE THAT LOCATION KNOWING HOW IT WOULD AFFECT YOU.
HE'S TRYING TO MANIPULATE YOU.
AND IT'S WORKING.
OF COURSE IT'S WORKING! I CAN'T JUST SIT HERE, SAFE AND SOUND, AND LET HIM KILL MORE PEOPLE.
PEOPLE I CARE ABOUT. PEOPLE I **LOVE**!
I'M TIRED OF ARGUING ABOUT THIS. UNLESS ANYONE HAS A BETTER IDEA, I'M GOING TO FARAFRAH AND I'M RESCUING OUR FRIENDS.
I GUESS . . . WE SHOULD . . . MAKE A PLAN?

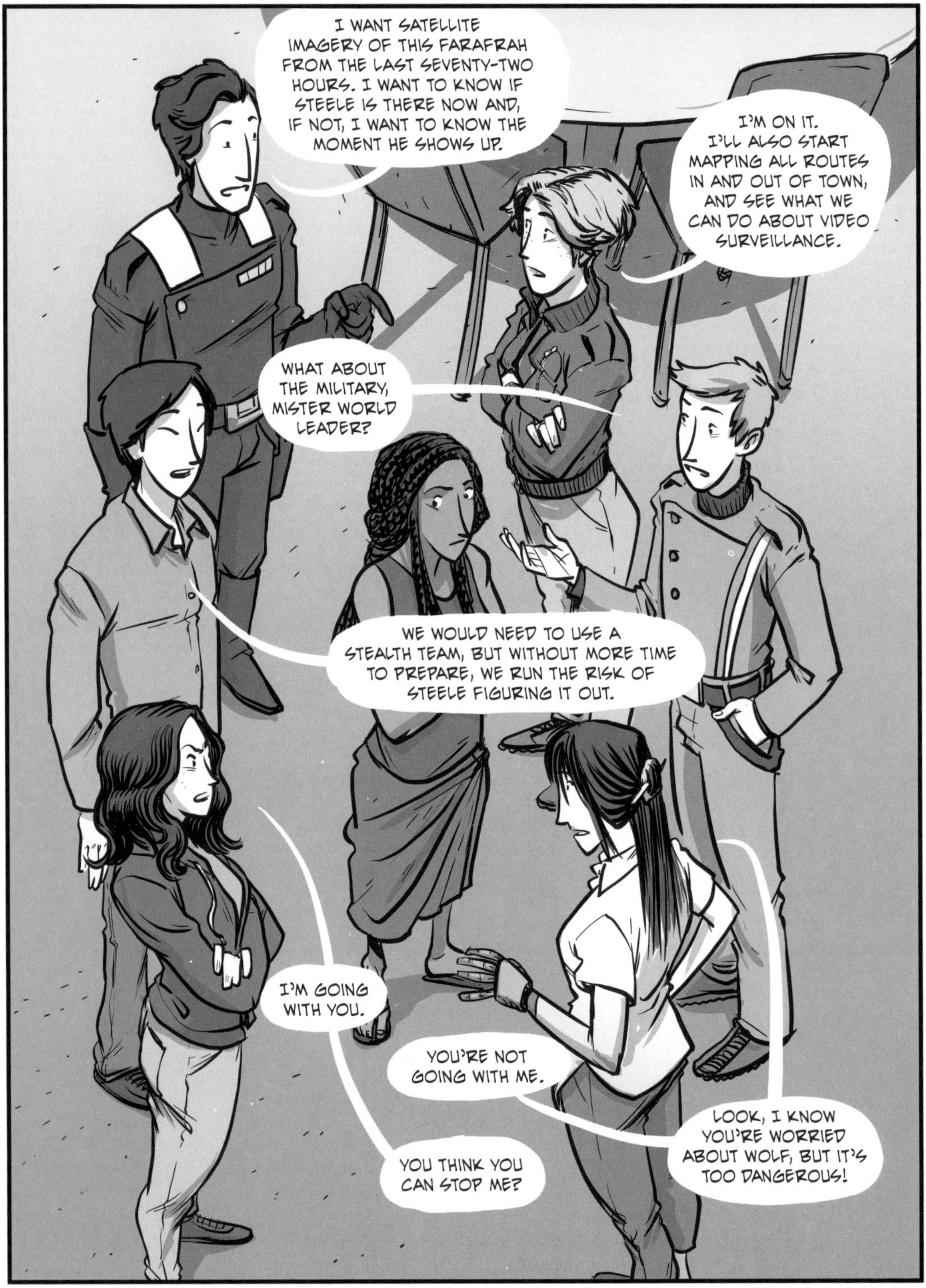

I WANT SATELLITE IMAGERY OF THIS FARAFRAH FROM THE LAST SEVENTY-TWO HOURS. I WANT TO KNOW IF STEELE IS THERE NOW AND, IF NOT, I WANT TO KNOW THE MOMENT HE SHOWS UP.
I'M ON IT. I'LL ALSO START MAPPING ALL ROUTES IN AND OUT OF TOWN, AND SEE WHAT WE CAN DO ABOUT VIDEO SURVEILLANCE.
WHAT ABOUT THE MILITARY, MISTER WORLD LEADER?
WE WOULD NEED TO USE A STEALTH TEAM, BUT WITHOUT MORE TIME TO PREPARE, WE RUN THE RISK OF STEELE FIGURING IT OUT.
I'M GOING WITH YOU.
YOU'RE NOT GOING WITH ME.
YOU THINK YOU CAN STOP ME?
LOOK, I KNOW YOU'RE WORRIED ABOUT WOLF, BUT IT'S TOO DANGEROUS!

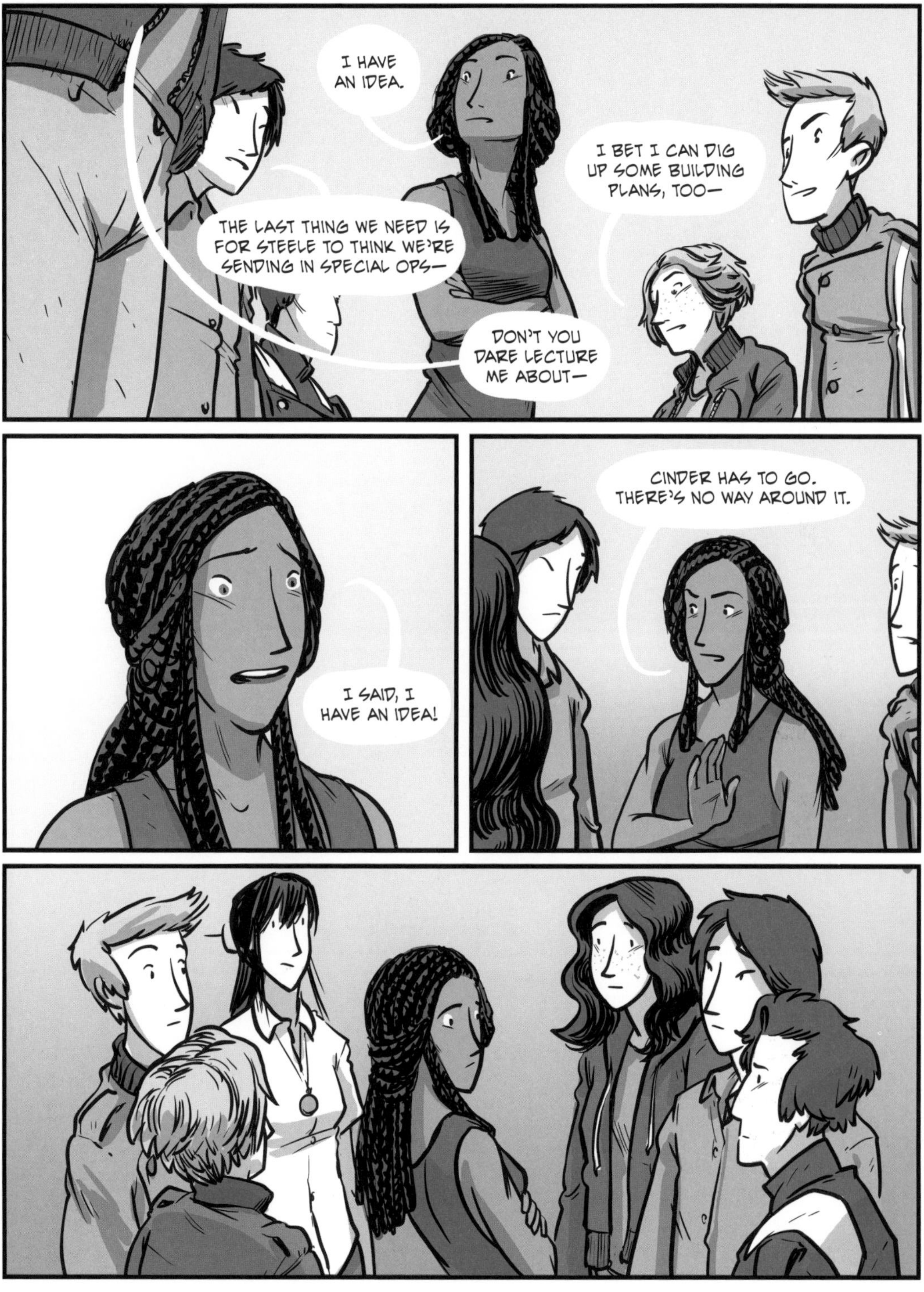
I HAVE AN IDEA.
THE LAST THING WE NEED IS FOR STEELE TO THINK WE'RE SENDING IN SPECIAL OPS—
DON'T YOU DARE LECTURE ME ABOUT—
I BET I CAN DIG UP SOME BUILDING PLANS, TOO—
I SAID, I HAVE AN IDEA!
CINDER HAS TO GO. THERE'S NO WAY AROUND IT.

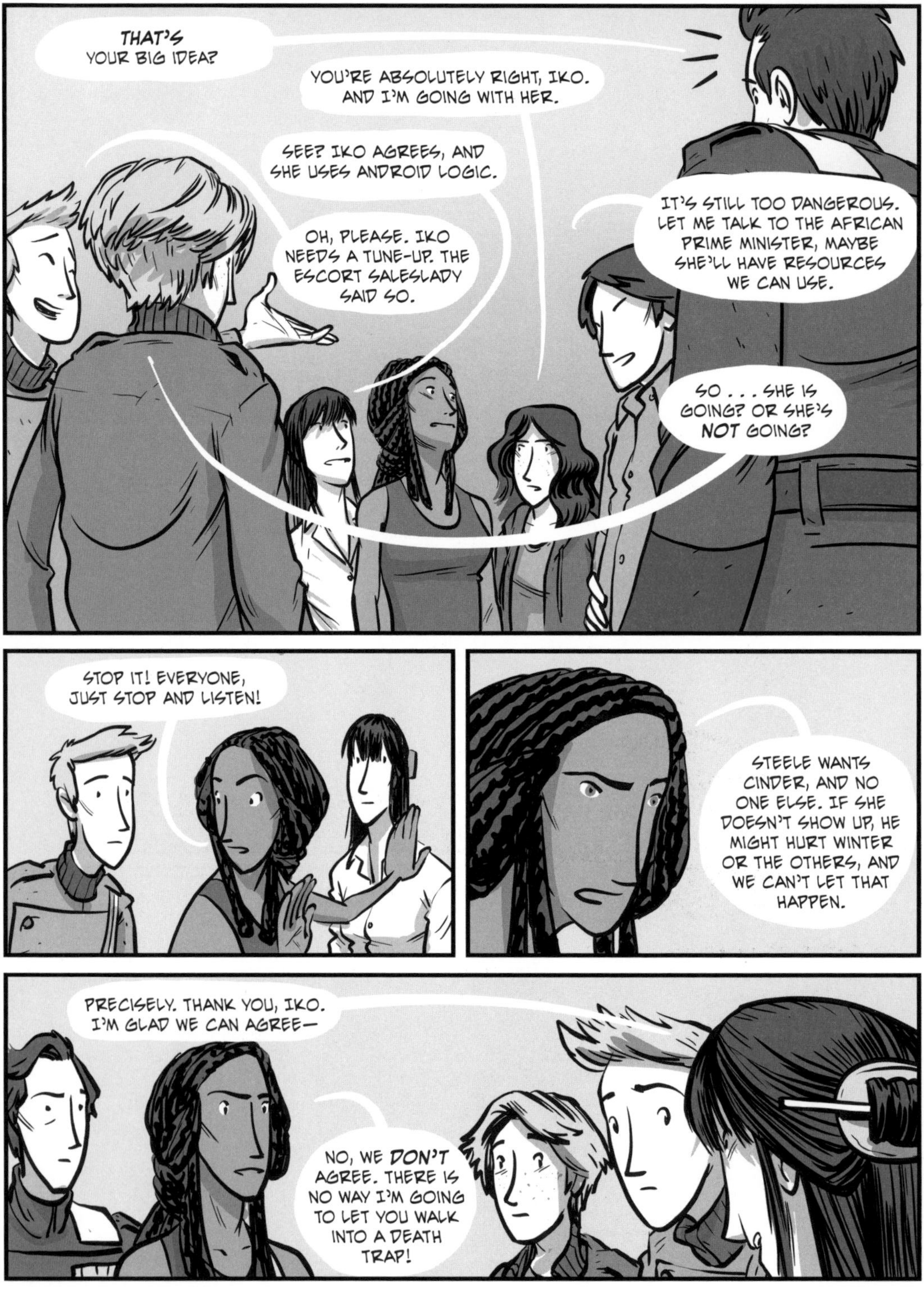
THAT'S YOUR BIG IDEA?
YOU'RE ABSOLUTELY RIGHT, IKO. AND I'M GOING WITH HER.
SEE? IKO AGREES, AND SHE USES ANDROID LOGIC.
OH, PLEASE. IKO NEEDS A TUNE-UP. THE ESCORT SALESLADY SAID SO.
IT'S STILL TOO DANGEROUS. LET ME TALK TO THE AFRICAN PRIME MINISTER, MAYBE SHE'LL HAVE RESOURCES WE CAN USE.
SO . . . SHE IS GOING? OR SHE'S NOT GOING?
STOP IT! EVERYONE, JUST STOP AND LISTEN!
STEELE WANTS CINDER, AND NO ONE ELSE. IF SHE DOESN'T SHOW UP, HE MIGHT HURT WINTER OR THE OTHERS, AND WE CAN'T LET THAT HAPPEN.
PRECISELY. THANK YOU, IKO. I'M GLAD WE CAN AGREE—
NO, WE DON'T AGREE. THERE IS NO WAY I'M GOING TO LET YOU WALK INTO A DEATH TRAP!

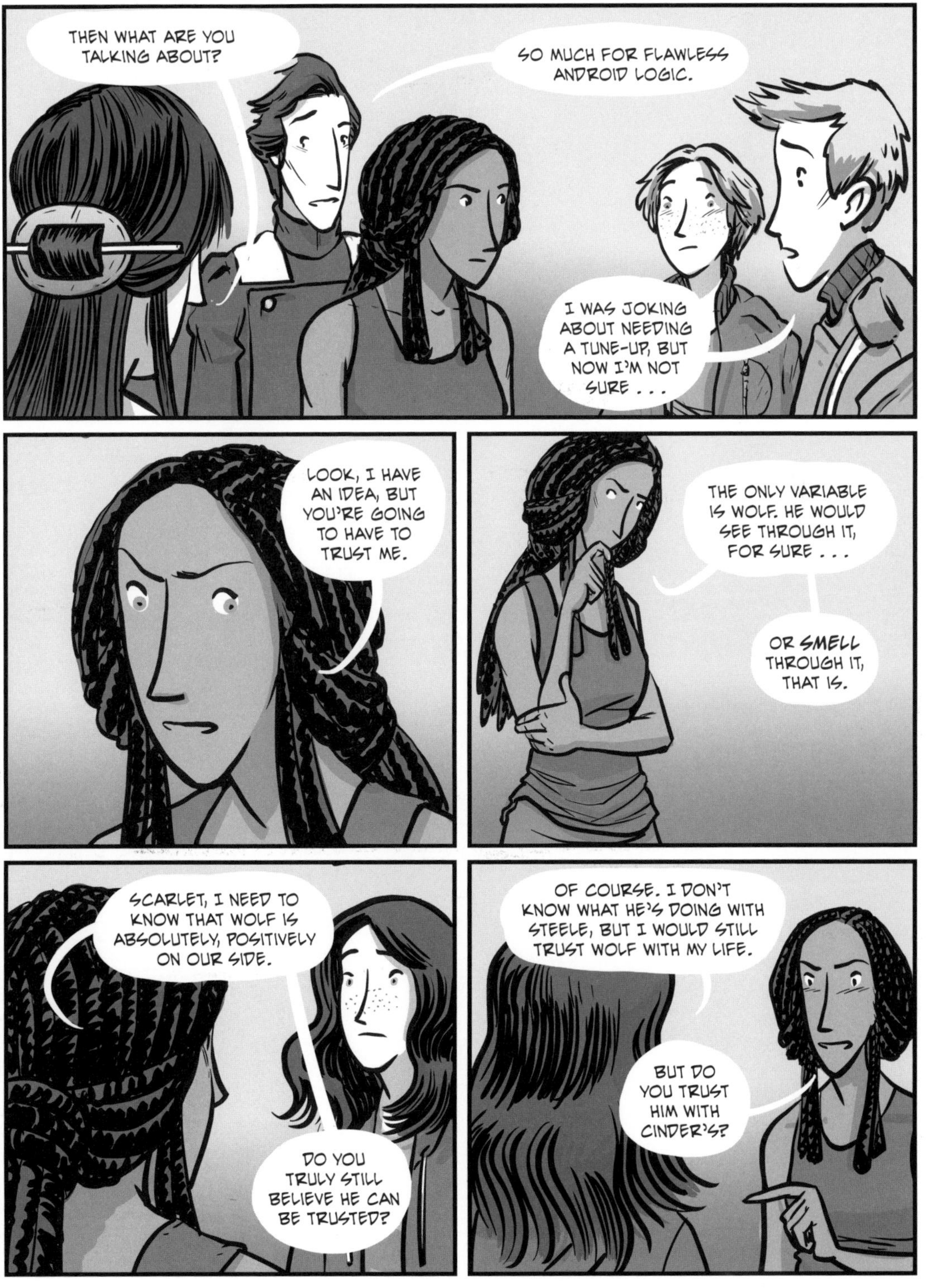
THEN WHAT ARE YOU TALKING ABOUT?
SO MUCH FOR FLAWLESS ANDROID LOGIC.
I WAS JOKING ABOUT NEEDING A TUNE-UP, BUT NOW I'M NOT SURE . . .
LOOK, I HAVE AN IDEA, BUT YOU'RE GOING TO HAVE TO TRUST ME.
THE ONLY VARIABLE IS WOLF. HE WOULD SEE THROUGH IT, FOR SURE . . .
OR SMELL THROUGH IT, THAT IS.
SCARLET, I NEED TO KNOW THAT WOLF IS ABSOLUTELY, POSITIVELY ON OUR SIDE.
DO YOU TRULY STILL BELIEVE HE CAN BE TRUSTED?
OF COURSE. I DON'T KNOW WHAT HE'S DOING WITH STEELE, BUT I WOULD STILL TRUST WOLF WITH MY LIFE.
BUT DO YOU TRUST HIM WITH CINDER'S?

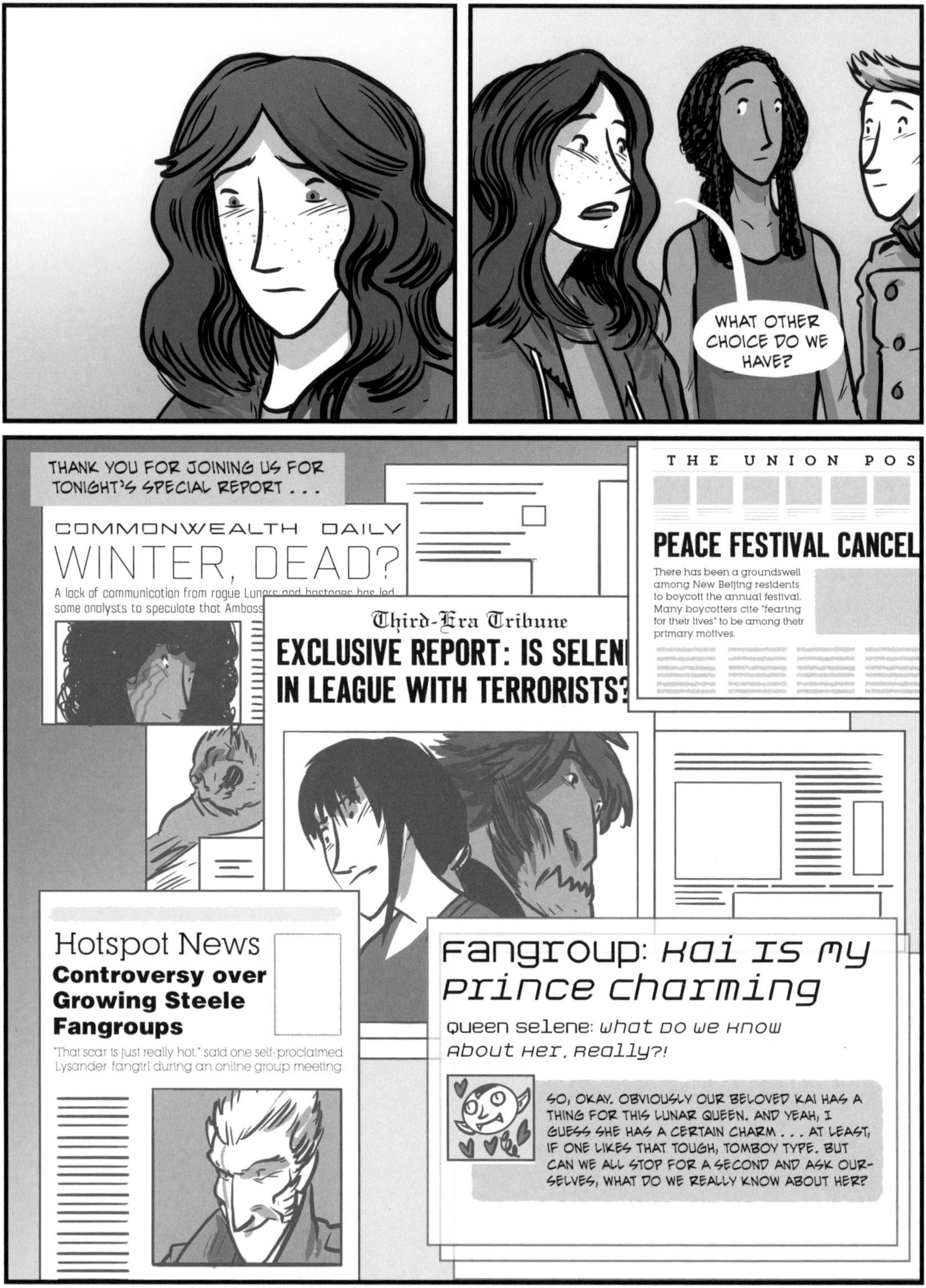

WHAT OTHER CHOICE DO WE HAVE?
THANK YOU FOR JOINING US FOR TONIGHT'S SPECIAL REPORT . . .
COMMONWEALTH DAILY
WINTER, DEAD?
A lack of communication from rogue
some analysts to speculate that Ambass
THE UNION POS
PEACE FESTIVAL CANCEL
There has been a groundswell among New Beijing residents to boycott the annual festival. Many boycotters cite "fearing for their lives" to be among their primary motives.
Third-Era Tribune
EXCLUSIVE REPORT: IS SELEN
IN LEAGUE WITH TERRORISTS?
Hotspot News
Controversy over Growing Steele Fangroups
"That scar is just really hot," said one self-proclaimed Lysander fangirl during an online group meeting.
Fangroup: Kai Is my Prince charming
Queen selene: what do we know About Her, Really?!
SO, OKAY. OBVIOUSLY OUR BELOVED KAI HAS A THING FOR THIS LUNAR QUEEN. AND YEAH, I GUESS SHE HAS A CERTAIN CHARM . . . AT LEAST, IF ONE LIKES THAT TOUGH, TOMBOY TYPE. BUT CAN WE ALL STOP FOR A SECOND AND ASK OURSELVES, WHAT DO WE REALLY KNOW ABOUT HER?

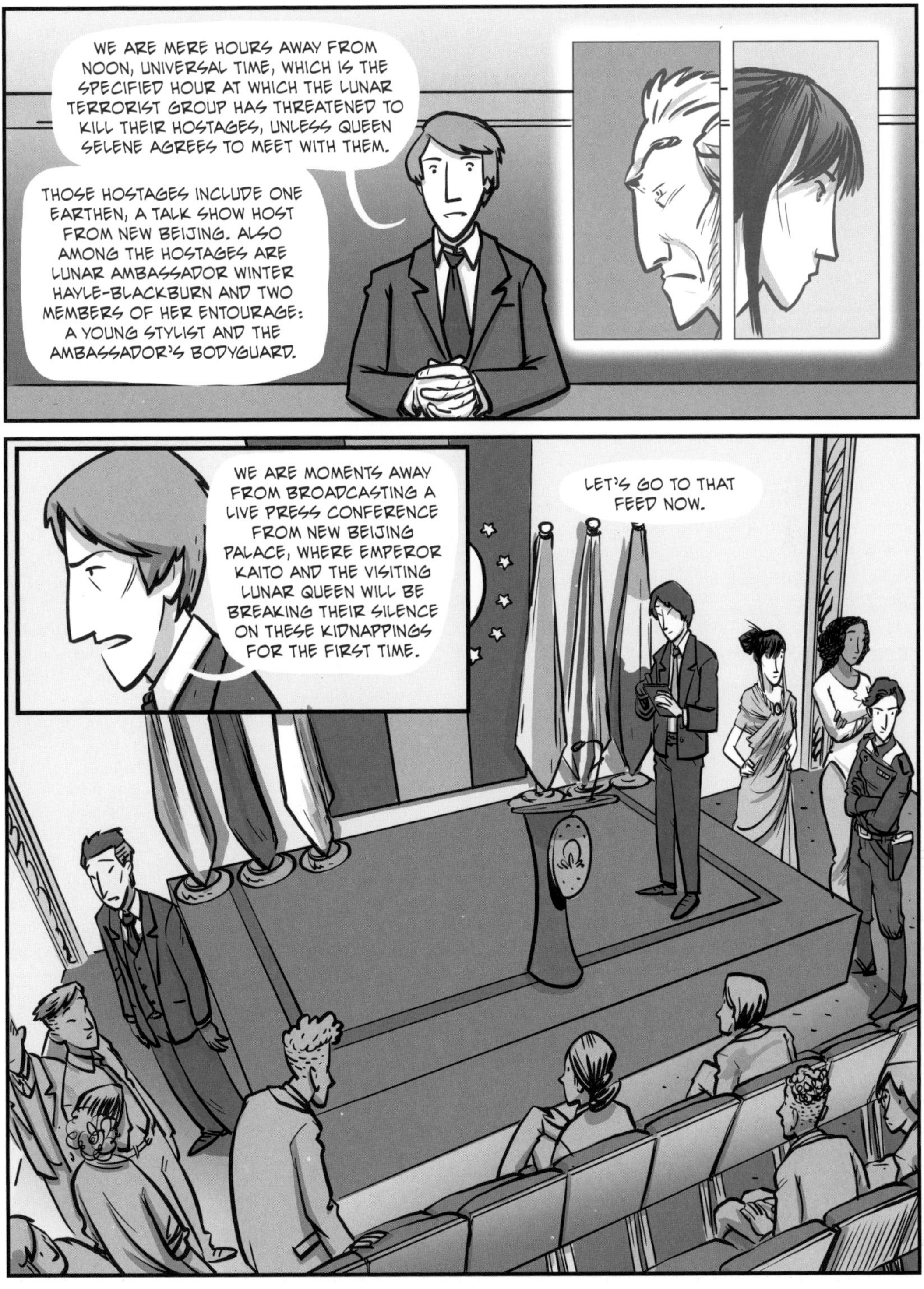
WE ARE MERE HOURS AWAY FROM NOON, UNIVERSAL TIME, WHICH IS THE SPECIFIED HOUR AT WHICH THE LUNAR TERRORIST GROUP HAS THREATENED TO KILL THEIR HOSTAGES, UNLESS QUEEN SELENE AGREES TO MEET WITH THEM.
THOSE HOSTAGES INCLUDE ONE EARTHEN, A TALK SHOW HOST FROM NEW BEIJING. ALSO AMONG THE HOSTAGES ARE LUNAR AMBASSADOR WINTER HAYLE-BLACKBURN AND TWO MEMBERS OF HER ENTOURAGE: A YOUNG STYLIST AND THE AMBASSADOR'S BODYGUARD.
WE ARE MOMENTS AWAY FROM BROADCASTING A LIVE PRESS CONFERENCE FROM NEW BEIJING PALACE, WHERE EMPEROR KAITO AND THE VISITING LUNAR QUEEN WILL BE BREAKING THEIR SILENCE ON THESE KIDNAPPINGS FOR THE FIRST TIME.
LET'S GO TO THAT FEED NOW.

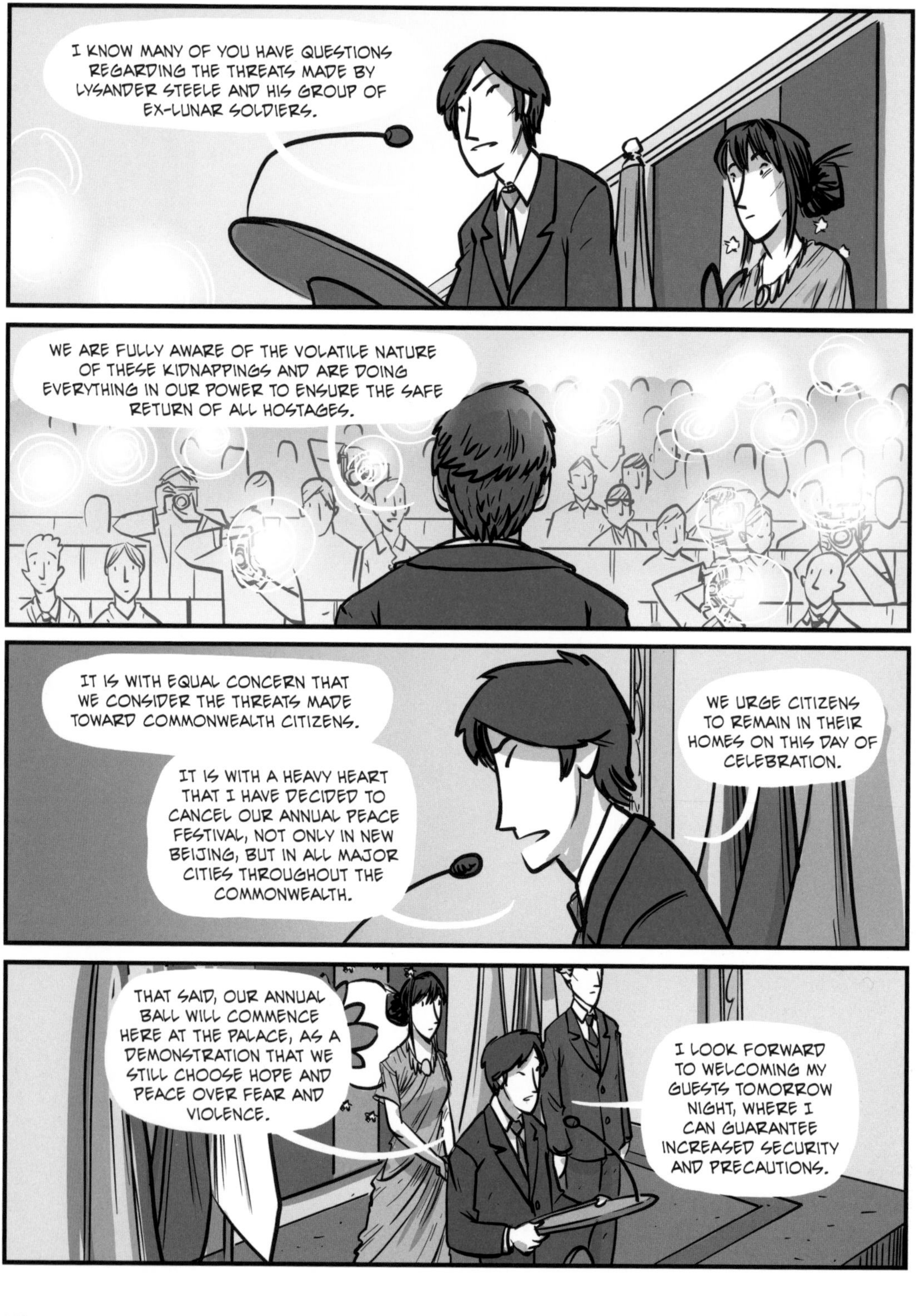
I KNOW MANY OF YOU HAVE QUESTIONS REGARDING THE THREATS MADE BY LYSANDER STEELE AND HIS GROUP OF EX-LUNAR SOLDIERS.
WE ARE FULLY AWARE OF THE VOLATILE NATURE OF THESE KIDNAPPINGS AND ARE DOING EVERYTHING IN OUR POWER TO ENSURE THE SAFE RETURN OF ALL HOSTAGES.
IT IS WITH EQUAL CONCERN THAT WE CONSIDER THE THREATS MADE TOWARD COMMONWEALTH CITIZENS.
IT IS WITH A HEAVY HEART THAT I HAVE DECIDED TO CANCEL OUR ANNUAL PEACE FESTIVAL, NOT ONLY IN NEW BEIJING, BUT IN ALL MAJOR CITIES THROUGHOUT THE COMMONWEALTH.
WE URGE CITIZENS TO REMAIN IN THEIR HOMES ON THIS DAY OF CELEBRATION.
THAT SAID, OUR ANNUAL BALL WILL COMMENCE HERE AT THE PALACE, AS A DEMONSTRATION THAT WE STILL CHOOSE HOPE AND PEACE OVER FEAR AND VIOLENCE.
I LOOK FORWARD TO WELCOMING MY GUESTS TOMORROW NIGHT, WHERE I CAN GUARANTEE INCREASED SECURITY AND PRECAUTIONS.

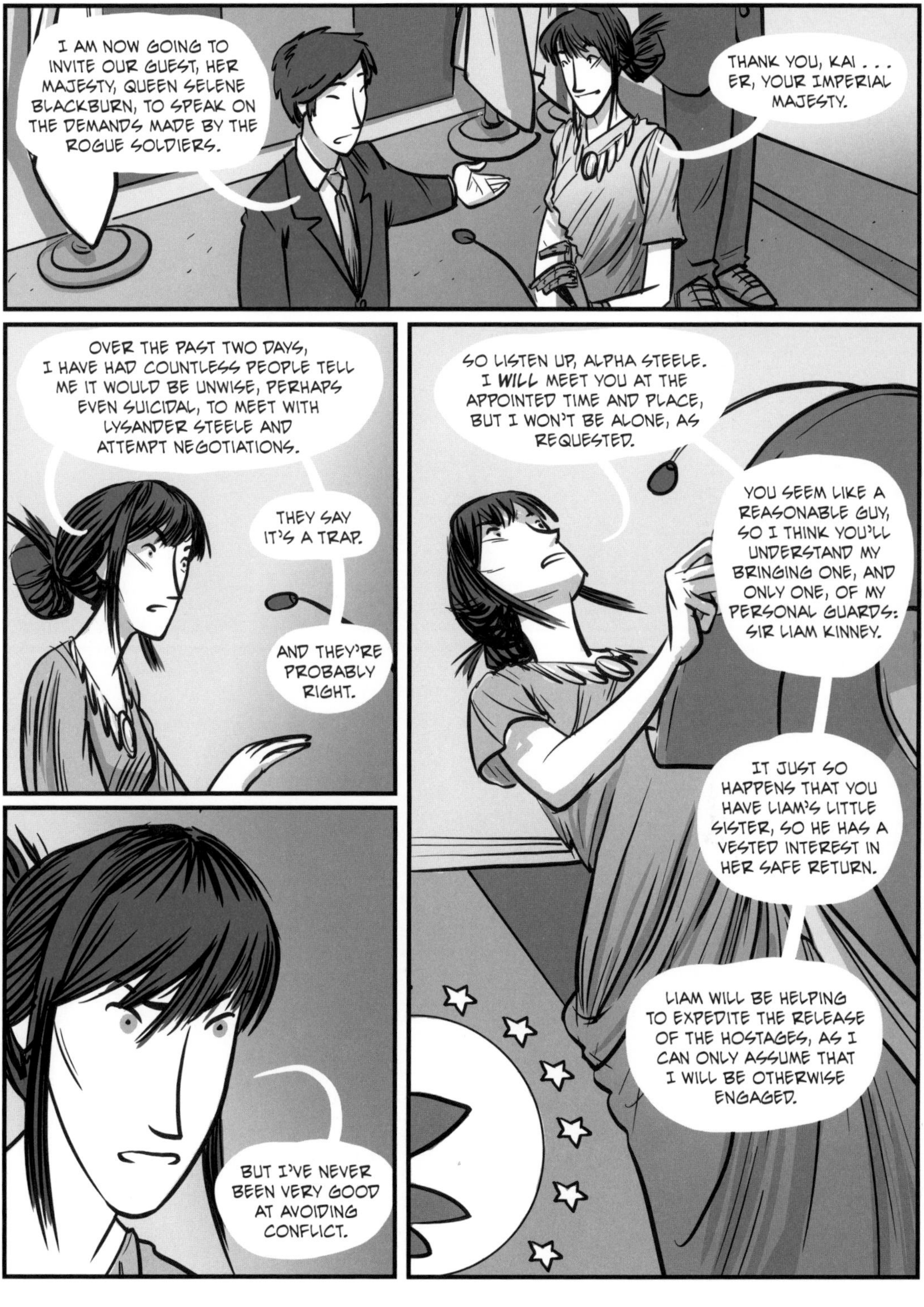
I AM NOW GOING TO INVITE OUR GUEST, HER MAJESTY, QUEEN SELENE BLACKBURN, TO SPEAK ON THE DEMANDS MADE BY THE ROGUE SOLDIERS.
THANK YOU, KAI . . . ER, YOUR IMPERIAL MAJESTY.
OVER THE PAST TWO DAYS, I HAVE HAD COUNTLESS PEOPLE TELL ME IT WOULD BE UNWISE, PERHAPS EVEN SUICIDAL, TO MEET WITH LYSANDER STEELE AND ATTEMPT NEGOTIATIONS.
THEY SAY IT'S A TRAP.
AND THEY'RE PROBABLY RIGHT.
BUT I'VE NEVER BEEN VERY GOOD AT AVOIDING CONFLICT.
SO LISTEN UP, ALPHA STEELE. I ***WILL*** MEET YOU AT THE APPOINTED TIME AND PLACE, BUT I WON'T BE ALONE, AS REQUESTED.
YOU SEEM LIKE A REASONABLE GUY, SO I THINK YOU'LL UNDERSTAND MY BRINGING ONE, AND ONLY ONE, OF MY PERSONAL GUARDS: SIR LIAM KINNEY.
IT JUST SO HAPPENS THAT YOU HAVE LIAM'S LITTLE SISTER, SO HE HAS A VESTED INTEREST IN HER SAFE RETURN.
LIAM WILL BE HELPING TO EXPEDITE THE RELEASE OF THE HOSTAGES, AS I CAN ONLY ASSUME THAT I WILL BE OTHERWISE ENGAGED.

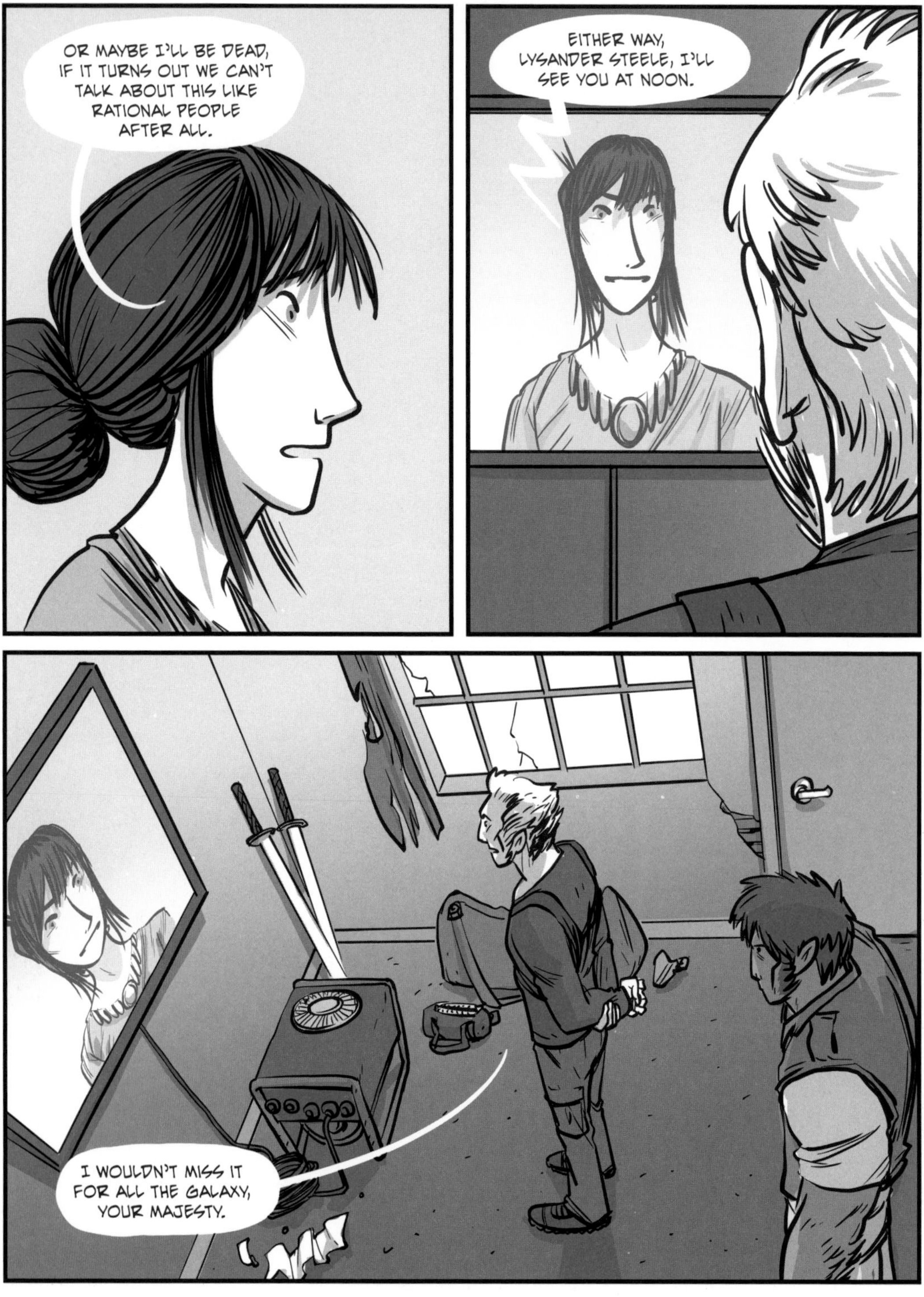
OR MAYBE I'LL BE DEAD, IF IT TURNS OUT WE CAN'T TALK ABOUT THIS LIKE RATIONAL PEOPLE AFTER ALL.
EITHER WAY, LYSANDER STEELE, I'LL SEE YOU AT NOON.
I WOULDN'T MISS IT FOR ALL THE GALAXY, YOUR MAJESTY.

CHAPTER VII

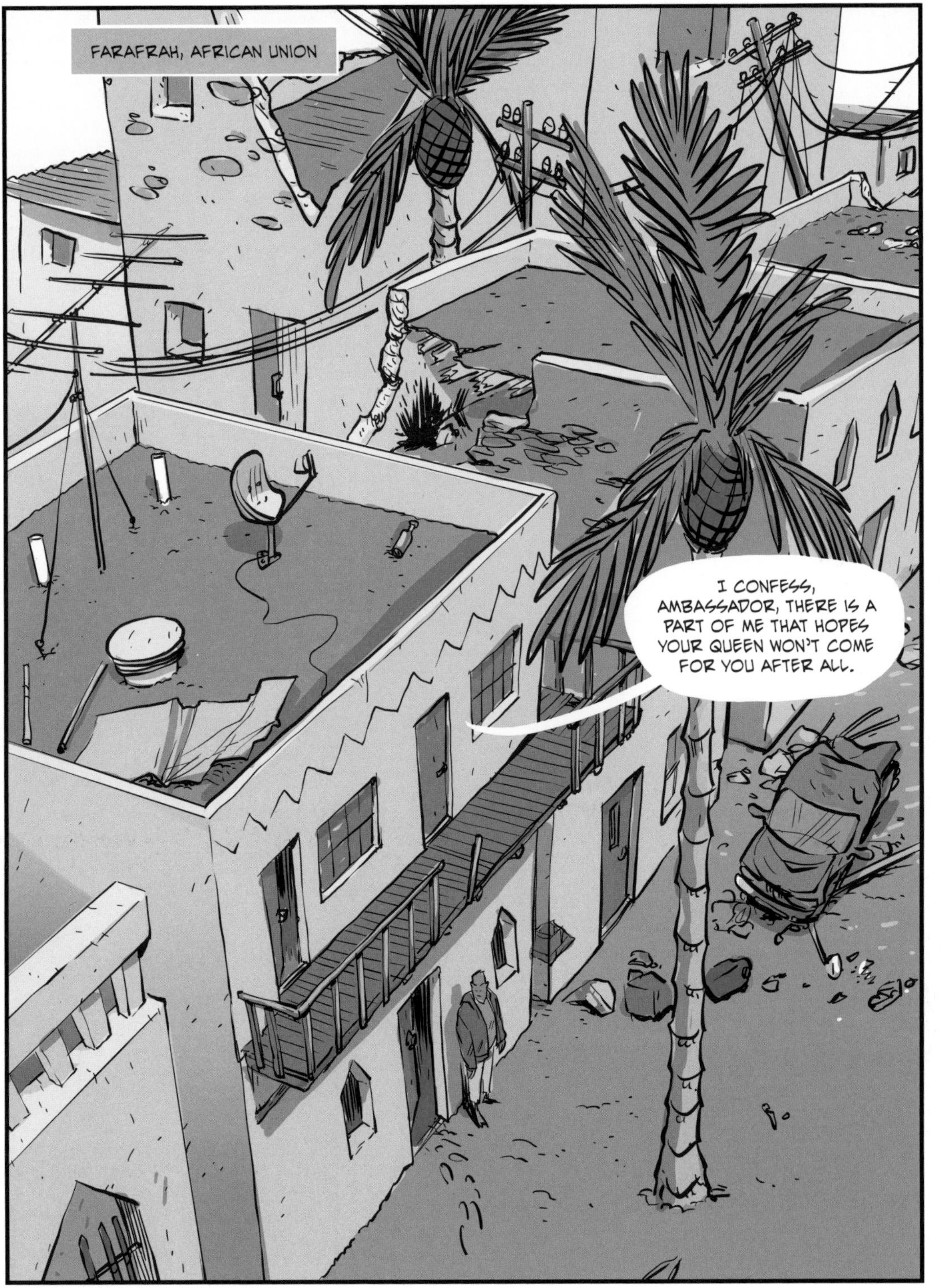
FARAFRAH, AFRICAN UNION
I CONFESS, AMBASSADOR, THERE IS A PART OF ME THAT HOPES YOUR QUEEN WON'T COME FOR YOU AFTER ALL.

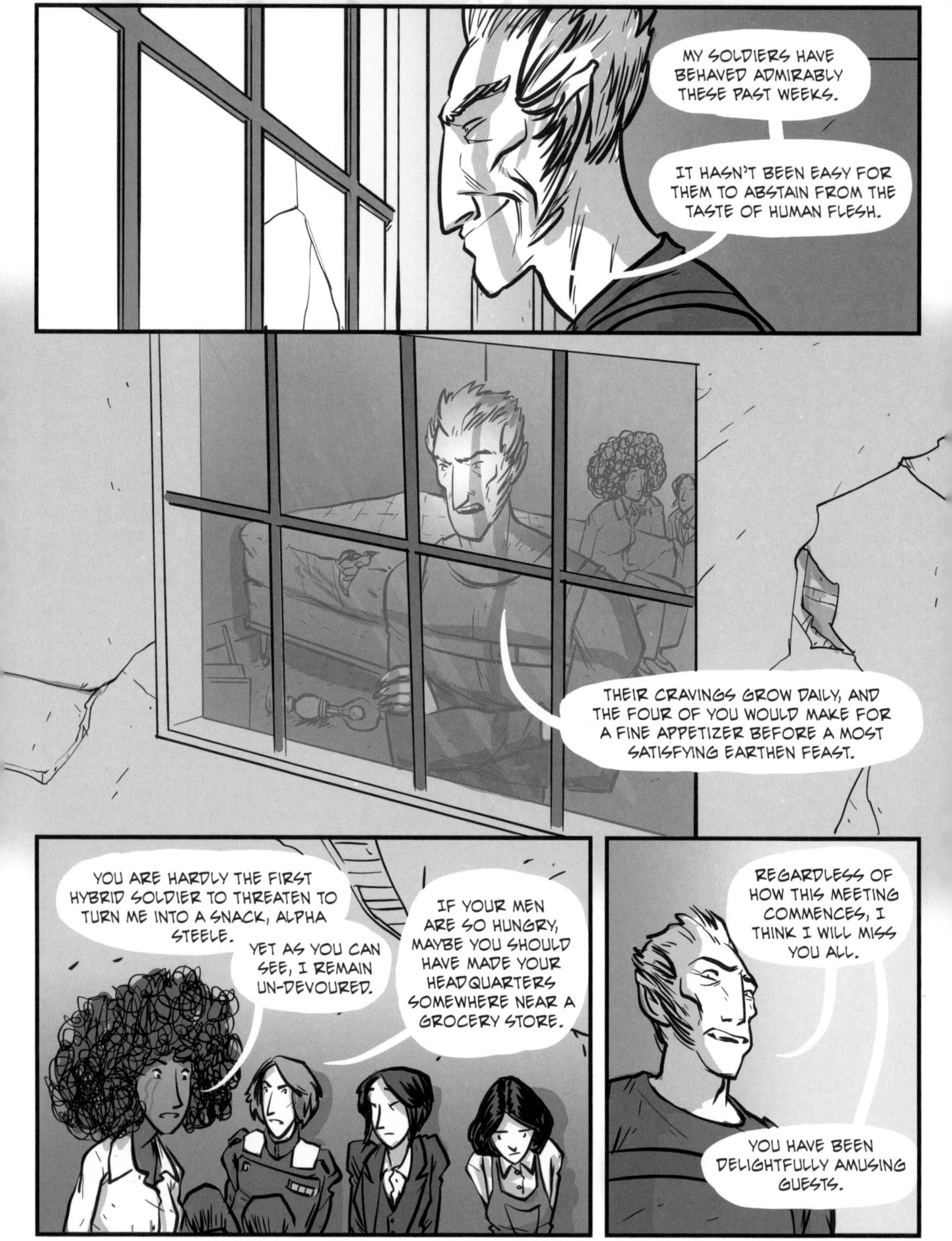

MY SOLDIERS HAVE BEHAVED ADMIRABLY THESE PAST WEEKS.
IT HASN'T BEEN EASY FOR THEM TO ABSTAIN FROM THE TASTE OF HUMAN FLESH.
THEIR CRAVINGS GROW DAILY, AND THE FOUR OF YOU WOULD MAKE FOR A FINE APPETIZER BEFORE A MOST SATISFYING EARTHEN FEAST.
YOU ARE HARDLY THE FIRST HYBRID SOLDIER TO THREATEN TO TURN ME INTO A SNACK, ALPHA STEELE.
YET AS YOU CAN SEE, I REMAIN UN-DEVOURED.
IF YOUR MEN ARE SO HUNGRY, MAYBE YOU SHOULD HAVE MADE YOUR HEADQUARTERS SOMEWHERE NEAR A GROCERY STORE.
REGARDLESS OF HOW THIS MEETING COMMENCES, I THINK I WILL MISS YOU ALL.
YOU HAVE BEEN DELIGHTFULLY AMUSING GUESTS.

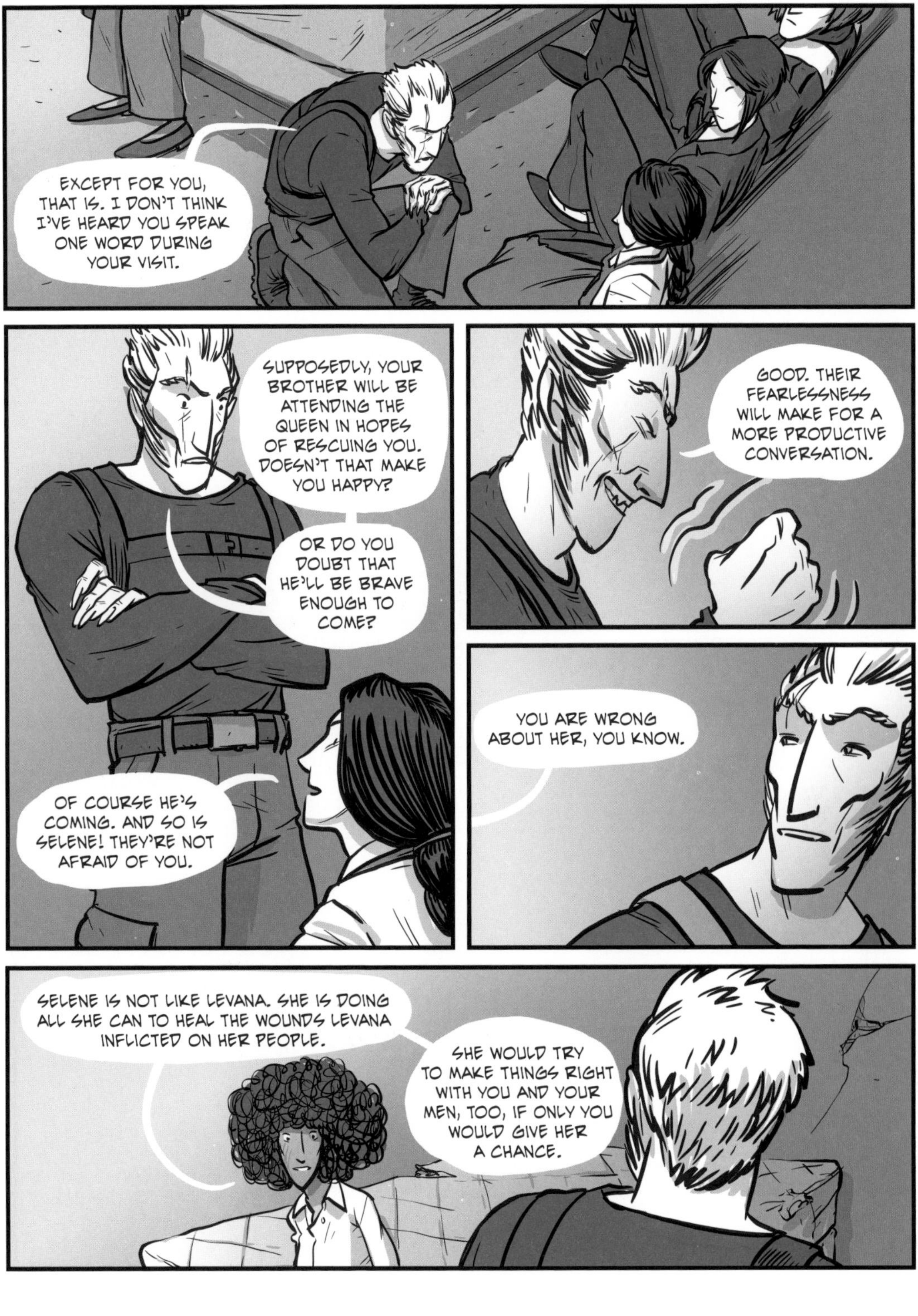
EXCEPT FOR YOU, THAT IS. I DON'T THINK I'VE HEARD YOU SPEAK ONE WORD DURING YOUR VISIT.
SUPPOSEDLY, YOUR BROTHER WILL BE ATTENDING THE QUEEN IN HOPES OF RESCUING YOU. DOESN'T THAT MAKE YOU HAPPY?
OR DO YOU DOUBT THAT HE'LL BE BRAVE ENOUGH TO COME?
OF COURSE HE'S COMING. AND SO IS SELENE! THEY'RE NOT AFRAID OF YOU.
GOOD. THEIR FEARLESSNESS WILL MAKE FOR A MORE PRODUCTIVE CONVERSATION.
YOU ARE WRONG ABOUT HER, YOU KNOW.
SELENE IS NOT LIKE LEVANA. SHE IS DOING ALL SHE CAN TO HEAL THE WOUNDS LEVANA INFLICTED ON HER PEOPLE.
SHE WOULD TRY TO MAKE THINGS RIGHT WITH YOU AND YOUR MEN, TOO, IF ONLY YOU WOULD GIVE HER A CHANCE.

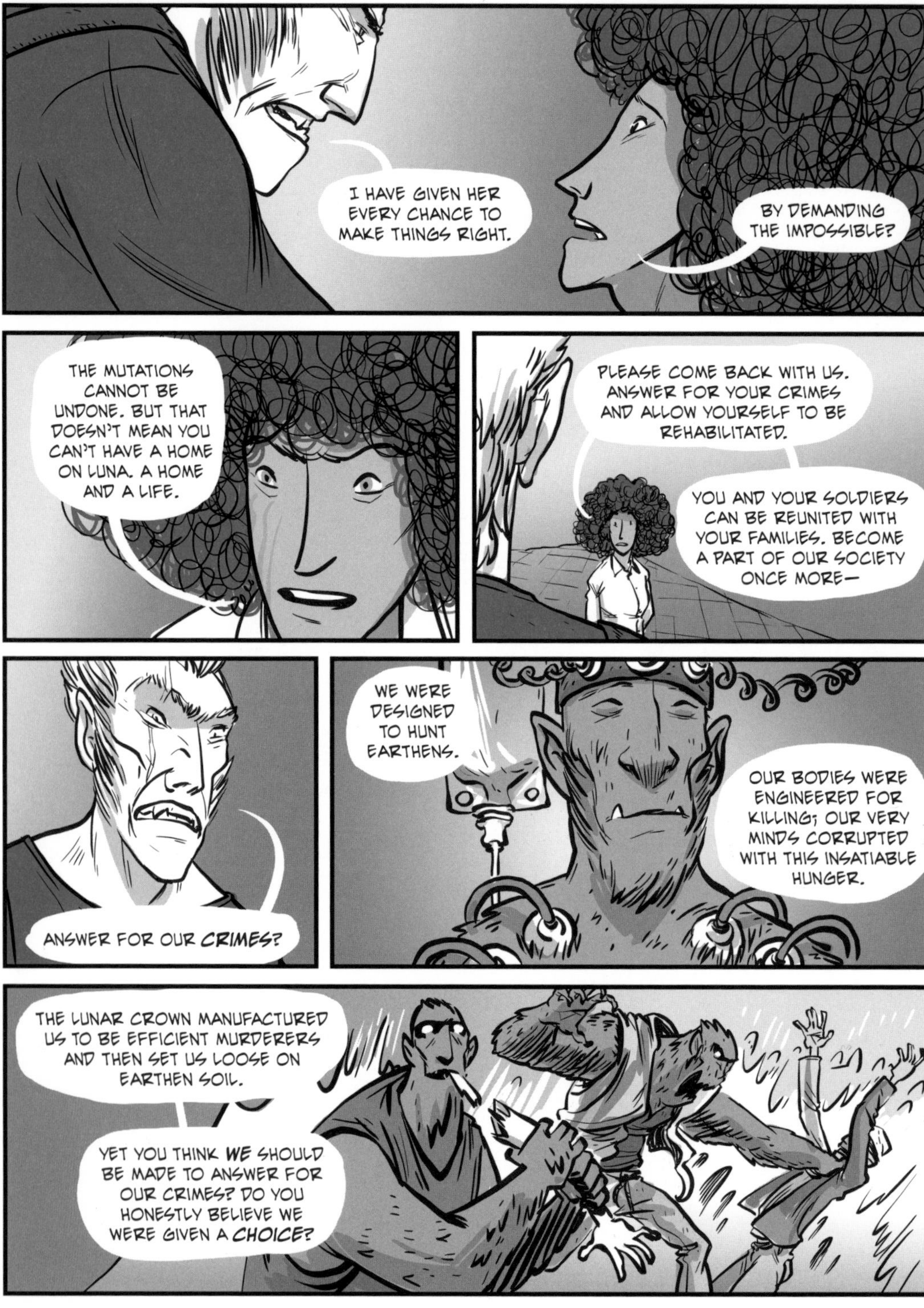
I HAVE GIVEN HER EVERY CHANCE TO MAKE THINGS RIGHT.
BY DEMANDING THE IMPOSSIBLE?
THE MUTATIONS CANNOT BE UNDONE. BUT THAT DOESN'T MEAN YOU CAN'T HAVE A HOME ON LUNA. A HOME AND A LIFE.
PLEASE COME BACK WITH US. ANSWER FOR YOUR CRIMES AND ALLOW YOURSELF TO BE REHABILITATED.
YOU AND YOUR SOLDIERS CAN BE REUNITED WITH YOUR FAMILIES. BECOME A PART OF OUR SOCIETY ONCE MORE—
ANSWER FOR OUR **CRIMES**?
WE WERE DESIGNED TO HUNT EARTHENS.
OUR BODIES WERE ENGINEERED FOR KILLING; OUR VERY MINDS CORRUPTED WITH THIS INSATIABLE HUNGER.
THE LUNAR CROWN MANUFACTURED US TO BE EFFICIENT MURDERERS AND THEN SET US LOOSE ON EARTHEN SOIL.
YET YOU THINK **WE** SHOULD BE MADE TO ANSWER FOR OUR CRIMES? DO YOU HONESTLY BELIEVE WE WERE GIVEN A **CHOICE**?

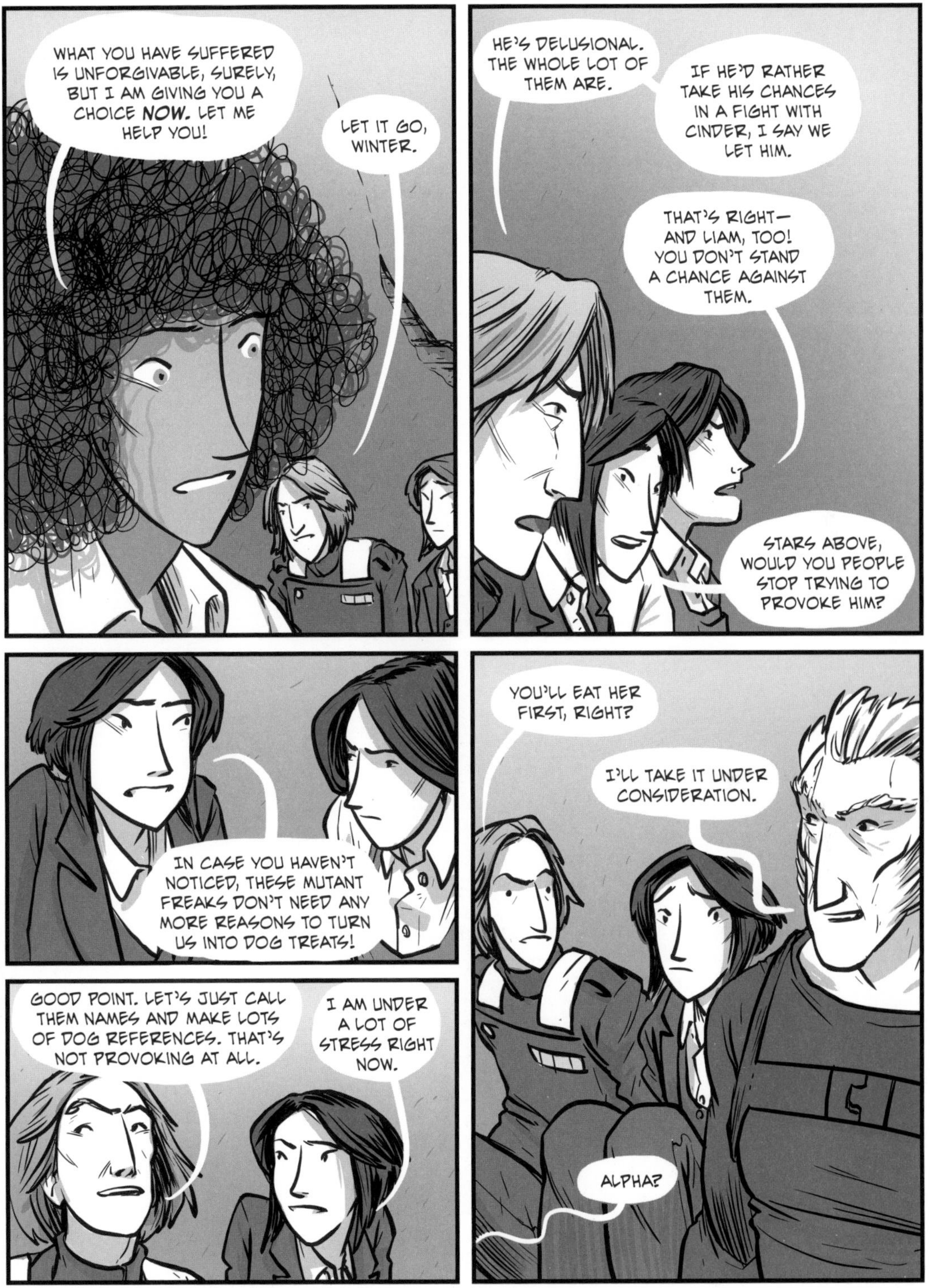
WHAT YOU HAVE SUFFERED IS UNFORGIVABLE, SURELY, BUT I AM GIVING YOU A CHOICE **NOW.** LET ME HELP YOU!
LET IT GO, WINTER.
HE'S DELUSIONAL. THE WHOLE LOT OF THEM ARE.
IF HE'D RATHER TAKE HIS CHANCES IN A FIGHT WITH CINDER, I SAY WE LET HIM.
THAT'S RIGHT— AND LIAM, TOO! YOU DON'T STAND A CHANCE AGAINST THEM.
STARS ABOVE, WOULD YOU PEOPLE STOP TRYING TO PROVOKE HIM?
IN CASE YOU HAVEN'T NOTICED, THESE MUTANT FREAKS DON'T NEED ANY MORE REASONS TO TURN US INTO DOG TREATS!
GOOD POINT. LET'S JUST CALL THEM NAMES AND MAKE LOTS OF DOG REFERENCES. THAT'S NOT PROVOKING AT ALL.
I AM UNDER A LOT OF STRESS RIGHT NOW.
YOU'LL EAT HER FIRST, RIGHT?
I'LL TAKE IT UNDER CONSIDERATION.
ALPHA?

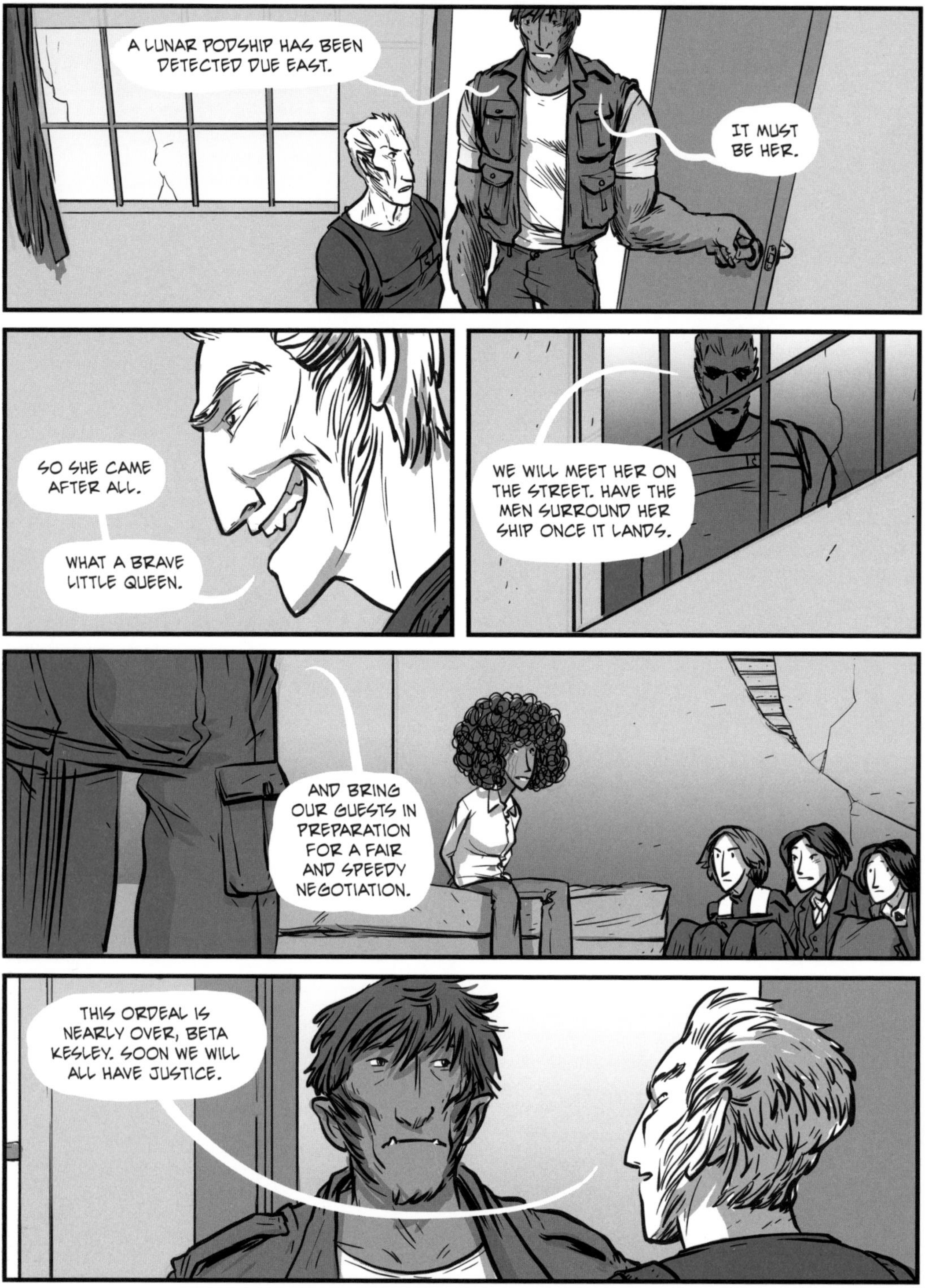
A LUNAR PODSHIP HAS BEEN DETECTED DUE EAST.
IT MUST BE HER.
SO SHE CAME AFTER ALL.
WHAT A BRAVE LITTLE QUEEN.
WE WILL MEET HER ON THE STREET. HAVE THE MEN SURROUND HER SHIP ONCE IT LANDS.
AND BRING OUR GUESTS IN PREPARATION FOR A FAIR AND SPEEDY NEGOTIATION.
THIS ORDEAL IS NEARLY OVER, BETA KESLEY. SOON WE WILL ALL HAVE JUSTICE.

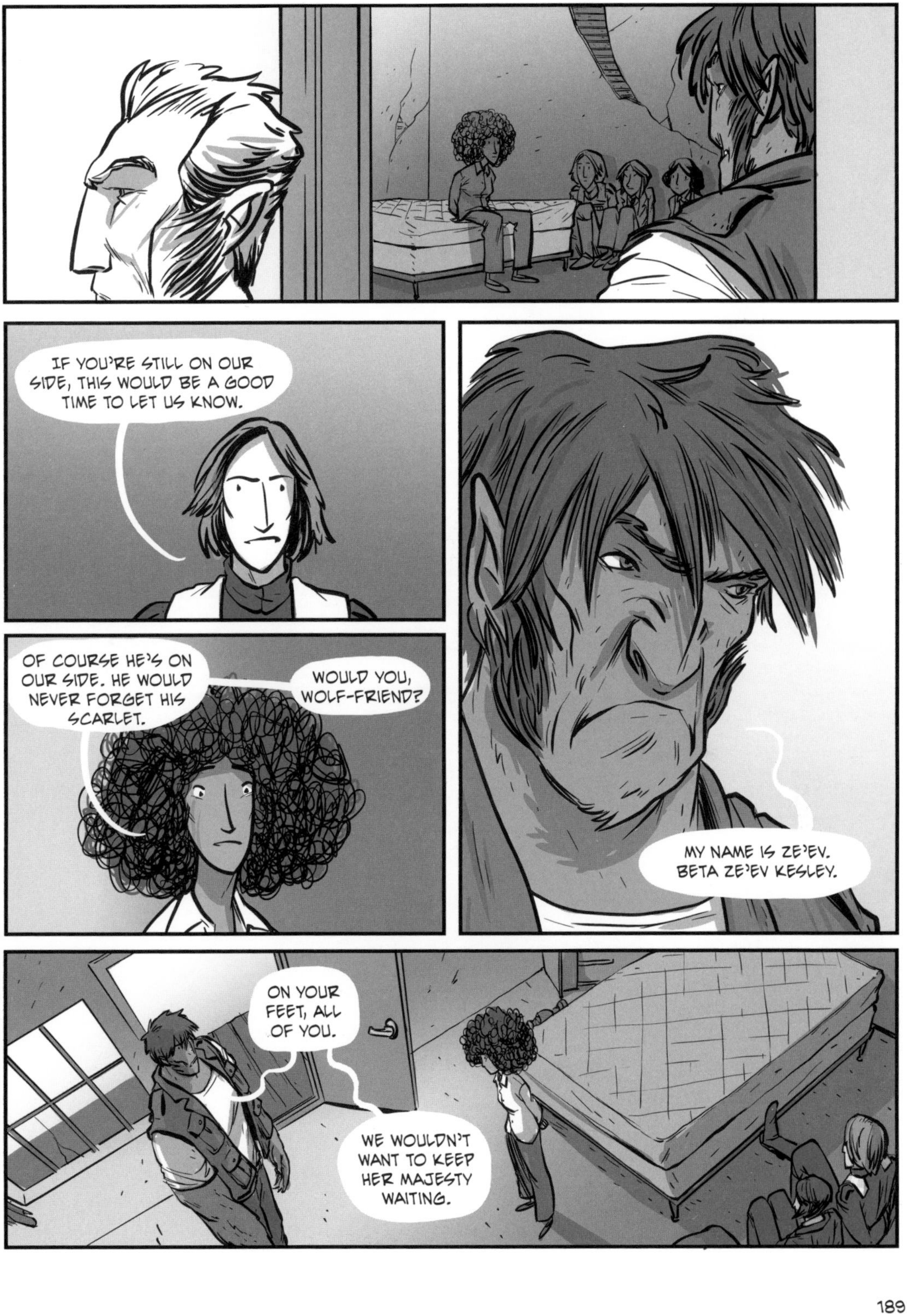
IF YOU'RE STILL ON OUR SIDE, THIS WOULD BE A GOOD TIME TO LET US KNOW.
OF COURSE HE'S ON OUR SIDE. HE WOULD NEVER FORGET HIS SCARLET.
WOULD YOU, WOLF-FRIEND?
MY NAME IS ZE'EV. BETA ZE'EV KESLEY.
ON YOUR FEET, ALL OF YOU.
WE WOULDN'T WANT TO KEEP HER MAJESTY WAITING.

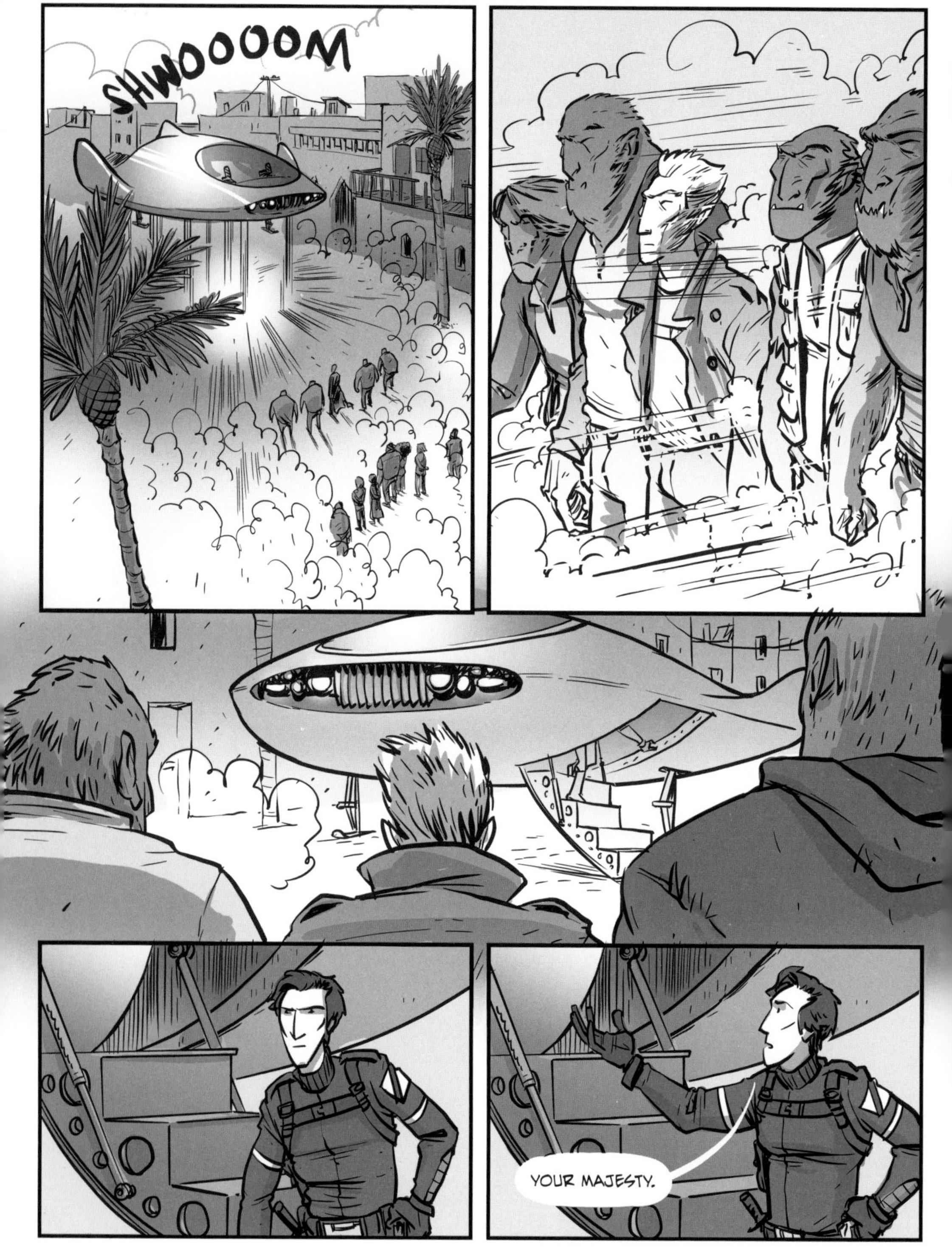
SHWOOOOM
YOUR MAJESTY.

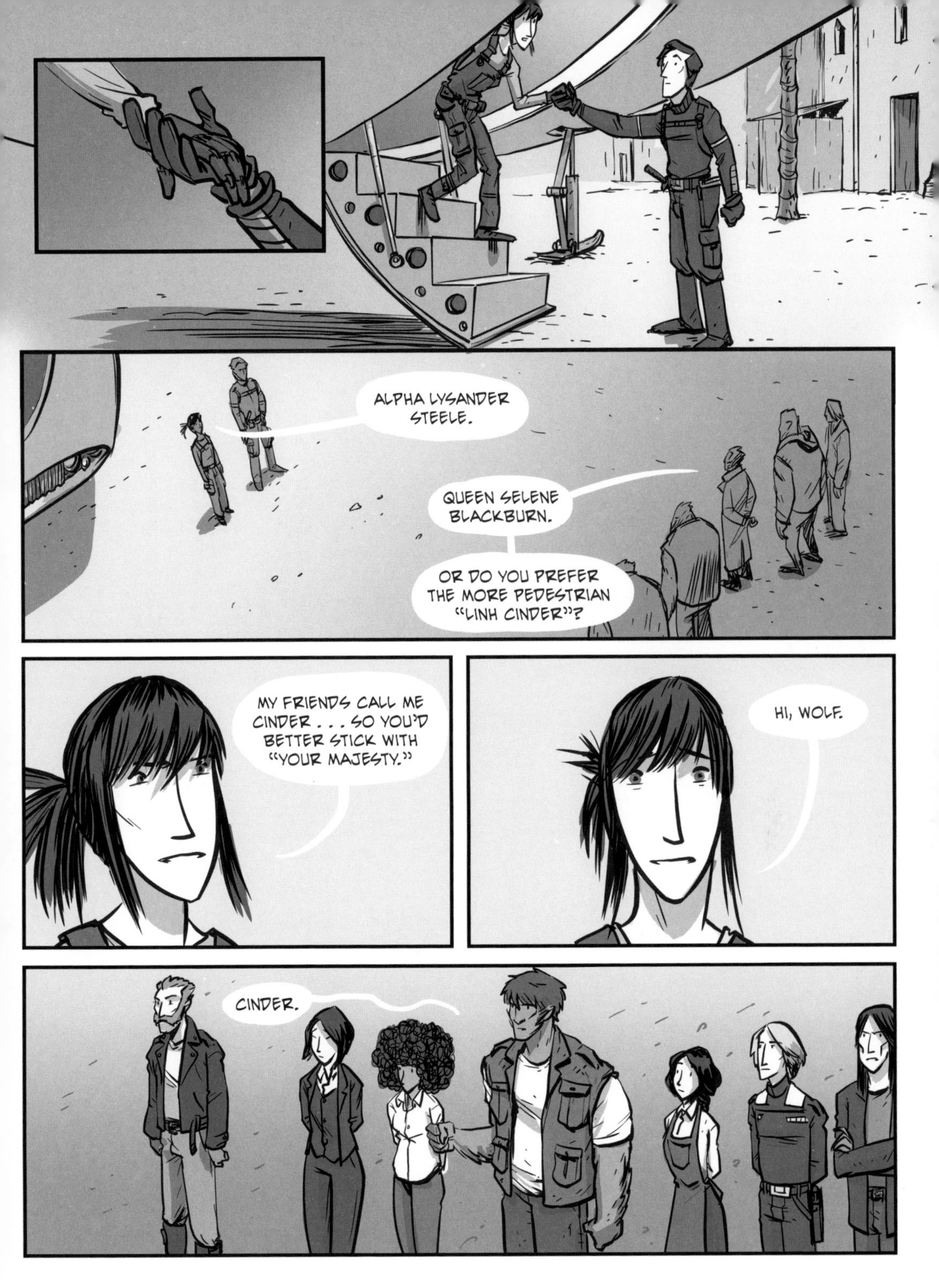
ALPHA LYSANDER STEELE.
QUEEN SELENE BLACKBURN.
OR DO YOU PREFER THE MORE PEDESTRIAN "LINH CINDER"?
MY FRIENDS CALL ME CINDER . . . SO YOU'D BETTER STICK WITH "YOUR MAJESTY."
HI, WOLF.
CINDER.

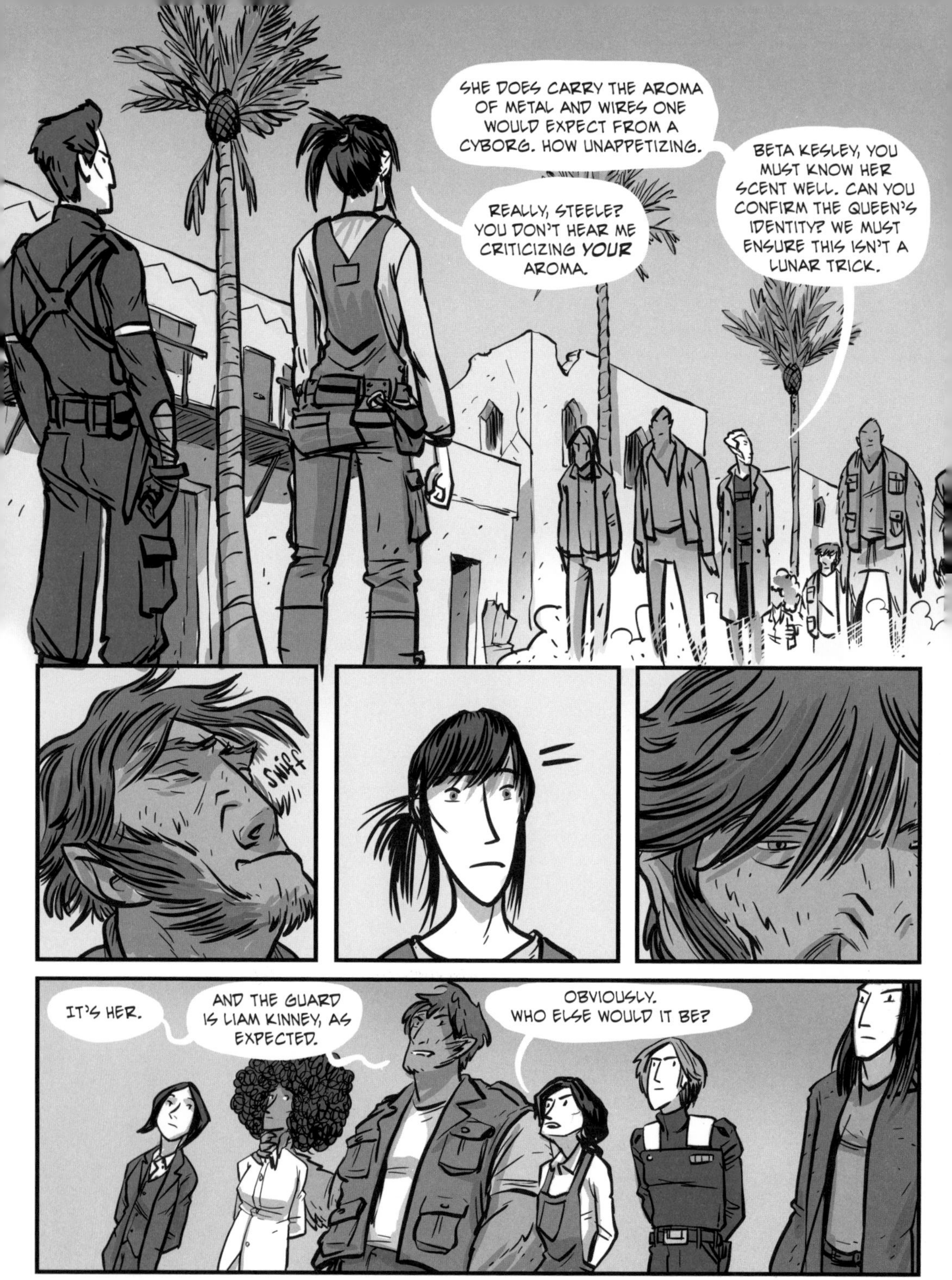

SHE DOES CARRY THE AROMA OF METAL AND WIRES ONE WOULD EXPECT FROM A CYBORG. HOW UNAPPETIZING.
REALLY, STEELE? YOU DON'T HEAR ME CRITICIZING *YOUR* AROMA.
BETA KESLEY, YOU MUST KNOW HER SCENT WELL. CAN YOU CONFIRM THE QUEEN'S IDENTITY? WE MUST ENSURE THIS ISN'T A LUNAR TRICK.
sniff
IT'S HER.
AND THE GUARD IS LIAM KINNEY, AS EXPECTED.
OBVIOUSLY. WHO ELSE WOULD IT BE?

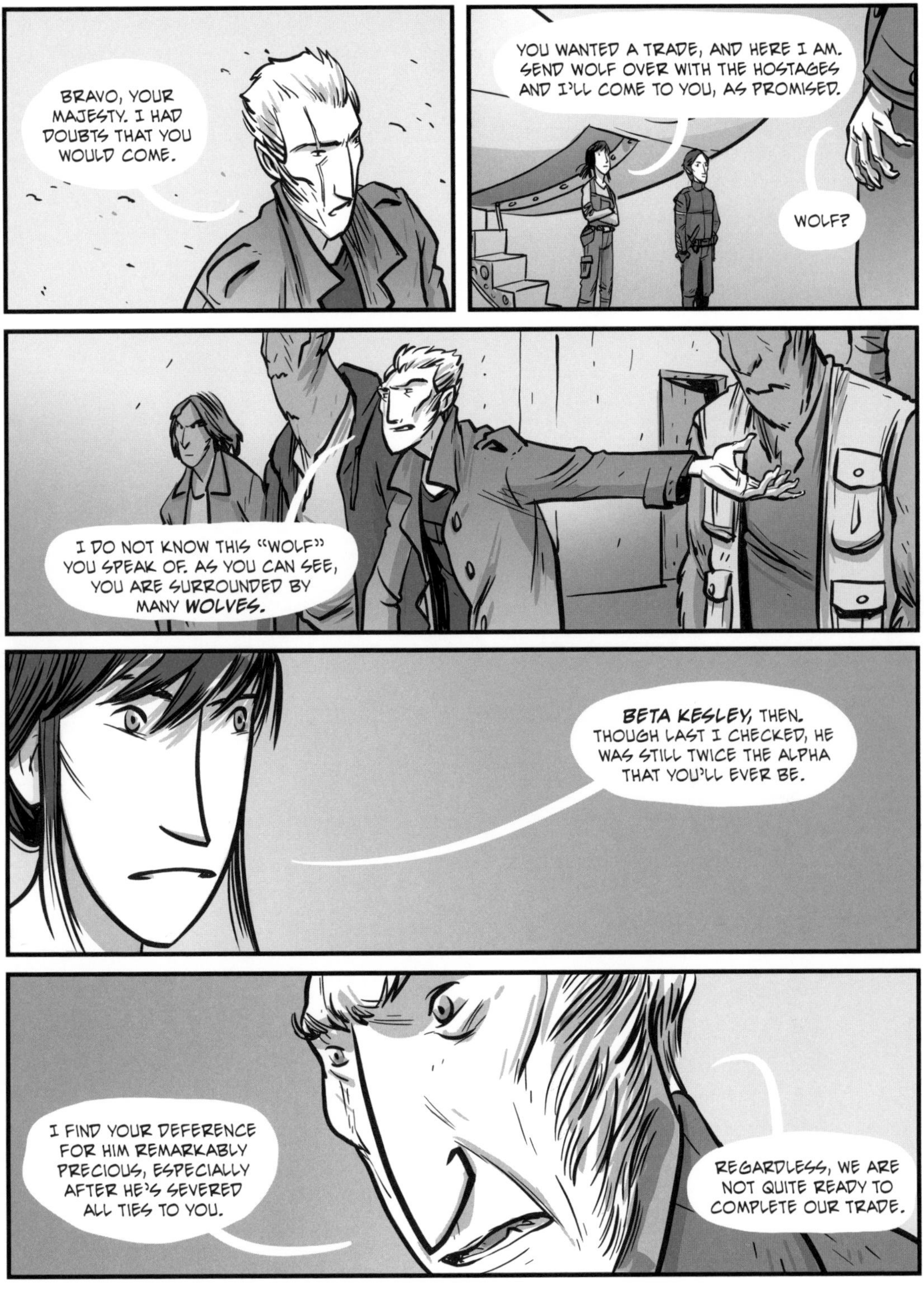
BRAVO, YOUR MAJESTY. I HAD DOUBTS THAT YOU WOULD COME.
YOU WANTED A TRADE, AND HERE I AM. SEND WOLF OVER WITH THE HOSTAGES AND I'LL COME TO YOU, AS PROMISED.
WOLF?
I DO NOT KNOW THIS "WOLF" YOU SPEAK OF. AS YOU CAN SEE, YOU ARE SURROUNDED BY MANY WOLVES.
BETA KESLEY, THEN. THOUGH LAST I CHECKED, HE WAS STILL TWICE THE ALPHA THAT YOU'LL EVER BE.
I FIND YOUR DEFERENCE FOR HIM REMARKABLY PRECIOUS, ESPECIALLY AFTER HE'S SEVERED ALL TIES TO YOU.
REGARDLESS, WE ARE NOT QUITE READY TO COMPLETE OUR TRADE.

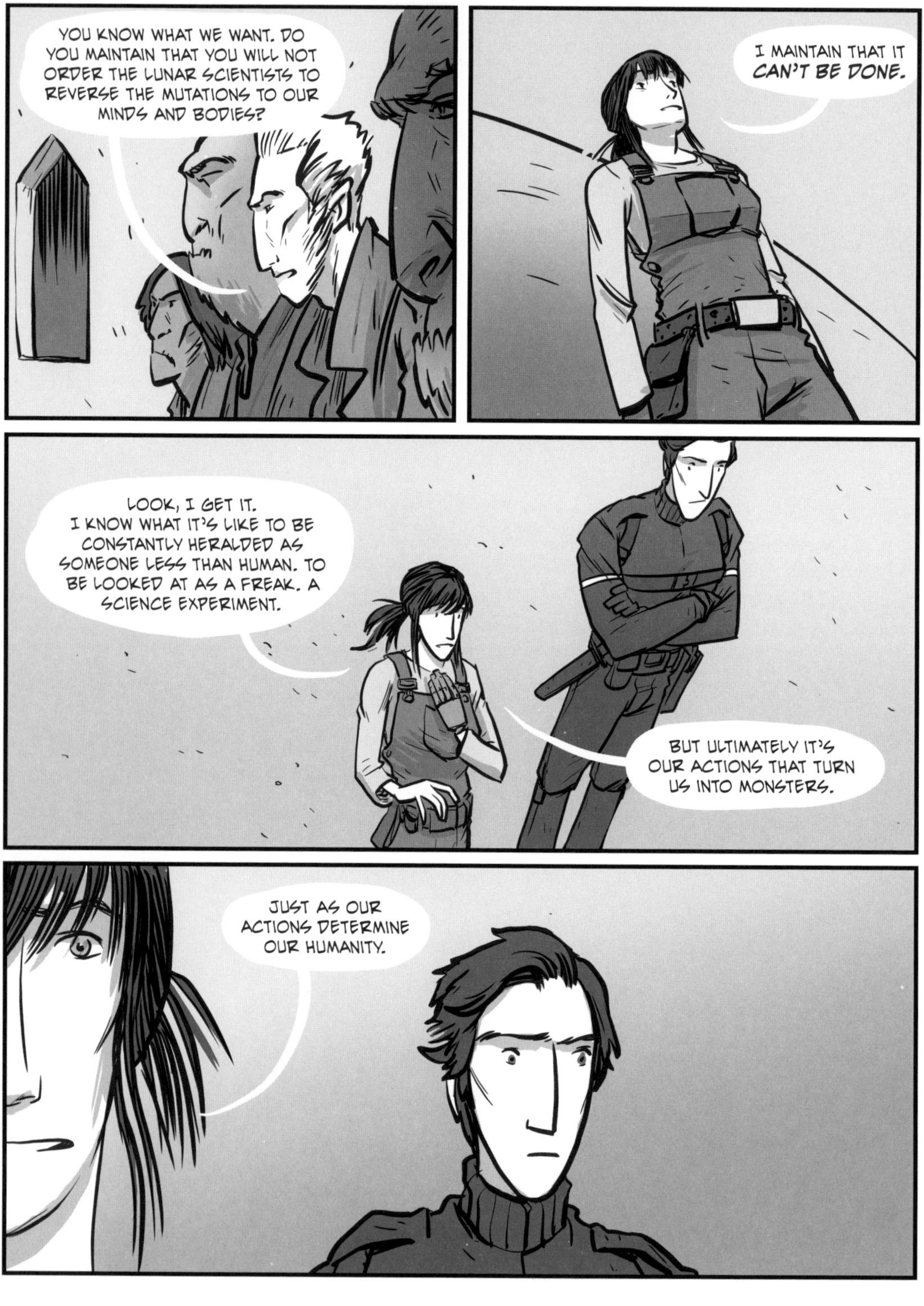
YOU KNOW WHAT WE WANT. DO YOU MAINTAIN THAT YOU WILL NOT ORDER THE LUNAR SCIENTISTS TO REVERSE THE MUTATIONS TO OUR MINDS AND BODIES?
I MAINTAIN THAT IT *CAN'T BE DONE.*
LOOK, I GET IT. I KNOW WHAT IT'S LIKE TO BE CONSTANTLY HERALDED AS SOMEONE LESS THAN HUMAN. TO BE LOOKED AT AS A FREAK. A SCIENCE EXPERIMENT.
BUT ULTIMATELY IT'S OUR ACTIONS THAT TURN US INTO MONSTERS.
JUST AS OUR ACTIONS DETERMINE OUR HUMANITY.

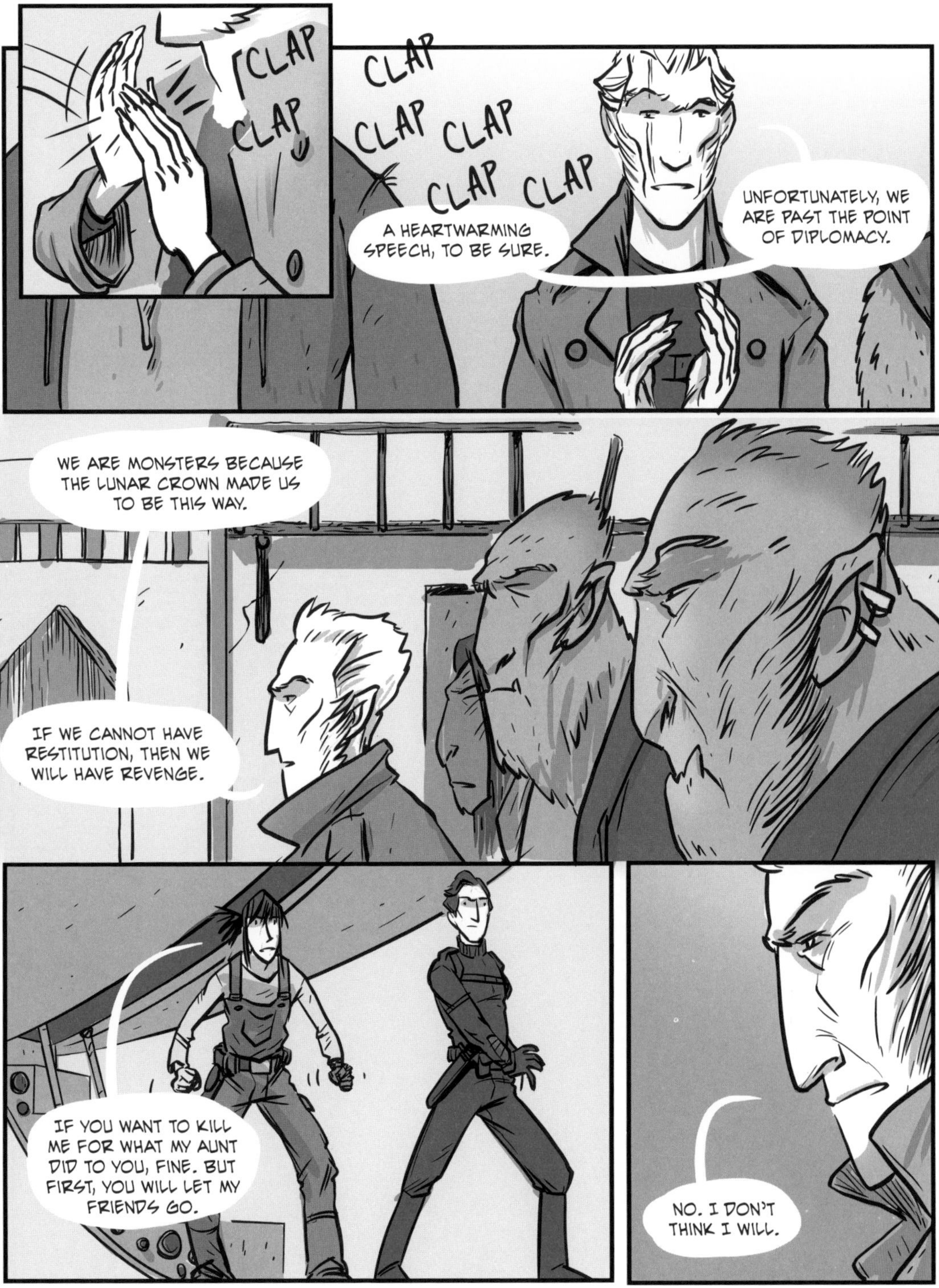
CLAP
CLAP
CLAP
CLAP CLAP
CLAP CLAP
A HEARTWARMING SPEECH, TO BE SURE.
UNFORTUNATELY, WE ARE PAST THE POINT OF DIPLOMACY.
WE ARE MONSTERS BECAUSE THE LUNAR CROWN MADE US TO BE THIS WAY.
IF WE CANNOT HAVE RESTITUTION, THEN WE WILL HAVE REVENGE.
IF YOU WANT TO KILL ME FOR WHAT MY AUNT DID TO YOU, FINE. BUT FIRST, YOU WILL LET MY FRIENDS GO.
NO. I DON'T THINK I WILL.

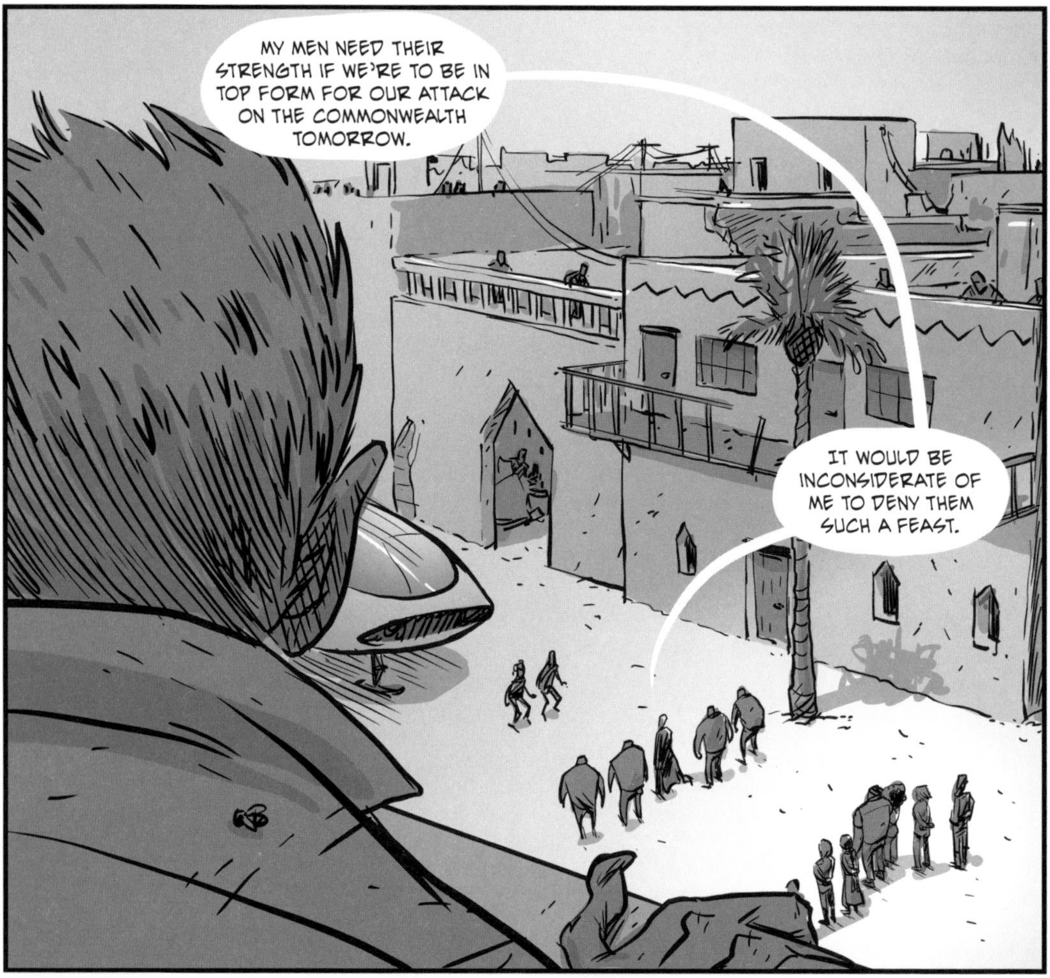
MY MEN NEED THEIR STRENGTH IF WE'RE TO BE IN TOP FORM FOR OUR ATTACK ON THE COMMONWEALTH TOMORROW.
IT WOULD BE INCONSIDERATE OF ME TO DENY THEM SUCH A FEAST.

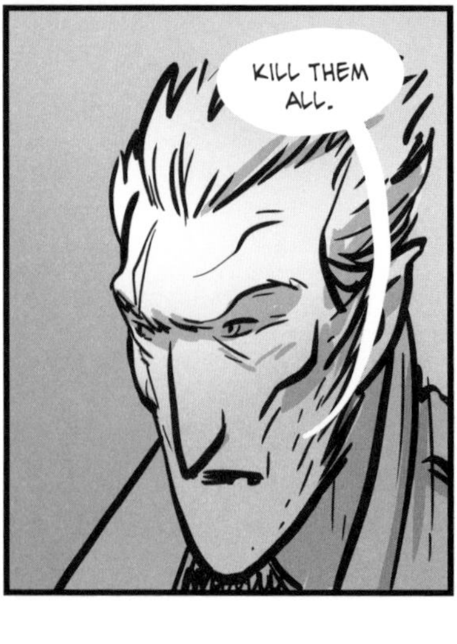
KILL THEM ALL.

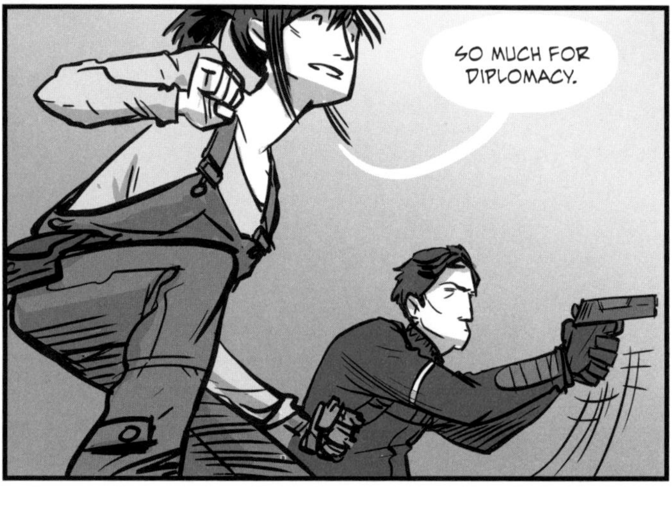
SO MUCH FOR DIPLOMACY.

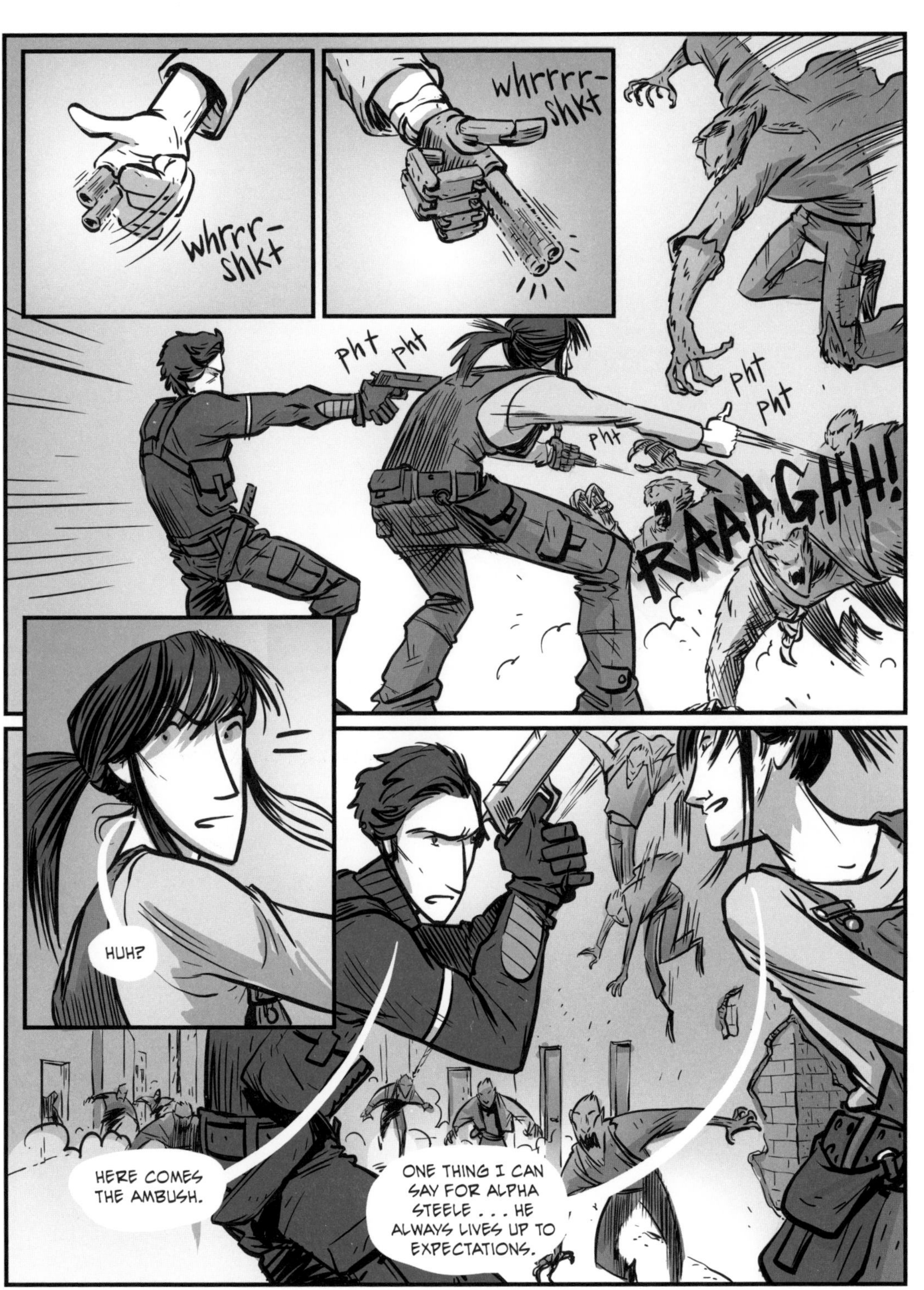
whrrr-shkt
whrrrr-shkt
pht pht
pht pht
pht
RAAAGHH!
HUH?
HERE COMES THE AMBUSH.
ONE THING I CAN SAY FOR ALPHA STEELE . . . HE ALWAYS LIVES UP TO EXPECTATIONS.

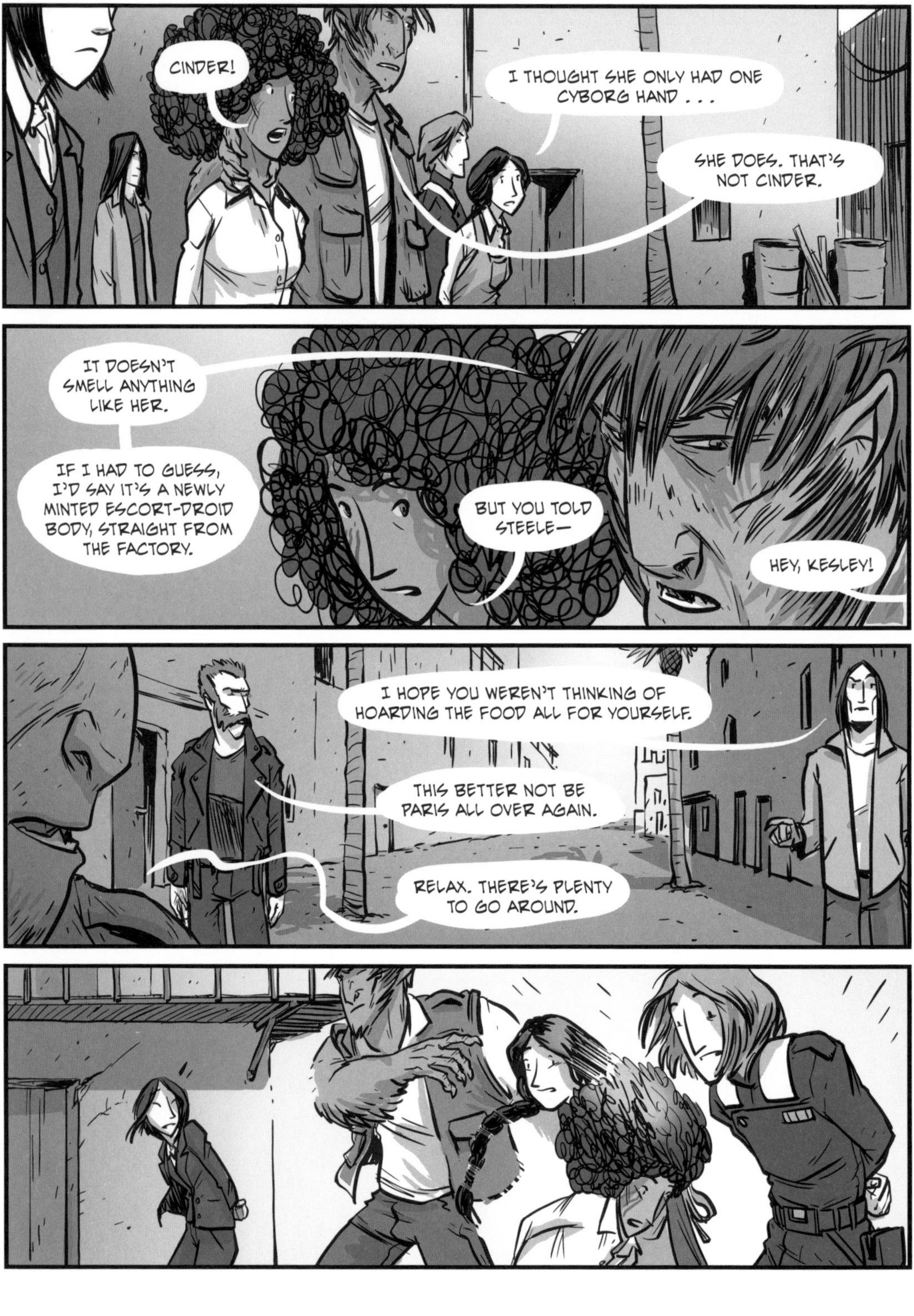
CINDER!
I THOUGHT SHE ONLY HAD ONE CYBORG HAND . . .
SHE DOES. THAT'S NOT CINDER.
IT DOESN'T SMELL ANYTHING LIKE HER.
IF I HAD TO GUESS, I'D SAY IT'S A NEWLY MINTED ESCORT-DROID BODY, STRAIGHT FROM THE FACTORY.
BUT YOU TOLD STEELE—
HEY, KESLEY!
I HOPE YOU WEREN'T THINKING OF HOARDING THE FOOD ALL FOR YOURSELF.
THIS BETTER NOT BE PARIS ALL OVER AGAIN.
RELAX. THERE'S PLENTY TO GO AROUND.

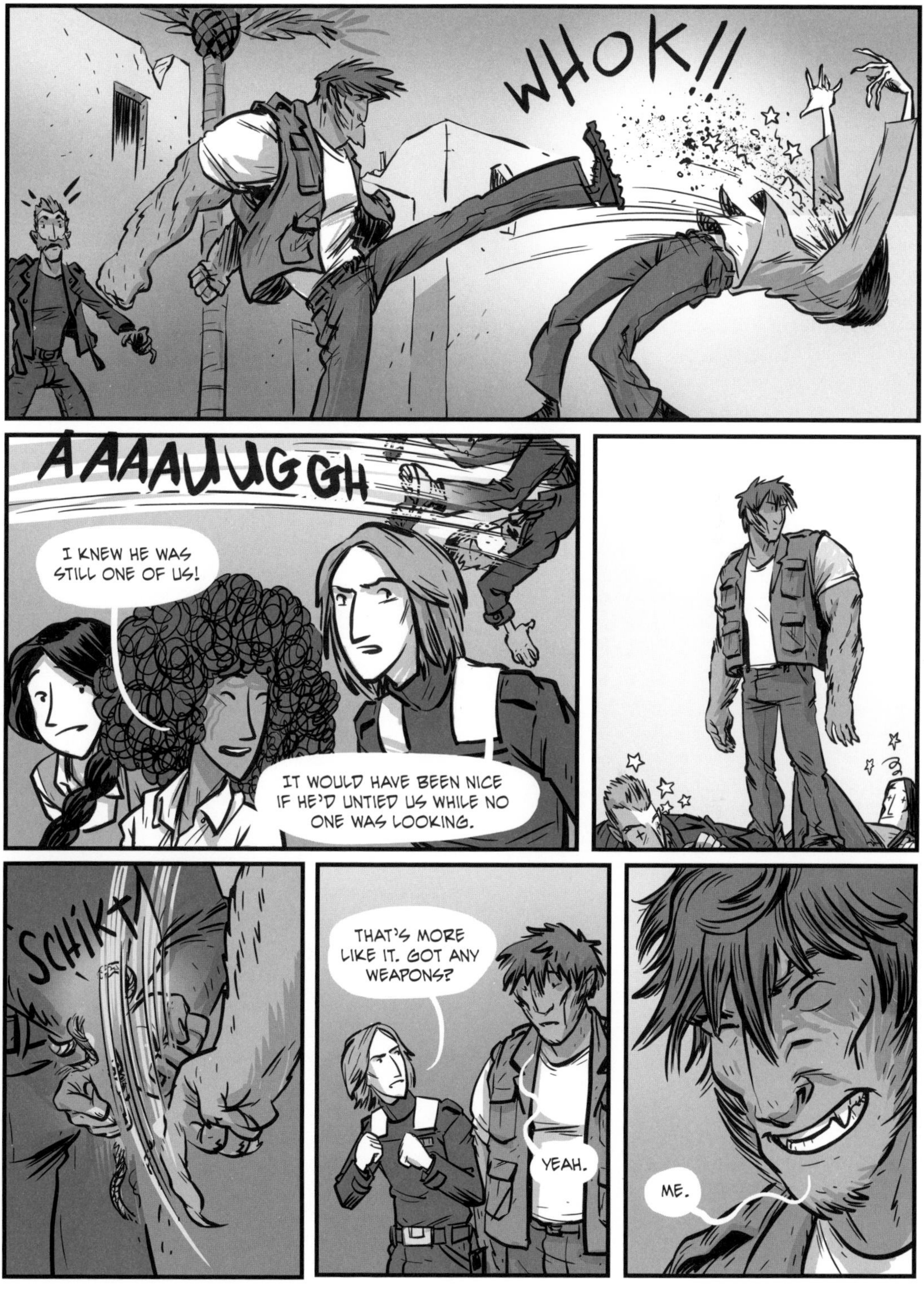
WHOK!!
AAAAUUGGH
I KNEW HE WAS STILL ONE OF US!
IT WOULD HAVE BEEN NICE IF HE'D UNTIED US WHILE NO ONE WAS LOOKING.
SCHIKT
THAT'S MORE LIKE IT. GOT ANY WEAPONS?
YEAH.
ME.

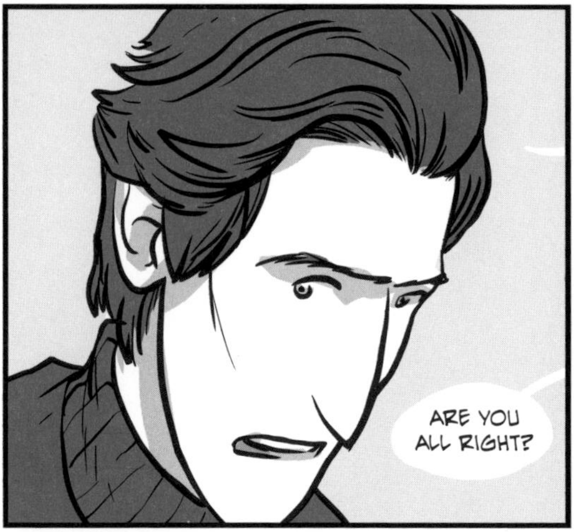
ARE YOU
ALL RIGHT?

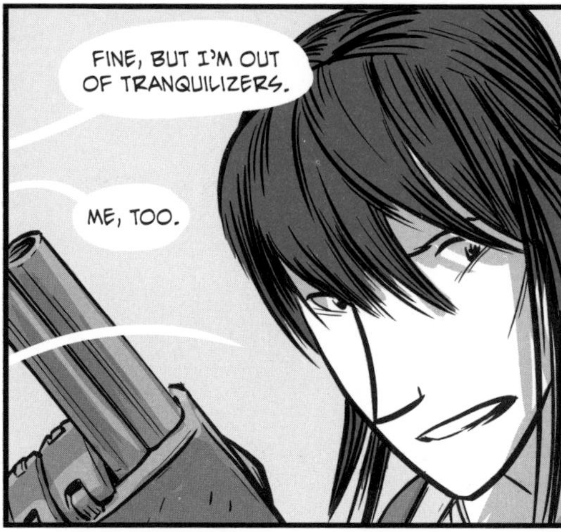
FINE, BUT I'M OUT
OF TRANQUILIZERS.
ME, TOO.

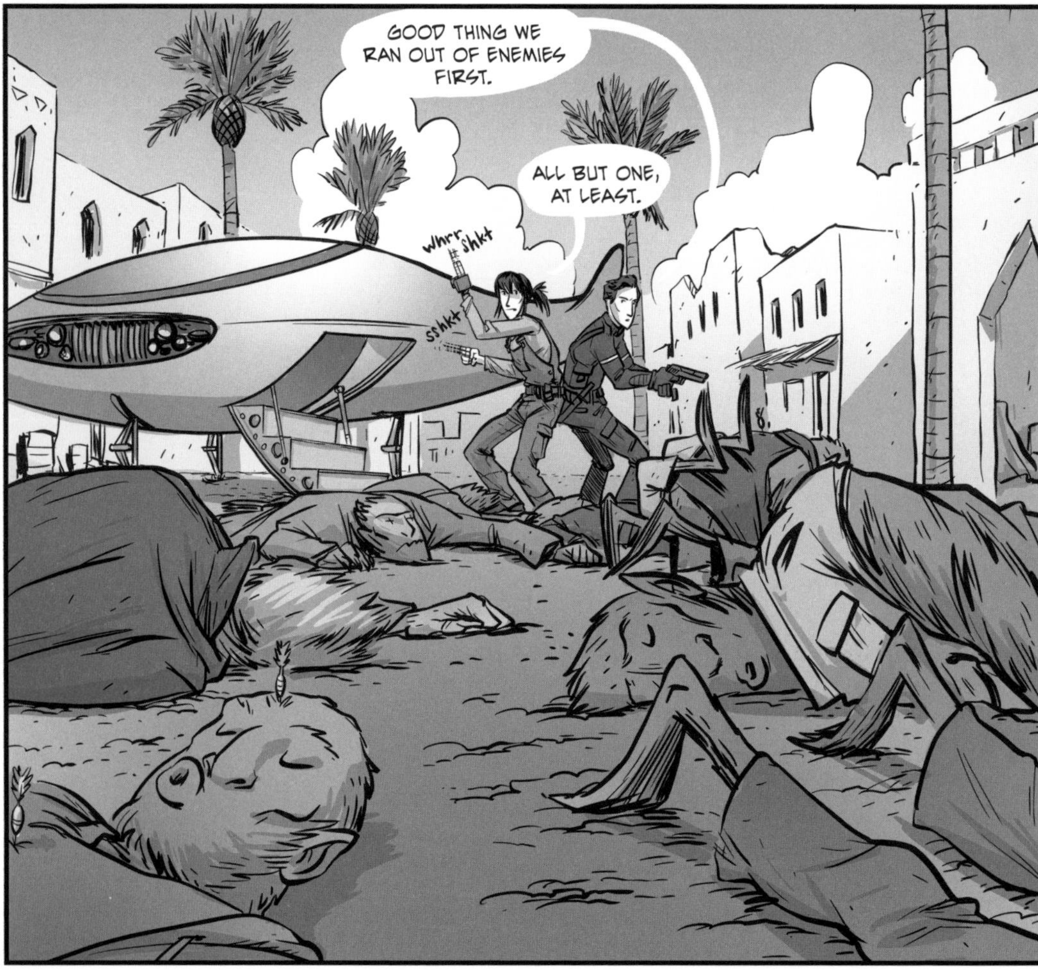
GOOD THING WE
RAN OUT OF ENEMIES
FIRST.
ALL BUT ONE,
AT LEAST.
whrr shkt
sshkt

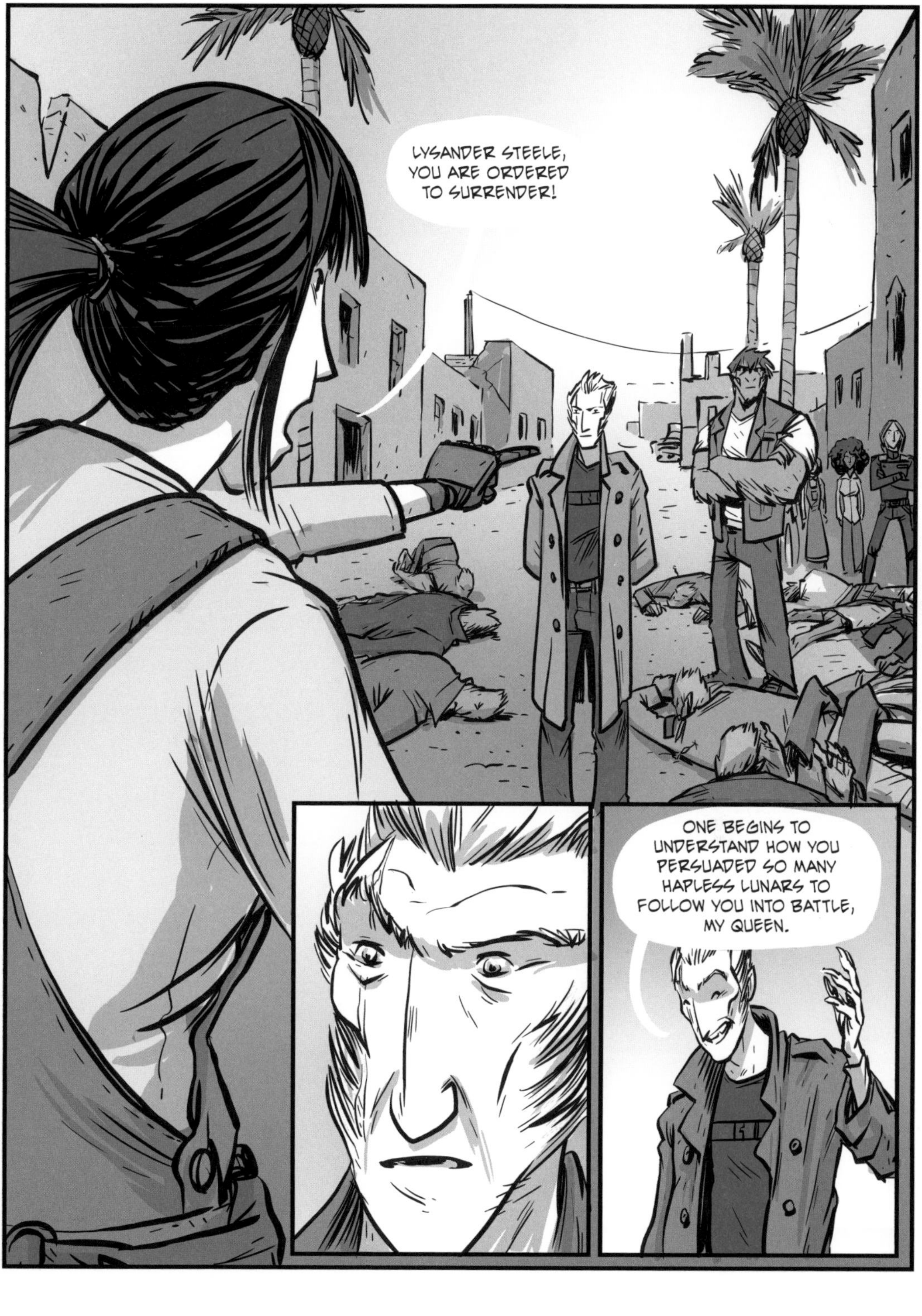
LYSANDER STEELE, YOU ARE ORDERED TO SURRENDER!
ONE BEGINS TO UNDERSTAND HOW YOU PERSUADED SO MANY HAPLESS LUNARS TO FOLLOW YOU INTO BATTLE, MY QUEEN.

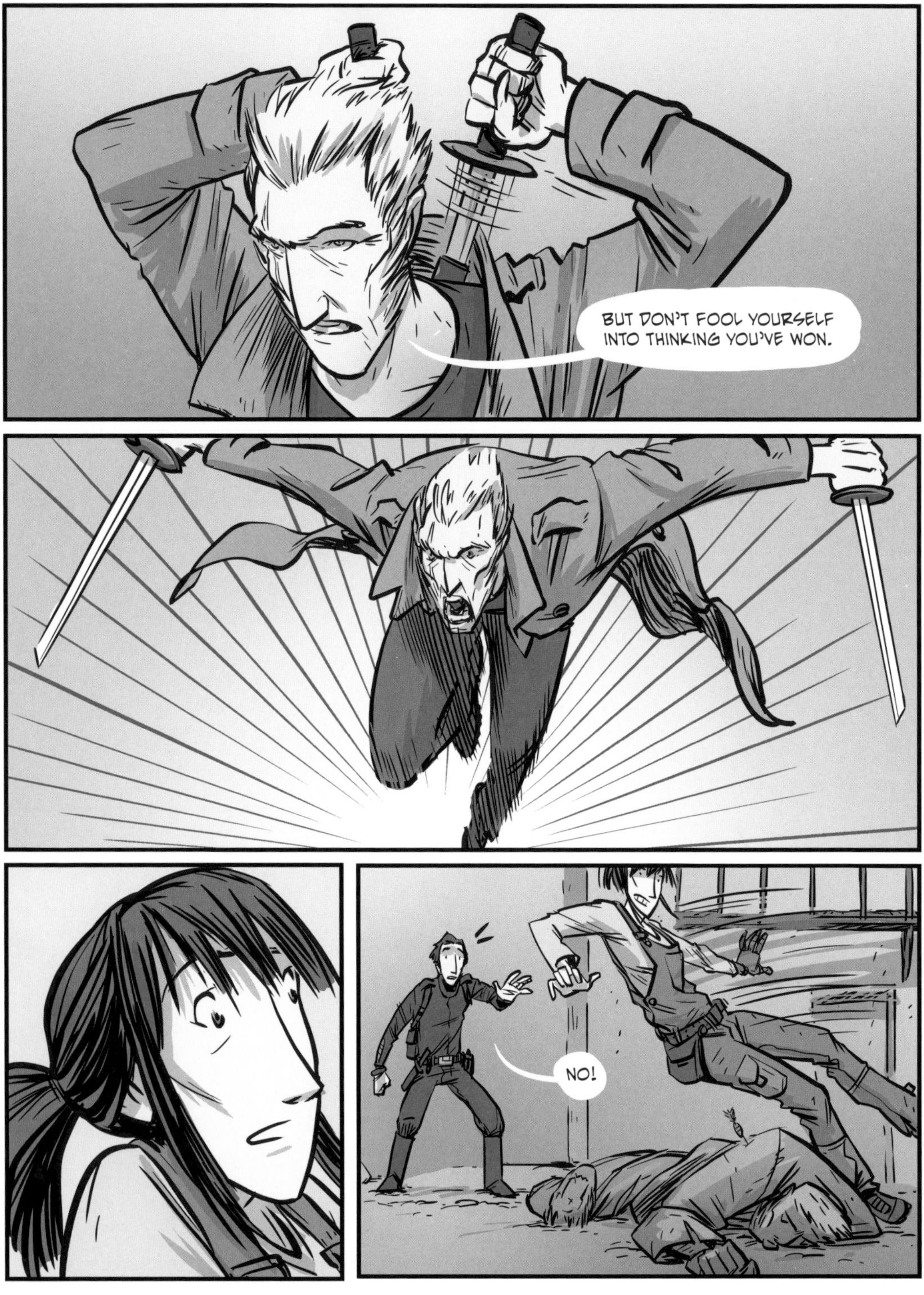
BUT DON'T FOOL YOURSELF
INTO THINKING YOU'VE WON.
NO!

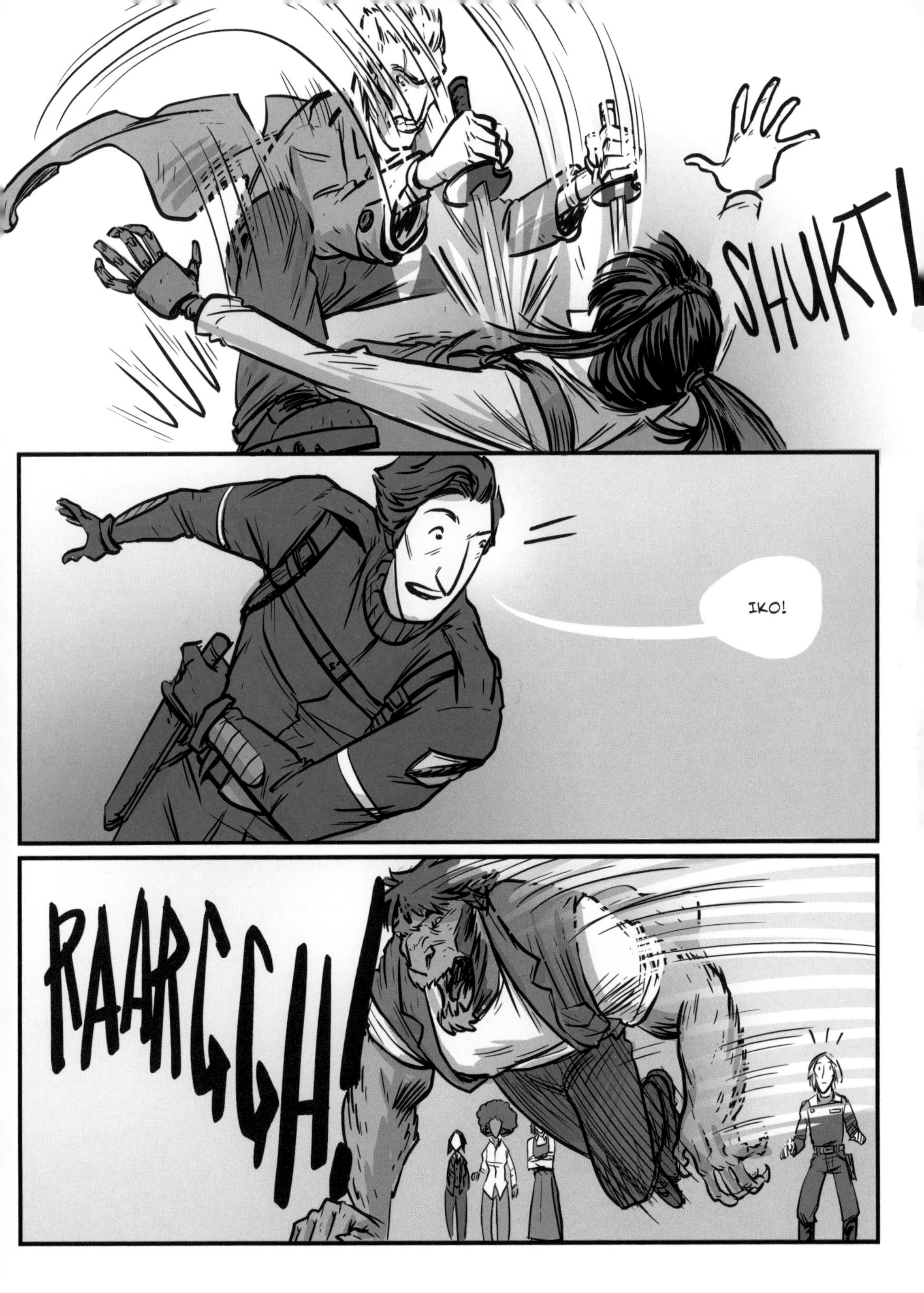
SHUKT!
IKO!
RAARGGH!

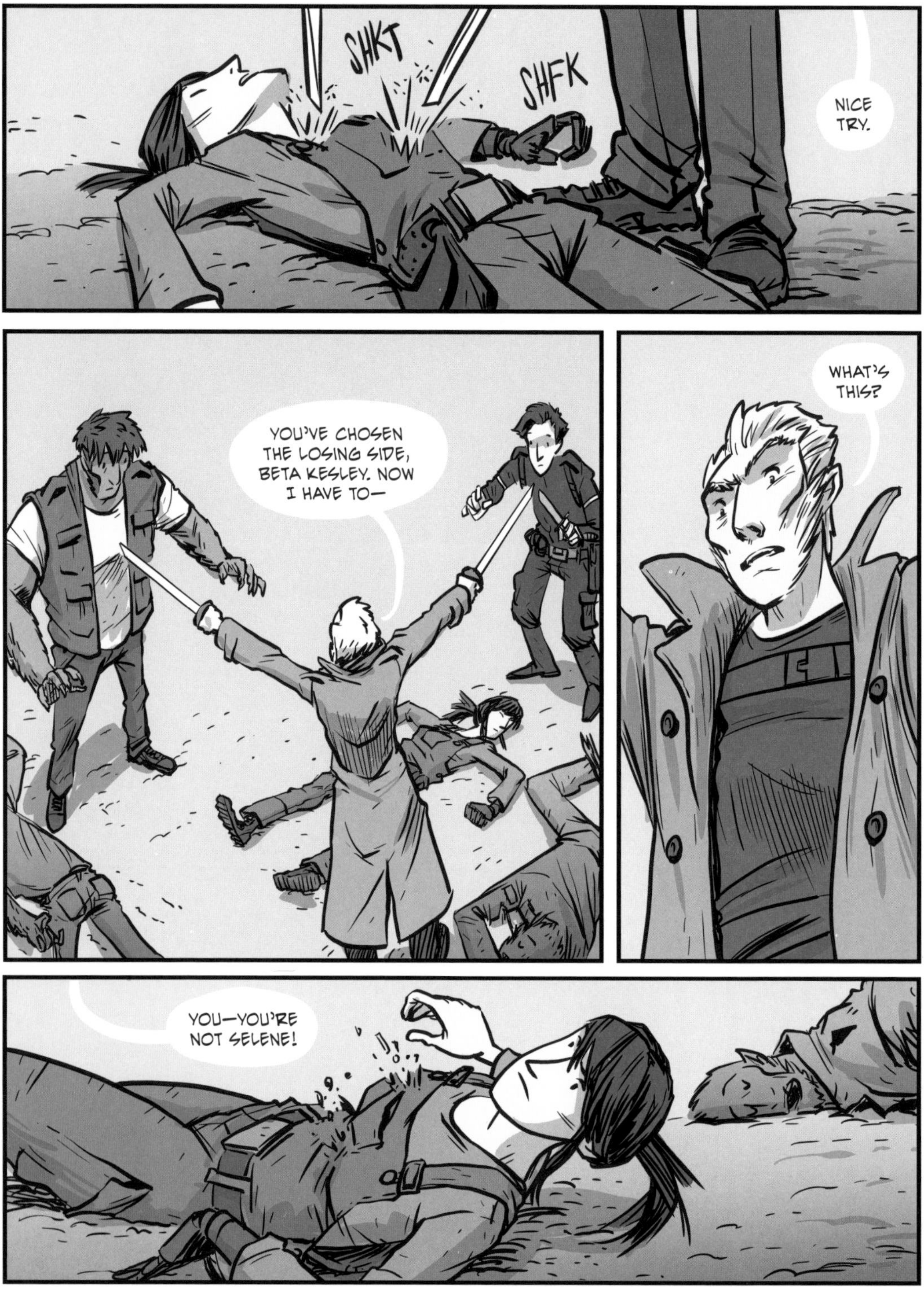
SHKT
SHFK
NICE TRY.
YOU'VE CHOSEN THE LOSING SIDE, BETA KESLEY. NOW I HAVE TO—
WHAT'S THIS?
YOU—YOU'RE NOT SELENE!

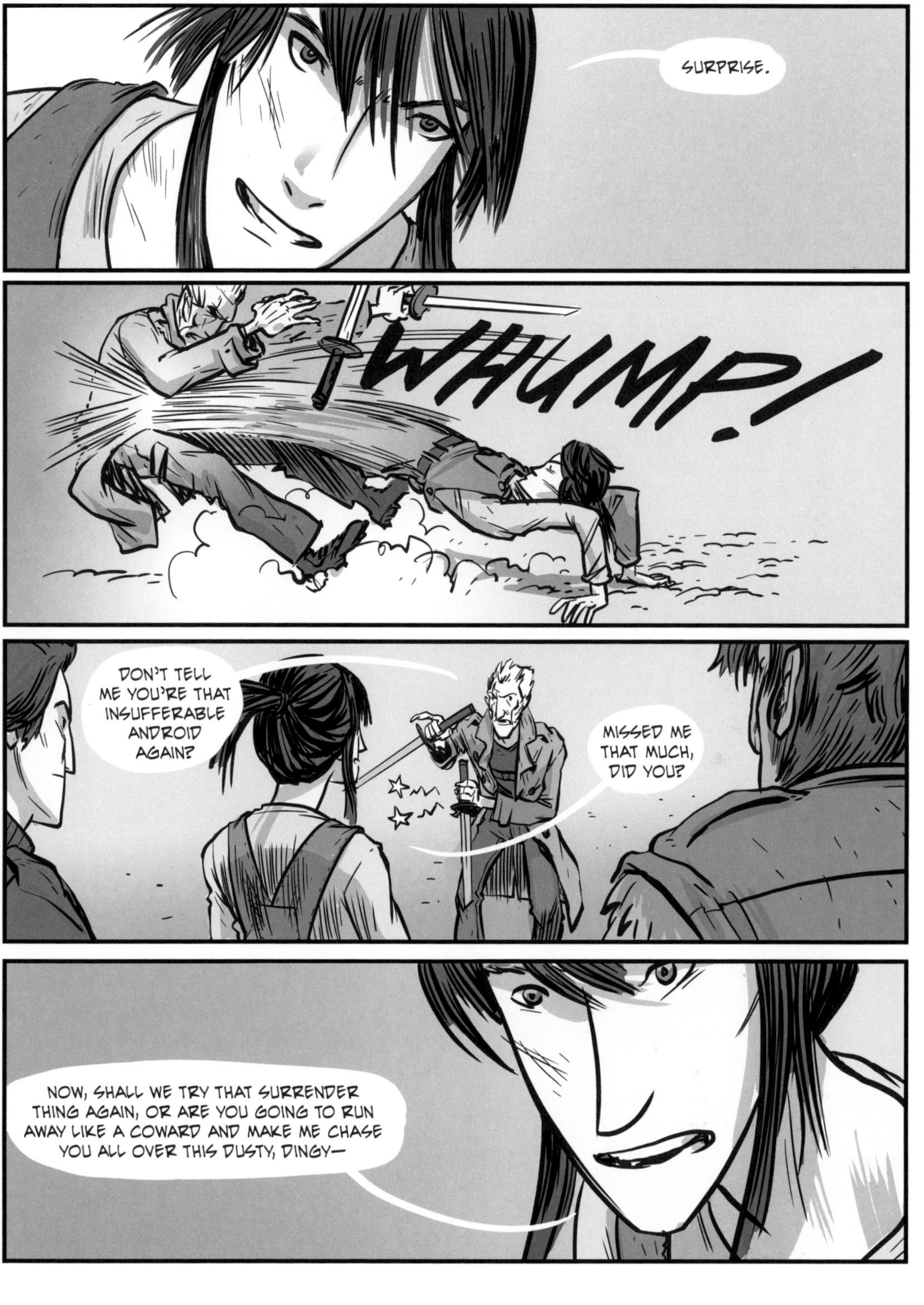
SURPRISE.
WHUMP!
DON'T TELL ME YOU'RE THAT INSUFFERABLE ANDROID AGAIN?
MISSED ME THAT MUCH, DID YOU?
NOW, SHALL WE TRY THAT SURRENDER THING AGAIN, OR ARE YOU GOING TO RUN AWAY LIKE A COWARD AND MAKE ME CHASE YOU ALL OVER THIS DUSTY, DINGY—

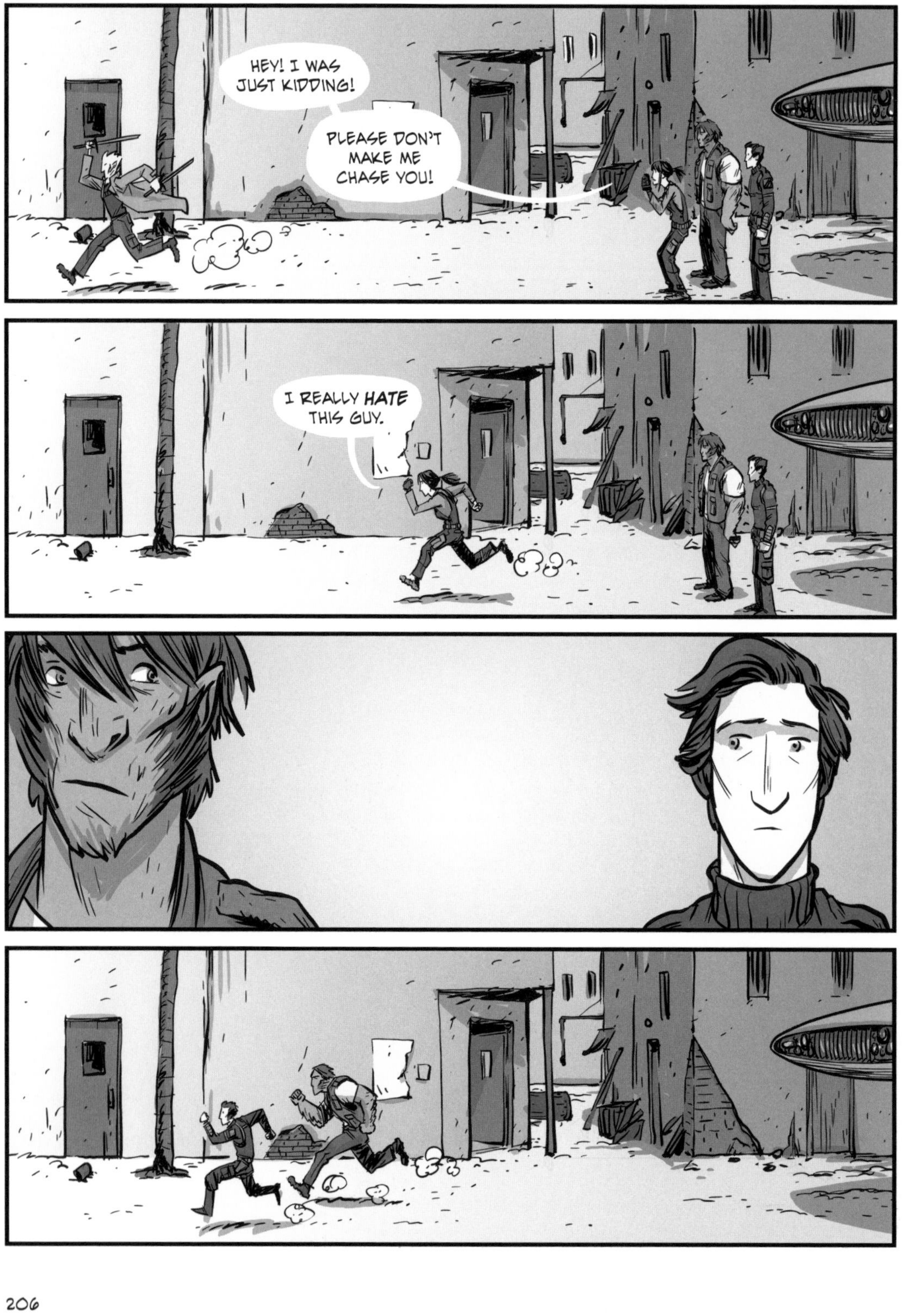
HEY! I WAS JUST KIDDING!
PLEASE DON'T MAKE ME CHASE YOU!
I REALLY **HATE** THIS GUY.

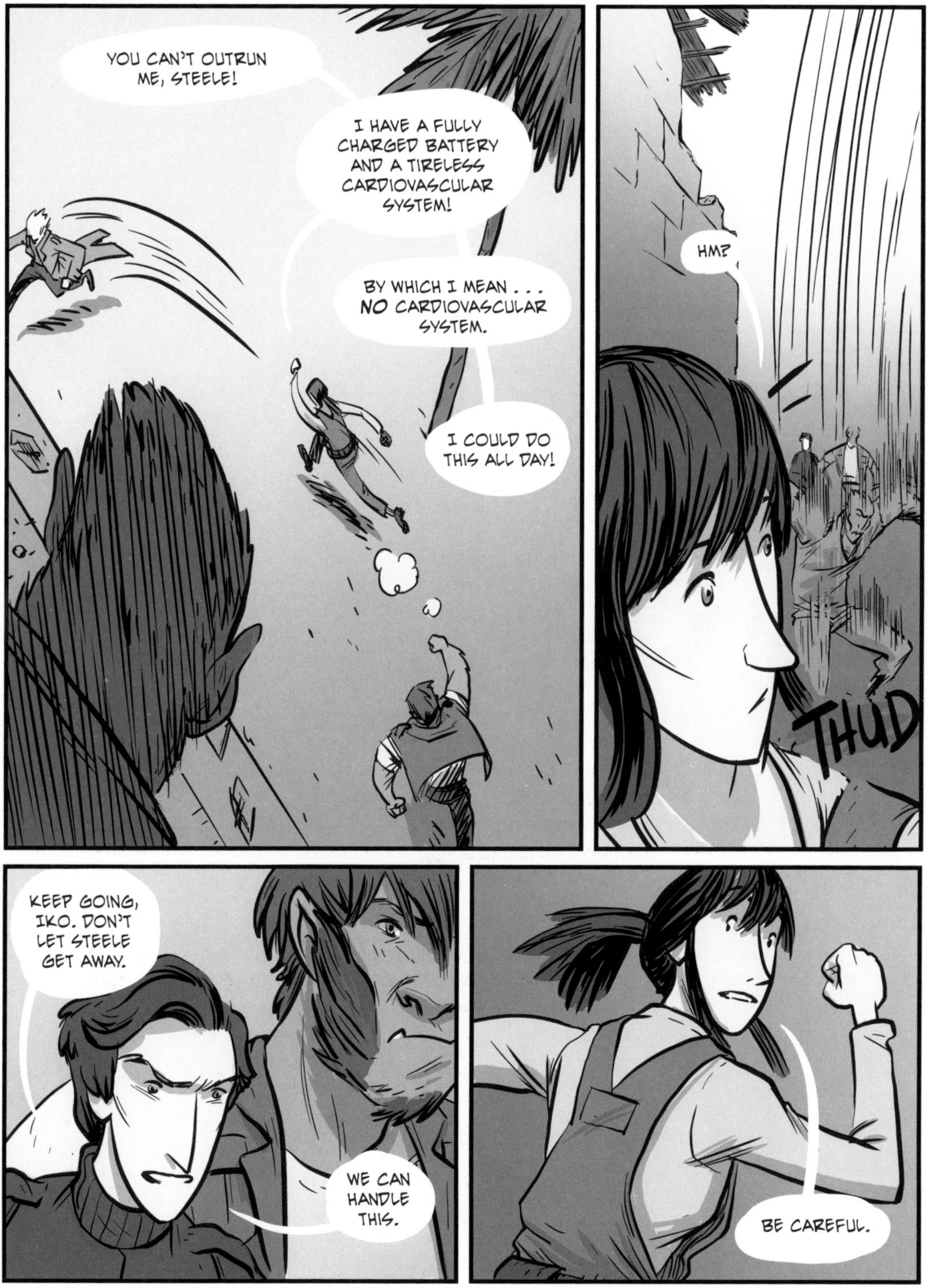
YOU CAN'T OUTRUN ME, STEELE!
I HAVE A FULLY CHARGED BATTERY AND A TIRELESS CARDIOVASCULAR SYSTEM!
BY WHICH I MEAN . . . NO CARDIOVASCULAR SYSTEM.
I COULD DO THIS ALL DAY!
HM?
THUD
KEEP GOING, IKO. DON'T LET STEELE GET AWAY.
WE CAN HANDLE THIS.
BE CAREFUL.

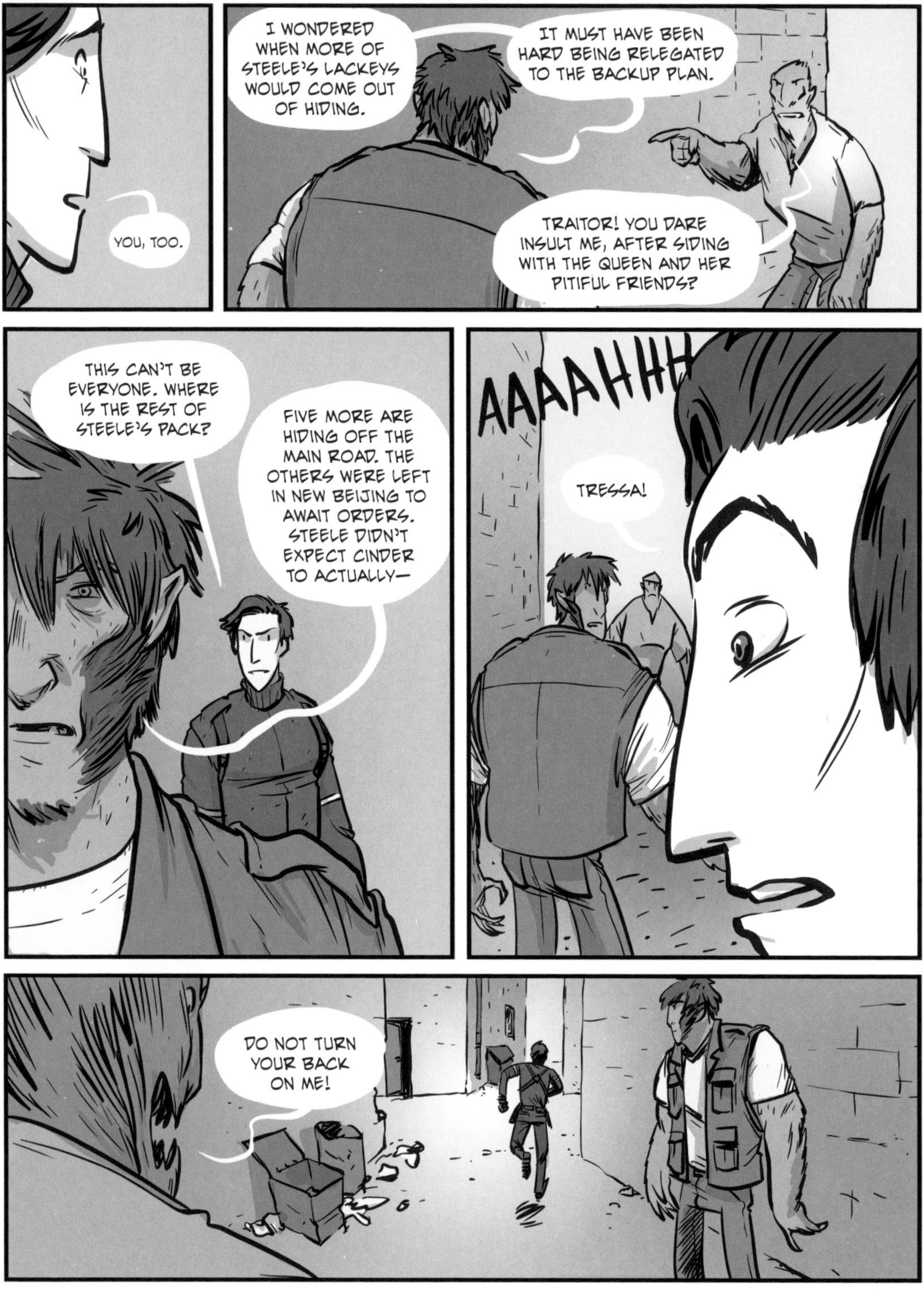
YOU, TOO.
I WONDERED WHEN MORE OF STEELE'S LACKEYS WOULD COME OUT OF HIDING.
IT MUST HAVE BEEN HARD BEING RELEGATED TO THE BACKUP PLAN.
TRAITOR! YOU DARE INSULT ME, AFTER SIDING WITH THE QUEEN AND HER PITIFUL FRIENDS?
THIS CAN'T BE EVERYONE. WHERE IS THE REST OF STEELE'S PACK?
FIVE MORE ARE HIDING OFF THE MAIN ROAD. THE OTHERS WERE LEFT IN NEW BEIJING TO AWAIT ORDERS. STEELE DIDN'T EXPECT CINDER TO ACTUALLY—
AAAAHHH
TRESSA!
DO NOT TURN YOUR BACK ON ME!

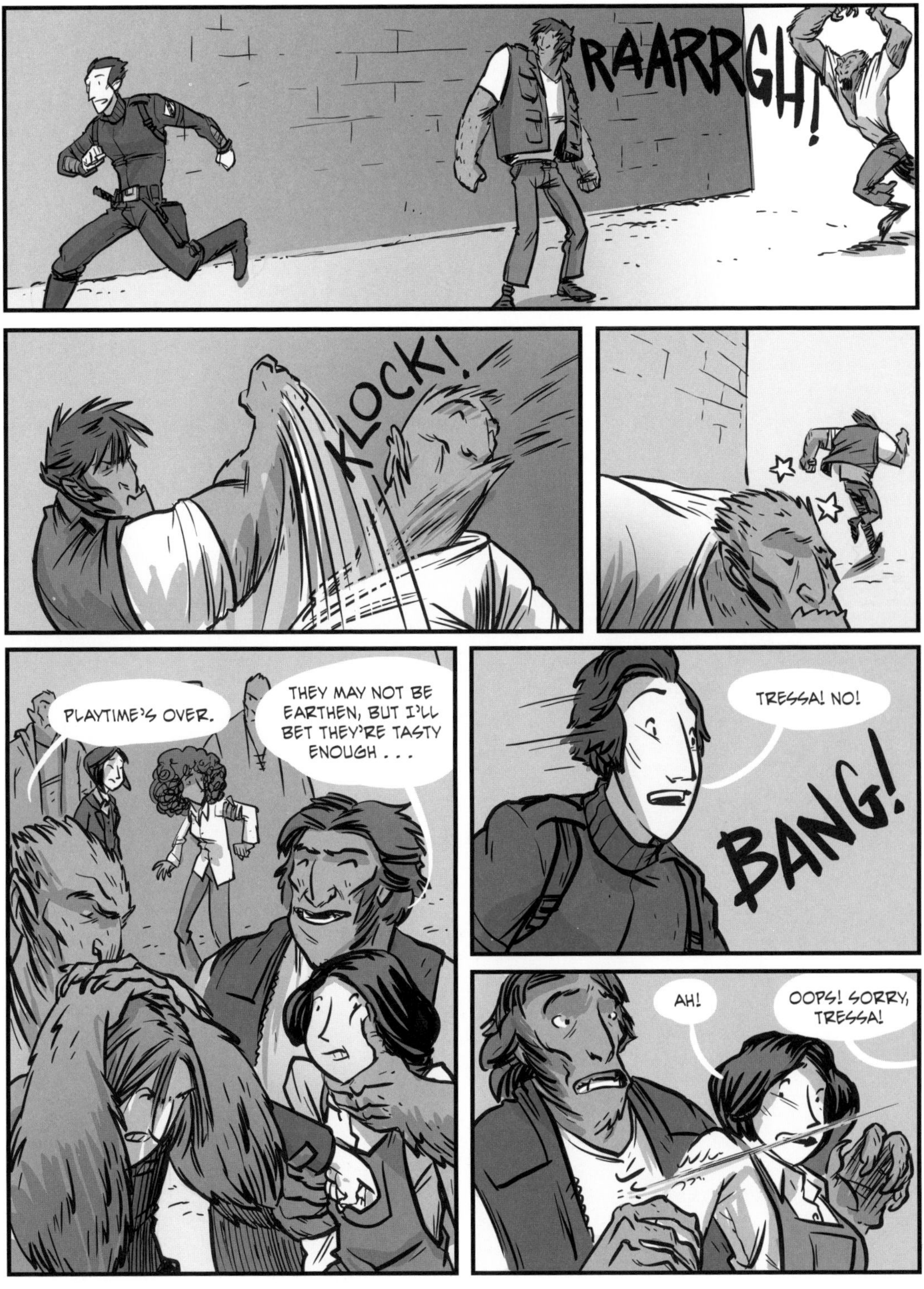
RAARRGH!
KLOCK!
PLAYTIME'S OVER.
THEY MAY NOT BE EARTHEN, BUT I'LL BET THEY'RE TASTY ENOUGH . . .
TRESSA! NO!
BANG!
AH!
OOPS! SORRY, TRESSA!

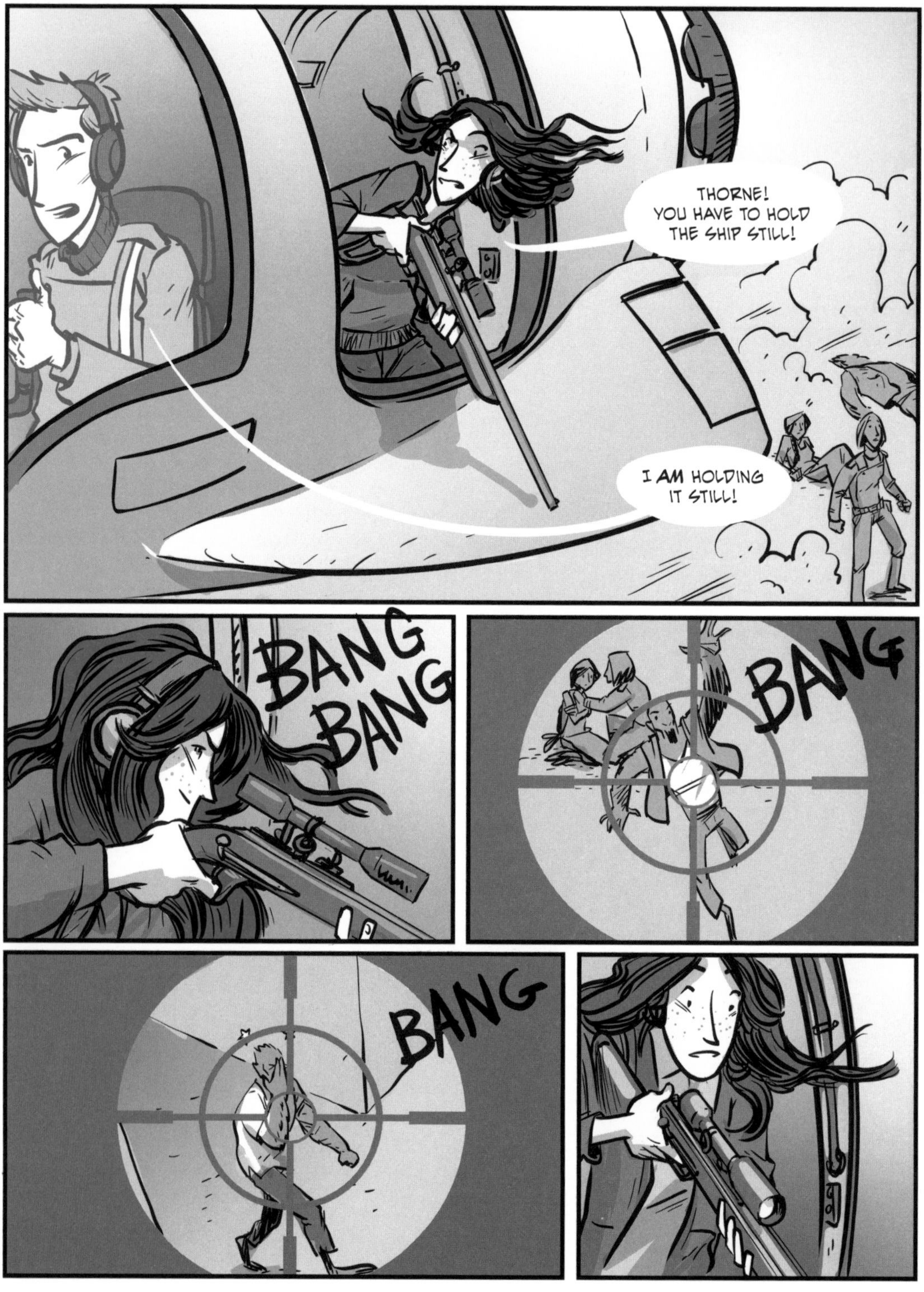
THORNE! YOU HAVE TO HOLD THE SHIP STILL!
I AM HOLDING IT STILL!
BANG BANG
BANG
BANG

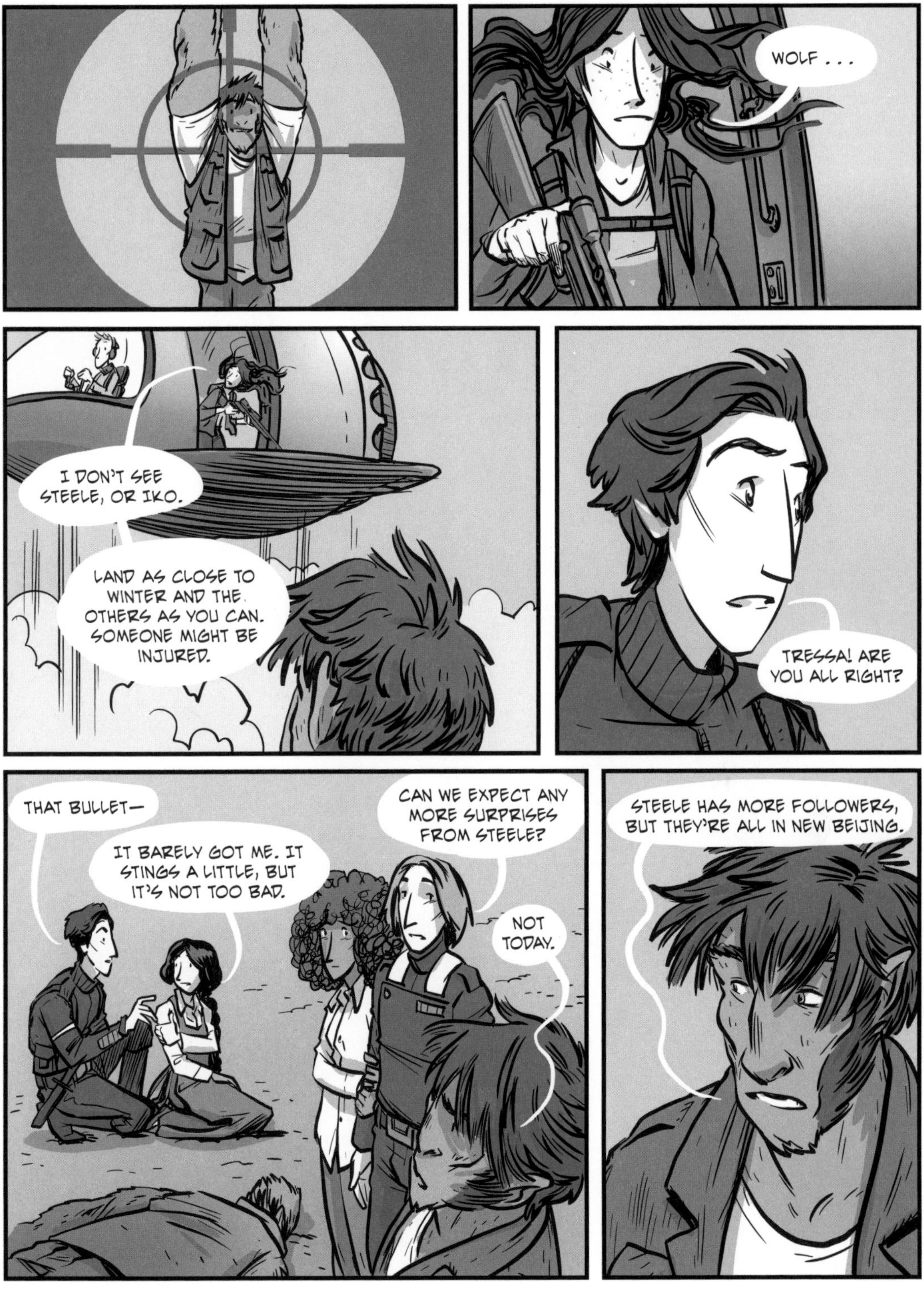
WOLF . . .
I DON'T SEE STEELE, OR IKO.
LAND AS CLOSE TO WINTER AND THE OTHERS AS YOU CAN. SOMEONE MIGHT BE INJURED.
TRESSA! ARE YOU ALL RIGHT?
THAT BULLET—
IT BARELY GOT ME. IT STINGS A LITTLE, BUT IT'S NOT TOO BAD.
CAN WE EXPECT ANY MORE SURPRISES FROM STEELE?
NOT TODAY.
STEELE HAS MORE FOLLOWERS, BUT THEY'RE ALL IN NEW BEIJING.

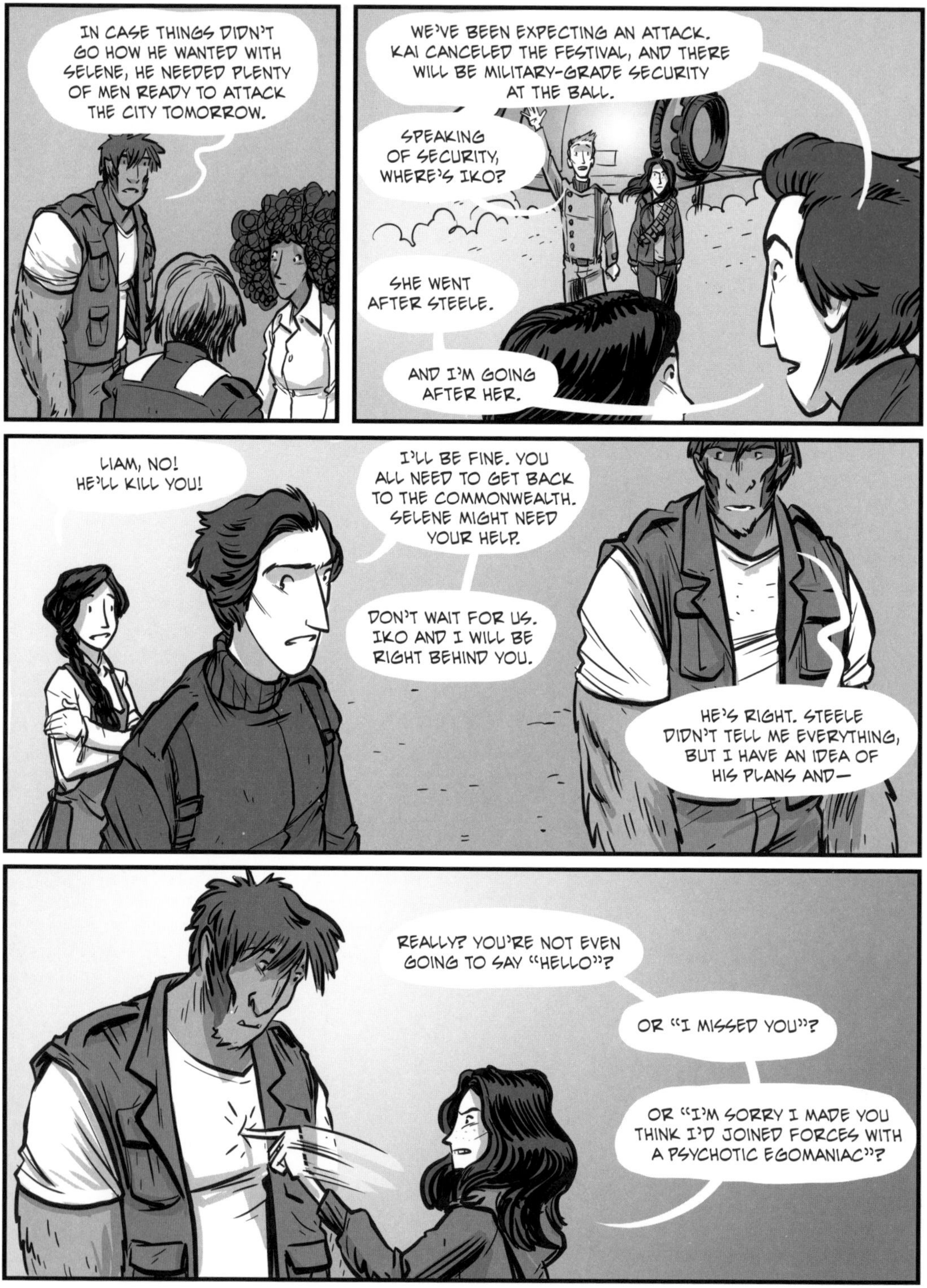
IN CASE THINGS DIDN'T GO HOW HE WANTED WITH SELENE, HE NEEDED PLENTY OF MEN READY TO ATTACK THE CITY TOMORROW.
WE'VE BEEN EXPECTING AN ATTACK. KAI CANCELED THE FESTIVAL, AND THERE WILL BE MILITARY-GRADE SECURITY AT THE BALL.
SPEAKING OF SECURITY, WHERE'S IKO?
SHE WENT AFTER STEELE.
AND I'M GOING AFTER HER.
LIAM, NO! HE'LL KILL YOU!
I'LL BE FINE. YOU ALL NEED TO GET BACK TO THE COMMONWEALTH. SELENE MIGHT NEED YOUR HELP.
DON'T WAIT FOR US. IKO AND I WILL BE RIGHT BEHIND YOU.
HE'S RIGHT. STEELE DIDN'T TELL ME EVERYTHING, BUT I HAVE AN IDEA OF HIS PLANS AND—
REALLY? YOU'RE NOT EVEN GOING TO SAY "HELLO"?
OR "I MISSED YOU"?
OR "I'M SORRY I MADE YOU THINK I'D JOINED FORCES WITH A PSYCHOTIC EGOMANIAC"?

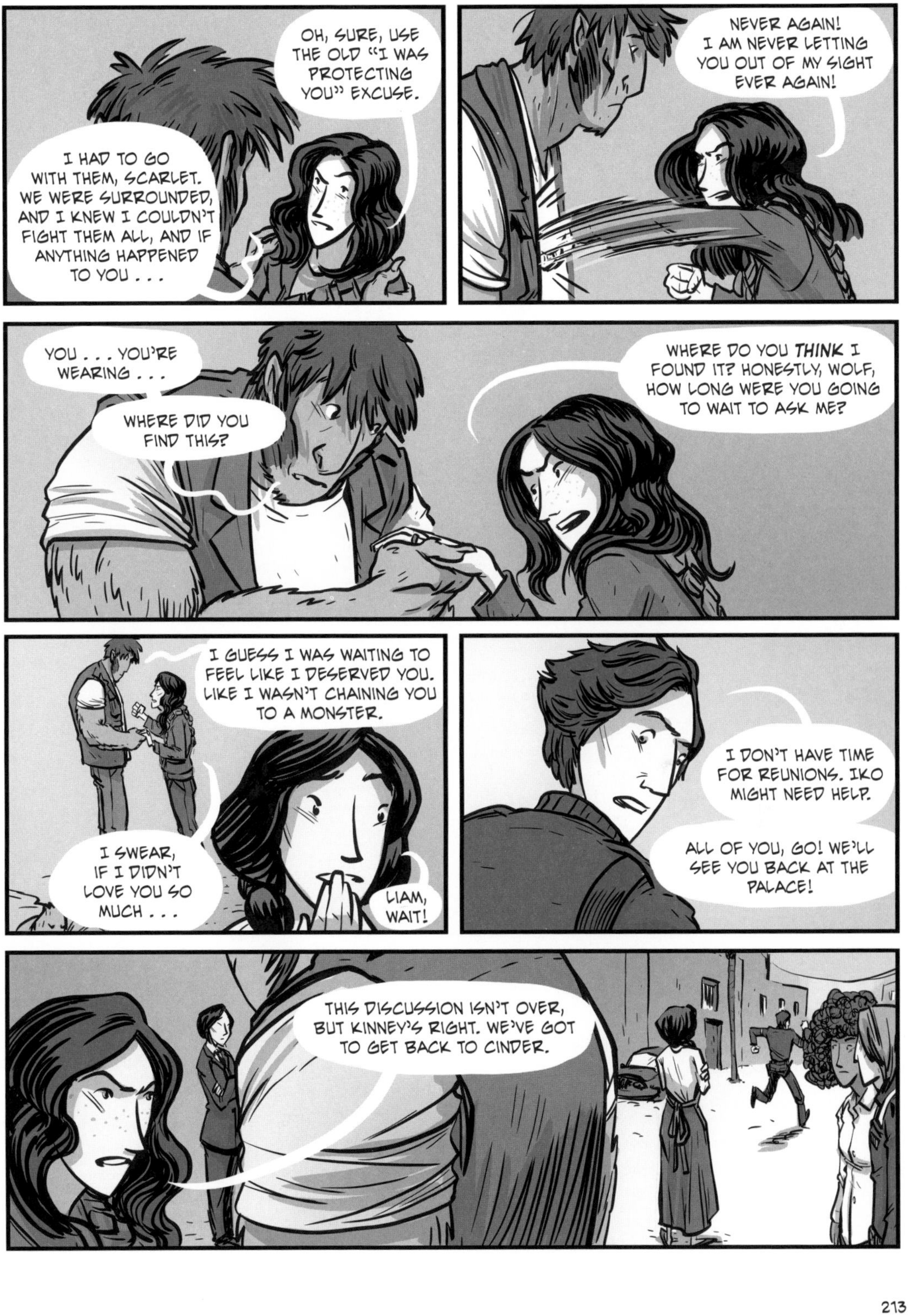
OH, SURE, USE THE OLD "I WAS PROTECTING YOU" EXCUSE.
I HAD TO GO WITH THEM, SCARLET. WE WERE SURROUNDED, AND I KNEW I COULDN'T FIGHT THEM ALL, AND IF ANYTHING HAPPENED TO YOU . . .
NEVER AGAIN! I AM NEVER LETTING YOU OUT OF MY SIGHT EVER AGAIN!
YOU . . . YOU'RE WEARING . . .
WHERE DID YOU FIND THIS?
WHERE DO YOU THINK I FOUND IT? HONESTLY, WOLF, HOW LONG WERE YOU GOING TO WAIT TO ASK ME?
I GUESS I WAS WAITING TO FEEL LIKE I DESERVED YOU. LIKE I WASN'T CHAINING YOU TO A MONSTER.
I SWEAR, IF I DIDN'T LOVE YOU SO MUCH . . .
LIAM, WAIT!
I DON'T HAVE TIME FOR REUNIONS. IKO MIGHT NEED HELP.
ALL OF YOU, GO! WE'LL SEE YOU BACK AT THE PALACE!
THIS DISCUSSION ISN'T OVER, BUT KINNEY'S RIGHT. WE'VE GOT TO GET BACK TO CINDER.

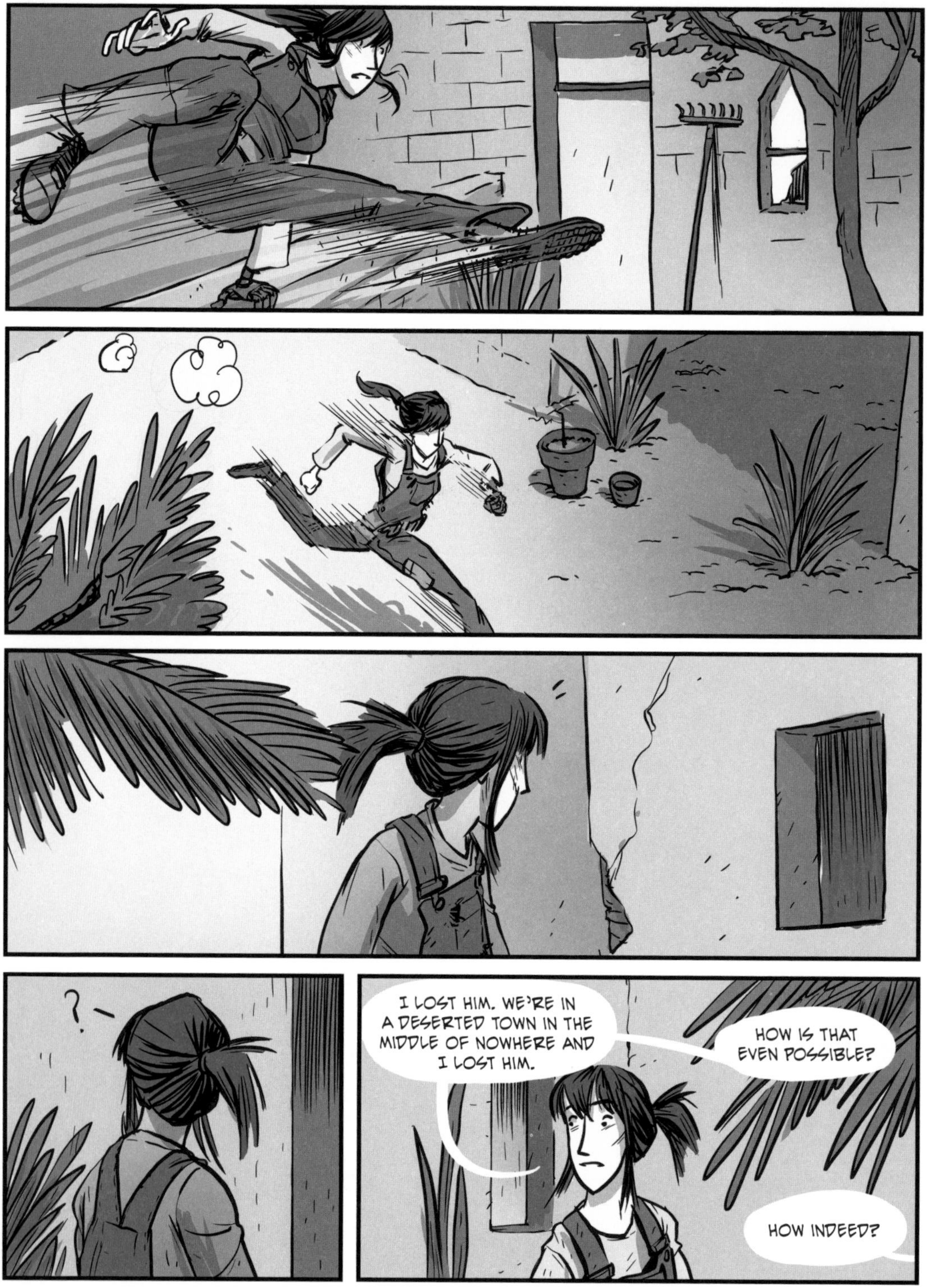
?
I LOST HIM. WE'RE IN A DESERTED TOWN IN THE MIDDLE OF NOWHERE AND I LOST HIM.
HOW IS THAT EVEN POSSIBLE?
HOW INDEED?

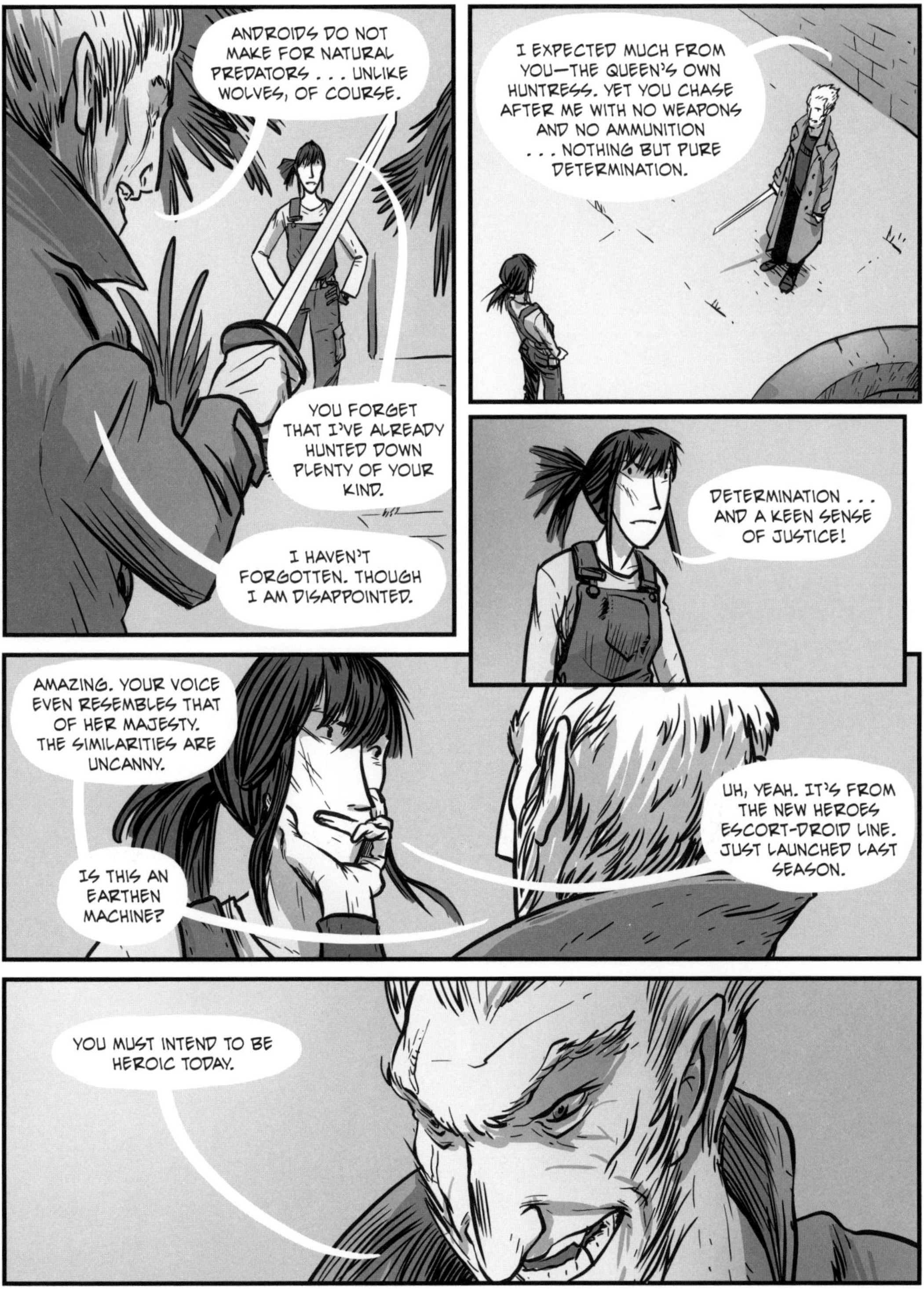
ANDROIDS DO NOT MAKE FOR NATURAL PREDATORS . . . UNLIKE WOLVES, OF COURSE.
YOU FORGET THAT I'VE ALREADY HUNTED DOWN PLENTY OF YOUR KIND.
I HAVEN'T FORGOTTEN. THOUGH I AM DISAPPOINTED.
I EXPECTED MUCH FROM YOU—THE QUEEN'S OWN HUNTRESS. YET YOU CHASE AFTER ME WITH NO WEAPONS AND NO AMMUNITION . . . NOTHING BUT PURE DETERMINATION.
DETERMINATION . . . AND A KEEN SENSE OF JUSTICE!
AMAZING. YOUR VOICE EVEN RESEMBLES THAT OF HER MAJESTY. THE SIMILARITIES ARE UNCANNY.
IS THIS AN EARTHEN MACHINE?
UH, YEAH. IT'S FROM THE NEW HEROES ESCORT-DROID LINE. JUST LAUNCHED LAST SEASON.
YOU MUST INTEND TO BE HEROIC TODAY.

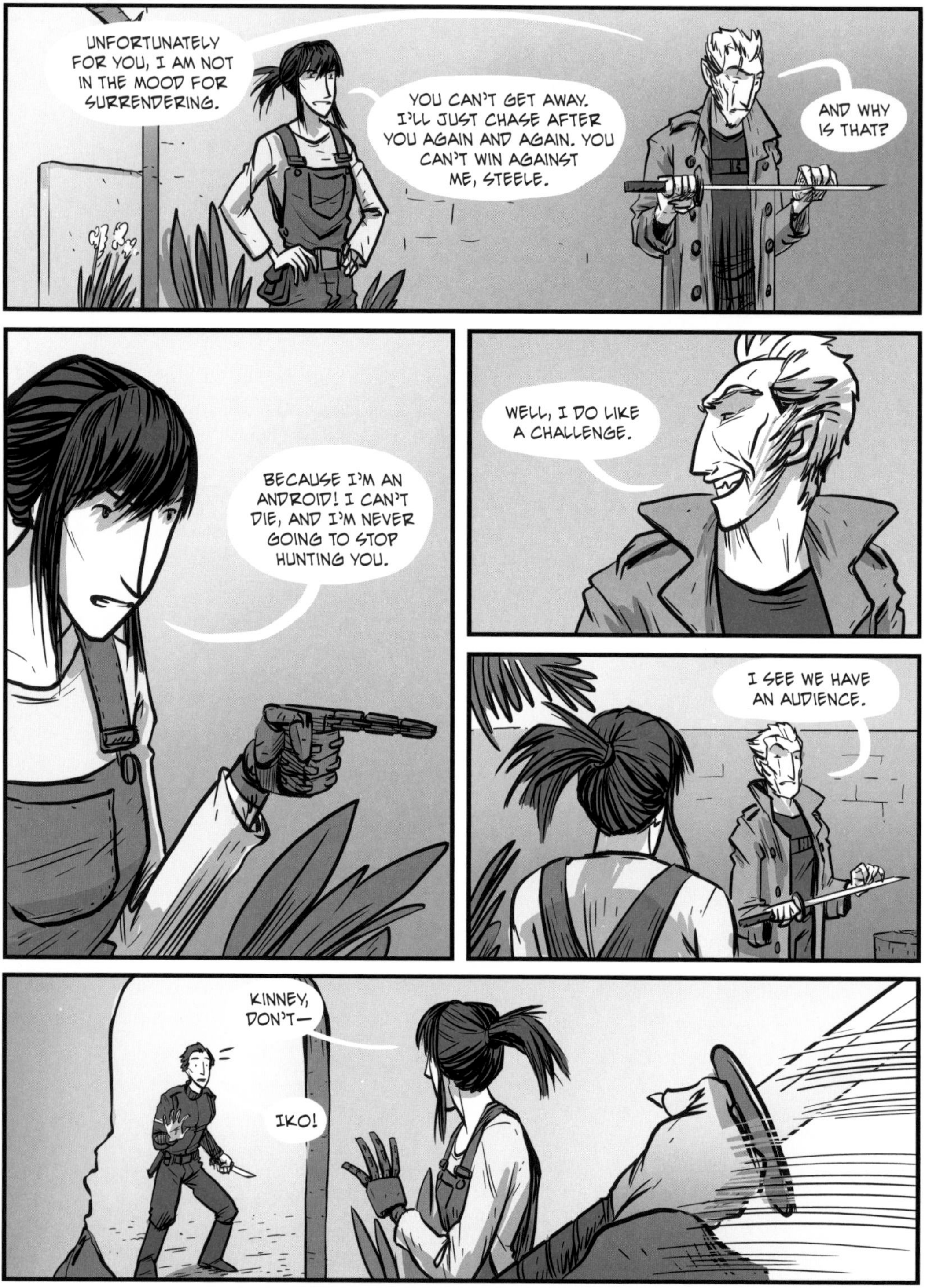
UNFORTUNATELY FOR YOU, I AM NOT IN THE MOOD FOR SURRENDERING.
AND WHY IS THAT?
YOU CAN'T GET AWAY. I'LL JUST CHASE AFTER YOU AGAIN AND AGAIN. YOU CAN'T WIN AGAINST ME, STEELE.
BECAUSE I'M AN ANDROID! I CAN'T DIE, AND I'M NEVER GOING TO STOP HUNTING YOU.
WELL, I DO LIKE A CHALLENGE.
I SEE WE HAVE AN AUDIENCE.
KINNEY, DON'T—
IKO!

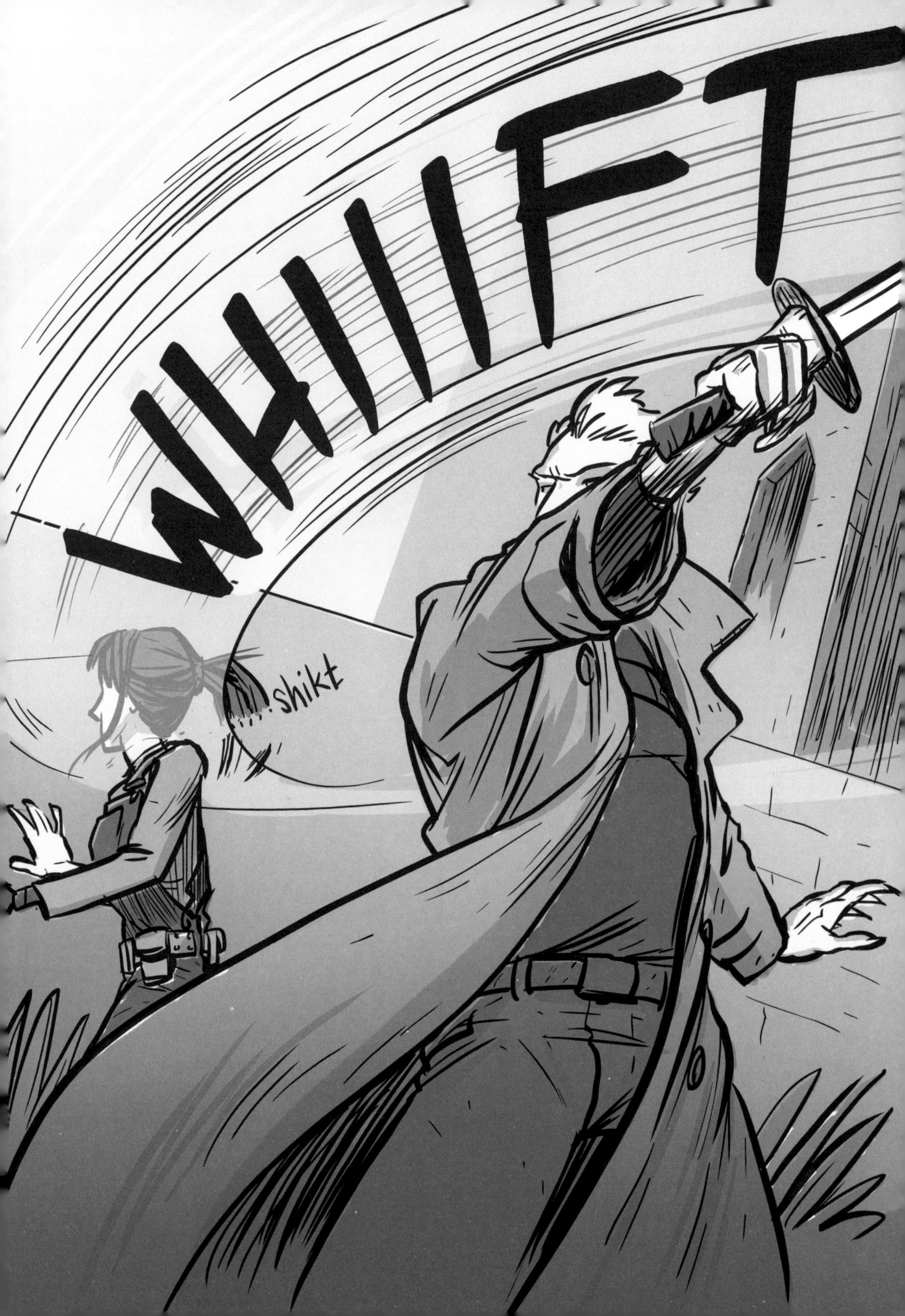
WHIIIFT
shikt

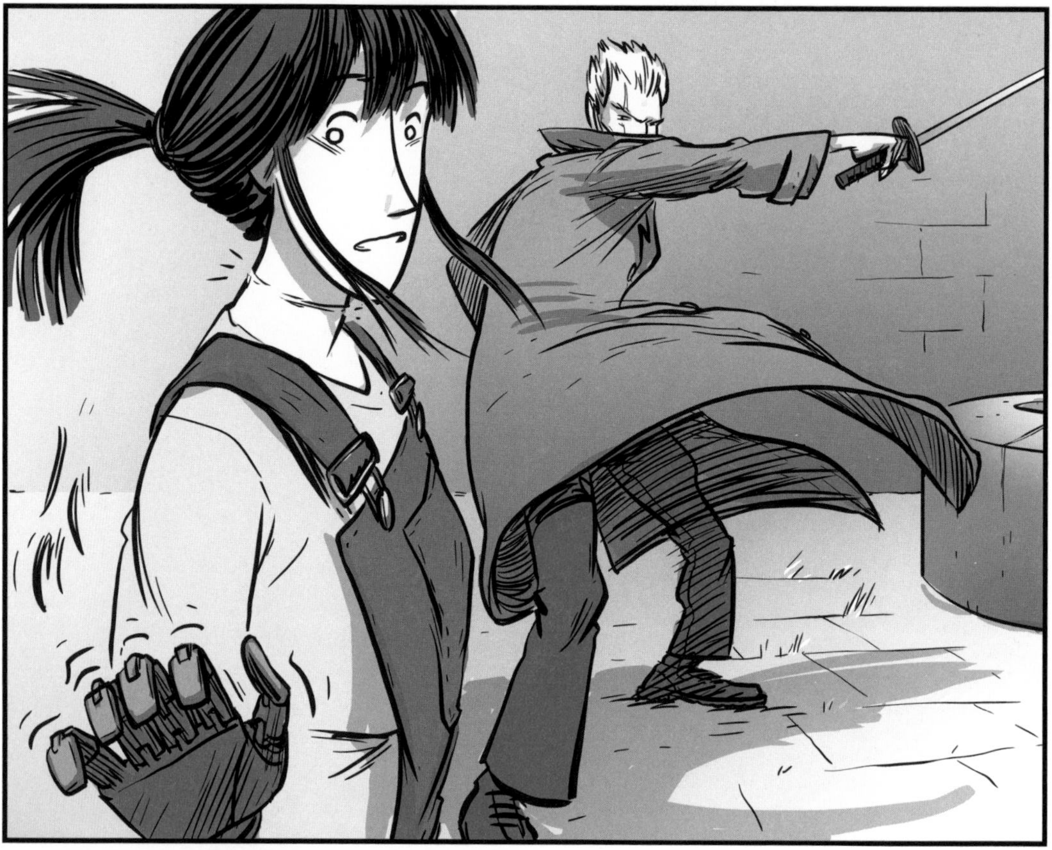

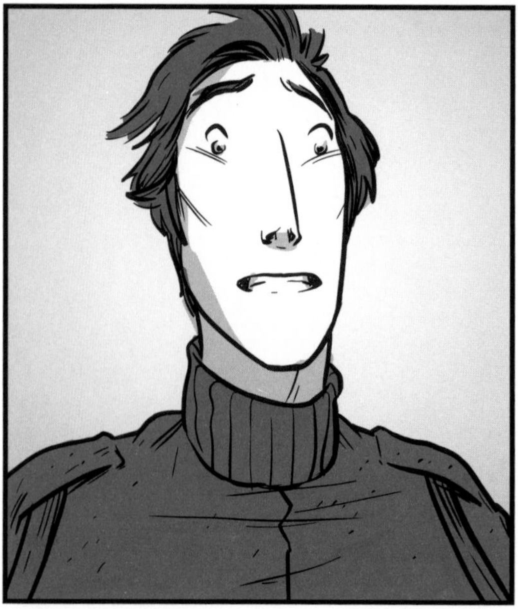

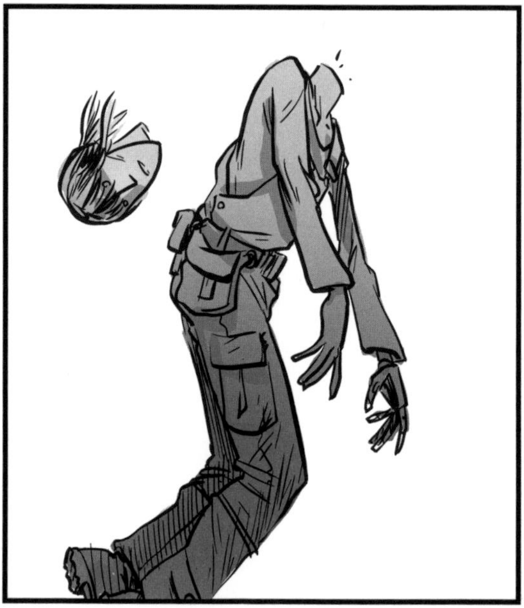

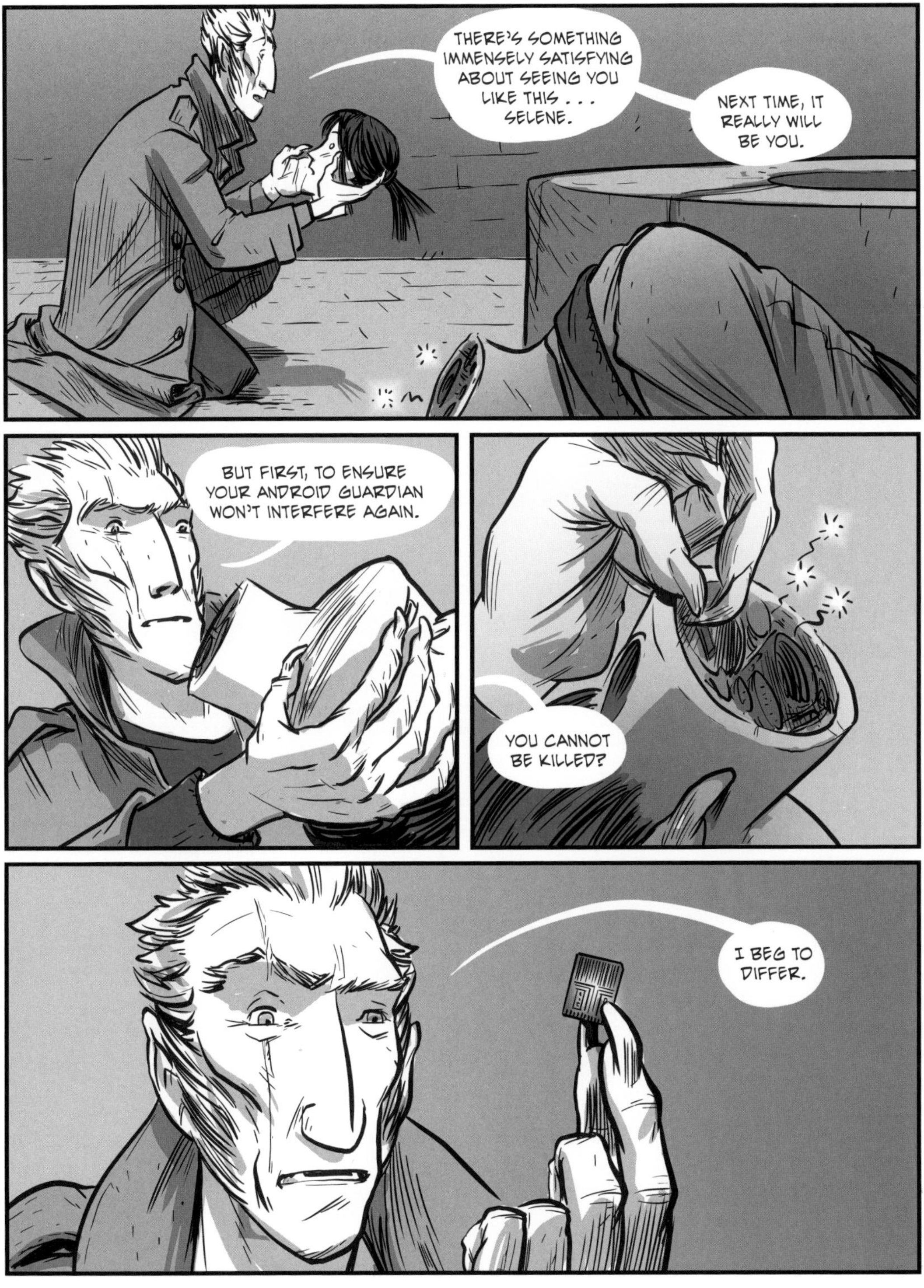
THERE'S SOMETHING IMMENSELY SATISFYING ABOUT SEEING YOU LIKE THIS . . . SELENE.
NEXT TIME, IT REALLY WILL BE YOU.
BUT FIRST, TO ENSURE YOUR ANDROID GUARDIAN WON'T INTERFERE AGAIN.
YOU CANNOT BE KILLED?
I BEG TO DIFFER.

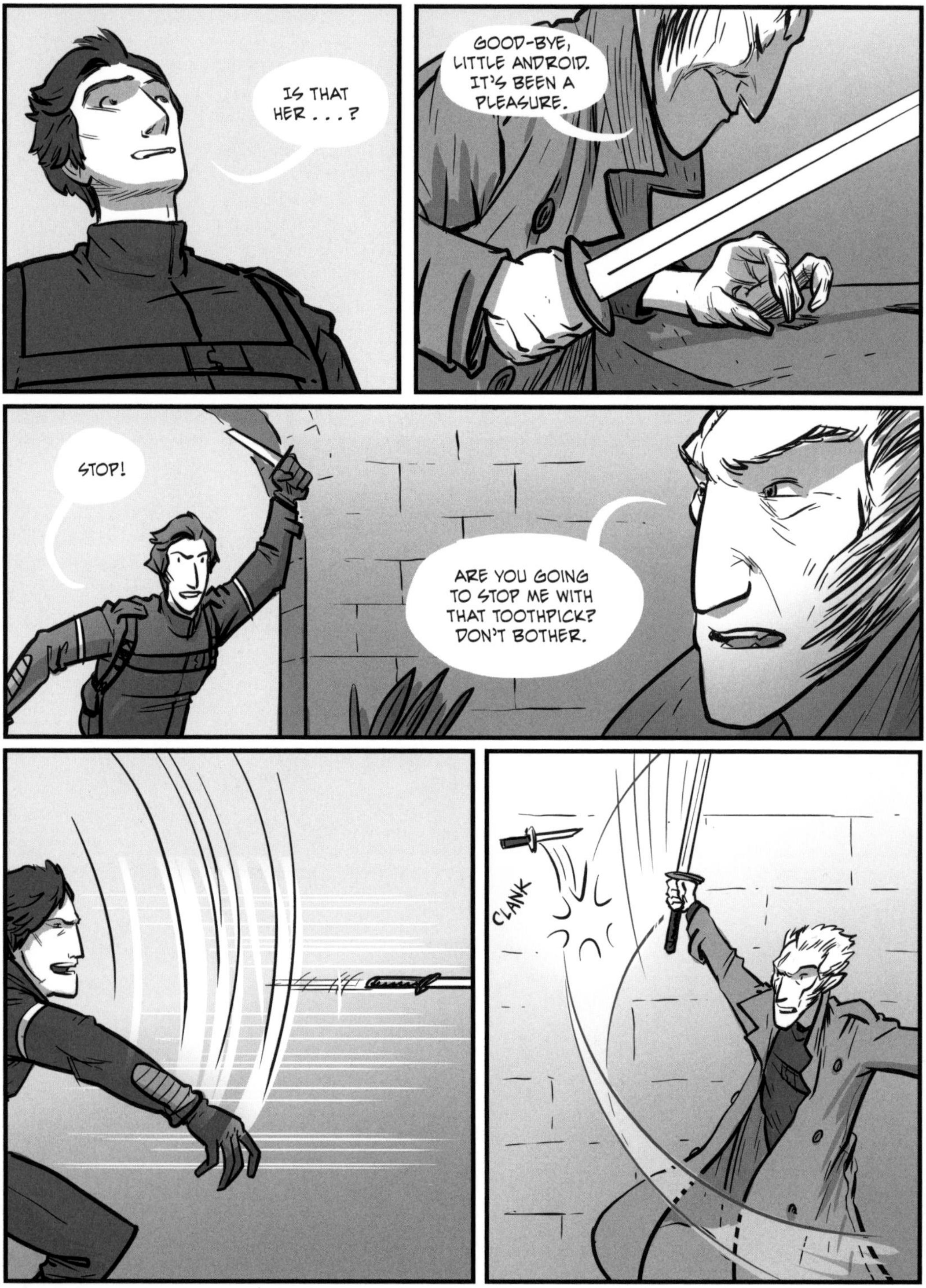
IS THAT HER . . . ?
GOOD-BYE, LITTLE ANDROID. IT'S BEEN A PLEASURE.
STOP!
ARE YOU GOING TO STOP ME WITH THAT TOOTHPICK? DON'T BOTHER.
CLANK

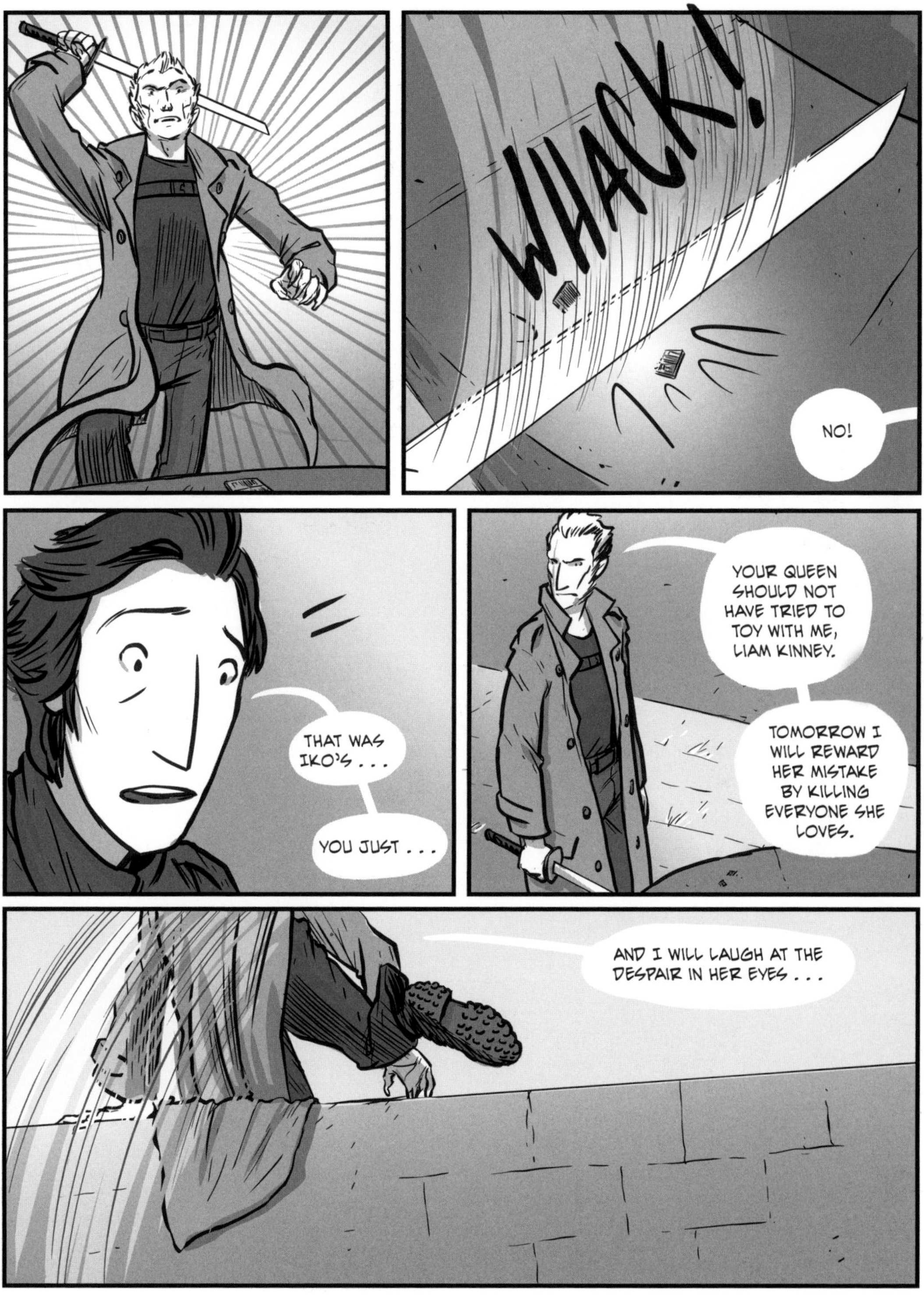
WHACK!
NO!
THAT WAS IKO'S . . .
YOU JUST . . .
YOUR QUEEN SHOULD NOT HAVE TRIED TO TOY WITH ME, LIAM KINNEY.
TOMORROW I WILL REWARD HER MISTAKE BY KILLING EVERYONE SHE LOVES.
AND I WILL LAUGH AT THE DESPAIR IN HER EYES . . .

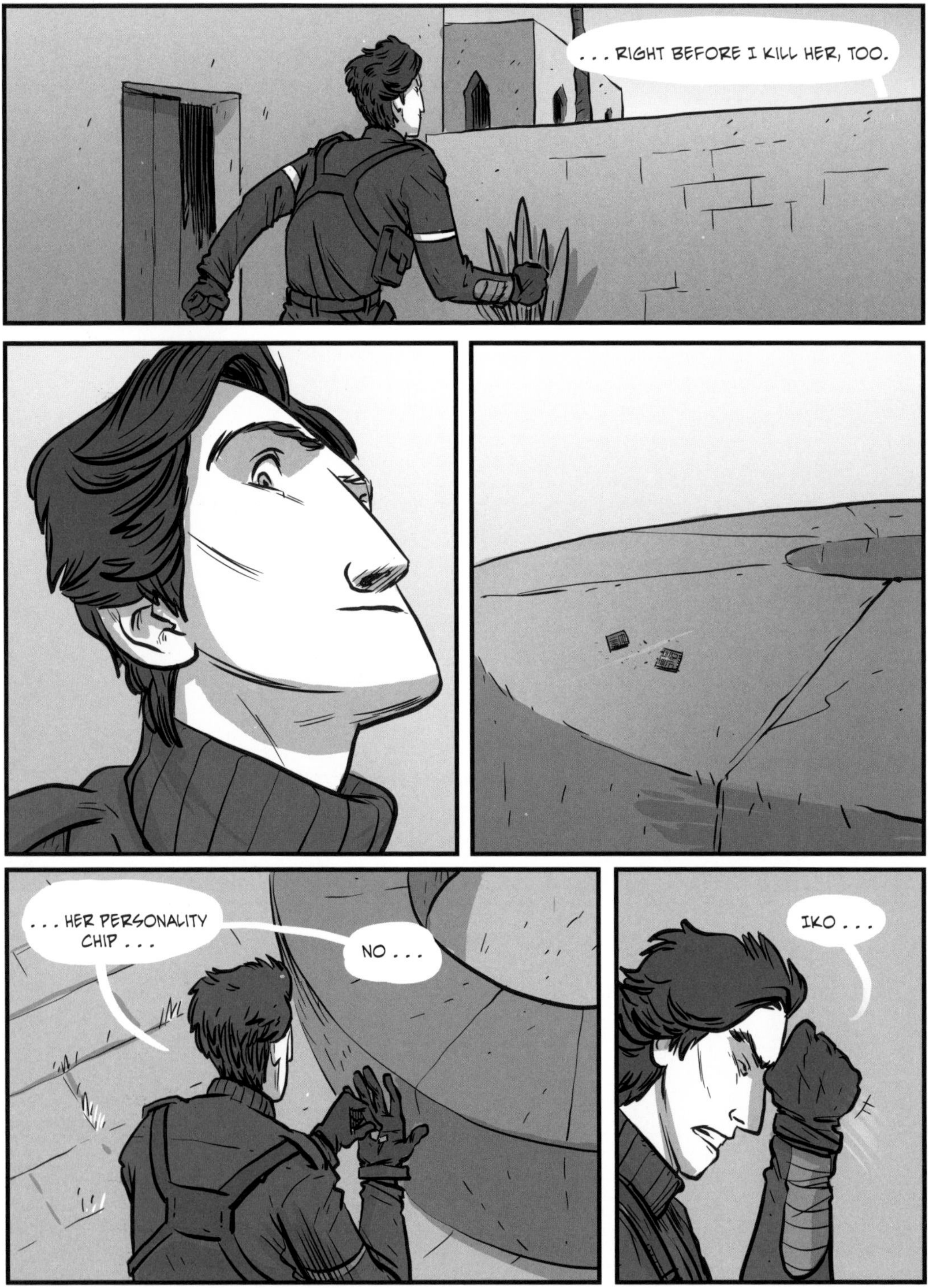
. . . RIGHT BEFORE I KILL HER, TOO.
. . . HER PERSONALITY CHIP . . .
NO . . .
IKO . . .

CHAPTER VIII

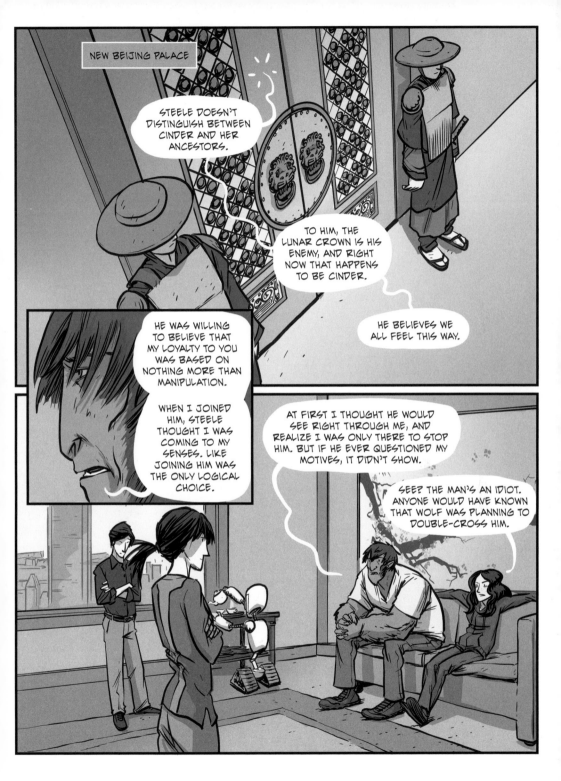

NEW BEIJING PALACE

STEELE DOESN'T DISTINGUISH BETWEEN CINDER AND HER ANCESTORS.

TO HIM, THE LUNAR CROWN IS HIS ENEMY, AND RIGHT NOW THAT HAPPENS TO BE CINDER.

HE BELIEVES WE ALL FEEL THIS WAY.

HE WAS WILLING TO BELIEVE THAT MY LOYALTY TO YOU WAS BASED ON NOTHING MORE THAN MANIPULATION.

WHEN I JOINED HIM, STEELE THOUGHT I WAS COMING TO MY SENSES. LIKE JOINING HIM WAS THE ONLY LOGICAL CHOICE.

AT FIRST I THOUGHT HE WOULD SEE RIGHT THROUGH ME, AND REALIZE I WAS ONLY THERE TO STOP HIM. BUT IF HE EVER QUESTIONED MY MOTIVES, IT DIDN'T SHOW.

SEE? THE MAN'S AN IDIOT. ANYONE WOULD HAVE KNOWN THAT WOLF WAS PLANNING TO DOUBLE-CROSS HIM.

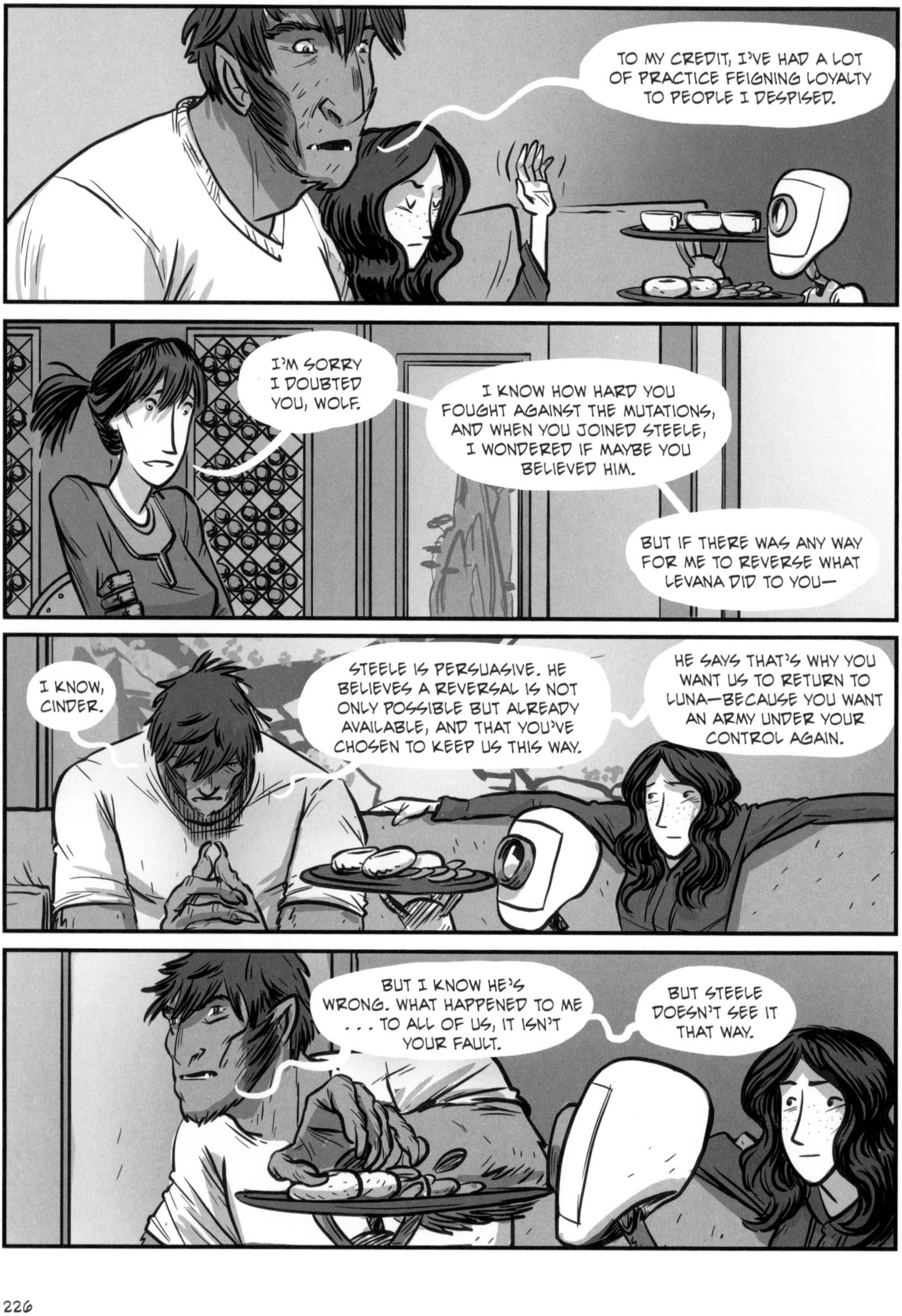
TO MY CREDIT, I'VE HAD A LOT OF PRACTICE FEIGNING LOYALTY TO PEOPLE I DESPISED.
I'M SORRY I DOUBTED YOU, WOLF.
I KNOW HOW HARD YOU FOUGHT AGAINST THE MUTATIONS, AND WHEN YOU JOINED STEELE, I WONDERED IF MAYBE YOU BELIEVED HIM.
BUT IF THERE WAS ANY WAY FOR ME TO REVERSE WHAT LEVANA DID TO YOU—
I KNOW, CINDER.
STEELE IS PERSUASIVE. HE BELIEVES A REVERSAL IS NOT ONLY POSSIBLE BUT ALREADY AVAILABLE, AND THAT YOU'VE CHOSEN TO KEEP US THIS WAY.
HE SAYS THAT'S WHY YOU WANT US TO RETURN TO LUNA—BECAUSE YOU WANT AN ARMY UNDER YOUR CONTROL AGAIN.
BUT I KNOW HE'S WRONG. WHAT HAPPENED TO ME . . . TO ALL OF US, IT ISN'T YOUR FAULT.
BUT STEELE DOESN'T SEE IT THAT WAY.

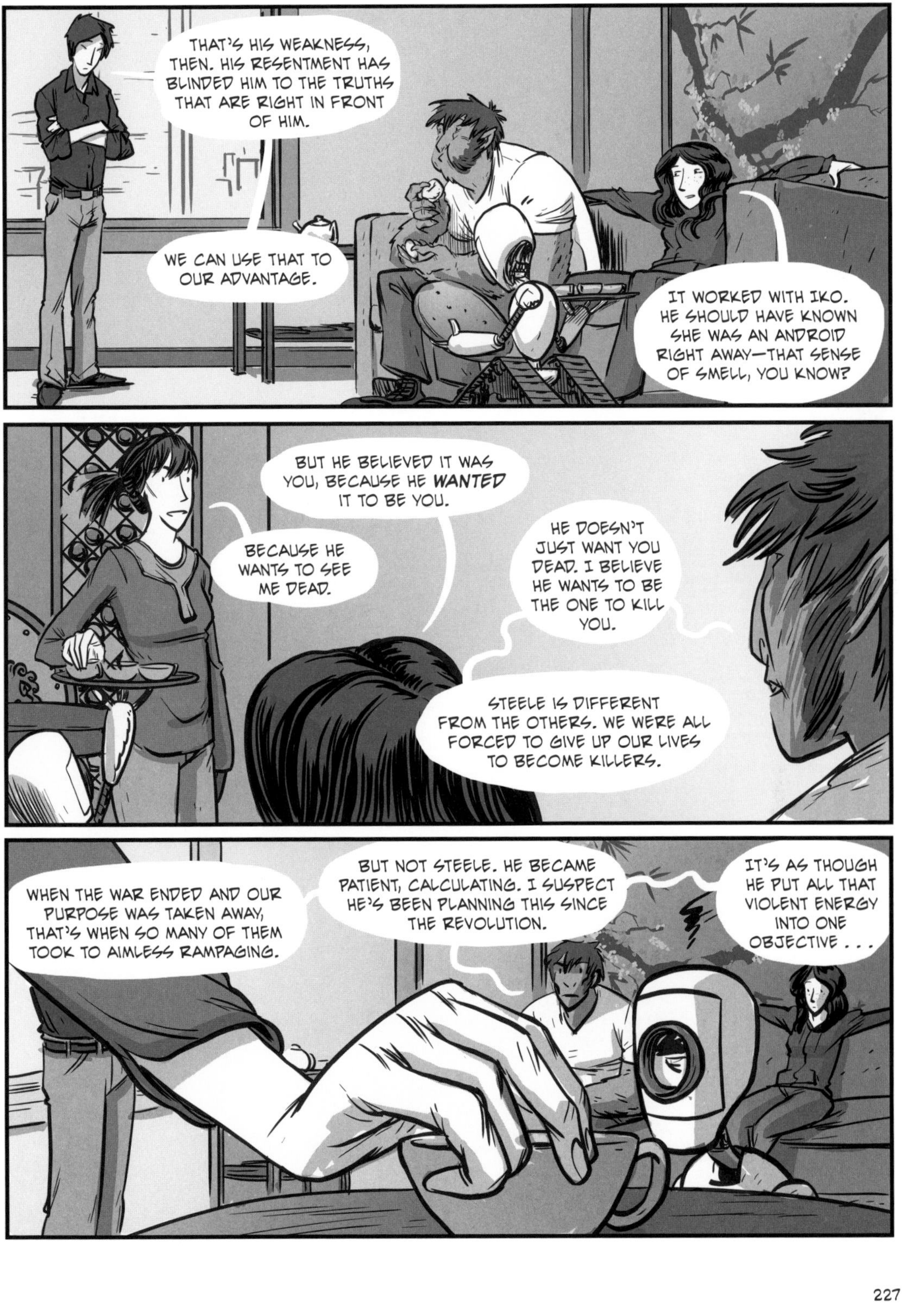
THAT'S HIS WEAKNESS, THEN. HIS RESENTMENT HAS BLINDED HIM TO THE TRUTHS THAT ARE RIGHT IN FRONT OF HIM.
WE CAN USE THAT TO OUR ADVANTAGE.
IT WORKED WITH IKO. HE SHOULD HAVE KNOWN SHE WAS AN ANDROID RIGHT AWAY—THAT SENSE OF SMELL, YOU KNOW?
BUT HE BELIEVED IT WAS YOU, BECAUSE HE **WANTED** IT TO BE YOU.
BECAUSE HE WANTS TO SEE ME DEAD.
HE DOESN'T JUST WANT YOU DEAD. I BELIEVE HE WANTS TO BE THE ONE TO KILL YOU.
STEELE IS DIFFERENT FROM THE OTHERS. WE WERE ALL FORCED TO GIVE UP OUR LIVES TO BECOME KILLERS.
WHEN THE WAR ENDED AND OUR PURPOSE WAS TAKEN AWAY, THAT'S WHEN SO MANY OF THEM TOOK TO AIMLESS RAMPAGING.
BUT NOT STEELE. HE BECAME PATIENT, CALCULATING. I SUSPECT HE'S BEEN PLANNING THIS SINCE THE REVOLUTION.
IT'S AS THOUGH HE PUT ALL THAT VIOLENT ENERGY INTO ONE OBJECTIVE . . .

REVENGE.

TOO BAD THE ONE PERSON WHO DESERVES HIS REVENGE IS ALREADY DEAD.

HE SHOULD BE KISSING CINDER'S METAL TOES AFTER ALL SHE DID TO GET RID OF LEVANA!

Shudder

I'D REALLY RATHER HE DIDN'T.

EITHER WAY, IT SOUNDS LIKE STEELE HAS HIS HEART SET ON A FIGHT, AND I PLAN ON GIVING HIM ONE.

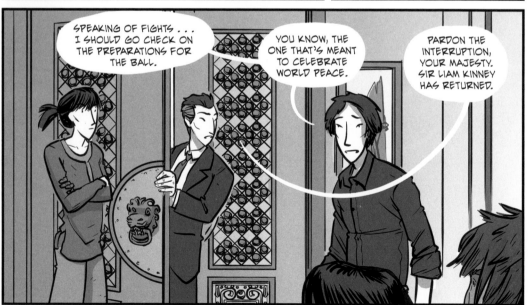

SPEAKING OF FIGHTS . . . I SHOULD GO CHECK ON THE PREPARATIONS FOR THE BALL.

YOU KNOW, THE ONE THAT'S MEANT TO CELEBRATE WORLD PEACE.

PARDON THE INTERRUPTION, YOUR MAJESTY. SIR LIAM KINNEY HAS RETURNED.

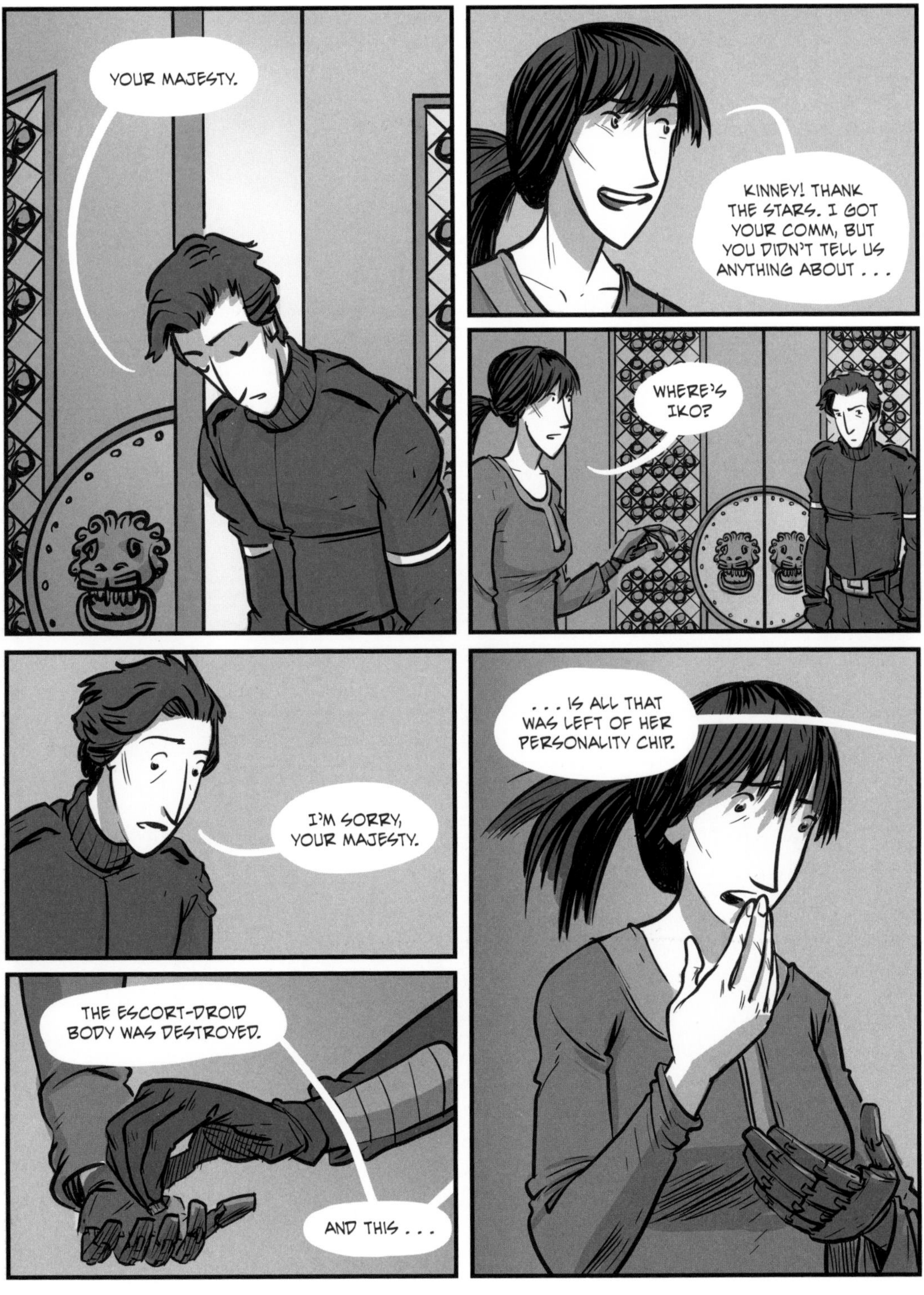
YOUR MAJESTY.
KINNEY! THANK THE STARS. I GOT YOUR COMM, BUT YOU DIDN'T TELL US ANYTHING ABOUT . . .
WHERE'S IKO?
I'M SORRY, YOUR MAJESTY.
THE ESCORT-DROID BODY WAS DESTROYED.
AND THIS . . .
. . . IS ALL THAT WAS LEFT OF HER PERSONALITY CHIP.

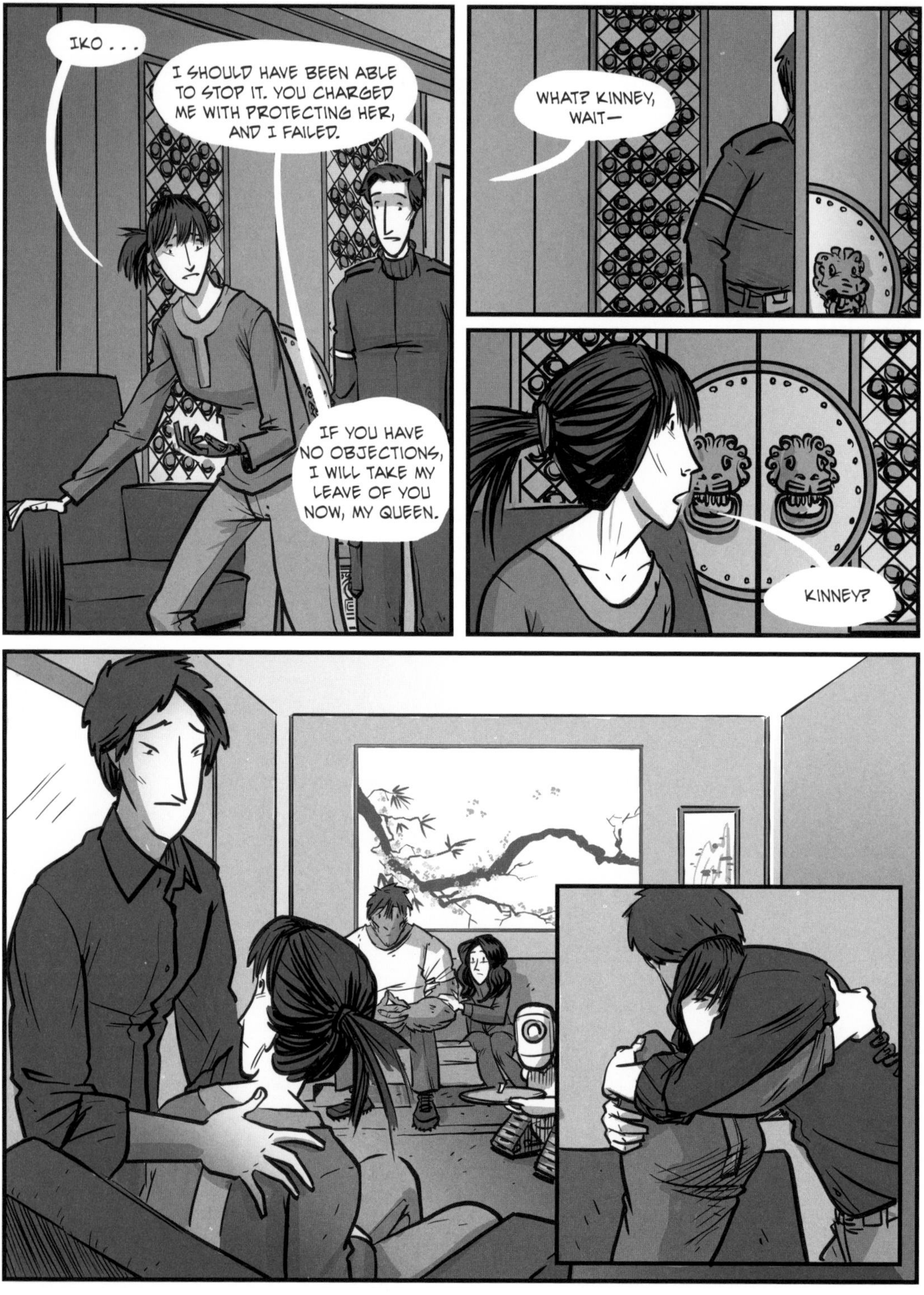
IKO . . .
I SHOULD HAVE BEEN ABLE TO STOP IT. YOU CHARGED ME WITH PROTECTING HER, AND I FAILED.
IF YOU HAVE NO OBJECTIONS, I WILL TAKE MY LEAVE OF YOU NOW, MY QUEEN.
WHAT? KINNEY, WAIT—
KINNEY?

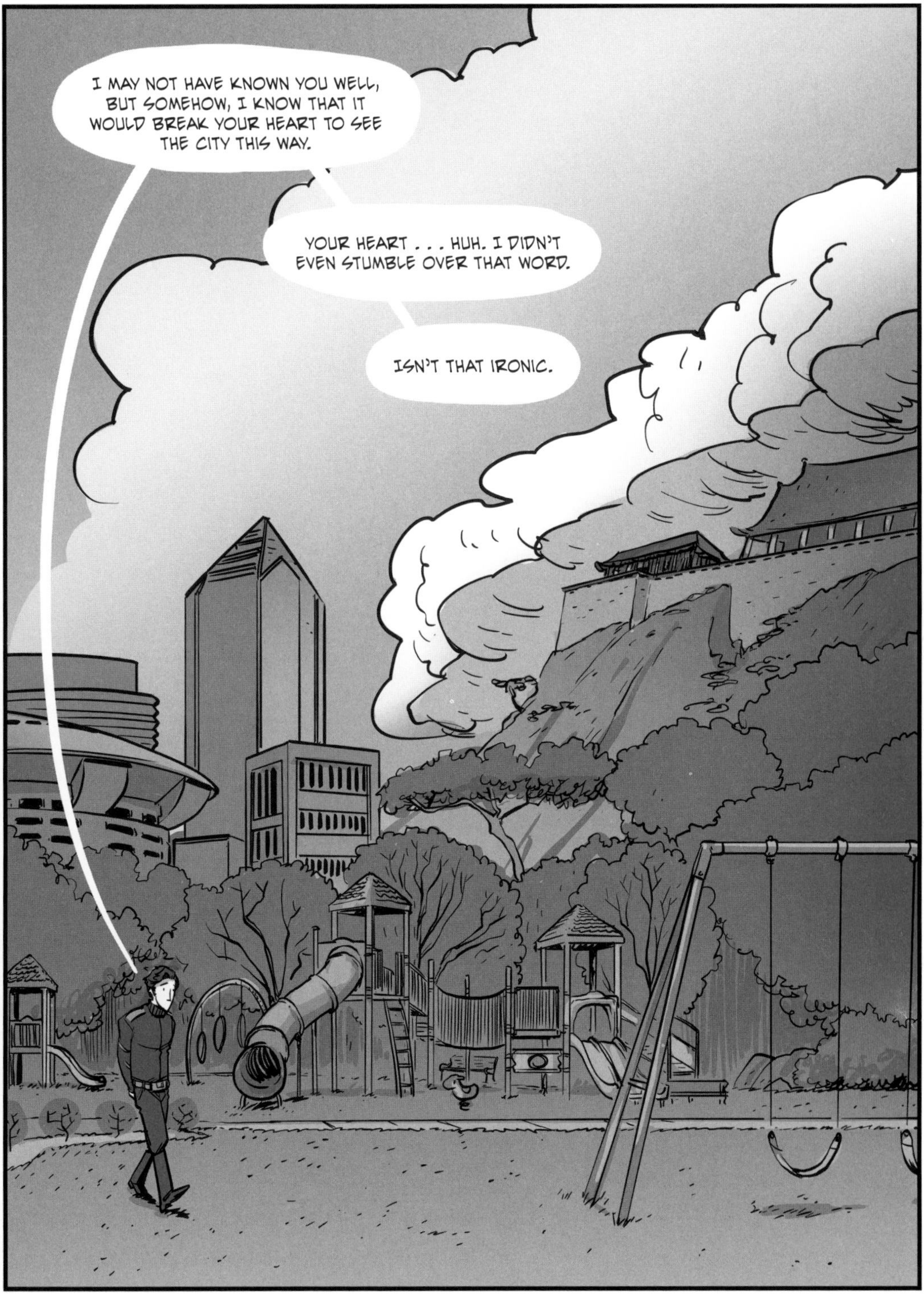
I MAY NOT HAVE KNOWN YOU WELL, BUT SOMEHOW, I KNOW THAT IT WOULD BREAK YOUR HEART TO SEE THE CITY THIS WAY.
YOUR HEART . . . HUH. I DIDN'T EVEN STUMBLE OVER THAT WORD.
ISN'T THAT IRONIC.

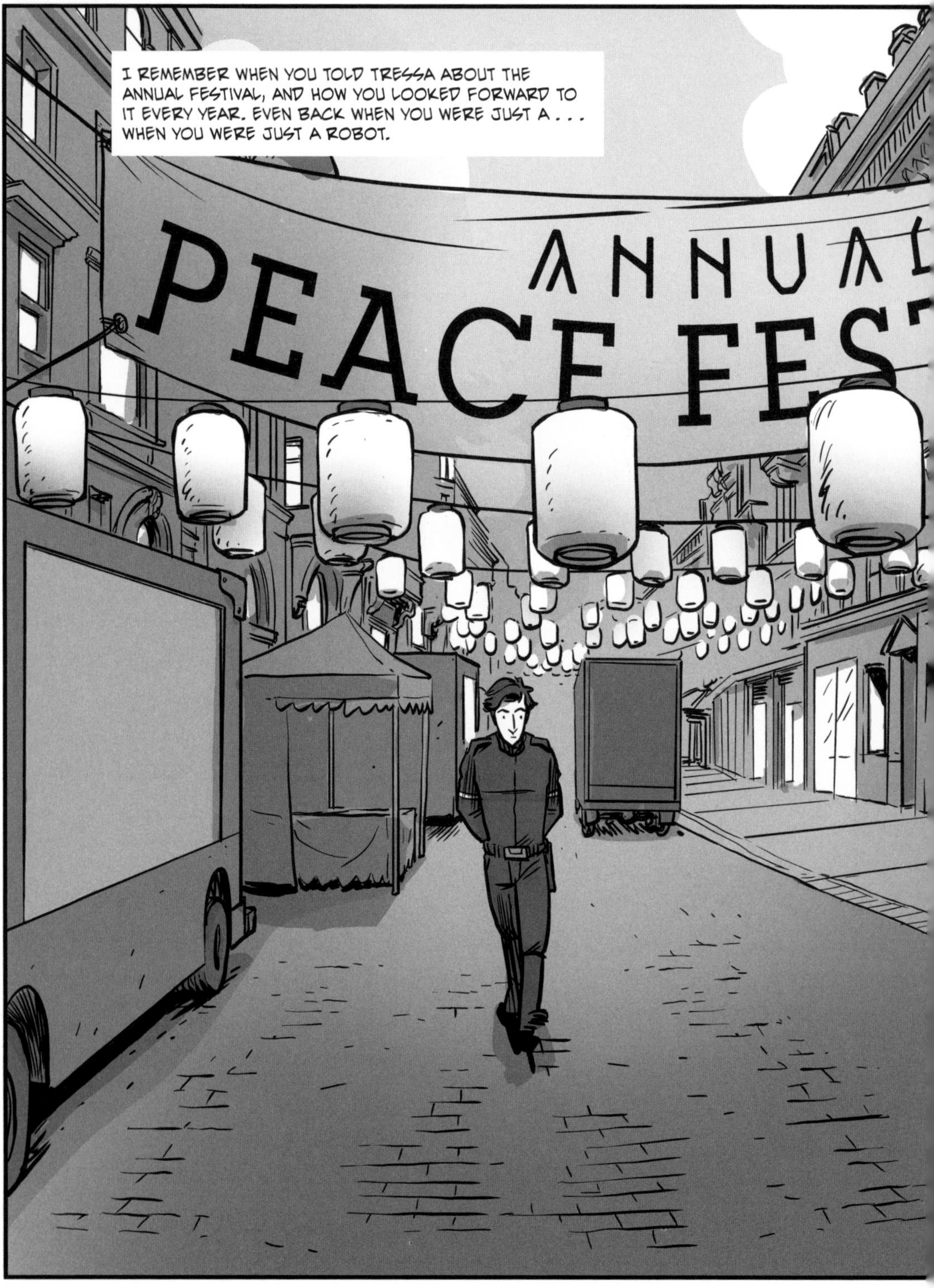
I REMEMBER WHEN YOU TOLD TRESSA ABOUT THE ANNUAL FESTIVAL, AND HOW YOU LOOKED FORWARD TO IT EVERY YEAR. EVEN BACK WHEN YOU WERE JUST A . . . WHEN YOU WERE JUST A ROBOT.
ANNUAL
PEACE FES

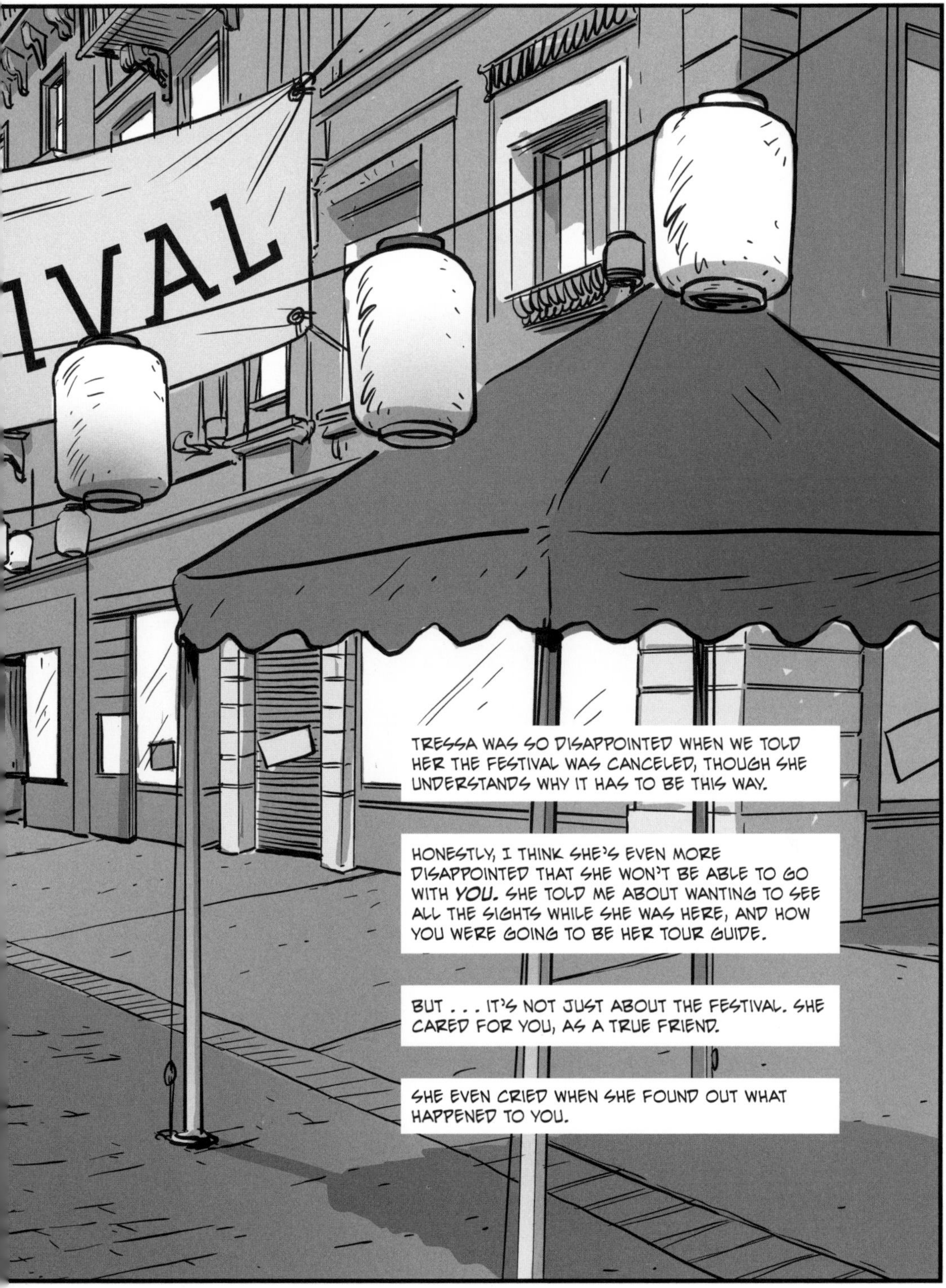
IVAL
TRESSA WAS SO DISAPPOINTED WHEN WE TOLD HER THE FESTIVAL WAS CANCELED, THOUGH SHE UNDERSTANDS WHY IT HAS TO BE THIS WAY.
HONESTLY, I THINK SHE'S EVEN MORE DISAPPOINTED THAT SHE WON'T BE ABLE TO GO WITH ***YOU.*** SHE TOLD ME ABOUT WANTING TO SEE ALL THE SIGHTS WHILE SHE WAS HERE, AND HOW YOU WERE GOING TO BE HER TOUR GUIDE.
BUT . . . IT'S NOT JUST ABOUT THE FESTIVAL. SHE CARED FOR YOU, AS A TRUE FRIEND.
SHE EVEN CRIED WHEN SHE FOUND OUT WHAT HAPPENED TO YOU.

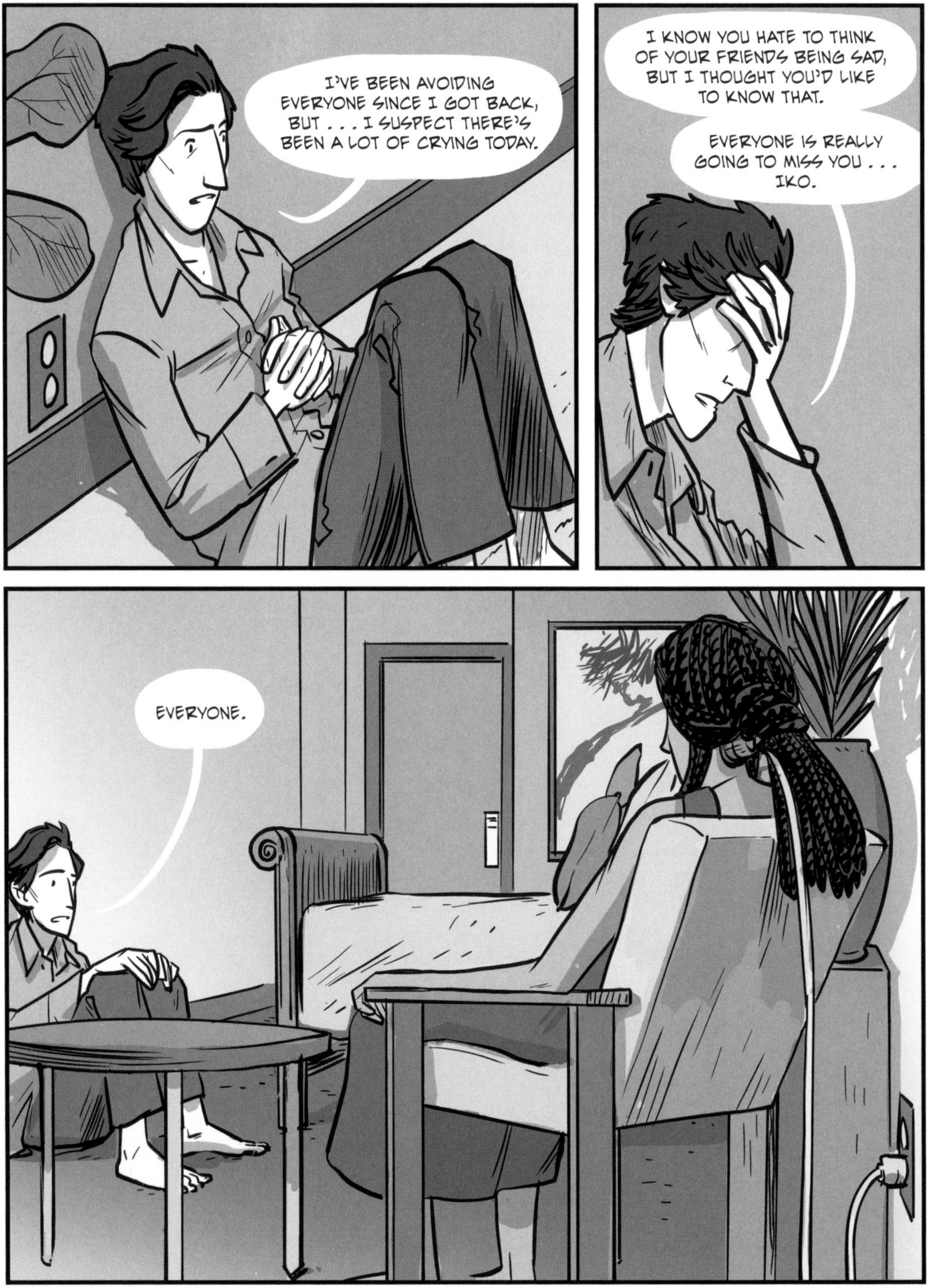
I'VE BEEN AVOIDING EVERYONE SINCE I GOT BACK, BUT . . . I SUSPECT THERE'S BEEN A LOT OF CRYING TODAY.
I KNOW YOU HATE TO THINK OF YOUR FRIENDS BEING SAD, BUT I THOUGHT YOU'D LIKE TO KNOW THAT.
EVERYONE IS REALLY GOING TO MISS YOU . . . IKO.
EVERYONE.

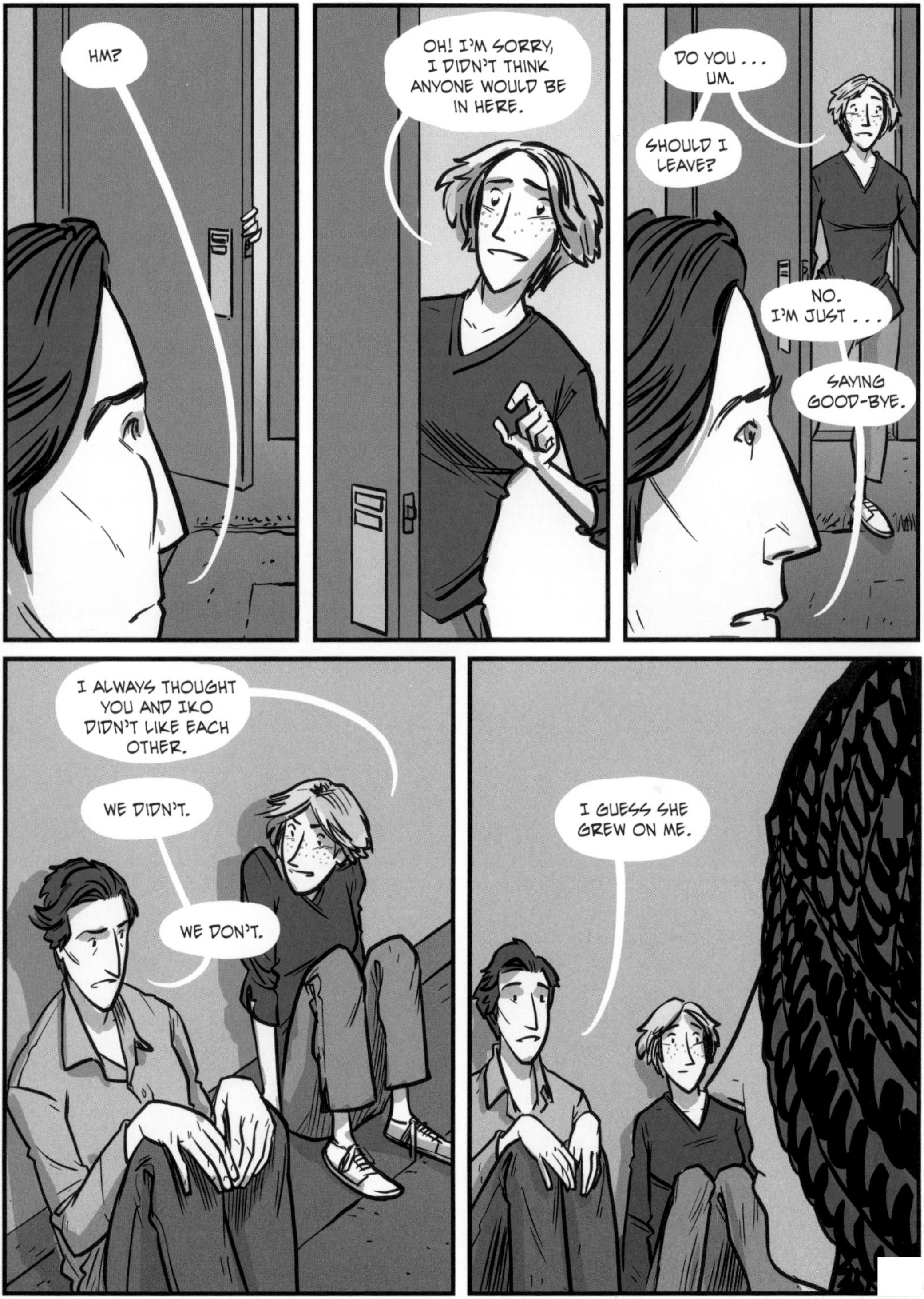
HM?
OH! I'M SORRY, I DIDN'T THINK ANYONE WOULD BE IN HERE.
DO YOU . . . UM.
SHOULD I LEAVE?
NO. I'M JUST . . .
SAYING GOOD-BYE.
I ALWAYS THOUGHT YOU AND IKO DIDN'T LIKE EACH OTHER.
WE DIDN'T.
WE DON'T.
I GUESS SHE GREW ON ME.

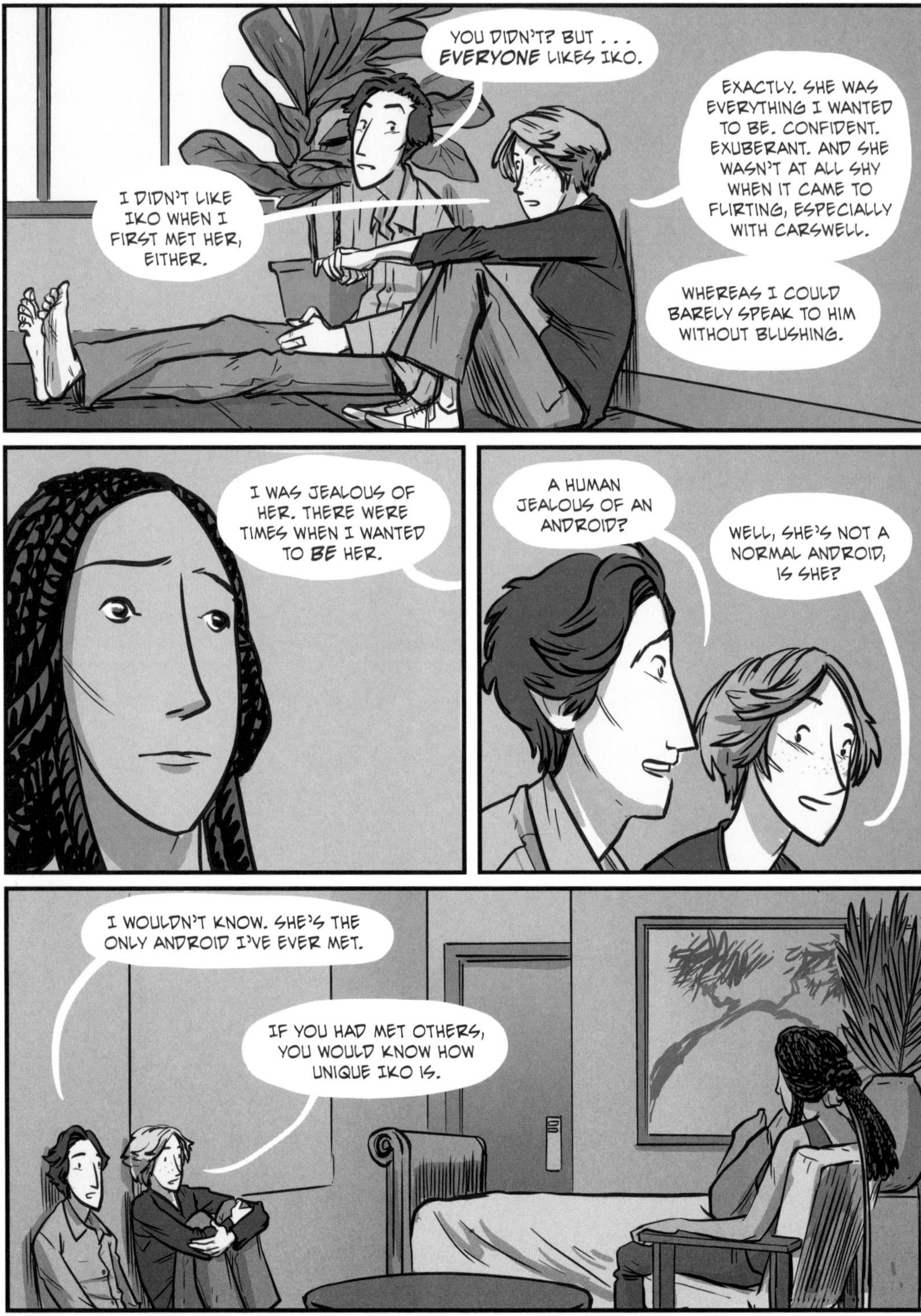
I DIDN'T LIKE IKO WHEN I FIRST MET HER, EITHER.
YOU DIDN'T? BUT . . . EVERYONE LIKES IKO.
EXACTLY. SHE WAS EVERYTHING I WANTED TO BE. CONFIDENT. EXUBERANT. AND SHE WASN'T AT ALL SHY WHEN IT CAME TO FLIRTING, ESPECIALLY WITH CARSWELL.
WHEREAS I COULD BARELY SPEAK TO HIM WITHOUT BLUSHING.
I WAS JEALOUS OF HER. THERE WERE TIMES WHEN I WANTED TO BE HER.
A HUMAN JEALOUS OF AN ANDROID?
WELL, SHE'S NOT A NORMAL ANDROID, IS SHE?
I WOULDN'T KNOW. SHE'S THE ONLY ANDROID I'VE EVER MET.
IF YOU HAD MET OTHERS, YOU WOULD KNOW HOW UNIQUE IKO IS.

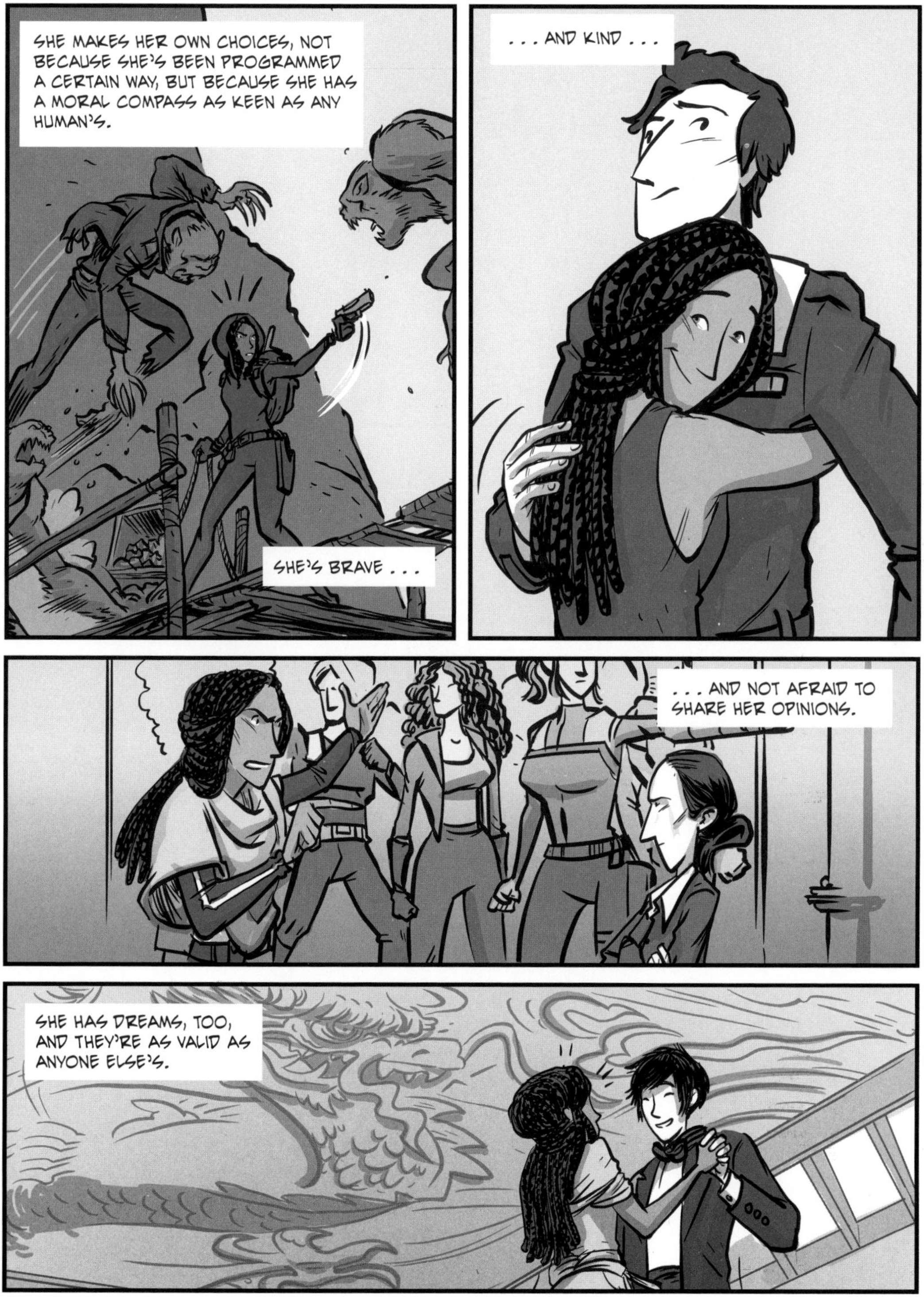
SHE MAKES HER OWN CHOICES, NOT BECAUSE SHE'S BEEN PROGRAMMED A CERTAIN WAY, BUT BECAUSE SHE HAS A MORAL COMPASS AS KEEN AS ANY HUMAN'S.
SHE'S BRAVE . . .
. . . AND KIND . . .
. . . AND NOT AFRAID TO SHARE HER OPINIONS.
SHE HAS DREAMS, TOO, AND THEY'RE AS VALID AS ANYONE ELSE'S.

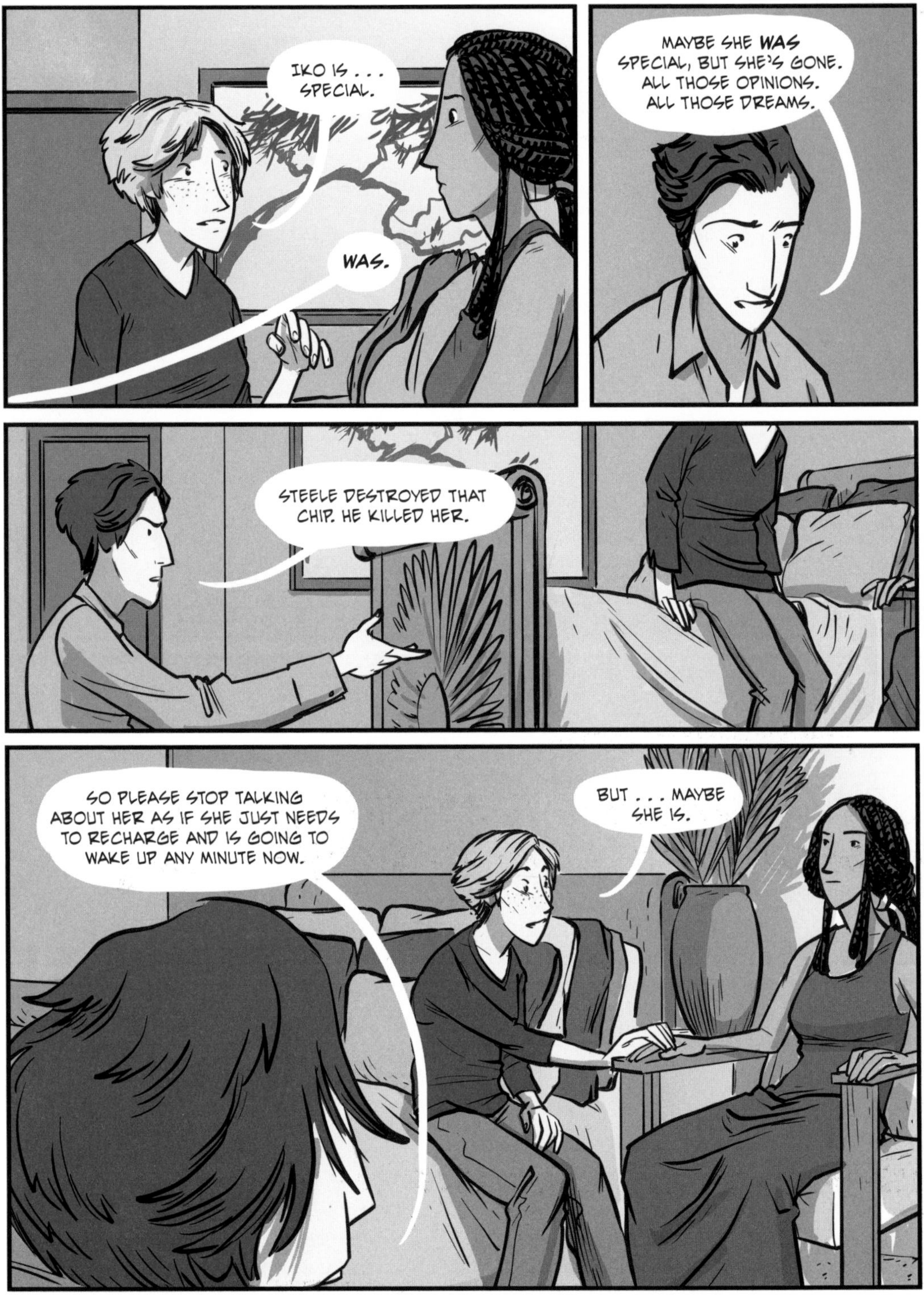
IKO IS . . . SPECIAL.
WAS.
MAYBE SHE **WAS** SPECIAL, BUT SHE'S GONE. ALL THOSE OPINIONS. ALL THOSE DREAMS.
STEELE DESTROYED THAT CHIP. HE KILLED HER.
SO PLEASE STOP TALKING ABOUT HER AS IF SHE JUST NEEDS TO RECHARGE AND IS GOING TO WAKE UP ANY MINUTE NOW.
BUT . . . MAYBE SHE IS.

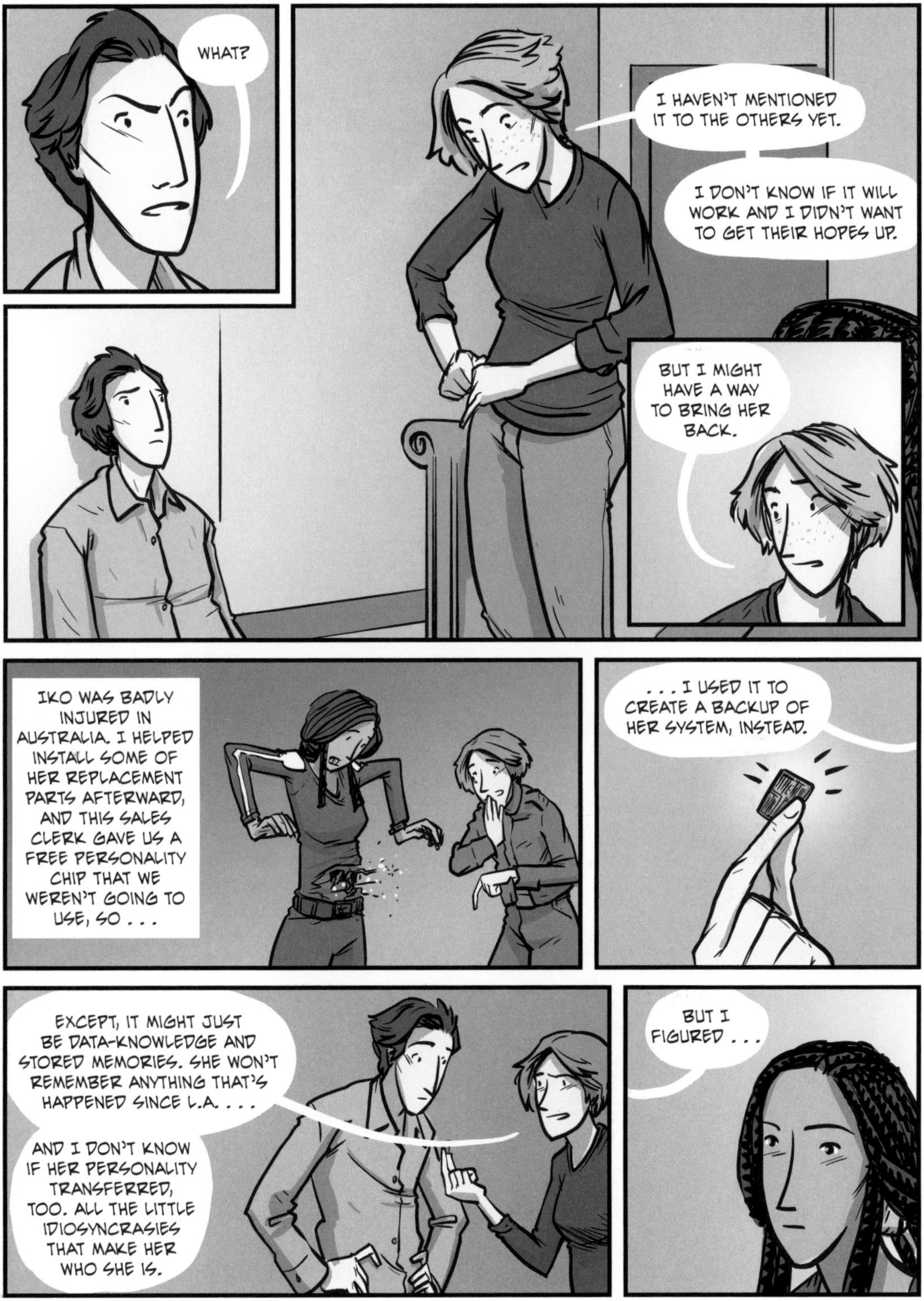
WHAT?
I HAVEN'T MENTIONED IT TO THE OTHERS YET.
I DON'T KNOW IF IT WILL WORK AND I DIDN'T WANT TO GET THEIR HOPES UP.
BUT I MIGHT HAVE A WAY TO BRING HER BACK.
IKO WAS BADLY INJURED IN AUSTRALIA. I HELPED INSTALL SOME OF HER REPLACEMENT PARTS AFTERWARD, AND THIS SALES CLERK GAVE US A FREE PERSONALITY CHIP THAT WE WEREN'T GOING TO USE, SO . . .
. . . I USED IT TO CREATE A BACKUP OF HER SYSTEM, INSTEAD.
EXCEPT, IT MIGHT JUST BE DATA-KNOWLEDGE AND STORED MEMORIES. SHE WON'T REMEMBER ANYTHING THAT'S HAPPENED SINCE L.A. . . .
AND I DON'T KNOW IF HER PERSONALITY TRANSFERRED, TOO. ALL THE LITTLE IDIOSYNCRASIES THAT MAKE HER WHO SHE IS.
BUT I FIGURED . . .

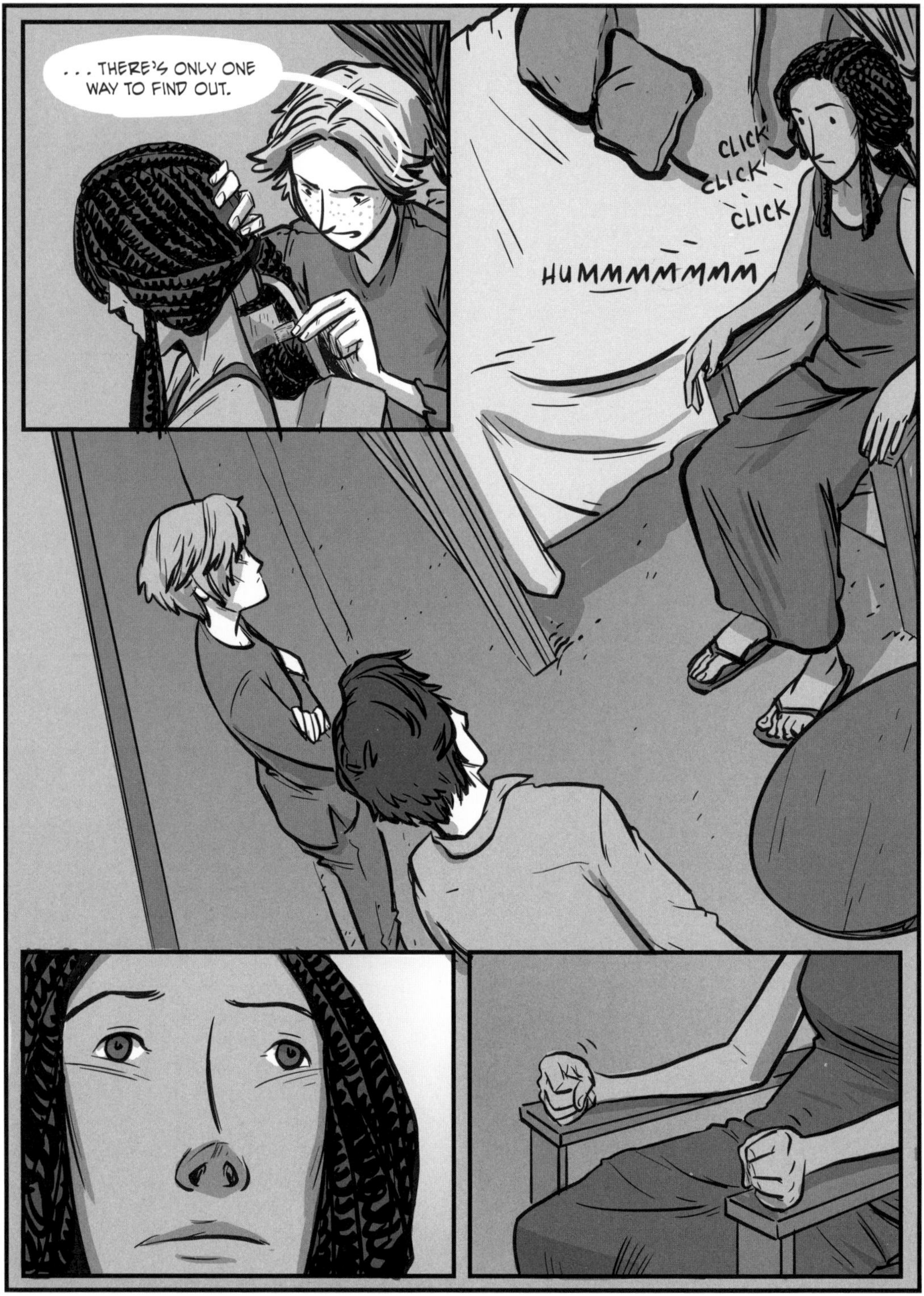
. . . THERE'S ONLY ONE WAY TO FIND OUT.
CLICK
CLICK
CLICK
HUMMMMMMMM

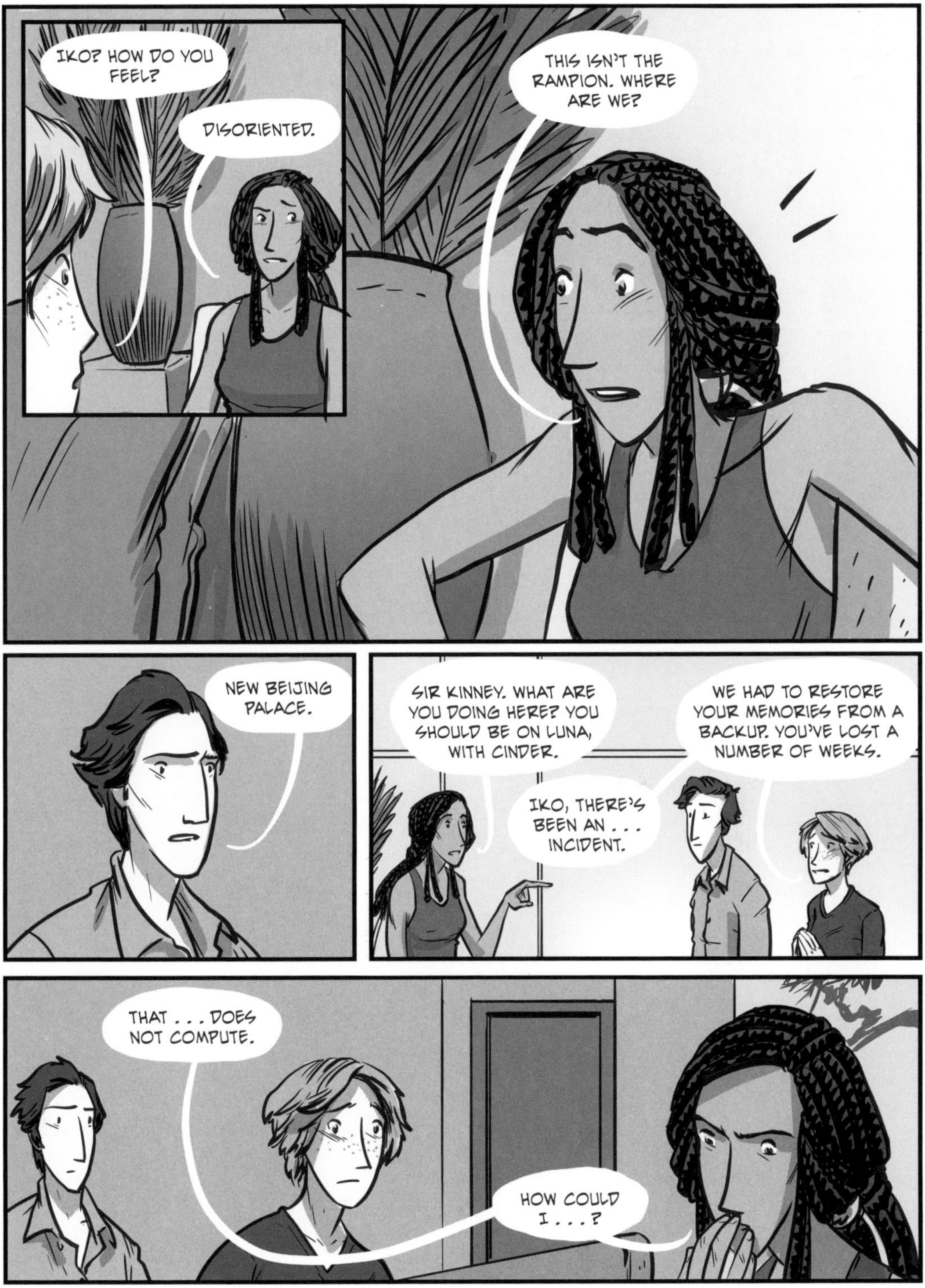
IKO? HOW DO YOU FEEL?
DISORIENTED.
THIS ISN'T THE RAMPION. WHERE ARE WE?
NEW BEIJING PALACE.
SIR KINNEY. WHAT ARE YOU DOING HERE? YOU SHOULD BE ON LUNA, WITH CINDER.
IKO, THERE'S BEEN AN . . . INCIDENT.
WE HAD TO RESTORE YOUR MEMORIES FROM A BACKUP. YOU'VE LOST A NUMBER OF WEEKS.
THAT . . . DOES NOT COMPUTE.
HOW COULD I . . . ?

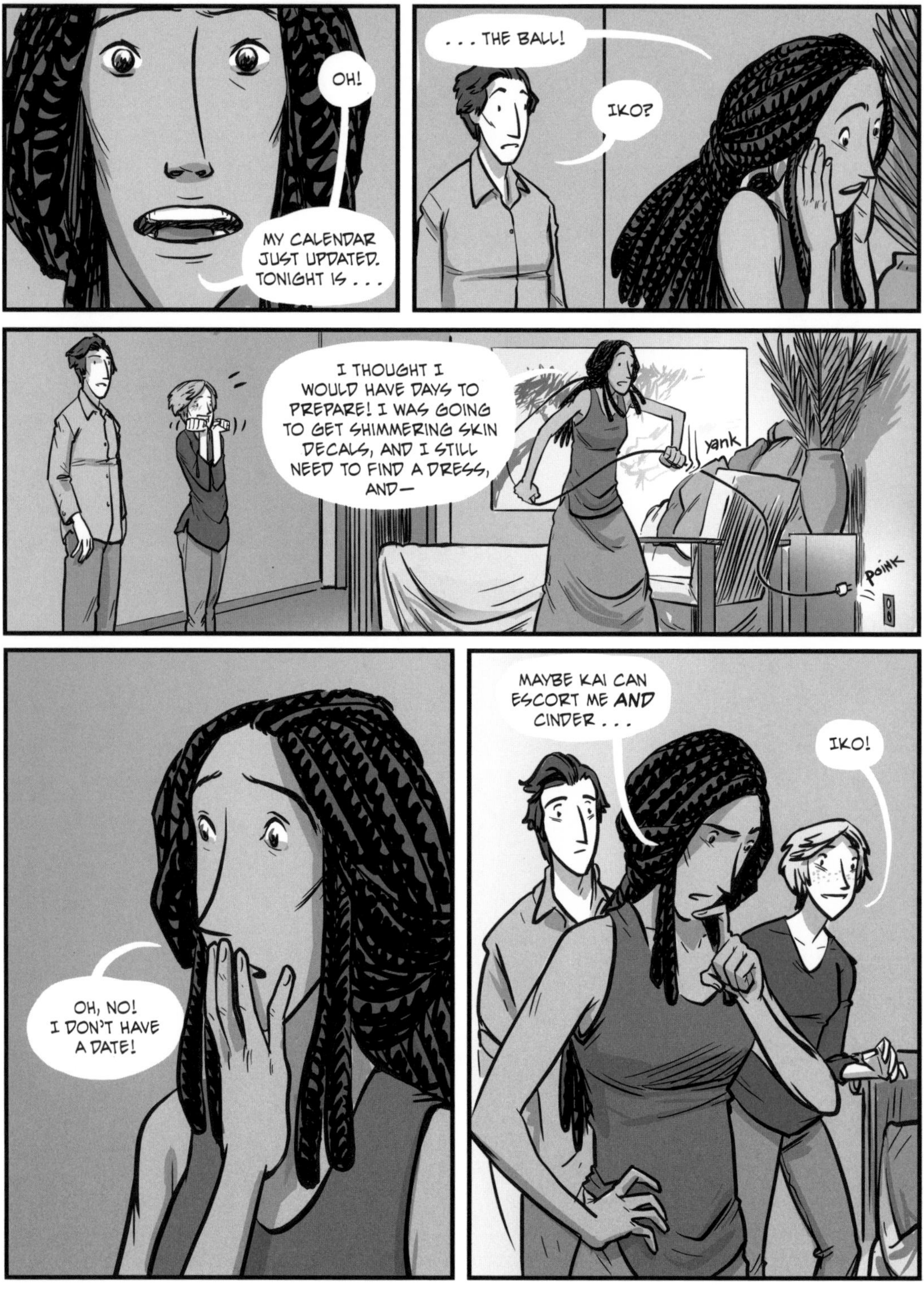
OH!
MY CALENDAR JUST UPDATED. TONIGHT IS . . .
. . . THE BALL!
IKO?
I THOUGHT I WOULD HAVE DAYS TO PREPARE! I WAS GOING TO GET SHIMMERING SKIN DECALS, AND I STILL NEED TO FIND A DRESS, AND—
yank
POINK
OH, NO! I DON'T HAVE A DATE!
MAYBE KAI CAN ESCORT ME **AND** CINDER . . .
IKO!

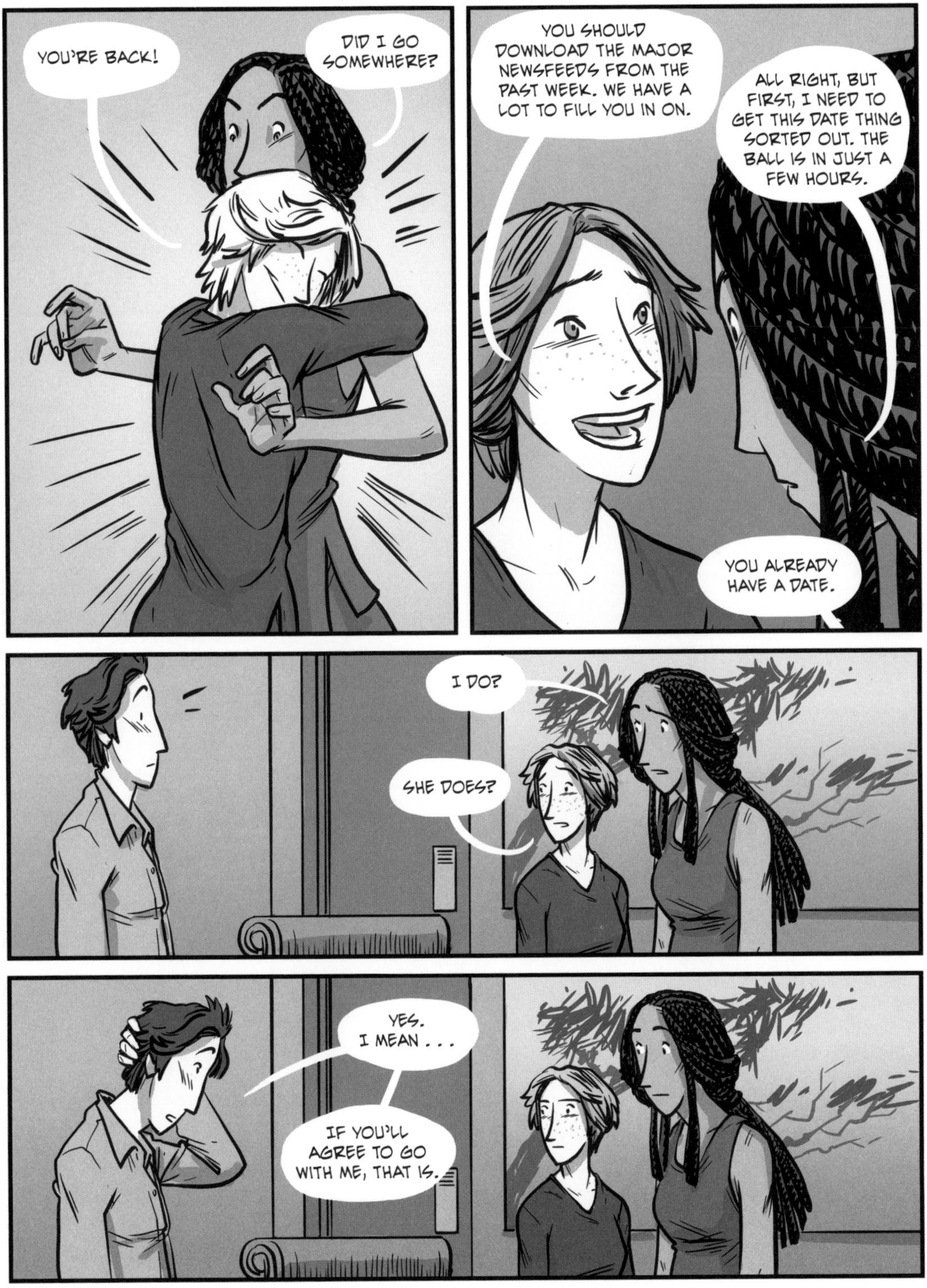
YOU'RE BACK!
DID I GO SOMEWHERE?
YOU SHOULD DOWNLOAD THE MAJOR NEWSFEEDS FROM THE PAST WEEK. WE HAVE A LOT TO FILL YOU IN ON.
ALL RIGHT, BUT FIRST, I NEED TO GET THIS DATE THING SORTED OUT. THE BALL IS IN JUST A FEW HOURS.
YOU ALREADY HAVE A DATE.
I DO?
SHE DOES?
YES. I MEAN . . .
IF YOU'LL AGREE TO GO WITH ME, THAT IS.

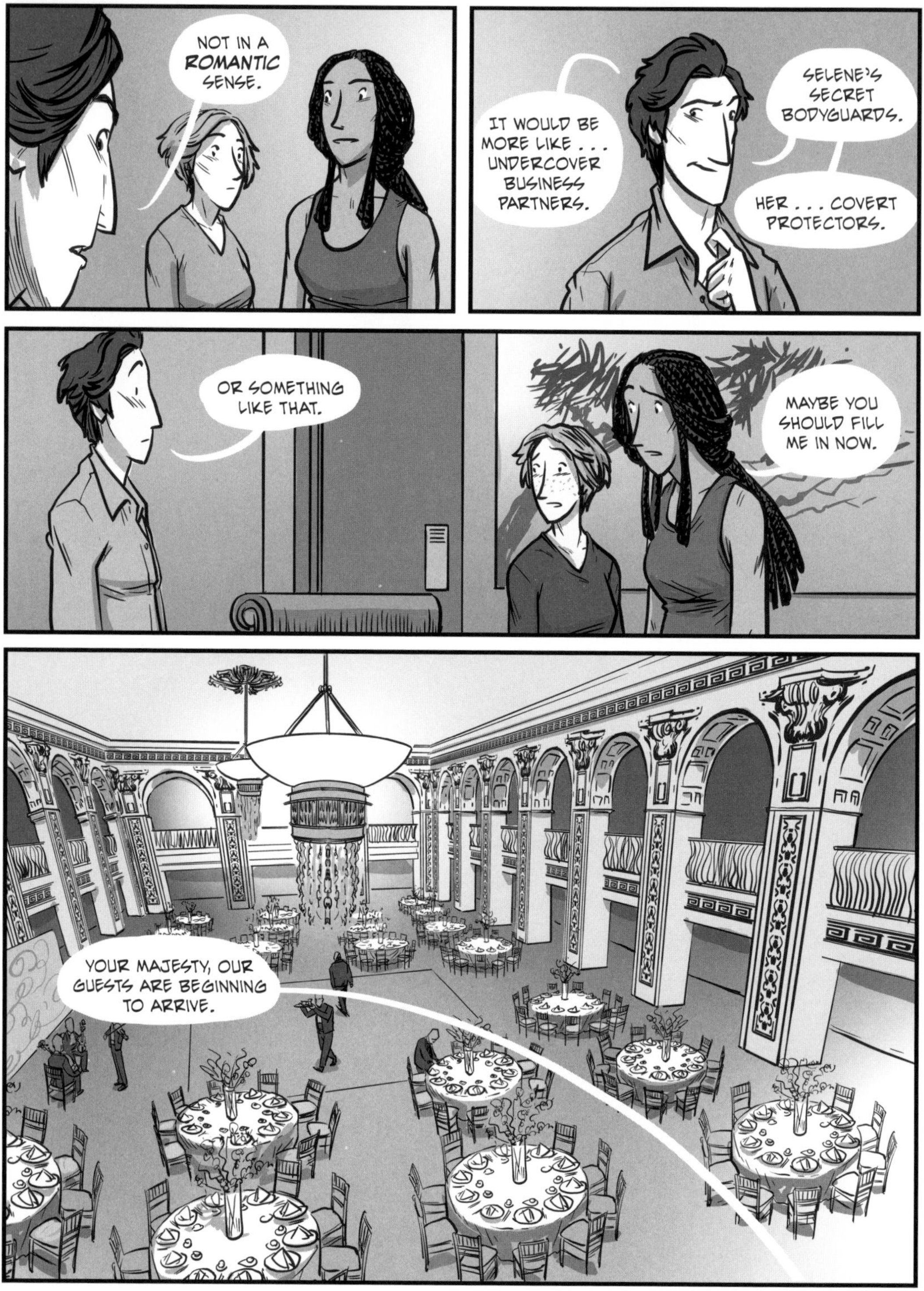
NOT IN A ROMANTIC SENSE.
IT WOULD BE MORE LIKE . . . UNDERCOVER BUSINESS PARTNERS.
SELENE'S SECRET BODYGUARDS.
HER . . . COVERT PROTECTORS.
OR SOMETHING LIKE THAT.
MAYBE YOU SHOULD FILL ME IN NOW.
YOUR MAJESTY, OUR GUESTS ARE BEGINNING TO ARRIVE.

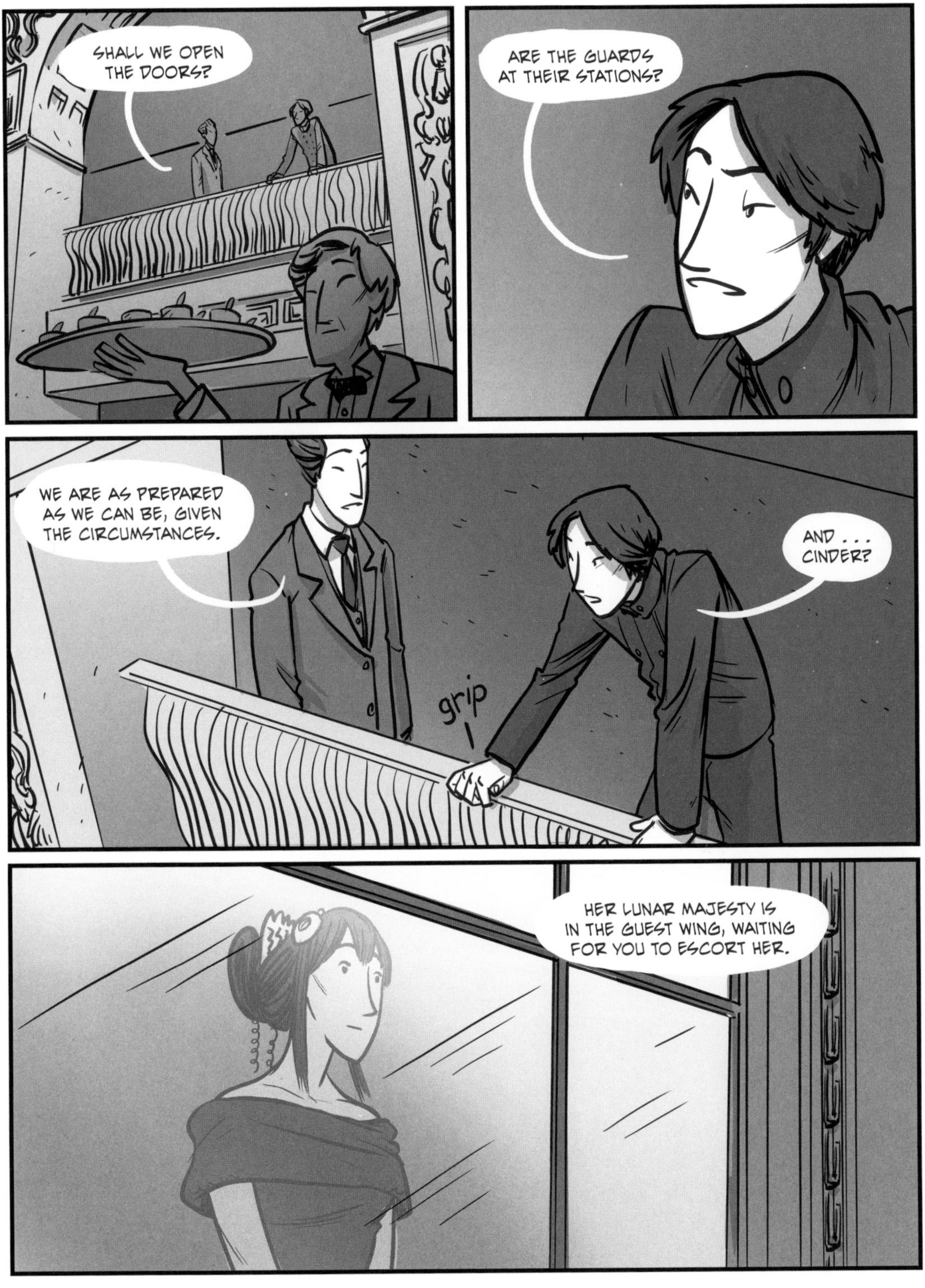
SHALL WE OPEN THE DOORS?
ARE THE GUARDS AT THEIR STATIONS?
WE ARE AS PREPARED AS WE CAN BE, GIVEN THE CIRCUMSTANCES.
AND . . . CINDER?
grip
HER LUNAR MAJESTY IS IN THE GUEST WING, WAITING FOR YOU TO ESCORT HER.

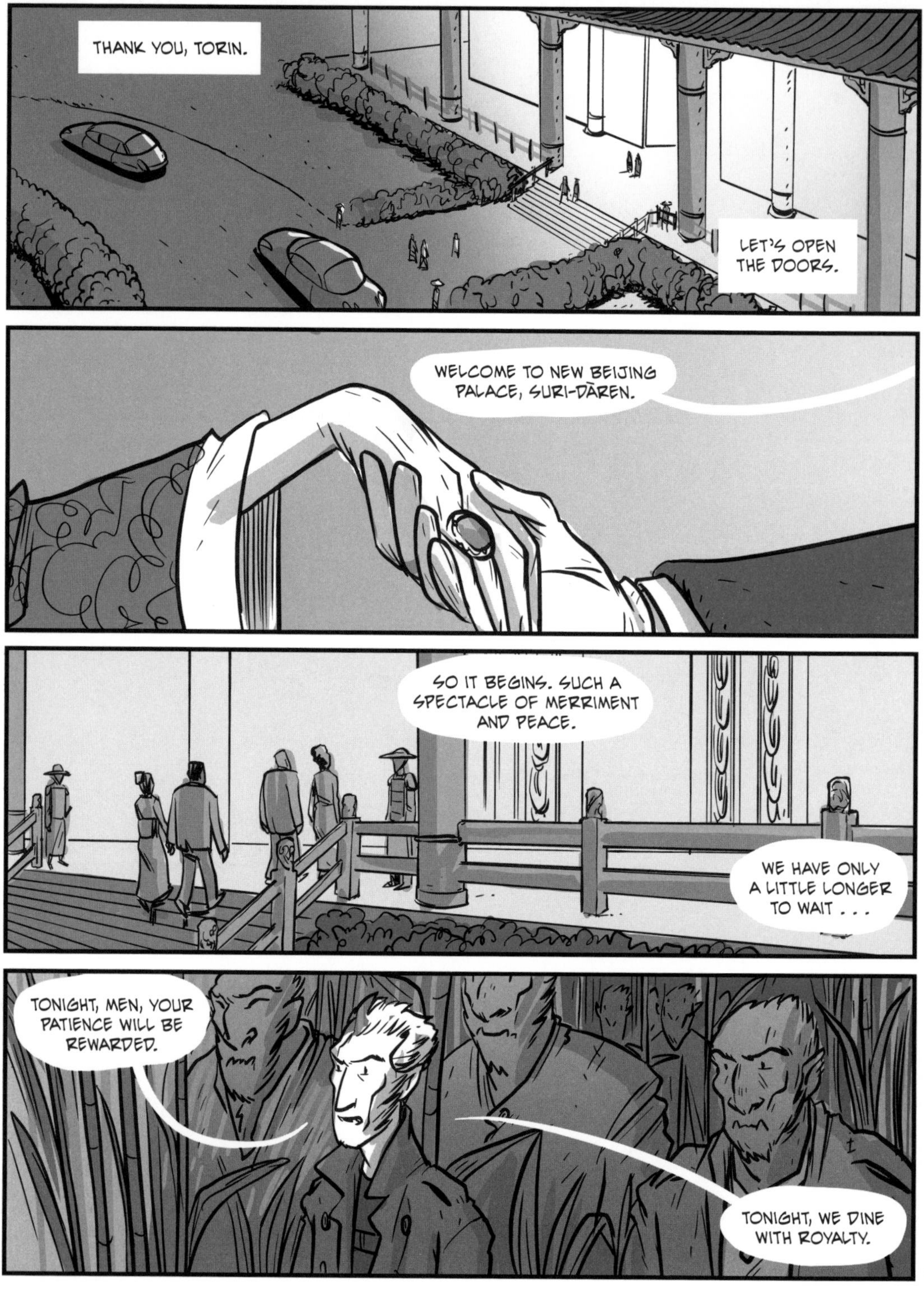
THANK YOU, TORIN.
LET'S OPEN THE DOORS.
WELCOME TO NEW BEIJING PALACE, SURI-DÀREN.
SO IT BEGINS. SUCH A SPECTACLE OF MERRIMENT AND PEACE.
WE HAVE ONLY A LITTLE LONGER TO WAIT . . .
TONIGHT, MEN, YOUR PATIENCE WILL BE REWARDED.
TONIGHT, WE DINE WITH ROYALTY.

CHAPTER IX

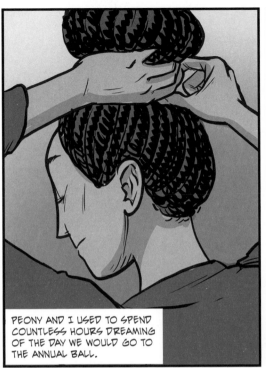

PEONY AND I USED TO SPEND COUNTLESS HOURS DREAMING OF THE DAY WE WOULD GO TO THE ANNUAL BALL.

PEONY WOULD DRESS UP IN ADRI'S SILK KIMONOS, AND I WOULD DRAPE STRANDS OF PEARLS OVER MY SERVANT-DROID BODY.

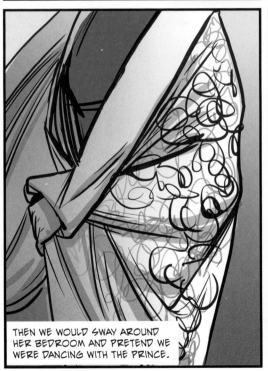

THEN WE WOULD SWAY AROUND HER BEDROOM AND PRETEND WE WERE DANCING WITH THE PRINCE.

I WISH SHE WERE HERE NOW. I WISH SHE COULD SEE ME LIKE THIS—A REAL PERSON WHO DESERVES TO GO TO THE BALL.

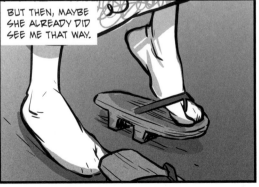

BUT THEN, MAYBE SHE ALREADY DID SEE ME THAT WAY.

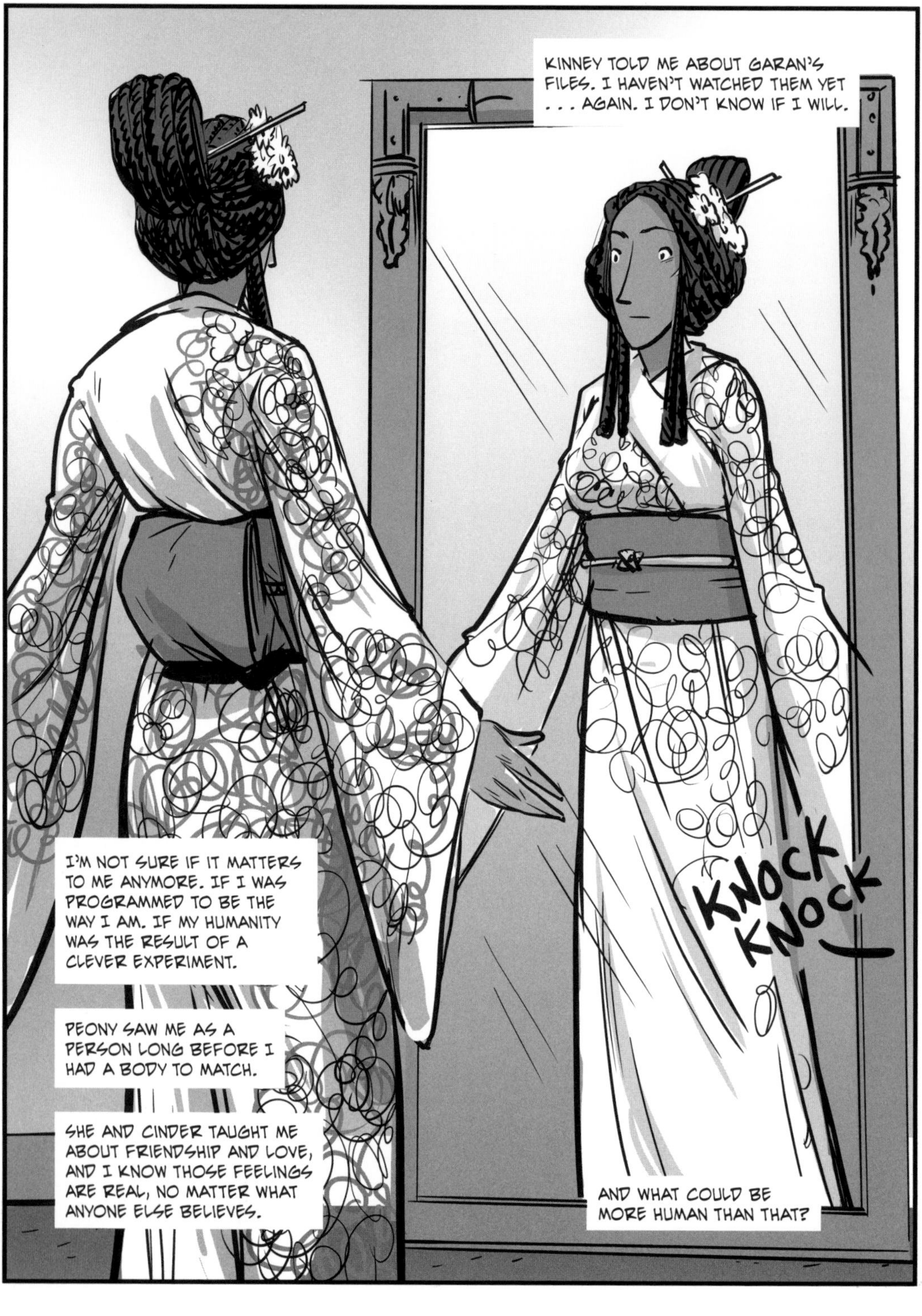
KINNEY TOLD ME ABOUT GARAN'S FILES. I HAVEN'T WATCHED THEM YET . . . AGAIN. I DON'T KNOW IF I WILL.
I'M NOT SURE IF IT MATTERS TO ME ANYMORE. IF I WAS PROGRAMMED TO BE THE WAY I AM. IF MY HUMANITY WAS THE RESULT OF A CLEVER EXPERIMENT.
KNOCK KNOCK
PEONY SAW ME AS A PERSON LONG BEFORE I HAD A BODY TO MATCH.
SHE AND CINDER TAUGHT ME ABOUT FRIENDSHIP AND LOVE, AND I KNOW THOSE FEELINGS ARE REAL, NO MATTER WHAT ANYONE ELSE BELIEVES.
AND WHAT COULD BE MORE HUMAN THAN THAT?

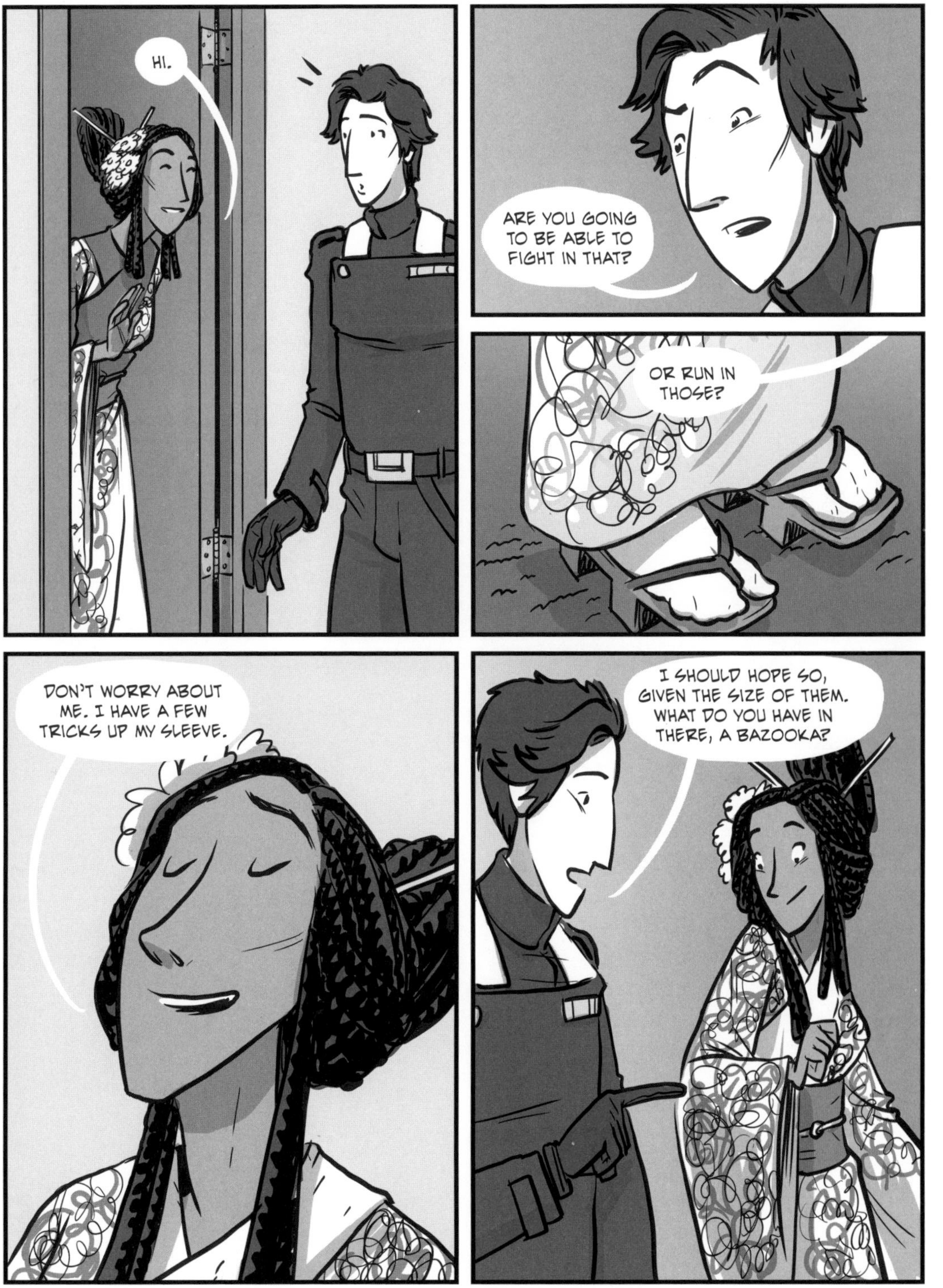
HI.
ARE YOU GOING TO BE ABLE TO FIGHT IN THAT?
OR RUN IN THOSE?
DON'T WORRY ABOUT ME. I HAVE A FEW TRICKS UP MY SLEEVE.
I SHOULD HOPE SO, GIVEN THE SIZE OF THEM. WHAT DO YOU HAVE IN THERE, A BAZOOKA?

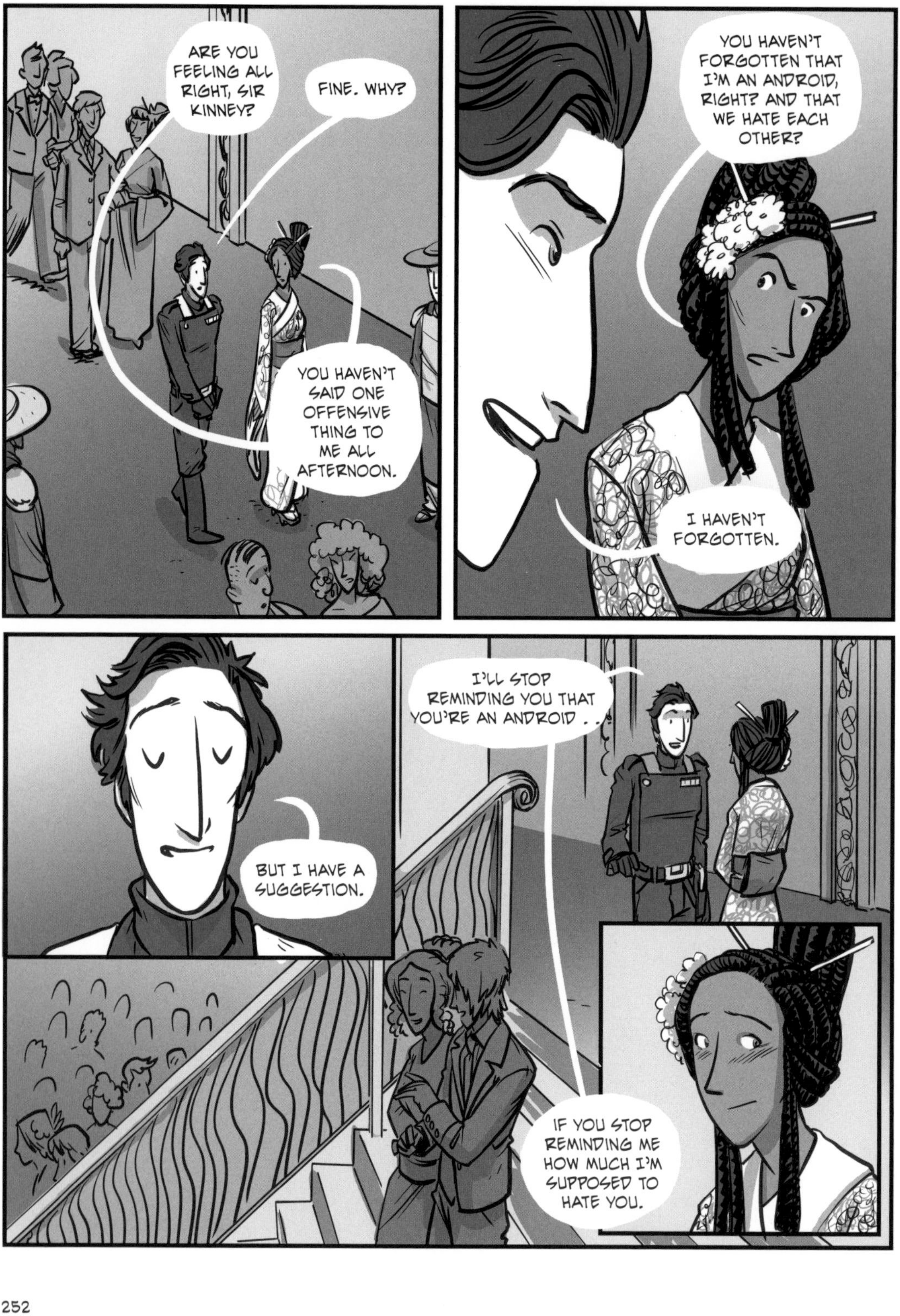
ARE YOU FEELING ALL RIGHT, SIR KINNEY?
FINE. WHY?
YOU HAVEN'T SAID ONE OFFENSIVE THING TO ME ALL AFTERNOON.
YOU HAVEN'T FORGOTTEN THAT I'M AN ANDROID, RIGHT? AND THAT WE HATE EACH OTHER?
I HAVEN'T FORGOTTEN.
BUT I HAVE A SUGGESTION.
I'LL STOP REMINDING YOU THAT YOU'RE AN ANDROID . . .
IF YOU STOP REMINDING ME HOW MUCH I'M SUPPOSED TO HATE YOU.

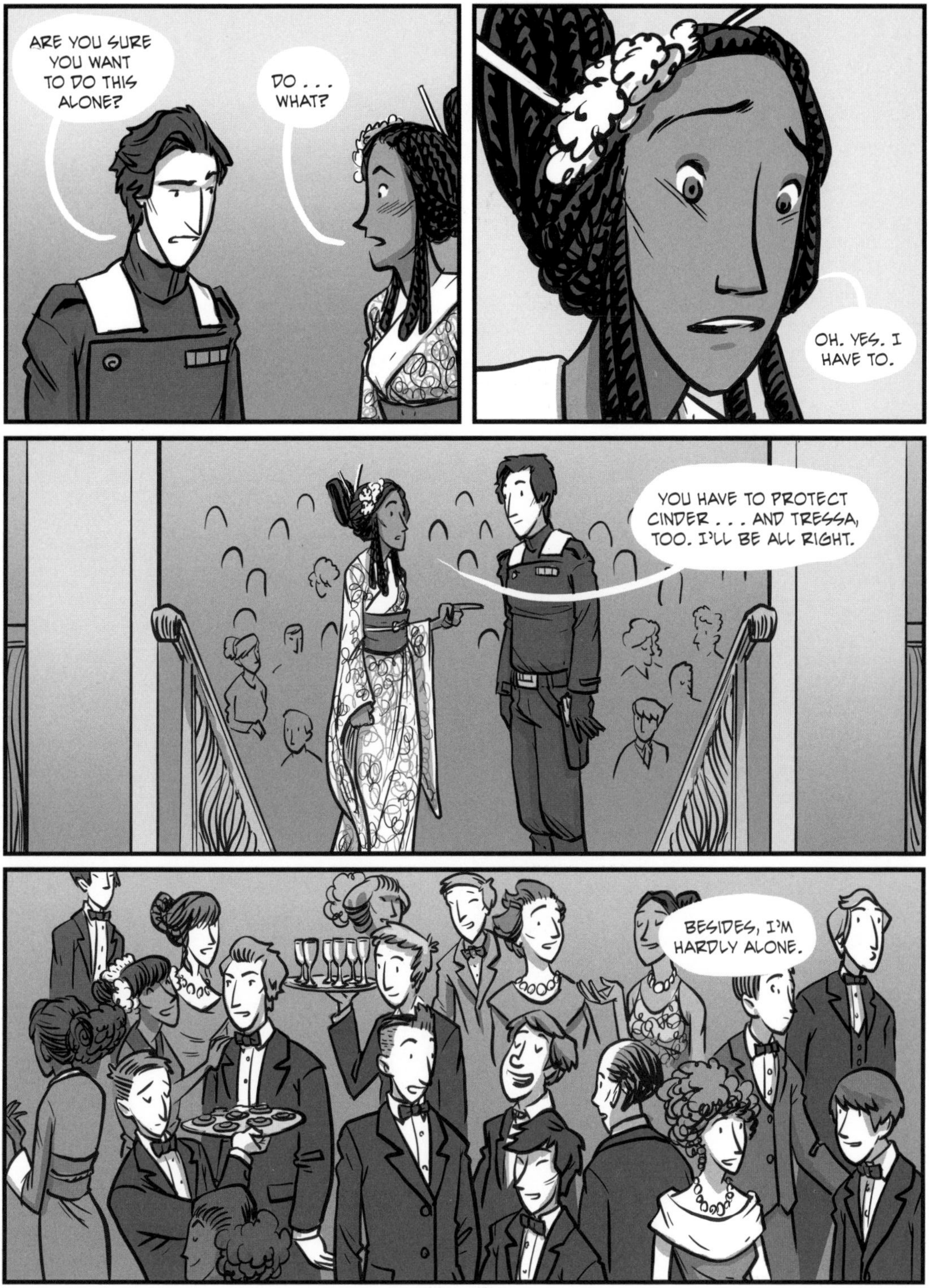
ARE YOU SURE YOU WANT TO DO THIS ALONE?
DO . . . WHAT?
OH. YES. I HAVE TO.
YOU HAVE TO PROTECT CINDER . . . AND TRESSA, TOO. I'LL BE ALL RIGHT.
BESIDES, I'M HARDLY ALONE.

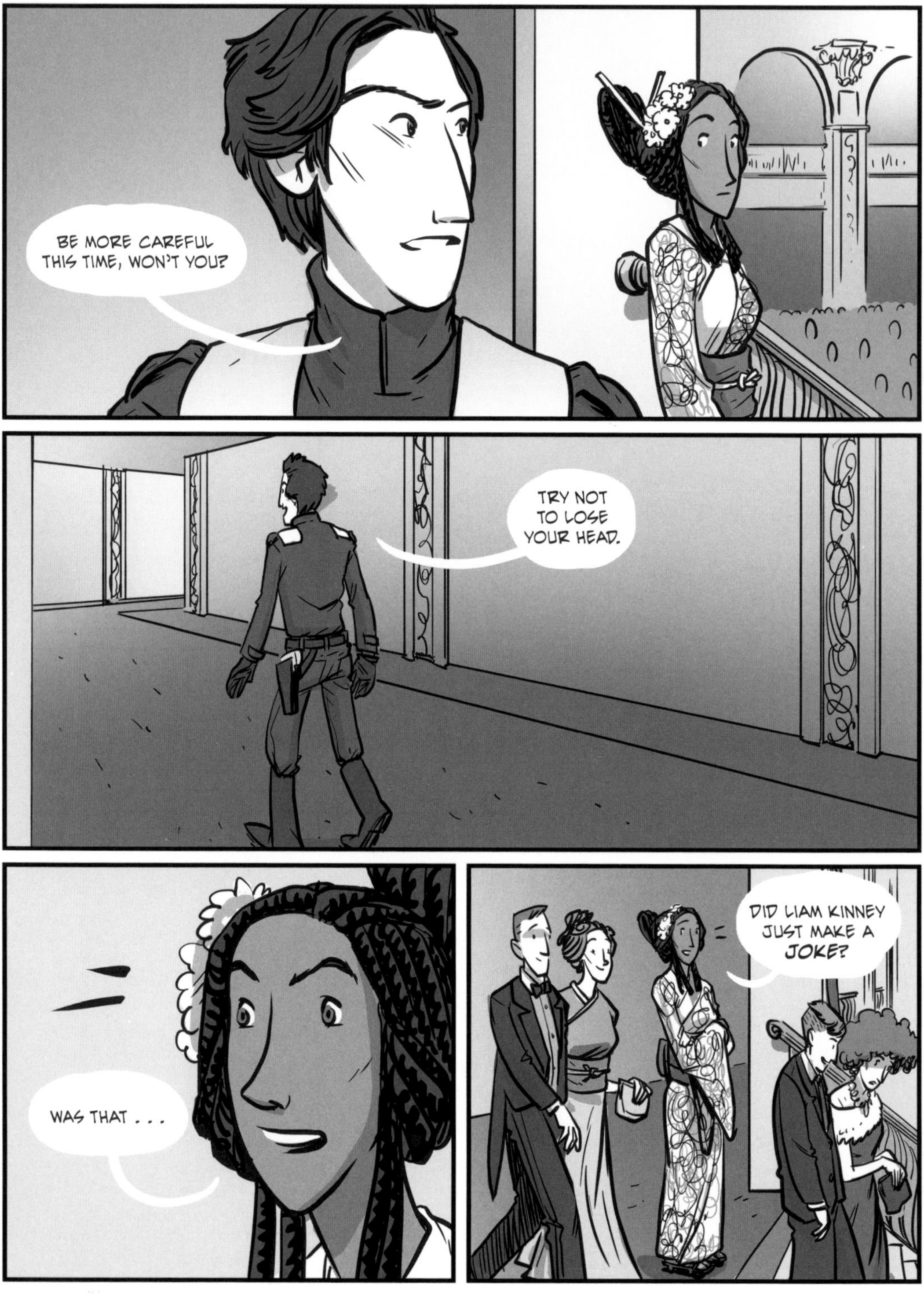
BE MORE CAREFUL THIS TIME, WON'T YOU?
TRY NOT TO LOSE YOUR HEAD.
WAS THAT . . .
DID LIAM KINNEY JUST MAKE A JOKE?

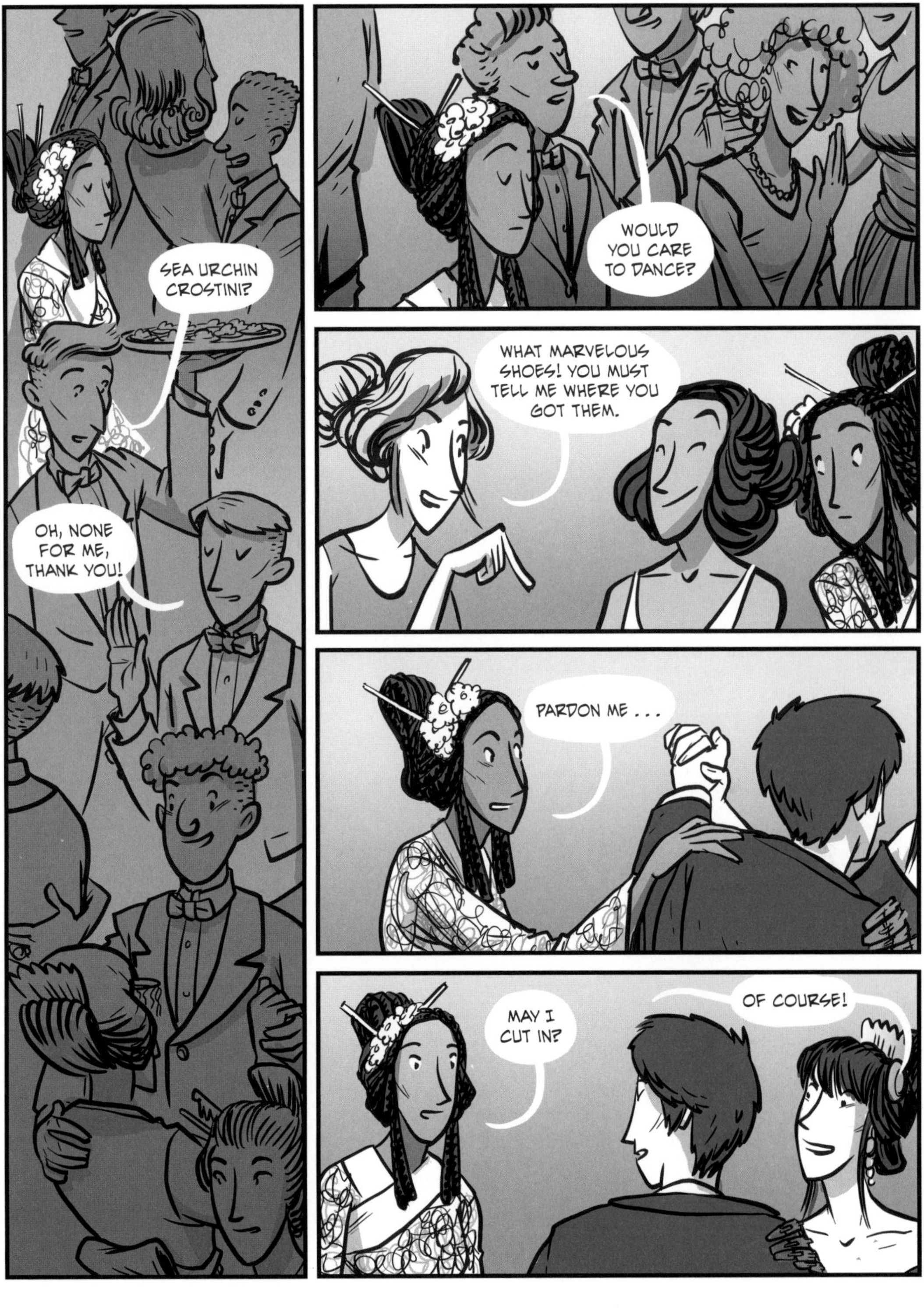
SEA URCHIN CROSTINI?
OH, NONE FOR ME, THANK YOU!
WOULD YOU CARE TO DANCE?
WHAT MARVELOUS SHOES! YOU MUST TELL ME WHERE YOU GOT THEM.
PARDON ME . . .
MAY I CUT IN?
OF COURSE!

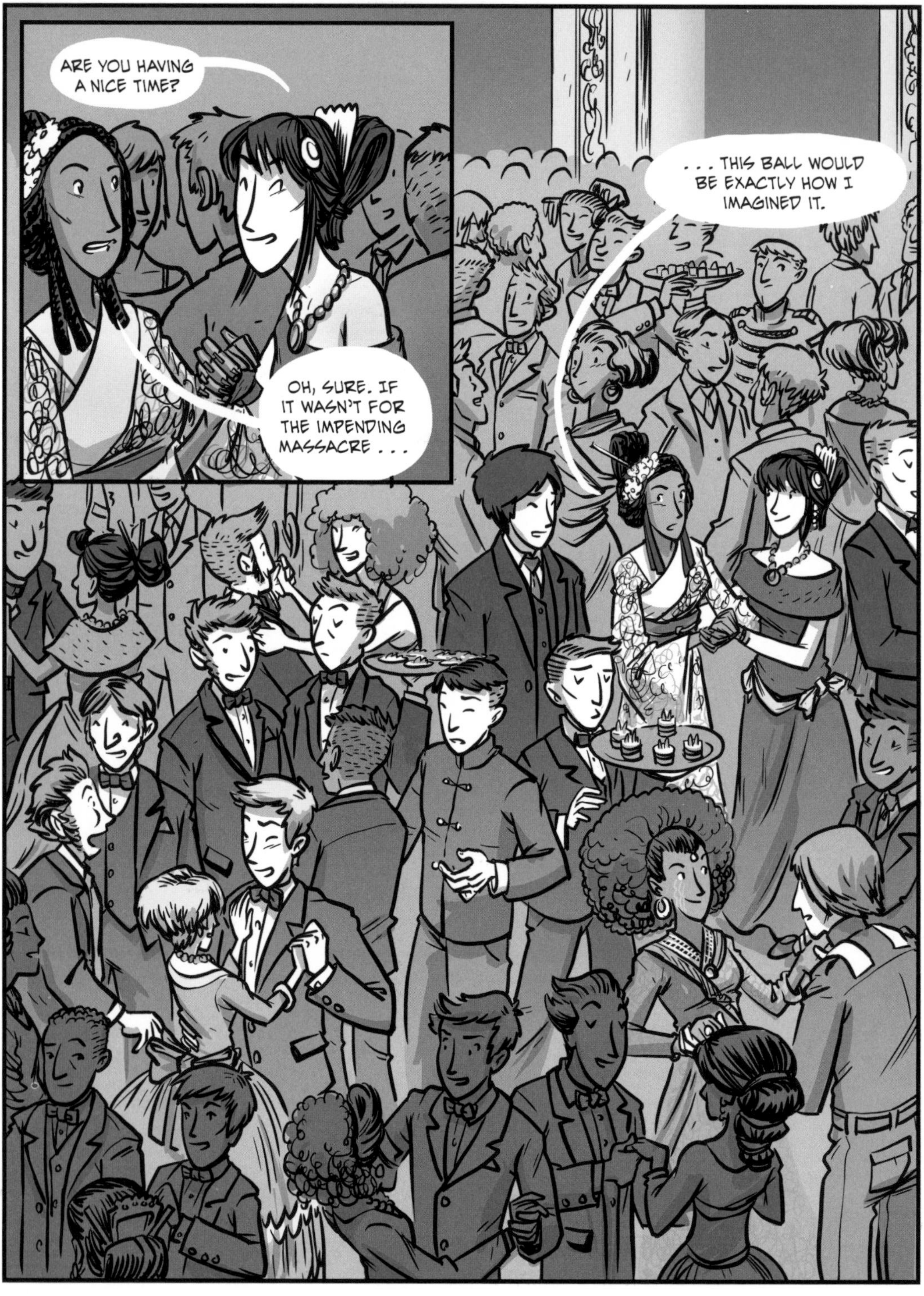
ARE YOU HAVING A NICE TIME?
OH, SURE. IF IT WASN'T FOR THE IMPENDING MASSACRE . . .
. . . THIS BALL WOULD BE EXACTLY HOW I IMAGINED IT.

IT IS A DAY WORTHY OF CELEBRATION!

127 YEARS OF WORLD PEACE! THE WHOLE WORLD SHOULD—

AAAOOOOO

AAAAOOO OO OO OO OOO

THEY'RE HERE! THE MONSTERS! THE WOLVES! THEY'RE—

SCHUCKK!

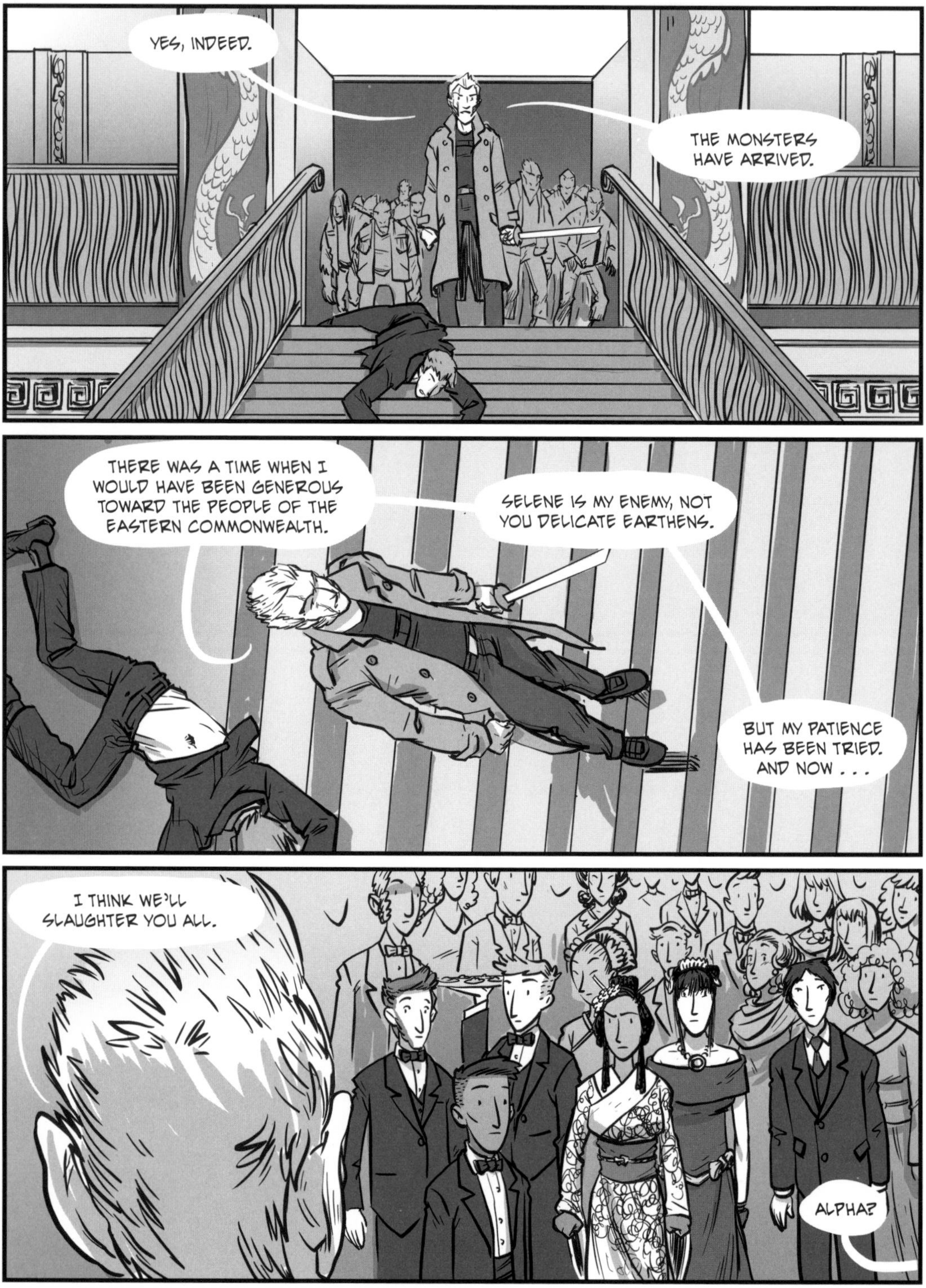
YES, INDEED.
THE MONSTERS HAVE ARRIVED.
THERE WAS A TIME WHEN I WOULD HAVE BEEN GENEROUS TOWARD THE PEOPLE OF THE EASTERN COMMONWEALTH.
SELENE IS MY ENEMY, NOT YOU DELICATE EARTHENS.
BUT MY PATIENCE HAS BEEN TRIED. AND NOW . . .
I THINK WE'LL SLAUGHTER YOU ALL.
ALPHA?

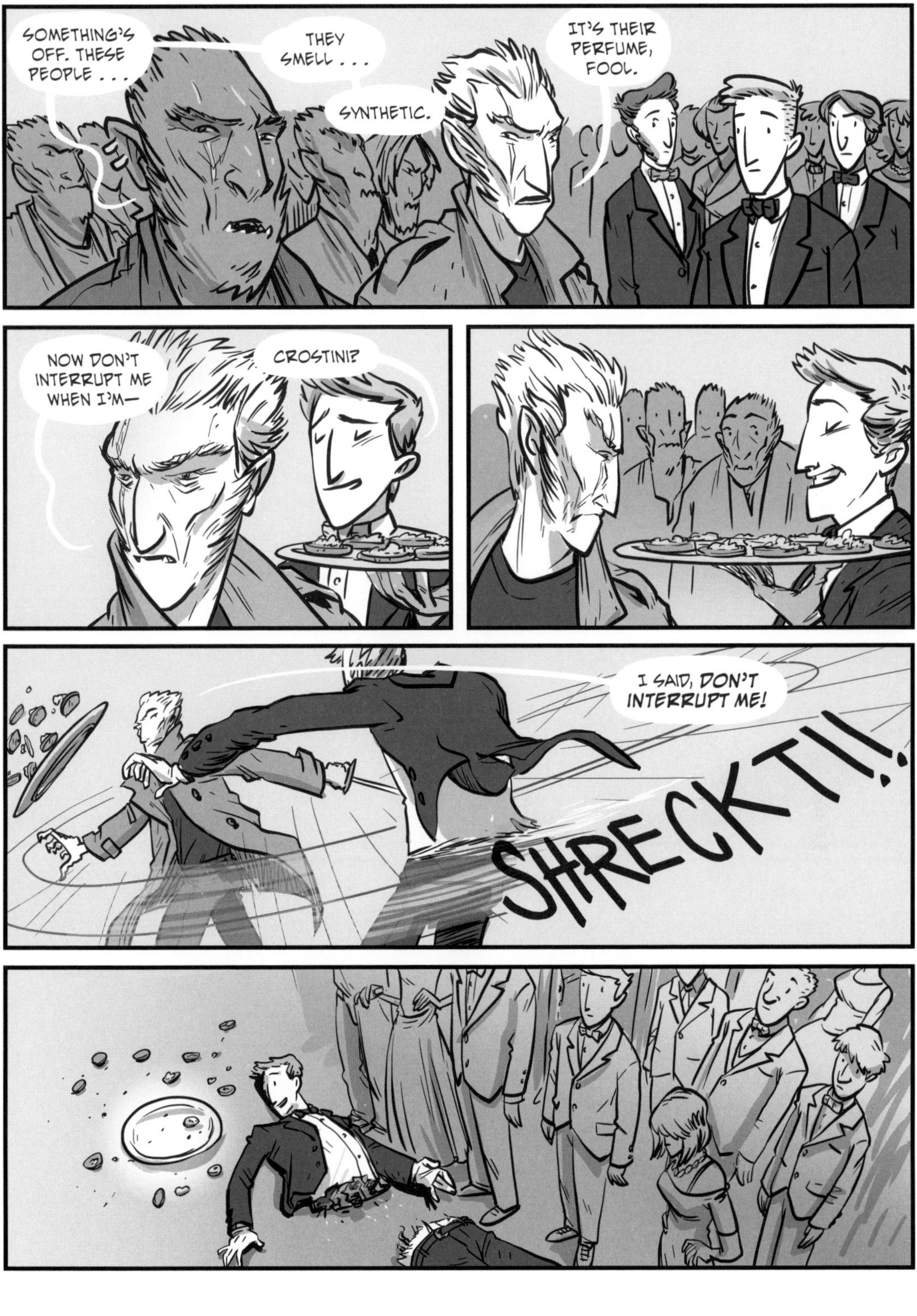
SOMETHING'S OFF. THESE PEOPLE . . .
THEY SMELL . . .
SYNTHETIC.
IT'S THEIR PERFUME, FOOL.
NOW DON'T INTERRUPT ME WHEN I'M—
CROSTINI?
I SAID, DON'T INTERRUPT ME!
SHRECKT!!

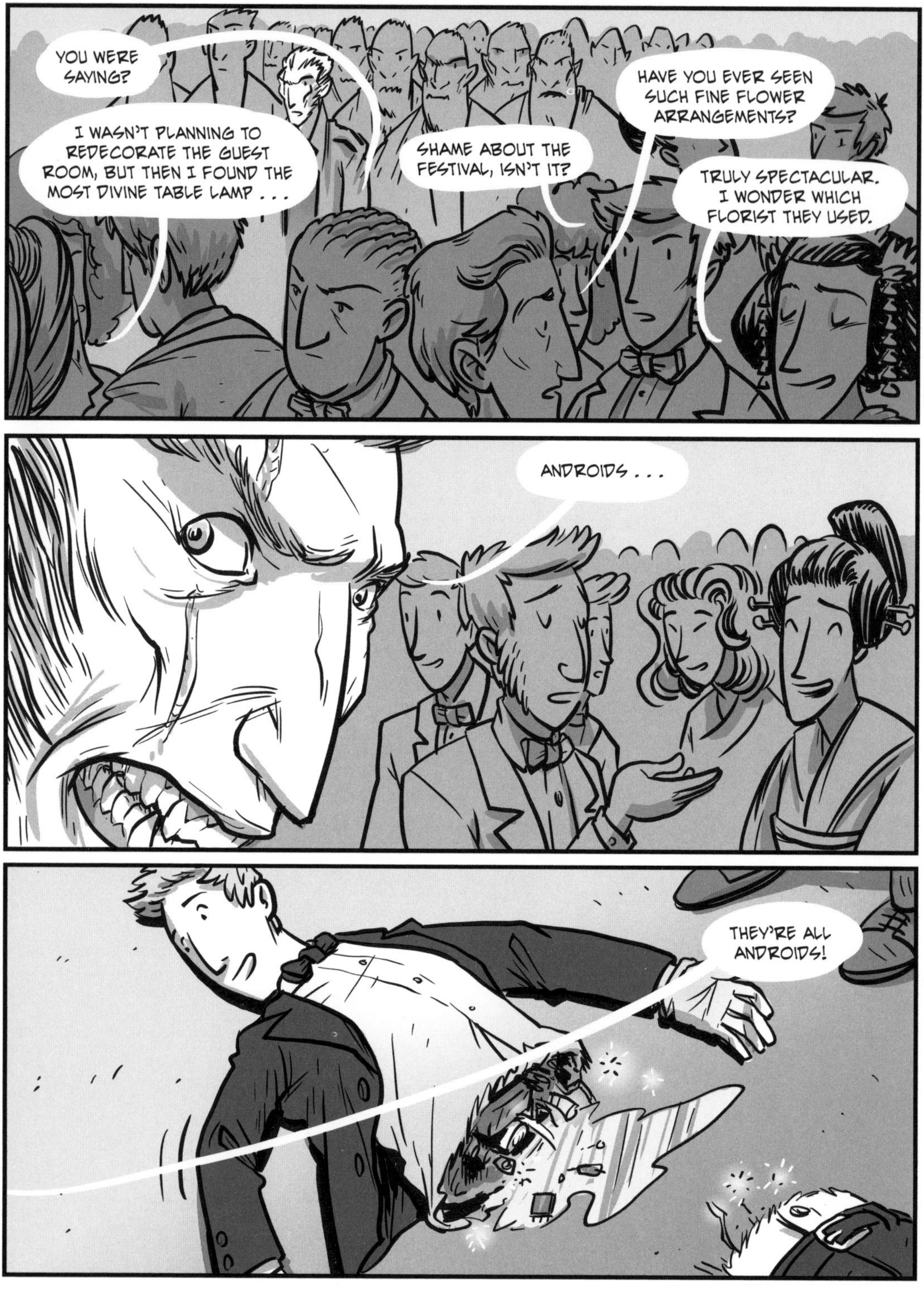
YOU WERE SAYING?
I WASN'T PLANNING TO REDECORATE THE GUEST ROOM, BUT THEN I FOUND THE MOST DIVINE TABLE LAMP . . .
SHAME ABOUT THE FESTIVAL, ISN'T IT?
HAVE YOU EVER SEEN SUCH FINE FLOWER ARRANGEMENTS?
TRULY SPECTACULAR. I WONDER WHICH FLORIST THEY USED.
ANDROIDS . . .
THEY'RE ALL ANDROIDS!

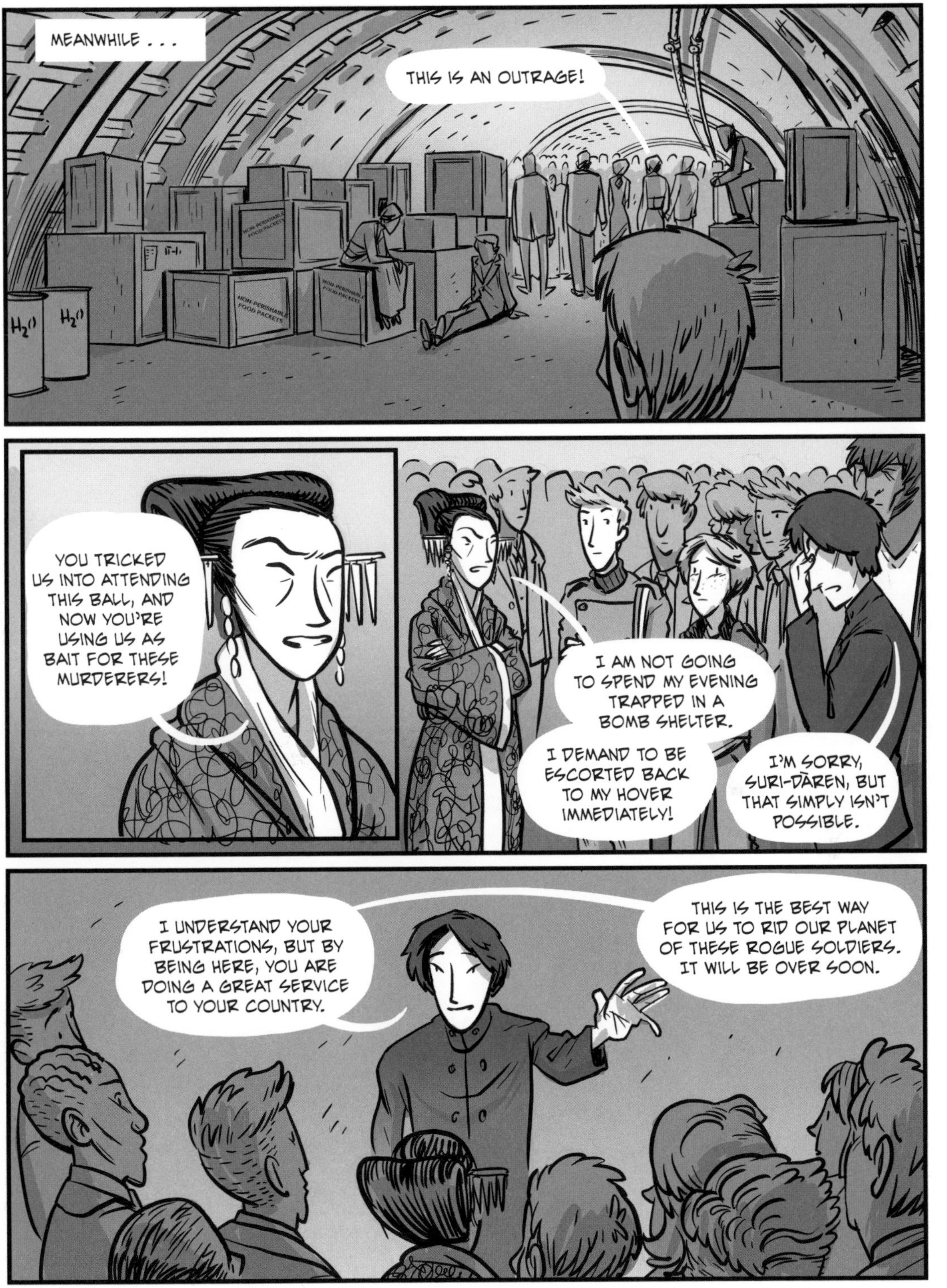
MEANWHILE . . .
THIS IS AN OUTRAGE!
NON-PERISHABLE FOOD PACKETS
YOU TRICKED US INTO ATTENDING THIS BALL, AND NOW YOU'RE USING US AS BAIT FOR THESE MURDERERS!
I AM NOT GOING TO SPEND MY EVENING TRAPPED IN A BOMB SHELTER.
I DEMAND TO BE ESCORTED BACK TO MY HOVER IMMEDIATELY!
I'M SORRY, SURI-DÄREN, BUT THAT SIMPLY ISN'T POSSIBLE.
I UNDERSTAND YOUR FRUSTRATIONS, BUT BY BEING HERE, YOU ARE DOING A GREAT SERVICE TO YOUR COUNTRY.
THIS IS THE BEST WAY FOR US TO RID OUR PLANET OF THESE ROGUE SOLDIERS. IT WILL BE OVER SOON.

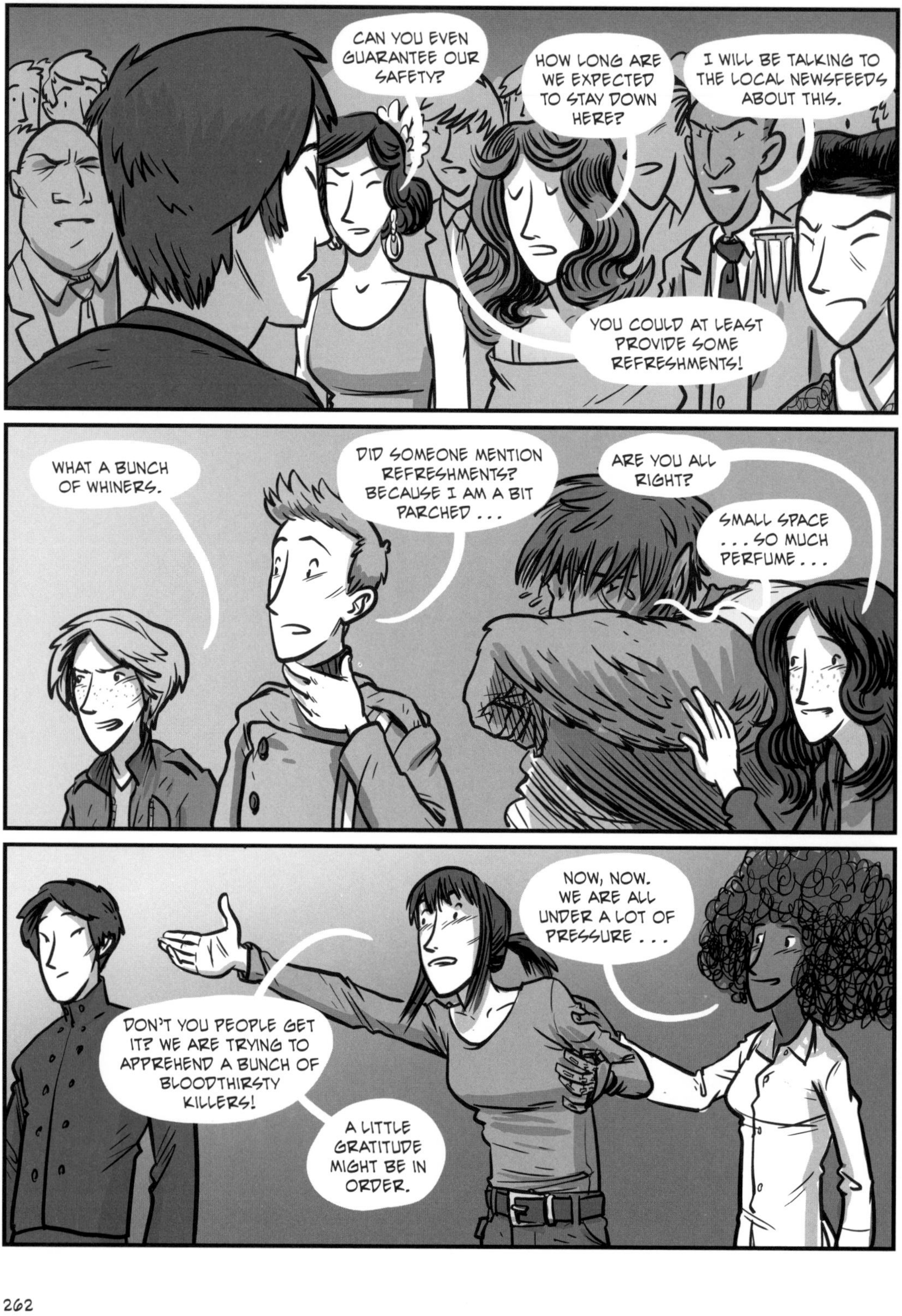
CAN YOU EVEN GUARANTEE OUR SAFETY?
HOW LONG ARE WE EXPECTED TO STAY DOWN HERE?
I WILL BE TALKING TO THE LOCAL NEWSFEEDS ABOUT THIS.
YOU COULD AT LEAST PROVIDE SOME REFRESHMENTS!
WHAT A BUNCH OF WHINERS.
DID SOMEONE MENTION REFRESHMENTS? BECAUSE I AM A BIT PARCHED . . .
ARE YOU ALL RIGHT?
SMALL SPACE . . . SO MUCH PERFUME . . .
DON'T YOU PEOPLE GET IT? WE ARE TRYING TO APPREHEND A BUNCH OF BLOODTHIRSTY KILLERS!
A LITTLE GRATITUDE MIGHT BE IN ORDER.
NOW, NOW. WE ARE ALL UNDER A LOT OF PRESSURE . . .

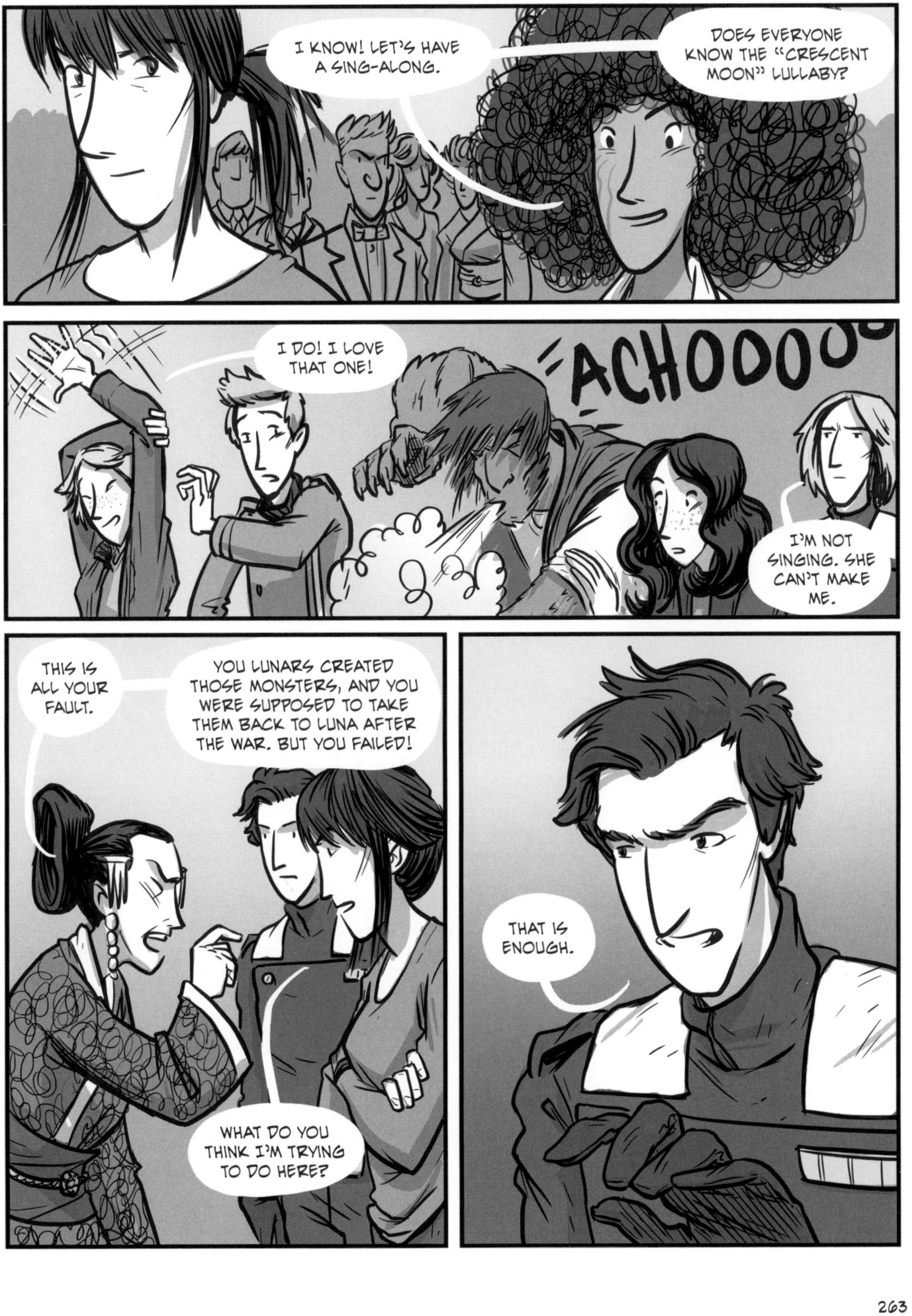
I KNOW! LET'S HAVE A SING-ALONG.
DOES EVERYONE KNOW THE "CRESCENT MOON" LULLABY?
I DO! I LOVE THAT ONE!
ACHOOOO
I'M NOT SINGING. SHE CAN'T MAKE ME.
THIS IS ALL YOUR FAULT.
YOU LUNARS CREATED THOSE MONSTERS, AND YOU WERE SUPPOSED TO TAKE THEM BACK TO LUNA AFTER THE WAR. BUT YOU FAILED!
WHAT DO YOU THINK I'M TRYING TO DO HERE?
THAT IS ENOUGH.

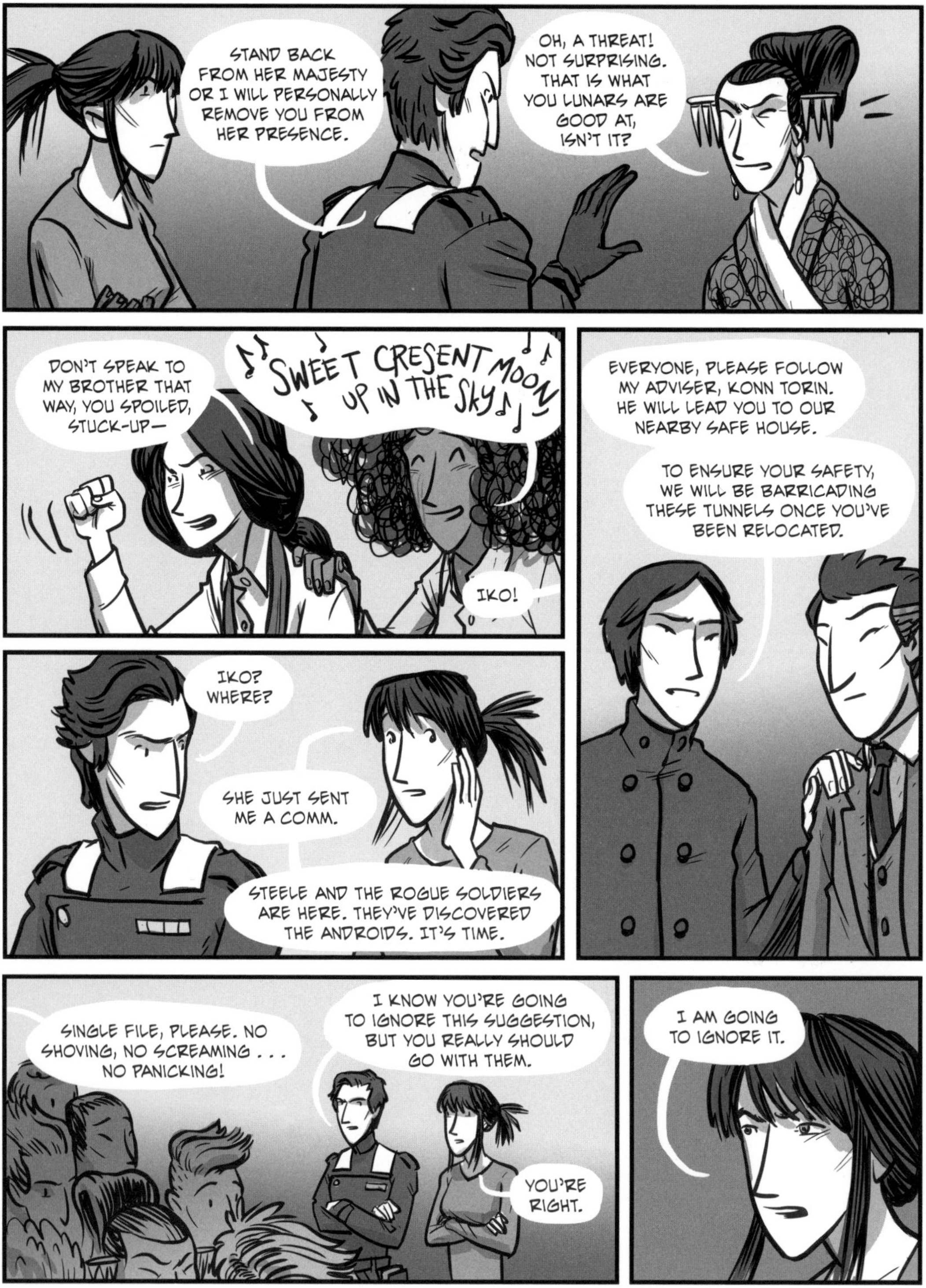
STAND BACK FROM HER MAJESTY OR I WILL PERSONALLY REMOVE YOU FROM HER PRESENCE.
OH, A THREAT! NOT SURPRISING. THAT IS WHAT YOU LUNARS ARE GOOD AT, ISN'T IT?
DON'T SPEAK TO MY BROTHER THAT WAY, YOU SPOILED, STUCK-UP—
SWEET CRESENT MOON UP IN THE SKY
IKO!
IKO? WHERE?
SHE JUST SENT ME A COMM.
STEELE AND THE ROGUE SOLDIERS ARE HERE. THEY'VE DISCOVERED THE ANDROIDS. IT'S TIME.
EVERYONE, PLEASE FOLLOW MY ADVISER, KONN TORIN. HE WILL LEAD YOU TO OUR NEARBY SAFE HOUSE.
TO ENSURE YOUR SAFETY, WE WILL BE BARRICADING THESE TUNNELS ONCE YOU'VE BEEN RELOCATED.
SINGLE FILE, PLEASE. NO SHOVING, NO SCREAMING . . . NO PANICKING!
I KNOW YOU'RE GOING TO IGNORE THIS SUGGESTION, BUT YOU REALLY SHOULD GO WITH THEM.
YOU'RE RIGHT.
I AM GOING TO IGNORE IT.

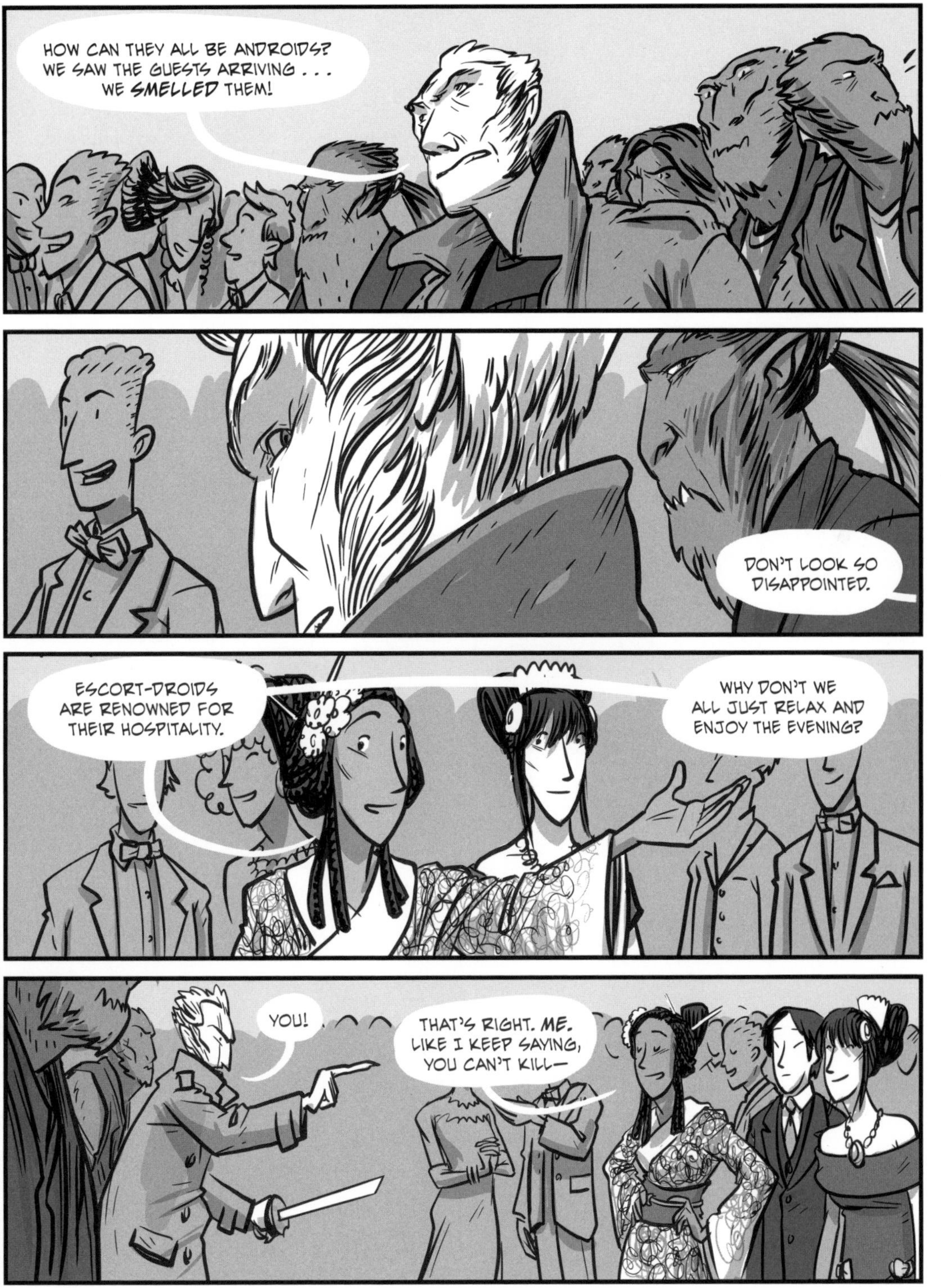
HOW CAN THEY ALL BE ANDROIDS? WE SAW THE GUESTS ARRIVING . . . WE **SMELLED** THEM!
DON'T LOOK SO DISAPPOINTED.
ESCORT-DROIDS ARE RENOWNED FOR THEIR HOSPITALITY.
WHY DON'T WE ALL JUST RELAX AND ENJOY THE EVENING?
YOU!
THAT'S RIGHT. **ME.** LIKE I KEEP SAYING, YOU CAN'T KILL—

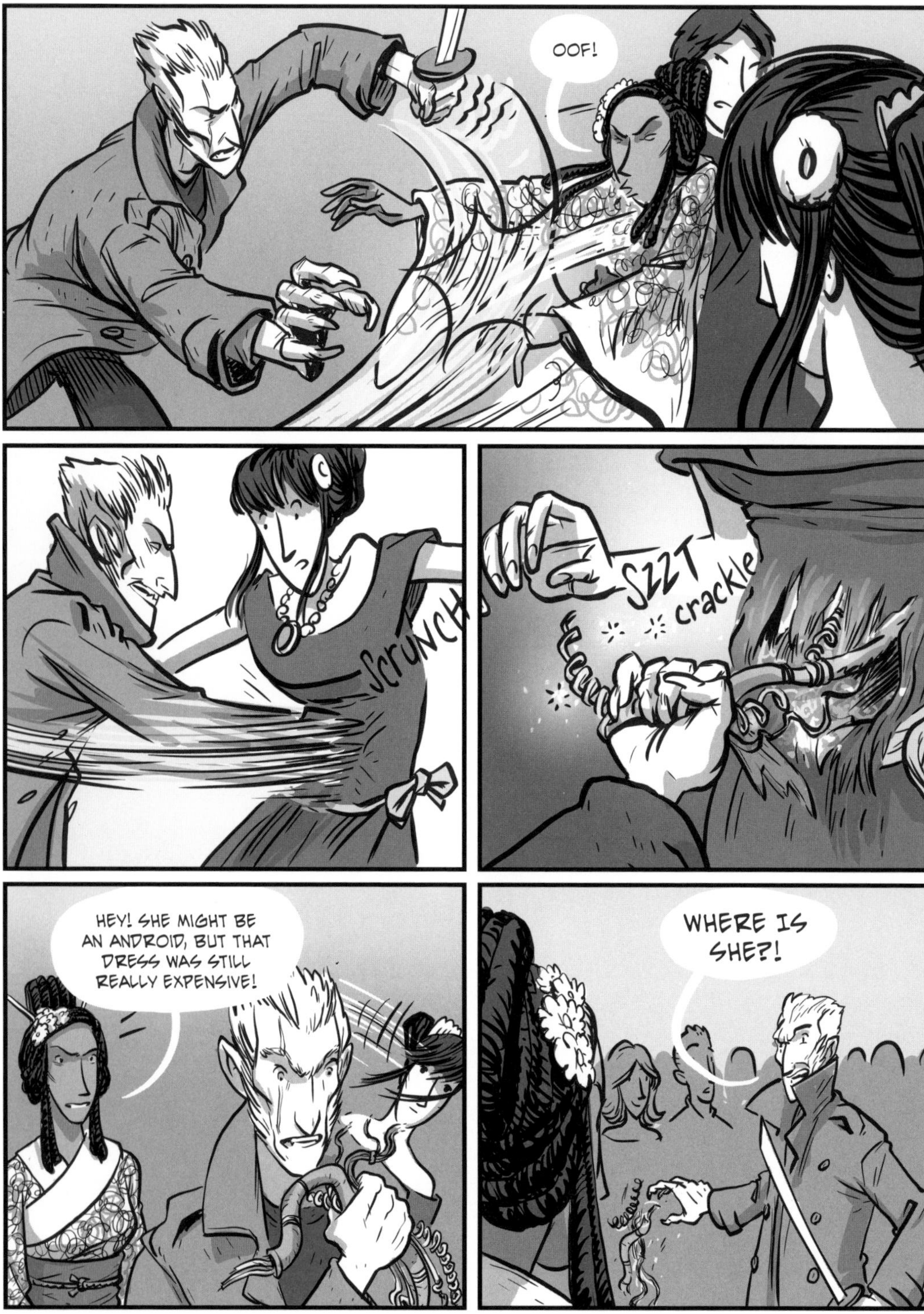
OOF!
SCRUNCH
SZZT
crackle
HEY! SHE MIGHT BE AN ANDROID, BUT THAT DRESS WAS STILL REALLY EXPENSIVE!
WHERE IS SHE?!

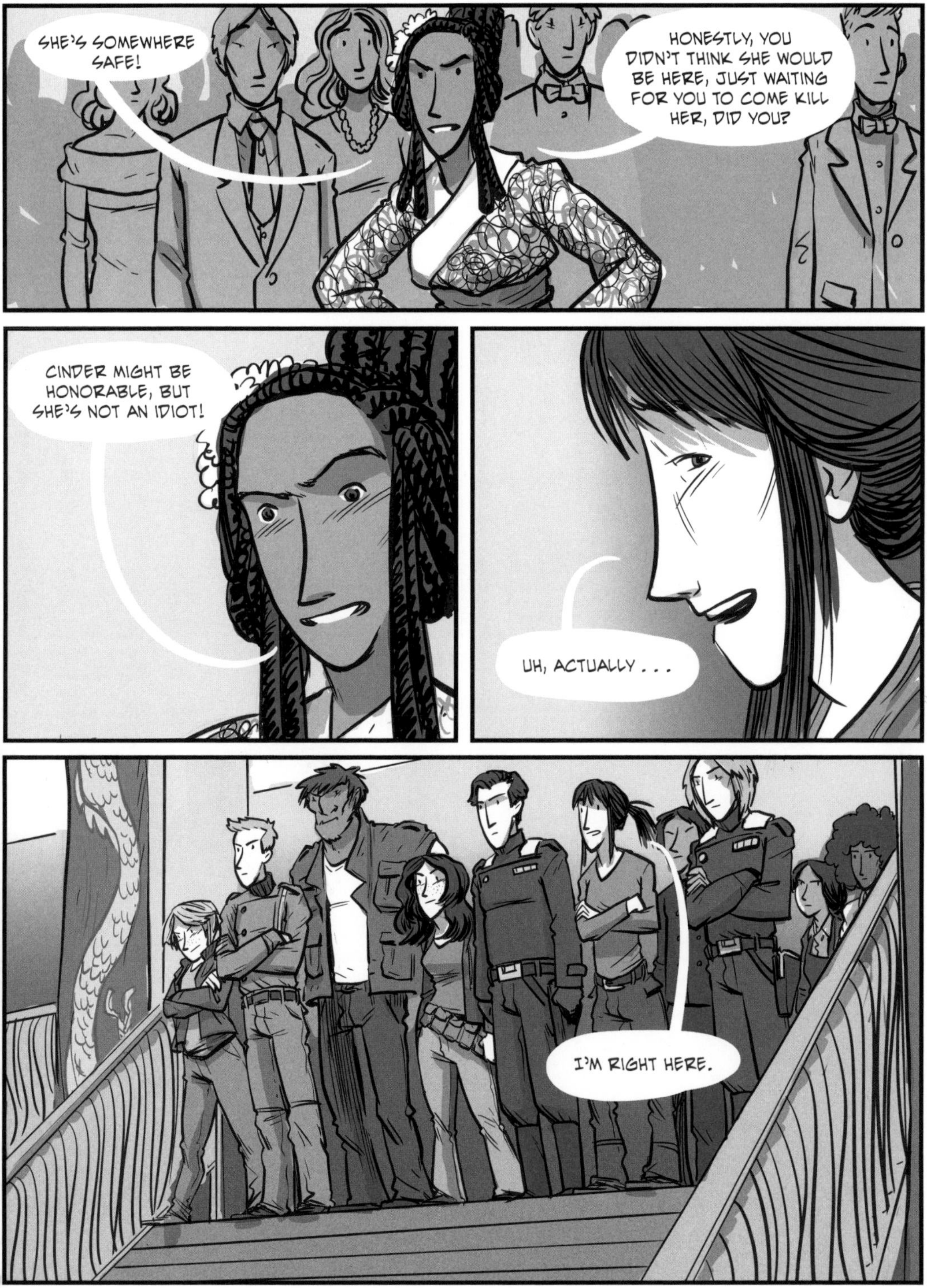
SHE'S SOMEWHERE SAFE!
HONESTLY, YOU DIDN'T THINK SHE WOULD BE HERE, JUST WAITING FOR YOU TO COME KILL HER, DID YOU?
CINDER MIGHT BE HONORABLE, BUT SHE'S NOT AN IDIOT!
UH, ACTUALLY . . .
I'M RIGHT HERE.

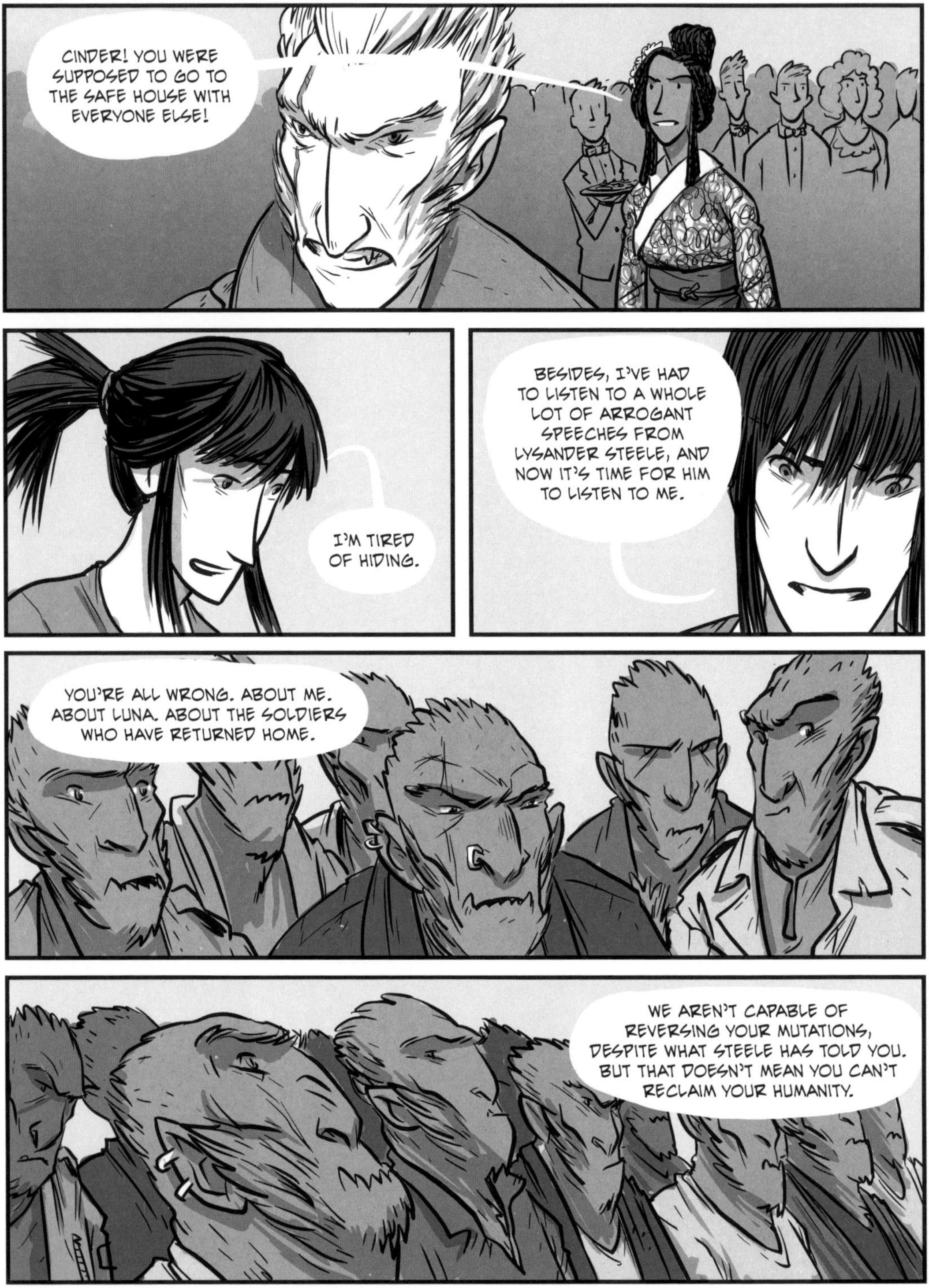
CINDER! YOU WERE SUPPOSED TO GO TO THE SAFE HOUSE WITH EVERYONE ELSE!
I'M TIRED OF HIDING.
BESIDES, I'VE HAD TO LISTEN TO A WHOLE LOT OF ARROGANT SPEECHES FROM LYSANDER STEELE, AND NOW IT'S TIME FOR HIM TO LISTEN TO ME.
YOU'RE ALL WRONG. ABOUT ME. ABOUT LUNA. ABOUT THE SOLDIERS WHO HAVE RETURNED HOME.
WE AREN'T CAPABLE OF REVERSING YOUR MUTATIONS, DESPITE WHAT STEELE HAS TOLD YOU. BUT THAT DOESN'T MEAN YOU CAN'T RECLAIM YOUR HUMANITY.

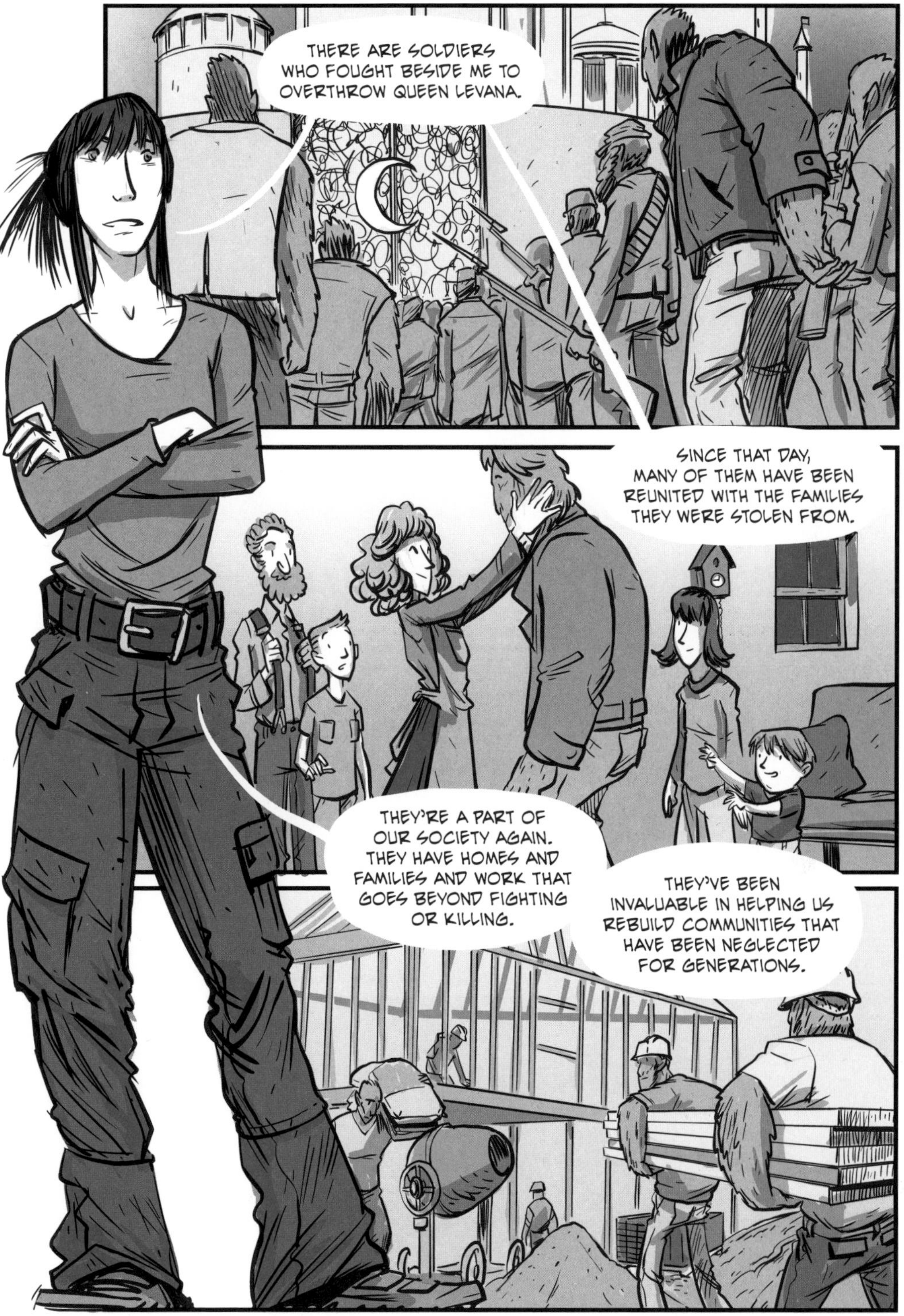
THERE ARE SOLDIERS WHO FOUGHT BESIDE ME TO OVERTHROW QUEEN LEVANA.
SINCE THAT DAY, MANY OF THEM HAVE BEEN REUNITED WITH THE FAMILIES THEY WERE STOLEN FROM.
THEY'RE A PART OF OUR SOCIETY AGAIN. THEY HAVE HOMES AND FAMILIES AND WORK THAT GOES BEYOND FIGHTING OR KILLING.
THEY'VE BEEN INVALUABLE IN HELPING US REBUILD COMMUNITIES THAT HAVE BEEN NEGLECTED FOR GENERATIONS.

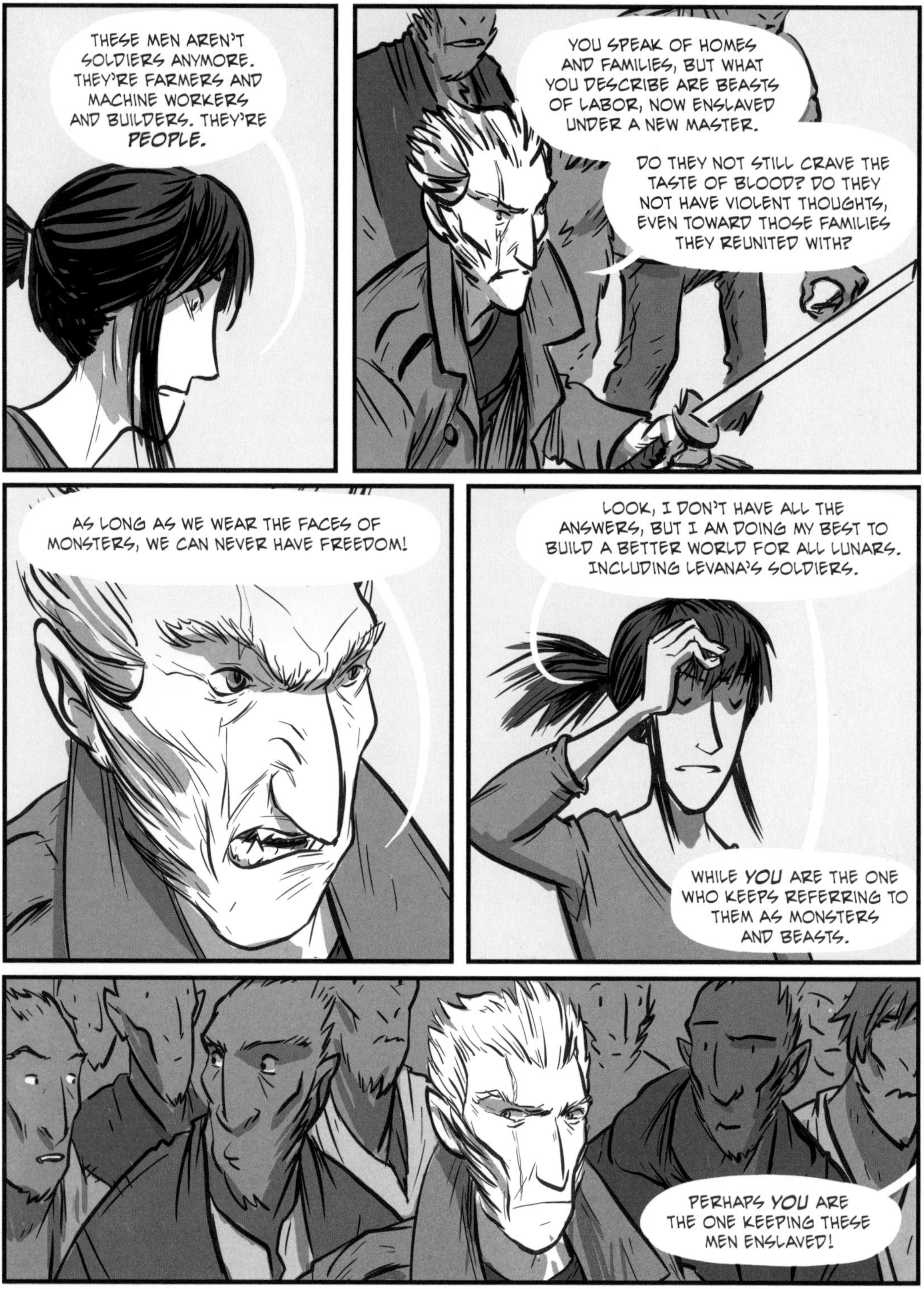
THESE MEN AREN'T SOLDIERS ANYMORE. THEY'RE FARMERS AND MACHINE WORKERS AND BUILDERS. THEY'RE *PEOPLE*.
YOU SPEAK OF HOMES AND FAMILIES, BUT WHAT YOU DESCRIBE ARE BEASTS OF LABOR, NOW ENSLAVED UNDER A NEW MASTER.
DO THEY NOT STILL CRAVE THE TASTE OF BLOOD? DO THEY NOT HAVE VIOLENT THOUGHTS, EVEN TOWARD THOSE FAMILIES THEY REUNITED WITH?
AS LONG AS WE WEAR THE FACES OF MONSTERS, WE CAN NEVER HAVE FREEDOM!
LOOK, I DON'T HAVE ALL THE ANSWERS, BUT I AM DOING MY BEST TO BUILD A BETTER WORLD FOR ALL LUNARS. INCLUDING LEVANA'S SOLDIERS.
WHILE *YOU* ARE THE ONE WHO KEEPS REFERRING TO THEM AS MONSTERS AND BEASTS.
PERHAPS *YOU* ARE THE ONE KEEPING THESE MEN ENSLAVED!

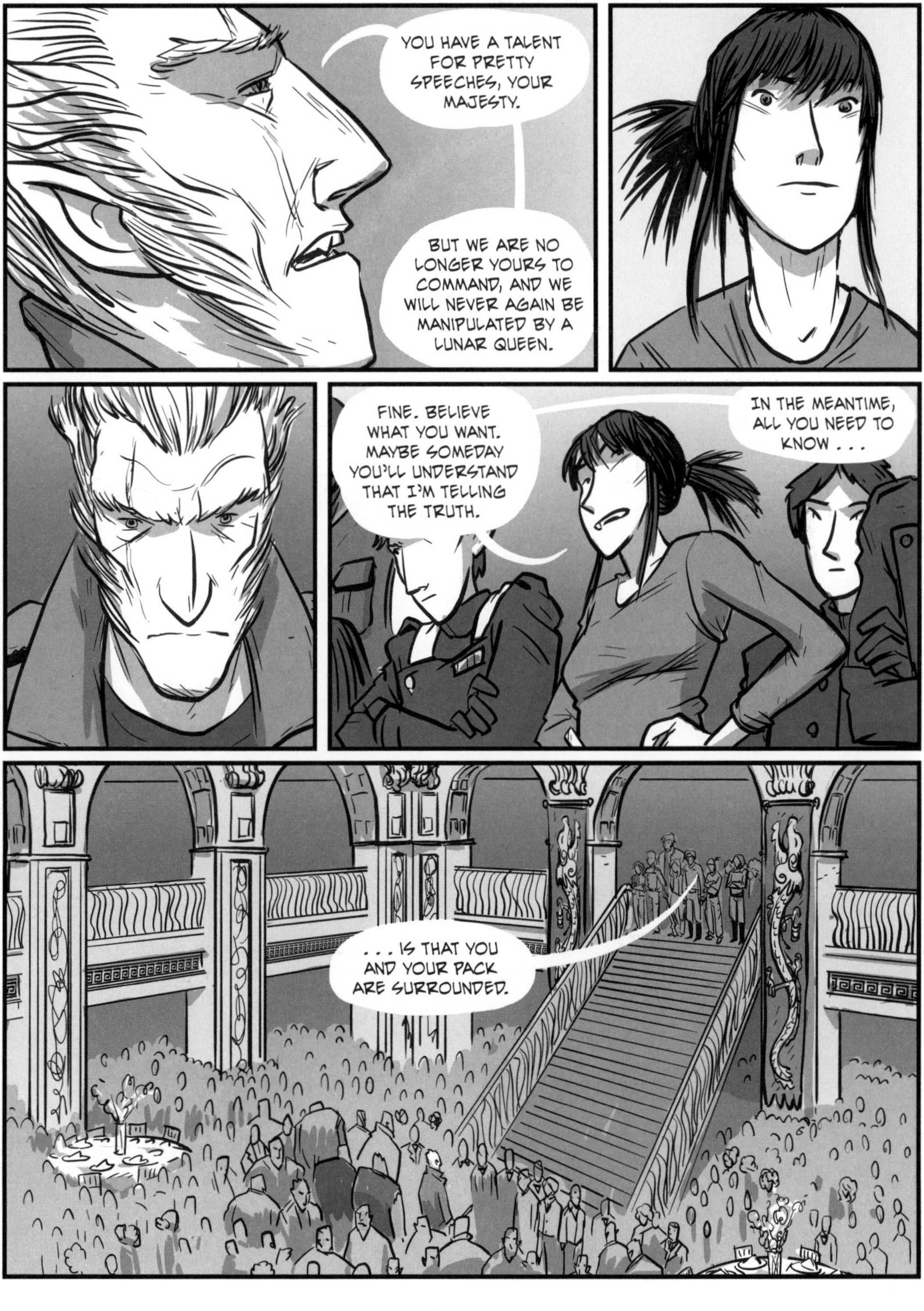
YOU HAVE A TALENT FOR PRETTY SPEECHES, YOUR MAJESTY.
BUT WE ARE NO LONGER YOURS TO COMMAND, AND WE WILL NEVER AGAIN BE MANIPULATED BY A LUNAR QUEEN.
FINE. BELIEVE WHAT YOU WANT. MAYBE SOMEDAY YOU'LL UNDERSTAND THAT I'M TELLING THE TRUTH.
IN THE MEANTIME, ALL YOU NEED TO KNOW . . .
. . . IS THAT YOU AND YOUR PACK ARE SURROUNDED.

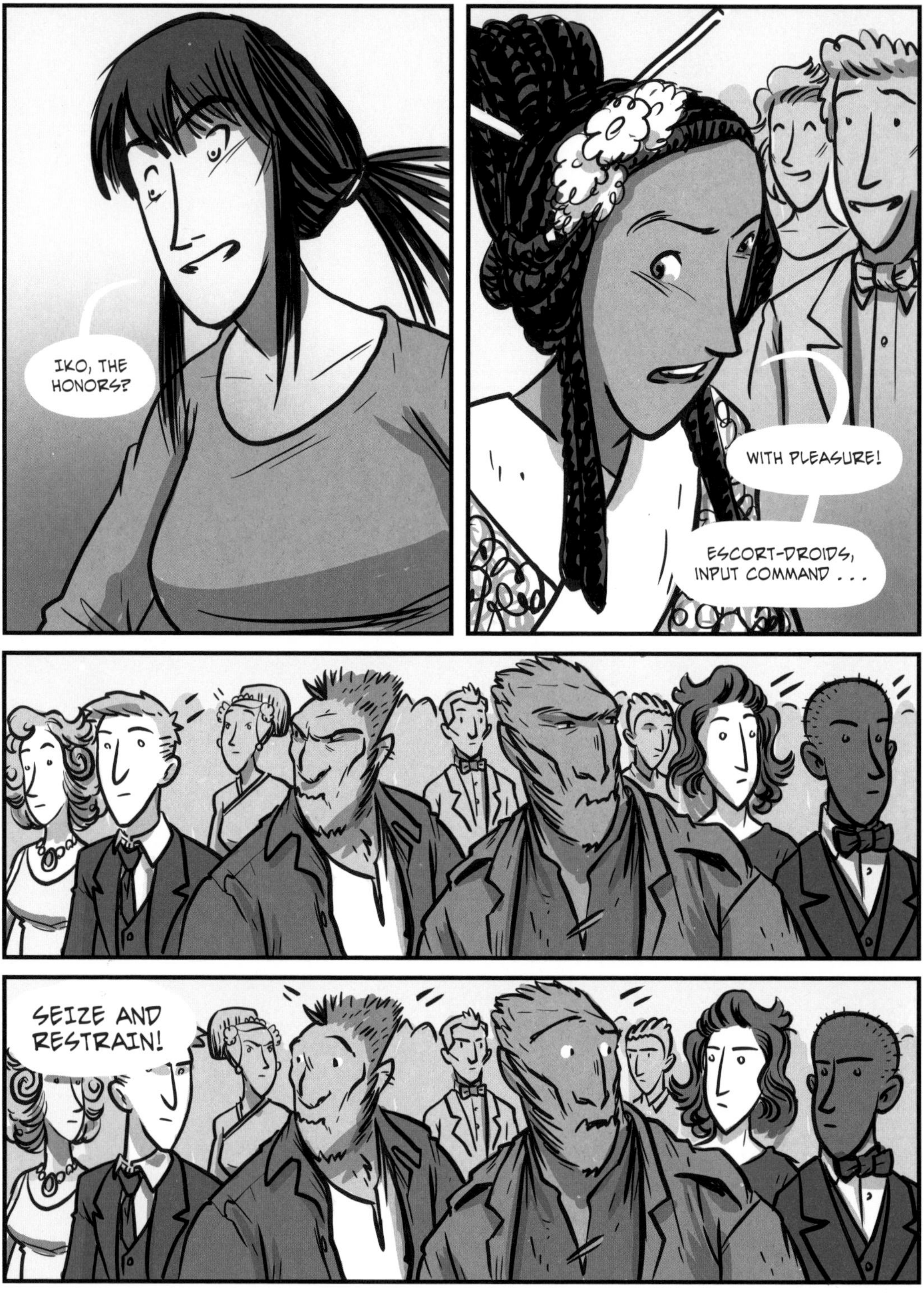
IKO, THE HONORS?
WITH PLEASURE!
ESCORT-DROIDS, INPUT COMMAND . . .
SEIZE AND RESTRAIN!

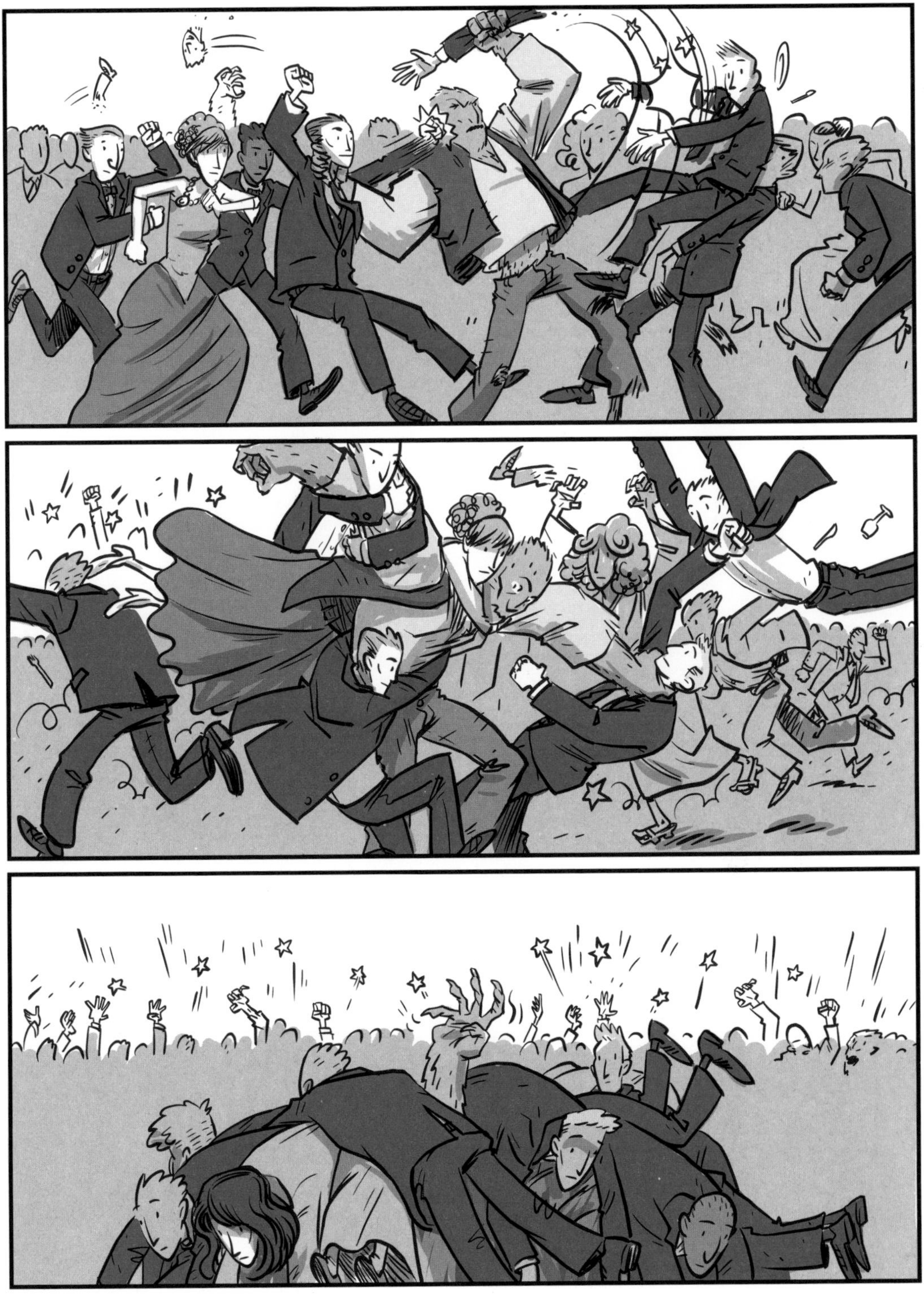

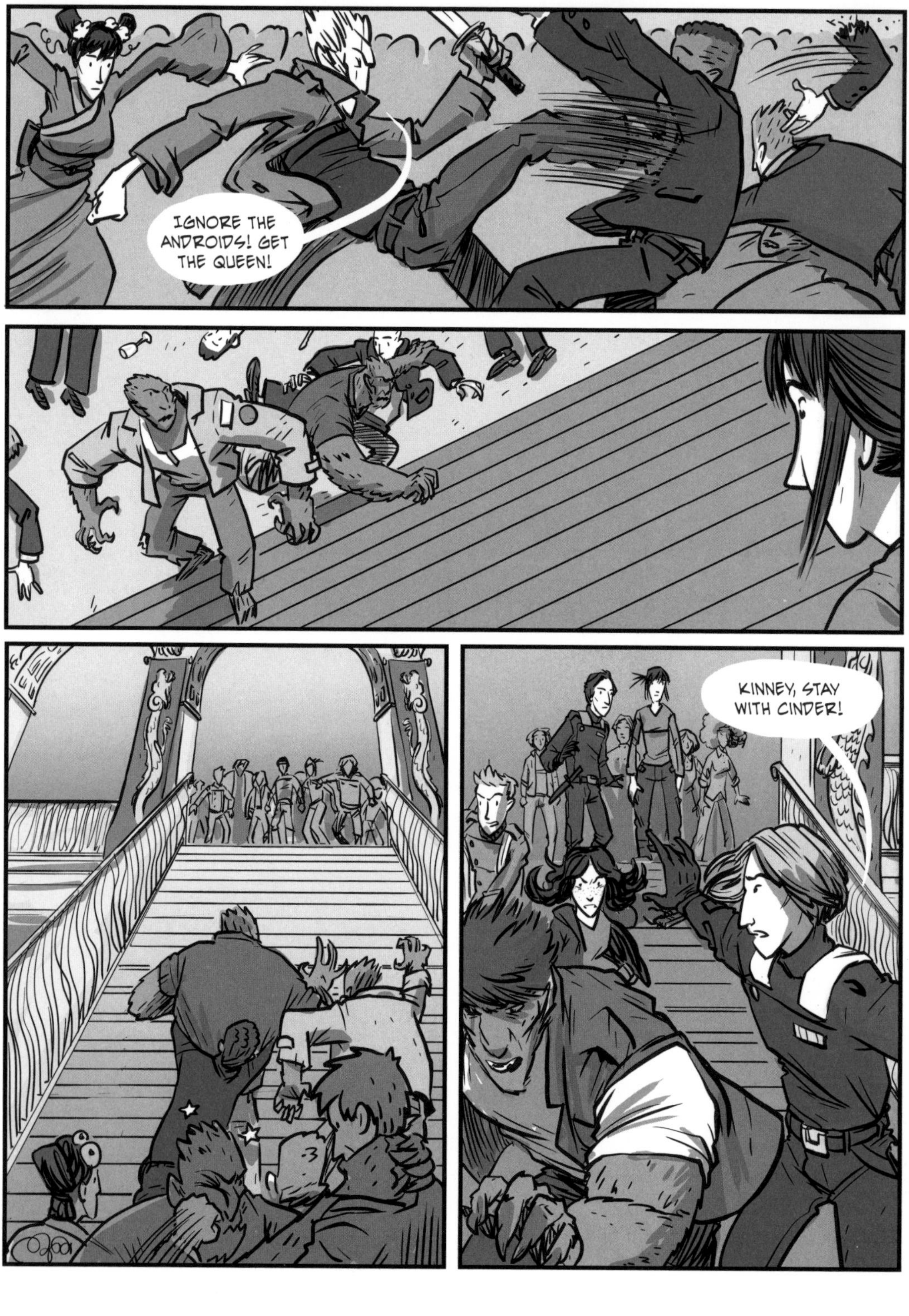
IGNORE THE ANDROIDS! GET THE QUEEN!
KINNEY, STAY WITH CINDER!

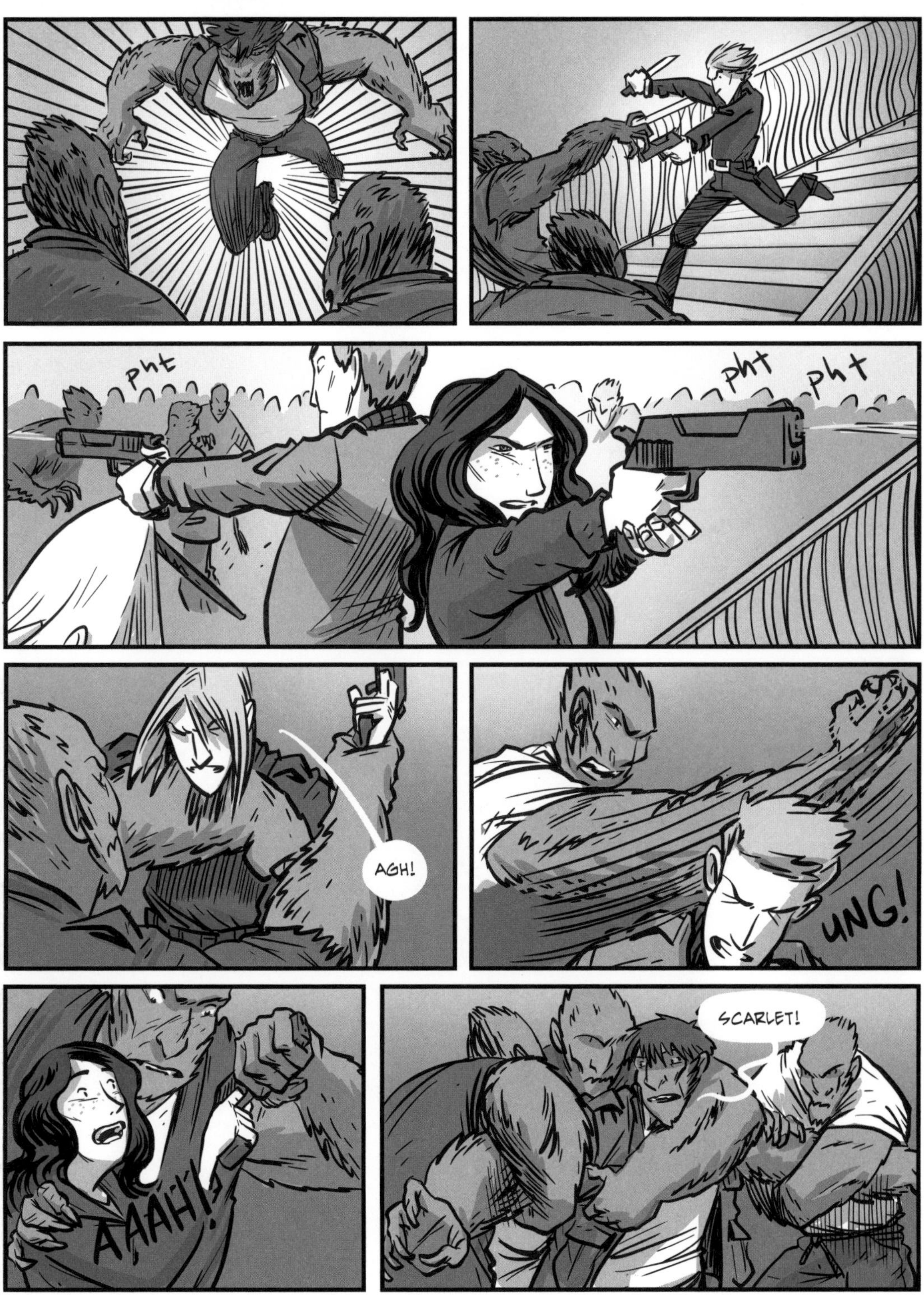
pht
pht
pht
AGH!
UNG!
AAAH!
SCARLET!

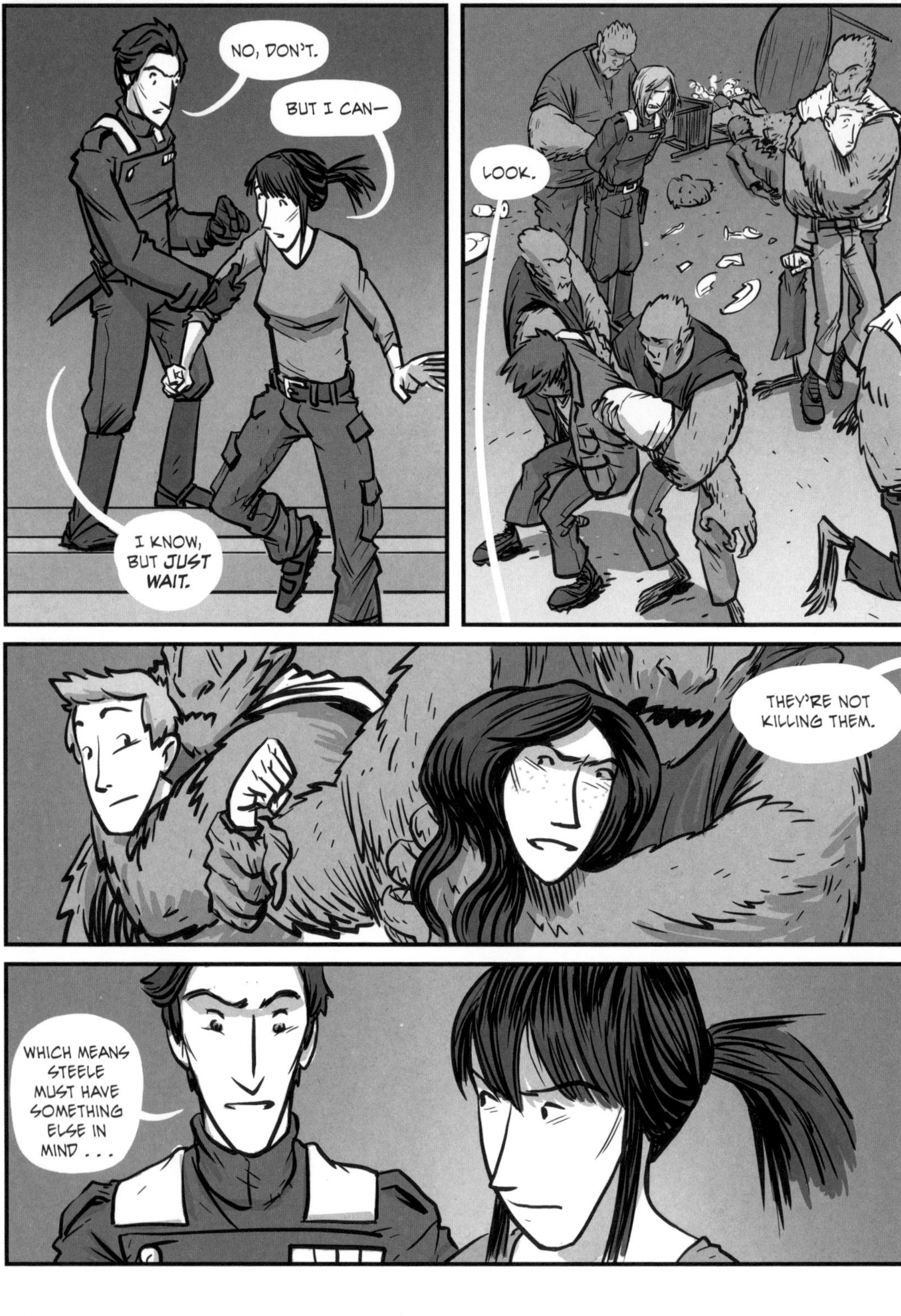
NO, DON'T.
BUT I CAN—
I KNOW, BUT JUST WAIT.
LOOK.
THEY'RE NOT KILLING THEM.
WHICH MEANS STEELE MUST HAVE SOMETHING ELSE IN MIND . . .

CHAPTER X

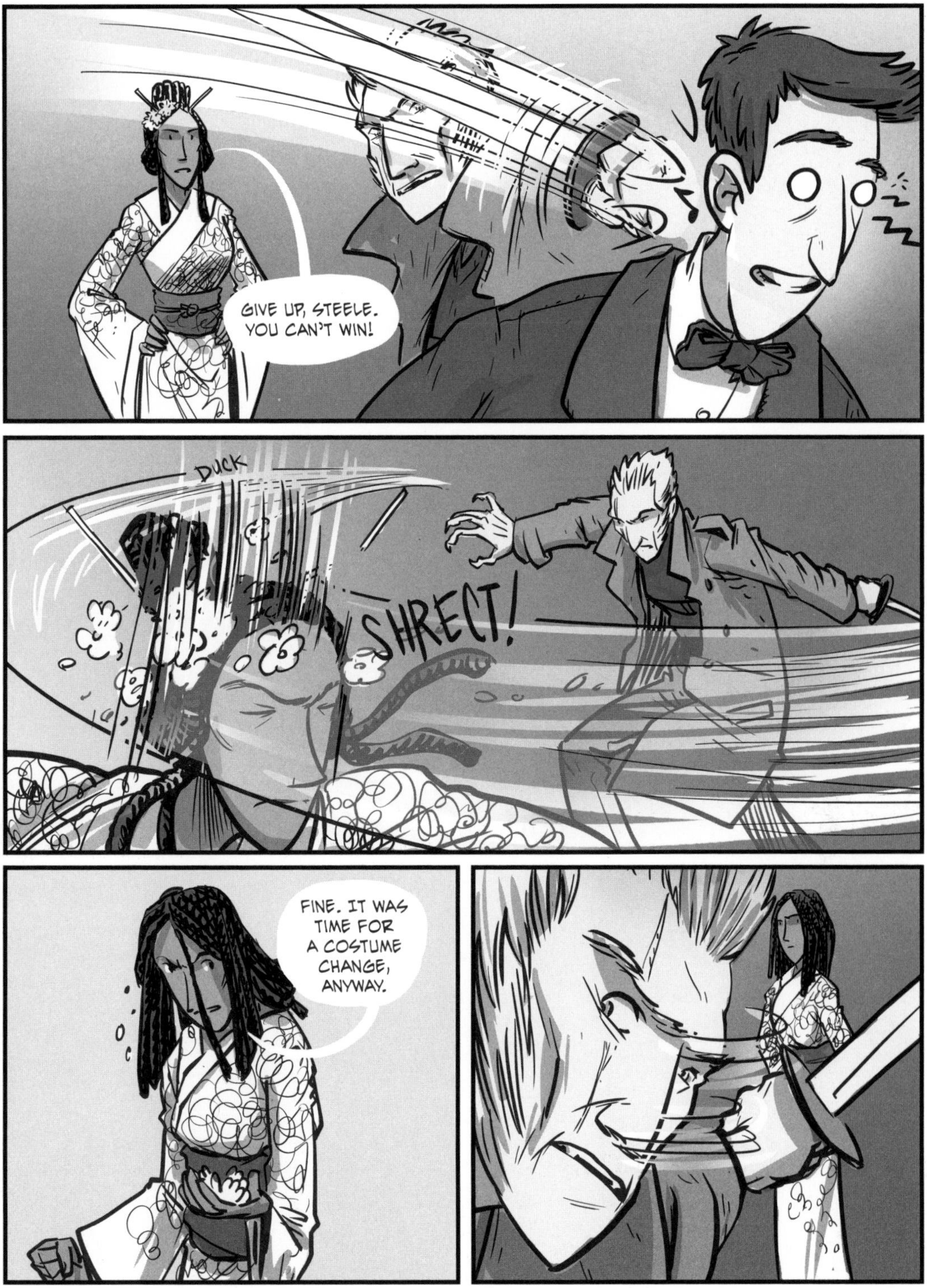

GIVE UP, STEELE. YOU CAN'T WIN!
DUCK
SHRECT!
FINE. IT WAS TIME FOR A COSTUME CHANGE, ANYWAY.

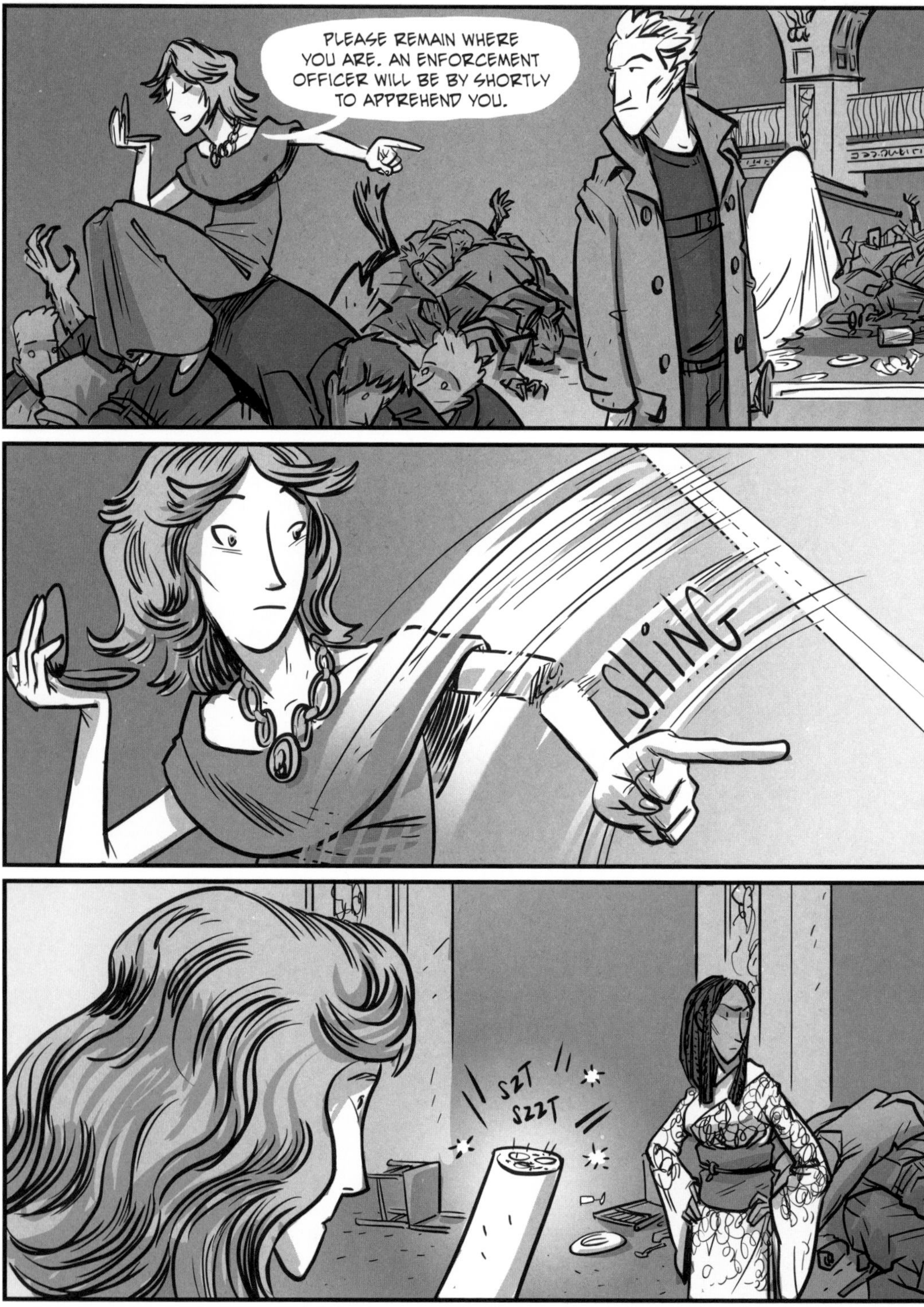
PLEASE REMAIN WHERE YOU ARE. AN ENFORCEMENT OFFICER WILL BE BY SHORTLY TO APPREHEND YOU.
SHING
SZT
SZZT

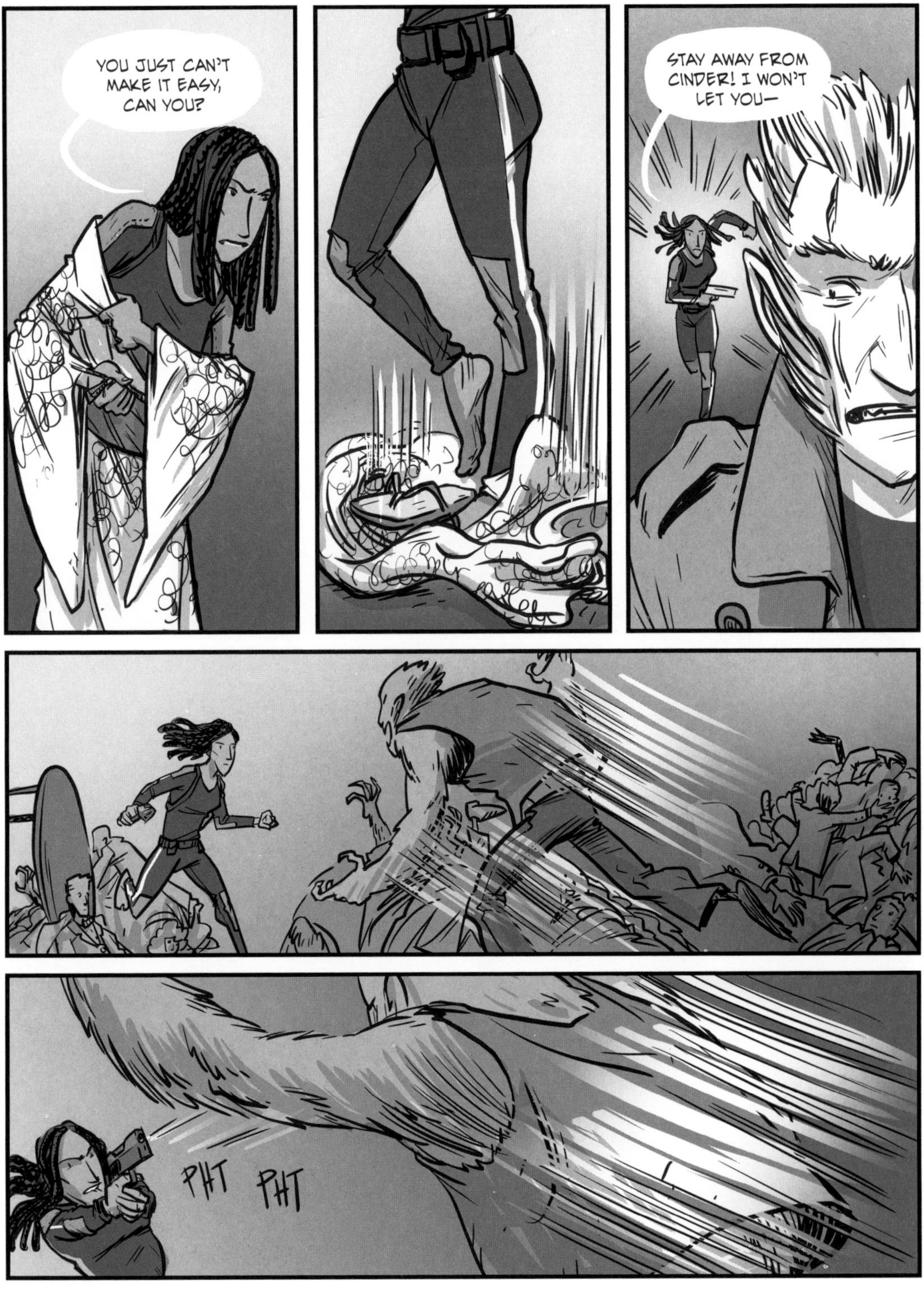
YOU JUST CAN'T MAKE IT EASY, CAN YOU?
STAY AWAY FROM CINDER! I WON'T LET YOU—
PHT
PHT

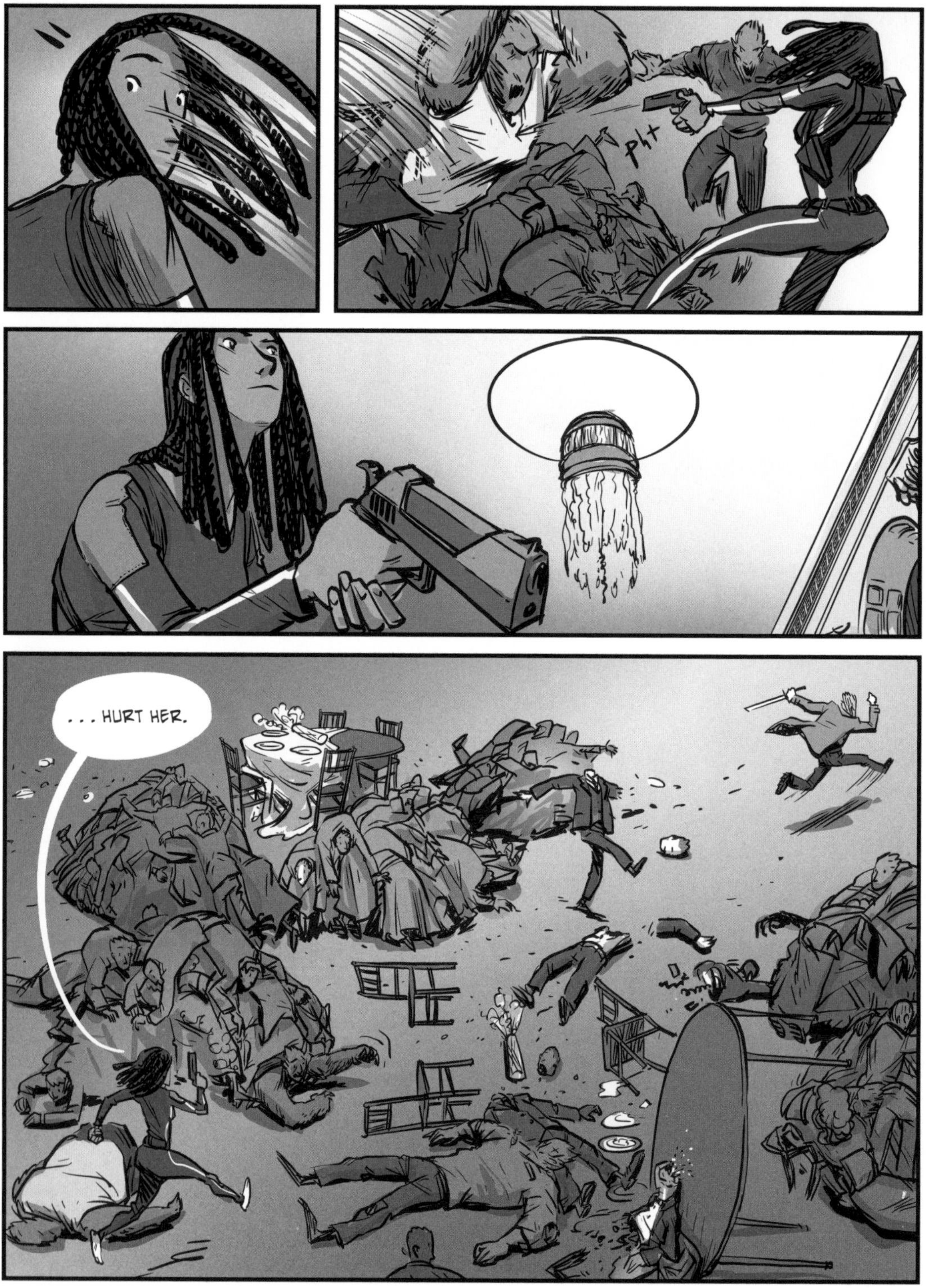
Pht
. . . HURT HER.

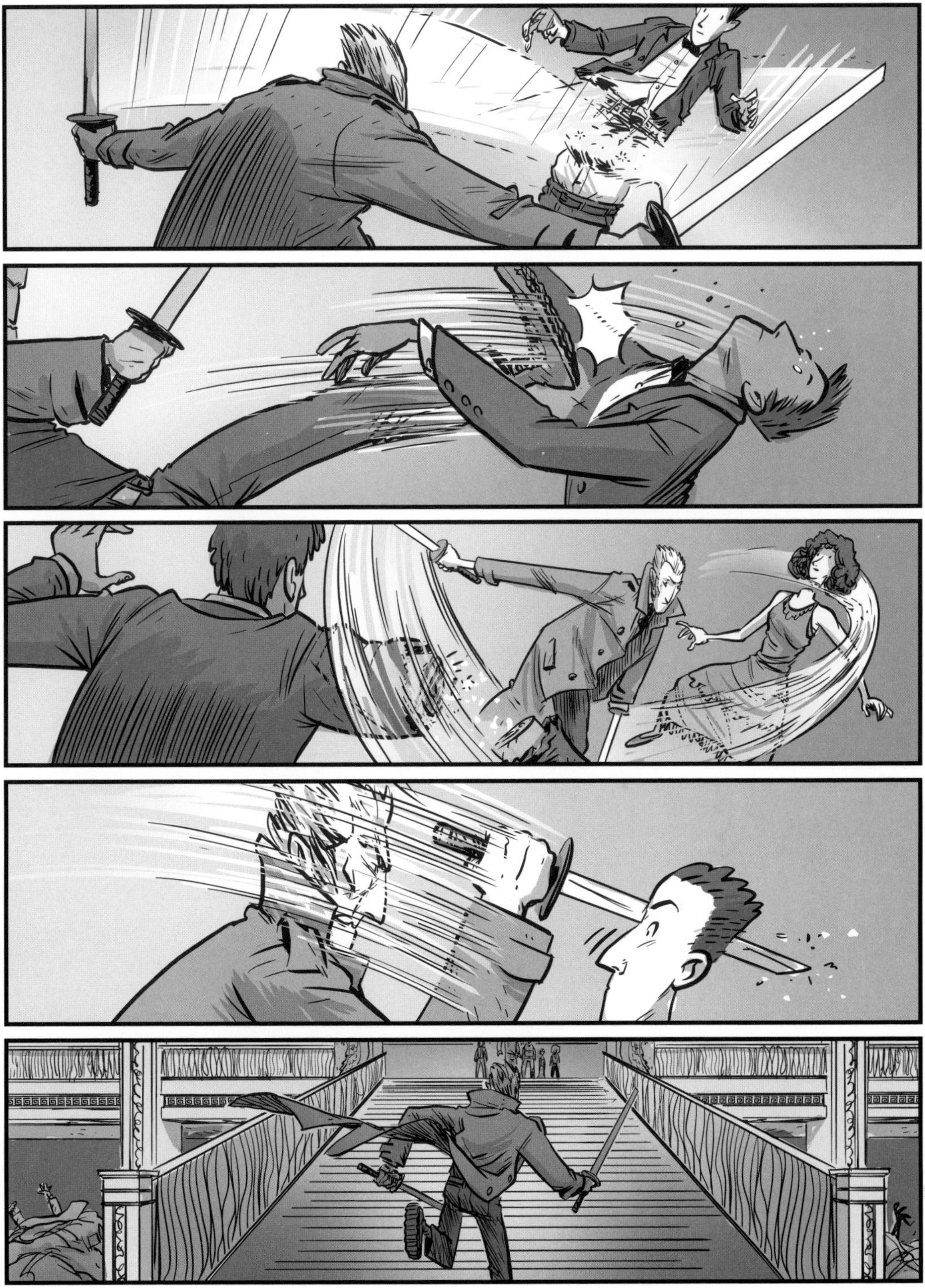

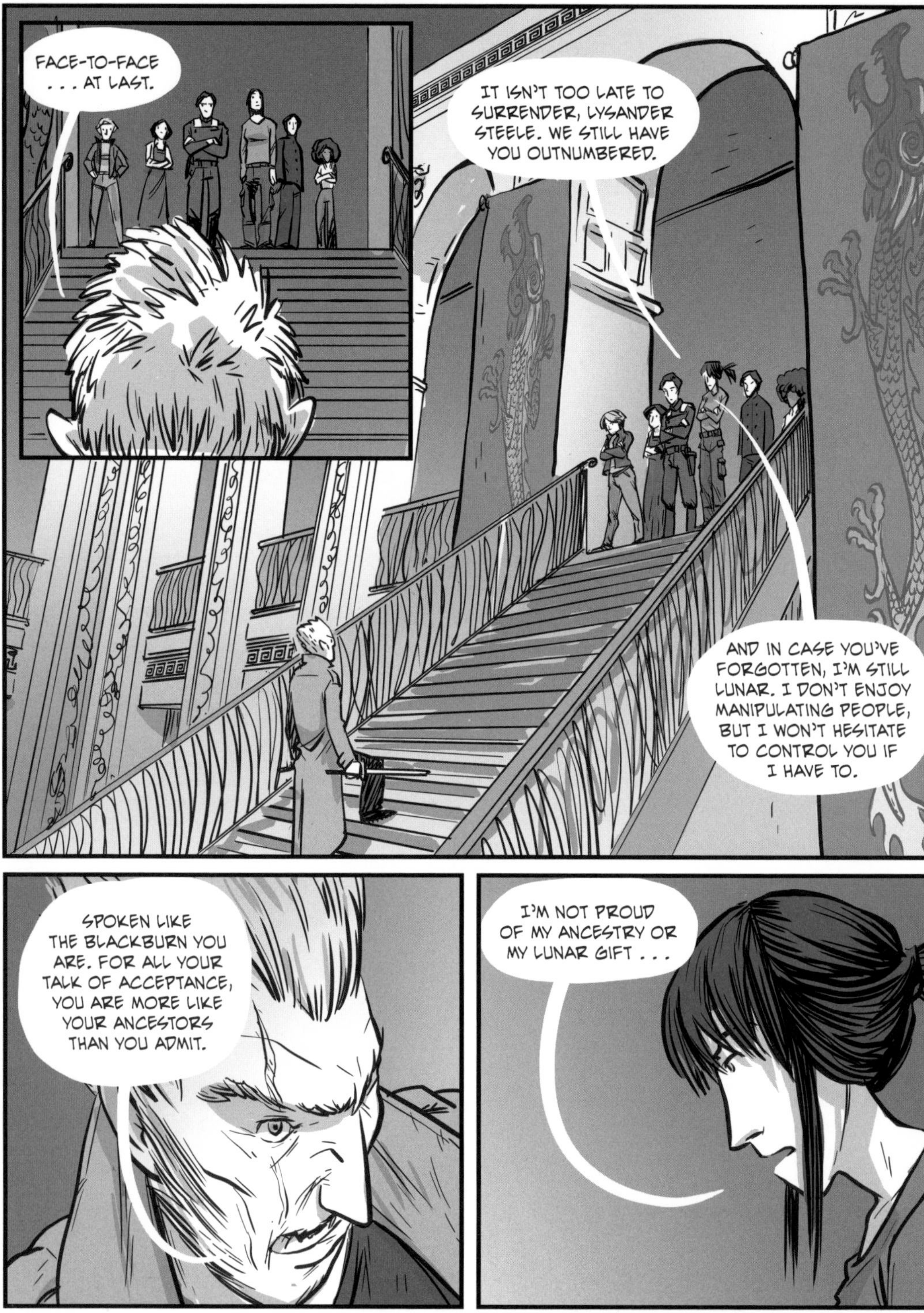
FACE-TO-FACE . . . AT LAST.
IT ISN'T TOO LATE TO SURRENDER, LYSANDER STEELE. WE STILL HAVE YOU OUTNUMBERED.
AND IN CASE YOU'VE FORGOTTEN, I'M STILL LUNAR. I DON'T ENJOY MANIPULATING PEOPLE, BUT I WON'T HESITATE TO CONTROL YOU IF I HAVE TO.
SPOKEN LIKE THE BLACKBURN YOU ARE. FOR ALL YOUR TALK OF ACCEPTANCE, YOU ARE MORE LIKE YOUR ANCESTORS THAN YOU ADMIT.
I'M NOT PROUD OF MY ANCESTRY OR MY LUNAR GIFT . . .

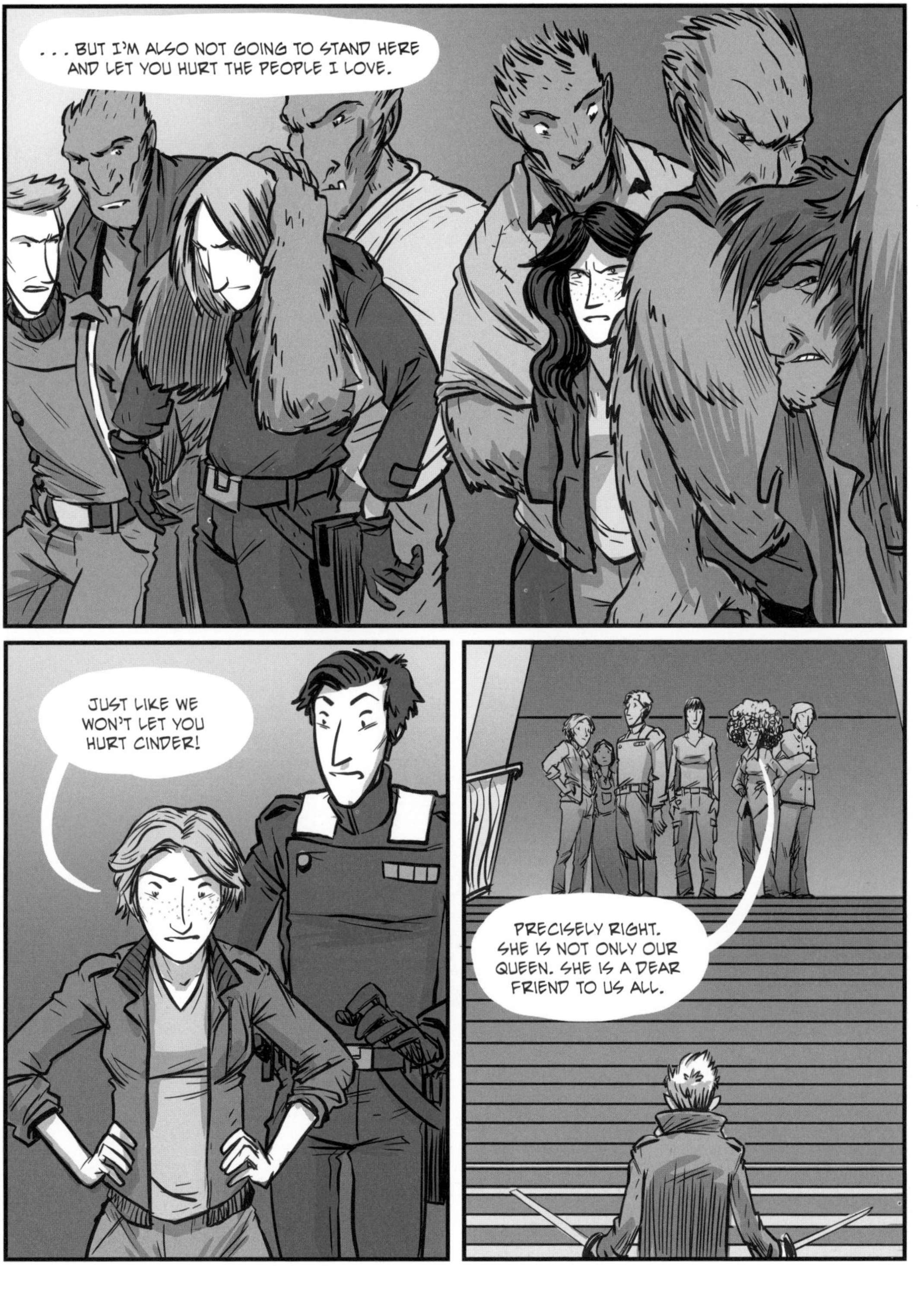
. . . BUT I'M ALSO NOT GOING TO STAND HERE AND LET YOU HURT THE PEOPLE I LOVE.
JUST LIKE WE WON'T LET YOU HURT CINDER!
PRECISELY RIGHT. SHE IS NOT ONLY OUR QUEEN. SHE IS A DEAR FRIEND TO US ALL.

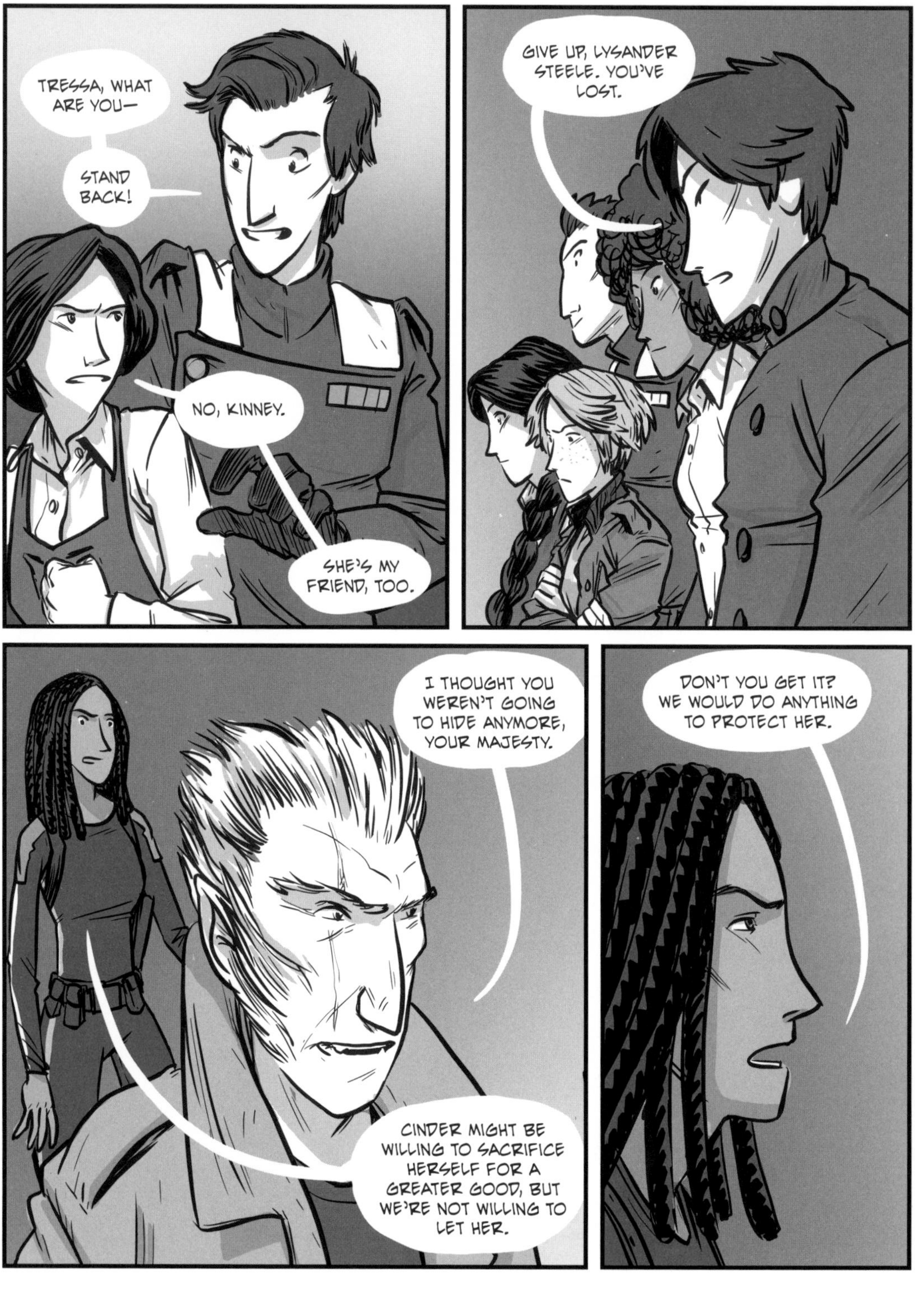
TRESSA, WHAT ARE YOU—
STAND BACK!
NO, KINNEY.
SHE'S MY FRIEND, TOO.
GIVE UP, LYSANDER STEELE. YOU'VE LOST.
I THOUGHT YOU WEREN'T GOING TO HIDE ANYMORE, YOUR MAJESTY.
CINDER MIGHT BE WILLING TO SACRIFICE HERSELF FOR A GREATER GOOD, BUT WE'RE NOT WILLING TO LET HER.
DON'T YOU GET IT? WE WOULD DO ANYTHING TO PROTECT HER.

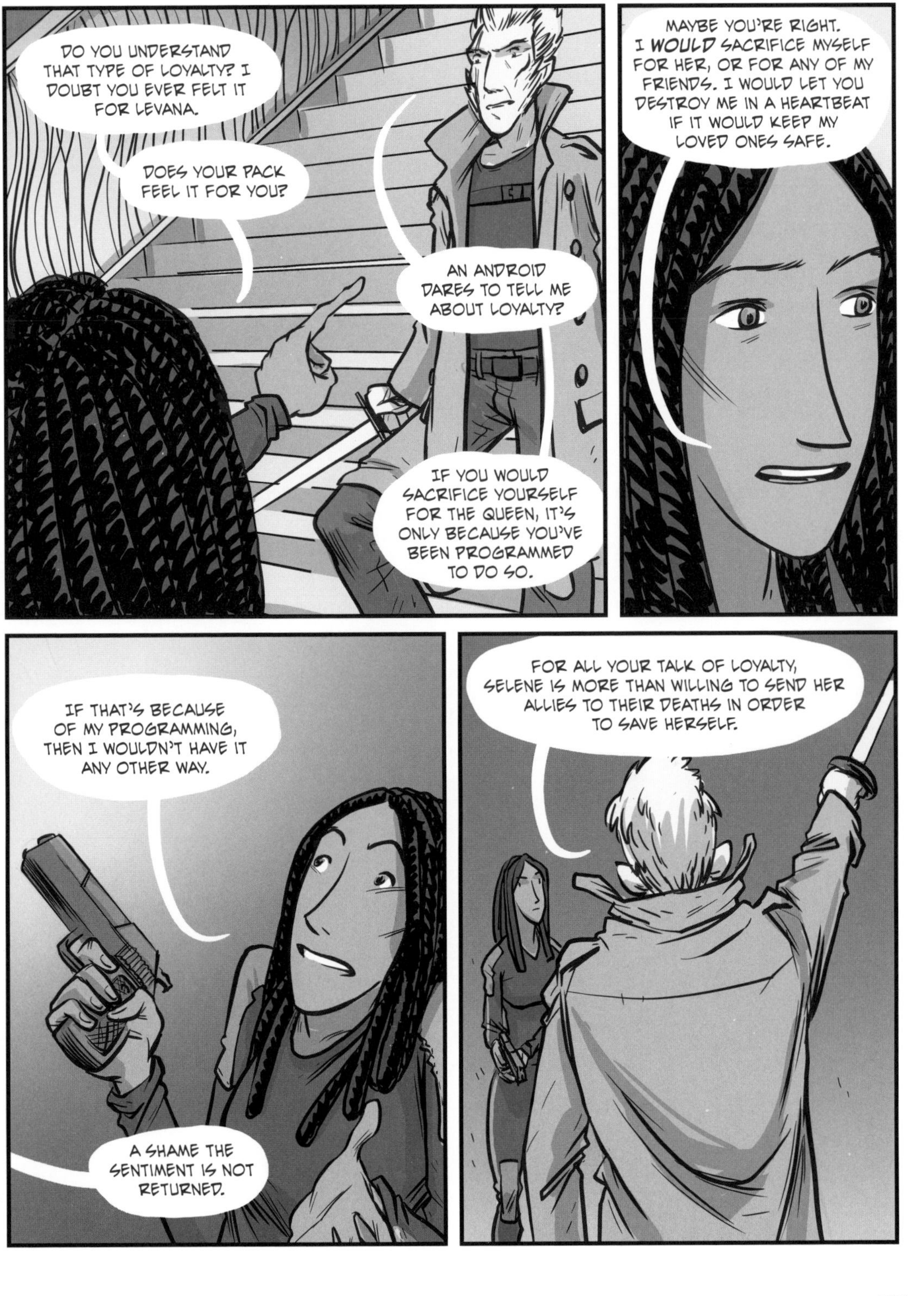
DO YOU UNDERSTAND THAT TYPE OF LOYALTY? I DOUBT YOU EVER FELT IT FOR LEVANA.
DOES YOUR PACK FEEL IT FOR YOU?
AN ANDROID DARES TO TELL ME ABOUT LOYALTY?
IF YOU WOULD SACRIFICE YOURSELF FOR THE QUEEN, IT'S ONLY BECAUSE YOU'VE BEEN PROGRAMMED TO DO SO.
MAYBE YOU'RE RIGHT. I ***WOULD*** SACRIFICE MYSELF FOR HER, OR FOR ANY OF MY FRIENDS. I WOULD LET YOU DESTROY ME IN A HEARTBEAT IF IT WOULD KEEP MY LOVED ONES SAFE.
IF THAT'S BECAUSE OF MY PROGRAMMING, THEN I WOULDN'T HAVE IT ANY OTHER WAY.
A SHAME THE SENTIMENT IS NOT RETURNED.
FOR ALL YOUR TALK OF LOYALTY, SELENE IS MORE THAN WILLING TO SEND HER ALLIES TO THEIR DEATHS IN ORDER TO SAVE HERSELF.

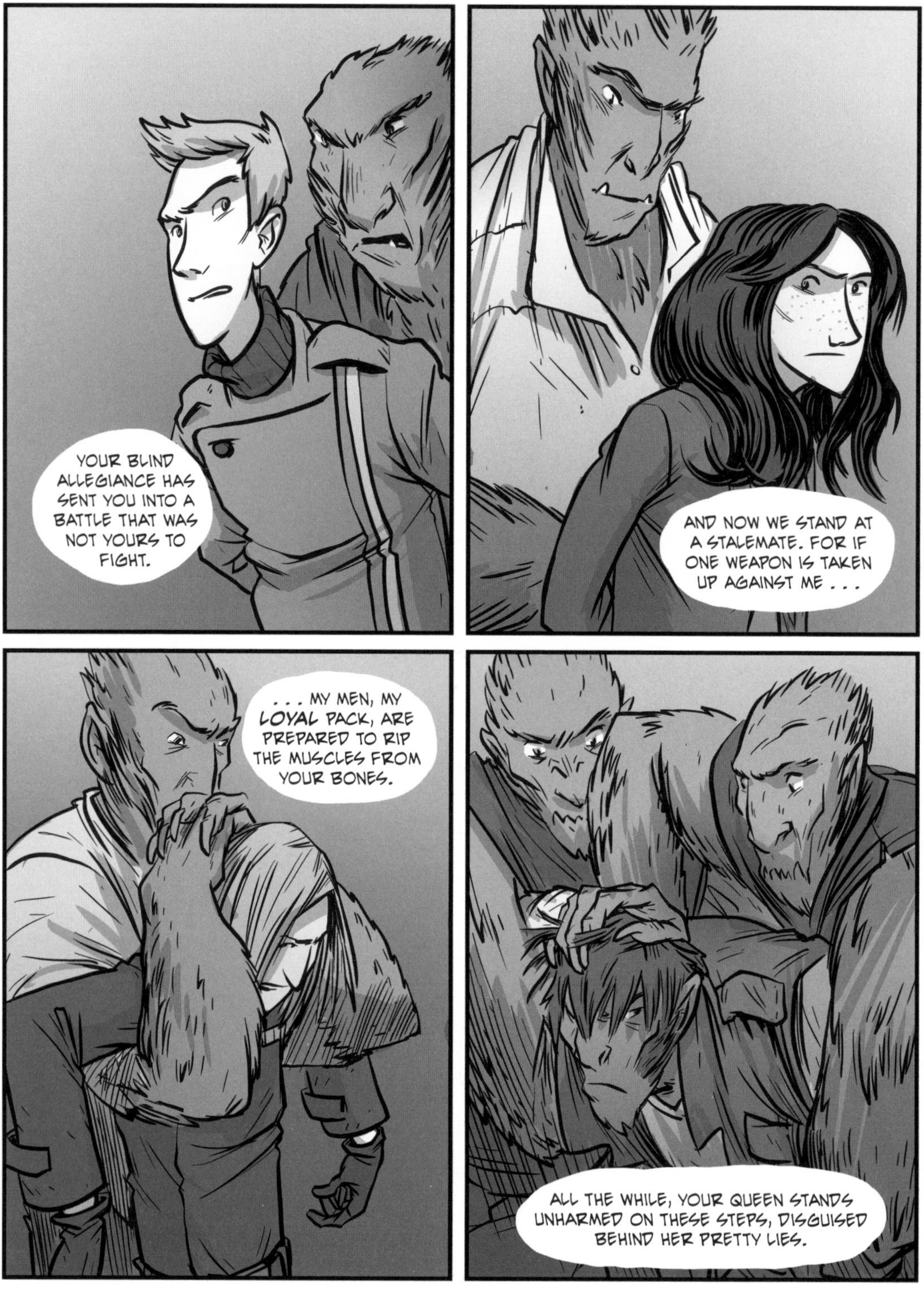
YOUR BLIND ALLEGIANCE HAS SENT YOU INTO A BATTLE THAT WAS NOT YOURS TO FIGHT.
AND NOW WE STAND AT A STALEMATE. FOR IF ONE WEAPON IS TAKEN UP AGAINST ME . . .
. . . MY MEN, MY *LOYAL* PACK, ARE PREPARED TO RIP THE MUSCLES FROM YOUR BONES.
ALL THE WHILE, YOUR QUEEN STANDS UNHARMED ON THESE STEPS, DISGUISED BEHIND HER PRETTY LIES.

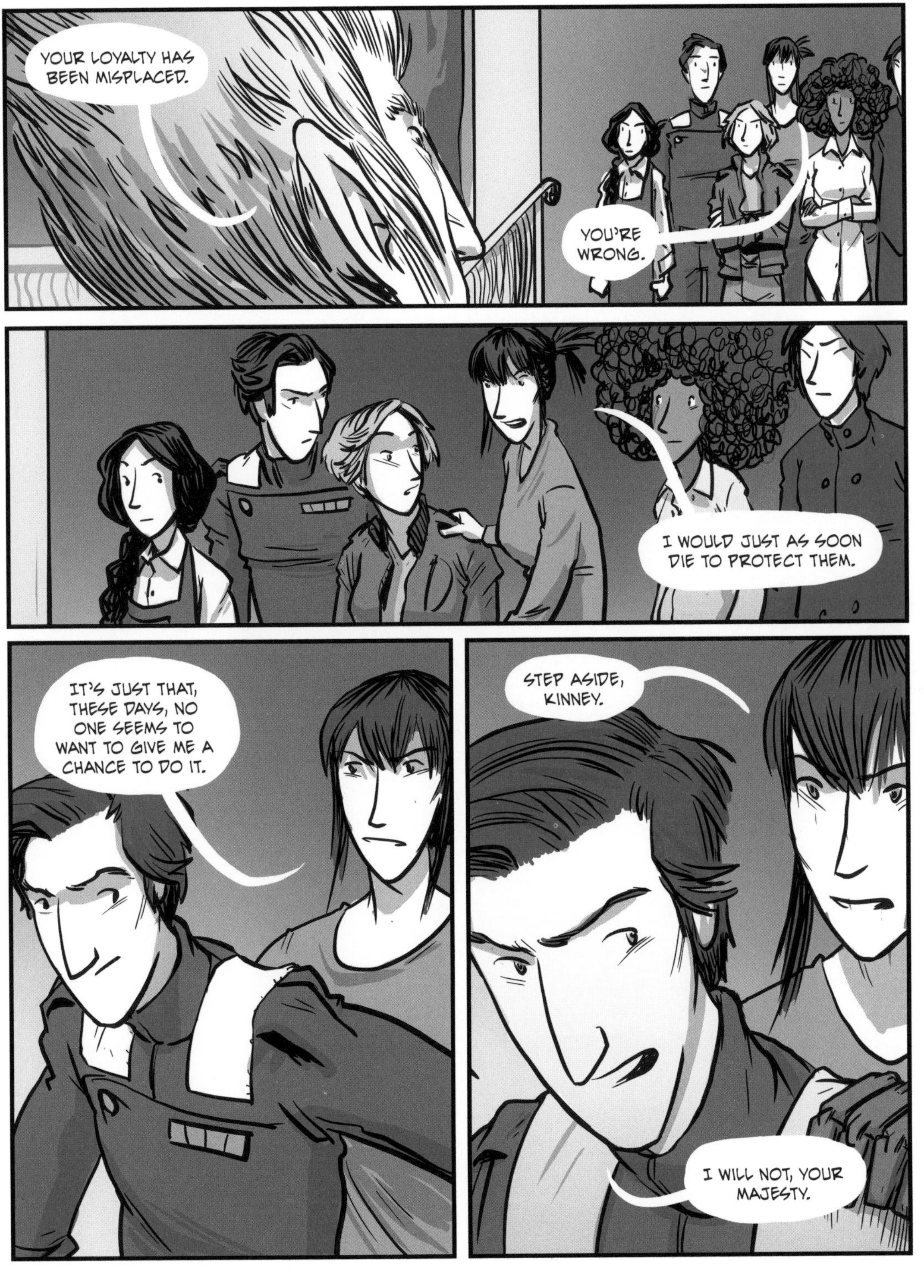
YOUR LOYALTY HAS BEEN MISPLACED.
YOU'RE WRONG.
I WOULD JUST AS SOON DIE TO PROTECT THEM.
IT'S JUST THAT, THESE DAYS, NO ONE SEEMS TO WANT TO GIVE ME A CHANCE TO DO IT.
STEP ASIDE, KINNEY.
I WILL NOT, YOUR MAJESTY.

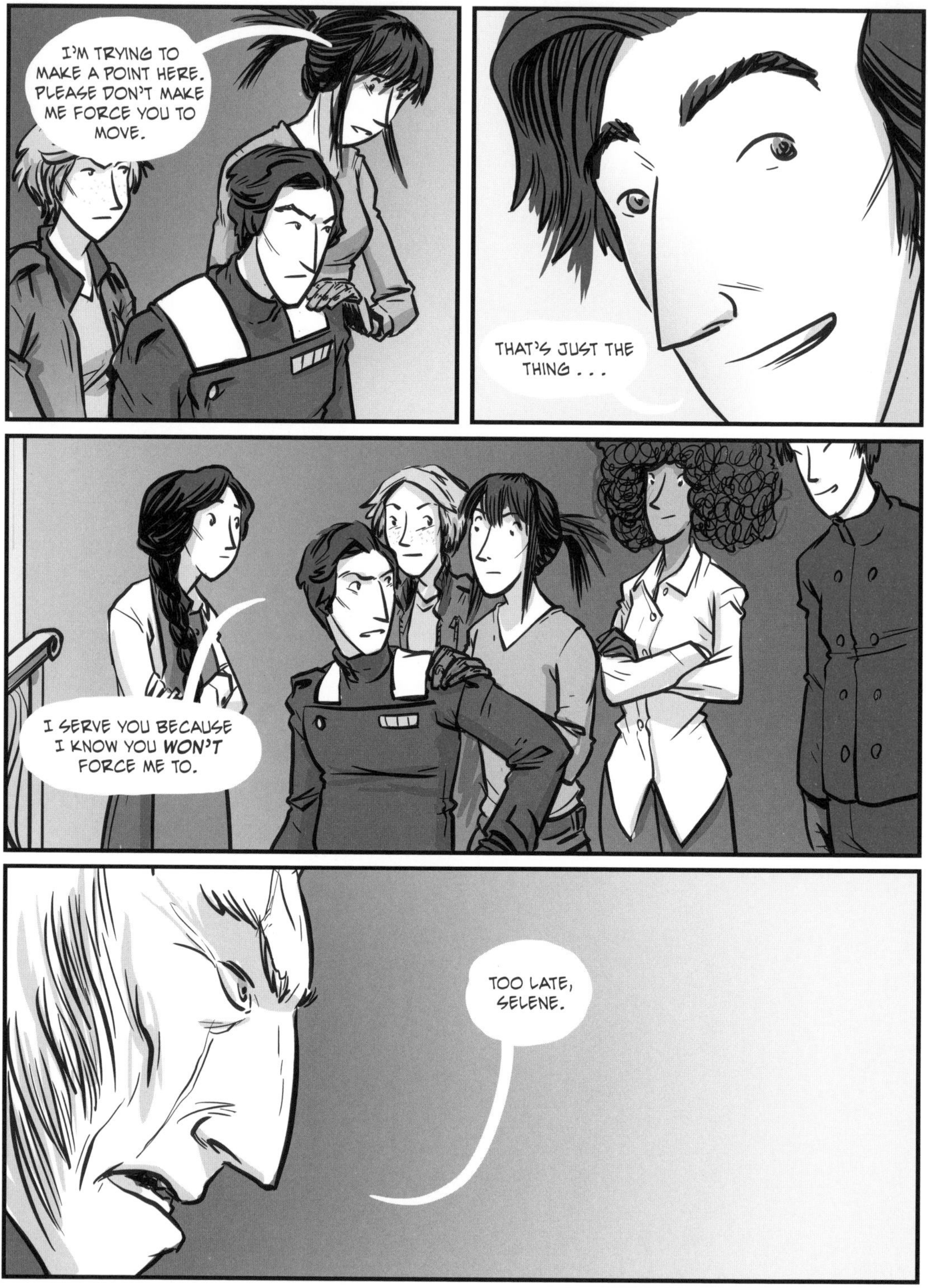
I'M TRYING TO MAKE A POINT HERE. PLEASE DON'T MAKE ME FORCE YOU TO MOVE.
THAT'S JUST THE THING . . .
I SERVE YOU BECAUSE I KNOW YOU **WON'T** FORCE ME TO.
TOO LATE, SELENE.

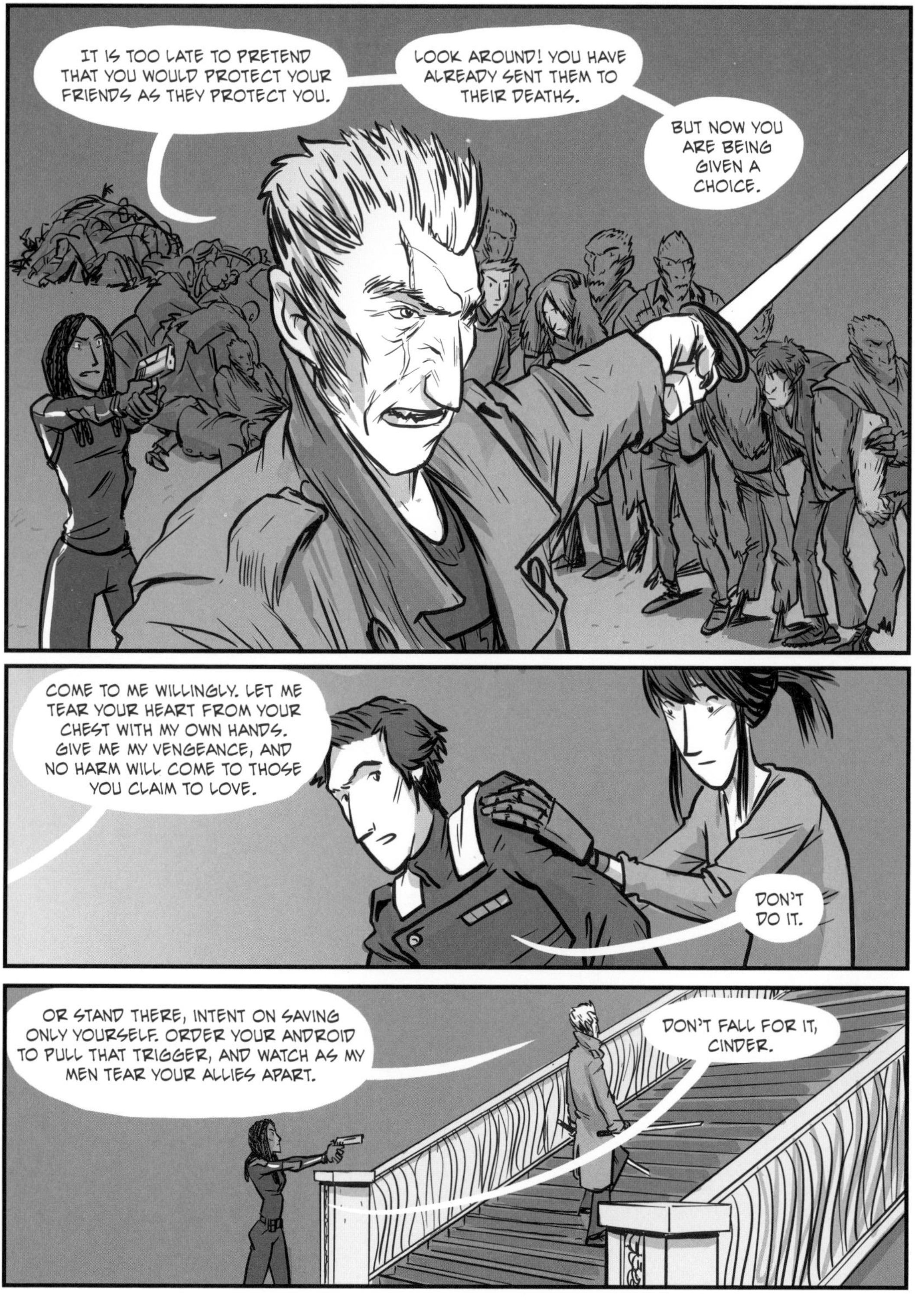
IT IS TOO LATE TO PRETEND THAT YOU WOULD PROTECT YOUR FRIENDS AS THEY PROTECT YOU.
LOOK AROUND! YOU HAVE ALREADY SENT THEM TO THEIR DEATHS.
BUT NOW YOU ARE BEING GIVEN A CHOICE.
COME TO ME WILLINGLY. LET ME TEAR YOUR HEART FROM YOUR CHEST WITH MY OWN HANDS. GIVE ME MY VENGEANCE, AND NO HARM WILL COME TO THOSE YOU CLAIM TO LOVE.
DON'T DO IT.
OR STAND THERE, INTENT ON SAVING ONLY YOURSELF. ORDER YOUR ANDROID TO PULL THAT TRIGGER, AND WATCH AS MY MEN TEAR YOUR ALLIES APART.
DON'T FALL FOR IT, CINDER.

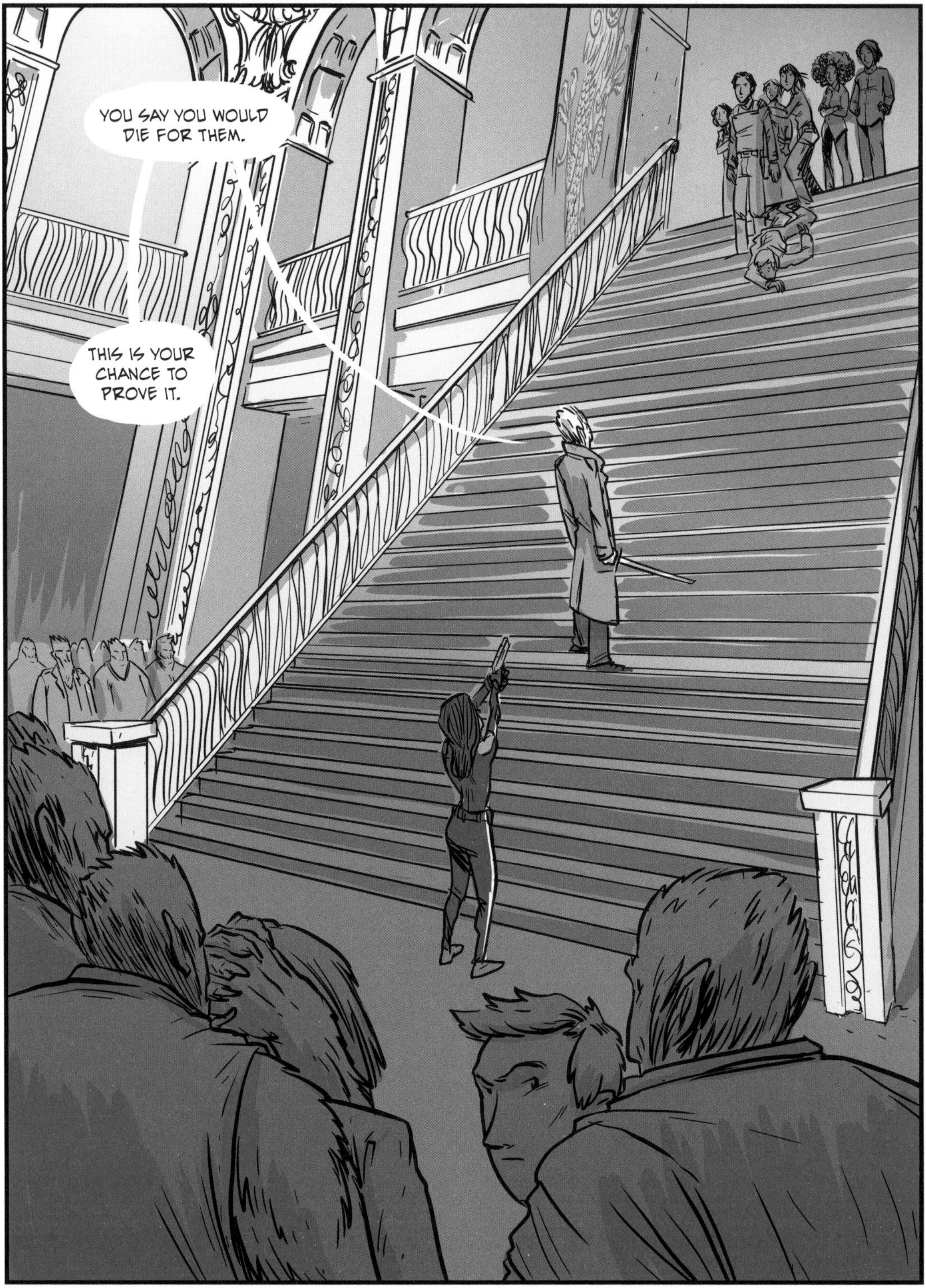
YOU SAY YOU WOULD DIE FOR THEM.
THIS IS YOUR CHANCE TO PROVE IT.

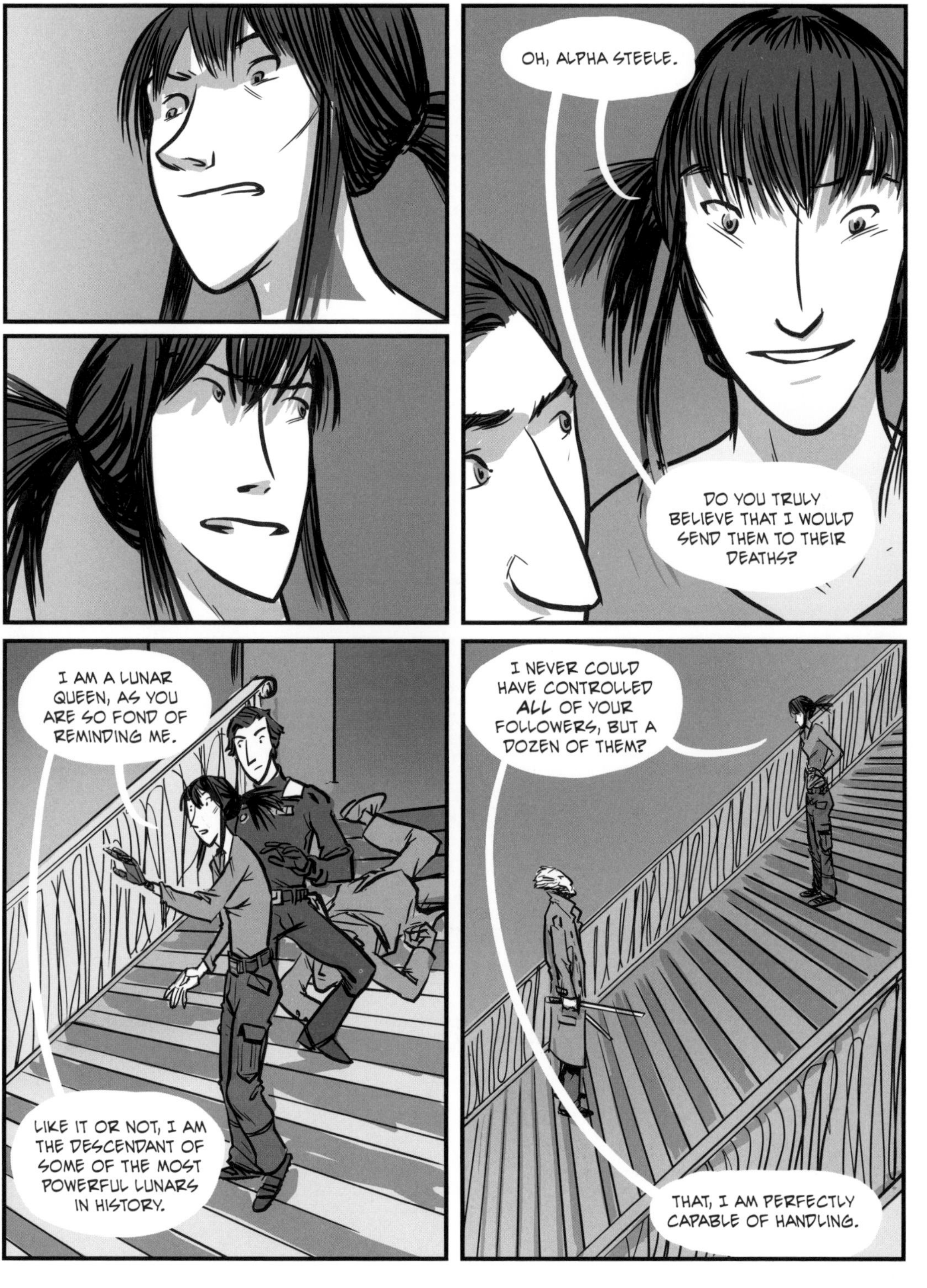
OH, ALPHA STEELE.
DO YOU TRULY BELIEVE THAT I WOULD SEND THEM TO THEIR DEATHS?
I AM A LUNAR QUEEN, AS YOU ARE SO FOND OF REMINDING ME.
LIKE IT OR NOT, I AM THE DESCENDANT OF SOME OF THE MOST POWERFUL LUNARS IN HISTORY.
I NEVER COULD HAVE CONTROLLED ALL OF YOUR FOLLOWERS, BUT A DOZEN OF THEM?
THAT, I AM PERFECTLY CAPABLE OF HANDLING.

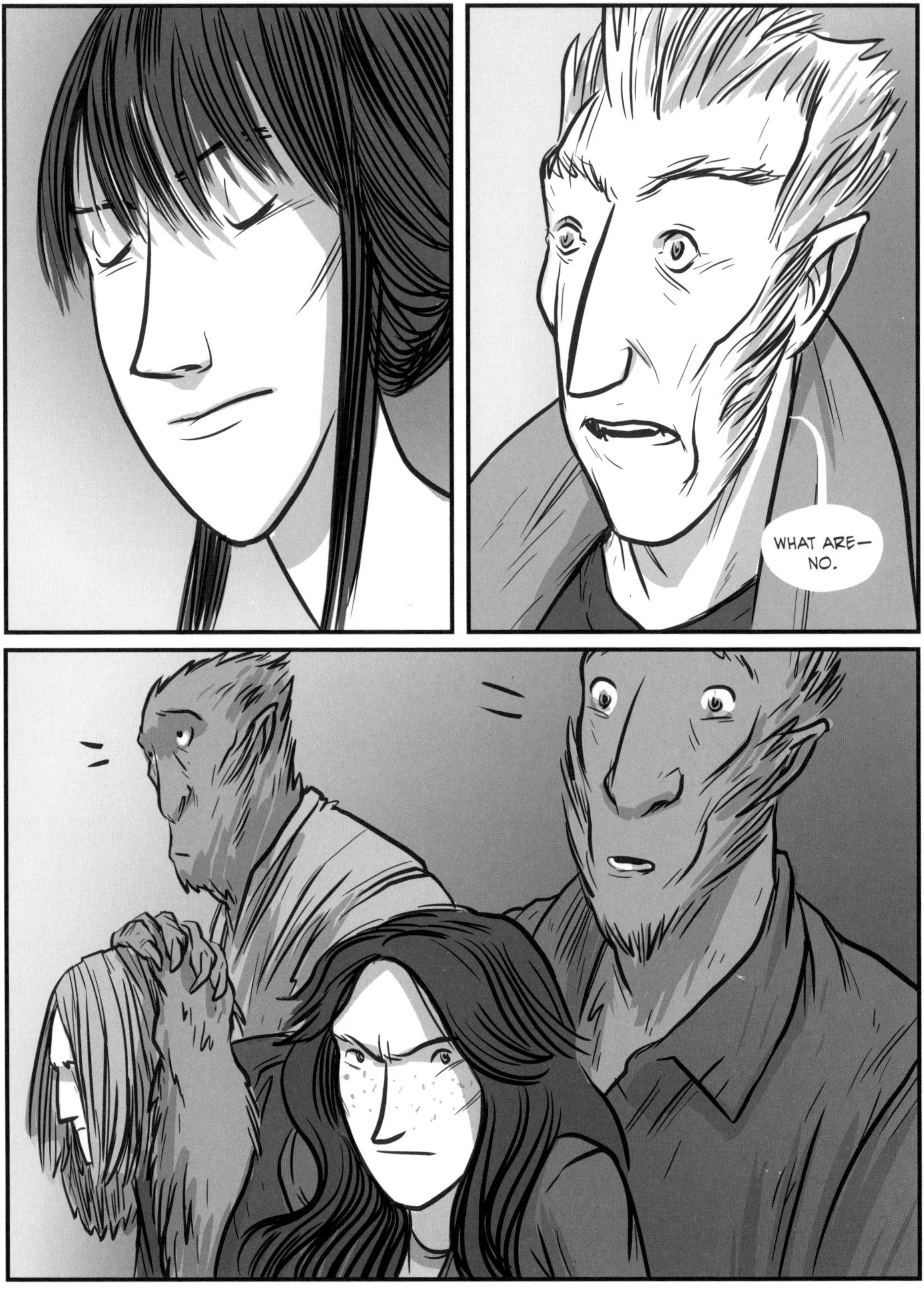
WHAT ARE—
NO.

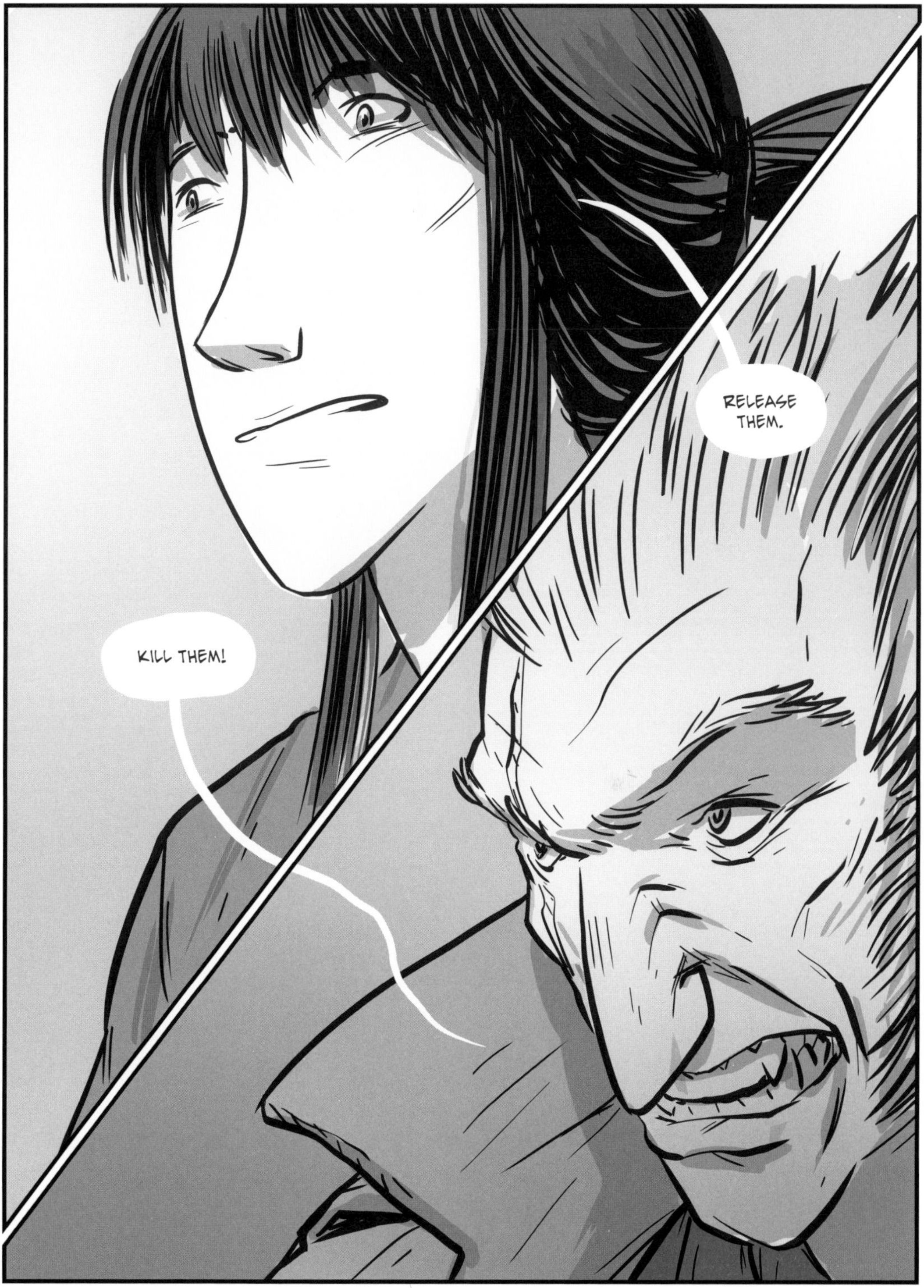
RELEASE THEM.
KILL THEM!

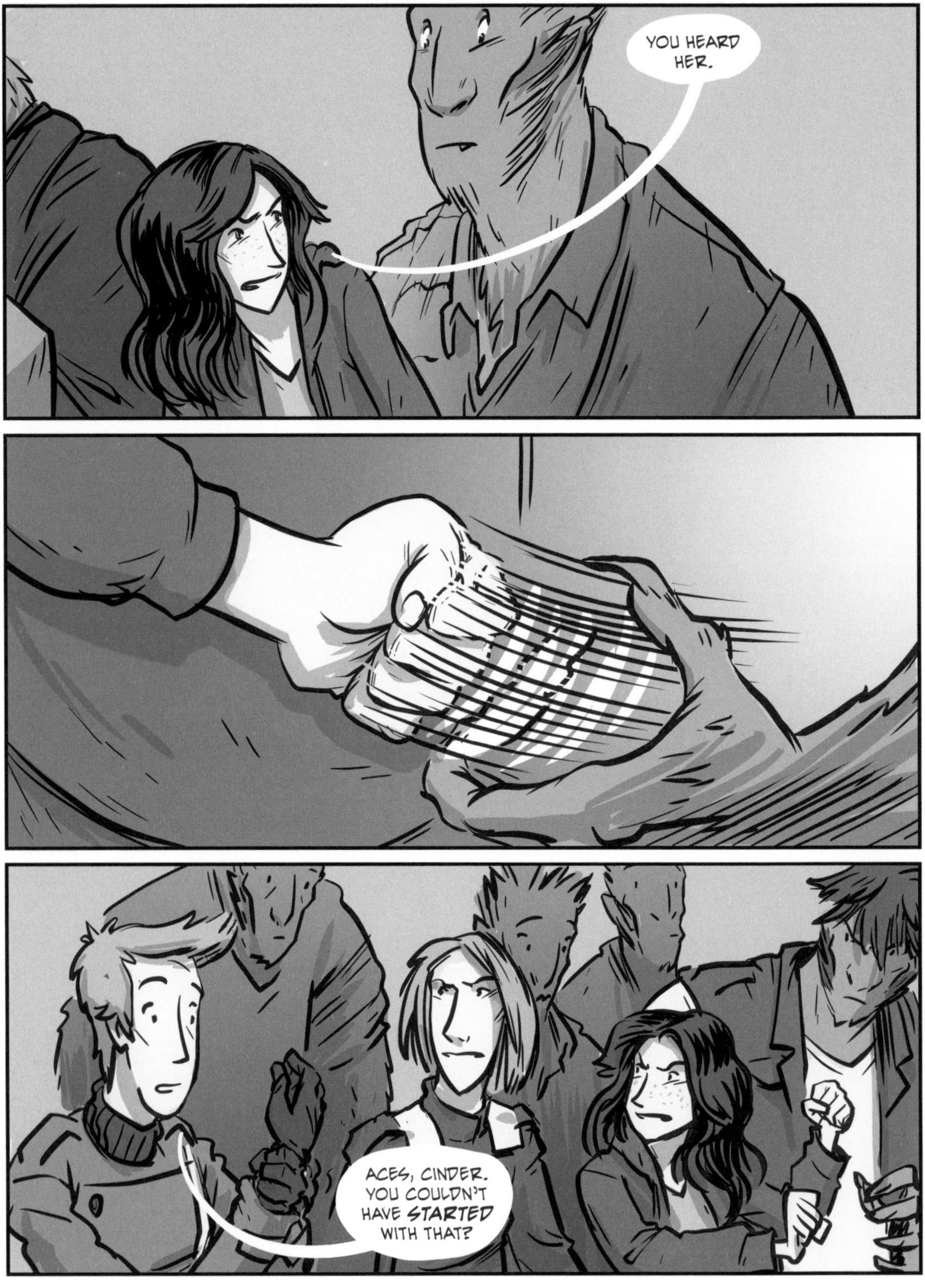
YOU HEARD HER.
ACES, CINDER. YOU COULDN'T HAVE **STARTED** WITH THAT?

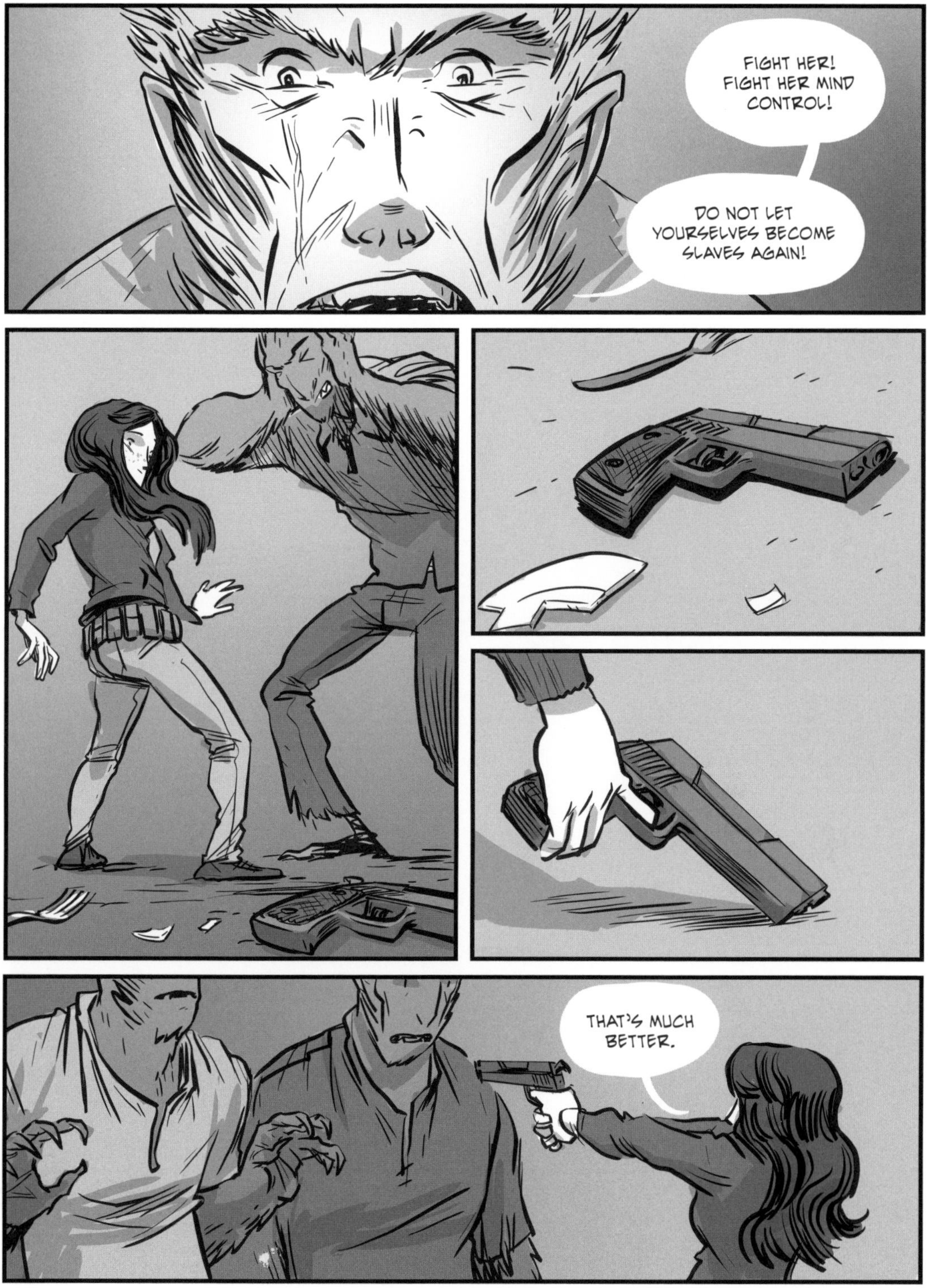
FIGHT HER! FIGHT HER MIND CONTROL!
DO NOT LET YOURSELVES BECOME SLAVES AGAIN!
THAT'S MUCH BETTER.

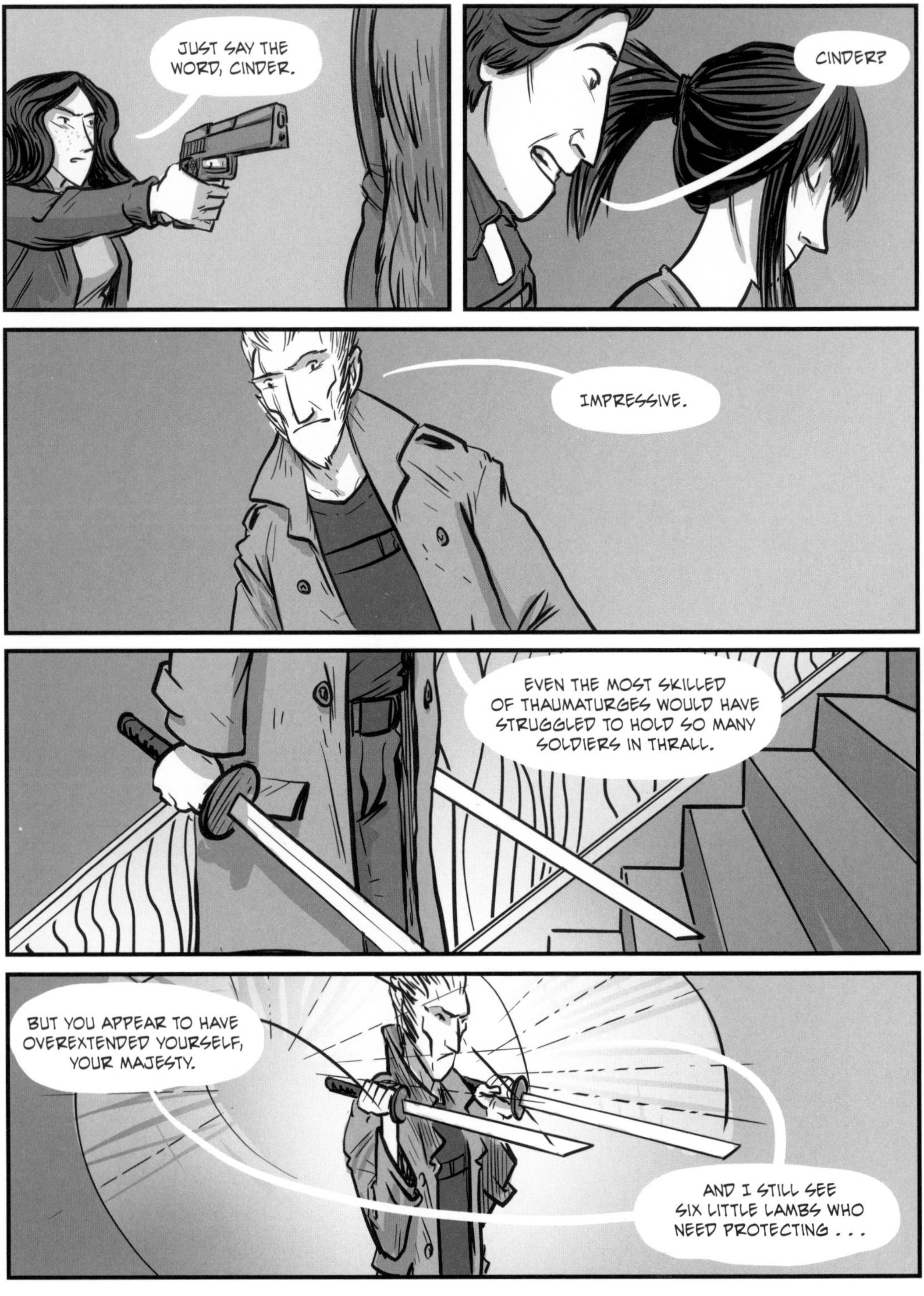
JUST SAY THE WORD, CINDER.
CINDER?
IMPRESSIVE.
EVEN THE MOST SKILLED OF THAUMATURGES WOULD HAVE STRUGGLED TO HOLD SO MANY SOLDIERS IN THRALL.
BUT YOU APPEAR TO HAVE OVEREXTENDED YOURSELF, YOUR MAJESTY.
AND I STILL SEE SIX LITTLE LAMBS WHO NEED PROTECTING . . .

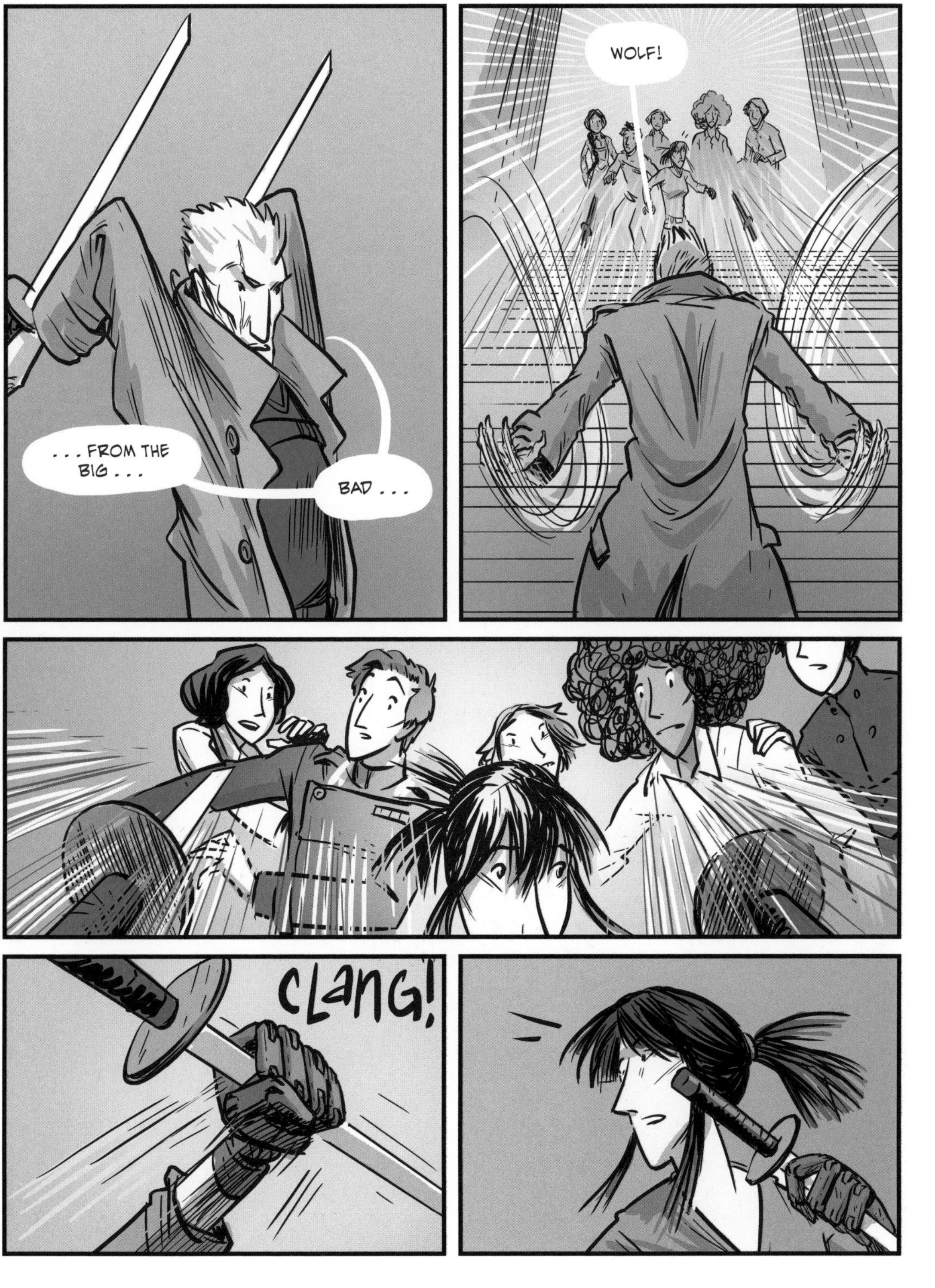
. . . FROM THE BIG . . .
BAD . . .
WOLF!
CLANG!

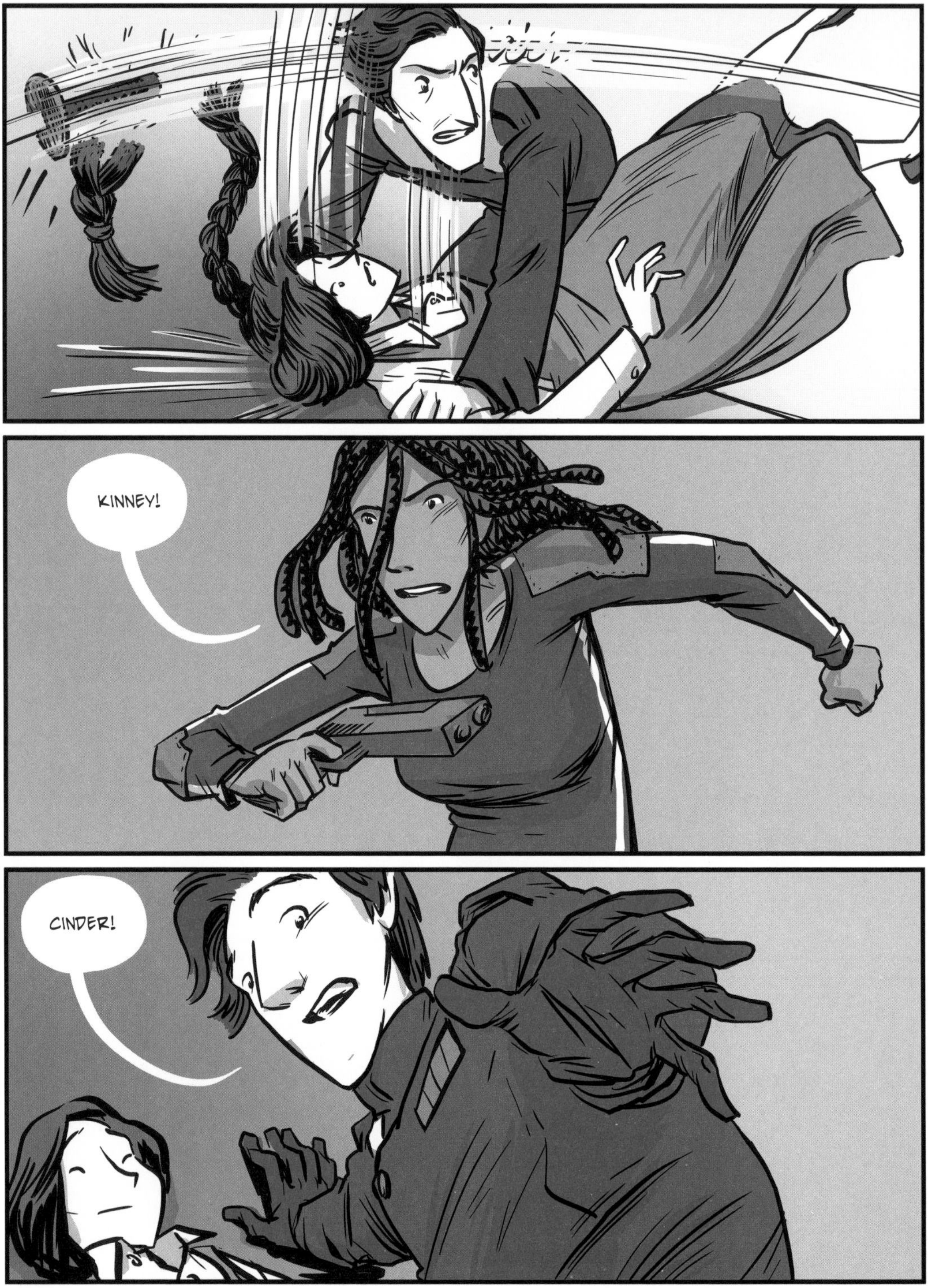
KINNEY!
CINDER!

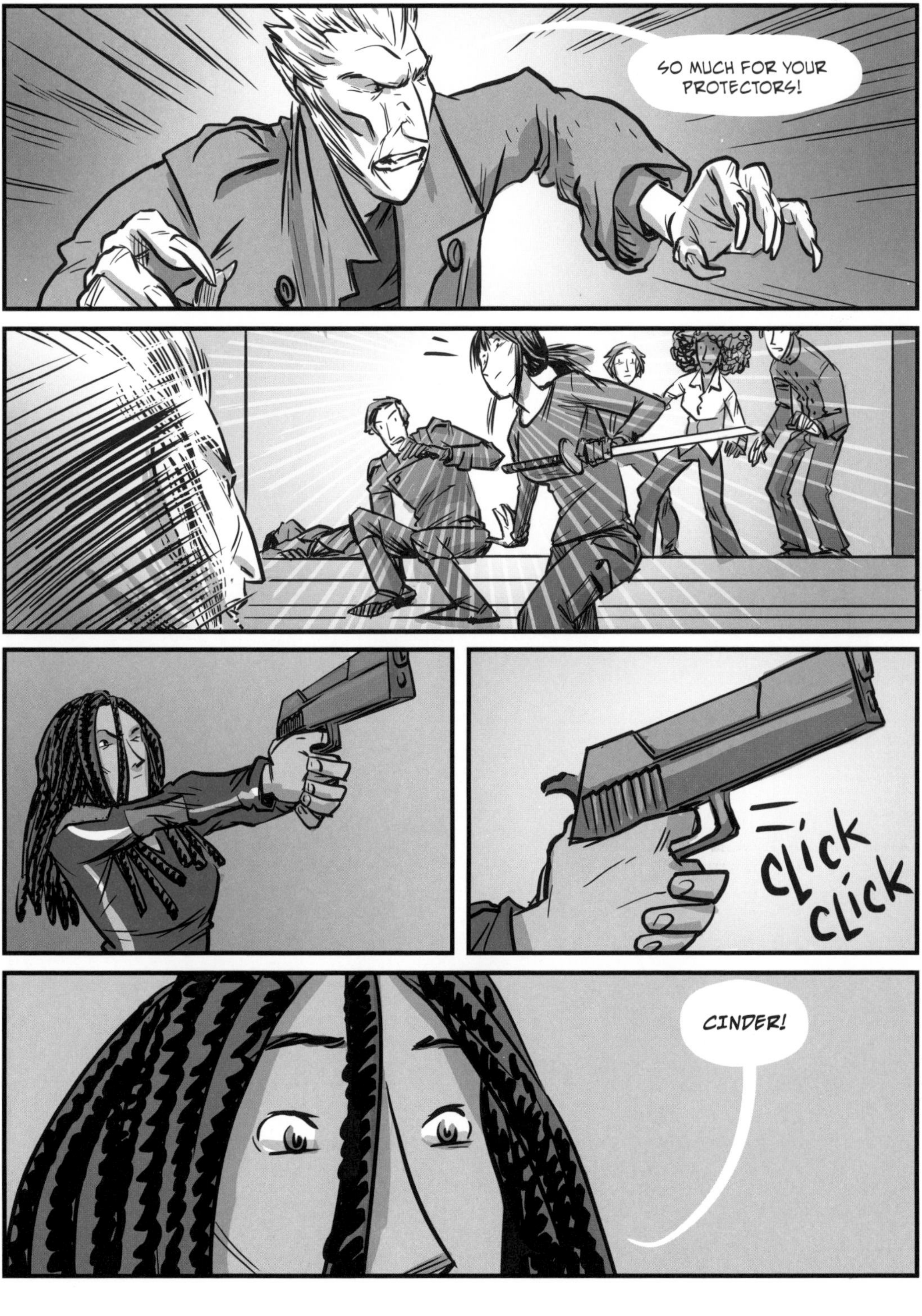
SO MUCH FOR YOUR PROTECTORS!
CLICK CLICK
CINDER!

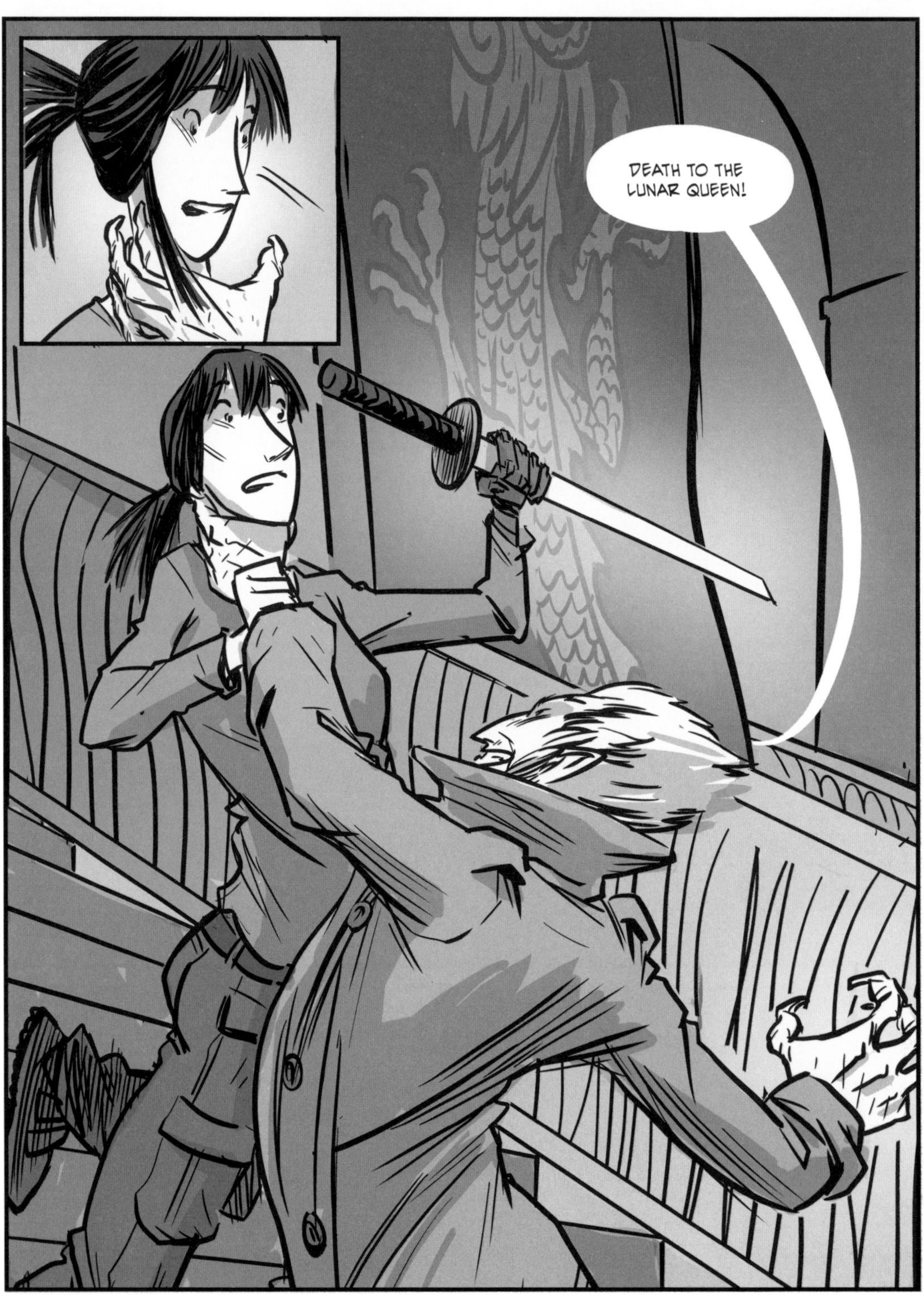
DEATH TO THE LUNAR QUEEN!

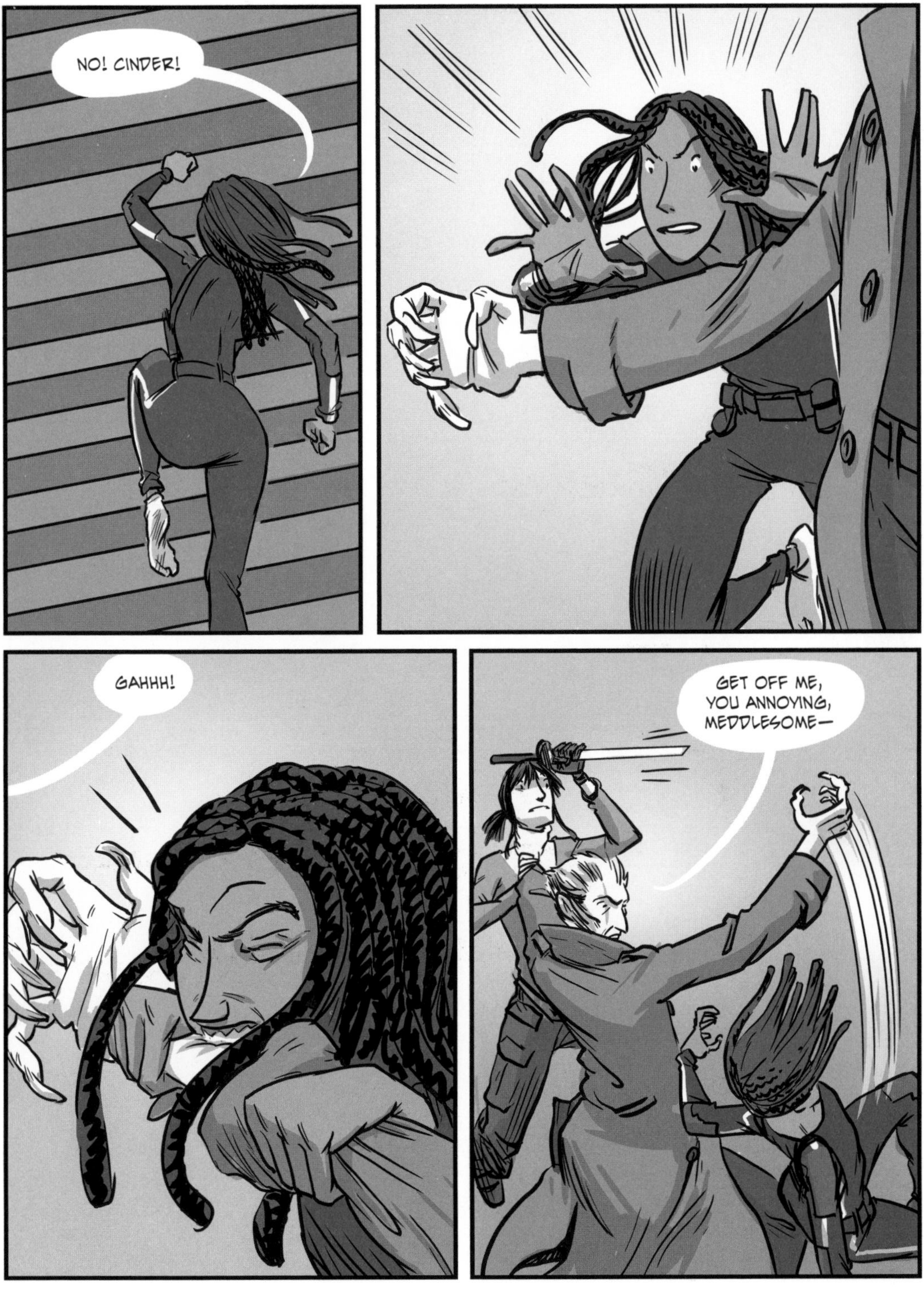
NO! CINDER!
GAHHH!
GET OFF ME, YOU ANNOYING, MEDDLESOME—

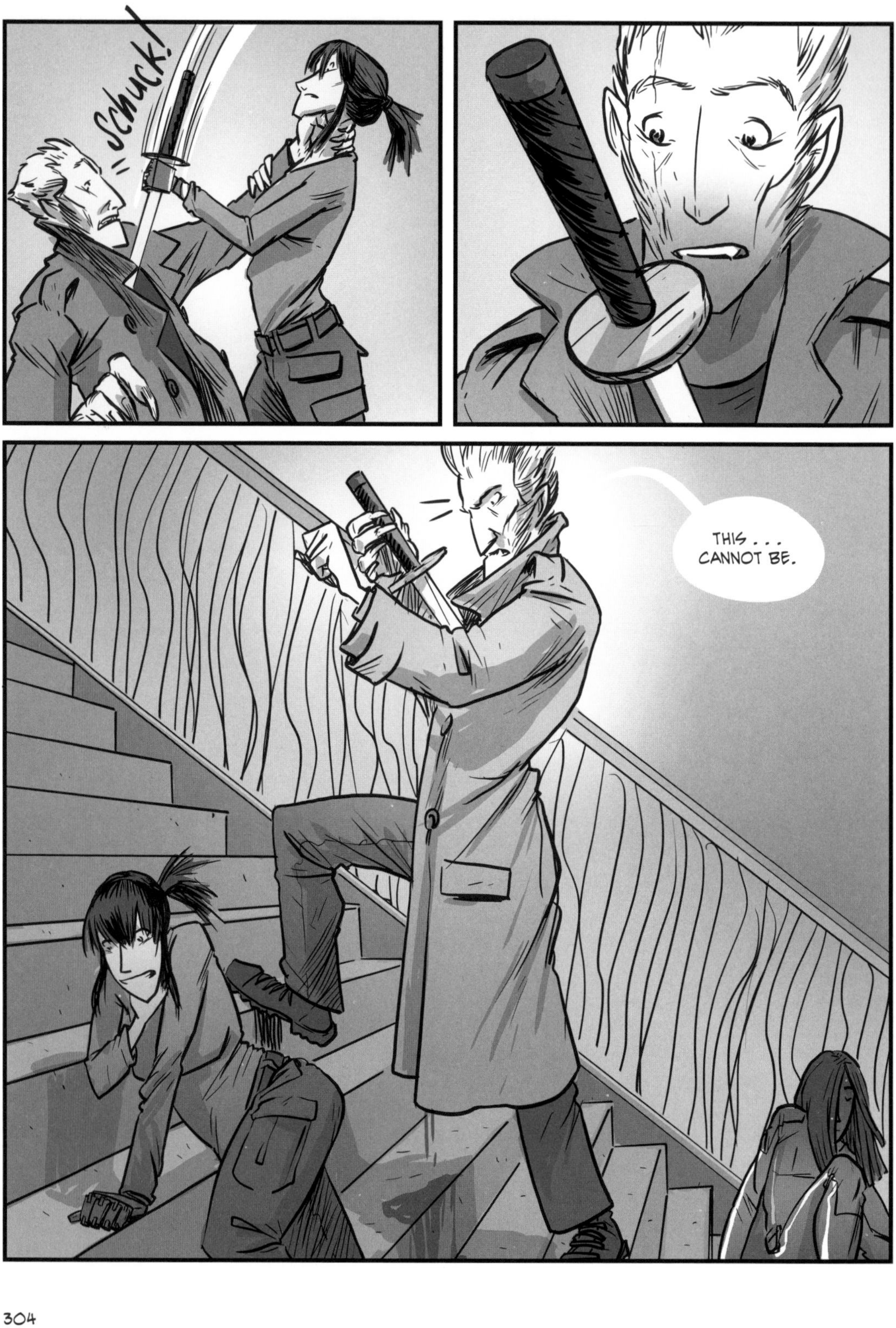
Schuck!
THIS . . .
CANNOT BE.

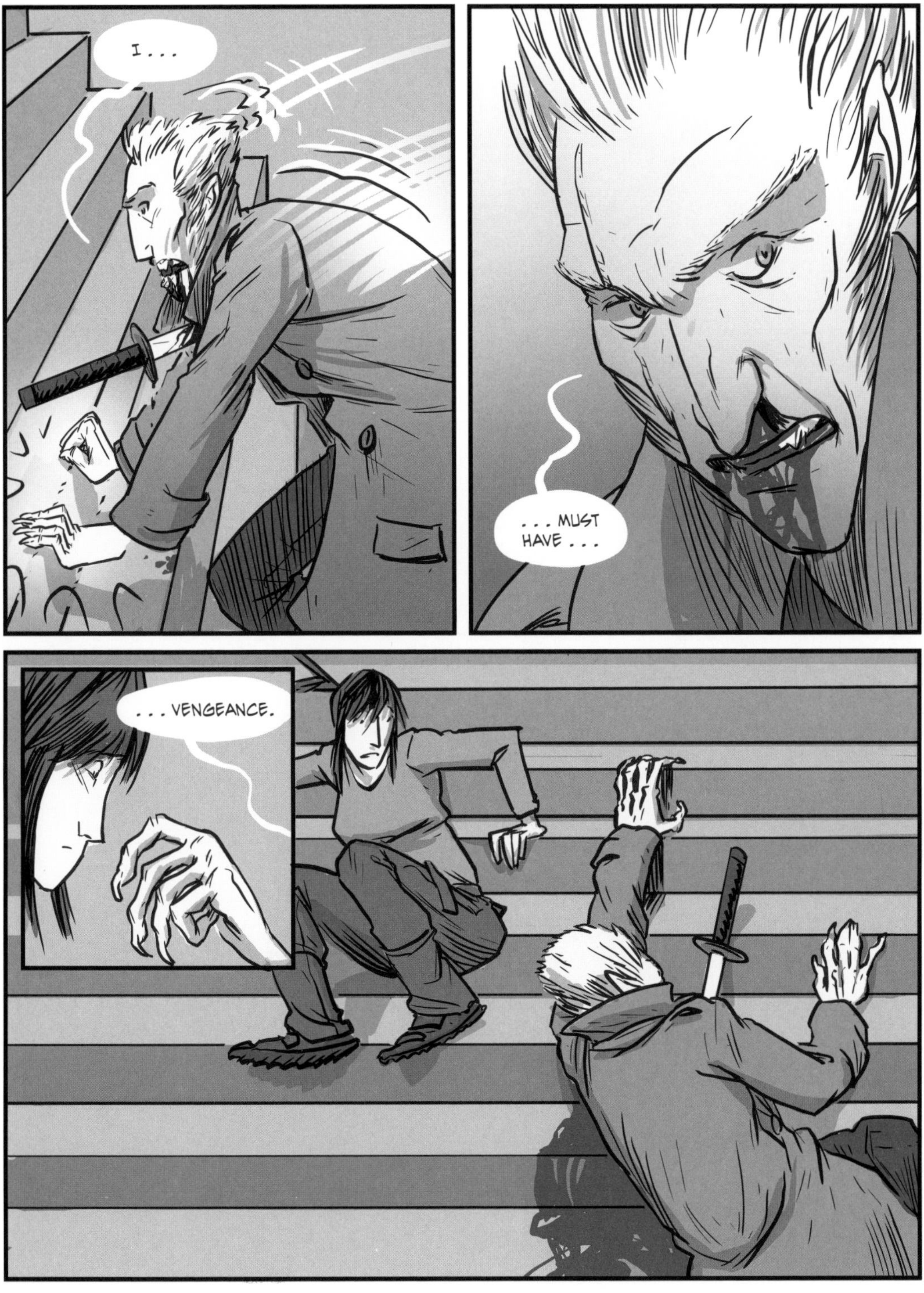
I . . .
. . . MUST HAVE . . .
. . . VENGEANCE.

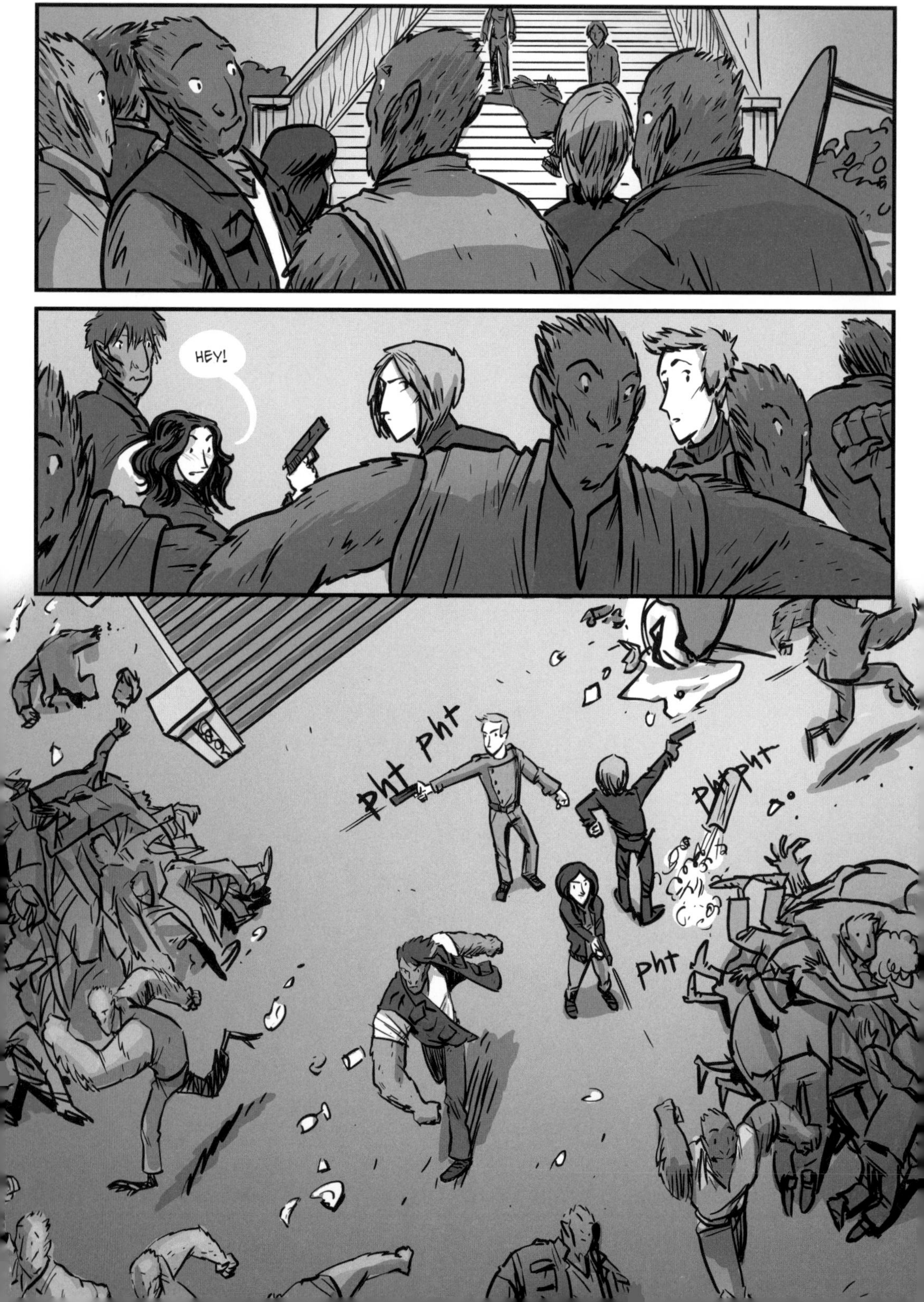
HEY!
pht pht
pht
phtpht
pht

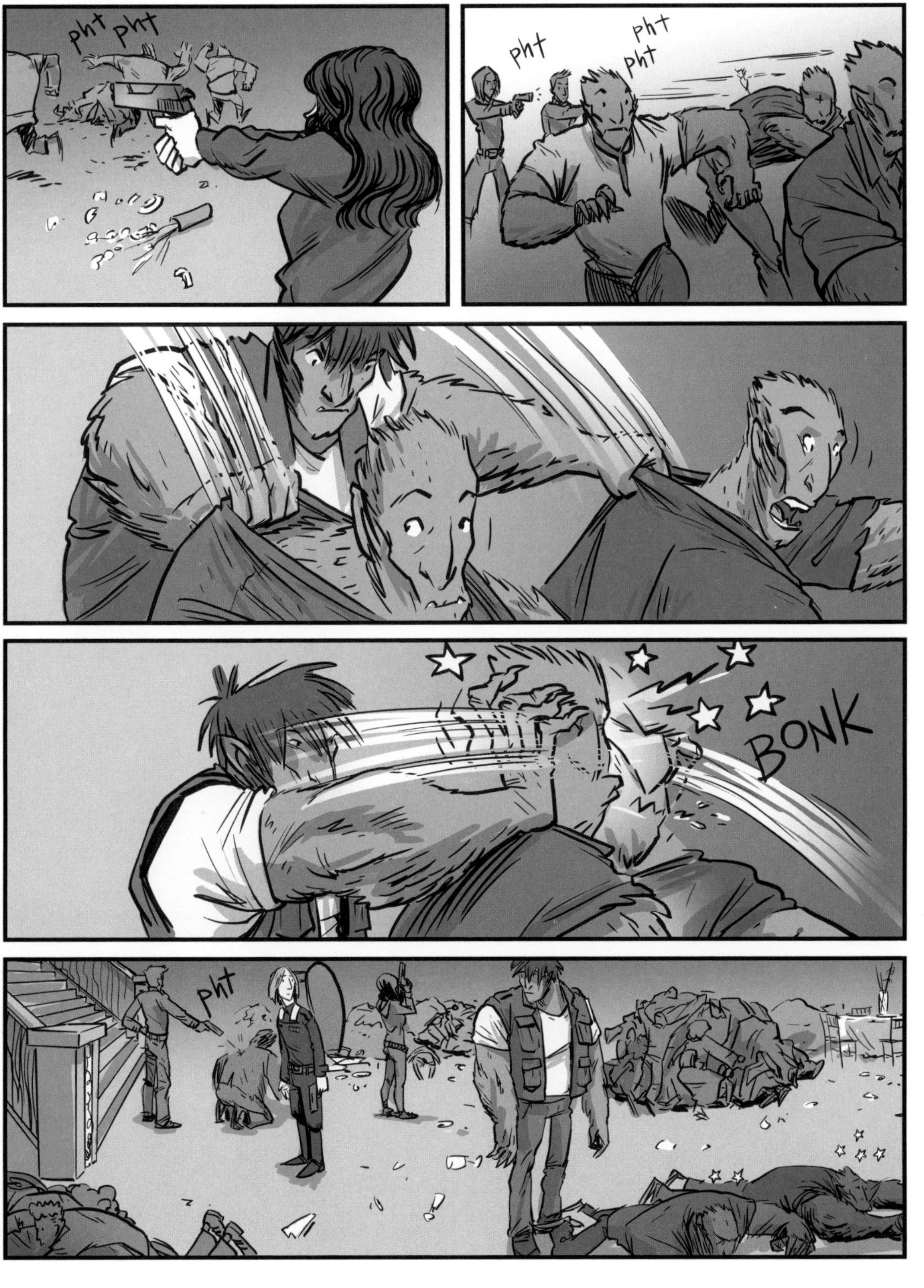
pht pht
pht
pht
pht
BONK
pht

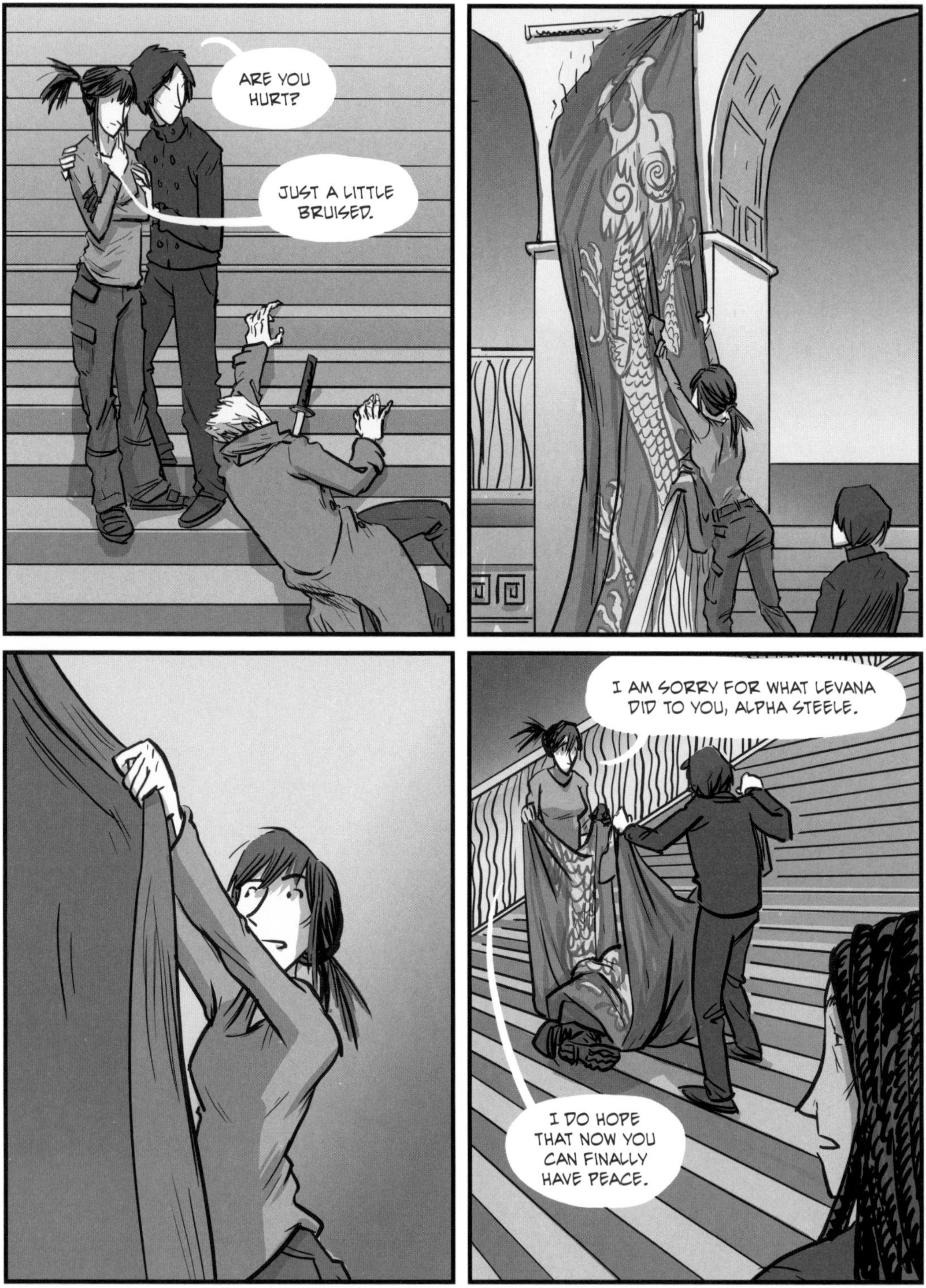
ARE YOU HURT?
JUST A LITTLE BRUISED.
I AM SORRY FOR WHAT LEVANA DID TO YOU, ALPHA STEELE.
I DO HOPE THAT NOW YOU CAN FINALLY HAVE PEACE.

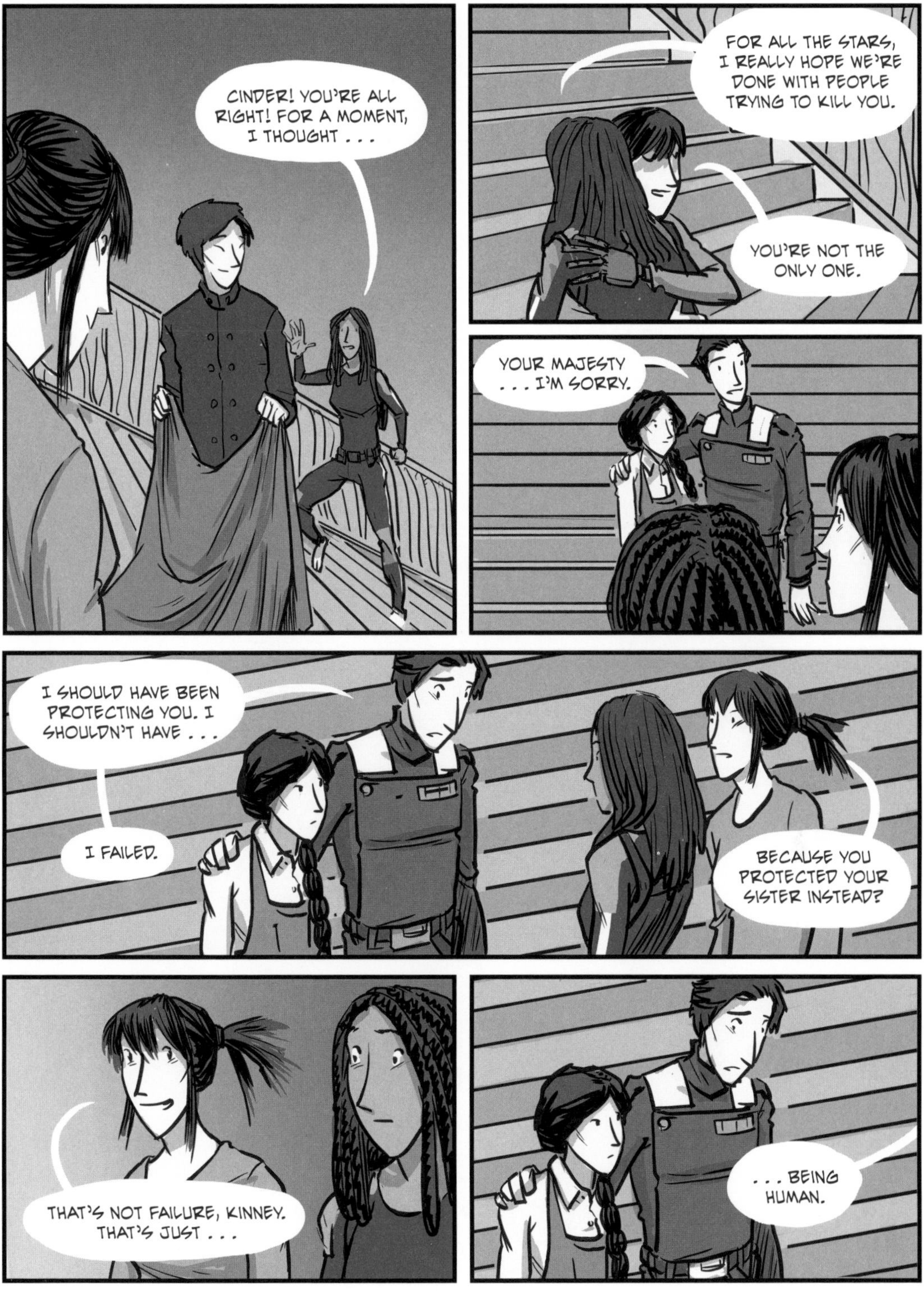
CINDER! YOU'RE ALL RIGHT! FOR A MOMENT, I THOUGHT . . .
FOR ALL THE STARS, I REALLY HOPE WE'RE DONE WITH PEOPLE TRYING TO KILL YOU.
YOU'RE NOT THE ONLY ONE.
YOUR MAJESTY . . . I'M SORRY.
I SHOULD HAVE BEEN PROTECTING YOU. I SHOULDN'T HAVE . . .
I FAILED.
BECAUSE YOU PROTECTED YOUR SISTER INSTEAD?
THAT'S NOT FAILURE, KINNEY. THAT'S JUST . . .
. . . BEING HUMAN.

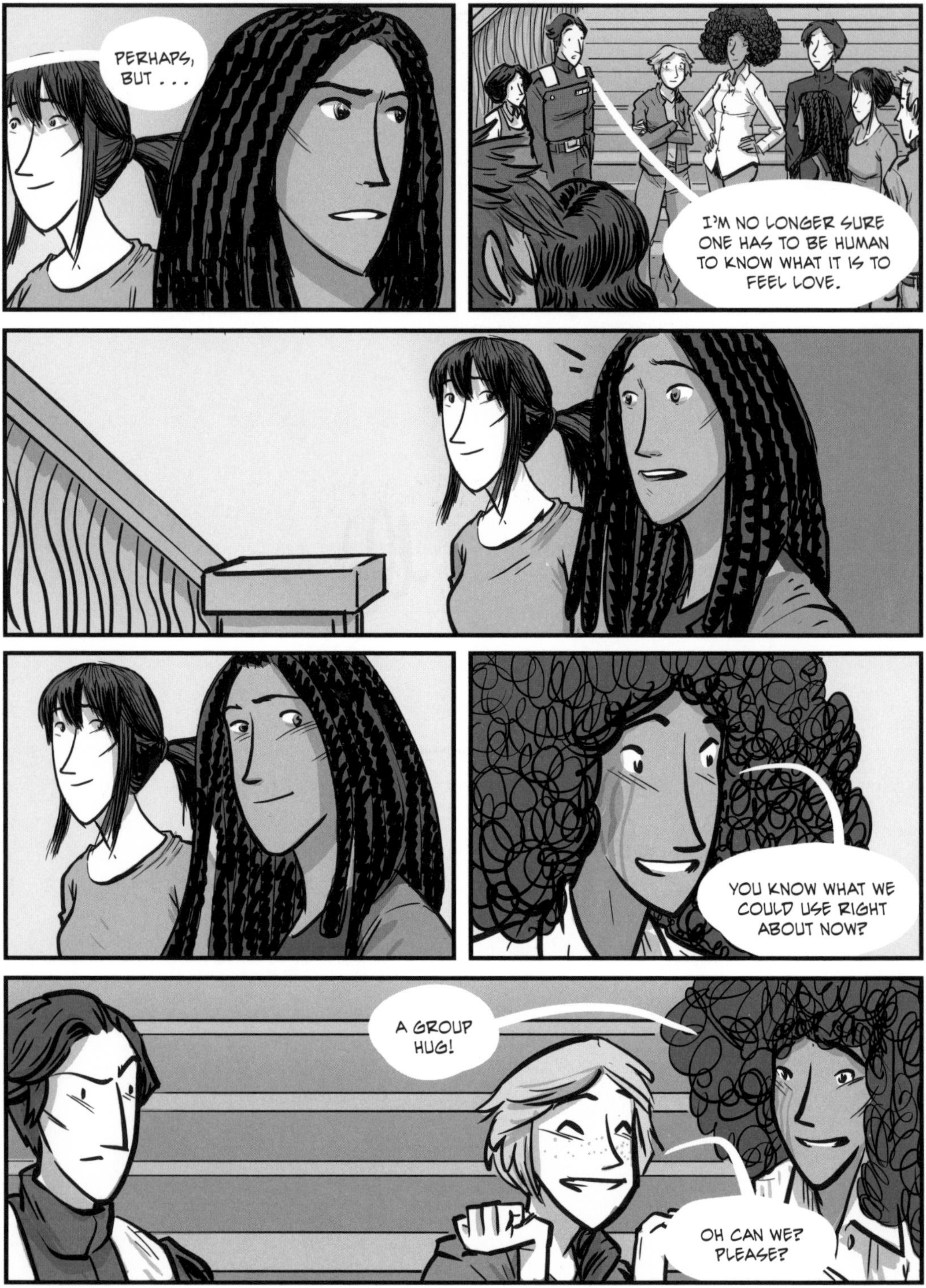
PERHAPS, BUT . . .
I'M NO LONGER SURE ONE HAS TO BE HUMAN TO KNOW WHAT IT IS TO FEEL LOVE.
YOU KNOW WHAT WE COULD USE RIGHT ABOUT NOW?
A GROUP HUG!
OH CAN WE? PLEASE?

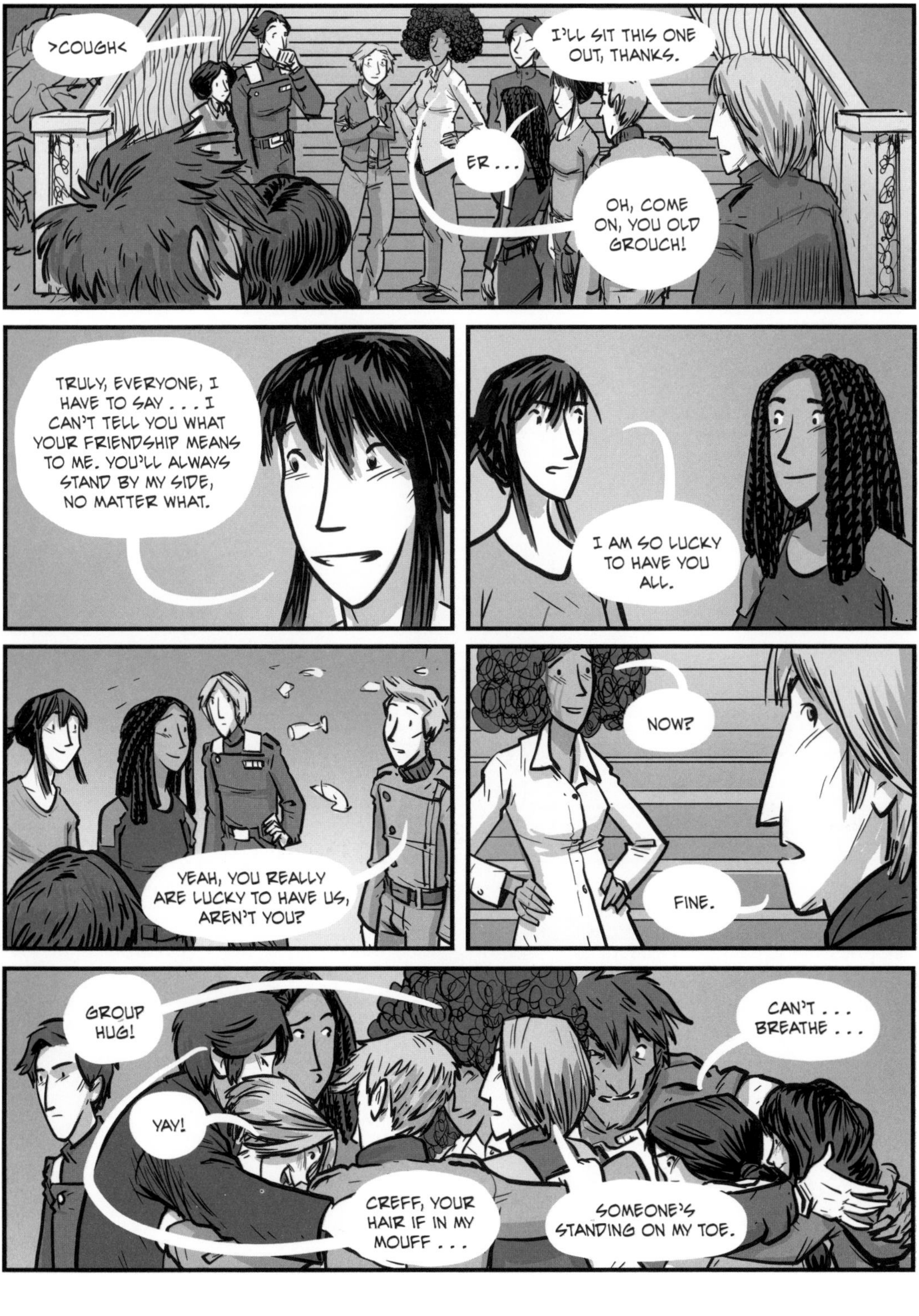
>COUGH<
I'LL SIT THIS ONE OUT, THANKS.
ER . . .
OH, COME ON, YOU OLD GROUCH!
TRULY, EVERYONE, I HAVE TO SAY . . . I CAN'T TELL YOU WHAT YOUR FRIENDSHIP MEANS TO ME. YOU'LL ALWAYS STAND BY MY SIDE, NO MATTER WHAT.
I AM SO LUCKY TO HAVE YOU ALL.
YEAH, YOU REALLY ARE LUCKY TO HAVE US, AREN'T YOU?
NOW?
FINE.
GROUP HUG!
YAY!
CREFF, YOUR HAIR IF IN MY MOUFF . . .
SOMEONE'S STANDING ON MY TOE.
CAN'T . . . BREATHE . . .

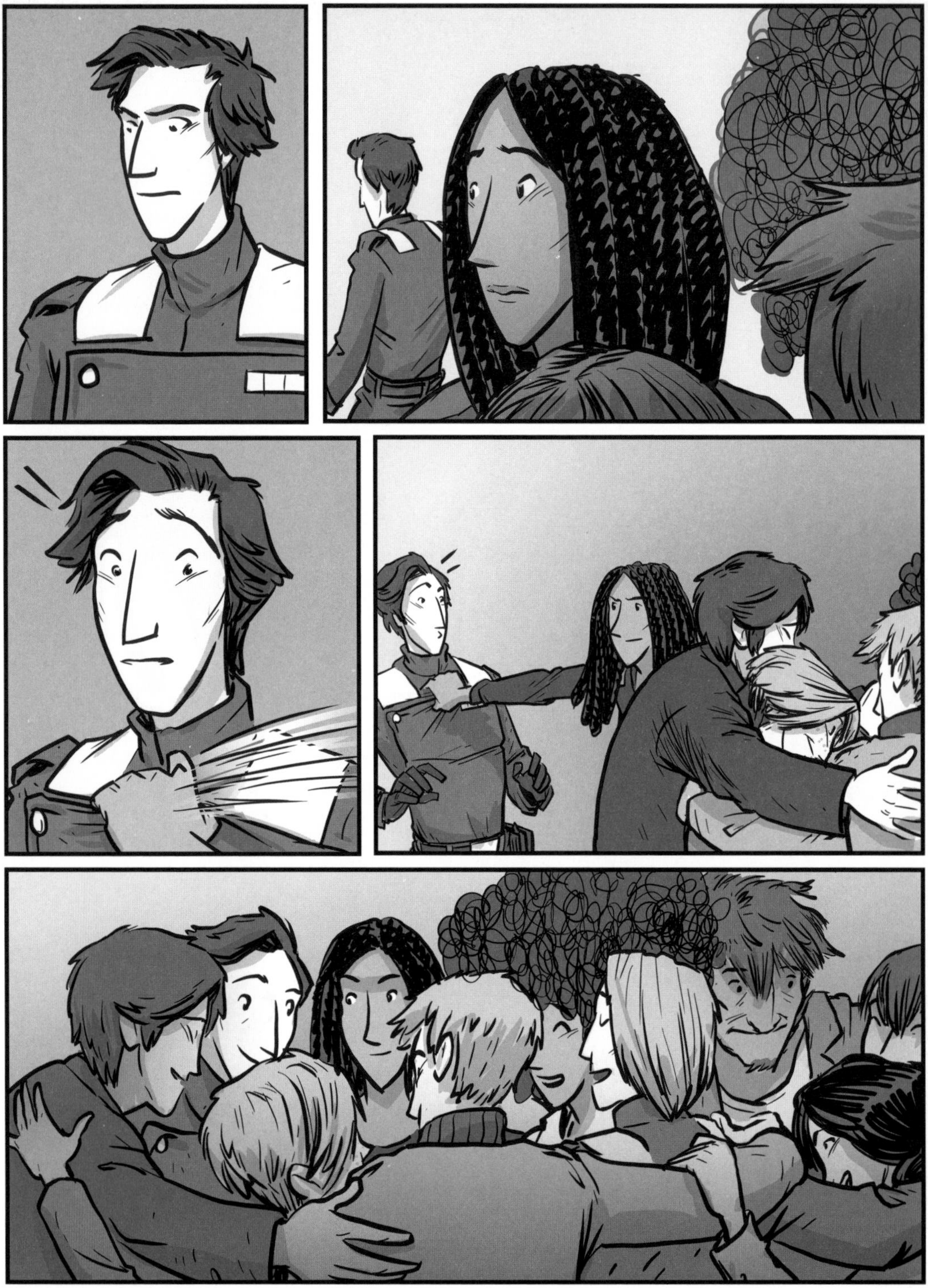

EPILOGUE

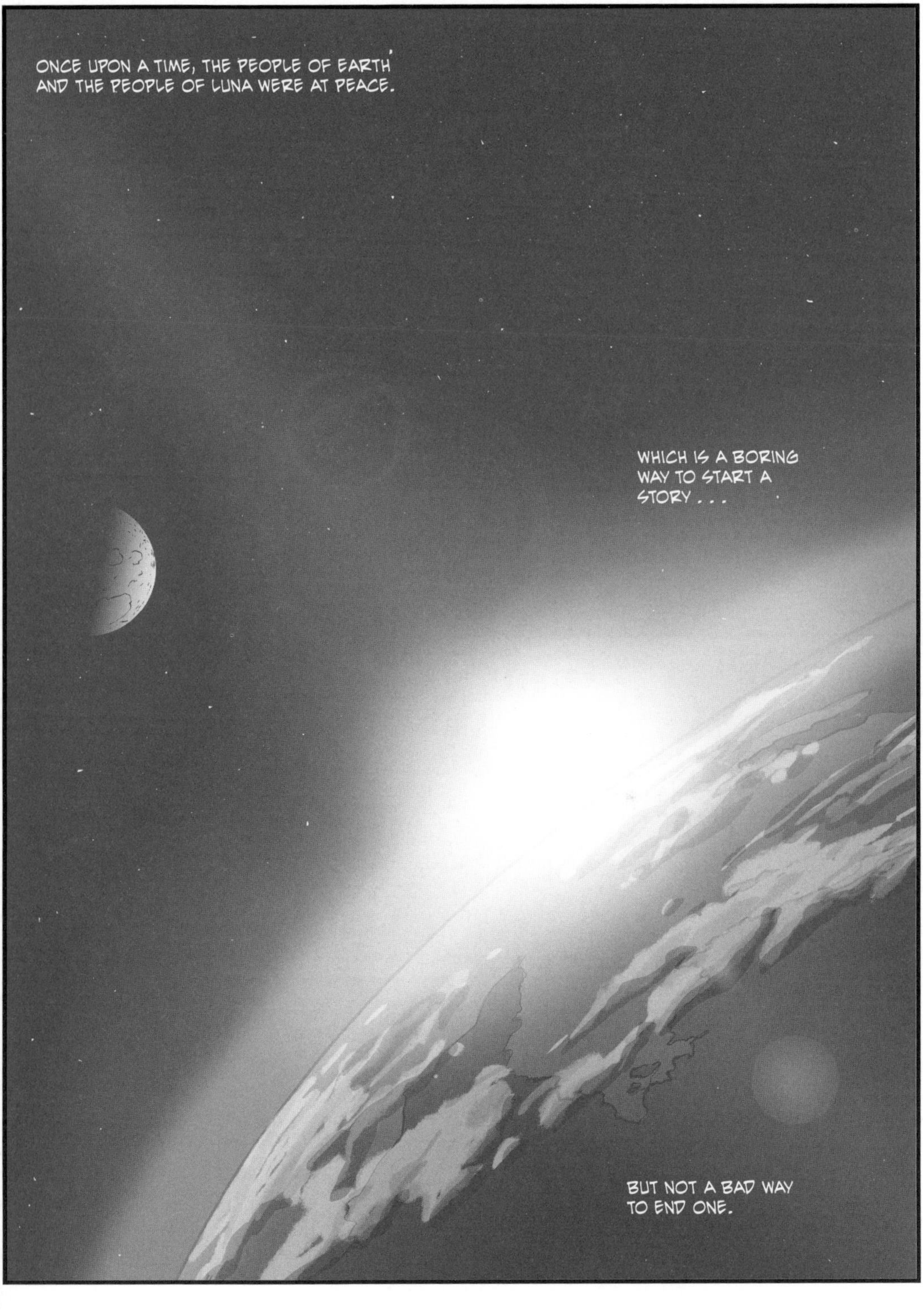
ONCE UPON A TIME, THE PEOPLE OF EARTH AND THE PEOPLE OF LUNA WERE AT PEACE.
WHICH IS A BORING WAY TO START A STORY . . .
BUT NOT A BAD WAY TO END ONE.

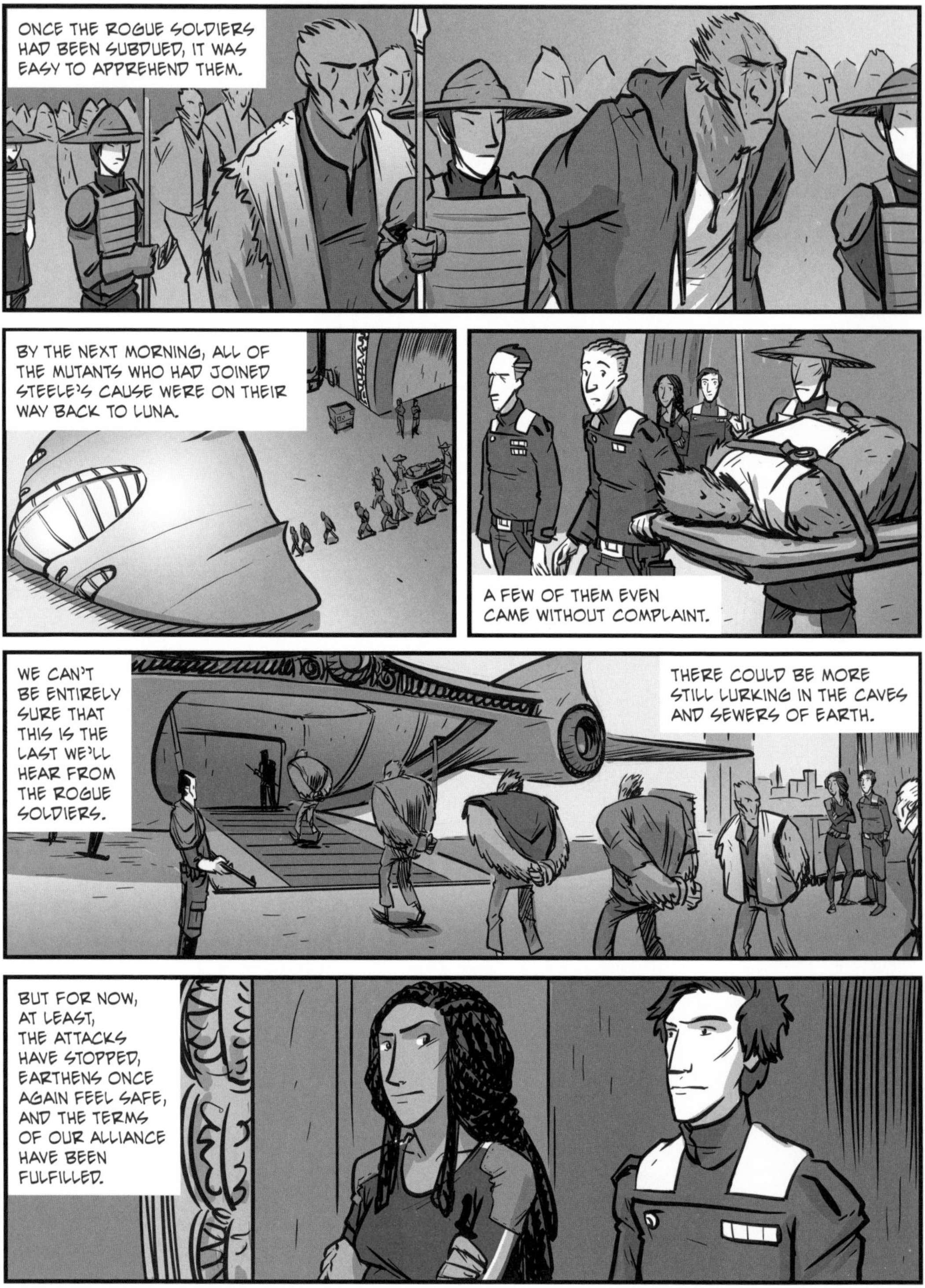
ONCE THE ROGUE SOLDIERS HAD BEEN SUBDUED, IT WAS EASY TO APPREHEND THEM.
BY THE NEXT MORNING, ALL OF THE MUTANTS WHO HAD JOINED STEELE'S CAUSE WERE ON THEIR WAY BACK TO LUNA.
A FEW OF THEM EVEN CAME WITHOUT COMPLAINT.
WE CAN'T BE ENTIRELY SURE THAT THIS IS THE LAST WE'LL HEAR FROM THE ROGUE SOLDIERS.
THERE COULD BE MORE STILL LURKING IN THE CAVES AND SEWERS OF EARTH.
BUT FOR NOW, AT LEAST, THE ATTACKS HAVE STOPPED, EARTHENS ONCE AGAIN FEEL SAFE, AND THE TERMS OF OUR ALLIANCE HAVE BEEN FULFILLED.

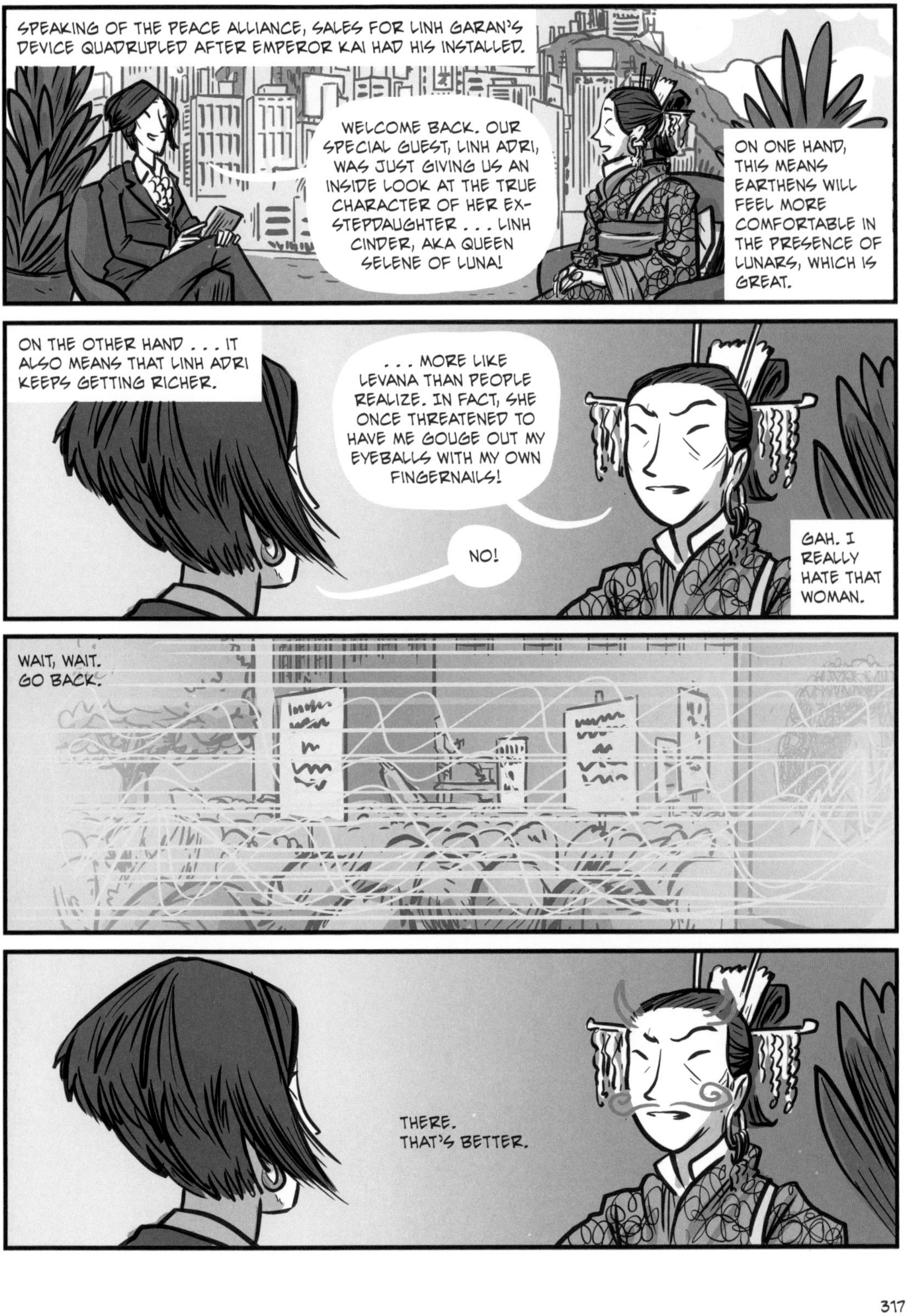
SPEAKING OF THE PEACE ALLIANCE, SALES FOR LINH GARAN'S DEVICE QUADRUPLED AFTER EMPEROR KAI HAD HIS INSTALLED.
WELCOME BACK. OUR SPECIAL GUEST, LINH ADRI, WAS JUST GIVING US AN INSIDE LOOK AT THE TRUE CHARACTER OF HER EX-STEPDAUGHTER . . . LINH CINDER, AKA QUEEN SELENE OF LUNA!
ON ONE HAND, THIS MEANS EARTHENS WILL FEEL MORE COMFORTABLE IN THE PRESENCE OF LUNARS, WHICH IS GREAT.
ON THE OTHER HAND . . . IT ALSO MEANS THAT LINH ADRI KEEPS GETTING RICHER.
. . . MORE LIKE LEVANA THAN PEOPLE REALIZE. IN FACT, SHE ONCE THREATENED TO HAVE ME GOUGE OUT MY EYEBALLS WITH MY OWN FINGERNAILS!
NO!
GAH. I REALLY HATE THAT WOMAN.
WAIT, WAIT. GO BACK.
THERE. THAT'S BETTER.

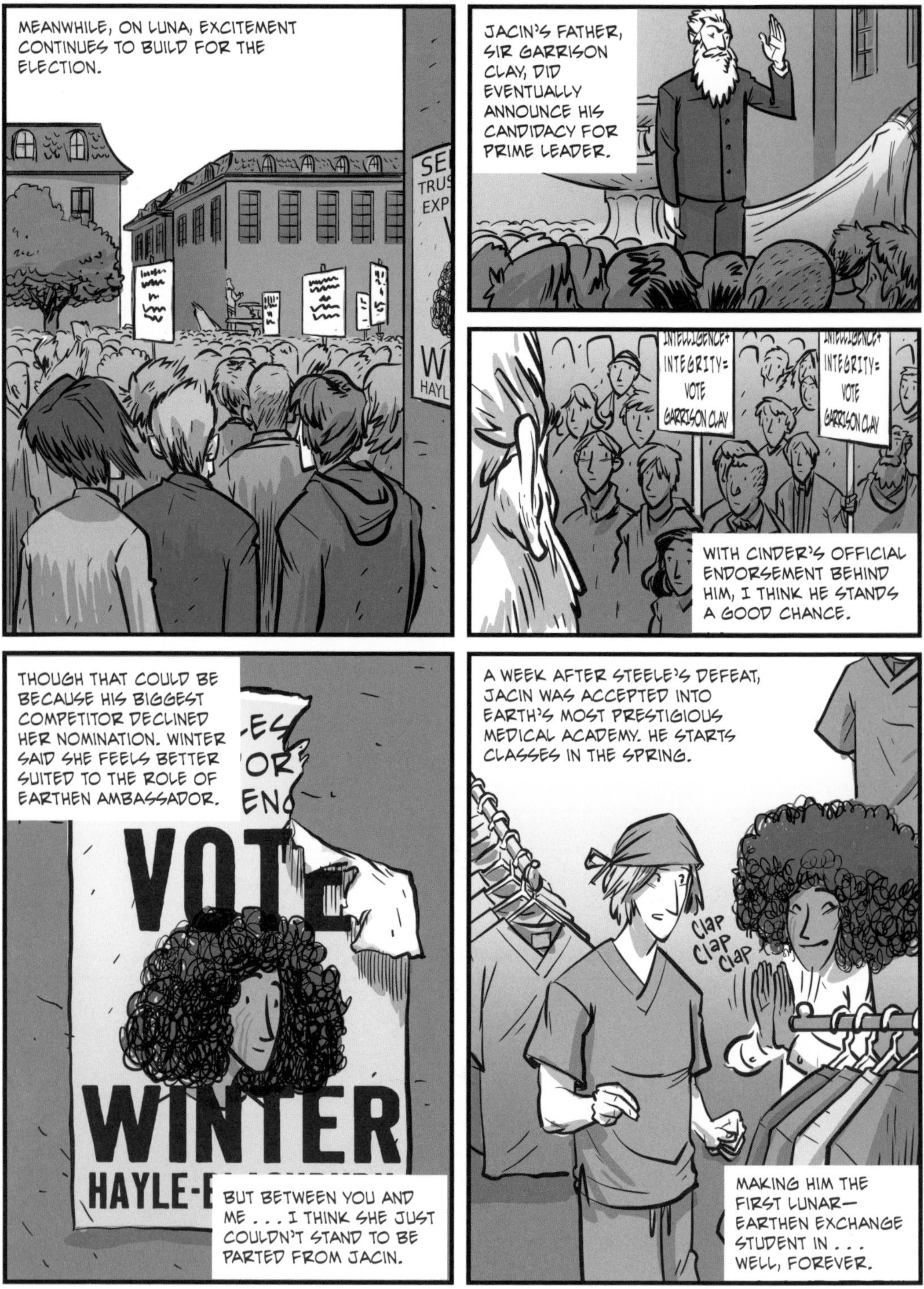
MEANWHILE, ON LUNA, EXCITEMENT CONTINUES TO BUILD FOR THE ELECTION.
JACIN'S FATHER, SIR GARRISON CLAY, DID EVENTUALLY ANNOUNCE HIS CANDIDACY FOR PRIME LEADER.
INTELLIGENCE+ INTEGRITY= VOTE GARRISON CLAY
INTELLIGENCE+ INTEGRITY= VOTE GARRISON CLAY
WITH CINDER'S OFFICIAL ENDORSEMENT BEHIND HIM, I THINK HE STANDS A GOOD CHANCE.
THOUGH THAT COULD BE BECAUSE HIS BIGGEST COMPETITOR DECLINED HER NOMINATION. WINTER SAID SHE FEELS BETTER SUITED TO THE ROLE OF EARTHEN AMBASSADOR.
VOTE
WINTER
BUT BETWEEN YOU AND ME . . . I THINK SHE JUST COULDN'T STAND TO BE PARTED FROM JACIN.
A WEEK AFTER STEELE'S DEFEAT, JACIN WAS ACCEPTED INTO EARTH'S MOST PRESTIGIOUS MEDICAL ACADEMY. HE STARTS CLASSES IN THE SPRING.
CLAP CLAP CLAP
MAKING HIM THE FIRST LUNAR—EARTHEN EXCHANGE STUDENT IN . . . WELL, FOREVER.

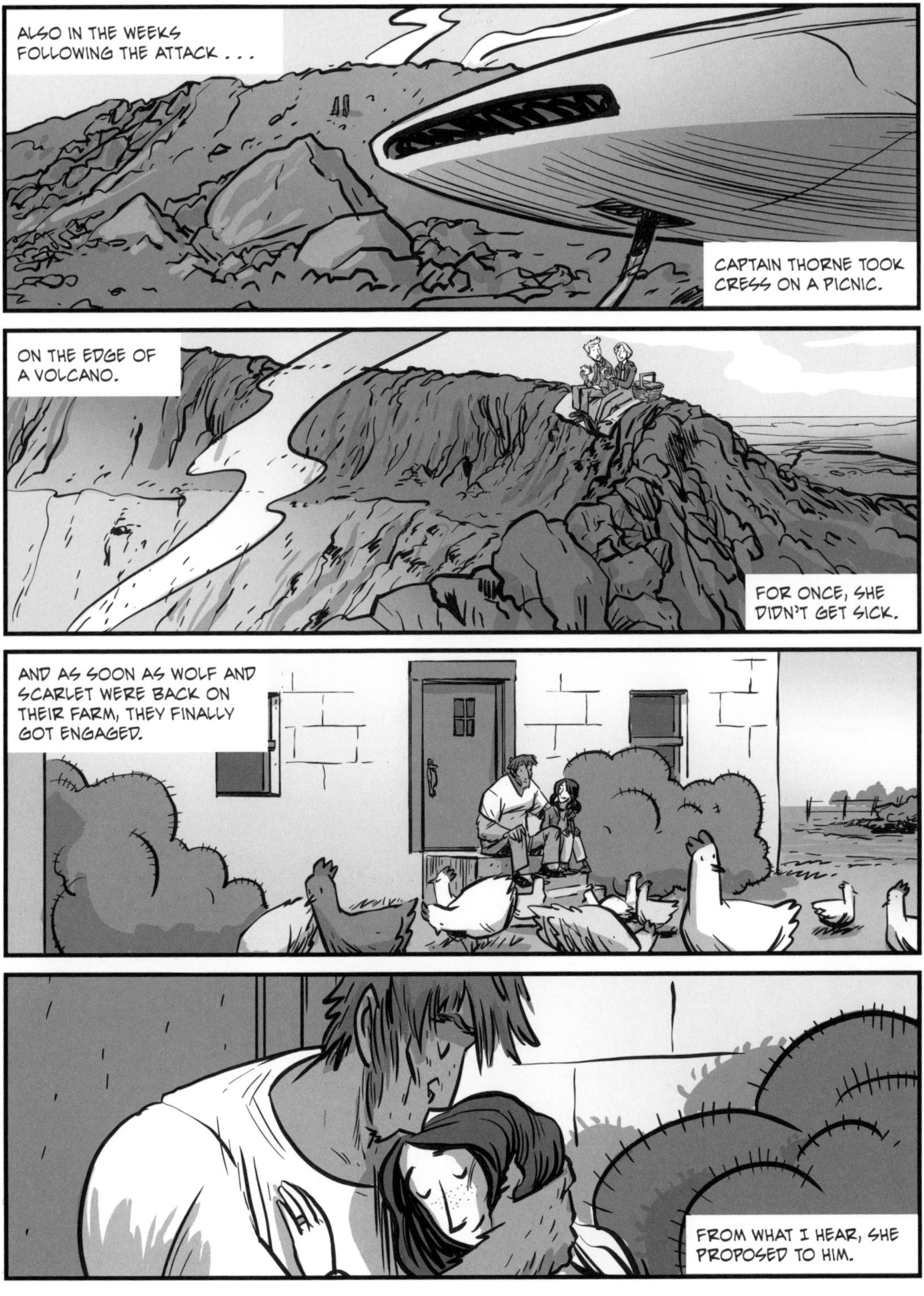
ALSO IN THE WEEKS FOLLOWING THE ATTACK . . .
CAPTAIN THORNE TOOK CRESS ON A PICNIC.
ON THE EDGE OF A VOLCANO.
FOR ONCE, SHE DIDN'T GET SICK.
AND AS SOON AS WOLF AND SCARLET WERE BACK ON THEIR FARM, THEY FINALLY GOT ENGAGED.
FROM WHAT I HEAR, SHE PROPOSED TO HIM.

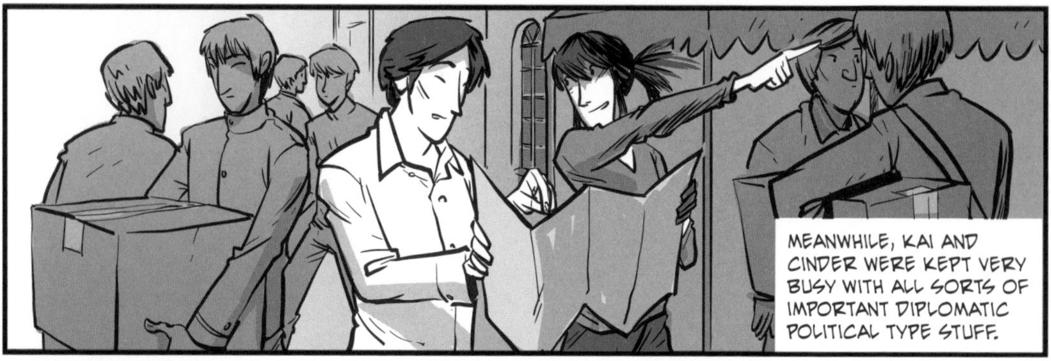
MEANWHILE, KAI AND CINDER WERE KEPT VERY BUSY WITH ALL SORTS OF IMPORTANT DIPLOMATIC POLITICAL TYPE STUFF.

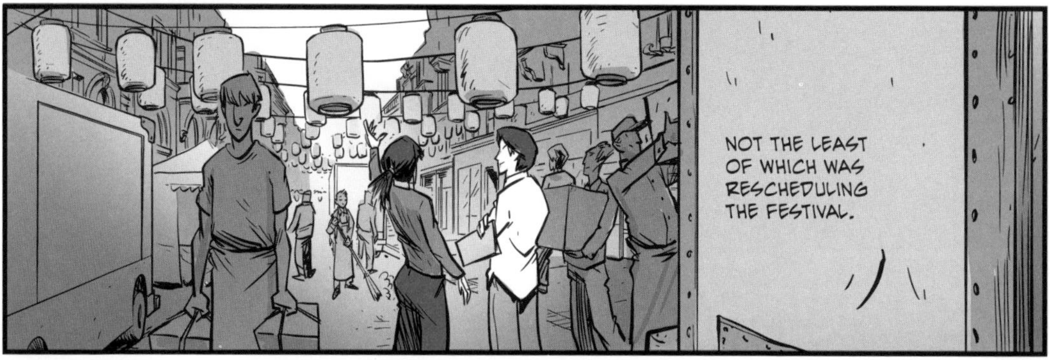
NOT THE LEAST OF WHICH WAS RESCHEDULING THE FESTIVAL.

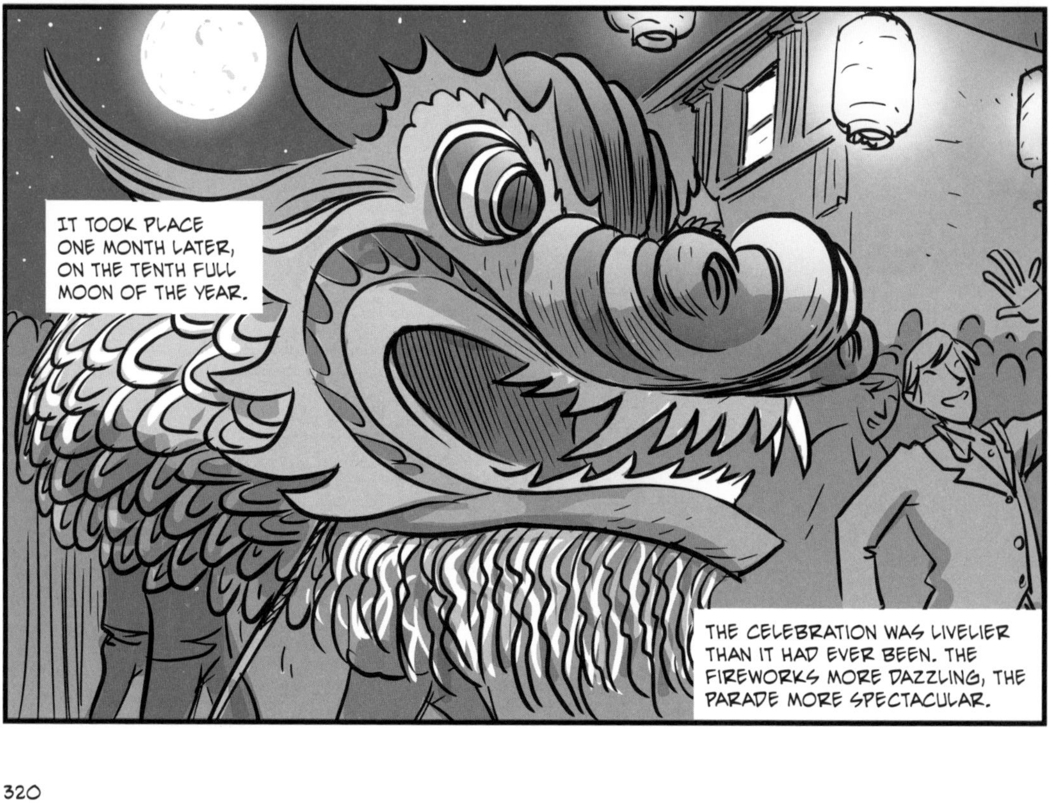
IT TOOK PLACE ONE MONTH LATER, ON THE TENTH FULL MOON OF THE YEAR.
THE CELEBRATION WAS LIVELIER THAN IT HAD EVER BEEN. THE FIREWORKS MORE DAZZLING, THE PARADE MORE SPECTACULAR.

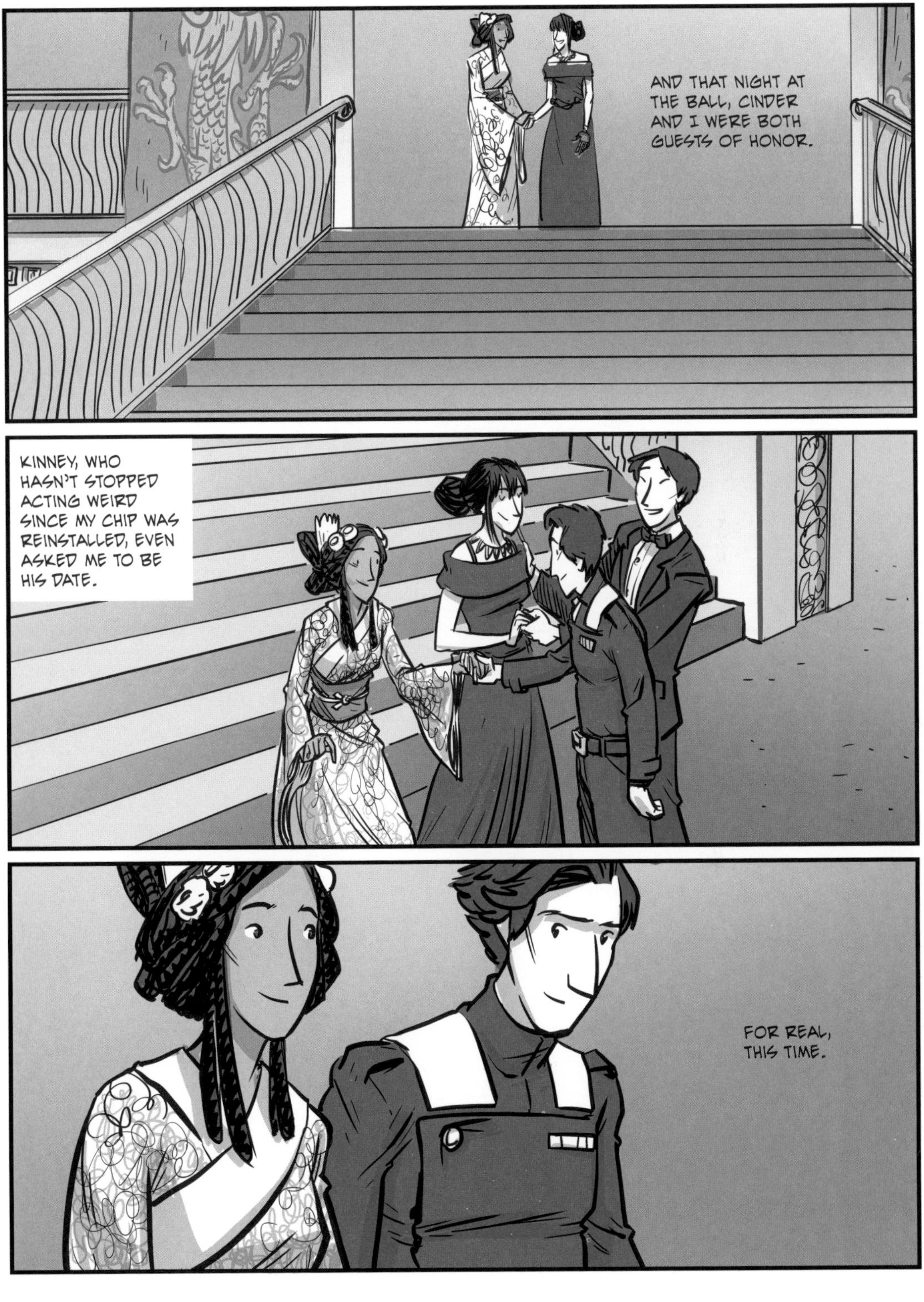
AND THAT NIGHT AT THE BALL, CINDER AND I WERE BOTH GUESTS OF HONOR.
KINNEY, WHO HASN'T STOPPED ACTING WEIRD SINCE MY CHIP WAS REINSTALLED, EVEN ASKED ME TO BE HIS DATE.
FOR REAL, THIS TIME.

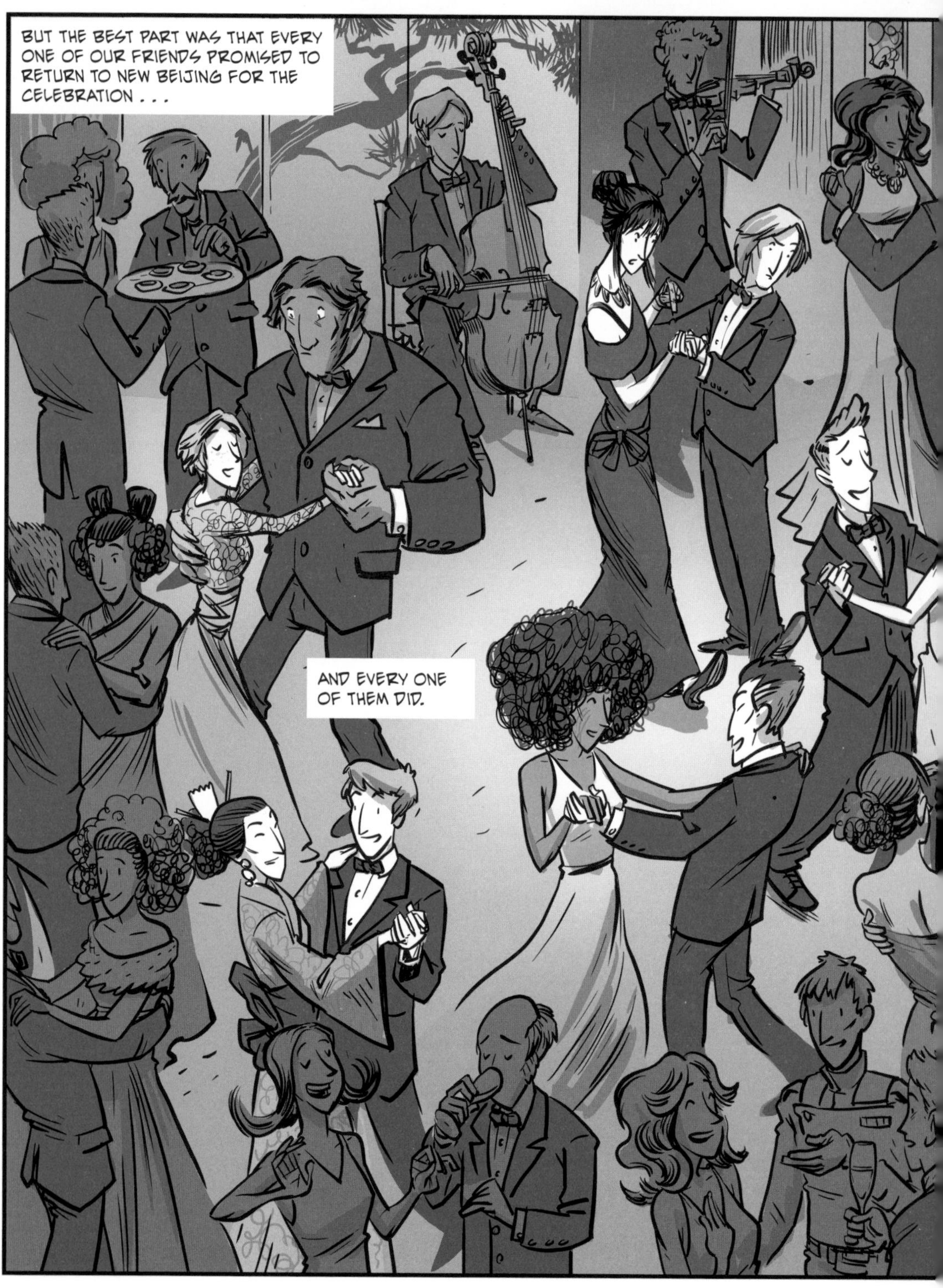
BUT THE BEST PART WAS THAT EVERY ONE OF OUR FRIENDS PROMISED TO RETURN TO NEW BEIJING FOR THE CELEBRATION . . .
AND EVERY ONE OF THEM DID.

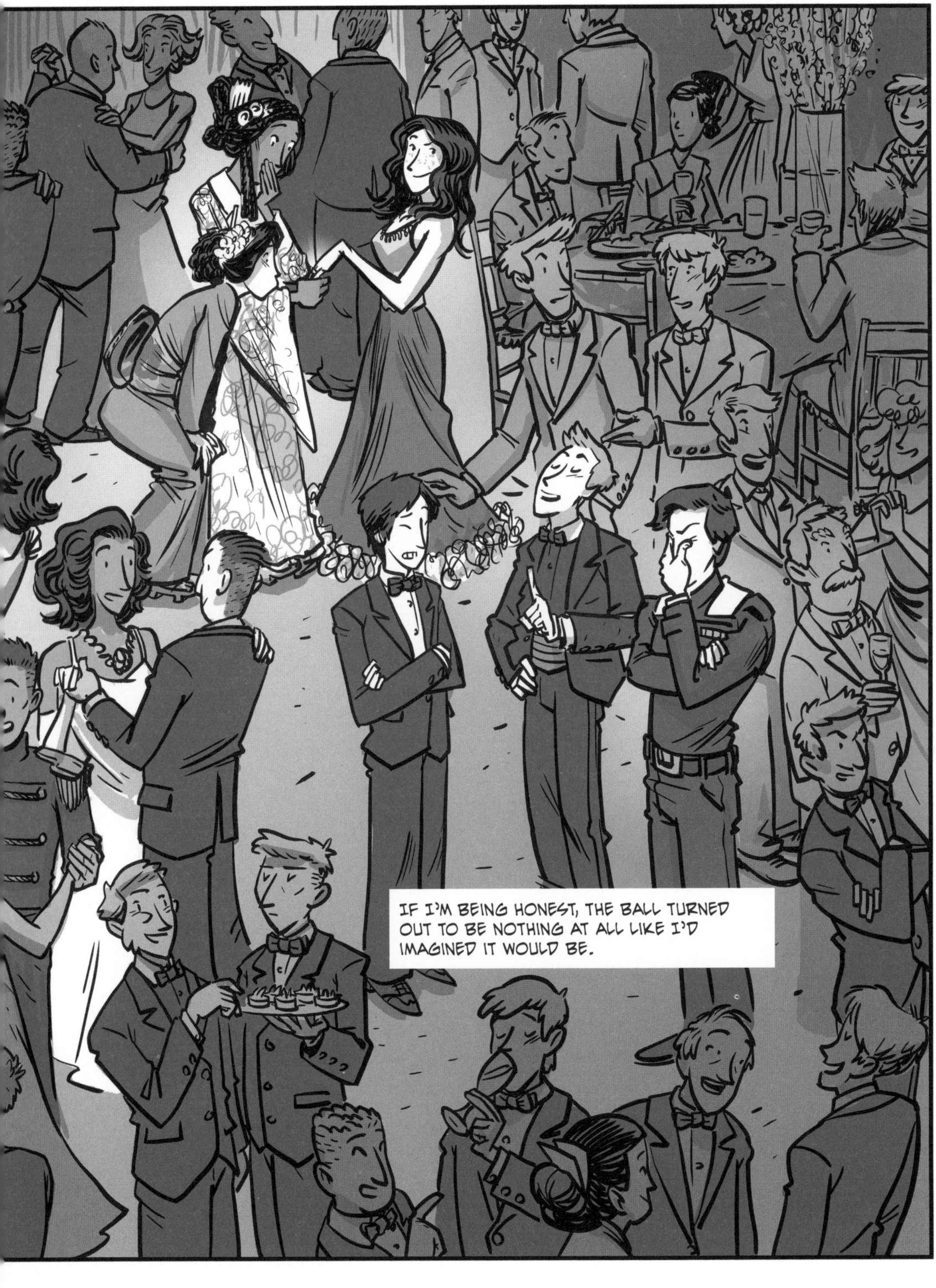
IF I'M BEING HONEST, THE BALL TURNED OUT TO BE NOTHING AT ALL LIKE I'D IMAGINED IT WOULD BE.

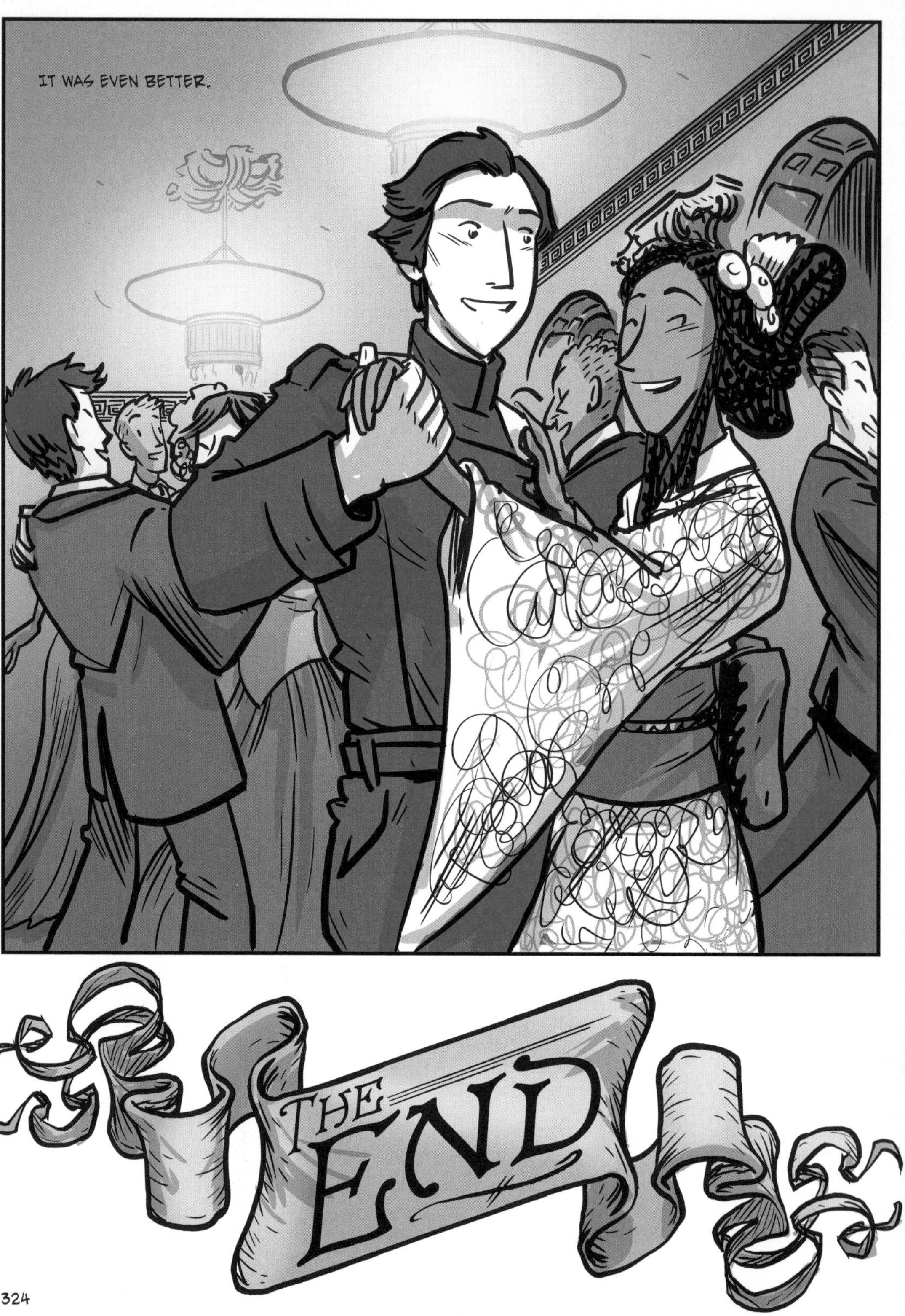
IT WAS EVEN BETTER.
THE END

PRAISE FOR

WIRES AND NERVE

VOLUME 1

#1 NEW YORK TIMES BESTSELLING AUTHOR
MARISSA MEYER
WIRES
AND
NERVE
the Lunar Chronicles series
ART BY DOUG HOLGATE

"THE LUNAR CHRONICLES CONTINUE in this entertaining graphic novel sequel to the existing volumes. This follow-up to the futuristic fairy-tale retellings centers on Iko, cyborg mechanic Cinder's best friend. . . . Newcomers will be helped by a prologue that introduces all of the main characters and flashbacks that are sprinkled throughout. This first volume in a duology is split into seven chapters, each action-packed and fast-paced. The romantic tension building up between Iko and a protective royal guard not only is juicy but also speaks to deeper themes—humanity, loyalty, prejudice, sovereignty, and more. . . . The diverse cast, the charming dialogue, and the clean design make this sci-fi fantasy sequel a must-have for graphic novel and YA collections."

—*School Library Journal*

"This story doesn't require preexisting knowledge of the series, easily catching up fans and new readers alike with capsule introductions to Cress and other members of the Rampion crew in a prologue. Iko is an entertainingly flippant yet formidable heroine, a former servant droid who now inhabits an escort's body and takes on bloodthirsty enemies as though she were invincible. . . ."

—*Publishers Weekly*

★"Fans of the Lunar Chronicles and new readers alike will be delighted. . . . Beloved worlds and characters have smoothly transitioned into graphic format, and a thorough character introduction and quick recap will help new readers feel right at home. . . . Energetic and entertaining with the right balance of action, humor, and romance."

—*VOYA*, starred review

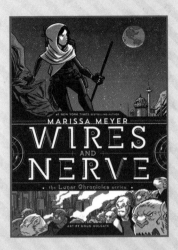

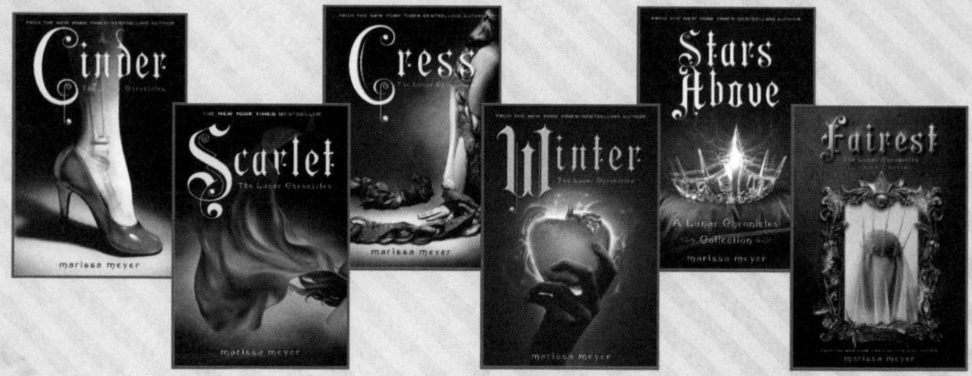
Cinder
marissa meyer
Scarlet
marissa meyer
Cress
marissa meyer
Winter
marissa meyer
Stars Above
A Lunar Chronicles Collection
marissa meyer
Fairest
marissa meyer

PRAISE FOR

The Lunar Chronicles

#1 *NEW YORK TIMES*–BESTSELLING SERIES
***USA TODAY* BESTSELLER**
***PUBLISHERS WEEKLY* BESTSELLER**

"A mash-up of fairy tales and science fiction . . . a cross between Cinderella, Terminator, and Star Wars."
—*Entertainment Weekly*

"Prince Charming among the cyborgs." —*The Wall Street Journal*

"Terrific." —*Los Angeles Times*

"Marissa Meyer rocks the fractured fairy tale genre." —*The Seattle Times*

"Epic awesome." —*Bustle*

"A binge-reading treat." —*MTV*

"Takes the classic to a whole new level." —*NPR*

Thank you for reading this **FEIWEL AND FRIENDS** book. The Friends who made

WIRES AND NERVE
VOLUME 2: GONE ROGUE

possible are:

Jean Feiwel, Publisher

Liz Szabla, Associate Publisher

Rich Deas, Senior Creative Director

Holly West, Editor

Anna Roberto, Editor

Christine Barcellona, Editor

Kat Brzozowski, Editor

Alexei Esikoff, Senior Managing Editor

Kim Waymer, Senior Production Manager

Anna Poon, Assistant Editor

Emily Settle, Administrative Assistant

Danielle Mazzella di Bosco, Senior Designer

Follow us on Facebook or visit us online at mackids.com.

OUR BOOKS ARE FRIENDS FOR LIFE.